A **DARWIN'S WORLD** Novel

BURNING LANDS

By Dominic Covey

RPGObjects

Burning Lands
Copyright 2008 RPGObjects

All rights reserved under international and Pan-American Copyright Conventions. Published in the United States by RPGObjects, Eden Prairie, Minnesota.

No part of this book may be reproduced or transmitted in any form or by any means, graphic, electronic, or mechanical, including photocopying, recording, taping, or by any information storage or retrieval systems, without the permission in writing from RPGObjects.

This book is a work of fiction. Names, characters, places and incidents are products of the author's imagination or are used fictitiously. Any resemblance to actual events or locales or persons, living or dead, is entirely coincidental.

RPGObjects
www.rpgobjects.com

ISBN-10: *0-9743067-9-7*
ISBN-13: *0-9743067-9-7*

Cover Art by Jason Walton
Map Art by Dominic Covey
Layout by Chris Davis

Burning Lands is dedicated to the following people:

To my father, even though you aren't here to read it.

To Sheena, since it was you who got me to pick up the pen again and finish.

And to all the fans of *Darwin's World*.

CHAPTER 1

Rickety towers of ash-blackened steel rose towards the heavens, though they seemed to be nonsensically placed out here in the broad open flats, with nothing else around. Without perspective, they seemed enormous, gigantic, and unearthly. Without scale, everything seemed larger and more powerful; the wind, blowing with unchecked force across the desert wastescape, picked up to a full gale of biting grains, which quickly became a deafening, agonizing roar as it swirled and disappeared into the dead red sky above.

Discoloring the black steel of these purposeless monstrosities was a bleak red glow, an awful alien color that choked the air. It clung to everything; it hovered over the entire landscape as far as any eye could see. The sun, unfettered by an atmosphere that could no longer protect the world, beat lethally down on the vastness of sand and dust, turning the earth into a mirror image of mythical Hades.

Though the wind howled and roared with anger, the huge metal towers, affixed with multitudes of pipes, of metal shoring, of scaffolds rusted and worn, remained still and silent. Utterly still. They did not move, they only sat there, their tops exposed by the sands. Fixtures that might have once jingled, rattled, or clanged had long been stripped by wind, by time and by scavengers long since dead.

The only noise, other than the sighing and whipping of the terrible storm, was a strange, haunting, disembodied howl. It was a low sound, perhaps more like a groan, a distant, lonely moan; but it was just the same wind that raged night and day, only speaking with a different voice, blowing through the pipes, the tubes and the holes in the old metal towers. The wind, channeled through this maze of ancient structures, now long gone to decay and rust, made a strange and frightening noise in the eternal twilight of that red, eerie glow.

Burning Lands

From a distance, that is all that could be seen, a collection of black metal, like the half-revealed bones of some ancient skeleton-ship adrift in a sea of sand. Like the headstones of huge giants, buried just beneath the earth eons ago, great handfuls of junk metal seemingly dropped from a great height across the landscape without thought or care.

The howling wind and the groaning murmur, which had raged alongside one another for countless years, unchallenged in their lonely fury, suddenly submitted to a distant, soft sound that seemed to stand out between their mighty bellows. It must have been a sound which had not been heard by the lifeless titans of steel for decades.

It was the sound of feet, walking steadily across the sands. A sole figure moved across the desert, casting a deep shadow before it as it kept the sun behind. It was irregular, seemingly disfigured. It carried on its shoulder and back bags of gear, odd trinkets, and bits of shiny metal that glimmered intensely in the dying sunlight, shreds of worn-out leather and bleached cloth, pieces of wind-burnished steel and tin.

Up close, silhouetted by the sun's dim and darkening rays, the figure proved to be a man... or more accurately, the shadowy descendant of what once might be called a "man". Tall and narrow, with skin nearly as brown as his leather clothes from years under the sun, the man moved over the dry sand on supple moccasins made from a strange, well-worn hide. Stitches, wide and crude as if guided by a clumsy hand, nonetheless kept the shoes tight about the deformed and crooked toes beneath.

The wind, coarse and heavy with the particles of sand it drove before it, whipped at the face of the man. His lips were gray, parched and withered. His eyes were almost completely shut, only cracked open enough to permit a narrow angle of vision before his path. A scarf of soiled and blackened cloth whipped about him in the wind, draped loosely about his head and neck to protect against the harsh and deadly elements of his world. Leather pants, stitched and re-stitched to accommodate his growing body from an early age, still clung to his crooked hips as he shuffled down the last dune to reach the cool shadow of the huge metal towers. His entire garb bore patches and stains that spoke of old struggles for life and survival in this savage and lonely wilderness, but he was a survivor.

A loose collection of metal links and rings, either stolen or recovered from the junk and debris of years of scavenging, created a working belt around his narrow, malnourished middle. Anchored at one end by the jutting bone of his hip, it hung loosely to the other side. From its hanging end dangled the odd metal spar or jumble of what might have been keys, while all about hand-made leathered bags, half a dozen or so, crammed together around his unnaturally thin waist.

The man's chest was covered by a tattered old covering, something that may have once been a jacket taken from the dead of the desert. Bits of it were leather, true, some of it even fresh (in large, unsightly patches), but beneath, just vaguely, one could make out the old fabric that had once formed its base. It was now stained and bleached from decades of exposure to the desert sun. The bag over his back was packed with all manner of important things, bound tightly and stored out of sight but not out of mind. A chain, rusted and black, dangled from the bag to his waist, attached tightly to his makeshift belt. One hand, gnarled and brown, held tight to the bag's single shoulder strap.

Bitter and broken fingernails held in the other hand a wood and metal pole, itself cracked and caked with earthy stuff. His thumb moved over the metal face on one side, his calloused skin feeling the hot brass that was now blue and chipped from time and age.

Finally, dangling from his already burdened back was a small collection of canteens, mismatched and of odd colors, one or two just a simple makeshift water skin, swinging leanly and precariously as he trudged on with a wanderer's senseless drive.

The realization of the footsteps he himself made suddenly made him stop dead in his tracks. In an instant, with motions like a cat, the pole, actually some kind of shoddy "gun", was ready in his hands. The figure quickly dropped and scurried like a hunkering mouse, ears tweaked as the noise increased and became distorted, getting louder and louder.

A stronger gust of wind roared through the hellish sky, stronger than before. Motes of sand were picked up from the desert floor and skittered along like a gossamer tide just a foot or so above the ground.

A pair of dark brown eyes stared out from the shadows around his face, watching, alert. The air was quiet. But for the buffeting blast of wind, it was utterly, deathly, silent.

Yellow, chipped teeth gnashed against one another nervously. Bitter dry lips trembled momentarily, on edge. Dust collected on a beard covering his rugged face, disguising how many years this poor lonely individual had managed to survive in this lost, lifeless land of nightmares.

Still it was silent. The man, hiding behind an old oil drum, slowly moved one hand from the end of his shoddy musket to his belt. Quietly, his movements masked by the repetitive sigh and heave of the wind, his rough and ugly hand, covered in thick callous tumors that made it look like an old catcher's mitt, fished into one of the small sacks at his side and retrieved a small, faded yellow tennis ball. His rough fingers played with the soft fuzz on the surface of the ball nervously. Weighing it, considering it. His dark eyes stared out again.

The tall metal towers, whose shadow stretched on for dozens of paces in this dead oasis amid the sands, stared back in silence.

With a quick toss, the man hurled the ball across the sands, to a place some twenty paces or so between the towers, the path which he had been on, the path his senses had been warned against. Instantly he ducked, prone against the spilled drum, watching as his tennis ball bounced once on the sand, leaving an impression, slowing and rolling with the wind's influence.

Eyes, staring down at the crude iron sights of his weapon, watched and waited for a response. There was none. The only sound was a strange distant echo of the bouncing ball, which was soon lost and carried away by the winds among the towers.

He blinked. Still he waited; it seemed like an eternity. Then, after a long cautious wait, the man rose, re-assured that he was alone again in the world. Weapon held firm in hand, he walked across the sand towards his ball.

Suddenly, that same noise that had unsettled him thundered out. He grasped his musket and readied himself for a flight back to cover. But then he just smiled.

His eyes darted about, staring in every direction, but cautiously, and with some amusement, he stomped his foot down on the wind-packed sand. That noise again.

An echo. An echo of his own footsteps, snared and multiplied and magnified by the ghostly metal towers of rust and decay.

The man, while relieved, only cautiously bent over, on one swollen knee, to fetch the ball in hand. His eyes constantly swept the tower tops, the shadowed underhangs. No movement was to be seen.

The sight that had drawn him, from atop a distant dune perhaps a mile away, now loomed in his eyes.

That feeling again. In his heart. He felt it beating quickly. His toes were trying to curl, if curl they could, inside his painfully tight moccasins. His teeth bared as his lips curled in growing anticipation and... excitement.

He walked, ever cautiously, towards the shapes lying in the sand in the large open clearing under the shadow of the metal towers. As he came into the shaded opening, the wind seemed to cease, quieting to a low hum. His scarf settled against his neck. The beating, vicious sun was cooled as he passed into the shadow of the largest of the metal derricks, shielded from its never-ending stare.

His footsteps no longer seemed to echo either. The sand was thin here; hard-packed earth, or more likely concrete, lay only a foot or so beneath the sand.

The sight of the shapes he had seen from afar, now up close, just a few paces away, made him smile with primitive glee. They were dead, decayed bodies. His smile grew larger still.

There was a buzz. The familiar sound of black flies, his constant companion it seemed, now clinging to the exposed and terrible wounds adorning the dead, spawning feasting maggots. He could detect the odor of the foul-smelling flesh, which now filled his widening nostrils and made his eyes water.

Nearby he saw a *rifle* of some kind, no musket, to be sure, but it was broken in two parts where it had been struck violently. The others must have had similar weapons, but these were conspicuously missing, leaving only the one shattered weapon.

He went over and toyed with the broken rifle, but ultimately dropped the pieces and returned to the corpses. With a wave of his tightly bound left hand, the man scared the flies from the first of the bodies. He only looked for a fraction of a second at the wounds, a huge explosion from the chest, leaving the cracked and broken ribs exposed to the drying sunlight; the head and exposed limbs, all but gone to the ravages of beetles, voracious sand mites, and the harsh flesh-stripping wind, before kneeling in the sand beside it to search.

His fingers moved quickly and with their own curious dance, hovering one moment and darting in the next like a wavering divining rod in the hands of a magician. His eyes, though now concentrating on the body and its tattered plastic clothes, were always moving; every second or so he looked up and about to watch for possible ambushers. He was like a predatory bird, head cocked, eyes moving, fingers darting in to explore and snapping back instantly to remain within reach of his weapon.

The corpse's costume, a shattered helmet and rubbery uniform, tattered and worn, was uniformly gray in color. The scavenger let its tough, torn material slip from his hands. No good. The rubber wouldn't breathe at all, and that meant it was unfit for someone living among the wide open spaces of the sweltering desert.

His hands instead moved down to the legs. They were clad in the same exceptional material, soft and slippery to his fingertips. A smile came over his face, but as he ran his palms gleefully over the surface, he stopped suddenly when they made contact with something at the corpse's side.

Ignoring the stench of week-old rot, the smell of churning maggots, and kneeling among the blown-out and blackened tissues of his abdominal cavity, the eager eyes of the man suddenly widened as they felt around and grasped a solid object attached to a broken plastic belt.

Ungraciously and excitedly the man yanked on the belt, trying desperately to pull it free. He tugged viciously, almost angrily, like a child denied a piece of tempting candy, until the belt finally snapped and with a jolt came free. The object, whatever it was, was in his hands.

It was heavy. His fingers roamed the cold plastic surface, running over the flap and to the brass snap. Popping it open, the man's eyes flared wide for a brief moment as they beheld the metal object within, until bit with flying sand from another gust of desert wind and closed shut again.

The man pulled the object out by its textured handle, as if fondling a relic of some ancient god. It felt warm in his hand, and heavier than expected. Its dimensions were unfamiliar, but he knew well what it was. An intact *pistol*. His eyes looked up and down its appreciable metal surface, black and cold and simple. He held it in hand, just staring.

The moment of awe finally ended with the realization that his search had only begun. The man replaced the pistol in its holster, and threw it and the broken belt over one shoulder. He patted the fragile cadaver quickly and excitedly.

A small collection of beautiful brass cylinders, no larger than his thumb, were found in one of the pockets in another belt hung with almost a dozen pouches. His fingers touched the metallic shells, worshipped them with a quick fondle. He scooped the dozen or so rounds (all of the same size) in his greedy hands and dropped them carefully into one of his own pockets. He checked again the dusty suit as well as around the corpse to see if any had fallen out, before moving on.

A canteen on another body caught his eye. Crawling over quickly on his knees, he almost fell over as he desperately grabbed it in his hands, tearing off the annoying screw-top. He stared in, shaking the can slightly, his finely tuned ears listening. His excitement dwindled and fell. He turned the canteen upside down and nothing poured from within but grains of the same reddish sand. He tossed the canteen over one shoulder, joining the bundle already dangling there on a chain.

A leather case sat nearby, partly buried in the sand, its lid hanging open and flapping methodically in the wind. The man picked the case up in one hand and looked inside, but it proved to be completely empty. He considered taking it for a moment, then nonchalantly dropped it.

He turned to the body. This corpse's garb was the same as the others. His hands moved and yanked the first of its thick-soled rubber boots off with violent effort. He grunted with annoyance, as the foot remained attached, inside. It took several long seconds to unfasten the plastic buckles and dump the rotten, pale-skinned extremity out and onto the dirt.

This done, he smiled, and took off his moccasin. The smell of his own dead skin and moldy feet made even his shielded nostrils reflex and turn away. Moving quickly, he pulled the boot on over his foot, relishing the coolness, the soft interior. But the boot was for a foot far larger than his. Without a moment of hesitation, he discarded the rubber boot and replaced his moccasin. Still he continued his search.

Moving on all fours over the body, he came to the final two corpses, lying almost side-by-side. The smell was overpowering, so he pulled his scarf tight over his mouth and nose. The bodies were noticeably bloated. Again, to his surprise, they seemed to wear the same clothing, a coverall of unbroken gray plastic, and a strange helmet with a dusty glass faceplate.

His fingers dangled in sudden apprehension over the corpses. A strange feeling began to rise within him. Reaching down slowly, he took one of the lifeless arms in hand. This one was covered in dried blood. He pulled off the glove unceremoniously and peeled back the sleeve to see the arm itself. He stared at the metal jewelry around one wrist. It glimmered softly and beautifully in the reddish sun. Small stones, turquoise and rough corals, dotted its surface. *Useless*. He dropped the dead arm without a second thought and kept searching.

The first body had proved empty, except for another empty canteen, which he subsequently kept. He reached towards the head but found inside the shattered helmet only a crumpled, broken tangle where the face had been.

He turned his attention to the final body. A strange metal plaque was grasped in the corpse's hand. The man worked to free it. For a few moments he touched it, prodded it, played with the unintelligible buttons on its surface, but it remained non-functional. Still, he kept it.

The man saw the same familiar uniform cloaking the body. He tugged at the leggings, but they resisted him. He moved up to undo the synthetic plastic belt, but his eyes widened again. Immediately he jumped back, grasping his musket in hand. He glared at the intact face that stared back at him through the faceplate, his eyes filled with surprise and confusion. His heart was racing.

Slowly he realized that this place was as empty as before. Only the wind came to his ears. Only the dead sight of the metal towers, of the decaying bodies, came to his nervous eyes. He looked back on the fourth corpse. Moving forward, cautiously, he examined what he could see through the glass with his keen vision. The face inside was intact. But it was *perfect*. No flaws. Not like any other person he had ever seen, not in his entire life. There were no tumors, no aberrations, no deformities, no skin welts, rash, warts, or even the beginning of scale-like shingles present on so many survivors these days.

With a sudden boldness he reached around and fumbled with the helmet until it came off with a barely-perceptible "hiss" of compressed air. He could see it now, the body within. The corpse's eyes, while shriveled, were white, not tinged yellow like most men he'd seen. The face, though now sunken from some internal corruption, was pale and soft; even with death considered, this person must have been fair beyond compare. Not a year exposed to the sun he himself had endured all his life. It was as if... as if this figure was not of his world at all. Its lips were soft and pink, though noticeably whitened from the days after its death. The hair, still affixed to the head, blew like spider webs in the wind. Each strand, which the searching man hesitantly ran his coarse fingers through, was soft. And *gold*.

Crouching over the face, he touched it. He ran his fingers through the hair, his other hand dropping the musket to just touch the skin. Stretched taught over the skull beneath, like the leather pulled tight over a drum, it was nonetheless soft and supple, not worn and weathered like his own. He played with the corpse's face for minutes, just staring at the dead eyes, at the open mouth, at the pearly white teeth, which were just now beginning to yellow in the sand and sun.

He brought his fingers, now oily due to something in the corpse's hair, to his own nose. His eyes widened again from the unexpected scent. There was a strange odor now lingering on his fingers, fingers which had caressed the cadaver's hair, that made him smile slightly. It was a strange smell, but one that he found he liked. A delicate, wonderful smell. He had never smelled anything like it before. He rubbed his fingers together, as if trying to capture the scent before it evaporated and blew away in the wind.

The man took a deep breath and crouched. He weighed his own delight in the fair hair with his better judgment. He wondered if he had room to spare. Desire, and childish greed, showed in his mottled, mongoloid face. He pulled out a long black knife from its sheath at his side, took the head by its wonderfully scented hair with a simple smile on his face, and went to *scalp it...*

Just then there was a horrified *gasp* from the nearby shadows.

The man, if one could call him that, suddenly gripped with surprise at being taken so off guard, leapt to the side, groping desperately for his gun. Grabbing the ramshackle rifle in his heavy mitts, his heart pounded in his ears, drowning out all other noises. His fingers, tripping over themselves, searched for the trigger, desperate to fire at what could only be a surprise attacker. Grunting, knowing his life may be gone in seconds, he whipped the musket up, his red-rimmed eye staring down the barrel and across the sights, at the origin of the sudden, foreign noise.

The man gawked as he beheld the origin of the sound, just a few paces away from where he crouched. There, encapsulated in the shadows of a tiny void in the industrial ruins, sheltered out of the wind, he saw a small shape... a young girl crouching, vainly attempting to hide behind a rusted metal pipe.

She stared back at him in horror. Paralyzed. His finger twitched, hanging just before the trigger. Her eyes, green like nothing he had ever seen, seemed to tremble in fear. His own eyes, glaring at her, blinked once, then twice. And softened.

The girl's hair, a mess of frizzy blond curls, billowed crazily in the wind. Her pale skin, what he could see of it, appeared pasty and white. Her attire, a diminutive uniform consisting of a similar rubbery coverall like the adult dead littering the site, seemed ill-suited and ridiculous on her. She appeared to have lost her helmet, and the neck of her suit crept up to her jaw and looked terribly uncomfortable.

She was a child.

The man slowly relaxed his tense finger. He lowered the gun slightly. He stared straight at the girl, eyes contemplating. The girl's mouth, hanging open up until this moment, clenched shut over white, unbroken teeth. Her eyes squinted in an attempt to shield themselves from the sun, which she seemed utterly and totally unaccustomed to, and her lashes beat furiously as particles of sand caught in them again and again, irritating her eyes.

The man cocked his head slowly to the side, finally appraising his find, a youngster, perhaps a third his age. She was so small; he had never seen anyone so short before!

Burning Lands

Her clothes, they weren't like his at all. They were... intact. His hand almost unconsciously wandered out to touch the rubbery sleeve, but her absolute fear of him caused her to quickly skitter back from his reach and against the far side of her tiny hiding spot.

The man blinked again in realization. He could see she was just as terrified of him as he had been of her. His hand came back to his side slowly. He reconciled to simply stare at her face and attempt to understand her presence in this place, of all places.

His mind wandered. She was soft-skinned. Not a scar or scab or fleshy obtrusion, unlike him. It was unnerving. It was haunting. For a moment he felt something akin to *shame*, as if he were looking at an image of what humans were once supposed to look like, and in comparison he knew he fell terribly short of such a perfect and unblemished mold. Some survivors of this tortured land had grown bitter at those they called "Ancients", cursing and lamenting the passing of What Had Come Before; but being a simple man, he could only stand mutely and marvel at this lost link to a human past that lay moldering in the ruins dotting the wastes.

Understanding that his statue-like demeanor wasn't earning her trust, he licked his dry lips with a clumsy white tongue, tasting the thick plaque on his teeth as it made contact, in deep thought. Eventually he dropped his musket to his side, and withdrew both arms.

The child watched, staring in defensive fright. Her gloved hand was ready to strike out at any unexpected move, knuckles clenched into a pathetic fist half the size of his. The man hesitated. He didn't know what to do. Then suddenly, he motioned to her. He extended his hand, rough and covered in thick skin that made it almost the appendage of a monster, out to her. The little girl's stare wavered in fear as they beheld the grotesque limb. Her eyes narrowed on the tumors and growths clustered on the fingers, each digit so ballooned that is was barely able to close tight enough to form a fist.

She looked up the arm, which just sat there, unmoving except for the slight bob as it fought to stay still in the desert wind. She saw the sand-blackened face, wrinkled and shriveled up. She saw him blink once or twice, watching her. His mouth, lips drawn back, revealed yellow, ugly teeth. The sight made the young child giggle. She thought, in a childlike way, that it looked like a funny attempt at making a *smile*.

The mutant saw the girl grin, then break out into soft, contagious giggles. She covered her face with her little gloved hands as she snickered. While her eyes remained on his, they softened, too. He smiled. He felt the lines in his cheeks form in ways he had never really felt before... beyond the slight grin of satisfaction he sometimes made when he found food, water, or shiny junk. His eyes involuntarily started to close. He felt a strange feeling. Strange noises, just like hers, came from within him.

The child only giggled more as the mutant stammered with his own alien laughter, as if he was just now discovering how to laugh. He was. His unpracticed laugh sounded like a chortle, like she had imagined Santa Claus would sound. In her short span of seven years, she had never heard anyone laugh like *that* before! It started slow, cautious, confused. But since she did nothing to dissuade him, he felt comfortable and laughed out loud, a rough, genuine burst of belly laughter.

When it was done, the man smiled broadly, and he began to breath heavier. He had laughed for a good few heartbeats. The child was now sitting back on her knees, like him, and no longer seemed so afraid. She removed her gloves clumsily and then rested her hands on her knees. Her mouth opened and he heard a soft noise.

"My name's Gale," she said in a beautiful sing-song voice, "what's yours?" The mutant's eyes went wide again and he lost his smile. The little girl, squinting and shielding her eyes from the sun, soon lost her own grin as she saw his reaction to her greeting.

The man just stared at her. She could see him staring at her lips. He looked... surprised. Angry? *Jealous?*

The man reached out, his fingers forward; she recoiled only slightly, but bravely stayed her ground. The mutant's fingers hovered before her lips, their tips tickled by her soft quick breaths. Slowly he touched her lips, his fingers shaking. The little girl stared at him, squinting. The mutant finally blinked. He brought his hands back to his own mouth, which was hanging open. He touched his own lips. The girl suddenly realized.

"You can't talk, can you?" she asked. Again the man reacted with surprise by backing away from her when she spoke. He felt his own lips. He looked up at her, eyes flickering.

"*Ooownngar*," he said, the sound distorted and uncontrolled, air just blowing madly through his throat. His lips and tongue struggled to create sounds he could never make. The little girl giggled; he sounded like an *ogre!* The man tried again, to imitate her words, but failed. There was a moment of awkward silence. Slowly, the smile returning to his face, he reached out for her hand again. After a long moment, the little girl didn't know why, but she took it.

The man retrieved his gear, and taking her hand in his own grotesque mitt, led her off into the desert. As the two figures walked off, it was a strange sight, almost comical. A tall, narrow, deformed man, bristling with rifle, rusty canteens, and scavenged gear. He walked with a slow step, keeping pace with the small child at his side.

Every now and then she wandered, or had to stop and rest. The man lingered nearby, leaned over to hear her, to attempt to understand her. Soon she was up again with a spring in her step, humming an eerie, discordant, five-note tune as she skipped along.

It was a strange sight indeed.

The sun beat down on the rough broken rocks. It was large, the sun, distorted as it loomed high in the sky. Something in the atmosphere, perhaps the flurry of distant sand, made it irregular and rough, undefined despite its deadly brilliance.

On one of the hot, baking rocks scattered about the craggy wasteland sat the same girl. She was older now, bigger than when the deformed man had first encountered her by the nameless towers, when he had first found his one and only *friend*. In many ways she was still the child she had always been, but she was taller now, tougher, and used to the solitary desert life they now shared. Her hair had grown out, her skin had tanned, and the lingering scars on her arms from strange injections, the only visible trace of her life before, had all but vanished.

The girl was pulling a patch of skin from some hairless desert creature tight over the face of the flat boulder, which proved to be quite useful for preparing such hides. She perched there, like some dexterous desert bird, with the skill and expertise of one who had done this for years. And she had. Her hands, once soft and white, delicate and frail, were now tough and calloused. They moved quickly and with greater strength; the years in this harsh wasteland had made her stronger, of course. Her legs, curled beneath her in a squatting crouch, were now golden and glowing, no longer white, pale, and frail as they had been.

The man took his eyes off her, still beaming with a father's pride. He breathed heavily as he heaved the skinned haunch of meat onto the makeshift fire just in the leeward side of the boulder, away from the blowing wind. Immediately smoke began to rise as the fatty parts of the flesh were singed by the heat. He took a moment to breathe, wiping the grime and sweat and blood from his face.

The girl smiled, breaking off her habitual humming, admiring the carcass. With an almost monkey-like agility she jumped down from her little perch, leaving the hide in the sun for future use, to land in front of their next meal.

"It's wonderful..." she said as she climbed down across from him. The mutant smiled as well. He sat back against the rock, searching for his canteen. His eye finally fell on her outstretched hand, which held the object in its palm. She was smiling as well, her warm, teenage face beaming. The wind blew a few strands of her sun-bleached blond hair across her brow.

She always knew exactly what he was looking for. He reached out for something, a smile of expectation on his face. She watched. He closed his eyes, still smiling, imagining in his mind the image of his horn knife, the one he used to cut bits of meat off with. He then opened his eyes.

She was still sitting there, staring. Her mouth was closed, as if in a contented contemplation. Peaceful. She just stared at him. She seemed distant. *Strange.*

This was a game they always played, it was one of her favorite tricks. It always made him smile as well, in pride, perhaps, but also out of simple, easily-awed amusement. He was as simple and innocent as he had been when they had first met and though his body had aged badly with the passing of the years since then, his mind had not advanced as appreciably as hers. He was stunted, retarded in many ways and she had come to realize he was a simpleton, but loved him no less.

The girl suddenly blinked, as if waking from a trance. The serene look on her face gave way to a devious smile. He grinned in return, wondering if she would guess right. The girl moved to their bundle of things, and searched only for a second. She turned, victorious, the horn knife in hand, blade pointed skywards. The man choked on a guttural chortle, the product of a deformed voice box that would never speak a word, and admitting defeat with a nod took the knife from her. She giggled and plopped down beside him. The man shook his head in an admission of his continued amazement, smiling, as he began to trim the slowly cooking meat. A few steaming slices plopped into the bowl she held in both hands, a bowl made from an old army helmet they'd found in the desert.

Later, as the sun began to set on the flat red horizon, the aging man sat back, finishing off the charred black flesh on the ends of a femur. His face was covered in oil and unsightly juices. A look of gratification spread across the narrow lips and caked, filthy face. The girl sat back as well, sitting cross-legged, watching with a peaceful look on her face. Her soft greenish eyes stared, her eyelids only partly closed to shield against stray sand. Finally gorging himself, the man grunted with satisfaction, filling his mouth with water from the water skin. He swished it around before swallowing and burping.

The girl frowned. "Manners," she said quietly to herself, watching him eat. The man pounded his chest, forcing the bubbles up his throat to form a string of small quiet belches, before getting up and moving over to the skin she had started work on. She just watched, contented, happy. It had been a particularly fortunate find, that beast. She was full, and there was time now to rest.

"Johnny," she said aloud, knowing he could never understand her, almost as if in a daydream, "tell me again about the day you found me..."

Johnny, the name she had given him years ago, made him look up. He knew that whenever she said that word, made those sounds, it meant she was referring to him. But she said nothing more, so he looked back to the unrecognizable piece of skin, rubbing the dried fleshy side with a rough white stone. The girl just stared, blinking.

"It was so long ago..." she mumbled, "... I don't remember anymore. I don't... remember *anything*..." She stared into the fire.

It wasn't completely true. Her mind remembered strange, fractured images. Blurry and distorted, old sights and sounds. Of many people, more like herself, not like Johnny; of happiness too, of songs and... music. But there were other memories as well, of tears and terrified weeping. Of her father and her mother... Tears formed in her eyes as she sought to fight off the memories that had plagued her ever since that day they had left the darkness for the light. In the past seven years, with their enigmatic visions and horrible dreams, the memories of that time had become duller and less vivid, but they still rose up now and again to remind her that while she was safe now, the past was still the hiding place of what she feared most.

She heard the sound of the wind and it consoled her. But the past wouldn't remain dead. She closed her eyes as she remembered her mother crying, screaming at her through her glass faceplate to run, to *flee*. The memory conjured up a long-forgotten terror, the knowledge that THEY were following, that they were close behind. She could hear the sound of her mother screaming. She could hear the ear-piercing shrillness of the weapons they used as they chased down her parents and the others. Even now the sounds were so vivid they made her skin crawl. She found herself rubbing her arms even though the evening was reasonably warm.

Her mind fought the confusing memories after that, memories of the night when she hid among the metal towers. She waited for them to find her. She knew what it meant, to be found; father and mother had told her. She remembered her fear, her tears, the feeling of being lost and all alone. Even now she could still hear the sound of the engines, the noise of their flying machines. The cold blue pinpoints of light that were their hunters' eyes. She couldn't forget the screams, the noise, the thunder of her heart pounding in her ears.

She remembered the sudden silence, and the deepening of night. An embrace of cold she had never before known, born from a bleak desert plain overlooked by emotionless stars billions of miles away. She remembered the dawn of the next day, how the light revealed to her young eyes the littered bodies of her family. She remembered, only vaguely, the few days she had spent, staring at them and not knowing what to do or where to go. She remembered the sole figure moving over the dune towards where she lay hidden.

Burning Lands 15

She blinked, her heart now cold and slow and quiet. Her eyes were heavy. She was too tired to cry anymore, so she drifted off into sleep.

The man, who had been watching silently on his side of the camp, sighed softly. He stared at her, wondering what it was that she always thought about before going to sleep. He snorted, clearing his nose of the annoying sand that ringed his nostrils from the past few days of hunting and gathering. He went to sleep as well.

Johnny sprang up suddenly, his eyes instinctively fluttering wide to take in the panoramic view their perch among the crags afforded them.

The night was dark, the broad open sky dappled with the glittering stars of distant constellations, lending the sweeping dunes and sporadic islands of rock of the desert their weak blue radiance. He waited, silent and still. Something had awakened him; his senses, sharpened by years of living alone in the hostile desert, had made him as jittery and skittish as a sand mouse, and even in sleep his ears were listening for the sounds of danger.

He remained still for several long moments, but the sky gave up no secrets, it seemed eager to lull him back to sleep. But his survival instinct was stronger than that. He sensed that, moments ago, the horizon had been alive, his acute ears picking up on a suspiciously lingering quiet, like the kind that sometimes follows thunder in a summer storm. But nothing called back, and while the surrounding miles of sand remained dark and dead, something about that distant, thin horizon seemed... ominous.

Johnny looked over at the girl, who lay there sleeping. A tight frown showed on her small face, and her legs coiled and curled as she slowly twisted and thrashed in her sleep. A nightmare of some kind had her in its grip, and wasn't ready to let her go. Johnny's eyebrows, until now arched in alarm, flattened as he reached over to stroke the girl's matted, sweaty hair in an effort to calm her. As his fingers moved towards her head, he suddenly snatched them back as the sky reverberated with a sound that, while distorted, echoed across the desert from a long way away... and to the east.

Moving on instinct Johnny dropped back down and rolled to one side, reaching for his musket, but by the time he had it in his hands it began to occur to him that the sound must have been ten miles or more away. He still held the gun in one hand, but ceased struggling to uncork the powder horn to load the thing. Instead he quieted again, held his breath, and listened. The sound was vague, indistinct. A *pop-pop-popping* noise. Moments later, a low rumble. A full minute passed, but he didn't move.

A high, drawn-out shrieking sound echoed in the darkness, one so unfamiliar that he almost leapt from his perch to hide among the rocks, only staying his ground because he wouldn't, couldn't dare leave the girl asleep and alone. The sound was alien, cold, mechanical and as it gained in pitch, seemed to fade into the night sky like a wisp of smoke swept up and away by a quiet wind.

Moments later the horizon was silent again. His eyes scanned for lights, for fires, for signs of anyone or anything approaching. His ears listened for the sounds of predators, animal and man, skulking about in the night. He spotted and heard nothing.

The strange sounds, perhaps some short, fierce battle played out just beyond the horizon, did not repeat themselves. Whoever had lost the struggle in the darkness was gone now; too late to be saved. The killers, whose cold and alien shrieks still haunted his mind, had moved on, roving in another direction after the small human prey they had originally been sent after to hunt.

Johnny batted his eyes for the first time in minutes; he'd been staring and his eyes hurt. The girl's sleep was less frantic now; her breathing seemed normal and her legs ceased writhing. The wind returned, gently and moved her blond hair about her forehead, but she slept soundly. Johnny laid back down and gripped one of the skins around him, eager to forget what he had heard and return to the comforting escape that sleep alone provided him.

The girl woke up the next day, the sun shining brightly overhead. She squinted, a natural response to waking in the light and rolled onto her back, her body bathed by the glow of the burning sun. Her friend was already awake, sitting high up on their rock. He was working on the tanned hide, his sparse bits of hair blowing in the warm morning wind.

She rubbed her numb mouth and nose as she got up, listening to the desert's silence. Only the man's hands moving, rubbing a porous rock over a stretched hide, made any noise until she decided to yawn. The man looked with a warm grin as he saw her rise. He sat up and held up the hides. He was beginning what would be a small-sized garment for her. His face beamed with silent, muted pride. She smiled. She moved over to the dead campfire, and fished about for the kindling pouch. The man motioned wordlessly to a nearby rock. She lifted it and pulled the kindling pouch from beneath it.

She had come to realize, over time, her friend's strange set of values. Over the years, he had taught her many things. For survival. Together the two of them had managed to make life easier for one another. He had saved her life by taking her under his wing; she had helped him, made his life easier by being a second set of hands.

They collected dew from under rocks in the desert each morning. He had taught her that. And she somehow intuitively knew, at times, exactly where to dig to find water beneath the surface. That always made him stare and wonder. He could use the ramshackle gun to acquire food when he went away into the desert for hours, even days. She was never sure what strange desert creature they ate; he always returned with the meat well chopped up and skinned, bundled up on his back, and from afar he looked comical like an overburdened, hunchback butcher coming to market.

She had learned to recognize what was useful and what was not. Although sometimes she lingered over a familiar piece of junk they found amid the desert sands (a bottle cap, the remains of a plastic doll, etc.) she never kept anything too conspicuous or too heavy. She knew enough to stay out of a fight whenever there was one, whether with the hideous animals of the desert or the tortured beasts that sometimes crept towards the firelight as night fell, their eyes glowing violet through the darkness, and who had to be killed if for no other reason that to put them out of their misery.

She had never really seen anyone else since they had met so many years ago. Her friend was always on guard; her own senses almost always presaged the approach of danger. He was often able to kill potential dangers, far off on the horizon, with his muzzle-loading musket. She never really saw the bodies of those he felled; he did much of the scavenging alone, cautious, keeping her away and out of sight in case of ambush or the unexpected. He was her protector from both danger and the violence that was necessary for their survival.

It had dawned on her some time ago that they had been following the course of a dry river for a long time, a dead waterway winding its way lazily through what seemed to be endless crags and desert. She had wondered at the length of such a waterway, until it became clear that they were simply moving up and down the same river for many months, perhaps years. She had wondered why Johnny stayed to this relatively small area and at times it almost felt like they were skirting the edge of something lying just beyond the horizon, staying out of sight but close enough for Johnny to sense its movement, hear its heartbeat... whatever it was. She, of course, heard nothing. But perhaps Johnny knew what lay out of sight and went there on his hunting trips and never told her about the wonders over the next hill. She wished she could understand him and at times even wished she could slip away to find out what lay beyond the limits of the dry river and the few miles surrounding it. Was there life out there? Were there other people somewhere, anywhere? Who were they; what were they like?

She trusted in Johnny's instincts, however, and was afraid of the world without him, and was content with the life he had chosen to share with her.

She started at the slow-burning kindling with bits of stone. She looked up at him. Johnny was flaying away, concentrating on his work, his swarthy body gleaming under the brilliant sun.

Suddenly she felt an assault of primal fear deep inside her. Her heart seemed to flutter; she found she couldn't move. Her head darted up as a distant sound erupted across the wind-swept desert sands. The roar of *engines*. Cheap, salvaged, oil-guzzling internal combustion engines.

Johnny looked up as if taken totally by surprise. Nothing harmful had ever come to him by surprise since he had met the girl. She had always known beforehand. He didn't even look afraid. He just squinted, staring off into the desert. He might have seen something, being on a higher perch than she, but he didn't have time to react to whatever it was that he saw.

There was a sudden, unexpected peal of thunder, but, oddly, the sky was clear. The girl screamed a tearful shriek.

To her, Johnny, sitting atop the rock, went into slow motion. She saw his head *explode;* the shot entered the front of his forehead and tore out the back. His skull shattered completely from the immense and sudden force of whatever struck him, showering her with a cascade of blood and bits of sharp bone before the tatters blew away as he jerked momentarily like a crazed rag doll. The upper part of his head was gone but his body still moved.

In a short moment the simple man, her one and only friend, fell back off the rock, dead. With a horrible sound his corpse landed in a heavy heap at the foot of the boulder, dragging with it the leathery buckskin he had been preparing for her. He collapsed atop his belongings, the pistol, the strange plaque and some of his own crude tools from a life spent among the sands. The girl screamed, crying, her eyes welling with tears and her throat tightening up like a vise. She stared at the remaining half of his broken face, her mind unable to comprehend what had just happened. *Johnny was gone.*

After the shot, the roar of engines became louder and sand billowed all around as unseen machines created an artificial storm with their noisy approach. An old pre-Fall motorcycle, rusty and black with oil and grease, covered in a patchwork of shaggy hides and wicked barbed blades, roared past only a dozen paces away, kicking up a cloud of sand and tiny rocks as it went. The girl stayed low, crying vainly to herself, holding her friend's dead body to hers, in a sad and futile attempt to cradle it from further harm and keep whatever life was left from leaking away.

Another roar, as even more cycles came racing by. She tore her head away from Johnny's corpse and looked up as one of the motorcycles raced close by her, its sole occupant firing a sawed-off shotgun right in her direction. His very appearance chilled her to the bone; she had never seen such a man before and even through the heavy cloak of gun smoke and dust she was staggered by the brutality so clearly visible in his face.

It was a man, maybe only seventeen or eighteen years old but to her just as much a monster as the unmentionable things that crawled along miserably in the desert in the hours before dawn. This man's face was completely hairless, bald, and he was covered in weird paint and markings, scars and jagged pits that spoke of past battles with others of his kind. His eyes were wild and sharp like the blades adorning his bike. Despite his savage appearance he was smiling with unbridled glee, jagged ugly teeth that had probably never been cleaned even once in his life and a careless grin splitting his face from cheek to cheek.

He fired in her direction again like a frenzied madman but he was a poor shot. The girl screamed, instinctively dodging aside. The buckshot missed widely and instead blasted sand from the boulder, leaving hot white gouges and flecks where it struck stone. As she fled for cover among the irregular rocks all around, the roars of the oily, metal machines seemed to fade from her keen ears. She stayed down, struggling to calm herself, hoping she might go unnoticed if she could stop her lungs from heaving and her heart from pounding.

There were some shouts. She heard deep, echoing voices calling out across the sands through the artificial haze of disturbed dust and swirling exhaust. With a combination of dread and curiosity she found the nerve to peek, to get a glimpse of this savage pack of beasts who had come and turned her life on its head.

The motorcycles had stopped roaring; only one or two raced in the distance as if prowling the outermost perimeter of their camp to see if there were more victims to hunt. The lead motorcyclist crept up the side of a nearby dune and came abruptly to a halt in front of two tall and very different men, who plodded slowly down the slope with guns relaxed.

The first of the two men approaching the camp walked with a heavy, plodding stride, his enormous feet trudging through the grainy dune of sand. He was completely bald like the motorcycle raiders, his skull burned to a deep tan by the sun. His almond-shaped eyes, squinting against the hard desert blaze, stared straight ahead with a no-nonsense glare, blinking now and again only to prevent themselves from drying out. But he was certainly different, his head was unusually small, his eyes were pale and viscid, without discernable pupils.

The sight of those eyes, even from such a distance, made the girl sink back for a moment, for fear he might somehow see her. Without knowing where his eyes were looking, it seemed as if he could see everything at once. In her eyes he looked less like a human and more like a freak. A monster. But her curiosity and fear kept her glued to the spot. She continued to stare with morbid fascination at these newly-arrived bringers of death.

Unlike his microcephalic head, the hulking bounty man's entire torso was broad like a barrel and his big, knotted arms hung loosely at his sides. Over his chest he had a covering of dirt-caked metal ringlets with trailing tassels along its edges where sleeves might have once been. He wore old stitched pants, mottled and dusty, over his powerful legs. A leather glove adorned one grossly misshapen hand, missing two of its fingers, while the other nursed a big black rifle. A belt of gleaming brass bullets was worn straight across his barrel chest along with a collection of knives, blades, and implements sharpened for the sole purpose of killing.

The second man, walking just a few strides behind his companion and more than a full foot shorter, wore a long, heavy overcoat of some indiscernible black material that fell almost to his ankles. It was soiled by dust and sand, but looked relatively sound for its apparent age. This latter figure's pants were black as well, bound together by hooks and pins; they made a noticeable noise as he walked, for they were tightly worn about his legs and waist, constrained by a pair of leather holsters hung low on his hips.

This second man wore a floppy, wide-brimmed fedora hat on his head, beneath which could be seen disheveled, bone-white hair that blew back from his face when caught by the desert breeze. A dark scarf covered his neck and, in fact, it looked like all of his body, except for his face, was meticulously and deliberately shielded from the sun. Where his skin showed, it was freckled and burned badly. His glare was hard and unmoved by the sight of bloodshed around him, his distant and detached eyes disguised behind a pair of black sunglasses. He walked alongside his companion with an almost "tired" gait, like a game hunter winding down at the end of an exhausting safari.

The two men came right up to the mounted rider, who revved his motorcycle's engine with a cheerful, carefree laugh as if signaling an end to a long and victorious hunt. From her hiding spot, the girl could hear them clearly. Voices. *She hadn't heard human voices for so long!*

"That's our *ghoul*," said the ghostly man with the fedora hat in a low, even voice, looking off in the direction of the dead body of Johnny, his glance only momentarily stopping on the corpse's one remaining eye and its lifeless stare.

"Finally caught the mother-fucker," the man on the cycle shouted over the roar of its engine.

The man with the hat opened the breach of his rifle, which was still smoking from the large-bore rifle shot that he had fired only moments before.

"You are one bad ass mother-fucking crack shot, man," repeated the mounted warrior, shaking his head in apparent disbelief. The putt-putt of his cycle's engine was now a low purr, but his whole body and posture seemed ready to race off at a moment's notice, as a panther might look when stopping just momentarily on a tree branch.

The man with the dusty hat just blew the powder remnants from the rifle bore and reloaded the empty chamber with a fresh round. He played with the single brass shell, from the first and only shot as if weighing the implications of his actions, but his eyes betrayed nothing, not pride, boasting, or even regret. The strange shades seemed to mask even their icy color from sight.

"That's..." mumbled his bald companion, counting on his few remaining fingers and speaking in a deep, rumbling pitch, "... four gallons, Buddy."

Buddy, the savage warrior squatting on the war-motorcycle, just laughed again. His face was rough and coarse, his features a conglomerate mix of the various ethnicities of the angry invaders who had despoiled this land generations ago, leaving their blood to mingle with the survivors. The girl knew nothing of the new races of the wasteland, of course, so to her his dark eyes and skin were merely curious. Unknown to her, like many other inhabitants of this part of the world, he could trace his ancestry back to the great foreign armies that once invaded this land, but interbreeding among their survivors left his ethnic heritage mixed, and indistinct.

Buddy flicked his dyed-green tongue out of his mouth imitating a hissing desert snake, his wild eyes rolling around in some weird display of excitement or simply drug-induced euphoria. The hunt was a prolonged ecstasy, the death a satisfying climax, but he had played no part in the kill and was maybe now regretting letting others do the job.

When no recognition was forthcoming from the mounted raider, the bald giant looked over at the albino in the long coat and fedora, then back again to the cyclist.

"Don't fuck with us, Buddy. We had a deal. We track down that ghoul, we get four gallons."

The arrogant kid on the motorcycle just smiled, enjoying this game tremendously. Keeping two seasoned bounty-men dangling on the end of a rope gave him a thrill, a rush. He bobbed his head about, as if considering, pretending the entire affair was in fact in his hands and hoping the two renowned hunters would ask, no, *beg* him to honor his people's end of the bargain.

"You wouldn't want me to go to your boss and claim you tried to cheat us, now would you, Buddy?" the ogrish man continued calmly, his flat voice a toad-like baritone. Buddy just looked past the hulking giant and to the silent man in the hat, summing him up, looking him up and down. He smiled, and his eyes darted back to the hulk.

"The water's back at Oasis. You want it, you're going to have to come back with us."

"Aw, damn," the big bald man started, "they *never* carry it with them."

"Alright," the man in the hat said finally, his voice smooth and velvety like wind through a reed, "fair enough." In a calculated show of good faith he lifted his rifle and rested it over one shoulder.

The girl looked away from the conversing men and felt about for any kind of weapon. Suddenly she heard footsteps nearby. Turning, she saw another raider just a few feet away, searching through what had been Johnny's belongings. This one wore some mangy pelt on his head as if it would hide his total lack of hair. His hairless eyebrows were pierced with chipped brass rings. His muscled and lithe body, leathery from the beating sun and riding shirtless on the back of a rumbling hog, was covered only in a web of decorative leather bands and belts, buckled about with metal snaps and clasps.

His tight leather pants, stitched with copper wire, shifted and stretched as he trudged into the camp.

Holding a much more primitive powder musket in hand, the newly-arrived raider immediately kicked the body of her beloved friend, simply out of malice. She looked away as it flopped about, as dead as any carcass left to rot on the plains. The man snorted deeply, and spat out a huge stream of phlegm-tinged saliva onto the lifeless corpse. He then used his black, dirt-encrusted boots to sift the canteens and other belongings, as if afraid to catch disease from rummaging through them.

She closed her eyes, hoping she would go unnoticed. But etched into her mind were the heart-breaking images of Johnny's body, kicked around like trash and spat upon with some unjustifiable hatred.

Suddenly, the man shouted. "Hey, boss! We got a musket! And an old-style pistol! And some rounds!" The engine roars finally ceased altogether. They were all around her now, dismounted and searching the crags and boulders where they had made camp. She heard some howls and laughter, some shouts and garbled commands, voices varying in pitch, near and far.

The searcher took the pistol from its holster much the same way Johnny had done so many years ago when she watched him loot the bodies of her pursuers. He didn't see the metal plaque that was now partly buried under the body, too consumed by the elegant craftsmanship of the strange pistol. She began to cry. She couldn't help herself.

The man with the pelt spun around. "Holy *fuckin'* shit..." he gasped. He saw, lying among the boulders, just a few feet from the bloody body, a girl, weeping. The other figures were now approaching across the sand. She looked up, staring, tearing up uncontrollably.

The man's eyes, pinched and narrow, were as alien as any she had ever seen. The mongrel looked at her, and dropped his gun. He fell to one knee, his hand wandering to his crotch to start undoing his leather pants.

The girl didn't know what he was going to do but stared with instinctive horror and trepidation as he slowly approached, a vile smile growing on his face, baring the yellow and brown ruins of what had once been teeth. His arms opened, his hands came forward, as if forming a "net" before him from which she couldn't flee.

She screamed as she felt his calloused hands grab her, violently, yanking her from her place amid the rocks and throwing her brutally down onto the hard-packed sand of the camp, just inches from the dead body of her friend.

"*Fuck yeah...*" she heard him gasp breathlessly, as if muttering aloud would alert the others and force him to share his "prize".

She cried in horror, not really understanding *why* he wanted her so badly but seeing in his eyes a crazed, violent lust that scared her to the bone. His jagged teeth, his wild, predatory eyes... the look impressed on his hard, unfamiliar face was terrifying.

Suddenly she heard a "crack" and a shrill cry of pain. Then a short scuffle. "Get off her, you dumb son-of-a-bitch." The voice was calm, cold, calculated. It didn't seem angry or surprised. Or even caring. She opened her eyes.

The searcher was wincing in pain, nursing his hand, cursing profusely. The bald giant stood there, watching the cretin retreat quickly on all fours and out of sight. The giant turned and looked straight at her, passing her an unblinking glare with those colorless white eyes. They were like the eyes of those radiated desert wolves, the ones that wander out of the desert's heart dying of hunger and thirst and insane from the heat. She felt a chill from his glance as if he were more animal than man and that he and the others were closing in for the final kill. She stared up at him, inching away, hands scrambling to find a rock, a bone or some other implement with which to defend herself.

The second man, the shorter one with the brimmed hat, was also standing there, watching the injured raider retreat from the presence of his gigantic companion, stumbling in agony and muttering curses as he went. This latter man's look was one of unemotional assessment. His eyes, staring through shadowy colored glass, moved over to her with a quick, passing glance. He played with a toothpick between his teeth, his tongue moving about unconsciously as he thought.

"A *survivor*." The man in the hat finally said flatly.

"You *trash*..." the bald giant spat, chasing after the raider and kicking him in the rear as he scrambled away, still trying to get to his feet. There was a cry of pain as he rolled a few more feet away down the rocky slope.

The man in the hat stared down at her, shaking his head. He finally called out to the man on the motorcycle, who was now walking happily across the sand, his musket draped over one shoulder.

"Look's like you hit it, Buddy," he said.

The bald motorcycle rider, hearing that, quickened his step and came quickly over, his bare chest glistening with sweat and colorful tattoos. He clapped his hands and shouted with glee when he laid eyes on the girl.

"No fuckin' WAY!" he cried out. "The ghoul had *toys!*" The girl pulled away from them, up against the rock. In her mind she kept thinking, *I have to get away.*

The man in the hat looked at her though, still using his tongue to play with that toothpick, not moving any closer or further. He reminded her of an iguana, dry rasping tongue licking back and forth over its lips.

The bald motorcycle rider, realizing his luck, turned and kicked the pained and retreating would-be rapist across the jaw. There was a final cry as the other man collapsed in an unconscious heap.

Buddy turned back and jogged over to the appraising rifleman's side. He looked the girl over, a smile of obvious delight creeping over his face. He turned to the man in the hat.

"Hell, Rider," he said, clenching his fists together happily, "Slug's gonna fuckin' have a cow when he sees this! A fuckin' *kid*, man. She's healthy... and she ain't ugly."

He reached out and grabbed the girl's jaw despite her attempts to flee, looking her soft face over with appreciating eyes.

"She's fuckin' *gorgeous!*"

The man in the hat, *Rider*, ignored the raider's comments and looked over at the hulk, whom she surmised was either his friend or simply a professional peer. "What's this kind of thing worth?"

The giant frowned, considering. He still seemed to be looking at the girl as if she were an object. Barter goods.

"Dunno. Slug?" the giant wondered. "He'd probably pay a lot. I dunno... thirty gallons? She's a little young for his purposes, though. Needs to ripen a few more years."

"Yeah..." Buddy, the motor biker, considered with a little disappointment, pointing to parts of her to indicate her undeveloped shape. "But *laozong* don't mind waiting. Call it an investment for the future."

Rider just stared at the girl through narrow squinting eyes. "Raise her to be his own..." he murmured.

"This is it, Rider," said Buddy, "this chick's gonna be the key to me being *numero uno* in the Oasis. You wait and see..."

"You keep dreamin', Buddy," Rider said, but though the words suggested he was familiar, almost "friendly" with Buddy, there was no sense of camaraderie or friendship whatsoever in his tone.

"You fuckin' bounty hunters are all the same," Buddy said with impatience, motioning for the distant bikers to come over, the sound of their roaring engines growing louder, "you don't see the big picture."

"Oh yeah, and what's that?" asked the hulking bald bounty hunter, almost laughing.

"The big picture is this, my man, *civil-i-zation*. Slug's draggin' us into a new age! The water merchants from down south are bringing new ideas to this land, a new way of living and people are *listening*. You can either be a part of it or be squashed by it. We're gonna make Oasis a trade town like Tucumcari, gentlemen. A motherfuckin' *nexus*."

"A *nexus?*" asked Rider, smiling for once. "I didn't know you knew words like that, Buddy." The smile was suddenly demeaning, patronizing.

"Aw, fuck you, Rider," Buddy said, almost like he was a boy pleading to an older brother. "You know, people like you guys fuckin' make me sick. You guys are worse than glue-sniffin' scavs, man. Fuck, if it were up to me, I'd say fuck your four gallons. Cap you guys right now. Less fuckin' mouths to feed."

The girl tried to fight as one of the bikers got off his bike and ran over to tie her up tightly with a length of plastic cord. The three men walked off, talking. The girl was an afterthought now.

"Won't have to worry about that," said Rider, staring off towards the horizon, "we'll be on our way soon enough. Just as soon as we conclude business with your boss."

There was a weird, metallic, gypsy-like music reverberating through the hot dry air as the hunting expedition returned that evening. It was approaching dusk and the dwindling vegetation ringing the settlement of Oasis provided cool relief from the merciless sun, even as it began to dip low in the sky. Instead of lush trees, a forest of white, yellow, and tan-colored tents lay sprawled about the settlement, clustered around a small body of still, glass-green water. Laughter and loud boisterous noise came from nearly every direction, weaving in and out of tents and the narrow alleys between them. A few malnourished goats sat in makeshift pens here and there in the few spaces left, their fences clumsily erected as if simply thrown together. Large groups of bald men wandered about this sprawling camp and if not for the drunken laughter and the strange music, one might mistake the entire settlement for some religious sanctuary by the numbers of bald men and the sole gender (male) seen on its streets. But these weren't members of some strange sect and their drinking, fighting, and crude tongue gave the place a violent and despicable energy.

Ironically the place may have once been a monastery of some sort. Though the buildings were gone, leaving only scattered stands of stone where pillars had been, a large statue of the Buddha loomed over the small lake at the town's center. Whether it had been here originally or had been erected by foreign invaders from the East, or had simply been built by survivors of the Fall seeking to emulate the gods of the past, could never be known. Wind-worn by the ages, the stone figure no longer looked serene and contemplative but rather toady and grotesque; its fine face, arms and extended belly were smoothed to a round shape so that now it merely looked like a featureless heap of bones and flesh on a pedestal, forever awaiting the worship and adoration of the desert's miserable denizens.

Whatever it once was, on the Twisted Earth this place was called a town, a den for people and while it was dangerous out in the desert, it could be even more so here in the shade among the jackals.

The girl finally woke up, secured on the back of one of the motorcycles, racing into the tent camp. Disoriented from being upside-down, she only had a moment to bat her eyes to fight the sand lashing at her face before she fell to the ground in a heap, unceremoniously flung off the cycle just outside one of the large tents.

Rider and his huge companion, "Tank", walked casually into the settlement, shielding their eyes from the setting sun and the clear sky. They walked confidently, their rifles put back into sheaths on their backs and as they approached, large groups of natives (raider warriors and their enslaved captives) began to gather as if the two men were soldiers returning from a long campaign.

Buddy walked in front of them like some kind of safari guide, but they already knew this town well; it was the camp of the *Scorpions*, one of the more significant bands of desert raiders now fighting for control of their particular corner of the American desert. Sure there were bigger, more vicious gangs out there like the *Doomriders* and the *Ravagers*, but the Scorpions were neither a mad cult nor a gang obsessed with conquering the world. Small enough to go unnoticed by their bigger "brothers", but large enough to make themselves known to the weaker inhabitants of the land, theirs was a commanding presence. And in recent months, they had become good bosses to work for as well. There was newfound wealth here, and wherever there was wealth there was always work. The two of them, Rider and Tank, had been here ever since they got word that Slug, the Scorpion's "king", was hiring to do away with a particular *ghoul* that had been preying on their trail scouts, leaving only scavenged and portioned bodies behind. It had been a minor problem for years, but now apparently Slug had wealth enough to lure bounty men to scratch that annoying little itch, as well as the desire to do so in the name of helping make the "Forbidden Lands" a safer place.

The *Forbidden Lands*. This was a region of what was once fertile plains skirting the eastern foothills of the Rocky Mountains, which the people of the south called the *Wei Shan*, from northern Wyoming to New Mexico, having turned almost entirely into a desert wasteland in the long generations since the Fall. It was here, to these plains, that the hardiest survivors of the Great Holocaust of Man had fled in the early years after the war, hoping to escape the boiling fires of the ruined cities of the east. They may have escaped death by fire and destruction, but radiation and disease tracked them across the miles to this land as well and tainted and changed them where it found them. Over time the land, too, became withered and corrupted, scarred from the toll the Final War took on the world, until all that was left was an unending sea of sand, its grains pushed and blown in unbroken cycles by an ever-present, angry wind.

Without civilization and law to guide them through that early age of darkness, humanity broke down; the mechanisms of justice and order ground into dust and forgotten. In the Forbidden Lands those who would hope to survive learned to live violently and stay mobile, adapting to an almost entirely nomadic existence. Their early ancestors learned the hard way that a law is only as strong as the man enforcing it. Even the land they had chosen to make their refuge from the devastated east seemed poised against them; the desert was ever-changing, devouring landmarks and burying the mistakes of the ancient past or revealing them suddenly like momentary glimpses into a forgotten world... before swallowing them up again.

Brutal towns rose and fell almost overnight in these hard lands, and nothing lasted long. "Trust" had become an impossible luxury; as such, communities remained close-knit and seldom reached out to others for more than a short-lived gathering to barter for the things vital to their survival. To facilitate these shaky trades, family groups (clans, tribes, and gangs) might come together briefly to erect temporary "trade villages" at convenient meeting places, like old crossroads, dry riverbeds or the rare oasis. These trade villages were often an uncanny reflection of the harsh and adventurous people who inhabited the Forbidden Lands. Their shoddy buildings rose quickly, their bazaars burned brightly in the night with torchlight, music, and laughter, and more often than not the entire settlement vanished by night's end in the fashion of a circus moving on by dawn. But during their short life, these towns became true havens for the desert's survivors, with drink passed around freely, women shared and traded, and violent gladiatorial games undertaken with a drunken obsession.

These were the lands of savages. Sure civilization in some rudimentary form did exist on the Twisted Earth but only outside this barbarian frontier. To the south it was a different story. There lay the great trade route of the Far Desert, a precariously thin vein connecting east and west, threading its way through the shadow of glowing ruined cities and the battlefields of ages past. New life was springing up along this vast artery; villages, towns, and fortresses belonging to the new powers rising to dominate the far ends of the wasteland. Some of these were merchants, others idealists with a cause and still many more simply marauding raiders adhering to the age-old adage that "might makes right".

But Rider's thoughts weren't with the geography or politics of the lands he lived in but rather circled around this newest trade town, "Oasis", which Slug and his Scorpions were trying to establish as a *permanent* settlement in the Forbidden Lands.

Rider took the toothpick from his mouth and spat. It looked no different than the many hells he had seen before. He watched as two men ran by, one chasing the other with his penis in hand. There was a loud outbreak of laughter as the two men raced off between two tents under the blazing sun, disappearing into the underbrush. Slave being chased by his master? Such things were common now, in this world where there were no universal laws; the land being one great big prison, with the strong enforcing their own rules, where the weaker sex, namely women, were a rare commodity to come by. In their absence, as it had been throughout history, men turned to each other to appease their animal nature.

He heard a chopping noise from above, which turned his attention from the raucous laughter of the natives. Several of the raiders were climbing the tall trees, wearing only canvas pants and cutting down miserable fruit and juice-bearing leaves with machetes and hatchets. The raiders who lived here liked to believe a veritable industry was growing in this place and it was true that Oasis was fruitful. It was just so damned depraved, wretched, moldy and sickly from within. Rider wouldn't stay long, not if he had any say in the matter.

Rider heard the sound of animals from the goat pens behind one of the tents, and of course, the pervasive gypsy-like music created by metal machine parts strummed and banged by primitive musicians in the large open-air tents set up by the edge of the watering hole from which the town got its name.

Men from all over ran up to the pile that was the girl. She screamed as the men gathered around her. Some hooted and howled; others watched, in closely-clustered groups, whispering conspiratorially amongst themselves and sneering at her.

Buddy shouted angrily, "FOR THE LAOZONG!" The assemblage scattered at once like roaches scrambling for cover as the lights come on. She felt Buddy grab her painfully by the arm and drag her to the shaded entry flap of the largest tent in camp.

"Well, well, well," came the rumbling voice of a taller warrior, standing with two other guards in front of the tent. She looked up and saw this new face, waiting there with a broad smile to greet her.

The warrior was bald like the other raiders of the camp; his chest was bare too. He looked built like a prize fighter, albeit one covered in many coiling scars and the puffed-out welts where countless old stab wounds had healed in the past. For all his battle injuries, he was not crippled and his body was in tremendous shape, preserved and maintained for the sole purpose of fighting and killing. Certainly born and bred for war, he wasn't like the others, who seemed like crazed and unsupervised adolescents. This one was calm and sure of himself, jaded and cold-blooded, a much more mature version of the thugs and punks in camp and, in a twisted way, the model of what each yearned to become should he survive long enough. One look at this man was to see the future of the drunken killers that made up the ranks of Oasis' ruling gang.

He wore old pants, torn and patched over and over, with a powerful Ancient-era pistol hanging around his hip. He bore a leather whip in his strong, scarred hands, holding it like a prisoner who had just taken it from his captors and would never willingly relinquish it. He had the lingering traces of past beatings etched into his back and chest, but these only seemed to make him tougher.

This new man, an underling of Oasis' ruling master but in reality an unrecognized leader of men in his own right, looked his raider cousin, Buddy, in the eyes before slowly shifting over to the girl.

Olive-skinned with gray-brown eyes, the champion of these thugs stood taller than the others, by several inches, drawing with his height a certain palpable aura of superiority to which even she yielded to. There was something overwhelming about him, a malevolent magnetism. With just a passing glance she was reduced to the status of an object, and despite her own sense of worth she suddenly felt insignificant in his presence and unable to speak.

"Let me through, Valero," Buddy contested, pulling the girl forward with a start. "Check out what I got for Slug."

Valero continued to look passively at the girl, the broad grin unchanging as his gaze slowly fixed on her tears, her frightened face. He must have seen girls like her before. The thought chilled her. How many captives had this man simply smiled at as they were dragged to their unmentionable fates? He didn't look impressed and worse, he didn't even look thrilled to see her like the younger warriors around him. He may as well have been a eunuch, since he bore the same terrible and unfaltering countenance, a detachment from the drunken lustiness that possessed his underlings.

Valero's gray-brown eyes gradually moved from her and looked at Buddy; he snorted as if to say, *big deal*. Instead he looked over to Rider who was just now casually approaching with Tank a few feet to his side. There seemed to be more interest there as he regarded the bounty hunters.

"Tank and Rider," he addressed them, almost gallantly, though his voice was noticeably icy, "I hear you've managed to get our ghoul?"

Rider motioned with his hand and Tank pulled the blanket off the fly-infested head taken at the site.

The girl stared at the head and while there was a deep pain at the loss, a cold realization spread through her. Yes, there *were* more men in the world; she had wondered what remained concealed over the horizon and why Johnny had kept them at arm's length from whatever lay beyond. Now that she was here, she knew why she and Johnny had lived in hiding these past few years.

Valero moved over, as the guards all around watched like a band of thieves ready to betray their "guests" at a moment's notice. He completely ignored the face, unconcerned about the kind human being to whom it had once belonged to, his only interest lying in the huge hole in the skull.

"What caliber of gun did you use, Rider?" Valero asked quietly, his voice even and level. The shot didn't impress him. Rider shifted his weight, trying to judge Valero. He was loathe to say too much about his capabilities as a "hunter", but Valero's presence was... intimidating nonetheless, and jerked a response from him.

"A big one," he said vaguely.

Valero turned, finishing his casual appraisal of the corpse. He looked at Rider. Suddenly his voice was amiable. "You know, Rider, I'm something like you. You know, a little education. I know... a little about... *before*."

Rider watched him with calculated eyes. *An educated raider?* No such thing. More like a dangerous liar.

Rider remained still as Valero paced around him slowly and with enough confidence that he even turned his back once or twice.

"Four-forty-four," Valero finally said, answering for Rider. *Had he snatched that out of thin air? If so, he was good...*

Valero looked back at the corpse. "Did you find anything on the ghoul?"

Rider shrugged and shook his head slowly. *Now where was this going?*

Valero raised an interested eyebrow, as if that meant something, then looked to Buddy, who confirmed with a wordless nod. "Then how do you know this is our ghoul?" Valero asked.

Rider and Tank both turned and looked at Valero in surprise. "How do you know it *isn't?*" Tank asked, almost insulted.

"Because," Valero began coolly, "four of our scouts have gone missing in the past few months and if this ghoul was responsible he probably would have taken something from them; their weapons and ammunition, or some token or another."

"Maybe he did," Tank said. "He *had* a musket."

"Not one of ours," Buddy interjected, suddenly picking up on his boss' line of reasoning.

"He would have at least taken a better-quality weapon, given the chance," Valero explained. There was something to what Valero was saying, but both bounty hunters were eager to be paid and leave this wretched place, and eagerly wanted to seal the deal.

"We searched for weeks along the edge of the Burning Desert and his was the only trail we found out there," Tank said, slight anger easily discernable in his voice. "If there was a person behind the disappearance of your men it was this guy, right *here*." He kicked the heavy head slightly to signify just which "guy" he was referring to.

"Look," Buddy blurted out impatiently, breaking the tension. He motioned to the girl, as if to remind everyone there was something more important to discuss. "The laozong's gonna want to see this, Valero. Can I go or what?"

Valero turned and stared at the comparatively weak, narrow-limbed and miserable "Buddy". It was like a career soldier looking down at a draftee. There was loathing in that long, penetrating stare but he finally chuckled, casually, letting the previous matter lie.

"Alright," Valero said, backing away from his veiled accusation. "Tank. Rider. Slug will see you."

Valero smiled at Rider expectantly, a canine gleam in his grin that Rider had seen before. It was the look of a prideful man who wanted to make an enemy even if there was no reason for conflict... exercise his muscles, prove his dominance, remain on top.

No matter how hard they might try, civilization wouldn't sit well with these types, Rider thought to himself. Slug was re-inventing himself and in the process forcing the Scorpions to do the same. He had grandiose dreams of turning Oasis into a respectable city where traders would come, but murderous scumbags like him don't, *can't,* change that easily. Slug was trying to remodel his army of rapists and thugs overnight and force upon them the mantle of civility. Valero, a career killer, itched for war; it was in his blood, it was the only sensation left that excited him. Slug's new vision was his antithesis, an affront to his being.

Rider knew Valero, or at least his type. After spending just three short weeks here, he had come to know the deal. Valero was smart. Considering that Valero had hinted as much, he suspected the veteran raider was probably not actually from *this* community, but more likely from another. Some called them "xenophobes", but those who couldn't pronounce that big word simply called them the "last vestiges", those who came from the few communities descended from those-who-came-before, little changed but unable to stem the tide of what was becoming of the world. Those few scattered groups of holdouts, who clung religiously to some scrap of the way things were (be it the technology to extract water from the air, or some moldy old collection of books) fell one by one with each passing year and little if anything was now left of the world of the past.

Then again, perhaps he was just another desert raider who got his hands on some ancient texts and studied up, hoping to lord it over others.

But Valero was also very dangerous, a fact Rider didn't even try to deny. In the wasteland bravado is good, it keeps you alive, keeps the mangy killers in place. But a gunslinger also had to recognize there was always someone better than him; hell, that was an age-old axiom! And Valero was just too damn sharp, formally educated or not. Valero played his cards well; Rider knew he had earned the command of Slug's guard not through loyalty but by being ruthless and cunning. He had survived a lot of raids where other men didn't. He brought glory and fear to the Scorps and before Slug's new quest for culture that was all that mattered. He was a trusted member of the gang because, in no small part, he *was* the gang, the embodiment of the feral killing spirit they all had... but were now attempting to hide. And as that made him an icon for both the young and the old, it made him *really* dangerous.

But more than having the respect of the gangers who followed him, Valero was waiting for his own big opportunity. He was a planner, Rider could see that. He was happy with his current position, for now at least, or at least he pretended to be. Maybe he wasn't sure where his strengths lay. Maybe he was only just now beginning to recruit allies among the camp.

Something was brewing in Oasis, it was palpable. Rider suspected that at least a dozen of the raiders of the Scorpions were secretly loyal to Valero. There was this shared "look", this kind of glance they cast towards each other every now and then. Certain groups of raiders hung out alone in the camp, separate from the rest. They talked with Valero in hushed whispers just before nightfall. He passed out the whiskey among the same crew and kept segregated company. It was obvious, at least to anyone who kept their eyes and ears open.

Normally, Rider wouldn't give a damn about the treacherous politics of a squalid hellhole like Oasis. He'd just collect his pay and beat it out across the desert, messing his tracks as he went to prevent his former employers from tracking him down and killing him to take back that very same pay a day later. But this time, he knew Valero had a thing for him. Valero was... "interested" in him. Valero didn't trust him. Valero knew Rider was just a little too good, just a little too quiet, just a little too much the "Lone Ranger".

Rider buried those thoughts and stood still as some of Valero's men patted him and Tank down, taking account of their hidden weapons and gear. They found the pistols at Rider's side and the compact, holstered submachine gun concealed beneath his long jacket. Valero looked at it for a moment, playing over its small surface, then gave it back. None of it seemed to concern him.

Rider and Tank walked as confidently as possible into Slug's tent, knowing full well that Valero and his own collection of personally loyal guards were still watching them with more than a passing interest.

Buddy and the others came into the huge airy tent. When a man lives his whole life on the hard seat of a motorcycle and the smell of a high octane gasoline was considered pleasant, this was like stepping through a portal into an alien world. Inside it was cool, shaded, and wonderful. Even Tank, normally quiet and withdrawn, exhaled deeply in the all-consuming comfort. Perhaps it was because his larger frame and huge bulk suffered more than others from the desert heat or perhaps it was just a reflection of the real fatigue that was just now beginning to show heavily on his small, distorted face.

Mats and rugs covered the entire floor of the huge airy tent, leaving no part exposed to the sands of the desert beneath. It was not unlike a real enclosed structure, something none of them had seen in a very long time. Huge hangings, made of pigment-painted hides stretched along old black and rusted chains, hid the real contours of the massive tent. Out of sight, in the shadows or beyond a gauzy curtain, might lie additional guards waiting to emerge and slay threatening transgressors.

Braziers made from old glass ashtrays and metal pots burned rare wood-chip embers, filling the air with a delicately scented aroma. It was an odd and luxurious touch that made each man feel miles removed from the hard, brutal life just a few feet outside. But most glorious of all the furnishings were the accoutrements of the place. Piles of the softest animal furs rose like a mountain in the center of the tent, in front of veiled lace partitions, probably once curtains taken from the ruins of some old motor home abandoned on a desert highway, that formed two or three separate "rooms" inside the tent. Their contents, no doubt the personal quarters, harem, and eating/bathing space of the tent's owner, were concealed just out of sight.

The mountain of furs served as the "throne" of *Slug*.

Lounging on the shapeless heap sat Slug, self-proclaimed chief, king and emperor of the Scorpions. A powerful leader, commanding many warriors and their machines and perhaps deliberately deluded by his own conspiring yes-men, he still managed to look regal despite what he had become. Just a few generations ago, those creatures called "mutants" had once been a rarity but now, in this era, they were everywhere, the norm. Thus a man as repugnant as Slug could become the leader of men, whereas in past centuries a man's looks were as integral to his charisma as his skill and magnetism.

Slug was bald like the other gangers but he suffered from probably the worst case of cleft lip that any of them had seen. A good portion of his upper lip was just a big gap in the loose flesh of his face, connecting his mouth with his left nostril. A steady flow of mucus oozed from the elongated gap, leaving his face slick and wet, forcing him to snort, snivel, and wheeze every few seconds just to breathe. This natural deformity did a lot to take one's attention away from the fact that Slug was grotesquely *gaunt*, probably the result of one STD or another picked up from his years of raping and pillaging. His loose, hanging flesh was covered in badly-done tattoos from his violent youth, tattoos that now seemed to vanish among folds of extra skin. As he sat there, his arms as thin as rails, his neck hanging with loose jowls and his stomach slightly distended, Slug reminded Rider of the great statue at the center of Oasis. With a little imagination, the one could easily be mistaken for the other.

Wearing only the slightest hint of clothes and bead-strewn with gaudy necklaces and bracelets that looked like they were cracked out of a department store candy machine, the once-infamous and dreaded Slug was now but a weak and withered leader of brigands. Rider's eyes wandered over the skeletal "raider lord". One of his pierced nipples were being played with by a beaten and bruised concubine (herself so drugged up she didn't care about her demolished face). A thick chunk of fruit was being offered by yet another. Two more slave women fanned him, while at least half a dozen armed guards with spears and axes stood by, watching quietly from the shadowy corners of the place.

Slug spoke quietly with a figure seated a few feet away to his side, an aquiline, middle-aged man dressed from head to toe in a flowing white robe and even gathered around his head in a bundled turban. As the bounty hunters entered their conversation ended, and both turned to meet the visitors.

"Laozong," said Buddy, lowering his head out of traditional respect, "Rider and Tank got the ghoul. And we found this in the ghoul's camp..."

Slug turned from the slice of fruit dangling before him and, with sickly yellow eyes, looked over the kid.

The girl, her eyes clouded with lingering tears, stared back, gulping down the knot that choked her throat. She felt the two raiders release her and quickly unbind her. Slug looked her over with an appraising glance. His wet lower lip, dripping with saliva, shifted and twitched.

"Buddy," he said through strangely choked vocal chords and chattering teeth, "you please me yet again. A find such as this is..." He raised his eyebrows in delight, and Buddy's lips parted in a huge grin, his mind already leaping ahead to the rewards he would receive from his predictably lecherous master.

"*Fay!*" the diseased raider chief shouted. As soon as he spoke a thin willowy man came from behind the curtains, his head and body lowered as if expecting a swift hit from his master. "I want you to take this child and appraise her."

His effeminate manservant moved and looked the child over. "Hmmmm," the servant mumbled, his voice unnervingly high-pitched, "she looks to be about... thirteen or fourteen at most. She won't be fit for your purposes for another year or so, sire."

Slug nodded mechanically and waved a hand in dismissal. "Take her away then. Brand her and put her with the others." He smiled at the girl, showing the ugly nubs of rotten teeth. "You will learn from them, *my sweet*." His statement made some of the guards present grin in amusement, but the man in white robes remained silent, watching, uninvolved. The girl was taken effortlessly from the tent.

Buddy stood slightly to the side as Rider came forward.

"Ah, *Rider*," said Slug, an almost friendly smile creeping across his aging features, "so you have done your part. I commend you!" His tone was grandiose, and to Rider seemed wrong, spilling from such a ghastly ruin of a face. He said nothing, of course, and instead leaned down to scrape some of the ghoul's dried and caked blood from his leather boot, using his long-bladed knife.

"That's four gallons, fresh, in water skins or canteens, *now*." The last word was subtly punctuated as Rider brought the knife back up to wipe the grime on a nearby tent post.

Slug chuckled and chortled grossly. Tank cast Rider a quick, surprised glance, as if to warn him about pushing the dangerous raider lord too far. He knew there was a little bit of showmanship in all negotiations but here, in this camp, Tank felt ill at ease and more than happy to get going.

"Rider," said Slug innocently, "why so eager to leave?"

"I'm not," Rider shrugged passively, "but I think my work here's done."

Slug ignored Rider's statement and motioned for one of the concubines. She looked hazily at her master for a long moment before his order finally sunk in, then walked straight over to Rider's side, stiff as a robot. Staring at him with her freakish, opaque yellow eyes, she played with the metal rings that ran through her large brown nipples while looking lifelessly at him, all in some frail attempt at being seductive. To Rider it was like gazing into the eyes of a crack addict on her last legs, or better yet, a corpse that just didn't know when to lay down and die. He looked at her for less than a second, then turned his head back to the onlooking raider-lord.

Apparently Slug hadn't seen Rider's disgust. "You know," he said, "you and your associate Tank here could gain a lot from staying among us. A fresh water source... no end in sight. A band of willing warriors, the finest and prettiest this side of the Wei Shan. And *women*..."

His veiny, mottled hand gestured to the collection of "furniture" lying about among the hides and furs. Even in this woman-starved world, where the gentler, victimized sex was rarer than water (and priced accordingly) Slug's collection was hardly a temptation. Though he said nothing, Rider hoped Tank was with him on that at least. A quiet, uncomfortable moment passed.

"Like the man said," Tank interjected in his usual low voice, "we're free men, Slug. With all due respect... *our water*." Inside at least, Rider sighed with relief.

Slug looked at Tank, considering. His size was impressive, his shot not too shabby but Tank lacked the same panache as his smaller companion, the one they called "Rider". Together they were a team to be reckoned with; even in his own abode, with all his men ready to protect him, breaking a deal with desert bounty men like those two was a bad prospect. Sure they'd go down quick; but ugly men like them, full of self-worth and angry pride, would take Slug down with them just for the principle of it. He snorted a thick, gurgling snort, then looked back to Rider.

"Rider, Buddy tells me that you killed this ghoul from half a mile away. And right to the head, eh? A once-in-a-lifetime shot..."

Rider stood without reaction. He was growing tired of the small talk and transparent flattery. *How did Slug become so powerful; surely not through such obvious designs and simple bribery?*

"I can use men with such skill at arms. And I also believe, Rider, that you possess other talents, too?" The assemblage of guards, a few of the near-lifeless women, and even the foreigner dressed in white, until now sitting quietly and out of the conversation, looked towards Rider.

Slug smiled a wet grin and continued. "Word has it that you, Rider, came from a lost *city?*" Rider just stared at the oozing raider boss.

"A 'last vestige'. Men such as you are rare these days... you hold *knowledge*... of what came before... of how things worked. Your people hold back when they could be helping raise the rest of the human race from barbarism."

Rider stared at him. There were many reasons to defy this monster, but he decided to be brief. "No, you heard wrong. My home was a city, yes. Did we have knowledge, no. We just lived there, among ruins, a small colony. Just a whole lot of broken stone but no less a desert than this place. And my people died out long ago."

Slug threw his head back with a chortling laugh that stopped Rider short, bringing a brittle hand up to his bony chest. "Was it raiders? Was it *me?* Where are you from, Rider? Raton? Or Folsom? Among the xenos living in that little shithole, Gila-Town? Or maybe it was that little fort, at Cimarron? Which one, Rider? There have been so many!" Slug smiled broadly; his conquests were many and despite advocating civilization these days, he still secretly liked the idea that his years of marauding may have left men like Rider all over the wasteland. Brooding men, broken men, men whose entire lives had been shaped by his own campaigns of mindless destruction.

Rider's voice diminished to a whisper but his stare was unwavering. "None of those. It wasn't raiders. We were just squatters, really. We certainly weren't guardians of some fabulous technology. What we knew is really nothing of use to you, to anyone."

"You sure, Rider? I know, I've *heard*, that many men who hold the knowledge of the Ancients are picky about whom they share this knowledge with. They say... men of knowledge only share their secrets with those they deem 'worthy'.

"And are we not worthy, Rider? Look around you! Civilization... all right here. We have a powerful base here, an army that grows by the day. My children are strong and fair! We have mounts of steel! And guns! True, we were once raiders but we invested the gains from those years of savagery to create something good and strong. We have a lasting stockpile of fuel for our war machines and the thinkers we took as slaves taught us the knowledge to craft our own things if we need them. We rule these thirty square miles with absolute certainty... and we have our 'culture'."

Rider found himself blinking all of a sudden, as if deep down he were offended by Slug's associating his group of rapists, murderers and thieves with the word "culture". But he stifled a disdainful frown, kept his face emotionless. He sensed where this conversation might lead and felt Tank might not back him if it came to blows.

"Culture, Rider. We are shavers, Rider, unlike the bearded barbarians of the deep desert. A ritual even the Conquerors proscribed to, yes? And we relish music and song, art and decoration, as they did. We savagely fight the urge to eat our own. That is, I believe, the greatest sign of civilization?"

Slug looked over to the white-clad visitor as if looking for confirmation, as if this man's opinion meant a great deal to the raider chief. But the visitor, whoever he might be, simply nodded to appease him.

Slug seemed greatly satisfied and continued. "All those others out there, in the deserts, they have no such qualms. *Ghouls*. And the oasis we hold has *water*... much of it." Slug motioned with one gaunt arm to the man in white. "The *Clean* traders have even sent a representative and now we work towards bringing more of their people here. There will be trade. An exchange of goods and ideas. They will help us become even more civilized."

Civilization, again. It was common knowledge that the illustrious "traders from the south" were bringing a new way of life to the northern wastelands but their reception among these untamed peoples (wild barbarians, raiders and rogue scavengers) had been mixed. Rider, for one, was not impressed.

"Tell me we are not cultured, Rider. Tell me we do not *deserve*."

Rider looked over to the figure in white, who returned the appraising gaze with strange, discerning eyes of silent wisdom. These two were of entirely different worlds and both knew it; respecting, in a way, each other from a detached distance. The

Clean agent was no doubt an elder of considerable years, having dealt with the worst of the desert scum and rabble to secure water rights for his, the greatest clans of water merchants, the "Clean". The way he sat there, inoffensively and quiet, spoke volumes of his own uncanny knowledge of raiders and their type; that is to say, how to act and how *not* to act. But Rider knew, deep down, this visitor was just as thinking, observant, and wily as himself. This diplomat, this merchant, was more likely scouting out the defenses and numbers of the oasis right under Slug's nose, all under the false pretext of being a "negotiator", recording this information to send back to his masters in the south.

Rider just stared blankly at the man, then back to Slug. "Like I said," he quietly persisted, "I have no knowledge to offer... whether or *not* I find you worthy."

Slug, still managing a sly grin, nodded as if accepting defeat but looked at Rider as if he didn't really believe him at all. His eyes twinkled with hidden plans.

Rider stared back, cold and assuredly. He was telling the truth. There was very little to say. While there were holdouts and "last vestiges" dwelling elsewhere in the desert, the cities of the past were really just ruins now and few had anything to offer raiders and their kind except for a few days of sport shooting up the lingering reminders of Ancient law and order. He and his people had lived among the ruins for a time, only to be wiped out by a terrible mistake. They had been simple and innocent, and had hoarded no secrets. He thought of the past, his earlier life, and the lessons learned in the varied trials of survival... and the tragedy that comes with failing them.

It was quiet. Slug finally breathed laboriously through a veil of mucus clogging his throat, and spoke again. "Well, I suppose I'm mistaken, Mr. Rider. Four gallons for you and your associate. Perhaps we will do business again."

With that, Slug dismissed them with a wave of his hand. Rider blinked and Tank exhaled noticeably. Buddy watched as some half-naked raiders came in with four one-gallon water skins, made from stretched goat hides from the animal pens of the camp and gave two each to Tank and Rider.

Rider and Tank openly checked the contents and threw each other accepting looks, but there wasn't a grin among them.

Rider was, however, slightly disappointed but he didn't let it show. In the end, they would not receive the reward for the girl, probably some tremendous amount that would instead be given to that worthless raider, Buddy. That was a shame. Where he planned on going, two gallons, even four, would only cover a few days.

That was something he and surely Tank already knew. For a moment Rider was already contemplating the next few days. Would Tank go his own way, or pretend to stay with him and wait for the right moment to strike? Or would he do it first? Both needed the water, one just didn't have enough.

But for now he put those thoughts out of his mind. Rider tipped his dusty old fedora and turned, leaving along with his "associate" through the flap in the tent.

Night was beginning to set in over the desert landscape. The enormous dunes clustered at the edges of the oasis like buttressing walls were beginning to draw deep cool shadows over the encampment, and the big crimson sun was now half obscured by the horizon.

Burning Lands

Rider heard laughter from one of several open-faced tents and walked over, listening to the crunch of sand and loose stones under his worn black boots. A thin splinter of wood hung from his parched lip like a toothpick, offering a cheap pleasure. It afforded a slight fragrant taste to his mouth, eroding the stench of his weeks-old breath.

A few men outside the tent were wrestling, grappling against each other as nearby warriors of the raider camp cheered, jeered and threw sand at them, arguing over bets in an almost equally violent manner. Winners would become "husbands" that night; losers would be the "wives".

Rider's eyes betrayed a poorly-withheld disgust and he strolled past into a nearby tent, moving past others in the lamplight and coming up alongside the low eroded table where his traveling company, Tank, sat talking with a tribal wanderer from the deep desert.

The tribesman facing him from the other side of the wooden table was the image of feral savagery in this day and age; thin but not malnourished, lean but not weak, with skin baked dark by the sun and decorated with organic pigments made from rare desert plants. The natives of this land were once civilized but their descendants, like this one, saw little need for clothing beyond the slightest shift of fur to cover his loins and a cape that doubled as his blanket during the night. He was burdened with traveling gear; plastic canteens, water skins and even a sturdy walking staff, with four pairs of spare pre-Fall shoes dangling by their frayed strings from his worn and dirty belt. Rider quickly guessed he was probably a junk peddler on some great journey or another, only stopping momentarily in Oasis to barter for food and water before hastily moving on and out of sight. Or he might simply be a wanderer, drawn by the sounds and sights of Oasis, who would pack and leave once he was satisfied he had seen everything there was to see in this awful little place.

"No, my friend, I'm not asking to hear your fancy tales..." Tank said, "... what I need are supplies to reach the Far Desert. Now can we trade?" The wanderer raised his head as if to object, but Tank lifted one large hand in the air, palm forward, to silence him so he could continue his pitch.

"Hear me out! This is what they call the 'Dream Leaf'. Other, earthy folk like yourself make it on the other side of the Wei Shan but it's really rare. Smoke it, and you'll see the gods... Got this bit from a Cartel caravaneer in Socorro who makes regular trips into the mountains to trade with the natives. As you can imagine it's *not* cheap stuff..."

The tribesman had watery blue eyes sunk into deep, wrinkled sockets, which seemed innocent yet at the same time acutely aware, boring into Tank and through his clumsy salesmanship. But the man didn't move, he simply listened, as if witnessing Tank weave his dubious tale was just as entertaining as actually using the Dream Leaf itself. Eventually the grizzled little tribesman sighed, mumbled something and let go of his half-shell cup of water to take the small grimy pouch of old leaf shavings from Tank's hand.

Tank chuckled grimly, rubbing his naked chin, and whispered to Rider with a grin. "*He's interested...*" Rider shook his head, a slight, nasty smile on his lips. He patted Tank on the shoulder as he wearily took a seat on the other side of him, motioning to a nearby youngster to pour some water from the communal gourd.

The deep desert tribesman opened his mouth to reveal an incomplete row of yellow teeth, worn to nubs from chewing hard plant fibers and softening leather for a lifetime of handmade shoes. In a soft, quick voice he said something to Tank and retrieved his own satchel, emptying a few things on the table. Tank fingered easily through the stuff, using one big, gnarled digit to push aside the worthless junk and separate the stuff that interested him. The old tribesman nodded, took the deteriorating sandwich bag filled with old marijuana leaves and then left, still chattering to himself disappointedly as he walked out into the night.

"Crazy old timer," Tank said, sighing once the savage tribesman was gone.

"What'd he say?" Rider asked, with only passing interest.

"Oh, just superstitious warnings. He said 'the gods' were angry and brought their wrath upon his village, killing man, woman and child alike, and stealing away the livestock. Said he was heading west into the Rockies, where they'd never find him."

"A lot of the frontier tribesman seem to be heading west these days," Rider murmured.

"I'll bet they're fleeing west to escape the Clean, and all their 'new ideas'!" Tank suggested with a laugh.

Rider shrugged and took the tin cup as the bartender, just a kid and no doubt someone's catamite here in this awful camp, filled it to the brim. The boy, despite being half Rider's size, held it back, awaiting payment. Rider smirked and placed a few inch-long chips of dried, leathery meat on the table. The boy bit one, his teeth leaving a white mark. The meat was odorous, tough, probably dog. He looked at Rider with eyes far too old for his age, as if to admonish him for the poor trade, but ultimately accepted.

Rider sipped from the cup, only wetting his lips. The water was warm but relatively clean, only a few particles churning in the cup. It was fresh. He closed his eyes, letting his tongue slip from his mouth and dart into the meager portion of water.

Tank scooped up the stuff the old tribesman had willingly relinquished, a few shavings from a cinnamon stick that he might use to flavor his water after a few weeks in the canteen, a couple of sticks of wood useful for kindling sometime down the road, a half dozen glass marbles streaked with faded color and a rusty straight razor.

Rider looked over at the collection of bits and snorted.

Tank turned, suddenly aware of Rider's amusement. "What?"

"*Junk*. What are you going to do with that crap?"

Tank smiled, putting the shavings and sticks away in his pouch. He let the cool marbles rest in the palm of his coarse right hand, closing his massive fist tightly and enjoying the cool sensation against his skin. He shrugged, as if embarrassed to explain. "I like them. They're... nice."

Rider shook his head and, seeing this, Tank chuckled. "How 'bout this?" Rider asked, motioning to the razor.

Tank chuckled again. "My blade's gettin' dull, Rider."

Rider shook his head. "You don't need a blade, Tank. Who are you kidding?" His voice was cold and insensitive. "You haven't got any hair to shave. You *never* will."

Tank just stared at the blade, his thick calloused finger running over the edge. "Maybe... someday..." he murmured.

Realizing he had struck a nerve Rider just stared for a moment, then looked away. He wouldn't pursue that any more. He took a drink.

Tank, and others born in recent memory among the wastes, were the refined product of generations in the desert. Refined! Oh, Tank had his share of "changes", alright. It was in him, from birth, gifts (wanted or not) passed down invisibly from his father and mother that, in them, had been vestigial and non-functional but which now worked actively and effectively within their son. Some of those gifts were good, some were bad. They were Nature's attempt to make something that would survive the nightmare that the world had become; they were *mutations*.

Surprisingly his were among the more useful of Nature's twisted adaptations. They called him "Tank" because he refused to go down in a fight. Rider hadn't been with him long in the grand scheme of things but in that time he'd seen Tank take a knife six inches deep in his back and continue fighting during a drunken barroom brawl and even survive a close-ranged shotgun blast to his chest, a hit that would've ripped a normal man in two. And Tank's body recovered quick too; even the worst wounds healed in a matter of days for Tank, given care and rest. Something in his blood refused to give up, spurred him on to *live*. He was truly a monster and also a *tank*.

But Tank also had that dwarfed head, the result of *microcephaly*, which over the years was actually getting smaller, enhancing the pitiful freakishness of his already troll-like appearance, while at the same constricting his brain. In a matter of years he wouldn't be so quick witted and might eventually even lose the ability to speak, or even to think like a human being. Given care, in a more caring world, he might have found peace and happiness in a hospital or asylum but on the Twisted Earth there was rarely any such compassion; turned out into the wastes, he would degenerate into a gibbering, slavering beast.

His microcephaly also left Tank without the capability to grow hair. But that was something Rider knew he could never say out loud. To Tank, it was the most visible sign that he was a mutant, a monster, a defective human being; not his freakish size or his diminutive head but his lack of hair. Unlike the raiders of Oasis, who shaved their heads to appear "wise" like the Buddha statue that loomed over the center of the village, Tank was ashamed of his baldness and he yearned with a childish hope that one day that would change.

What a dream. What kind of a world is it where the "dream" a man has, is to simply grow hair? Deep down, Tank knew how ridiculous it was too. But he kept on believing, hoping, that one day he'd "get better". Tank put the razor away without another word.

For a moment Rider felt almost sorry for what he was likely to do in a few days, either take the big lug's water at night before he even woke, or cap him as he walked point and take his goods then. It was an ugly thought but he knew Tank had thought it too, if not today then tomorrow. It was the way of men. Sure they were brothers in a sense, both being bounty hunters, but no one walked the sands as friends. It was just the way.

"But, hey," Tank said out loud, craftily changing the subject. "Here's to nabbing that *ghoul!* Hoorah!"

Rider grinned slightly but nodded. He raised his cup. The two chuckled and drank. As they laughed, the young bandit Buddy sat down beside the two men, breaking any possible chance of real camaraderie flourishing, merely with his presence.

"Boys!" he laughed, "I think I owe you a drink!"

"Why's that?" asked Tank.

"Well, Slug has seen to it that I be rewarded for *my* part in findin' that there ghoul. Seems Slug has a thing for old Buddy-boy. And he likes me, he really does. He says he's gonna put me in charge of breaking in new harem girls."

They could both hear the giggle growing under Buddy's breath. "At least for the next few weeks, anyway."

Buddy squealed with delight (despite the fact that no one shared it), and stole the water gourd, pouring himself and the others fresh cups of water in "celebration".

"Yep. You know that sweet little thing that Slug had come on to you in the tent, Rider?" Rider recalled that burnt-out, wasted bit of furniture with the ugly yellow eyes. He sneered but no one noticed.

"I'm gonna celebrate by bangin' her *tonight!*"

Rider went back to his drink without a word. Buddy, in the annoying way of little men, was obviously trying to get to him but that just wouldn't work·in this case. Tank went back to drinking too, reflecting a similar disinterest.

Buddy apparently didn't let their passiveness faze him because he slapped his dusty knee and laughed out loud. At least *he* was happy. He chugged his drink and let out a refreshed gasp of air. "So if you boys'll excuse me," he chortled, getting up, "I do believe I see the sun goin' down. Tonight's the night..."

Soon Buddy was gone. Rider saw that his own second cup was near empty. Soon it would be time to go and leave this pretty little place behind. He wasn't sorry to be facing the open desert again, though at present he was perhaps a bit too tired to head out straight away.

Just then, he heard the tent flaps open. Something made his spine tingle. Rider heard the boots, several pairs, and the quieting of the conversation in the now-crowded tent. He smelled the strong, unique odor of Valero, machine oil, sweat and lingering traces of high-quality gunpowder, coming up behind him.

"Well, Rider," came the familiar deep voice of Valero as he took a seat beside the bounty hunters, "I'm glad to see you're still here. Haven't left yet? *Good.*"

Tank turned and lost his unconscious smile as he realized the raider-king's chief bodyguard was not alone. There were some half-dozen other raiders with him, taking up places nearby, watching silently but appearing ready for any action into which their leader might order them. They had musket pistols, wiry spears and other weapons on hand, sitting at their belts, assuredly but their intended effect was the same - *intimidation.*

Rider just slurped another drop of water into his mouth. Only then did he turn to acknowledge Valero's presence.

"Just about ready to take off though," Rider said, sighing deeply to disguise the tension suddenly evident in the tent. Valero smiled slightly in a similar display, motioning for the gourd to be passed around once more in mock friendship.

Tank quieted. Free water? From raiders? The catch was no doubt soon to follow, and it was probably a BIG one.

"It's a shame you'll be leaving us tonight, Rider."

Rider knew that voice, that *tone*. It made his toes curl. Something *was* up. *Now*. And he was going to somehow be involved. Despite his better judgment, his best wishes, his most anxious attempts... by the end of the night one thing or another would be different.

Rider just listened, slowly unplugging the water skin and gently pouring the dwindling contents of the cup into his water skin, intent on saving the offering for later.

Valero didn't seem to notice. If he did, he would have assumed then and there that Rider would say no. But he was too eager. Despite all his other strengths of mind and wit, something at this moment excited him so that he overlooked Rider's discreet motions.

"*Tonight I'll be taking control of the Scorpions,*" Valero whispered sharply, his voice lingering in the still air, his eyes expecting a reaction from Rider that was, unexpectedly, not forthcoming.

Rider replaced the cork tightly and slowly let the water skin hang from his shoulder. Tank put his own cup back on the table, as if wanting to distance himself from the notion of indebting himself to the likes of Valero. He said nothing as well.

Valero blinked but his eyes remained locked on Rider's face. "We number over one hundred men. Slug has three hundred or so of his own, mostly on the pay, but *we* control the arms. Tonight, at midnight, my men will be ready and we're going to sack Slug's tent. It will be a big fight. It may be close..."

He heard the rasp in Valero's dry throat. "I could use a man like you, Rider. I need men like you to help me take over. You're good with the 'stick'. You've seen a fight or two. *What do you say?*"

The heavy question seemed to linger in the air like the distant crash of thunder during a summer storm. The kind that makes more sensible animals scatter and run. Rider stayed put, and exhaled a long deep breath.

Valero sensed Rider's unease and pressed further. "Rider, you knew it was inevitable. Slug and his dreams of trade and stability... it's all wrong and you know it. This land has seen hundreds of years of war and killing and he thinks he can change that overnight. He can't; not the land, not the people and certainly not their hearts. A permanent settlement? The land won't have it any more than the people will. The desert will come and sweep it away, just like it does all the camps in these Forbidden Lands. And who wants change, anyway? The Clean, sitting quietly in the shadows in their spotless white robes? Hell, they just want the oases that dot this desert and the natives be damned. You know that and I know that. To Hell with them! We need to skip this bullshit of resting on our asses in the sand, listening to diplomats do our talking and watching idly as our freedoms are taken away, one by one, in the name of 'civilization'. Negotiating with the Clean! Get real. Alliances and trade agreements, for the mutual benefit of all! Never happen. And all of this squatting in the shade, raising goats like tribesmen, my men being forced to take their brothers for wives because there's no women around. No. We need to move! Strike! There are lots of settlements out there, I know. They are all so weak, filled with weak men and frightened women. Women who'll spread willingly for real men! We'll find those settlements, take them. Take their wealth, dance and revel as they worship us, and drink their fear like wine! That is the way it *should* be for men."

Rider's eyes closed as he listened to the unfolding horrors that constituted Valero's "plan" for the future of the Forbidden Lands.

"No more living on fruit, no more cleaning the offal of penned beasts. Who is more domesticated now anyway, the livestock or us? We'll have animals hauled to us as tribute, paid by the cowering primitives living their pathetic lives on the fringe of the desert. Pigs and cows from those pitiful communes huddled in fear in the shadow of Midway. We'll sack the merchants for their goods, take what we want. The Clean, the Cartel! They'll have to pay *us* to move through these lands. We are too powerful to suffer the humiliation of bowing to their prices and demands anymore! We need not barter any longer. We will TAKE what we will. Women, food, medicines... weapons. We have the power here to do it.

"We will *rule*, Rider, from atop a throne of punishment and from a court of pain."

He had a flourish in his voice, but the tone of his wildly unbalanced tirade quieted now. "I will lead this gang but you have a place among us as well. You are too valuable a gun to lose to the senseless trails of the desert. I know you, Rider. You're not as quiet as you seem, you have so much to say but no heart to say it. What happened to make you turn your back on your ambition, to lock it away and deny it the light of day?"

He was mocking now. "Have you witnessed too much death? Cannot stand the suffering that you've seen and dealt?" His eyes bored into Rider. "I say commit the memory of each crying face to Hell, let the screams of those you've killed become a symphony, and rebel against your heart! Live for the moment, and take comfort in knowing that others suffer more than you! You have the potential to be my greatest advisor, my general. Ride with *me!*"

It wasn't a question, but a command. Rider saw the faces of the raiders in the tent. Quiet yet excited, knowing that if found out, they would surely be killed but compelled by and committed to their insanely charismatic war-leader. Rider sensed that Valero's confidence was contagious; Valero knew something, he had an edge, and the others sensed it and fed from it, finding the will to mutiny against Slug, their petty *laozong*.

Tank, too, was silent. He was certainly an outsider in this discussion. The deals pertained to Rider, not him. Sure he knew Rider from days before, hunting together for pay but what about now? If he said yes, they might give him work too and that'd be alright; but if Rider said no, his foolhardy defiance would bring him down as well. Quickly he looked about for the nearest egress, and his hand slowly, discreetly moved to secure his things for a quick flight.

Rider pushed his empty cup away on the table.

"No thanks, Valero," he said, standing. "Do what you want. This isn't my war. I'll be leaving. Just give me time to get my things and I'll be out before the first gunshots."

Valero watched with no expression as Rider departed, only his eyes gleaming with power like a man possessed. In the awkward silence, Tank rose quietly, threw his things hastily over his shoulder and followed before the tent flap could even swing back.

The air in the harem tent smelled rancid. The young girl's eyes welled with tears, not only from confusion and fear but from a sickly sweet smoke as it bit at her eyes. It mixed with the sweat of several dozen women and gross perfumes made from mixtures of animal sweat and tree oils. The strong thick musk from the wood chip braziers in the harem tent added further to the smothering stench. Beneath it all lay the subtle but noticeable reek of the opium fumes that perpetually kept the women docile, unafraid and tame.

Not that their masters really needed to keep them subdued any longer. By now, the women were a part of Oasis, an integral piece of the machine that was their raucous, decadent way of life. Whoever they had once been, the daughters and wives of other desert people, they had long been stripped of their individuality and minds. Raped, savagely beaten for years and kept as expendable treasures, they had regressed. They were simple and primitive; they knew no other way anymore. They hated their masters, despised their situation but an absence of any escape (even a dream) left them hard, shallow and complacent. Not one of the women had any sense of purpose beyond staying alive. And the drugs, they only added pungency to the strength of their adherence; addicted, deep down they didn't even *want* to run away.

The eerily thin and wispy man who had brought her here, the eunuch Fay, was no longer with her. After examining her briefly he had quietly taken her, without a word, and given her over to the harem girls to be branded. He left in a hurry, as if releasing her into their care had relieved him of some terrible and unwanted burden.

The girl crouched among other women, eyes wide and unblinking as if at any moment now she might see her chance to escape. No one in the smoky tent paid her any real heed; she was just the newest and there'd be many more like her to come. She in particular looked weak; she wouldn't last. Why get attached by offering a hand? No mentor approached her. No, the others kept away, smoked their opium and explored each other's bodies to find the ecstasy that they only feigned in the presence of their emaciated, diseased master.

The girl was content for a while to remain ignored and unseen but then a voice called out. She had been noticed. "What should we call you, little one?" asked one of the women, a wry smile curling across her lips, one as unsettling as the worst of the raider males. It had been many years since she had been in the company of so many people. Strange memories came flooding back; she couldn't fight them off... fractured visions, lost voices, screams, shouts. She remembered fleeing to the desert... so many years ago.

"My name is Gale," the girl suddenly said. She found herself surprised, as it was the first time anyone had asked. Though she had introduced herself, no one seemed to care. The women returned to whatever they had been doing before. Gale sat alone.

Time passed, and as minutes turned to hours the smoke of the harem tent consumed her completely as well, until she too passed out into a hazy dream. Sharp pain from the day's treatment faded into a dull throb and nausea, and hours seemed like days. The laughter of the harem girls became a swirl of slurred noise, like the calls of predatory birds echoing in some weird, dark abyss. From time to time they came at her, like lucid dream-like images, to taunt her in her sleep; but being only half-aware she was unable to turn away or crawl free. Sapped of strength and will, she could only cower and take whatever verbal abuse they could throw at her.

Some time later there was a slight sound of laughter from the other side of a few gossamer and animal skin hangings, makeshift "walls" in the harem tent. Gale awoke, a pile lying among odor-permeated skins in the harem. She could hear several other girls and women sleeping all around, their breathing shallow and weak, obviously lost in mind-numbing hallucinations. It was now night and except for the dying embers in the braziers, it was pitch black.

Her eyes fought to open. Smoke from the low burning braziers stung her nostrils. Her eyes struggled to adjust.

Gale skittered away and looked around, her back drawn defensively against a heavy curtain. Another girl rolled over in her sleep, sobbing quietly from some unknown nightmare. To her left she heard an unusual noise, turned, and looked. She saw the silhouettes of a woman and a man coupling through the curtain. A dim fire or lantern was burning on the other side of the screen, where the laughs and sounds were coming from. She backed away into the shadows, searching for a different way out.

Elsewhere, Rider packed an awaiting horse with the few most practical bags and sturdily-clamped bundles he had acquired over the years. His face was expressionless, even in the pitch darkness of the desert night. He was too busy to show his tension; he quickly checked and double-checked to make sure everything was there, intact.

Midnight was closing in. It was black out that night and few stars could be seen. The moon, usually brilliant out here in the Forbidden Lands, was just a shadowy sliver only just now waxing high in the sky. He heard the crack of the main campfire around which several unknowing and oblivious raiders sat; some asleep, others staring mesmerized into the flames.

Tank was hurrying too. He could taste his own growing excitement, his own apprehension. He was stuffing his few remaining trade goods and belongings into packs and harness pouches as well. Rider was no doubt doing the same elsewhere in the camp; he wondered if the uncanny albino was already gone, having slipped out sometime earlier when no one expected. Hmmm. If so, he'd better beat tracks soon as well.

Rider knew he had to leave. He was sure Tank knew it too. It was only an hour before Valero was going to make his move. Taking his horse by the reigns, whispering softly to it in a childlike banter, he led his burdened steed along the edge of camp, skirting through tall fronds and broad leafy bushes to avoid being caught in the campfire glow. At the edge of the light he lurked, guiding his horse towards the far side of the camp, on the other side of the oasis, where it was all dark and the stars lit the desert a little more brightly. There, hunkered down while gathering his things, he saw Tank quietly getting ready to leave as well.

"*Psst,*" Rider whispered softly. Tank moved with a start and spun, his lips formed into a little "o". Squinting, he recognized the long black coat and the chestnut horse following behind in his shadow. It was Rider. He turned back to load his own heavier white steed, now hastening.

Rider figured it was time to make his move. The big guy was a bit on edge, afraid... wanted to beat tracks and soon. Now was the time to suggest traveling together, getting out of Oasis as a team. He'd worry about getting Tank's water later. Now though, they had to go.

Just then, Rider's eye caught motion off to the side; instinctively he looked. Over across the camp, he saw several of the bald raider warriors sneak into the shadows, into the main armory tent. Several others now stood outside as well, well concealed in the shadows, hunched over and moving strangely. They were arming themselves.

"*Shit!*" Rider cursed in a sharp whisper.

Tank looked up. "*What?*"

Rider unbuckled his rifle holster. He began to race, sliding it out of the sheath and loading it up. "Valero *lied*. He's making his move now! We've got to hurry!"

Tank threw a frightened look over one shoulder and cursed too. More men now emerged from the tent. A chaotic mass was gathering muskets, axes, and spears. Their growing whispers were getting louder, sounding like hungry locusts gathering in a pack for their sudden swarm. Suddenly, one of the men at the campfire, groggy from his share of fermented goat's milk, rose and stared off into the dark towards the growing army of Valero's men.

"What the..." he murmured. "Hey!" he yelled, his voice slurred. "What're you... doin'?!"

Rider cussed and pulled his and Tank's horses around and further back into the foliage, sure to be out of sight. Though Tank muttered a protest, he realized what Rider was up to and went with him, hunkering down and retrieving his own stick from his steed's saddle.

Suddenly there was a shot that pierced the electric silence like a peal of solitary thunder, sure to be heard for miles and wake up everyone in camp. Rider cursed again, sharper, and dropped his last bundle of trade goods. Tank dropped to the earth, swinging around, taking advantage of some nearby rocks to scurry behind. The sound of the musket report indeed rang through the night with singular clarity and volume.

Knowing that they had no time to lose, Valero, somewhere out there in the camp's maze of tents and palm-shaded alleys, signaled for an all out coup. There was a surging roar of battle cries as Valero's men suddenly erupted forth from hiding spots all over Oasis, centered around the armory tent but also elsewhere in the tent town. Figures scrambled all across the dimly lit settlement.

The first few men at the central campfire rose wearily. They had no chance at all. Nearly a dozen men, most of them drunk, were suddenly hit by a volley of muskets cracking off balls from the front of the armory tent. Thick smoke filled the area; the pungent odor of black powder swirled in the cold night air. Six men fell, bodies broken and riddled with lead shot. The remainder squatting at the fireside either floundered in confusion, or raced and tripped going for their own firearms.

Rider peered around the trunk of a narrow tree and saw a wave of Valero's men charge into the confused survivors at the fire, hacking away with stone hatchets and metal knives. Just paces away he saw one of Slug's loyal men take an axe right to his head, a stream of red gore streaming across the naked chest of his attacker, bathing him in a fine red sheen.

Still Rider backed off, leading the horses and Tank scurrying low, close behind. Tank had his rifle out, watching defensively for anyone who might wander or flee into the overgrown side of the oasis where they were pulling back for cover.

Tent flaps flew open. Naked men ran out, wondering what was happening. Many were shot down as they stumbled foolishly out and into the open, falling to the ground in clouds of smoke and blood. Chests were pierced. Heads were cracked open by musket balls. Decrepit, useless lives ended abruptly in an enfilade from Valero's regiment of treacherous warriors.

Rider saw Valero among the men, moving back and forth. He shouted an order and a small group of five or so raiders charged into a tent. He could hear the gross sounds of hacking, as the sleeping occupants were literally chopped to pieces in their sleep.

More men raced by, close to the line of trees and abundant undergrowth, not seeing the two bounty hunters as they backed off into the night. Torches taken from the main campfire were tossed onto one of the tents, the main barracks of Slug's men. The tent flap tore open as the material caught fire and half-naked men came pouring out, armed and screaming with rage, firing off in uncontrolled volleys to make good their escape.

Valero seemed almost surprised but only for a moment. Muskets readily fired at the emerging raiders, taking off the front rank and injuring those behind with tiny shrapnel exploding from their comrades. More men poured out from behind, from the cloud of smoke belching out the sole exit, firing their own weapons at their ambushers. Valero's men began to fall, one by one.

In seconds, the mass of loyal soldiers swept towards Valero's now-scattered usurpers, entering into a chaotic, bloody melee.

Gale gasped with a start as shots rang out all across town. For a moment she thought she had been caught in her attempt to sneak away. But immediately she realized the sounds came from outside. Quickly she scuttled over across the skins and peeled apart a panel of the tent to peek through.

Outside she saw men running everywhere and nowhere. A thick cloud of gun smoke was already filling the air of the entire tent city, whirling primarily about the main camp, casting eerie shadows as unseen men ran to and fro. She heard screams nearby, cries in the distance, echoes sounding out across the black night sky as more muskets fired in an uncoordinated fashion all over Oasis.

Her bright, gimlet eyes stared straight ahead as her heart pounded. Some of the other girls were now waking and a confused mass of questions ran through them. Some departed, running off towards Slug's tent which was adjacent to theirs and connected by clever tunnels of fabric.

On the other side of the curtain from Gale, Buddy himself cursed. He too had heard the shots. He threw the woman draped over his chest off and scrambled clumsily for his clothes. He heard the other harem girls shouting and crying out in drugged and drunken confusion. *What the hell was going on?!*

Rider saw the edge of the camp and spotted the last few tents near the perimeter. The light from the many fires didn't pierce the darkness out there. Just a few dozen yards more and they would vanish into the night.

"Come on!" he shouted at Tank. Tank leapt up onto his horse's back and dug his heels into its sides. Rider followed suit, once Tank was safely ahead of him, riding through the last few yards of foliage and out past the perimeter tents. The village was left behind with their sudden burst of speed.

Burning Lands

Back in camp, Valero rose and fired his pistol, an old Wildey .44, into a loyal raider who charged him, screaming like a maniac. The man's head nearly exploded as the high-caliber shot ripped through his face, breaking bone and leaving a jagged stump. Men swirled all around. Brothers driven by the same passion as himself gathered about him to fight, butchering the men foolish enough to stay at Slug's side. The adrenaline raced through Valero's body.

Suddenly, out of the corner of his eye, he saw Tank and Rider racing off into the night. He cursed, his eyes flaring wide.

"SHOOT THEM!" Three of his men turned and saw the riders close to vanishing into the night. Unwilling to question his command, three shots rang out from muskets.

Rider heard his heart beating as his horse bounded off. He was catching up to Tank, now only a few yards ahead, heading towards the steep and barren face of the dunes bordering on the oasis. He heard the shots echo in the night and saw puffs of sand and dust erupt into the air as two out of three missed widely.

Just then, he felt a sudden and unexpected lurch, a sinking feeling as his horse simply dropped from beneath him into the sand, headfirst, sliding to a motionless pile feet away. In its dying collapse, Rider was thrown clear, sprawled out across the wind-packed sands.

"You missed one! Now get the other!" Valero screamed, reloading his smoking pistol. His men began reloading their muskets frantically.

Rider felt a choking sensation in his throat... *blood*. His head spun round and round but his feet kept moving, defiant, trained and instinctive. He kept running, low, making himself a harder target. His heart was pounding and as his eyes finally cleared and narrowed, he saw Tank in the distance, riding hell for leather over the crest of a far dune and into the open desert, almost a hundred yards away.

Turning on weak, bruised knees, Rider looked back and saw, even from this distance, Valero and his men frantically reloading among the mass of warriors battling it out. They were moving away from the battle, personally pursuing him towards the desert's edge. Valero stared at him, his hard expression turning into a challenging, ruthless grin.

Snapping his head back, Rider weighed the distance to the tall dune against the closeness of the trees. In an instant he knew that though the dune was closer, he'd leave his back wide open if he tried to scale its slippery sand; but the trees, the trees...

"HEYAAAAH!" he cried, forcing himself back towards camp.

"Come on boys ..." Valero murmured to his men, trying to get them to hurry. They scattered, knelt and took up firing positions. He raised his pistol towards the distant outline of Rider, making a direct line for the oasis' trees. Rider's hands were empty; he'd lost his rifle in the fall. He was a sitting duck.

Valero fired. Again. And again. Rider heard the shots, saw them directed right at him. He could hear the .44 magnum repeating over the warfare going on in the camp, as shots whizzed past his head or struck dully into the sand around his feet. Then, even that sound faded into obscurity, as his mind focused on the sound of his feet hitting sand with each harried step.

The line of trees was closer... closer. His heart raced, his throat burned from dryness and exertion. In one final burst he literally threw himself through the air and into the trees.

Valero saw Rider make it to the trees. He pulled his gun back, smoking, ejecting the last round and reloading like a practiced marksman.

"Which one got away?" one of his men asked.

Valero just grinned and motioned his men to follow. They had a battle to win.

Back in the heat of the conflict, Buddy threw open the tent flap to the harem, pulling his musket pistol out in front of him. His eyes widened in horror as he saw the battle raging outside.

Suddenly a few gunshots cracked through the air nearby. The harem girl following close behind him for a peek outside was struck, killed instantly. Blood spattered his bare back. He shouted nonsensically and dropped flat onto the sand, firing wildly back, the black powder smell stinging his nose. The few remaining harem girls screamed and panicked.

Gale, still hiding apart from the others in the darkness, quietly took advantage of the situation and raced out of the tent, past Buddy's prone shape, stepping on him gingerly as she went.

Buddy cried out again and spun, as more shots hit the tent. He began furiously reloading the clumsy flintlock, looking back and forth over his shoulders in total confusion. His few brief years as a brutal killer, always in control of his victims, laughing at their pleas for mercy, began to fade. He had never been in any sort of real large-scale skirmish or any situation where the outcome was unclear. He was terrified!

Gale ran at full speed and took cover in the shadows of an old decaying wagon, resting by the side of one of the many tents clustered at the heart of the village. She stared, confused but alert, watching with awe at the bloodshed and carnage but searching with hawk-like eyes for a way out.

A group of men charged with axes and stones into the ranks of a few gun-wielding warriors no more than a dozen paces away. She couldn't understand at all what was happening. They all looked alike, bald savages, just this morning laughing and celebrating together; now killing themselves in an orgy of pure madness. The men with guns fired one last volley, felling half their attackers, but the others continued through without hesitation. She gasped as she saw limbs taken from bodies and blood streaming in all directions, all amid smoldering fires and the ever-growing smoke from the hundreds of shots echoing out in the night.

In the dark, seemingly safe cover of the trees, Rider still felt exposed. Hunkered down as he caught his breath with what little time he could spare, he realized he'd lost his big stick when his horse got sniped. He slipped his dry tongue over his pursed lips as he assessed his situation. He wasn't hit, but he was hurting.

But his mind was focused on the steely eyes of Valero, who had taken it upon himself as a personal challenge to see Rider die. That pissed him off.

Reaching down, he checked his belt holsters, then opened his big panel jacket. Slipping out of the voluminous coat he brought a chromed, meticulously cared-for miniature submachine gun. He checked the clip, then slapped it back in. It was time to hunt that son-of-a-bitch.

Men of Slug's camp, bloody and recuperating, were retreating from the fireside's edge and deeper into the camp, firing as they went, and even lobbing stones from makeshift slings. They dragged their few living wounded with them to the line of tents. Valero was nowhere to be seen but his men were no doubt retreating with him. A few stray shots echoed through the din. The battle was moving on.

Rider could hear his own breathing. Heavy. Enraged. His breath was forming into short dying clouds in the icy night air. A cold sweat had formed on his gnarled hands and pallid face. Strands of his colorless hair stuck to his face but he took no notice. One by one, his fingers gingerly tapped the metal handle of his pocket-sized Uzi, as he slid off and ran towards a nearby tent, throwing his back against it as he slid to the dirt.

Somewhere else, the girl Gale, caught sight of shapes moving. From where she sat, under the cover of the wagon, she also saw that horseman, the one who had killed her only friend Johnny, up against a tent and attempting to steep himself in its shadow.

Back at the harem tent, Buddy got up. His mind had cleared; his fear had diminished to a grim, almost suicidal energy. He was ready to fight but where he was, all was now quiet. He stared with wide eyes, searching the night for any sign of movement. He nursed the big heavy flintlock pistol in one hand, ready to cap anyone moving through his line of sight. He felt the cold lifeless arm of the dead harem girl splayed out over his leg. Something about it was ghoulish; he kicked it sharply aside, muttering something akin to disgust.

Again he looked back. It was still quiet. He could hear, faintly, the sobbing and moans of the harem girls in the dark tent behind him. Slowly he got to his feet but hunched over as he dashed across a short expanse of sand to a nearby tent. Several other bald soldiers sat there, nursing gaping wounds, feebly reloading muskets and staunching the confusion and disarray, calling out to each other for reassurance.

Buddy ducked down and slid alongside them. "What the fuck's goin' on!" he yelled.

One of them, his eye missing from a stray shot, just screamed, his voice going hoarse mid-cry. Buddy crawled back, horrified.

"Valero's gone nuts!" said someone in the dark, pointing off into the night as if to punctuate the palpable division in the Scorps. "He's fuckin' *crazy!* He's gonna kill us all!"

"What the..." Buddy murmured. "Where the fuck is Slug?"

Suddenly, the silence was pierced by a growing noise. The men taking cover looked up in wonder.

The sound of motorcycle engines roared through the alleys that formed between the decrepit raider tents. Piercing headlights struck out through the darkness, illuminating astonished faces that took immediate cover.

Gunfire once more ripped through the night. A few unwary loyalists were cut down instantly. One crumpled body fell on Buddy, pinning him under its weight. He cried out in surprise but his voice was lost among the screams.

The roars of the rebel motorcycles took everyone off guard. A huge cloud of sand and dust followed them as they raced into the settlement from the distant corral just on the edge of the camp, spreading before them a billowing dust cloud like an enveloping wave of confusion.

Coughs and shouts echoed through the storm of sand. Buddy pushed the body off, only to find himself fighting to clear his eyes of biting dust particles.

Gale cried as the sand hit her too and like a strong gust of wind, knocked her back and onto her butt with a squeal.

Rider bit hard against his lip, but covered. He felt the dust cloud swarm around. He held fast to his Micro-Uzi, knowing any minute the motorcycles would be upon them and he'd better be ready.

And they were. In an instant the gust of biting sand was followed by roaring cycles which wove in and out of the dust fog, their riders firing wildly at any poor bastard they happened upon. Cries and screams were drowned out by the roar of the fiery engines.

Rider took aim, firing off at one of the headlights. The rattle of automatic fire rang out with a unique *rat-tat-tat* that few in the camp had ever heard. Men from both sides of the battle ran away from its chattering report. He heard the cycle, fatally stricken, crash into a tent, and heard more screams from within as it caught fire. He pulled back behind cover, and tightened the grip on his gun.

Buddy wondered what in the hell that noise was. He poked his head out quickly and then once more. He snapped himself up onto his knees and fired. To his surprise, over the small crest of sand, among bodies and fallen raiders, he saw a swarm of at least a dozen cycles, headed straight towards him and the few remaining loyalists of Slug's guards gathered outside this nameless abode.

Buddy shouted a choked cry of terror and bolted. A few tried to follow suit but were cut down as they emerged. Those that stayed bravely in place felled one or two of the riders but were soon either run over or cut down as the cyclists rode by with swords and whirling, spiked flails. He ran off, listening to the sound of the others being butchered behind him.

Gale, too, heard the grotesque cries and choked. She yearned to run out and help, even though these same men would have killed her or worse just this morning, but fear held her back, made her stay her place.

Suddenly she felt a strong hand grab her and throw her back to the ground, onto her back. She cried out as she saw several of Valero's men, armed with guns and axes, on foot. They were following behind the wave of motorcycles that had passed by, mopping up those few who had survived the "cavalry" charge. Most moved on, leaving just one straggler, who moved towards her. Yelling something incomprehensible, he raised his axe to cleave her.

Her eyes narrowed in concentration, and in doing so she stared directly at the man's contorted, cruel face.

Rider, across the way, popped his head out and let off a burst. He darted out again over a fallen raider and saw at a distance the young ghoul-girl on her back, about to be *killed*.

He looked, his finger hesitating on the trigger. A machinegun burst... he shouldn't waste it. Not to help a weak child. Certainly not. But he watched, fascinated perhaps in some cold inhuman way; concerned, of course not, but at the very least wondering with a lingering and morbid curiosity what that useless girl's ultimate fate would be.

"Nnnnnggggg ..." the guy cried, as his muscles strained to bring the axe into her flesh. The axe came down hard on the sand. He opened his eyes and saw the girl still lying there, just a few feet away. She was looking back at him with wide eyes and an almost apologetic expression, as if afraid her dodging would only infuriate him further. The raider swung again and Gale rolled once more with catlike grace out of the axe's path. The raider snarled and swung once more, but the girl seemed able to anticipate his every move and skittered aside without much exertion at all.

Rider's eyes widened as he watched. There was something unnatural about her ability to dodge this hulking raider's blows. Something very unnatural about the intense concentration in her eyes...

The raider, growing exasperated, turned white as he slowly realized what she was doing, at least as far as his simple mind could fathom. In seconds the raider took off after the others, stumbling over bodies and debris as he went, leaving the girl alive.

Gale shouted with a throaty growl as she ceased concentrating and her body slumped against the tent. Her whole form shook for a few drawn-out seconds.

Rider couldn't believe his eyes. He had seen it. With his own bloody eyes. Not just the inability of the raider to cleave her but the power in her eyes when she had stared him down. Making sure the others had moved on with quick looks in each direction, he ran over and with one quick motion threw the girl back against the wagon.

Gale cried out and screamed, striking out with weak arms. Whatever she had done to preserve her life against the raider had exhausted her because he was readily able to pin her with one hand.

Rider slowly crouched in front of her, his eyes searching her familiar face. This was certainly that grubby waste from the ghoul's desert camp but she didn't look so helpless now. For a moment he found himself looking at her with much more interest.

All was quiet. Rider sunk deeper onto his heels, watching for any sign of movement from the fog of powder smoke and churned sand, rattle-stick tight in hand. Gale no longer cried, having regained her composure. But suddenly, she jumped with surprise as another figure threw himself down in the small niche by the tent alongside them.

Rider spun, ready to pop off a burst, only to see Buddy's soot-stained, bloody face.

"... (huff) It's over, man! Rider! It's over! Slug's dead! I seen him! Dead with the others! They killed the Clean guy too. Valero's really cleaning up. He's got men... (huff) stickin' the dead and wounded to keep 'em all down. He's really out for blood, man!"

Rider looked back at Gale for a moment while he could. They had unfinished business. Had he really seen what he thought he had seen? No. She looked helpless again, just a worthless kid. She was scared. What had he been thinking! She was slippery to be sure, but not supernaturally. The raider had merely given up too easily; he would have had her eventually. She should consider herself lucky to be alive.

Buddy waited, grinding his teeth together noisily, staring out into the dark. He heard a distant series of cries as surrendering men were struck with axes and stuck with knife blades.

"We've gotta go, man! Rider! Do you hear me?!"

Finally deciding there was nothing special about Gale after all, Rider snapped out of it, grabbed Buddy and threw him forward. Buddy got to his feet and started running in Rider's chosen direction, towards the towering dunes seen over the sea of burning, abandoned tents.

Gale watched the two men run off together, presumably leaving her to die. Neither even looked back to see if she would follow. Rising to her feet, she looked around. Well, she decided, she certainly wouldn't die here. She raced off after them and towards the distant dunes.

Rider couldn't believe it was morning already. Or more accurately, that they had made it to even *see* the next morning.

Three isolated individuals walked over the sands, going up and down the mountainous dunes. Ahead of him, Buddy walked with a quick and eager step, driven by a lingering desire to put as much distance between them and the settlement of Oasis as possible. Blood stains all over the youth had turned him brown under the baking sun and the jingle of his chains and buckled semi-clothes twinkled in the air.

Although Buddy hadn't seen it yet, Rider had. Behind them, maybe a few hundred yards back, followed the girl. She rightfully kept her distance, keeping to the trail of tracks they had left, like a lighted highway, in their haste and fatigue.

Rider looked back and saw she did not stumble or fall behind like he half expected. No, her pace was practiced, competent, energetic. Though he refused to believe she had "powers", he realized that the grub might well know her way around the desert. Maybe. But the thought did not move him, did not impart any measure of respect by any means. That dot on the horizon following them was not a person, it was an extra mouth. It was begging and crying. It was pitiful attempts to gain his friendship, his debt. And when that failed, it was a knife in the back for his water or whatever else he had.

He turned away. Let her follow. And if she came close, he'd blow her away. Actually, he thought, this way she was actually of some use to them. If Valero and his men pursued, they'd get to her first. And the sound of her screams would give *them* some warning...

Hours passed. The sun rose higher into the sky. Now, the true desolation of the world outside the oasis was revealed like a glorious panorama all around.

Buddy came to the top of one of a million dunes of sifting sand, almost forty feet high. Below him lay another gulley where the sand would cool his burning feet. From up here it all looked like infinity, in every direction, and they were lost within its enclosing arms. He looked up, squinting, shielding his eyes from the huge disc of the fiery sun. Pitiful ribbons, the remnants of dying cloud formations, were framed against the yellow sky. A strong buffeting wind came over the haunting landscape of nothingness, pulled at him and brought with it the invisible particles of sand that once more began to sting at his eyes and motivate him onwards.

Rider followed, huffing and puffing. His few bits of exposed skin were burning as if on fire, his white hair billowing like cobwebs as he crested the peak. He too, stopped to look around, his eyes narrowing as he took in the vastness around them.

Burning Lands

It didn't used to be like this, a desert world with seas of sand. Below the endless dust were the bones of a futuristic civilization, the landscape crisscrossed by buried highways, mass-transit *maglev* railways connecting each metropolis with the next and the ruins of megalithic cities of stone, steel and silicon. The mile-high towers of ancient skyscrapers had mostly crumbled to dust; the cities were radiated ruins to which few dared to return. Battlefields where once gauss- and laser-armed war machines confronted surrogate legions of androids had been mostly swept away by the relentless sandstorms that now reigned in the skies. Those same legions, once they had ground themselves to dust on the frontlines of the Final War, had been replaced by their human controllers until they, too, had expended themselves in that last desperate defense of the American homeland. No amount of futuristic innovation (man-portable lasers, masers, powered armor) could stave off their eventual defeat; an earlier technology, the *nuclear weapon*, trumped it all. With a final whimper, their great civilization was gone at last, as subject as the ancient cultures of Egypt and Babylon to being lost to the ravages of time.

The desolation that surrounded them for miles was indeed breathtaking but Rider wasn't here to sightsee. He looked back over his shoulder and into the distance. It was clear. The smoke of the camp's burning cinders was long gone and dust clouds that might be kicked up by an army of raiders were, reassuringly, missing from the horizon. He took a moment to breathe. Then his eye caught sight of that dot again. Moving. He squinted to make sure he wasn't imagining things. She was there. That worthless kid was still with them.

Rider stood tall and fixed his hat tightly to protect from the growing wind. He turned away and kept walking in Buddy's path.

A few more hours slipped by.

"Where are we going?" The voice escaping from Buddy's mouth was weak and dry, as he faced into the wind and stared out into the sea of nothingness that was the Forbidden Lands. It wasn't so much the question itself but the way Buddy voiced it, that caught Rider's attention.

Buddy was thirsty. Not overwhelmingly thirsty. Not quite "water-mad". But his lips were dry. His throat was dry. They'd walked for hours under the beating sun and they had no water among them. The sound of his rasping lips made Rider take note, but he hid his caution well as he stopped beside the young raider outcast.

Rider stared out into the bleak wilderness of dunes. He could tell Buddy was looking to him for guidance, for reassurance, for some kind of a hope. He knew Buddy would quickly lose his cools now. They were tired and hungry and disappointment doesn't sit well with those two factors floating around.

He exhaled deeply and touched his dry tongue to his lower lip. "Tucumcari," he said, "the Trade City."

Buddy blinked once or twice as the wind picked up. "Trade City? Did you say, Trade City? That's over eighty miles!"

Despite Buddy's aggravation, Rider nodded slowly, his head scanning the horizon in front of them. They were already headed south. The watery blue outline of the Rocky Mountains could be vaguely seen, by anyone with eyes enough to look really hard, on the edge of the western horizon.

Buddy stared out across the sea of sand. For once he was quiet, his face all shrunk up in consideration. Sand particles clung to his bushy eyebrows. "We'll never make it..." he said softly, openly surrendering to defeat as his voice trailed off.

Rider kept staring out across the spaces, his eyes unconsciously counting the dunes one by one and the valley floors in between. "We will..." he said, starting out ahead of Buddy, "... and if we want to, we'd better keep moving."

Gale had been following now for three days. Her lips were dry and cracked but she held them tightly closed to keep out the dry air. She bit her cheeks now and again to stimulate some saliva production; it helped fight the cotton-mouth as spit welled up underneath her tongue.

For the past few nights she had seen the two men literally collapse among the dunes when exhaustion overcame them. The hideous raider was something of a "follower", she could only guess; he lagged behind the taller one in the long coat, like a dog. The tall one, he at least knew to shelter in one of the pitted valley floors so the wind wouldn't freeze them stiff. The coat, though it made him stink with day's-old sweat, kept him cool during the day and warm at night. The raider had no such luxury. At times she could hear him cursing about it even from so far away.

She also sensed other things. Every now and again, when they were within sight, she could concentrate on one or the other. She heard him. Talking. In his mind. The younger one was a simple, angry and violent creature; his thoughts were unfamiliar to her, and offensive. She avoided thoughts about him, for when she let herself slip she always experienced his anguish, hopelessness and feelings of abandonment. His was a shallow, ugly world, a vision of the here and now that reflected brutality, anxiousness and impatience. He was a creature born to live fiercely and die young; being left to dwindle in this void was a torture to his very being.

The other, the one she had heard called "Rider", seemed much calmer but veiled his emotions quite poorly to her prying mind. She could hear right through his collected and superior manner. He was afraid too, but he didn't let it show. He was tired, hungry and thirsty. Obsessed with thirst. He was a creature of constant survival, of day-to-day needs. Every now and then she could hear him whispering to himself in his own mind, as if he somehow thought someone was listening. Well, she was. But she was sure he didn't know. His thoughts were openly callous. Unfettered by any feeling other than fear for his own life. His eyes were glued to the raider, always expecting a surprise attack, a betrayal. Never letting his guard down. He was wary, suspicious.

Such an awful way to be, day in and day out. She also knew the extent of his contemptuousness for her and the fact that he knew she was following them.

She sat there, staring, under the mid-day sun. She had done a fine job of keeping her distance, only following them. She had fared the thirst and hunger far better than they. She'd had to do it plenty of times in the past, when her old friend (images flashed in her mind) sometimes came back empty-handed, sometimes for days. They had managed to survive, together. They had taught each other tricks of the desert and learned to cope; but now the thirst was reaching the point that even she could not deny. Her face was raw, dehydrated and baked. She had nothing on her except for a covering of thin clothes to keep her pitifully warm at night and to shield from the unrelenting sun. Now she sat in a more familiar, cat-like squat, staring out across the expanses towards the two distant men on a far away sand dune.

Across the way, on top of a huge dune, Buddy and Rider finally came to a stop. Buddy flailed his arms out pitifully. Miles and miles of sand lay beyond.

"This is it!" he shouted at the top of his burning lungs. "This is finally it! We're going to fucking die out here!"

This was dangerous, Rider thought. He could see the wild movements, the red-rimmed eyes. Buddy flopped around on weak legs, a half-cocked smile sweeping over his sun-blackened face.

"Keep going," Rider said, in a feeble attempt to distract him. It didn't work.

"No! I can't take it. I can't... go any more. Rider..." Buddy touched his swollen hand to his forehead, covering the breaking wave of emotion on his face.

Rider stopped, his legs spread to stabilize himself against the wind roaring at the top of the dune. His coat swung in the gale; the brim of his hat fluttered.

"Rider..." Buddy started, his left hand bringing up his pistol close against his chest. He kept his back to Rider, somehow thinking he could keep from Rider's eyes the sight of him loading the barrel.

Rider saw it and his eyes narrowed. It had come to that already. His hands drifted down towards his pistol holders.

"Rider," Buddy said, laughing, "I'm sorry I gotta do this. I'm sure you understand..." He turned slowly, raising in his weakened arm the big heavy pistol.

Rider was still standing there, in the same unmovable pose. In his hands he held two black automatics, already leveled directly at Buddy.

Gale sat up, far away. She sensed something. She turned her head towards the two men silhouetted on the hill. She had to tell them. *She had to tell them!*

Neither Rider nor Buddy saw the girl picking up speed as she ran in their direction.

Rider's eyes stared at the raider. His mouth was locked in a determined frown.

"What? You're not going to say anything? Not going to say... 'hey, Buddy, be reasonable. Hey, Buddy, we're gonna make it. Just hang in their pal?'"

Rider didn't move. His guns were already cocked.

Gale kept running, skipping over the dunes with puffs of sand.

"You gonna shoot me, Rider? You WANT to shoot me. You DO. Don't care that one of us has to die; just want that *fucking* thirst to go AWAY!"

Rider's fingers twitched.

"Well," Buddy said, his eyes tearing over, the pistol slipping willfully from his grasp, "go to it, crack shot. Better you than me, right? Better a guy like you to live and save the world from guys like me. Right? RIGHT?!?"

Rider's eyes darted to track the pistol as it hit the dune and slid away but snapped back to Buddy. His eyes were wild.

"NO!" Gale cried, coming up the final dune from its shaded side. "He's coming!!!"

Rider heard it only vaguely. The sounds outside his head were so distant. His own thoughts, his own condemnations, his own mind urging him to DO IT NOW, almost had him. They almost drowned out the sound that echoed on the other side of the hill.

His eyes blinked and his mind cleared. Suddenly, in the valley below, a mounted rider came galloping down the next dune, his white horse burdened with goods.

The girl came running up the hill between them, pointing past them to the very same figure on horseback as it drew nearer at a good pace.

"It's the giant!" she yelled, "He's brought water!"

By the time Rider's mind really cleared, it was much later that day. The sun still beat down menacingly upon the landscape, but now the fever of thirst had been quenched. Even now, as he quietly sat staring at the much more vocally-grateful Buddy, he knew that the thirst had gotten to him as well. His lips had been on fire, his throat cracked and inflamed. His eyesight, already bad from his acute albinism, had fared poorly and in a day or so they would likely have been dead... with or without that dramatic confrontation that would have claimed one of them.

Now, however, he sat with a renewed sense of vigor, some strength infused in him thanks to a few meager drinks of water bartered eagerly from Tank's supply. He was weak but at least he could think straight. He sat with the others in a loose circle at the foot of the far dune, under its cool, comforting shade. The sun, dipping lower in the sky, was off of their heads for the time being.

The giant, whom he thought deserted him at the oasis, was now carefully watching the laughing, doddering Buddy sip from his water skin. He stood close by his horse, his big hand assuring it that it was next. Rider knew full well that Tank valued his ride more than he did Buddy, but to diffuse the situation he had offered water to one and all.

Rider rubbed his sandy eyelids with his fingers, already flaking from sunburn. It made the effort all the more difficult, but it gave him a sense of relaxation that had been missing for the past few days.

"Looks like I came just in time," Tank finally said, his voice dull in the open area between the dunes. "Looks like you were both delirious."

His voice, though audibly amused, spoke the truth. Rider ran his finger along the rim of his dusty hat and looked up, staring at Tank. For a moment, though he held his tongue, his eyes reflected his own inner gratitude and heartfelt thanks. But Tank couldn't see that. Just the lenses of Rider's all-black sunglasses.

Tank reached over and pulled his water skin away from Buddy, who nearly fell over on his weak knees. Buddy instinctively tried to pursue and suckle more from its lip, but Tank was firm and pushed him over. He pulled away, swirled the heavy skin around to judge how much was left inside and retrieved a dirty metal pot from the goods burdening his horse. He poured some water into it and rested the container under his mount's muzzle so it could drink too.

As he waited for his horse to nourish itself, Tank's little white eyes swept over to the spot, just out of reach, where the feral girl squatted, watching. Her long blond hair was scraggly and covered much of her face when the wind blew, but he could see every now and again her dry, rasping tongue dart out to feebly wet her lips.

Her eyes were locked on the meager droplets of water spilling from the pot as the horse fed. But she kept her distance from them, by almost a full twenty yards, close enough to hear them talk, but far enough to scramble away if they made a move towards her.

Burning Lands

He turned back to Rider after only a second of acknowledging her presence, as the latter finally spoke. "Any sign of Valero's men?" Rider asked.

Tank looked up and took in a deep breath of desert air. His tiny, rabbit-like eyes fluttered as the wind picked up.

"No." He said this after some thought, as if considering some strange signs he had seen earlier that day or perhaps the night before. "A big group of them swarmed north with their vehicles the day after we left. Around dawn. Could see the dust cloud for maybe six, seven miles going north, northeast."

Rider considered their unexpected luck with a perched eyebrow. "That means they're going the opposite way..."

Buddy looked up for the first time from licking the evaporating moisture from his filth-caked hands. "Yeah? Alright then! Alright! We got a chance!"

Tank looked off to the northern horizon. Rider's gaze followed. Both were a little surprised at their fortune, and the revelation that Valero had erred in his calculated effort to hunt them down. But here they were, alive. Tank was a reliable scout, even more so on horse; if he hadn't spotted Valero's gang in the vicinity, then they just may have escaped without a hitch.

"But... but where do we go now?" Buddy asked. He rose to one knee.

"Camp's just a few miles southeast," Tank said, already beginning to mount his horse. Rider rose and gathered his coat about him, ready to plod off in the horse's shadow.

"Camp?" Buddy asked. "What camp?"

Tank looked back over one shoulder with a heavy groan, as he made the climb atop his steed. A smile formed on his bizarre-looking face. "You didn't think I'd share my last two gallons with you scum, did you?"

Buddy didn't necessarily know what he meant by that remark, or how to answer his question, but something about Tank's amusement at this most dire situation gave him hope. He stumbled on after them, chains and thorny spikes jingling as he went.

Tank looked over his shoulder once more at the girl, who had already gotten up with a start to follow them. Though she looked so young with that cherub-like face, she moved like a vulture perfectly poised, shadowing the dying man as he crawled through the wasteland. He gave her a long hard stare, not knowing what to do; he ultimately turned and slowly led the others off to the southeast.

The sun was getting low on the distant horizon; its reddish-gold light was now waning, turning the sky nearest to it a hellish amber, fading to a shade of wisteria and cold, desolate purple at its opposite horizon. No stars could be spotted at that hour, and only the murky crescent of the moon could be seen in the sky.

It wasn't night yet, but rather just the onset of another twilight in the Forbidden Lands. The wind was beginning to pick up once more, stronger and more defiant against those who braved the desert without its sovereign permission, carrying a biting cold as more and more of the sun's heat was sapped from the sands.

Up ahead a most curious sight was seen rising from a huge dune. Tank and Rider seemed unconcerned by the oddity of it, but Gale and even Buddy slowed to a stop to let their eyes explore its huge, unexplainable and ultimately bizarre shape and dimensions. Where the sun framed it against the sky, it looked like the angular fin of some colossal metal shark, the wind of decades having stripped it almost completely of paint and its fixtures, leaving only huge words in bright blue across one side. This huge "fin" was attached to a massive metal body, itself perched at an angle as it seemed to sink into the very earth like a knife hurled from the heavens. Riddled with holes in a regular fashion along one side, it was most curious indeed.

"What is it?" Buddy mustered, his voice carrying despite the wind.

Rider ignored the question and walked steadily over to a cache of heavy rocks concealed under the shadow of the great dune, which he noted was already disturbed. He kicked a few of the cairn's rocks over and rummaged through the contents protected within. Tank had taken his share; no more, no less. Rider was surprised.

Tank slid off his horse and took a turn looking at the mighty metal structure.

"Don't know what it *was*," he replied to Buddy's question. "But it *is* camp."

Buddy continued to stare upwards as he wandered forward. Tank, having spent a day or so here figuring out what to do, already knew where to set up a campfire where the wind was least likely to squelch it. After Rider retrieved a few sand-crusted belongings from the hollow cairn, he joined Tank in giving life to a meager but priceless fire.

Buddy came over, his face illuminated in the first flames of the camp. The cold was setting in quickly, but like the girl who sat far off with no such comfort, he was apparently consumed with imagining and wondering as to the great thing's origins and purpose. He moved from the fire to stare at the enormous object whose shadow they camped in.

Rider looked up at Buddy. Perhaps because he was annoyed at Buddy wandering off, or for daydreaming or simply because he let it slip, he muttered something aloud that all could hear.

"In the time of the Ancients," Rider said, "men flew about the world in airships of metal. They looked like birds, with huge wings," he pointed off to the barely-perceivable outline of broken wings some distance behind the craft.

"This one *crashed*," he said, turning from his explanation to finish the job he'd started. From among the cairn's rubble he had retrieved a can, which he opened with a knife at his side. He sat back on the cold sand and drank deeply of the nectar that flowed out.

Buddy's eyes swayed from the crashed airliner to the can. "What's that?" he asked, his eyes widening in realization.

"Peaches!" he shouted, stumbling over.

In a second Rider had swung out his knife and caught Buddy under the chin. He held his blade there momentarily as his eyes stared deep into Buddy's. He continued drinking the juice until the can emptied.

"Why should I feed you?" he quietly asked, pulling his knife back to open the rest of the lid. With his grubby fingers he pulled out the slender sliver of the quartered fruit, and dipped it into his mouth. He savored its sweet moist flavor for a moment before swallowing.

Buddy, on his knees, sank back, crestfallen. He had that frozen, trembling look on his face; his mind was working at a mile a minute to come up with some reason, some excuse, that Rider should share with him.

"Rider!" is all he could muster.

Burning Lands

Tank turned. "We've shared our water, we've spared your life, raider. Your people tried to kill us. Now get out of here." He punctuated this by swiping at Buddy, who tumbled aside. He was shocked, desperate.

"No!" he cried. "Valero's taken over the clan! He'd kill me, man! Come on, guys! You gotta give me some!"

"Take a hike," Rider said calmly between bites of sumptuous peach. A dribble of honey-like liquid trickled from his full mouth as he spoke.

"Come on man..." Buddy began. He was cut short as Tank pulled the rifle from his horse's back and fired a shot just in front of Buddy's skulking form. With a cry of fear Buddy leapt up and scurried off. Tank kept his rifle at hand, watching Buddy go, a look of half-disgust, half-uncertainty etched very visibly on his face.

Rider noticed it but didn't look up. "You did the right thing, Tank," he said, breathing a deep sigh of slow relaxation, moving closer to the fire as it began to grow. "He'd just be trouble. He's a rat by birth, and he'll stay that way."

Buddy, a dozen yards or so away, turned and threw out his arms. "What am I supposed to do, huh?" he called out bitterly. "Where am I supposed to go? What do I do for food and water?"

This last he punctuated by spitefully kicking a nearby rock with all his might. It took off and landed somewhere out in the sand. Neither Tank nor Rider answered his pointless question. Tank slowly retreated, soothing himself by muttering unintelligible sounds to his horse, sheathing the big heavy rifle in its weathered leather saddle-holster.

"Leave *me* to die..." Buddy hissed, walking away with the camp light to his back. He spotted the girl some yards away, in the shadows.

At once he started after her, hooting and hollering like a farmer chasing a greased pig.

"I'll eat *her!*" he shouted. "Here, piggy-piggy! Here piggy-piggy!" Gale let out a soft cry and scampered off, as Buddy half-heartedly gave chase, arms outstretched as he plodded after her. After a few moments he dropped to his knees and began to weep. Gale pulled back a few paces, out of arm's reach, terrified of him and watching his mental collapse.

Buddy fell over, weeping so bad he could barely be understood. *"Gonna... die... here... no... water... food... you fuckers..."* He curled up into a miserable ball and could be seen shuddering away even from back at the camp.

Tank was looking out at the sorry breakdown. Rider seemed as unconcerned as ever. His eyes once more settled on the girl.

"Where'd she come from?" Tank asked, almost indifferently. Something in his voice, however, seemed to give away a concealed interest.

Rider looked over, tossing the empty, licked-clean can away. "That's the ghoul-bait," he said, "the grub from the camp. Remember?"

It took a moment to sink in. Tank rolled his head back as it hit him. Before he could ask another question, Rider continued. "Just followed us out of camp. Not suited to be a slave, I guess. Can't find a way to get rid of her." With that Rider turned back to look into the fire, already drowsy. The contentment of a fine meal, water, and a fire to sleep by was setting in.

Tank was quiet for a moment, looking past Rider into the night. Slowly he let go of the horse's reigns and walked towards her distant, hunkered shape.

Gale saw him coming, and retreated slowly up the sandy slope of the dune. She was making little headway and slid slowly back. Tank moved closer, slowly and cautiously, opening his arms wide as if to say he meant no harm. But to her, his eyes, glossed over and white, looked like the eyes of a walking dead man, a zombie, getting nearer and nearer. She struggled to get away, rolling over now and attempting to crawl up the dune to escape. The little girl was deathly afraid of the huge man, and in the darkness, framed by the campfire, he reminded her of the Frankenstein creature she had heard of as a little child.

Just then, to her surprise, the man dropped to one knee and put down something he'd been hiding in one of his hands, right at her feet. A bundle wrapped in dirty cloth; a bit of crumbly bread and a thick-skinned orange gleaming with hidden inner moisture. She found herself turning her back on her better judgment, and sat squat on the earth savagely devouring the gift before her. With shaking hands she tore at the orange until she realized she was wasting more from the effort than she was getting.

Tank reached out then and took it from her, only momentarily, peeling it quickly and handing it back before her soft whimpers grew too loud. Taking it back, Gale tore at it with her teeth. In moments it was gone, and she turned to eat the bread too.

Buddy, rousing himself, saw this and came thumping over, grabbing her by the wrist in an attempt to steal it.

"Get away!" she screamed. Slashing at him with her rough, broken nails.

Buddy, remarkably, sunk away like a weaker dog that'd lost its bid for dominance, and into the shadows to sulk mournfully.

Gale didn't care. The animal in her, like never before, had taken over. She consumed each bite with feverish satisfaction, casting her angry eyes to the sides whenever she spotted Buddy moving near and around her.

"She can *speak*..." Tank muttered in surprise. He'd heard her before, but up close it seemed so strange.

Tank watched for a few moments, got up, and returned to camp. Rider watched him rummage through a few things on his horse. Looking around to see if anyone was looking, namely Rider, he poured from his water skin a pint of the clean, clear fluid into the same pot he had fed his horse. He turned, suddenly noticing Rider was staring right at him and the water.

Tank's face flushed momentarily. Rider's sunglasses were low enough on his nose that Tank could see his eyebrow shoot up in interest. Then Rider pushed the glasses back into place, pretending nothing was the matter.

Tank stared down at the precious stuff in the pot. He ignored Rider's burrowing glare and walked back to the girl. Kneeling, he offered the pot which she eagerly took and drunk to her heart's content.

Buddy stared, eyes dancing with greed, jealousy, and the sparkles of the dim firelight. His face changed into a smiling sneer that was much more reflective of his spite.

"He wants to *fuck you*, girl," Buddy hissed. "He wants to butter you up, fatten you good, and *fuck* you."

"You *trash*..." Tank muttered, rising to his feet in an instant. His voice was tinged with outright disgust.

Burning Lands

Gale didn't move, she just continued to drink away. Tank threw himself over towards Buddy, who tried to get away. The two scuffled for a few long minutes, rolling down the dune and punching away at one another.

Rider, at the fire, looked over only casually. For a brief second he watched the fight, but knew Buddy too weak to make a killing blow, and Tank too clumsy to get in a solid hit. He rested his hat over his face, crossed his arms behind his head, and lay back against the sand.

Tank collapsed to his knees, breathing heavily, as he watched Buddy run off into the night, yelling obscenities and curses back over his shoulder. Wishing them death, hexing them with an eternity of pain. Only when Buddy was good and gone did he look back at the girl.

"You can sleep by the fire," he said, looking at her. Gale stared back, but said nothing. Rising to his feet, he returned to camp with Rider.

It was now pitch dark outside, except perhaps for an eerie reddish glow on the horizon, a glow that never really left the face of the Twisted Earth completely. It was a strange glow, an odd iridescence that one unaccustomed to it could stare at for hours on end in fascination, like a frozen fire stretching from horizon to horizon, never moving. It looked like the sun rising, or setting, but it never faded or brightened more than a glow.

As it was, many appropriately called it "the glow", while others proscribed it magical powers and dire properties. Most likely it was the visible aura of lingering radiations that still bathed the planet, from the great cataclysmic wars of the Ancients that had ravaged the world and left it sundered. Its fire, which scorched the cities and nations and left them in ashes to be swept away by the winds, still seemed to be reflected in the very sky that carried their vehicles of destruction across the world in that time so long ago.

But these were the ponderings and thoughts of other men, of sandwalkers with the luxury of time to consider, and the rare philosopher or hermit with the inclination. To Gale, it was still a wonder, but to the two bounty hunters huddled by the dying fire, it was something they had always known and under which they had always lived.

The wind had picked up, and roared over the dunes. Rather unexpectedly it had gone from a tugging gale to a powerful driving force that brought waves of sand to crash down on the valley-like depressions between each mountain of dust. The sky bellowed with the thunder of its own winds.

In camp, Rider and Tank rose from their dreary, bone-numbing cold sleep as the sound reached its crescendo. Gale was already awake, attempting to pull a blanket from the cairn to cover herself from the blinding sand as it came at them like true wave heads, cresting the dunes and swirling about in chaotic whirls.

As he rose Rider shouted on sighting her, so close to the camp, her hands stealing one of his trade blankets, but the sudden realization that a storm was upon them dispelled his anger. Rolling over and getting to his feet, he was only barely able to shout the obvious:

"*Sandstorm! Bad one!*"

Tank, by virtue of his huge size, took longer to get to his feet but when he did, he seemed at best disoriented by the raging sounds about him. The wind, violently pulling at Rider and Gale, seemed to work vainly against the mighty mutant when he chose to stand.

Gale firmly wrapped the small blanket around her head, quickly and effectively reducing the sand hitting her square in the face, leaving only a narrow space for her eyes. She would breathe through the thin fabric, and felt at ease like this; she had had to face the storms of the Forbidden Desert on occasion before, and this was no different.

Watching Rider and Tank stumble about to get their bearings, she looked to the hollow wreckage of the airliner. The huge metal foil of the plane's tail creaked and reverberated with the wind, but seemed strong against it. Her eyes fell to the fuselage, and the windows, and the gaping hole where its rear boarding door had once been.

"To the ship!" she shouted, loud enough so the two men would hear her.

Rider heard her, and for a moment found himself stubbornly disregarding her advice, even as she led the way by first grabbing their canteens, then running full-tilt up the dune and to the darkened hole. Then, seeing the remainder of their belongings scattered and the fire completely wiped-out, he jogged after her, Tank in tow.

"My horse!" Tank muttered, looking back.

As he and Rider turned, they saw the horse suddenly attempt to bolt, for some unknown reason. Its eyes flared in sudden surprise, and it kicked up its front legs in an attempt to turn and flee. But something had its reigns. As they looked, they heard a strange gurgling, sandy noise, and the reigns being drawn under the sand by some unknown action. The horse reared in panic, but whatever had its reigns yanked it harder and harder. A fraction of the rope gave and for a moment it looked as if the animal would free itself. Then, suddenly, a grotesque yellow *hand,* riddled with ugly grayish veins that looked almost like cracks in a statue, shot out of the sand and grasped the rope, as another, and another burst from the sand itself and together they worked to pull the poor beast down.

Soon the entire area around it sank, and the horrified animal was sucked beneath the earth.

"My rifle!" Tank cried.

"*Run!*" It was the only advice his companion Rider could voice through the din, as he charged after the girl.

Despite the terrible effort of fighting the wind, running uphill and battling the knee-deep sand of the dune, the two big men made it to the fuselage hole and leapt through into the unknown.

Inside, the wind could still be heard raging at its tremendous volume, but the interior air was calm. As they went inside, Rider noticed that Gale's entrance had upset a thick layer of dust that now floated in swirling motes all about their heads.

The interior of the ruined structure was strange to all. It was much more cramped than they first imagined; though hollow, it was sectioned into tiny compartments at the point they had entered. At its steep angle of impact at about 45 degrees, it formed a sloping "tunnel" that fell into a void of blackness towards the front of the plane. One careless step, and they could slip and fall down the entire length of the angled fuselage.

Burning Lands   61

Rider turned and glared out into the dark, the thought of those ugly yellow hands rising from the sand still in mind. He struggled in vain to find a makeshift covering to bolt the entrance shut, until Tank came forward with a lopsided piece of bent metal and plastic, the plane's original doorway, in hand. Together they wrestled the thing in place, ramming it firmly against the hull until it was sealed as tight as it could be. As it shut, even the wind's tremendous roar seemed to diminish by degrees.

Tank fell against the bulkhead in exhaustion, and Rider slid off the side to likewise catch his breath. Their exasperated breathing echoed in the hollow, black interior, stirring up dead cobwebs, more dust, and fibrous clouds that wandered off and away from them as if suspended in space.

"We've boxed ourselves in," Tank stated the obvious. He turned and looked at Rider. "What *were* they?"

Rider stared at the door, sizing up its value as a barrier. He didn't answer Tank's question. He reached out with his hands for balance, resting them against opposite walls, and slowly made his way down the incline to the cabins beyond, and after the girl.

Rider found the elusive girl in the main cabin. It was hung at a precarious angle, but it was less narrow than the other space through which they had come. Dust and ash covered everything in a thick, yellow-black layer that felt like chalk wherever his hands came to rest. It unnerved him. The lingering smell of ancient death was subtly present here, but unknowable time had erased much of it from the furnishings. Long spidery strands of fiber ran from the broken ceiling panels to the many rows of seats running the length of the fuselage.

The angle here grew steeper, or perhaps the lack of abundant floor debris made the going harder, more treacherous. In either event, a rock skittered from Rider's feet down the aisle, picking up speed, and vanishing into the darkness down there. If he slipped, he'd slide effortlessly down into the unknown.

Gale was balancing herself on one of the mangy upholstered airline seats, oblivious to the choking dust she'd already kicked up around her. Her hands were covered in black ash from feeling her way through the dark. Her hair hung down at an odd angle due to the row's orientation towards up, so she repeatedly had to toss back her locks to continue focusing on what she was doing.

Rider looked around for a moment, his eyes adjusting now to the cluttered gloom, allowing him to take in the full grisly scene they had all stumbled upon. The entire cabin, and the forty or so seats in their neat rows, were filled with innumerable broken skeletons in rotten, ratty rags. Old bags were tossed about like toys throughout the place, collecting where gravity took them. Hanging from every panel on the roof was a plastic breathing mask, likewise dangling weirdly in this strange diorama of death.

The young Gale had given a cry of terror upon discovering the scene, but soon came to surmise that this vestibule to the deeper place, somewhere in the darkness below, was actually quite lifeless. The skeletons, each and every one, held a peculiar fascination for her, and she had moved closer to a particular one to stare with her wide eyes into its big empty sockets. She looked into them half-expecting it to come alive, but the dust and cobwebs certainly proved they were dead. She moved her hand close in a daring attempt to touch the bony features, but better judgment pulled her back.

Instead she looked at its ash-blackened clothes, long disintegrated except for the elastic straps that formed the framework of a summer dress; the floral design of the lacy fabric could still be seen in some lingering shreds, but these fell apart as she breathed near them. Crowning the skull were only a few hairs of gold, but those were remarkably long enough to reach beyond the skeleton's narrow shoulders.

She reached out... and touched the hair, which crumpled under her touch and fell apart. But something about golden hair froze her when her fingers touched them. Gale took her hand back, and turned slowly to the skeleton's side. There, sitting in the window seat next to it, was a diminutive skeletal form, a tangle of seatbelt around its waist. The skeleton was barely recognizable for all the ages since its terrible death, but the skull, big for its body, made it clear that this tiny figure was once a child. It wore a heavy fabric of jeans in an overall over its body that seemed to have weathered time perfectly.

Under its arm it firmly held a rotted, tattered doll, blackened on the face from some intense flash of heat.

Gale reached out and took the doll from the skeleton. She stared at it and a flood of memories came surging through her.

Suddenly, her mind was filled with terrible fear. Quick, shadowy images raced through her subconscious. Images of her mother, blond like her, blond like that dead skeleton. Clad in white, like an angel. Taking her by the hand, taking her away, fleeing. She saw a strange shape, a cold dead island at the center of a black underground lake, honeycombed with metal structures like a towering steel beehive that disappeared into a suffocating, dusty sky. It was home to her. She remembered living with others, others like her. Other little girls and boys, small and innocent.

A flood of sounds accompanied her crash of memory; she heard her voice with those of other children, singing nursery songs. She heard giggles and laughter, and strange musical notes. She heard her mother and father, teaching her and the other children about the City, about the great wars of the past, and about the future.

And then, through the dizzying whirl and confusion of her own unlocking thoughts, she heard those same voices, mother and father, talking in unison to a small gathering of friends. Something was terribly wrong! They had to leave! They had to run!

Others came. She remembered being taken by men in white uniforms, like the one she once wore, to the heart of the complex. Everything was bright and white and sterile. She was afraid. Faces of former friends, uncles and aunts, stared at her through protective glass. She remembered herself, just a child, restrained on a table and hooked up to terrifying machines. The awful, bright white light!

"Don't touch that!" came Rider's voice, piercing through the dusty darkness and breaking the girl's concentration.

All of the sudden she awoke from her trance, sitting there on her knees, holding the doll before her, staring into its eyes. One of its eyelids dipped mechanically; the other stared back at her.

Rider came forward and hissed his irritated command again. He also took the canteens she had taken, giving her a warning look, *never do that again!*

Gale let the doll go, placing it back with the skeletal baby. Rider moved past and looked down towards the front of the plane. He heard only creaking and the muffled sound of the wind.

Burning Lands

Suddenly there was a terrible noise that was heard by all three. It was a singularly disturbing noise, a terrifying noise, coming from outside the plane. At first it seemed only like a high point in the roar of the wind, a crescendo punctuating it as it came over the dunes. But then, again it came, this time louder, clearer. It was a shrill cry, an awful scream, but one whose voice was all too familiar. *It was Buddy.*

Tank, at the back of the wreckage, threw himself once more against the door to use his full weight against it, and also to better hear the noise he was sure he'd mistaken.

Gale sat up with a start and turned that way too. She slipped out and ran gingerly back up the difficult incline. Rider followed, all too aware. The girl hit the ground beside Tank and slid up against the wall to listen. Rider came up, hunkered down to avoid moving past the dusty windows, and locked eyes with Tank. He, too, was terrified.

They listened intently. Each ear was tuned to the wind, the raging storm outside. Each strained to pick up something, anything, that might dispel their first thoughts. Each vainly hoped it was just the wind.

Again the sound, almost drowned out by the ferocity of the storm, but performed so vigorously by the disembodied raider that it bypassed the wind and pierced even the hull of the wrecked airplane. It was a horrible scream, a pained, excruciating cry for help. One could hear him crying as he yelled, yelling for his very life. There was a sharp note of horrific pain in it, and of something else akin to true dread.

Tank slapped his pockets and made a motion to inform Rider he was unarmed. Rider nodded, reached down, and pulled out a pistol from one hip holster, passing it to the giant. With the other hand he took out the other pistol, cocked it, and listened again.

Gale couldn't bear it. Again Buddy screamed, this time louder, more injured, more desperate. It was like the cry of a man slipping slowly over the edge of a cliff, knowing he was going to die. Something had him, something had hurt him, badly. Each time he screamed she knew something had clawed him or taken a bite out of his struggling flesh. *They were eating him alive!*

Tank moved to pull back the door, but Rider grabbed him and threw him back. He raised his finger to his lips for silence.

Again the scream. Closer. Just outside. They could hear Buddy gagging on his own blood and tears, could hear him going hoarse in his own horror.

"Somebody..." they heard him cry, "... HELP ME! GET THEM AWAY FROM ME!!!"

This last was said with weakness, the result of blood seeping out of his many ghastly wounds. Then there was a gross "crunch", audible even on the other side of the metal hull, and Buddy screamed in a tempo of suffering. It was so shrill he lost his voice halfway, but the wind picked it up where he left off and roared like a taunting beast.

"We *must* help him!" Gale cried.

"No!" Rider exclaimed. "It's a trap! They've got him and they'll feast on him until we come out to help. Take small bites, one at a time, until we can't stand the screams anymore. There's a whole *pack* out there waiting for us to come to him!"

Tank slid away from the door. He stared in terror at both Rider and the girl.

"There has to be a way out of here!"

The only other option for the three trapped in the hollow tunnel of the crashed plane was to head downwards... down the sloping interior and into the darkness towards what, conceivably, had once been the plane's cockpit area.

Rider led the way, with Tank close behind, moving with purpose in the dark, ducking and bobbing to avoid the clouded, dust-crusted windows flanking the cabin. Gale, half-afraid the unknowable creatures outside would somehow sense their retreat, hurried along in their shadow and away from the creaking hatchway.

Outside, they could hear Buddy scream once again, his voice slowly diminishing as they increased their distance from the rear of the wreckage. The wind began to pick up once more, even stronger than before, and for the first time they heard the entire shell creak and reverberate. It suddenly became clear to all just how fragile this thing was that they had taken shelter inside.

Rider was the first to stumble upon something midway between the back of the plane and its bow compartments. Here, the wreckage of the plane's interior was almost complete, for only twisted metal, churned earth and sandy residue filled the corridor. Cracks in the ceiling of the fuselage had allowed, over time, grains of the stuff to seep through from the dune outside. By now, he surmised, they had entered the part of the plane that disappeared into the dune itself. They were underground.

At this point the cabin floor was torn apart; a huge gaping hole tore through and into oblivion, where sand and earth mixed to make an unstable tunnel wall that left the plane and headed directly down into the earth. A ghastly stench arose from this hole, a mixture of fresh soil, subterranean moisture, and something else...

Tank barreled into Rider in his own haste to catch up, picking up speed as he came down the incline, taking Rider completely off guard. With a jerk and an angry shout, Rider found himself tumbling forward and over the edge of the precipice of the hollowed floor, taking the off-balance giant with him.

There was a rush of loose gravel and sand, rocks and swirling cobwebs as the two of them slid down the unnatural tunnel to its soft padded bottom. Sand piled up from the slow erosion of the tunnel walls had left a bed of the stuff at its base that left the impact just short of painful. Though both men were disoriented and out of breath, taking a moment to rise to their wobbling feet from dizziness, each found the other to be okay.

The pit's bottom was dark, darker even than the fuselage above, since the dim starlight from the surface didn't even find its way here as it did through the windows in the wrecked plane. Here, only stone, rock and sand could be felt underfoot; nothing could be seen.

Rider hissed a curse under his breath as he fumbled for his pistol, which to his relief, he found only a foot or so away. Tank rose too, his hand still nervously clenched around the weapon his compatriot had lent him.

Overhead, Gale peered over the edge and stared down into the inky blackness. She couldn't hear either Tank or Rider. Turning her head slightly and brushing the hair back from her ear, she listened intently to the howling wind. Oddly, she heard a noise in the distance, like the sound of many humanoid creatures beating rocks against stone; howling, shouting and shrieking like unseen banshees just outside their refuge. Thinking the invisible outsiders were about to assault the portal they had so feebly barred, Gale, in a fit of panic, took to the lip of the yawning tunnel and carefully slid down the sandy slope after the two men.

Tank spun as the girl slid the last few feet and was dumped into the sand of the tunnel's recesses, just a few paces away from him. Reaching back he felt a length of her long hair and grasped out, taking her by the wrist as she began to flutter her arms before her to clear the cobwebs. He yanked her arm, picking the girl up with an easy motion and setting her down on her feet beside him despite her furious protests.

Rider stood and sharply commanded for both to be quiet. He knelt down to pick up his tatty wide-brimmed hat, but as he took it in hand, something caused him to stop dead, and turn his head slightly as if listening. For a moment he simply knelt there, alert.

Tank barely let his breath escape, in an attempt to maintain the silence. Gale, struggling to keep her balance on the shifting sand pile, wondered what was going on that had frozen the two men so.

Rider held up a hand as he fixed his hat quietly. "They're..." he muttered softly.

Tank finished his sentence. "Calling out..."

Gale snapped her head in sudden realization of her mistake. "No," she protested, "they're coming!"

Tank shook his head. "No, child," he said, "they're calling... *something*."

Rider stood, drawing back to within arm's reach of the other two, instinctively seeking protection among the group. Whether he considered the girl an equal or not, he was instinctively glad she was there to put his back up against.

"It's a trap," Rider said flatly, irony unerringly reflected in his voice, "they've tricked us again."

In the distance, all ears could hear the unknown creatures outside the wreckage celebrating, banging rocks against stones, crying and shouting, as if summoning with their chants something yet to be seen.

"They *wanted* us to take refuge in the wreckage. And they wanted us to fall in here. They must have spotted our rush towards the front... and knew we'd all go in."

"But why?" asked Tank, already knowing full well the answer to his question. Both large men turned to face the wall of darkness, moving unconsciously backwards with a slight step to keep their backs closer to the pit wall behind them. Gale sunk in between the two, peering cautiously upwards for a moment before following their gaze back to the tunnel leading into the dark.

The cacophony of the things celebrating outside now began to have an effect. Not only were the three huddled at the pit's floor sweating and afraid, fully aware of their calamitous situation, another being, a creature that had long lived in the bottom of the lightless pit, could hear, smell and *feel* their presence. The noise, of banging rocks and guttural cries had attracted something from the depths of the burrow to the pit's floor, an oubliette from which nothing ever escaped and where it often came to feed when those sounds rung out in the night.

"They won't follow us in..." Rider continued, though there really was no need; everyone knew instinctively what exactly was happening. They had been pushed into a trap, a bottle-neck, to face some tragic conclusion at the hands of something as yet unseen. No doubt those pale-skinned shadows would later brave the wreckage and descend the tunnel after the "thing" had fed, taking their share from the scraps it would leave behind.

The evidence was everywhere. As their eyes were slowly getting accustomed to the swallowing darkness, they could just now see bones and skeletal fragments littering the cave floor everywhere. Tank, whose eyes fared much poorer than his smaller companions, did not see the broken skulls and shattered limbs, but under his heavy broad feet, he could hear the all-too unsettling sound of bones skittering away on the sandy slope, or breaking under his tremendous weight. Many had been there before them. *Damn*, he thought to himself. He and Rider had only given this site a cursory look when they first planned it as a refuge so many weeks ago. Now, however, he cursed himself for not taking more care to explore the environs with scrutiny.

Though his eyes were sharper in the dark due to his particular adaptations, Rider busied himself with retrieving something from deep within his burdensome black coat to aid the others. In an instant he had it out, a rectangular electric lantern of great power, missing the handle by which it was once carried, forcing him to hold it like a baseball in his full grip. With his twitching thumb he flicked the switch and in an instant a brilliant beam of blue-white light pierced the black wall of shadow in a broad arc.

Tank wondered at the intensity of this "pocket torch", never having seen something quite so powerful in so small a size; his experiences in the dry desert towns of the Forbidden Lands and elsewhere had only revealed to him the sights of natural lights; fire, torches and the odd resurrected lantern.

There, before them, could be seen a rough tunnel, much more rocky now, leading at a slight angle down into the dark. But, just as the light swept the passage, it caught sight of something already moving up towards them at a great speed, now more than ever attracted to their position by the presence of Rider's blinding beam.

The thing was unlike any creature they had ever seen, and that fact sent a wave of terror through them, one and all. Burdened only by its sheer size, the beast looked like a perfect killing machine; riding on two sets of spidery legs of iron-hard chitin, its tall body seemed made of inter-connecting plates of solid organic armor. Ribs of overlapping armor plate and bizarre crests ringed the thing's upper body like the segments of a worm, with thorny protrusions here and there that resembled sharp white teeth erupting from its hide.

Two powerful appendages swept before the massive pit beast, each shaped like the curved blade of a reaping scythe, already wavering in the air in an unsettling motion that almost seemed to beckon them to it. Pitted with marks and notches, the bone edge of each harvesting scythe showed signs of countless victims before them. Above these extended claws, set into the bizarre body of the beast, sat a huge yellow eye, cyclopean and horrific, glaring outwards without the usual motion of most living things, like the dead eye of a predatory shark focused solely on the kill. Glistening with wetness, it seemed to glimmer like an open sore running with pus.

Then, suddenly, as their eyes met its and the light covered its entire shape, a huge maw dropped open just beneath the solitary eye, ringed with innumerable teeth both jagged and sharp, and an avalanche of hungry saliva drooled forth in anticipation of its next gory meal.

Burning Lands 67

The many bizarre life forms of the Twisted Earth all shared some common ancestry with the creatures that once lived before the Fall; even the worst mutants were once men, and the ravening hounds of the desert dunes were clearly descended from dogs. But this creature, to all eyes, seemed impossible to trace to any terrestrial creature of the pre-Fall world.

Rider, without a word, pulled his arm close to his hip and fired away with his pistol, getting off two quick shots as the thing lurched forward to close the few remaining yards between them. Up it came, through the descending tunnel, rushing forward on sword-like spider legs and bringing with it the dense stench of the world below. Each *crack-crack* of hammer fall and chamber explosion lit up the air even more, sending a whirl of moving shadows throughout the narrow abyss.

Tank blasted away, firing aimlessly towards its lumbering shape; it was impossible to miss. Gale, seeing the thing move directly towards Tank and Rider, leapt aside and tumbled off down the sandy pile and out of sight.

What happened for the next few seconds was only seen through hazy eyes by the young girl as she rolled away, out of control, into the dark. Rider's light remained firmly in hand, which he struggled to keep on the beast so all eyes could train on its quick and darting motions. Like looking through a peephole, the only thing she could really see was its massive form moving about, dancing a whirling dirge of violence, as her two companions battled it furiously. Now and again its single eye was caught in the light and its huge black pupil narrowed, reminding her of the beasts of horror stories from the distant past.

As it barreled into the pair from the onset, the creature used its sheer weight and girth to send Rider flying. With a sweep of one arm it gathered Tank up like a doll, despite his great size, and whipped the blade back in a deadly motion. Tank cried out an agonizing yell, as the bony claw left a brutal gash running the entire length of his torso.

Tank fell aside only momentarily, his mind consumed by the struggle for life and death. Blasting away, his shots echoed like distorted thunder in the pit's enclosing confines. Bullets prickled the thing as they impacted, leaving puffs of gun smoke and tiny sparks where they hit.

Rider maintained his light on the thing as he got to one knee, emptying the rest of his pistol into it before tossing the useless thing at the creature out of pure desperation. With haste he next brought out his Micro-Uzi, trusting in the efficacy of its jacketed ammunition, and trained it on the monster as it moved past in pursuit of the weakening Tank.

Tank, backing away from the two huge appendages that now came for him with deadly speed, fired the last shots from the pistol into the mighty creature. More sparks and smoke rose from its seemingly impenetrable hide as it continued to advance, until at last its thorny shape was all his eyes could see.

Gale rose to her feet, consumed by an unfamiliar desire to kill the abomination. Despite her small size, she knew there was something she could do to help. She knew she had the capacity to use her mind to do extraordinary things, and while reading thoughts and invading a mind with the intention to kill were two very different things, she knew she had to try. Narrowing her eyes on the creature's single cyclopean eye, she focused her entire will in an attempt to thrust pain and confusion into its mind, overload its alien thoughts and scatter them into oblivion.

In that instant the massive organic killing machine spun about on its spindly legs, its luminous eye narrowing on her with undivided attention. Her efforts had merely distracted it from Tank momentarily, not hurt it nor even clouded its senses; in that fraction of a second she had also foolishly linked her mind to its. A flood of sensations overpowered her thoughts, and she suddenly realized that this thing was as much animal as it was man, an impossible combination of both, with an animal's lack of conscience and a man's capacity for intelligent and willful cruelty.

Gale stood dumfounded by the experience and could easily have been torn apart had it been poised to do so, but the creature's unexpected interest in her faded as the intrusive mind link snapped like a faltering tether. Instead its animal instincts once again took over and it whirled back around to the greater threat. Suspecting a sudden strike from the larger mutant now behind it, the beast spun about, giving Tank that one brief moment to slip aside and down the slope away from its murderous attention.

As Tank slipped away into the dark, Rider rose and lunged forward, coming up from behind the thing and along side it, until the snub barrel of his submachine gun was against its hide. Before it could spin and rend him in two with its incisor claws, Rider pulled the trigger and cried out in anger and defiance.

The chamber flashed with light and the sound of automatic fire. Jacketed, steel-core bullets bored into the creature's chitin, breaking through and sinking into its bony mixture of flesh, tendon, and brain. The entire clip expended, Rider threw himself back and away from the wavering menace.

Tank, attempting to rise, found his back too badly injured and instead slumped against the pit wall. Blood poured out everywhere, all over his torso and onto his hands. His small white eyes fought desperately to stay open, fluttering like a panicking moth's wings.

Gale and Rider fell back, as in an instant the huge spidery thing fell simply to its side in a crumpled heap. Smoke, smelling of charred and burned gore, billowed out of the hole Rider had blasted in its armored body. It was dead.

Gale cried out to relieve her exasperation and fear. With an eye carefully locked on the thing, Rider quickly reloaded with his spare clip and moved over towards Tank, who now rested just feet away from its lifeless corpse. Gale, suddenly realizing the hulking mutant was badly hurt, rushed over and skidded to his side.

Rider put down his flashlight so that it illuminated the area near the wall where they sat, crouched. Tank looked up at both of them with a flat expression, his small white eyes still blinking.

Rider pulled Tank forward with all his might so he could examine the wound. There, Tank's chainmail vest had been torn apart, its little loops nothing more than half-circles where the bladed claw had simply sliced through. The flesh underneath was completely stripped, like a crimson swath across the man's big brawny back.

It was one of the worst wounds Rider, or Gale, had ever seen.

"Oh no..." Gale whispered.

"You're dead," Rider said, resigning Tank's fate effortlessly, as if it didn't matter one way or another.

Tank grunted. "Maybe not," he murmured matter-of-factly.

Rider stared incredulously. He knew the giant healed quick, but a wound that spanned his entire chest? *The giant was just too stupid to realize he was dead!*

Then, reaching out, Rider's hand traced something on Tank's chest. There, under the cursory blood brought up by the opened flesh, he saw that the hulking brute's entire torso was, unbelievably, a barrel of bone. Not a cage of ribs and cartilage, leaving gaping spaces open to deep injury like other men, but a solid casing of rock-hard bone. The abomination's slash, though powerful and razor-sharp, had only sliced the skin and tendon away, scraping the bony armor beneath. It must have been painful, and he would bleed, but his inner organs were preserved by his deformed bone structure.

Rider blinked with disbelief. Gale was dumbfounded. Tank rose with a pained gasp, but seemed more than able to support his own heavy weight once he got to his feet. He reached back and touched his own blood, glared at it, then cursed as if the entire affair was merely an inconvenience.

"Damn," he chuckled, "chainmail isn't easy to come by."

Rider rose without another word, forcing himself to look away from the grotesque bone showing from beneath the wound. Tank was already ripping strips of cloth to create a bandage. He was going to be alright.

Rider collected his two pistols, checked them and put them back in their heavy holsters. Tank, lumbering still from a lingering pain, would trail behind, and wouldn't need his anyway. Gripping his Uzi tightly in one dry calloused hand, Rider readied it as he led the way down the slope.

Against her better judgment Gale found herself following. On one hand she was terrified that another such monstrosity might dwell deeper below, but on the other she knew no other way to escape. The pit walls, the desolate wreckage, the fiendish things outside; yes, this was the only way!

Though cautious in his descent, keeping an eye out for any slight movement, any minor shift of rocks or skittering debris that might warn of an ambusher, Rider found his thoughts suddenly drawn to the girl. Following close behind, hunkered down as if her five feet of height might be too tall for this gigantic tunnel, in his eyes she suddenly fell somewhere between "hired help" and "friend". It was an odd realization, almost a sense of betrayal by his own being, that she should now no longer offend him or prick his impatience. Though she was no doubt a grub and a piece of someone else's furniture, she had proven her worth beyond a slab of begging, wailing meat.

But despite his hesitation to acknowledge her aid he found himself trusting more and more in the girl, even over his own intuition. Perhaps it was just desperation from being here, in this dark hole, but because Tank was too weak to back him up, he let the girl come alongside and guard the left, as he looked right. When she closed her eyes for a moment to think in that odd way, and then opened them again with that eerie look etched in her face, he found himself listening. When she said "turn right", he turned right, without question. He followed *her*, as the girl led them successfully through a nightmarish collection of tunnels and chambers to a yawning hole nearly a half mile distant... and into the night.

It had been a hard night, making progress over the uneasy sand during the storm. Gale had somehow led them out of the creature's tunnels beneath the desert and to an unexpected country of canyons and dry riverbeds, edged in on all sides by the ocean of dunes amidst which they had formerly been lost. Here in the shadow of the dune sea, among rocky gorges and valleys, the wind could not reach them in force, and instead made a heavy fog overhead through which the moaning wind sounded distorted and shrill.

They had run for miles and marched with quick steps beyond even that. Every effort was made to increase the distance between them and the nightmare of unseen creatures and pit beasts they left behind.

Several days passed. The three-person party moved among colossi of stone and exposed rock, staying on the natural trails of the valley floor and gorge ruts cut through the southern Forbidden Lands. Here, rolling sand dunes were only seen to the east and west; behind them, from where they came, the week-long sandstorm was now just a smudge on the horizon. They had escaped the worst and by chance, had evaded a death fated to many in the Forbidden Lands.

Rider and Tank were thankful that Gale had had the foresight to steal away the canteens before fleeing their camp those nights past. They knew well the need to reserve their water only for when they needed it most; both were quite surprised to see Gale shared the same recognition of the stuff's priceless value in the wilderness. Each time it came to drink, Rider expected the girl to beg for "one more sip", only to find her even more frugal than they were. This one had lived long in the desert, he concluded, but said nothing.

They discussed amongst themselves their options, now that they had sufficient water to make a trip through the wasteland. Two destinations seemed most likely; Trade City, to the south, or Midway, the Cartel's outpost in the Forbidden Lands, further to the northwest. This latter, they surmised, was a good idea, but an idea that ultimately seemed unlikely. Though Midway was an "open town" not unlike Trade City, rumors were already circulating that the Cartel was coming down hard on locals in response to growing banditry along their trade routes. Rider and Tank feared they might well be mistaken for raider scouts by some half-cocked Cartel soldier, and sniped on approach. Also, the Scorpions were out there, as were other raider bands, and moving through any of their lands without permission was a death sentence in itself.

Trade City, however, was to the south, and closer to the heart of what people were now calling "civilization". Trade City was big, really big. The Cartel had a base there too, but the city was largely dominated instead by the Clean, that water merchant house that brought the life-giving stuff for hundreds of miles throughout the Twisted Earth, from locations far and wide. Under their strict but efficient rule, Trade City had grown to something more like a sprawling "bazaar", of many colors and uncountable opportunities. This would certainly be the best place to go.

Gale contributed little to their nightly discussions, ignorant of these place names or the groups mentioned, either appraisingly or disdainfully, by the two more seasoned desert travelers. Instead she spent her time at night staring up at the stars, watching the phases of the blue moon and dreaming of the cities her parents once claimed were still scattered across its surface.

Days and nights passed, until at long last the three huddled on a towering dune overlooking a great plateau, a marker of sorts, where the Forbidden Lands ended and the Far Desert began. There, laid out like a paradise under the stars, spread out like a

Burning Lands

welcome mat to all who could see it, was a city of stucco buildings, bright and white; tents, teepees of tanned hide and ramshackle barrios of corrugated iron huts and clay structures ringed it like a choking noose of chaotic slums. From this distance they could not make out individual figures on the urban plateau, but they could see electric lights crowning many wall towers and some interior buildings. They glistened like weak stars lighting the way to this desert sanctuary, beckoning for all to come and get lost in its seedy promise.

Tank and Rider quietly set up camp without lighting a fire that night, just a few hundred feet from an old highway billboard that screamed "TUCUMCARI TONITE" in fading art deco lettering. Despite the sign's tempting offer, instead of pressing on they would wait out the darkness and approach the city only during the day, when the gates were open for all to come inside. Tonight they would sit in silence with patience and vigilance, for just outside, among the dunes and canyons all around, also waited predatory people spying for folk just like them. If they made themselves seen, other, darker sorts would find them and attempt to murder them and take their trade goods before the coming of the next dawn.

Cold and shivering, they waited out the night.

Gale was only barely awake when she found herself walking behind Tank and Rider towards the huge gates of Tucumcari, the Trade City. She had that foul taste of morning in her mouth, and dust bit her eyes. The sun was already high overhead, shedding its blinding radiance over the rough country. They had left the dunes and canyons behind and were now coming to the open passage leading into the great metropolis.

As she became more cognizant, Gale suddenly found herself in a world of unexpected wonders; they were a part of a great mass of other people, more people in one place than she had ever seen before (Oasis included). Here there were men of all colors talking and bartering outside the great gates; men in long robes, others with towels wrapped about their heads to shield from the sun. Men baked and toughened by the elements, with bearded faces full of hair, wild eyes lost in concerns beyond her ken, and speaking at such speed as to leave even her sharp mind behind. Over there her attention was drawn by a man leading a train of curious shaggy beasts, walking on tall spindly legs and with humped backs. Each of the ugly beasts was burdened with a tower of goods, carefully packed and balanced on its hump like a tower of teetering junk. Young boys, some her age or even younger, ran about the line with wands of metal, clicking their tongues and snapping their sticks to keep the *bawthoks* calm and patient.

These masses passed by two men standing on scattered boulders, each of them shouting out above the din like old-tome carnival barkers but in two very different languages:

"Come on in, ladies and gentlemen! To Tucumcari, the Trade City! Famed across the desert!"

"Mao yi! Zhi ming pu ji!"

"Jewel of the southern wastelands!"

"Bao shi nan fang bu mao zhi di!"

"Oasis among the dust seas!"

"Lu zhou dang zhong fen hai!"

"The birthplace of civilization, folks!"
"Chu sheng di wen ming!"
"Safety and security behind these great walls!"
"An quan xing hou zhe bi!"
"Law and order!"
"Fa lu bing zhi!"
"Come see the future!"
"Du qian tu!"
"Water enough for everyone!"
"Shui gei mei ge ren!"
"Opportunities for all!"

Beyond them could be seen a mass of others, a gang of horse riders and raiders bringing weird goods from all over the land to this safe-haven of trade. Dressed in heavy leather attire speckled with chains and metal spikes, covered in grime and dust, they looked like the worst the desert could offer; guns, rifles and axes poked out from among their goods, along with grisly trophies taken from their lives of predation - skulls, bone necklaces and desiccated heads mounted on pikes or from the hoods of their rickety cars. Through them came a meandering group of motley shapes, all of them clad in long purple robes that stood out vividly amongst the dusky mass; a gathering of strange monks, their unseen heads cloaked in hoods, their vision obscured as they walked and their minds leading them as they went.

This group Gale found most curious and she found herself wandering in their direction, lost in wonder at their hodge-podge of strange body shapes, tall and short, angular and stocky, all of them hidden beneath robes of a deep twilight color. She felt drawn by the rustling sound of their quiet chanting and the purpose with which they proceeded towards the gate. At that she felt a snap, which broke the trance. Rider called to her with a motion of his hand and beckoned her to remain at their side.

"They're with the *Brotherhood...*" Tank said in a hushed voice, seeing the procession she'd been staring at. He left it there as if mere mention of this "Brotherhood" should be reason enough to keep Gale away. Then he turned to Rider. "If she gets lost out here she'll never get in. She's got nothing to give..."

"*Nothing to give but herself*," Rider countered. Tank gave him a look.

Gale looked down at herself and realized the two men had wrapped her up good and tight in a long cloak from head to toe. Her entire face was concealed like a desert Bedouin, as was her body, keeping her from the prying eyes of cruel men in the crowd and among the packs of trade-jackals all about them.

"Keep that on," Rider cautioned, removing his sunglasses to look straight into her eyes, "or we won't be able to help what happens."

At that, the sound of painful cries came to their ears and they turned as a narrow merchant raised his whip once more to lash a weakened slave. Surrounded by a tight line of hired hands, the slavemaster drove forward through the crowd a mass of skinny, brutalized and hollow women. Running on bare blistered feet, bloody from miles of hard-driven travel, the collection of poor souls looked anything but appealing to the eye. These women, meant for the decadent and nightmarish pleasure markets, were each the strongest and most enduring of their kind; any others perished long ago. No, there were no beauties among them (or perhaps it only seemed so) only those who could survive through sheer physical will.

But to the mass outside the gates, it was a glimpse of heaven. These women were their next entertainments, and already the pack of leering men moved to within arm's reach of the slavemaster's train to taunt, heckle and threaten the slaves. Promises of finding them, buying them and ravaging them were exchanged in a nauseating clamor before the weeping women were driven on.

Gale shuddered. She knew little of what the actual words meant, but the violence, greed and lust in the men's eyes gave her some understanding of what she was seeing. She knew the fate of those women was death, either by some drunken "master" somewhere down the line... or at their own hands.

Rider's eyes followed hers, as the slavemaster was given privilege to enter with haste before the disorder at the gates grew out of control. Tall guards in spotless white armor allowed him and his party entry, before barring the great portal once more and returning to the business of demanding revenue from the outsiders gathering at their doorstep.

This was the *true* Tucumcari, the famed "Trade City".

"That's right," Rider said, "so keep your clothes about you. You're a boy, understand that? You're a boy, a scav like us. Nasty case of the White Skin, like me, but worse. No one will take your robes. Got it?"

Gale looked at Rider for a moment, regarding his lily white skin, carnation-colored lips and the thin strands of hair that peeked from beneath his hat. In this light his eyes looked blue but when his head looked up they turned gray and then red like coals in a raging furnace, as his eyelids narrowed to shield from the bright rays of the sun. She saw for the first time his soft white eyelashes, which gave his features a strange innocence. In that moment she didn't regard him as either repugnant or monstrous, but Rider took offense regardless, frowned angrily and pushed her forward so that she was no longer staring at him.

Instead Gale's eyes looked at the others moving towards the gate; raiders in leather with horses and cars, merchants with oxen and stranger beasts of burden, monks from bizarre desert cults and rough loners ("*scavs*") moving through the mass freely, burdened like human mules with goods stolen from all over the wasteland. These last were a common sight here, coming once every few months from the desert to the city to trade for bullets, food, water, a night with some terrified woman (no doubt from his own grotesque and unkempt appearance) and drugs to dull their pain and diminish the hopelessness of their lost lives.

"Don't make me repeat myself! Did you hear me?" Gale snapped out of it and nodded.

At long last it came to be their turn, and Tank and Rider did all the talking. The guards at the gate kept a keen eye on them even as they scanned the masses, while some indistinguishable Clean or Cartel representative made demands of her companions. Rider and Tank produced what goods they had to offer and stated their desire to bargain for water and, after days in the wasteland without it, food as well. Warily, but with relative expedience, a compromise was struck, and goods were given to the guardians and levy man. They especially desired Tank's meager supply of cinnamon, which all but paid for their entrance.

The "tax" paid, their party was motioned on through the towering gates of dusty wood and into the city's crowded, noisome interior.

Had Johnny known the world was so populated? Gale thought to herself, as they walked through the streets. *Had he just been trying to keep her safe or had he really been the outcast creature the Scorpions had branded him?* If he had merely been sheltering her, she could understand why, as they walked through the packed streets of the city.

Tucumcari was, to the eyes of Gale, a world within walls. It was by far the largest site she had seen since her flight so many years ago. What was once long ago a small town before the Fall of the Ancients, had been left to decay in their wake during the Final Wars. Ruined and burned to the ground, over time traders made the ashes and crumbling supports of old buildings a haven from the open road on their journeys throughout the land. In time, with the passing of decades, these minor merchants gave way to larger interests, the more numerous, foreign-blooded Clean and Cartel from across the deserts east and west, and the ruins were rebuilt. Now, a maze of streets, newly-erected buildings of mud, stucco, and brick, and towers to watch the wasteland for miles, stood loftily over its congested cityscape.

While the gamboge blazon of the Cartel, with its odd four-armed symbol of bright red representing the highways of the great western trade routes could be seen in abundance about town, this was surely a settlement run and directed by the Clean. Water was the predominant trade here; fresh drinking water, sold in small quantities to the desert scavs and wanderers doing minor trade in the barrio districts, or *en masse* to community representatives coming in from the desert. The sight of huge beasts of burden, oxen, heavy horses, and the curious *bawthoks*, burdened with plastic tanks of water, jerry cans, and a menagerie of glass beakers and jars, was quite common. So much glass gleamed in the streets, in fact, that in the open squares and bazaars the sun scintillated off nearly every surface, making it hard for the unaccustomed eye to remain focused for long.

Towering over the buildings were willowy flagpoles, hanging rectangular flags of pure white that snapped smartly in the plateau's relentless wind. One word was emblazoned on each in either a black, blue, or silver color: "CLEAN", a testament to the most significant product bartered here, and those who controlled its life-giving flow.

"*Ni he shui ma?*" came the beckoning of strangers' voices as she passed by, here, there, everywhere; leaving Gale to stare in wonder at what the repetitive words meant.

This was the birthplace of a new civilization, alright, brought and built by the toils of the descendants of those who had invaded this land. Gone were the old ideologies and nationalistic fervor of the past world. This great ark of mixed-blooded peoples was as "native" as any other tribe inhabiting the desert, only they sought to create something *new* here. This city, as it was, beamed brilliantly as their crowning achievement in the quest for this goal.

Gale, Rider and Tank made their way through crowded markets and bazaars, led by a shared intuition between Tank and Rider to find the best deal on water for what few goods they had left to trade away. The loss of Rider's horse at the oasis, as well as

Burning Lands 75

Tank's at the wreckage, meant they had little to go on. Gale, for her part, wandered close behind them, listening, learning and watching.

She found that each time they entered into trade, either Tank or Rider would switch into a fast-paced, blurred slang of tongue that was hard for her inexperienced ears to manage. She came to surmise that the merchants, here and elsewhere, had come to develop their own more efficient language, a pidgin variant of Chinese, Arabic and English full of contractions and shortened words to make speaking fast, furious and productive in as little time as possible. Although she had never herself witnessed one, it was like listening to two auctioneers battle it out to determine a mutually-agreeable price for the goods at hand.

Amid the confusion of the speech, shouting, bartering and bantering going on around her, Gale was well aware of the physical differences in these people as well. Outside, in the desert, most men were clad in heavy robes or clothes to cover their bodies, to shield from sun and whipping sand. But here, in the cool shadows of the tall stucco buildings of town, men moved about with much less on their bodies. Her eyes took in a flood of sights and visages; horribly deformed men and mutants, one and all. Faces missing eyes or mouths filled with peg-shaped teeth; the trace of mongoloid features in many others doing business in stalls or just walking down the streets past them. Entire groups of affiliated men, whether raiders of a common band or members of the same trade house, might have a dozen or more different features and gross deformities. None were complete, none were "whole" men. Bodies broken by a lifetime of hardship and born with ghastly aberrations like tumors, growths or deformed limbs. Though she had known Johnny was a hideous deformity himself, she had always hoped there were others out there like *her*. Seeing the city from afar, she had half-expected to stumble upon someone, somewhere, who resembled her.

But now she wasn't sure. It was as if she had awoken in a twisted little world where everyone was a monster, a ghoulish parody of humankind. In time, the sights that assailed her began to have little effect, though instinctively, perhaps for no reason, she kept her distance from all that came near. Knowing her own body, and its relative physical perfection, she realized all too well that she was a different kind of creature indeed. No one could see, of course; she was too bundled up for that, and she realized that years in the desert had made her filthy and crude to the eye. Not even Rider and Tank, who had seen her before she had donned the robes, could have recognized that she was hardly touched by mutation at all.

The square they had finally come to was dominated by a cracked stone elevation, a kind of raised area where goods could be sold up and out of the sand and dust. Flanking the square were all manner of buildings, and from the rooftops, windows and balcony-overhangs, a mass of people stared out at the goings-on below. All over, people of varied colors and creeds had gathered to hear the message of a small group of folk occupying the square.

There, addressing the amused onlookers was a collection of plain, humble and seemingly vagrant folk. Leading the congregation was a humble-looking fellow, maybe thirty at most, with sun-bleached hair and a face creased with wrinkles from years among the wastes. He wore a long tunic of discolored cloth with sleeves that fell past his wrists, and sack cloth pants that were just a few sizes too large. He was otherwise barefoot, and her eyes were drawn to his feet, which had only two large, fused toes on each. The man stood at the fore of others equally as unappealing; these included a few younger, spirited folks, beaming with smiles, and an old woman, hair long and white like a spilled bushel of cotton, holding herself up with a gnarled oaken staff. The youngish man spoke:

"This is an old land, a land that once stood for something! Not merciless trade! Not endless toil! It stood for life! It stood for liberty! It stood for happiness! Will you join us? We gather at our side members of all races, of all species, and we march forward into a brighter future! Come, join us! Or simply hear what we have to say! Brothers! Sisters!"

Rider shook his head and laughed. Tank, however, seemed drawn by their words... but he pretended not to be, instead hastening to close the final deal for a few cups of water. Every now and again there was a roar of laughter from the assembly, and one by one a handful here, and a smattering there, would wave the barefoot speakers' idiocy off and walk away chuckling.

"Who are they?" Gale asked, hurrying to keep pace with Rider and Tank as they moved along.

Rider just shook his head again. "Dreamers," he said sarcastically. "Believers in a 'better way'. They want to see their own particular vision of the future become real, and they want *you* to build it. You'll find people like them in every village, in every town, all over the wasteland. Problem is, they all have different ideas and 'visions' of what the future should be." Tank said nothing.

The trading continued for a full hour, moving from vendor to vendor, stall to stall. They passed grimy men looking for crudely-forged weapons, tinkers looking to buy even the oldest and most questionable machine parts, and vendors trading disintegrating books and magazines filled with lewd images and erotic depictions. Many of these were simply adult novels, only useful to those who could read, but some precious ones had actual *pictures*. As they passed by, a merchant held up a centuries-old, dog-eared catalogue once meant to advertise the latest "pleasure" androids available to John Q. Public; the lewd picture on the cover was the closest thing most scavs and visitors would get to a real woman in this female-starved age, and the prices for such picture-books (even those depicting human-mimicking *machines*) were exorbitantly high.

At long last they had all the water they could afford. Then, at some point, Tank turned to Rider and the two briefly exchanged some quiet conversation. After a few moments they nodded in agreement, and Tank turned to her. His small featureless eyes came to rest on her, his brows becoming flat with a sorrowful expression.

"Child," Tank said in his deep voice, "we've got to go our own ways now." He said this as if she were just a baby girl, somewhat to her chagrin. But she could somehow sense a poorly-concealed feeling of regret in his voice, which made her look harder and listen more closely as he spoke.

"We've traded for some water, Rider and I. I'm going to give you some... enough for a few days. But that's all. We've got things to do, each one of us. I'm going my own way."

"But what..." Gale chimed.

"Rider's going to take you to the Clean, they might have a use for you, beyond a piece of furniture."

Burning Lands 77

"But I want to go with you!" she said, looking as pitifully as she possibly could through the heavy covering of robes and veils. Tank turned the corner of his lips up in slight amusement.

"You're a good little grub," he said, "maybe even saved my life. That's why I'm giving you half of all the water I've got. The Clean should take it as a dowry. It's as good as *corium* to them."

Gale's lips trembled as a wave of tears began to well in her eyes. Big and green, they stared up into those monstrous pale orbs that seemed to get less and less menacing the more she knew the gentle giant. Tank shifted uncomfortably. Rider just watched, quietly waiting for Tank to say his sentimental goodbyes.

Tank knelt with a huff, touched her arm, and stared into her eyes. He reached out with his fat grubby hand and clumsily brushed the tears from her soft eyelashes, almost poking her eye out with his uncoordinated gesture. Though it had hurt, Gale knew he had meant well and stifled a wince of pain.

"The Clean will give you a good life here. You can't follow me around. Rider can't take you either. But they'll be able to take care of you. They'll put you to work, and in no time, you'll be big and strong and safe. They'll *keep* you safe. Someday you'll marry a high ranking minister and you'll be set like a queen!"

Though Tank smiled at this, Gale frowned in disappointment and anger. She didn't want his patronizing promises; she wanted to go with them! A single tear started trickling down her cheek, but with so much clothing on no one could see.

Tank rose and turned to Rider, extending his big hand. Rider considered for a moment, and a brief smile shot across his face. The two shook hands, before the former finally gathered his goods and left, casting one last glance over his shoulder at Rider and Gale before vanishing into the crowds of Tucumcari.

Gale walked quietly and obediently behind Rider as they made their way through the lower quarter towards the heart of Trade City. Although the din of the town had only grown exponentially since their arrival, she felt detached, alone, betrayed. Odd feelings, stacked up high upon the emotional baggage she already carried; fear, dread, isolation and abandonment. She walked quickly to keep up with Rider, who to her seemed quite willing to let her wander off now that Tank was gone.

But that was far from the case. Rider walked quickly because he walked with purpose; he was taking Gale to a better place, where he could get rid of her and make a quick buck; all while preserving what little semblance of a conscience he had left. The Clean were good people; well, not "good", but powerful, stable, and had prospects for a great future. They were life in the desert, they controlled the flow of water (with only a few competitors of equal standing anywhere in the wasteland) and their might was unquestioned here in Trade City. Yes, this was better for everyone.

As they entered another marketplace towards the heart of town, Rider turned to make sure Gale was close at hand. He looked down at her, awkwardly, as if trying all of a sudden to make up for his cruel callousness before. He forced a comforting smile, which only made Gale stare at him suspiciously and with resentment burning in her red, fatigued eyes. Seeing it had no effect, Rider sighed, turned and continued on.

Just then, as she began to follow, Gale stumbled into a tall robed figure. Looking up, she saw the strange face of a thin, angular man looking down at her, clad in a familiar purple robe. It was one of those strange monastic types they had seen at the front gates, though this one walked freely with his head exposed. Completely bald, his ears were mere slits on the sides of his head and his mouth was unusually small. The fingers of his hands were connected by thin membranes of flesh, the web-like manifestation of *syndactyly*, which without even the simplest medical know-how of days past, was a common sight in this dark future.

The mutant turned and looked down at her. Slowly his mouth formed into a haunting smile, as if his mind looked right into hers and could sense her fear and uncertainty. The smile grew broader, as if the two of them shared some special secret; that both were mind-readers, pretending to be simple wayfarers in this built-up city. He moved his hand up to touch her chin almost like a father, as if attempting to pass on to her some kind of strength to survive the trials that would meet her in the years to come. As he came close his smile flattened, his eyes widened, as if suddenly the man saw something *else* in Gale's face, in her eyes, *and the revelation stunned him.*

At that moment Rider turned and saw the monk leaning over her; he came quickly over to pick her up and drag her off. Gale, stunned by the look given her by the willowy mentalist, could barely break eye contact until at last they were once more part of the crowd.

Through the masses they weaved, passing down a narrow street until they came to the back entrance of a grandiose palace, its many crystalline domes gleaming in the mid-morning light and shaded by hundreds of pure white banners. Its upper stories, built in the fashion of some ancient slave-fortress, glowed brilliantly under the sun; but here, in the alleys leading to its rear, shadows kept it cool and its entrances discreet.

They came up to a stepped portico leading to a pair of huge natural wooden doors, each fitted with heavy wooden rings that served as hinges. Near the top of these doors were decorative wave-like symbols of a blue and green glass-like resin that served as translucent portholes for the guards within, and through which stray beams of colored light could shine into the gatehouse. On either side of the great portal stood men in long cool robes of white, wrists bound by thick leather bracers, armed with muskets and swords at their sides (a rare concession to sensibility for a people who usually decried the use of metal). Overhead, by almost a full twenty feet, hung a massive banner of white fabric, casting a deeper shade over the entrance and leaving the air cool and crisp.

Rider wet his lips in anticipation, weighing the situation. He had to make as good an impression as possible if he was going to do this right. The Clean were excessively particular, and not just any scum from the desert could impress them easily. He knew this from past experience, hard-earned experiences which kept him humble in the face of greater men.

Rider exchanged a few words with the guards, motioning to Gale in her long robes of mismatched cloth. Speaking from the start in the Trade tongue, he attempted to detach himself from his physical appearance as a mere desert wastrel, to suggest he was in fact a merchant or trader, in possession of something of potential use to the Clan. Remarkably, his fast-talking worked.

In ten minutes Rider and Gale were issued into the fortress, and to a cool, shaded corner somewhere within. The place was a small, secluded garden, no doubt an elegant meeting place visited by many on whom the Clean wished to impress their resources, for at its center was a cracked marble fountain through which water, real *water,* flowed.

Beds of fragrant flowers were meticulously cultivated in patches in the shade, and gracefully arched doorways and passages made from the curved trunks of trees led off in all directions to various quarters of the palace, quarters whose purpose he could only guess at. He heard voices some distance away, and over a low wall braided with flowered vines, in some unseen courtyard beyond, the sound of palace guards drilling for the day.

Rider's eyes found it hard to tear away from the sight of water being spilled from the stone fountain's huge figurehead, a rough statue of the same vague, Buddha-like deity, sitting cross-legged. It was a figure duplicated in a thousand modified forms by the survivors of the Fall. A benevolent smile showed on its cherub-like face, and from a great gourd at its side it spilled water freely as if generously filling the cups of all the world's impoverished, waiting at its feet. Statues such as this one were considered good luck all over the wasteland, even though few men could trace the origins of such figures. Knowledgeable sages suggested they weren't from this land originally, instead a custom transplanted by ancient invaders. This particular statue probably dated to the founding of the settlement of Tucumcari and the Clean's ability to maintain it in working order found some admiration in the otherwise uncaring man.

A pair of large double doors opened onto this sheltered courtyard, where he and Gale found themselves led by a palace guard and a minor household steward, who quietly informed the albino and his begrudging charge of the Clean's distaste for all things metal, the crude mechanical contraptions of the Ancients that had only brought harm and misery to the world. He gestured with one sweeping arm to the palace that had welcomed them, which itself personified this philosophy in every facet of its construction; curved and elegant walls made of mud, pipes and aqueducts made from clay, windows made from hardened tree sap that cast a rich golden-amber light on the palace's internal halls and chambers, and tree trunks grown and nurtured to serve as living doorways or pillars to support even larger structures of stone. The palace was a living, breathing monument, a forest of trees and plants and other organic things, woven together with a combination of skillful artistry and a sacred reverence for the enduring cycle of growth. The Clean truly were masters of bringing life out of the desert, and the palace served as a testament to their close symbiotic relationship with nature.

Rider conceded and surrendered most of his metal belongings to a servant, with the understanding that they would be returned when his business in the palace was concluded. He craftily bluffed the man, however, and chose not to mention the pistols hidden beneath his heavy coat. He didn't intend on getting into any trouble, but a man like him was never comfortable without a weapon somewhere on his body.

A few minutes later a willowy woman of no little beauty, something that took Rider slightly off-guard, emerged from a nearby corridor, brushing aside a curtain of thin vines woven with a veil of fragrant fig leaves and blossoms. Holding it open with her hand, showing the faintest traces of *syndactyly*, she stepped obediently aside and lowered her head in respect for the man emerging from beyond.

This was no ordinary woman. She had long, slicked-back hair of a chocolate color, icy white skin and glittering dark eyes shaded behind thick black lashes. Her features were exceedingly fine, giving her an inherently "refined" air, with a slender nose, small mouth and thin dark eyebrows. She evasively avoided eye contact when Rider looked upon her.

Rider moved his gaze from the figure of the woman, whose exciting shape could be seen vaguely through the gauzy fabric of her long white gown, to that of the elderly man who came forward to meet them.

The elder was just a few inches shorter than Rider and despite his age of perhaps sixty, seemed virile, vital and strong. Though his face was wrinkled and his features bronzed from the sun like anyone else, he was rather well-muscled, of comfortable shape, and healthy. He was utterly bald, but unlike the pathetic raiders of Slug and Valero's band, his baldness was a natural thing, not something done to appear "wise" or to copy the look of the deformed good-luck statues that dotted the desert's oases like the megaliths of prehistory. He wore a sweeping, elegant robe of a soft white fabric that swished behind him as he stepped forward in soft leather shoes. Extending his arms, he nodded politely and briefly to Rider and his charge before turning and motioning to his mistress to retrieve refreshments. Never once did a smile form on his face, however, and the look in his steel gray eyes was discerning, severe and yet calmly restrained.

"You've brought me a scav?" he suddenly said, his voice tinged with an unfamiliar accent. His voice had a trace of the accent of the Asian invaders of the past, but it also spoke of comfortable living, education and poise. Rider knew the sound well, what it meant, and the arrogance and disdain to which it was often mated.

"He said he had something to offer the Clan," the steward replied, bowing his head slightly in respect to his master. "A trade..."

The bald-headed mandarin looked to Rider and formed a brief smile. "What business do you bring?"

Rider calmly opened his hand and gestured with his open palm to his diminutive robed companion.

"I offer an *oblate*," Rider said, remembering the correct word, "an offering to join the noble ranks of the Clean."

The tall figure moved forward, pushing the sleeves of his robe up his arms like some Roman senator coming forth to have his hand kissed. Instead, he walked over and with a gentle but firm tug pulled away the scarf that covered Gale's face.

Eyes of alien, conniving interest stared at her for a moment, searching the young lines of her face, the dirt, the grime.

"How old?" was his first question, looking to Rider for answers.

Rider hesitated momentarily. "Certainly not *too* old..."

The mandarin looked back at her, touching her face with his fingers. "Fourteen, fifteen at the most," he deduced finally. He seemed relatively pleased. "Tribal?"

"No," said Rider. "Feral. But quick to learn..."

The mandarin looked displeased. "A feral mind breeds a savage body," he said, "and there is little that can be done with a savage..."

Rider moved slightly forward, then remembered where he was.

"*A jade stone is useless before it is polished*," he said, offering a Clean proverb he had once overheard. The mandarin looked at him momentarily, surprised that Rider knew such an ancient saying.

Just then the mandarin, looking back into the girl's frightened eyes, smiled broadly in realization that there was more to this oblate than the scav let on. He reached out and uncoiled Gale's entire headdress, finally letting her curly blond hair free.

The mistress, returning with water and ripe fruit, stared over at the girl, before shying away and offering water to Rider. He found himself looking at her, trying to catch her deep, gloomy eyes for just a moment. The woman defied him and stepped quietly away.

"A *girl*..." the mandarin said, smiling in amusement. "Interesting..."

Rider watched.

"Can she talk?"

Suddenly Gale opened her mouth and surprised one and all. "Yes, I can. And I can also speak for myself, sir." The man's eyes widened in further amusement and surprise. The serving girl looked over at this, as if trying to read into Gale's mind with a stare. Gale didn't notice.

"Why of course you can, little one," he said, then turned to Rider. "And a girl with defiance... will. Fascinating!"

Rider grew impatient. Though they were making headway, he felt as if his promise of payment was somehow avoiding him. He held his tongue.

"I find that quite odd," the Clean merchant said, "quite odd indeed. I've never heard of such a thing, outside of the amazons of the desert. Tell me, little one, were you born to those wild women? A fatherless bastard, hmm?"

Gale stared at him. Something about his arrogant, practiced manner annoyed her; she hated him. He could sense her antipathy and it only made him smile.

"No..." she said, her voice lingering. "... I don't remember where I was born..."

This seemed to satisfy the merchant, who now stood. He began rubbing his fingers in thought, as if pondering the child's future use to the Clan.

Rider jumped in, knowing that it was now or never.

"She has... mind powers."

All heads turned to Rider, then back to Gale. Gale looked over at him, staring at him as if he'd betrayed her too. *Now she'd never escape.*

"Truly?" The man knelt in front of Gale, his tone mildly patronizing and amused. "Tell me, child, what 'tricks' can you do with your mind?"

Gale just stared, her lips held tight in defiance. But Rider would have none of that, and spoke for her.

"I don't know how she does it, but I've seen her dodge a crazed killer's attacks as if she was *seeing* where his every strike was going," he said. "And I've seen her rattle a cave *terrolops* with a glance." The latter was a little white lie, but he knew she had tried some mind trick or another back there in the cave with the armored devil. And, after all, Rider felt it was in their best interests to sell her as well as they could.

The merchant looked at her with renewed interest, but one that was fast waning. "Perhaps of some value then," he said. "A talking, defiant girl with powers of the mind. Interesting. Perhaps we could sell you to the Brotherhood. If what this man says is true, you might have some talent for *precognition* and *telepathy*. Those are rare gifts on this side of the Wei Shan..."

Precognition and *telepathy*. Gale had heard those words once or twice before, long, long ago in her past. Whispered with a cold fascination that had chilled and frightened her. Suddenly she trembled, wavered in her stoic countenance. At once she could see into the man's eyes, and sensed his sheer capacity for ruthlessness; he was a broker, a miser, a pompous and arrogant capitalist who cared nothing for her, for Rider, or for anyone around him. He looked at each as a mere object, for his or her value, and for whatever he could get from them before passing from their lives.

"You're a beastly man!" she said, staring into his eyes, "I can hear your thoughts, I can smell your greed! You disgust me!"

He could see her anger, her hatred, etched in her obstinate face. The man laughed. "You most certainly *can* read minds, can't you... That, in itself, has just saved you, girl."

The merchant looked up at Rider. "Yes. Yes! I accept her among us!"

With the formal acceptance of a deal out of the way the steward came forward and took Gale away, forever, for all Rider knew. He watched with a mild sense of guilt, but quickly smothered that and turned to the canny merchant.

Once Gale was gone, Rider partook of more drink and food from the wooden platter. The merchant watched him with interest but seemed either oblivious or uncaring as to who or what Rider was - a bounty hunter and a trained killer. For the time being, Rider didn't let it phase him.

"And just what do you ask in return?" After only a few minutes the mandarin had finally come to the important matter at hand.

Rider stared at the man's mistress, standing nearby, and the mandarin noticed. The old man regarded the concubine with raised chin and spoke of her as an art dealer might speak of his most prized centerpiece.

"She *is* quite lovely. Her ancestors joined ours on the Fleet of A Thousand Ships when it crossed the oceans to land on these shores. But their stock all but diminished over the generations, too arrogant to integrate in their new homeland, until they were too few to avoid becoming prey. Her kind were once hunted almost to extinction in this land. She is a true rarity...

"So what does the petitioner ask for in return?" he said, returning to business.

"A month's water ration," Rider began, "ammunition for all my weapons, a healthy, swift horse and some food. I also want a new rifle, large bore, breech-loader, no muskets."

He shifted his attention to the girl. "And a night with *her*."

The bald mandarin bent his head backwards in a rolling laugh. "The water, the ammunition and horse, and food as well. That is *all*."

Rider ground his teeth, considering the pleasures lost. "No, the woman too," he demanded.

The woman, this whole time, remained at her master's side, head bent downwards, her face completely unflinching. Her thin black eyebrows were knit, however, as if concerned by the petty bartering that centered squarely on her. It struck Rider as odd somehow that she seemed unusually eager not to exchange hands, as if she *dreaded* a night with him.

Ultimately the mandarin smiled a final smile that dictated the course of the negotiations. "You are in no position to make demands, scavenger," he said, "and the offer I present is exceptional in its own right. I shall even go so far as to throw in the paltry dowry of the water she came in here with; that should be good for a few weeks in itself. Now, do we have a deal?"

After a moment of silence, Rider relented and nodded. The woman seemed relieved but said nothing, only closing her eyes. He had no choice but to accept the mandarin's offer and for the time being bury whatever desire she had aroused in him.

The mandarin sat deeply in an elegant chair fashioned to resemble a large leaf, its tip curling up in back to provide the mandarin with something to recline comfortably against. He watched Rider for a moment, then gestured for his mistress to depart; no point in her presence any longer, after all. He ordered a recently-arrived lackey to go and fetch the things that they had agreed upon, and another soldier joined the first to escort Rider out.

As he turned to leave, the aging mandarin asked over his shoulder. "I don't believe I got your name."

"Rider," he replied, looking back.

The mandarin quickly looked up. For a moment he just stared at Rider, before raising a finger to his guards. "The *bounty-hunter?*" Something sinister rose from the pit of his throat as he asked.

"Yes..." Rider replied, suddenly aware of a very perceptible danger.

"You're the fellow who was involved with the 'Slug' gang, the 'Scorpions', to the north in the Forbidden Lands?"

Rider's eyes narrowed. "Not involved. Working for. Briefly. *Very* briefly. Hired to hunt a ghoul in the area..."

The mandarin stood up, his eyes suddenly burning with interest. "Our diplomat among those raiders was *murdered*. A blooming alliance was thwarted by a renegade among the Oasis-dwellers, and now months of effort are in ruins. We have sent an army north to dash your fellows and their camp, and teach the dissenters a lesson. Our soldiers have orders to behead every last member of those treacherous bandits and leave none to mercy."

Rider heard the soldiers bring their muskets to bear from behind. His hands wavered, the instinct to draw his pistols in defense overcome by his better judgment and fear.

"I wasn't with them," Rider stated firmly, "my companions and I got out of there just before..." He was interrupted by the mandarin, who snapped his finger. The distinct sound echoed like a gunshot in the courtyard.

"The Clean care not to whom the knife belonged, but *you* were among those savages that butchered him. You were in their employ. You will pay like the rest. *Guards.*"

The two guards moved forward with a step, forcing Rider's hands into the air. As one held him subdued at the end of his willowy musket, the other patted Rider down and quickly stripped him of his concealed arms.

The mandarin quieted for a moment, watching the removal of his ingeniously-hidden weapons. He took the pistols himself, looked them over and examined them with something akin to a collector's interest.

"Ah, automatic pistols. Artifacts. Relics. These things did nothing for the Ancients but bring death and sorrow. It was things like these that brought about the end of their civilization. How dare you bring such wicked things into my home." He handed them off to one of the guards, relinquishing them with a distasteful look as if he was getting rid of something diseased.

"Don't take this personally," the mandarin said, returning to the unpleasant task at hand. "You're just one of many. The wasteland cannot afford to be wild forever, its people living off discarded things and playing like children in the garbage heap of the ancient past. The Clean brings with it a new civilization. And *order*. And profit. Wastrels like you and the scattered tribesmen of the north, Scorpions included, will soon be a thing of the past. Be thankful that you will serve as an instrument of a better future." This last he said with a modicum of amusement glowing in his smile.

"For his part in killing a sacred envoy of the Clan," the mandarin stated aloud, as if announcing Rider's crime to some invisible courtroom and its phantom jury, "a punishment fitting his crime. Take him to the slave market and sell him to the first bidder from Little Vegas. *Let him live out his remaining years in the corium mines...*"

The young speaker who'd spent the day in the city square passed through a heavy oaken door and immediately began to descend a tight set of stone stairs, spiraling into the darkness below the streets of the merchant quarter. In the cellars the noise of the textile factory above was diffused by the maze of dark earthen tunnels, until the sounds of primitive industry were entirely lost.

The young barefoot man, Karos, walked with a crude tallow candle in hand, its insignificant flame sputtering in an effort to hold back the enveloping darkness. He continued on, eyes wide, into a deep chamber where he knew he was expected.

He stepped through the entrance to the dark cave and saw the rough stone walls, the irregular level of the rocky floor. He'd been here before, for past meetings with his mysterious patrons from over the mountains, but in their presence he was always humbled and in awe. Unlike himself, who had only the simple deformity of fused toes to show for mutations, he knew the robed ones who came to speak with him were true "mutants", creatures blessed in body, and in *mind*, with the most unusual adaptations.

He was no longer afraid. Long ago, when he had first laid eyes on the robed ones, he had been aghast, terrified of their freakish faces and garbled, choked voices. But over time, working with them and *for* them, he had come to know them, understand their vision, and he realized the purpose behind their infiltration across the great mountains and into the lands of the Jia Lang.

At the edge of the candlelight, there was a soft shuffling, of crude cloth robes, bare feet, deformed legs and monstrous appendages too hideous to describe. While the sounds echoed in the darkness, from directions all around him, Karos stood bravely and spoke appealingly to the shadows.

"I am here as you've asked. You've called for me, yes?"

It was quiet and dark, but he could hear at least a dozen figures shamble around him, and in a moment saw the vague shapes of creatures in deep purple robes at the edge of the light. They hid there, slinking in the darkness, never truly comfortable with revealing their ghastly forms to anyone. Even a trusted and devoted agent like Karos.

"*Yesss...*" came a chorus of whispers, sounding like the scuttling of a hundred subterranean insects over bare stone. "We have something important to discuss..."

Karos listened. "Please, tell me," he said, eager to do what he could for the 'cause'.

Burning Lands

Again, silence, but this time he sensed an urgency despite their hesitation, and he knew that their next words were indeed of great importance. Important to the cause, to all mutantkind. The chorus of low voices slithered from the darkness to his ears.

"Some dark 'thing' has roused from a deep sleep..." the voices said mysteriously. "Something ancient, something evil. We first sensed its awakening three years ago, at the very edge of our perception, but its emergence was felt like nothing before or since."

"A *thing?*" Karos asked curiously.

"Yes, something great and powerful and alive... And somehow *dead* at the same time. A malignancy whose mind shines like a dark beacon... A thing from the past... A remnant of the ancient world that must be found to cement the future of our cause..."

"A remnant of the ancient world? Vital to the cause?" Karos muttered, finding himself babbling aloud.

"Something very important to the future... to the *cause*..." the creatures whispered softly.

The young man now listened without comment, unable to follow where this was headed, or what exactly they were talking about. He was in the dark, literally and figuratively, but he felt compelled to remain quiet and simply *listen*. They spoke of the cause, and that was enough.

"It hunts a thing, a piece of itself, a *girl*. She was here, today, in the city square, among the streets. She walked right past us, slipped from us before we even realized what she was, and now she has been given over to the Clean for safekeeping."

Karos thought for a moment, then nodded.

"Yes, I heard something like that," he said. "My sources say a bounty hunter sold a nameless waif to the palace just a few hours ago, that the mandarin has a new *oblate*. But beyond that I know very little."

More silence. For a moment he felt somewhat ashamed, wondering if he had disappointed the robed ones by offering so little information.

"We must find her, we must... *acquire* her..." they whispered.

Karos' eyes widened, suddenly imagining they might ask him to send some of his men, or even *himself*, to go and get the child. To attempt a raid on the palace would be suicide, with its tall ramparts, hundreds of guards and the muskets and swords they would have to battle against with their pitiful sticks and slings. He immediately appealed to the shadows.

"The palace is a fortress, buttoned up good and tight. I beg of you, we *cannot* be asked to go in there. It would cost many, many lives. And expose our cell to the Clean and their allies. We wouldn't stand a chance, we'd be rooted from the city!"

"Do not be afraid, Karos," the voices interjected calmly, soothingly. "We do not speak of today. Nor of tomorrow. Nor of anytime soon. We will wait, patiently, just as the ancient 'remnant' waits for her eventual return... to *it*. We will find our window of opportunity, in the coming years, when she is ready. But until that time, continue your work and know that you have done so very, very well..."

Karos nodded, suddenly put at ease. One by one the robed ones stepped back into the shadows. They would be leaving soon, their agents moving on, but he would continue their clandestine work here in the city of trade, Tucumcari.

Gale had wept for hours before the mandarin's mistress returned, this time with a plate of hot food, drink and fruit. It was the second time since her official "adoption" by the Water Clan, and though earlier she had refused, she was too hungry and tired to resist any longer.

The woman no longer scrutinized Gale for lice, or signs of disease. This time she allowed a brief smile of sympathy to show on her lovely, yet hard face. She reached out as if to stroke Gale's hair as she devoured a plump ripe pear, but seemed to catch herself and momentarily pulled back, as if resisting some vague temptation to mother her. But when she remembered it was just the two of them alone, she relaxed slightly and brushed her fingers through Gale's hair.

"It's alright," she said in a surprisingly soothing voice, "you're in better hands now. I'll take care of you. We can be friends. I won't hurt you, no one here will. Your days of being scared are over."

Gale still looked frightened despite the calm, reassuring words. Seeing this, the woman touched Gale's chin and brought her eyes to hers.

"What's your name?"

Gale hesitated for a moment, searching the woman's dark eyes for hidden motives. For some reason she felt compelled to say as little as possible about herself, as if divulging anything, anything at all, was to admit that she was, in fact, here to stay. But the woman seemed friendly and her calming approach genuine, and though she was older by at least ten years, the strength in her stare gave Gale reason to feel at ease. She looked back for only a moment before finally breaking the silence with a soft whisper.

"Gale."

"*Gale...*" the woman muttered, "... like a storm... You are a talented one, Gale. The Clan will see to it that those talents are put to use and perfected. They will educate you, as they did me. They are not the worst of masters, but their kindness must be earned and their rules respected."

It seemed like a lot to demand from the young girl, who again looked afraid.

"My name is Kseniya," she said. "I will be your older sister. In time you won't be afraid anymore, and as you grow older you will serve the Clean well. Don't cry now..."

A few minutes later the rustling of flowery curtains could be heard throughout the sanctum, and entering the cozy apartments came the elderly mandarin, dismissing the remaining guards so that he, his mistress and his new oblate sat alone. He took a seat behind Gale on a wooden divan draped with the downy fibers of a *synoro* plant, reclining and fanning himself for a few moments as he assessed her in silence.

As he looked at her a slight glimmer of amusement showed in the corners of his mouth, but he soon spoke in level tones. "It's good to see you eating, child," he said. "And clothed no more like a savage of the Forbidden Lands. Kseniya has picked out something nice for you, I see, and you wear it well. Do you like it? There are many other gowns like it for you here. You will learn to wear them *all* well."

As he spoke Kseniya got up and prepared her master a drink in a hollowed gourd to whet his thirst. She served him something fragrant from the fist-sized vessel before leaning to whisper in his ear. The man smiled.

"Your name is Gale. A good, simple name. We shall dispense with the Clan tradition of changing your name on adoption. You are perhaps a bit old for that, anyway. So we will call you Gale. A fine name indeed, child."

Gale looked afraid of him, chilled by what she knew was a patronizing approach. Her mind raced between the two of them, master and servant. Her eyes bore through the savvy mandarin's genteel veneer and into his gray, despotic heart; she felt entirely alienated by the cold detachment that ruled his being. Here was something she had never witnessed before, a man who by virtue of his years had come to terms with the reality of this dark life and thus turned his energies to ruling it. Instead of finding a shelter from the darkness, instead of creating a haven from the suffering and cruelty around him, this man made the void his home, his kingdom. All of the beauty of this place seemed wasted; the effort to create a living garden, a palace whose walls, doors and pillars were made by cultivating trees until they took on useful shapes, only to be ruled over by a soul-less despot. It seemed... false.

The woman, however, was quite the opposite; a servant and experienced concubine, she was not destitute or barren-hearted like the other harem women Gale had seen. Kseniya was strong of will and still had hope for something, though what exactly Gale couldn't see even with her prying. And for some reason Gale found herself relieved that Kseniya was here, now. Her presence at the mandarin's side seemed to somehow temper the merchant in some fashion, and gave him reason to maintain his air of faux civility (Gale could sense that under that thin surface lay an untapped ruthlessness). Perhaps he had once truly desired Kseniya, when she had been new, and had only recently grown accustomed to her like a child grows bored of a new puppy, but the fire that he had felt for her in the past must have been a hot one, because he clearly still regarded her fondly and, remarkably, even *trusted* her.

The mandarin was apparently oblivious to her probes and continued to speak, this time wandering the clay-walled room at a slow pace, looking upwards at the coils of tightly-knit tree branches that came together to create the roof. In the few gaps between them, tear-drop shaped panes of sap allowed sunlight to filter through and wash the chamber with a rich, coppery color.

"No, my child, don't be afraid. Though I do have a harem, I think Kseniya is about all I can manage at my age. Indeed, to pollute you so young would do the Clan a disservice; you will make someone a wonderful bride someday."

Gale was brought back to the conversation by the sudden revelation that she was to be a "bride". She looked over at the mandarin, who had stopped in front of a large hourglass, almost as tall as she, upon which he placed one hand as if its cool glass comforted him. Seeing her look of bafflement, the mandarin obliged her by explaining.

"As a woman in the household of the Clean, you will no longer need to be afraid of the predations of savages. Here, I am ruler, and my relations from across the desert are our allies. We are a unity, a great power. We will keep you safe, as we keep all our own safe. However, there are certain... obligations for one such as you. You see, we cannot afford to allow just anyone amongst us; you, however, are different, exceptional. I think we would do best to train and educate you. Considering your particular skills, you would certainly make a fine diplomat or..."

He let that unknown thought linger before trailing off. He quickly changed the subject.

"In addition to giving your life meaning beyond a simple 'harem girl', we will give you culture and refinement. Kseniya, here, will no doubt be an icon for you to model yourself after."

Kseniya did not respond to the unintentionally complimentary comment and kept her eyes away from her master as he spoke.

"But you will have even more; you show such great promise! No, Gale, there will be better things. We will find you a husband someday and you will marry, and you will serve the cause of civilization well."

All this seemed to satisfy the mandarin quite well, as if he felt good for the boon of "generosity" he offered her. Strangely, this imprisonment was, in a way, a great step up from the lives of the savage feral women of the desert; what he was offering was membership in a community, a home, a family, protection and a *future*.

He pushed the large hourglass on end and sand began to sift through the narrow neck and into the bottom.

"Your new life begins here. Now."

She watched, mesmerized by the grains of sand slowly draining away; but one question hung in her mind. "What about Rider?"

The mandarin hesitated for a moment before speaking. "He took a fair amount of water and a horse. He said he wished nothing more than to plunge headfirst into the wilds. Such is the way of scavs, my dear."

He expertly veiled his lies with a false look of sympathy and pity. Gale didn't even attempt to see through his words, because it fit the vile vagabond too well. But though she couldn't explain it, her heart sank even lower, to the pit of her stomach. *Rider, too, had left her.*

Leaving her with that last bit to ponder as the sand slipped away, the mandarin left, taking with him whatever strange thoughts were brewing in his head, leaving his mistress to tend to the confusion and dizzying fear in Gale's mind.

CHAPTER 2

Time moved quickly. Gale spent three years in the household of Margus, mandarin of Tucumcari and one of the greatest trademasters of the Clean Water Clan. With time, the child blossomed into a young woman, and the memories of her violent, fragmented past became lost, lost in a thick, smothering regimen of speech lessons, language lessons and instruction in the ways of the Clan woman. She lived in a world previously unfamiliar to her, confined to a wondrous walled compound of hidden gardens and courtyards, lush apartments and fine food. Water, which had long been something of value to her growing up, was now freely given, and she learned how integral water was to the Clean's philosophy of life, survival... and domination. Over three years her entire life was turned upside down, and with care and gentle grooming bleached clean.

With her passing into maturity, and the erasure of her frightened self, Gale grew to become a woman worthy of intense speculation and admiration, which came her way in droves. Kseniya, now headmistress of the harem, groomed her beauty and helped her learn the ways of a noblewoman. Unlike the barbarians of the wasteland, to whom only bawdy pleasures held any appeal, Gale learned to entertain a more civilized household and was instructed in how to play the *pipa* and the *sihu*. She often amused her "father", Margus, as well as bands of visiting dignitaries hailing from the allied desert villages with her fine playing. Her blooming physical beauty too, became the reason many older chieftains and leaders brought their sons with them to these gatherings, to see, and possibly court, the mysterious young woman.

In time, Gale forgot who she was and who she had been, and memories faded into obscurity. Yet, on restless nights, she dreamt of a shadowy past only thinly covered by her new life of luxury and care, and memories of who she had been, where she had been born and raised, and how she came to be in this savage world, escaped into her subconscious. She was never satisfied, always aware she was not complete, aware she was "different", and unconsciously seeking a means of escape to find her destiny among the sands.

Gale, now entering the prime of womanhood, walked quietly down the sunlit promenade within the palace of Trade City. She looked nothing like the grubby child she had been when she first came here. She was a woman, a lady, and a potent resource to her Clan.

She was a vision, framed as she was in the sun. She wore her normally unruly hair drawn up into a tight topknot, its blond curls spilling free behind her. Her sharp green eyes showed only the vestiges of her former innocence and youth; now they were more aware, always observing, and guarded. Make-up designed to please men's eyes contributed some to her beauty, but her natural features alone were striking enough that she never needed it, beyond a mere accentuation of the traits with which she had been born. The brilliance of her eyes were draw enough for most men, but to complement them she wore a sleeveless cyan *cheongsam*, as was the custom of Clan women, and a thin diadem about her forehead set with a piece of jade to match their striking color.

Today was Gale's seventeenth birthday, and she was to be married in a matter of days to the nephew of Margus, the mandarin who had first purchased her and brought her into his house. His nephew, Alin (whom Kseniya reminded her was both handsome *and* the closest suitor to Gale's age) hailed from some distant corner of Clean-held lands, and had himself just reached maturity as well. Their marriage would cement friendships within the Clan and facilitate an alliance that meant a lending of troops and trading of goods. Margus sought, it seemed, to bring not only the region around Tucumcari more firmly under his control, but also to unify the Clean Water Clans more solidly.

The first effort would not be an easy task, as Trade City was still co-dominated by the Cartel, a people who didn't share the anti-metal/anti-Ancient philosophies of the Clean, only wanting to stay in control of the wasteland's markets. They were more industrious people, perhaps blind to the machinations going on under their nose, theirs being a straightforward trading house that had steadily used the city as a stepping stone to strengthen their oil routes north into the Forbidden Lands. Even now the skyline grew darker each month with the arrival of more frequent motorized caravans, convoys of old scavenged trucks and fleets of scrap-metal cars, as Cartel oil tankers used the ancient highways of the Far Desert and even the city itself as a stopping point before heading north to Midway. They, the Cartel, would certainly have a say in any expansion here, but would they care... or would they simply grin and enjoy the profits it brought to their doorstep?

As for unifying the Clean Clans, they were traders and merchants who had become complacent eating and drinking the respect and awe of the natives around them. Their enclaves were scattered all across the desert, affiliated by relation and marriage. They were already powerful, and every year the effort to bring the Clean's civilization to the wasteland seemed to flourish more and more.

But these were matters Gale honestly cared little for, though she knew soon enough she would be a part of it all. In her three years she had learned her lessons remarkably well, and proved to be more than just an entertainer for distant family members drawn here at the behest of her powerful "father". No, she had shown a willingness to be part of her foster father's every meeting, secretly using her ability to read thoughts and emotions to better his deals and trade agreements. She had done so well that Margus brought to the city, under a veil of secrecy, a small coterie of the infamous crones known as "Mothers of Fate", to tutor her in private. Known far and wide in this part of the wasteland, these ancient women were said to possess the most potent precognitive and telepathic abilities (rivaling even the mentalists of the Brotherhood) and had served as advisors to many of the great kings and leaders that had come and gone in the history of the Far Desert. Gale had found herself strangely compelled to listen and learn from the matrons who came to teach her, just as she had been drawn to the purple-robed monks years ago (whom she had since learned had been Brotherhood missionaries passing through the region), but in these women she found no comfort or companionship. They had left her life, leaving her with more questions than answers about who she was and what would become of her.

Her lessons were not entirely for *her* betterment. They had been invaluable in making Margus personally wealthy, which in turn made his house wealthy and influential. For once in her life she felt a definite purpose and sense of worth, but oddly, even now, poised to become a bride and a valued strategic tool of her foster people, she felt utterly and completely dissatisfied.

She found herself *thinking* a lot more these days, her thoughts deep and complex like a river that had, over the last three years, come to wash away the child-like innocence of her youth and reveal an entirely different girl, no, *woman*, underneath.

"Mind you pay attention," came the teasing voice of *Sarah*, her only real friend other than Kseniya here in this palace of seclusion. Sarah was one of the few people around her age in Margus' household, one of the progeny born (and in turn raised) in his harem; she had been conceived as an accident and now maintained her livelihood as a pretty adornment, no more valuable than the ornate candelabras and furniture of the palace corridors.

Her intrusion was enough to shake Gale from her trance and back to the present. Sarah laughed at Gale's expression of surprise, and immediately sat with her.

"You must be excited," she said with a grin, borrowing Gale's comb to brush her own long black hair. Of course she was referring to Gale's coming marriage, which to Sarah seemed thrilling. Sarah, a menial, would never know such a life and like others in her caste would have to content herself with dreams, using Gale's fortunate life as a proxy for her own fantasies. Her brown eyes sparkled as she imagined the coming ceremony.

"If we could swap places I would," Gale said somberly, only slightly exaggerating her misery.

Sarah noticed, then laughed in an effort to lighten the mood. "You're crazy, Gale! Think of the new life you're about to adopt! So many women would give anything to be in your shoes!"

Sarah kept her smile but her eyes conveyed an underlying feeling. Gale assumed it was just Sarah's fascination with marrying a far-away prince, but she sensed it was deeper than that. Sarah was referring to the alternative to marriage... a life in the harem.

"I want to give you something," Sarah said. "In case we never see each other again." Before Gale could question why such a token was necessary, Sarah pulled from her pocket a small ring.

"It's a *promise ring*," Sarah said cheerfully. "It symbolizes a promise that we'll never forget our friendship."

Recognizing Sarah's intentions, Gale took the ring, unable to conjure a smile but trying it on to humor her nonetheless. It was a snug fit. "Alright, an exchange," Gale said, taking off one of the small rings she sometimes wore before handing it to Sarah.

Sarah smiled again and was about to put it on when another person's footsteps echoed in the shaded garden.

"Are you two conspiring again?" came Kseniya's familiar voice, as the matron of the harem approached. Often times Gale and Sarah's surprisingly philosophical conversations got them into trouble, but today Kseniya's usual tirade was held back; she had a glimmer of excitement in her eye, and an unusual patience.

Sarah got up when Kseniya entered, quickly smothering her grin and lowering her head before departing in a hurry. She cast Gale a sideways glance and the two shared a momentary, secretive wink.

"Today is your last lesson, Gale," Kseniya said once Sarah was gone. She took out a textbook and put it before Gale as she came over and knelt at the garden table. "You're beyond these things now. You've been an exemplary student, and you know far more than I ever will. But your new husband arrives today. You're ready for a whole new life."

Kseniya looked like she wanted to add something more, but she didn't. But Gale could imagine what it would be. *I'll miss you, Gale.*

She would miss Kseniya too. Kseniya had turned out to be all that she said she would be, an older sister who had taken care of her almost as a foster mother would. In a fashion, at least as best she could considering the circumstances. She had not been close, but neither had she been cold, and even now it was like the teacher looking on her last and favorite pupil, who was soon to leave for good. She wondered, quietly and only to herself, what would become of Kseniya now?

Kseniya turned the large hourglass over. Despite her thoughts Gale said nothing and opened the book to its last lesson, an ancient poem scripted centuries ago:

The night was long and dawn came slow to the Crimson Land.
For a century demons and monsters whirled in a wild dance,
And the five hundred million people were disunited.

Now the cock has crowed and all under heaven is bright,
Here is music from all our peoples, from Yutien too,
And the poet is inspired as never before.

"A poem by Mao Tse... tung..." she finished softly, reading the last line aloud as she fumbled with the name, but in her head she heard her adopted father's voice, having recited it a hundred times as an affirmation of the righteousness of his mission to tame the wildlands around them.

Burning Lands

She took out her quill and began to translate the words, aware of the time remaining for this, her final exam. Yet though she attempted to look fixated on the seriousness of the task, her mind was drifting again.

Across the lovely garden the familiar, methodic "whoosh, whoosh" of the palace's wooden water wheels could be heard in the distance. It was a rhythmic pulse that forever pervaded the terrace of the mandarin, echoing from the depths of the deep wells of the great Hydro Station, the building that stood over the deep water vaults that sunk into the mountain's core. With that mechanical drone setting the meter of her mind, she completed her lessons with swift strokes of the pen, while at the same time began plotting a way out.

As Gale pondered her escape from lavish seclusion to the unknown future of a life of freedom, all to the sound of the Hydro Station's mechanical pumps, another rhythmic pulse reverberated through the searing, poisonous rock almost two hundred miles to the west-northwest. This unnatural rhythm was caused by no machine, at least not in the traditional sense, and it brought forth no life-giving waters. It was the rhythm of thousands of human hands working bitterly against unforgiving walls of stone, trading in years of their condemned lives to wrestle nuggets of white-hot *corium* from the bedrock of deep underground caverns.

This was the sick and dying heartbeat of Little Vegas, home of the infamous corium mines of the Far Desert.

This was a place of death, a place where condemned men were sent by the new powers of the "Twisted Earth" to give the last years of their lives some worth. Here the scores of human lives lost each day to the high temperatures of the deep mines, and to the radiation sickness brought with the extraction of every corium nugget, were just part of daily operating costs. Ten, twenty, even fifty men was a small price compared to the metallic wealth dug, picked and indeed clawed out of the rock by the dying population, each and every day.

Little Vegas was not the great city of Las Vegas, Nevada. That was another sick and twisted town all its own, far on the other side of the Wei Shan, the spine of forbidding peaks that split the two worlds of the Twisted Earth into east and west. No, Little Vegas was something a bit more laughable, if true squalor, misery, and hopelessness could ever be laughed at. In a distant, previous life Little Vegas had been a mining boomtown of the Old West, turned into a ghost town well before the 1900s. Its dilapidated false storefronts and corral-lined streets had been nothing more than a curious draw for motorists heading along the highways of the desert for distant locales during the time of the Ancients, until one day it became the site of a nuclear power complex of unprecedented size constructed deep beneath the earth. Stories were still spoken of this once-legendary power station, built to power the four surrounding states, but at the twilight of the Ancients it, like all of their monumental structures, was sundered by their folly and arrogance. Rent and broken by the cataclysm of the nuclear holocaust, the facility had sunk deeper into the earth, spewing its radioactive fuel throughout its complex of tunnels, passages and man-made caverns. It is said that thousands of workers died in seconds as the white-hot gasses, vaporized radioactive graphite, billowed to every part of the facility before exploding onto the surface. Entombed in their own monument, the scientists and technicians became trapped as tunnels and chambers were encased in the deadly glowing metal that, when cooled over time, would become the precious substance known to the survivors of the apocalypse as "corium".

Few could say with any real certainty when the secret bounty beneath Little Vegas was first discovered, but it was no doubt some poor wandering prospectors who first found it. Corium was long the medium of this part of the desert, a rare metal that, while it had no intrinsic value, was impossible to reproduce. Slightly luminous, and only mildly radioactive (a year's worth of natural *rems* were far more threatening than a sizable chunk of the stuff), and given to eerie, almost organic shapes when it cooled into elongated "nuggets", it was something from the ancient world that could not be forged, created, or duplicated by mankind's ignorant descendants. It was also exceedingly rare, only found in the ruins of ancient reactors that had melted down in the chaos of the Fall. Prospectors wandered the deserts seeking out these lost reactor complexes, extracted the metal, and used it to trade with the wide-eyed and awed tribal folk who saw it as wonderfully magical stuff.

Little Vegas of the future was no longer a motorist's stop, a quaint ghost town with a gift shop and museum; it was a corium mill, a human grinding stone that ate the prisoners of other wasteland settlements and spat out luminous, radioactive "gold".

Hammers hit chisels, and chisels bit rock, and rock shuddered defiantly.

Deep beneath the squalid surface town, a mass of naked bodies writhed as they crawled against the burning stone of a cavern wall. Some two hundred feet underground, in an abscess in the ground created by hot expanding gasses hundreds of years ago, the slaves worked feverishly to take what they could from the rock for their masters, the corium miners of the town above.

One of just two dozen in the tight dark confines of the cave, working solely by the hot blue light coming from tiny globules of glowing metal peeking through the crumbling rock, was a naked man whose pale white skin had become soiled with dirt, sweat, and the chaotic red stripes of a hundred lashings. A tangle of limp white hair went all the way down the back of his neck, and hung in loose oily curls in front of his face. Heavy rusted shackles on his neck and ankle looked ridiculous because he had lost so much weight that they barely stayed on, but like the others in the mine that day, his will to try and escape had been brutally beaten out of him long ago. But it wasn't *entirely* broken.

A few men coughed, choking on the hot air as it robbed their mouths of moisture. Others, the dying among them, simply lay against the bare hot rock, on their skinned and bloody knees, moving their tired hands about in weak mimicry of digging, hoping their overseers would be fooled. The other miners clustered around them to hide them, giving false hope that they'd regain their strength once their shift was over. Even now a few bodies could be seen just on the edge of the continuous blue glow, shrunken and lifeless.

Just then there was a shout that echoed down the tunnels to this abysmal place. Then another. Then more, a chorus of laughs and cries of elation. A trio of guards wearing leather armor and masks to cover their badly mutated faces casually overlooked their work. When they heard the sound they turned, scrambled to the cave exit and shouted back down the tunnel. None of the three had guns, only whips, but they turned their back on the mass of exhausted workers with confidence. One of the guards raised a hand and the workers in the cave fell silent. A few bold ones took the sudden interruption as an opportunity to collapse against the rock and breathe, but their rest was short lived.

"Come on, you dead-weights," yelled one of the guards, "Stop what you're doing! This way!"

With the lash of their whips the guards rounded up their slaves like animals in a herd, goading them on with savage beatings to scurry off down the narrow, winding tunnels. Their group joined other groups of workers being moved from various parts of this level of the mines. They pushed on towards a deeper cavern that marked the end of one of the lowest workable pits of the mines, and the beginning of the collapsed regions of the old complex that were so radiated they still hadn't been touched by the explorations of the miners.

The crowd of destitute slaves surged forward, a flood of naked misery pouring into the huge cave, their eerily-distorted shouts and cries reverberating like a raging river in a gorge. Already a mass of miners were busy working on the far wall of the chamber, the black sooty walls of which extended up and out of sight. Tiny fragments of fluorescent blue corium, looking like odd watery shapes, peeked through cracks in the rock giving the place its only illumination. Enough ambient light filled the cave so that the new arrivals tossed their torches as they entered, and pushed like a sea of bodies towards the far wall to join in the fevered work.

Just then a pickaxe hit something that made a high-pitched metallic "twang". The rock chipped and fell away, and a stronger, brighter glow poured into the cavern from beyond.

One of the guards at the head of the mass pushed the miner who had hit pay dirt to the ground with a hard shove. The old man fell and stayed down for good. The guard stepped up onto his back in an effort to get closer, wavering as the old man fluttered until a good stomp put an end to the shaky movement. He then reached forward using one hand, in a heavy leather glove, to finish what the old miner had begun.

"A hand!" the guard shouted over the cacophony, his garbled voice partially masked by the bizarre protective apparatus around his head. He motioned for the other guards, who found the effort of speaking in their masks too cumbersome and so simply nodded their excitement.

"Clear this, *now!*" he commanded, stepping back. The bulk of the miner pack crashed inward at his order, slamming against one another in a desperate struggle to please him and avoid his wrath.

Among the herds stood Rider, survivor of the mines, who in the chaos of the frenzy stole a moment to take a breath and watch with hateful, red-rimmed eyes. But the respite was momentary at best, and he quickly hurled his axe to the earth with a short grunt to begin helping as baskets of chipped stone were passed back through the crowd to be taken away.

In moments the "artifact" was uncovered. It was a life-sized metallic statue in the vague shape of a human. Its arms were partially raised, as if trying to shield its face from some terrible fate. The gender was indeterminate.

"Clear it off!" shouted one the high-ranking guards watching from the rear, and the men almost trampled one another to comply.

Like the mummified remains found in ancient Pompeii, the "statue" was gradually revealed in its entirety as it was worked free from the surrounding rock. It was a man, or a woman, who had been incinerated in the white-hot gaseous graphite of the reactor core during the Fall and mummified in a shell of solid corium. Even now the few onlookers who took a moment to stare could see and almost *feel* the horrific terror and pain the figure might have felt in its last moment of life. It was still etched on its face and visible in the blue, mirror-like metal of its crusted surface.

"Don't just stand there," shouted the guard in the rear, pushing his way past Rider and other rock bearers. "Start breaking it down!"

Wiry-armed chisel men moved in and immediately began the work of rendering the dead Ancient's mummified remains into portable slivers of corium fragments. As for Rider, he continued to carry his rock-laden basket down the tunnel and away from the scene. Head bent to one side, the basket cradled on his shoulder, he kept his face down as he passed the streams of workers being shepherded back towards this new mother lode.

The heat from the radiated rock around him scalded his feet, but by now he was used to it. Some of the other workers weren't so lucky; many hadn't adapted so well. As he followed the man in front of him, Rider heard the bearer behind him collapse with a pained sigh. Rider turned and saw the old man slumped against the wall, his rock load scattered on the tunnel floor. Others squeezed past, afraid to suffer the consequences of causing a backup. Rider spat out a curse and came over, kneeling at the old man's side.

It's always the old ones, he thought. "Get up, old man, you're choking the flow. Get up! You know what the guards'll do if they find a worker missing, don't you? It'll be hell on all of us! Now get *up!*"

For the first time Rider saw the old man's face. He turned, his sickly gray features exposed to the thinning light of the tunnel. His pupils were dilating, his lips shivering out of control. Deep rings framed his sunken eyes; he was leaving this place soon. The man tried to speak, but couldn't. He waved one feeble arm about as if trying to dispel Rider's eerie face from his vision, but it fell weakly to his side. He exhaled deeply, his bony ribcage rising momentarily, then falling abruptly.

"Get up!" The old man didn't move. Rider tried a different tone. "Look, you're on the next elevator up. You don't want to miss your ride!"

The old man looked to each side and seemed to realize he was lying against the wall. He smiled, and began picking up rocks from his spilled basket but instead of putting them back in, starting placing them on top of his body.

"*Crazy old...* what are you doing?!?" Rider reached down to slap some sense into him but the old man suddenly found enough strength to knock Rider's hand away. He wheezed with the effort, but went right back to *burying* himself. Rider was stunned. He sunk back, lips drawn tight, and put the sight out of his mind as he retreated down the tunnel after the others.

The droning trickle of free-flowing water filled the courtyard as a small group of men walked through the lush gardens on the High Terrace of Tucumcari, the Trade City. Fragrant blossoms just now coming into bloom created a tide of refreshing smells that wandered freely throughout the place. The men's chatter quieted as Margus Han, their respected scion, approached with an entourage of his own servants and advisors. A welcoming party for arriving guests who had traveled a great distance to be here, in answer to Margus' summons.

Margus, at the lead, opened his arms in a polite gesture... and smiled. The dark-haired youngster in the midst of the small group of visiting dignitaries grinned a broad and handsome grin and came forward quickly, almost forgetting the more senior men in front of him. His actions raised an amused chuckle from the group.

"Alin," Margus said with uncharacteristic warmth, "the image of your father. Tell me..."

"He is well, uncle," Alin said, looking at his uncle's familiar face with true affection. "He sends his best wishes."

"And, more importantly, he sends more supplies from our people," mused one of the older men accompanying the young prince, to which all of the men present laughed.

Margus embraced each of the elders momentarily, taking a few moments to greet each and reaffirm their friendship through reminders of experiences they all shared. These men were old friends, veteran trademasters from the allied families of the Clean Clans, his trusted associates and correspondences of many, many years.

Alin was quiet as the older men talked and walked through the gardens underneath a series of looming archways made from living trees bent inward, their tops gracefully intertwined far overhead. But the unshakable smile on his face spoke volumes of how much he admired his uncle. Perhaps unconsciously, Margus stayed near the young man, never allowing Alin to fall behind or become marginalized by their private jokes or alienated when the conversation spoke of things that occurred well before he was born.

It was almost a full hour before the men finally came to the shaded part of the garden where the fountains flowed and the giant orchids shed their petals to create a perfumed carpet to walk on. Margus motioned for each man to sit at a low wooden table, as timely servants moved unobtrusively from nearby places to begin serving refreshments.

"Trade is expanding," said one of the men matter-of-factly, after they had relaxed for some time and the conversation turned inevitably back towards business, "and with it so does *civilization*. The savages in the north country become more tame each day. Soon their war-like ways will be over."

"Fascinating people," one of the elders, Hamut, interjected with an off the cuff comment.

"Oh?" asked another suddenly. "You sound like you *admire* them, Hamut. Is this true?" There was some laughter, but the elder in question grinned and took a sip of wine.

"I've read of their ways," Hamut said, "and they do fascinate me."

"They are wild and untamed," another stated confidently, "and they offer nothing to the advancement of society. To them civilization is just a string of difficult syllables, not a dream worth achieving."

Hamut considered, knowing he addressed an audience hostile to his reasoning. "I'm only playing Devil's advocate," he reminded them. "Some of their notions, traditions, are worthy of merit."

"Such as?"

"I choose the one greatest example: *Democracy*."

"Democracy?" exclaimed Margus, speaking for the first time since they had relaxed under the orchid grove. His posture reacted almost defensively to the comment as he sat up with a start. The other elders quieted and looked his way.

Hamut said nothing but grinned again. He alone among the assembled elders could risk raising Margus' ire, but even he recognized it was not always wise to do so when speaking of *ideology*.

"The tribesmen of the north rule by vote," Hamut explained, "so that every decision serves the interests of the majority. Where to migrate during the winter months, where to set up camp, which herds to slaughter, which leader will lead them. When they commit themselves, they commit their entire people to the task."

The men were quiet, unsure of how to respond in the presence of the mandarin.

"That's true," Margus admitted, breaking the silence, "I suppose there is merit in that." The elders murmured quietly, not sure what to say. But Hamut sensed that Margus wasn't finished. He was right.

"For instance," Margus continued, "when you do go to war against a democracy you can be confident your swords always kill an enemy. Because it was the *people* who chose to fight you, by their own free will; they do not march unwilling or at the command of some tyrant. So there are no innocents to be spared when one wages war against a democratic people." A few sycophants among the elders took the opportunity to agree with Margus' ruthless take on the concept of "rule by the people". But Margus wasn't satisfied with mere utterances of agreement; he continued, making sure there was no misunderstanding his stance on the subject.

"In an oligarchy, an autocracy, only one man is held responsible for the crimes of his people, and as a result, he alone must be punished for peace and reconciliation to flourish. Killing one man versus exterminating an entire people for the sake of peace? I ask you, which way is more humane?" The other men drank uncomfortably.

"No, they need our way of rule, our civilization, and with it they shall be enlightened," Margus reaffirmed.

"What of competition these days?" one elder asked, changing the subject.

"The *Far Traders* have returned to the deserts east of here," Margus said dismissively.

"They are scattered, disorganized," said another, a look of disdain on his wrinkled, aged face. "The Far Traders are cheap peddlers, sideshow merchants who still sell miracle cures alongside their cheap water and impure gasoline."

"That's the attraction, you see!" said Margus. "The barbarian chiefs know they aren't a threat, and humor them. And what do they get for their effort? They trade water away for beads and baubles. We give too much credit to those impoverished fools and their 'crawling cities', and far too much significance to their contribution to the civilizing of the wasteland."

"Perhaps when you're our age, Alin," said one of the elders, "the time will be ripe to sweep the Far Traders' crawling cities from the eastern routes and take that part of the world as our own."

A few of the men laughed, wistfully savoring the idea of curtailing the Far Traders, their only real competitors left in this part of the world. They were a people long driven to the fringes of the wasteland by the aggressive expansion of the Clean so that their entire race remained mobile, living in great sprawling communities on wheels.

"Never underestimate the competition," Hamut reminded, raising a finger.

"Hamut is afraid of gypsy-nomads!" A few laughed.

Hamut, who had brought up the cautionary note, smiled. "They have not only the business, but the *friendship* of their patrons. Something *we* cannot always claim to have..."

"We can't afford to," Margus said suddenly. "Our customers are different customers entirely. Friendship? Nonsense. The Far Desert and the Forbidden Lands, and even the lands over the Wei Shan, are a far cry from the pathetic little villages the Far Traders choose to pander to. Here it is the rule of violence, of *might*, that we contend with, on a daily basis. Simpering tribal bands looking for hope versus raider armies seeking only blood and glory? The Far Traders are coddled in their backwater world where all men think the same, of mere survival. We are stronger from the adversity *here* at the edge of the Forbidden Lands, invincible by the sheer factional nature of the wasteland that surrounds us, like a gauntlet. While they gather their 'friends', we build alliances of steel with the raiders and the Cartel. We will one day see which way is superior."

There was a strange tone in his voice that, if any of the half-drunk men had been listening closely, could have been construed as Machiavellian.

"You always speak so highly of alliance-building," said Elder Hamut, casually picking at a handful of grapes before devouring the polished purple bulbs one by one, "you always were one of our greatest diplomats, Margus".

At this comment Margus turned to his nephew. "Alin," he said, "if there is one thing your uncle will leave you with, it is advice, something that in the end is often far more precious than weapons, war or even water. While some will pursue victory for their own survival at the cost of many lives, winning can be achieved more readily, and without the cost, through the relentless enforcement of *relations*. Why stand opposite an enemy for the sake of pride when you stand to lose so much in the bargain? Instead, draw him in, soothe him, make him your most loyal, lasting friend. Then let him fight your battles for you."

"Let the coyote die defending his prey," Alin said slowly, and Margus chimed in as he guided his nephew through the recital of this ancient Clean proverb.

When the last word was spoken Margus' eyes gleamed. *Had Alin been his own son, he could be no prouder.*

The men's laughter quieted as a member of the rarer sex approached. Kseniya, wearing semi-transparent clothing as always to please the eye, walked over to Margus and stood behind him. Her face was serene, but her tightly-knit eyebrows showed how intensely she fought to contain her emotions. Margus let his hand rest on hers, patted it, then turned to the others and raised his water goblet in a wordless toast.

Hamut looked at Margus as he drank, then laughed. He rose and, with Margus' leave, took Kseniya's extended hand.

"I think I'll join you, Hamut," said one of the merchants, as did another, and together the rest of the elders departed with Kseniya, leaving Alin and his uncle alone as she led them to her master's harem, and the bevy of women waiting to entertain them.

Alin watched the other men depart, but remained quiet. Sensing the awkwardness, Margus also said nothing, and merely put his empty water glass down on the table.

After a measured moment he asked quietly, "Alin, your father's letters have grown infrequent these last years, even as you have become more of a reason to make him proud and boastful. A shame. But if I may ask... have you yet known the company of a woman?"

Alin blinked with surprise, and embarrassment.

"If you're to be married, you must know what to do..."

For the first time Alin spoke up before Margus had finished speaking. "Uncle... where is Gale? I would very much like to meet her."

Margus sat back and looked at Alin in a new light, as he secretly recoiled from this sudden revelation that young Alin possessed the amorphous beginnings of a more "moral" character. In that instant he wondered if the boy was up to the tasks of the Clan after all, if such qualms were admirable or condemnable in a future trademaster. He wondered if the boy was a little "off", more fond of men perhaps. Then, as he disregarded this thought as a frivolous concern, he consoled himself with the thought that maybe the boy was just eager to impress his uncle that he was a young man of virtue, worthy of marrying Gale, his charge.

Margus settled on the latter and smiled, amused at what he assumed had been an amateurish attempt to impress him.

"Patience my boy," he said.

With an exhausted gasp Rider fell against the warm blue rock, which despite its unusually high temperature was much cooler than the rock in other parts of the underground complex. He closed his eyes for a moment to catch his breath, even as other workers around him unloaded baskets of broken stone onto the ever-growing pile at the bottom of the deep, gloomy elevator shaft. As he gradually opened his tired eyes Rider looked up; in the distance the warm orange glow of torchlight could be seen above. Down the chute came cooler air, pumped lazily and irregularly down into the lower tunnels to keep the air from becoming suffocating, at least when it suited the guards to push the slaves on the upper levels to move from the corium-laced walls to operate the bellows.

A ramshackle gridwork of wood, corrugated iron and other scrap from the desert around Little Vegas shored up the vertical shaft. High above, a heavy wooden elevator was already being lowered to the level below to start bringing up the loose rock before it piled too high.

A smooth operation. He wondered if anyone would notice if the old man who usually rode up with the gange seemed a bit whiter than normal and more than a few years younger...

He decided finally that he didn't even care. He wet his parchment-dry lips with his tongue as the elevator drew nearer, the chains hanging beneath it rattling wildly and the wood creaking and buckling as it came. As the elevator hit the bottom of the shaft it echoed like thunder; the feeble workers who had also taken a moment to rest in the shaft's deep shadows moved into action as the single guard on the elevator stepped off and simply began unfurling his whip. The guard, looking for all the world like a monster of medieval nightmares in his armor made of hides and stitched human flesh, and his rusted and ornately-decorated breath mask, simply watched like a little god as the men cringed in his presence, and worked feverishly to load the elevator before his patience ran thin. Rider watched with keen interest from the shadows, wondering if this was a new hire, or a veteran of the mines who might suspect the disappearance of the old man whom he was now going to impersonate.

Rider joined the others, saying nothing, trying to remain unseen among the mass of naked, working bodies. The guard watched, the lenses of his mask reflecting their toil with cold detachment.

From behind, a few more miners came down the tunnel, led by a pair of guards. On their backs two of the guards carried dead bodies; another four carried sacks, burdened by some unknown shapes inside. As these loads were deposited on the flat elevator floor, the guard with the whip clearly looked like he'd had enough, and lashed one of the workers to show that he was ready to return to the surface. Immediately the rest of the slaves scrambled to get clear.

The guard coiled the whip at his waist and, once his hands were free, yanked a rope with both, and the sound of pulleys being tugged far overhead echoed down the shaft. A few rocks skittered off the vertical tunnel as the elevator began to rise.

"One of you get up here and keep this load from falling!" called the guard, his voice sounding alien as it passed through his leathery mask. He went to uncoil his whip again, but stopped as Rider leapt up without hesitation, grabbed hold of the elevator's edge and climbed on board like a limber gecko before the rickety platform disappeared back up the shaft. As it cleared the ground, the workers rushed back to the bottom of the pit to watch the elevator rise up, their faces overcome by shadows until they vanished entirely in the darkness.

Rider used his bare hands to gather the sharp and prickly splinters of rock to keep them from falling over the edge. This had been the old man's job, but apparently the guard was either unfamiliar with the workers on this shift, or never really cared to look at them to get to know their faces. Once the rocks were secure, Rider crawled over to the blanket-covered bodies. As he struggled to move one to better center it on the elevator, the flap fell open revealing the old man's dead face, staring up at him.

Terrified that the guard might see, Rider moved in between the dead body and the guard. Slowly, cautiously, he looked over one shoulder, ready to be struck down if the guard realized what was going on.

The guard had unzipped himself, and was urinating through the cracks of the wooden elevator down the shaft and onto the workers below. He wasn't watching Rider. Quickly Rider secured the blanket over the old man's head, and tied a rope tight around his neck. He closed his eyes to regain his composure, before moving to the next heap.

"Not that one," the guard suddenly said behind him in a hollow tone, and Rider found himself flinching.

The guard zipped himself up and turned. "That one is a *real* mess, another one they dragged out of the deep. They say he was *dissolved*. Something is down there, they're saying. Something really nasty living at the bottom of the mine and killing those who go too deep..." The guard moved over, putting his whip on Rider's shoulder.

"Hey, you tell anyone I said anything..." he let the threat rest there. Rider gnawed at his lip and nodded without turning. This one was a new hire; any other guard who'd been in the mines a while wouldn't hesitate to kill a slave, whether he felt threatened by him knowing too much or not. So Rider played along.

As they came to the level above, he immediately joined the slaves at the top of the shaft in unloading the elevator. Using bare hands, shovels and sticks, the men moved the rubble to an ancient ore cart that sat on rusted tracks. The elevator guard watched for a few moments, then wandered over to another small group of guards to steal a cigarette for later.

When the offloading was done, a group of miners waiting nearby climbed aboard the elevator at the insistence of their own masters, waiting to be taken down to the level below. Normally Rider would have been expected to follow, but he watched, waiting to see if the elevator guard would return. When he didn't, and the elevator started descending under slave power, Rider hunkered down and joined the other laborers as they started pushing the laden carts down the westbound tunnel and towards the *surface*.

Although it was bad down below, one really had to struggle to find reasons why the depths of Little Vegas were any worse than the surface. At least down below, more men died than lived. Up here they were forced to drag out their existence in the twisted carnival atmosphere of this hideous place, their cries of suffering drowned out by the drunken laughter of the ever-present guards, the canned Old West music pouring out of revived saloons and brothel-houses that adorned the town like towering landmarks to depravity, and the noise of countless more of their brothers being marched off towards the gaping maw of the corium mines.

What was worse was the knowledge that the town was a *trap*, a devious and deliberately-designed trap intended to lure people in and never let them go. It worked on all levels; the town itself was an oasis, kept illuminated at all times, night and day, by miles of multi-colored Christmas lights strung up on buildings and along the ramshackle walls that surrounded it. Dimwitted desert people, tribesmen and scavs, were drawn to its fancy lights like moths to a flame, sucked in by their own curiosity over the imagined wonders on the other side of the towering walls. But they were never allowed to leave once they crossed the threshold of the town gates. Hunters and survivalists who came only to trade for water and other supplies, found themselves sucked in and imprisoned against their will.

Word was spread on printed fliers, and on the lips of unscrupulous demagogues handsomely paid to take the message to Tucumcari and beyond, that work was to be had here, that the corium mines were so rich and that there was so much of the stuff to go around that everyone who came could share equally in its bounty. Remarkably, even in this day and age when men would seem to be more guarded and cautious than ever, the fools came from every corner of the wasteland, led by their dreams of a better life. Hungry to fill their bellies with more than just sand, and believing for some reason in the validity of a poster with fancifully-printed words, they came in small bands, large groups and veritable armies, hoping to leave as wealthy as kings. But all were broken, enslaved once they arrived, and condemned to die a wasting death of fever and radiation sickness in the deep mines of Little Vegas.

To ease the sting of their suffering the rulers of Little Vegas made some concessions to their slaves, including the brothels that outnumbered the watering holes almost three to one. But women were hard to come by these days, and so many miners who couldn't hack it down below ended up being forced into costume as saloon girls or working in wretched little peepshows. Some patrons secretly knew the difference, others didn't; but since most men lived their days either drunk, drugged, or so sick from the "red fever", they eventually gave up any notions of caring. It was Sodom revisited, reborn, remade.

Making good use of the old ghost town's existing structures, the town behind the walls looked like a built-up, overflowing, and overcrowded version of the legendary Deadwood. Saloons churned out distorted music from warped player piano rollers, while raucous chorus lines of transvestites shouted out bawdy songs that found their way out into the streets, at all hours. Herds of miners moved about the crowded town, clutching "pay stubs" in hand and just being thankful they had 24 hours before they were being pushed back into the mines. Twenty-four hours to drink, take whatever home-brewed drugs they could get their hands on, sniff glue, kill one another in brawls, and engage in all manner of unmentionable affairs.

Rider moved through the relative cover afforded by twilight. It was the best time, the *only* time, he could feel confident of moving unseen. Not that anyone would really recognize him (or care) if they spotted him. Few people were lucid on the surface, and even if they were, they had no idea he might be a man hell-bent on escaping.

Rider crouched in the shadows of one of many alleys winding through town, pulling on a shift of clothes he'd snatched from a laundry line elsewhere closer to the mines. A fight was already breaking out in the saloon across the way; miners were stumbling into the street, some clutching wounds, others being chased out by cross-dressing floosies hobbling after them on ill-fitting high-heeled boots. Elsewhere it might have been comedic, something to watch, but for Rider it was the distraction for which he'd been waiting.

He slipped out of the alley, keeping to the shadows, and entered in through the back of another drinking establishment down the street. A ramshackle sign hung over the door, reading "Torak's Hole".

Inside it was heady with smoke from dubious sources, as shadowy customers sat quietly in the corners or in niches, engaging themselves with the collection of bizarre pipes and alien hookahs arrayed about the place. Quiet conversations took place here and there, but most of the miners visiting the "Hole" came here just to lose it. Rider closed the door behind him, letting his eyes wander over the ash-gray faces of the people gathered there and adjust to the dim light coming from the smoldering red tips of cigarettes, pipes and the low flame of a few opium braziers strategically placed in corners.

Content that no guards were present, Rider moved to the bar and sat. Though he raised a finger to summon the bartender, he wasn't really here for a drink. Weeks before in the mines he had heard a rumor, had caught just a fragment of a passing conversation between miners returning from the depths. Nothing much, and certainly not enough to raise the alarm of less astute men, but he came here to test a suspicion that he just couldn't dispel. Besides, his plan of escape depended on him being right...

With a long brown smock sweeping behind him, the bartender eventually found his way over once his other customers were set up. A tall man, he was middle-aged and lean, like a man who'd perhaps indulged in a little too much of his own addictive product. He was completely hairless, without so much as an eyebrow or eyelash on his head. In the weird orange light of the fluorescent elixir he began to pour in front of Rider, his eyes, and even his bald pate, seemed to glow.

"Gomorrah's Grog," the man said with a slight grin, looking into Rider's eyes without watching what he was doing, but not spilling a drop. "I bet it's been a long time..."

Rider nodded; it was true. Not bad stuff, and though he hadn't come to drink, he reached out and took the glass.

The man extended a wrinkled hand for payment. Rider raised a finger as he drank the liquor, then brushed the man's hand away.

"On your tab then..." the bartender said with an unsettling grin, turning to walk off.

"Wait," Rider said, gasping for breath. "You're *Torak?*"

The bartender said nothing for a moment, continuing to methodically clean a glass, then looked back to Rider.

"I am. Can I help you?"

Rider considered his words, then spoke. "I want out of this town and I think you can help me," he stated quietly. Torak's eerie orange eyes shifted, then he grinned a forced grin, revealing brown teeth beneath his lips.

"Sorry, child, you're mistaken."

Rider felt ill at ease speaking with the bartender, as if there were other voices listening in. He took a moment to look around again, but no one was close; even the men at the other end of the bar were too far away to hear them clearly.

"I'm not here to plead with you or bargain with you. But you're going to help me whether I have to..."

Torak leaned close before Rider could finish. "Such talk is likely to get innocent people in danger, hurt. I don't know what you've heard, but I can't help you. Now unless you want more grog..." At that moment Rider felt a strange sensation, as if his mind was being peeled open and examined. Shrugging off the eerie sensation of being scrutinized, he continued:

"You don't look *too* badly mutated, Torak. Does that put a limit on how high in the hierarchy of the Brotherhood you can go?" Rider asked quietly, but just loud enough to be sure the bartender heard. Torak seemed oblivious as he cleaned a cup and served another patron a drink. Once the miner stumbled off, he returned to Rider.

"Brotherhood? Here in Little Vegas? No, you're mistaken." Even while he denied it Torak's eyes seemed alight not with the glow of his curious drinks, but with a strange evasiveness that was triggering Rider's sixth sense. And on top of that, each time the bartender spoke, it felt like the man was speaking on behalf of someone else, serving merely as a mouthpiece. It was uncanny.

Rider ground his teeth nervously as those eyes bore down on him. But the bartender's elusiveness convinced him to press on.

"I just wonder," Rider said, refusing to break the bartender's strange and intimidating stare, "what in the Hell Brotherhood *spies* are doing running a saloon in Little Vegas? Are they *spying* on the people of the east? Are they looking to bring their religion to the Jia Lang?" At that instant Rider thought he heard distant whispers in his mind. Could it be the bartender was reading his thoughts openly now?

Burning Lands

Torak smiled another false smile, a dry grin pulled forcefully across his angular face.

"It's not nice to throw around accusations, even when you're drunk. Some people might get the wrong impression. Besides, where did you get such a preposterous idea?"

Rider grinned and leaned forward. "It wasn't really hard, you know. The upper ranks of your cult may be subtle, but your footmen are a bit more obvious. Sometimes comically. Robed figures seen shambling about town at night. Sneaking from alley to alley. All of them coming here, slipping in through the back door. The miners in town have seen you guys and know you're up to *something*. I'm just surprised the town guards haven't heard about it. Wonder what they'd do if they knew there was a cult in town..."

Torak continued to clean the glass behind the counter, his face a perfect mask of calm, despite Rider's insinuated threat. It made Rider falter for a second... but only for a second.

"You know, I always thought the Brotherhood remained largely neutral in things. If word got out they were planning to take over Little Vegas, imagine what it would do to their relations elsewhere. Doesn't the Brotherhood have 'missionaries' in Styx, Socorro, even Tucumcari? I imagine the Clean and Cartel would be shocked, no, *appalled* to find out the Brotherhood's peaceful preachers were moonlighting as *spies...*"

The whispers ceased altogether, and at that moment Torak shook his head. "You're on a mission of vengeance," he finally said, replacing the top on one of the bottles behind the counter, "but I'm quite sure it hasn't anything to do with *my* establishment. Now you've come in here and made some outrageous claims, claims that, while certainly are unfounded, could put unwanted scrutiny on my business, my *friends*."

Now it was Torak's turn to lean close. "What do you *want?* Just to escape? If you'll allow me to quote an old cliché, 'Escape is easy, but surviving the desert, that's another story altogether.'"

"I can handle the desert," Rider said, and he looked almost insulted at the implication.

Torak nodded most seriously. "You look like proof that a man can subsist on willpower alone," he said, but then added, "but you're a man cursed with 'White Skin'. Oculocutaneous albinism type one, if I were to hazard a guess. And you've only got rags, and exposure to the sun on such a long trek is certain to kill you."

Rider stared resolutely ahead, but said nothing. This man, whoever he really worked for, knew mutants alright. Long ago *albinism* wasn't entirely unknown as far as genetic mutations went, but these days, in a world slowly being overrun by broad open deserts, it was one of the worst defects with which anyone could be born. Few sufferers survived long, and as a result *albinos,* and the knowledge of what it meant to be one, were vanishing from the world. Yes, this man knew mutantkind well, which made Rider even more confident in what he had surmised was true. Torak, and perhaps a few of the other men lingering in the bar (and no doubt watching him now), were in fact members of the Brotherhood, that alien cult only whispered about in these lands but who held terrible sway like a "neo-Rome" in the lands of Old Nevada, across the mountains. A religion based on the principles that the splitting of the atom and the nuclear wars had created mutation as an answer to the human race's inability to drag itself from wallowing in the mud of mediocrity, to create new and fantastic strains of mutantkind to populate the earth. Their zealous followers, from the lowest degenerate cretin to the strangely-alluring mind masters and the whispered-of "Illuminated", were always searching for lost sources of radiation which they coveted like gold, and hunted down moldering texts on technology and nuclear physics with the obsession of those sorcerers who once sought out the lofty *Key of Solomon*. Their presence here, in Little Vegas, was a sure sign that the distant cult of the Nevada desert was no longer so distant, they were here, among the men of the cities and trade towns on the eastern side of the Great Divide, and lurking with a sinister agenda.

"Tell me, Rider," Torak said, suddenly finding an opportunity to inquire, "why do you go off to take the life of a powerful unifier of the desert people, the architect of civilization? What possesses you to become an assassin, to kill the one man who seems actually capable of creating a land where peace is the order of the day? And to become a killer who will certainly never make it out alive?"

Though he seemed to lavish praise on Margus Han, Rider sensed that Torak did not for a moment believe the ruthless mandarin could ever deliver "peace" and "civilization". At the same time Rider was more than a bit annoyed that his mind had been penetrated so quickly and easily!

Rider snorted. "Unifier? Look at me! He did this to me. We made a deal and he betrayed it..."

Suddenly Torak's face grew blank, as he realized who exactly Rider *was*. In that second the whispers in Rider's mind intensified, he knew he was being probed with renewed interest, but he didn't know why the Brotherhood might be so interested in him and so he simply kept going:

"... he took a girl in exchange for goods then had me taken away and sold to the mines. He took everything and consigned me to this Hell. *Margus Han has to pay.*"

Torak was quiet for a long moment, as if listening to voices in his own mind, then slowly nodded as if what Rider said was sound logic. "True... but I remind you that you can't get away. Even if you survive, even if your skin resists the cancer... Even if you succeed, this man's death will mean a great deal to the wasteland. Are you prepared to be held responsible for whatever fills the void when he's gone?"

"Who, the Cartel?" Rider asked.

Torak grinned, and again Rider felt he was being watched through Torak's eyes by other sentiences elsewhere.

"No, not the Cartel..." Torak said in a sinister whisper.

"Just help me escape, Brother Bore-Me-To-Death, or so help me your little operation will become public knowledge faster than you can..."

Torak raised his hand for silence. "I insist you're wrong," he said, a sly grin on his face, "but if it'll get the dog to stop barking, we'll do what we can."

Rider was surprised; all in all it had been surprisingly simple getting Torak's help. Of course, that made him feel uneasy. Torak turned away, yet for a moment Rider swore he heard the man's voice in his mind:

"By the eastern gate at midnight. Don't be seen."

Burning Lands

"Gale..." came a strangely comforting male voice, echoing through the din of her dreams, "...You can find out what happens to 'Alice' later. Right now I want you to pay attention. This is very important, and we don't have much time. Try to remember: two, three, six... Gale, are you listening to me?"

"Yes, Daddy," she replied.

"Oh no you're not!" came the man's voice again, followed by laughter, a childish squeal, and sounds of happiness that were so unfamiliar that they yanked Gale from the murky depths of sleep.

Batting her eyes, Gale looked around and recognized the hanging ivy of the gardens. Kseniya was gone, and her books were packed away. Several of her master's cats lounged nearby, watching her strange fitful rest with passing fancy. As she rose from the cushions, the cats quickly lost interest and returned to their self-grooming.

Getting up, she realized it was early dusk; golden rays of sun were setting outside, framing the towering white clay walls in a warming aurora of light. She wondered what a full sunset looked like these days; though she was sure they hadn't changed in two years, she yearned to see it with her own eyes, without the walls of the palace to obstruct them.

Gale wandered the corridors, slowly reviving herself. Tonight was a big night, and she had to be refreshed when mandarin Margus introduced her to her future husband. That thought alone made her heart race, not from some giddy, girlish excitement, but from the fate to which that the meeting was likely to consign her. A fate someone else was deciding for her.

Down a nearby corridor Gale thought she heard Kseniya's voice. Approaching, she was about to say something when her keen instincts caused her to fall silent. Taking cover among the shadows of a nearby archway made from two fused *Barek* trees, she listened for a moment.

"... but you took the corium..." she heard Kseniya say, in a hushed but desperate whisper, pleading to someone just out of sight, "... you must give me the key, *we agreed!*"

There was a low chuckle, from some man Gale couldn't see, but who seemed familiar. A palace guard? "It'll take more than your body and a sack full of corium for any man to betray Margus Han. I honor the clan first, my master second, and you... well a treacherous whore hardly rates at all, now does she? Even one who holds the mandarin's eye."

"I can always find someone else," Kseniya retorted angrily, "Give me the money back!"

The man immediately laughed, albeit quietly. "No, woman, I'll hold onto the money," he said with amusement, and Gale could hear the clink of corium nuggets being coyly toyed with through the folds of a burlap sack. "Consider it a payment, you've at least bought my secrecy. After all, if milord were to hear you wanted this key, he'd certainly wonder why. And unlike me, he might ask questions. And I don't think even a deceitful slut like you could fool one so discerning as the mandarin, especially with that *mind-reader* of his at his side."

Gale was eager to peek around the corner, but she couldn't tell how far Kseniya and her unknown conspirator were down the hall. For all she knew they could be right around the corner.

Kseniya said nothing, and in seconds the man's laughter trailed off into a barely audible chuckle. Footsteps echoed, getting louder, and Gale sunk deeper into her niche, terrified. Just then a man rounded the corner, the armory master, but he kept on going, not noticing her there in the shadows. After a few moments, Gale patted down her dress, then walked out as if she had just arrived.

Kseniya was standing in the center of the candlelit hall, wringing her hands with worry. As soon as she saw Gale appear she turned around with a forced smile on her face.

"There you are," Kseniya said, her voice only slightly faltering, "we must get you ready for your meeting with Alin!"

"Kseniya," Gale said cautiously, "is there something wrong?"

Kseniya shook her head. "Nothing, Gale, nothing at all. I'm just... afraid to lose you."

Gale stared, eyes fixating on Kseniya. *She was lying.*

"Mistress, I want to help," Gale said, reaching out and taking Kseniya's hand, "what is going on?"

Kseniya stood back, pulling her hands free. She looked both ways down the corridors. "Gale, I don't know what you think you heard, so I won't even ask."

"I want to help," Gale insisted.

"No!" Kseniya snapped, and Gale could tell she was serious. She considered attempting to use her special skills to learn Kseniya's thoughts even against her will...

"Don't attempt to read my mind, for your own sake, child." Apparently Kseniya had anticipated her without the aid of second sight.

Respecting her mistress' wishes, Gale frowned. "If you're in some kind of trouble..." she started, and suddenly Kseniya laughed, swallowing the last of her tears. It was a laugh that almost seemed to pity Gale for her clumsy attempt to reach out to her more mature "sister".

"Oh, Gale, you mean well, and I'm sorry for snapping. My worries are *my* worries, and not yours. Come on, we don't have the luxury of standing here all evening. The mandarin's guests have traveled a long way and are looking forward to being entertained by your music. Don't be difficult, alright?"

In a few moments Kseniya had led Gale to her quarters, where Sarah and the other handmaidens waited for her at the door, ready to dress her for the evening. Gale went in first, disappearing into the room and behind a dressing screen. Once she was out of sight the handmaids looked expectantly at Kseniya, who closed her eyes momentarily, then shook her head. The others looked to each other with worry, but stayed silent due to Gale's proximity just a few feet away. Sarah nodded gravely to Kseniya, then went behind the screen to help Gale get dressed.

"Say nothing," Kseniya said in a whisper that only she and the menials outside could hear, *"there may still be another opportunity. We may have to get our hands dirty to do it, but there's still a chance. We just have to wait a few more days..."*

The moon was full and blue over the wretched rooftops of Little Vegas. Blinking lights of green, orange, and red cast eerie shadows that danced up and down the narrow alley skirting the eastern wall. Even in this gaudy light Rider was barely visible, concealed near a barrel and watching the wall from hiding.

Guards armed with muskets walked up and down the wall, returning every now and again to the small huts built atop the low towers to share a cigarette with the next sentry down the line. In the crisp night air the men had stripped their masks, revealing their truly gruesome faces: monstrous, with heavy folds of skin, broken teeth that on some erupted through their cheeks like stray tumors, and large multi-faceted eyes that glittered in the moonlight like the eyes of enormous, hungry insects. Surely with eyes like those they could see even better than he in this darkness, so Rider waited patiently, resigned to watching.

Considering the layered presence of sentries, he wondered just how Torak would engineer his escape. He shrugged, ultimately surrendering this one unknown variable to chance. It wasn't something he did often, especially when his own fate lay in the balance.

"It *does* look formidable," came Torak's voice and Rider almost jumped when he realized the bartender, now clad in a darker robe, was standing right behind him.

"Don't fucking do that," Rider said, shaking his head to show he was annoyed. Torak merely stared out at the night.

"Are you ready?" Torak asked. Rider looked back.

"Are you kidding? There's two guards in each tower right now and another walking patrol on this stretch of street." He pointed to the alley that ran along the base of the wall.

"No," Torak whispered, "the one on patrol is distracted right now. Actually, he's probably obsessing over the idea of getting something to eat. You have a few minutes before the compulsion fades and he returns." Rider looked incredulous, but said nothing.

"As for the guards up there..." Torak raised his head and stared for a few seconds at each tower in turn. "... no, it looks like they're a bit mixed up about what time it is. They're probably getting impatient waiting for the relief shift to show up. If you look now you'll notice they're getting a bit angry, probably accusing their fellow guardsmen of getting drunk without them. Ah yes, and now they're climbing down, saying,"

"'To Hell with it...'"

Torak seemed to speak with several voices, deep and soft, male and female. Rider watched him cautiously, suddenly questioning the sanity of being here, but his attention turned back just in time to see the tiny pinpoints of light from the guards' cigarettes go out. Then, one by one, the four watchmen descended from their posts and began walking away down the street.

When Rider looked back Torak was smiling.

"I do believe you're *gaping*," Torak teased, speaking in his normal voice.

"How did..." Rider started.

Torak quietly replaced his hood, then turned. But before he left, he turned his head back slightly.

"Travel quickly, Rider."

Rider watched for a few moments as Torak walked off, with the strange feeling that he was slowly becoming the pawn in someone else's game. He then remembered he only had a short time to enact his escape. Getting up, with only rags on his back, he scurried over to the wall, found suitable handholds, and began climbing. In just moments he found himself on top of the wall, catching his breath. He looked back, his eyes sweeping over the panoramic view his perch afforded him of the entire town. From up here he could see why savages and others were drawn here; it was somehow alluring, like a glittering jewel, with all its lights and the sounds of drunken laughter and wanton merriment spilling over the walls and into the desert. But as a survivor of Little Vegas, he now knew better. This was a place he was eager to leave behind.

With a grunt Rider scaled down the far side, dropping the last fifteen feet to the loose sand dune on the far side. Instantly he sprang to his feet, took just a second to find his bearings, and began jogging towards the east-southeast.

Somewhere far away a lone shepherd walked the last half mile towards his small village, moving hastily on crude sandals to cross the rocky, unforgiving plain. His quick, plodding footsteps were accompanied by the continuous "clack-clack" of his wooden crook hitting the solid earth as he pushed onwards. He pulled about him a coarse woolen robe to keep him warm, as the heat of the day had all but been leeched from the air by the onset of night. The sun was well beyond the horizon now and the sky was already cold and dark. Stars sparkled in the heavens, and the thin crescent of the moon lent only a passing light to the wild country below.

As he went, he took care to push along his livestock, a small herd of goats, keeping the distant glow of the eastern horizon to his back. His village, a nomadic settlement of only a hundred or so tribal inhabitants, sat just ten miles from the edge of the region known as the "Burning Lands", a barren wasteland that skirted the edge of their small world. To them it was a desolate place where no one went, a dreaded land of which many wild campfire tales were told. But despite its sinister reputation its light, emanating from the strange aurora that hovered over its radiated wastes night and day, was as sure and reliable as the movement of the stars. Even in the darkest of nights that eerie orange glow remained constant, lighting the way for any traveler or herdsman finding himself out and about under the stars.

The shepherd moved quickly, however, not wanting to be out too late regardless of the distant glow that graced the desert with its weak color. It was never wise to wander alone among these sands, and foremost on his frightened mind were thoughts of sandmen, the legendary *shadow people*, hunting things like the wild *carnages*, and worse.

He led the last few goats over the field of shale-like stone and into his clan's enclosure on the outskirts of the settlement. The tired, wiry animals still bleated stubbornly in the dark, and their tin bells jingled over the methodic chirping of the desert crickets that, while unseen, were no doubt out there in great numbers.

At long last he secured the ramshackle pen door, taking a moment to catch his breath from the hasty last mile or so over the rough terrain. His heart stopped racing, now that he was safe at home. Strolling away from the pen, he took a moment to look back out into the night he had just escaped, his eyes sweeping over the barrens lit gloomily by the undulating light of the distant Burning Lands. He could see for miles.

Burning Lands

He was distracted when, towards the center of the village, he heard indistinct laughter, music, and song. Tonight the warriors drank beer in celebration of their people's great king, chief of all the northern tribes, and toasted his continued well-being. There was drunken bragging as well, of course, and vicious rumor-mongering freely blurted out that slandered the foreign merchants of the south and their "suspicious ways". Here among savages, there was no need to speak delicately or diplomatically, and the shared distrust, and sometimes hatred, of the Clean and the Cartel was spoken of openly.

They also spoke of war, which seemed imminent to most. Rumors were spreading that the merchants of the Clean Water Clans had begun sending their janissaries to raid neighboring villages up and down the trade route, all under the pretense of finding "escaped criminals" in their midst. It was an outrage that riled most northerners, to the point of threatening to take up arms themselves and strike back. Only the level head of the northerners' king, whom they affectionately titled "Uncle Sam", kept them from rising up and starting a war.

The shepherd knew little of what went on beyond his village; instead his mind was filled with the thought of the revelry and the wanton women that were bound to be there. The best looking females of the clan were no doubt at the gathering tonight, fawning over the bravest and putting themselves out for display. He wondered if he might steal into the camp and get some beer and mutton for himself, sneak a peek at the amorous women all dressed up and painted for their men, but even as he considered a short walk towards the center of town, he found he was stifling a tired yawn.

That little vision of heaven could wait. He turned to go back to his mud hut for the night, using his long crook to support his tired body as he went. He skirted around the pen, at the edge of the village and approached the hide curtain that screened the entrance to his humble home. Just then he thought he heard something in the distance, in the night, and so he turned to get a better look, his hand clenching instinctively around the wooden crook.

The wide open plain was still and dark. In the distance he saw the same stony mesas that had stood there for eons, the same slight hills and rises that periodically dotted the rocky flats. The distant hellish glow of the Burning Lands was unchanged, its ribbon-like aurora pulsing with insubstantial orange-red-yellow fire. He strained his ears to listen. The crickets continued their racket... until all at once they ceased, stripping the night of all sound.

Only when it fell silent in the village did he finally hear it; in the distance, a steady high-pitched whine that seemed miles away. There was no other sound like it, nothing he had ever heard, no natural animal nor mutant beast. It grew louder, emanating from somewhere in the night sky, thundering across the plains. It was moving southwest, getting nearer and passing close to his small village.

He heard voices behind him. Other men were emerging from their homes; the warriors left the warmth and comfort of the central campfire and were now walking steadily towards the edge of the village as well, drawn by curiosity. The eerie keen was loud enough that the revelry ceased altogether and as one, the tribesmen took up places nearby, looking out into the darkness.

Livestock became skittish in their pens; the goats began to bleat nervously. A cow brayed, followed by another, then another and the herd pressed against the corral in a futile attempt to get away. A horse reared in panic, triggering a few cries. It reared again, this time breaking its corral door and running off into the night.

"What *is* that?" someone asked over the fearful murmurs. There was frantic talk and whispers. A few warriors took the first steps back towards their homes to fetch their spears and axes.

Over a mile away the thing that controlled the great flying machine awoke from its trance. Withdrawn into a partly-comatose slumber, guided only by instinct and its enhanced, inhuman senses, a beacon of many cries and terrified whispers called out to it. Like a lighthouse beam piercing the void of an impenetrable night, the being sensed the sudden rise of fear and panic nearby.

The ear-piercing shriek became a roar in the distance. The terrified people assembled at the village's edge were buffeted as the wind began to pick up, blowing dust and tangles of sagebrush past them. A few began to fall back; though they couldn't see the shrieking banshee that howled from the darkness, they knew well enough to get away, to *run*.

All of a sudden a brilliant light flickered on in the night, just five hundred yards away. The light concealed the bloated craft that carried it, flying in the sky not far from the village, its enormous wing-mounted turbofans shrieking as it hovered momentarily in the air.

The spotlight caught the fleeing horse as it ran off into the night. As the broad circle of light illuminated it, the horse reacted by bolting in another direction, whinnying in panic as it went, desperate to get away.

"Run! *Run!*" someone screamed. The suggestion was like a match put to a powder keg, because as one the remaining population began fleeing in a great rout, pushing and trampling one another while scrambling for cover.

The spotlight swept the dry rocky outskirts of town, zigzagging rhythmically back and forth, until its light touched the beginnings of a fence line, washed over a herd of frightened goats trapped in their pen and caught the shepherd and a few stragglers as they, too, began to run.

The partly-dead controller of the craft could sense the fear in the air, the aura somehow drew its predatory attention, and together it and the identical creature sitting in the seat behind it came back to life. Two by two their mechanical eyes flickered on, washing the cockpit of their ancient craft with a cold blue light. They were awake.

With a sudden reflex, the pilot reached out and flicked a dusty switch, while the one behind gripped a handle and instantly pressed the firing button.

While people ran everywhere, suddenly the night came alive with the sounds of a one-sided slaughter. Vivid lances of focused laser light struck out from the craft concealed by the bright glow of the searchlight, tearing into the shepherd, his neighbors and the elderly who had fallen behind the rest of the fleeing inhabitants. One by one they were cut apart, or three-inch holes bored cleanly through their bodies. Beams of brilliant red light swept horizontally through the mass of fleeing villagers, cutting grown men in two and decapitating two, three, heads at a time. It was a stunning spectacle, as a single craft reduced huts and tents to raging pyres, as instantaneous beams of light cut entire bodies apart and left the paths of the village strewn with crackling, burning corpses.

"Run!" came a panicked shriek from one of only a handful of survivors, but there was nowhere to flee. In a matter of minutes the entire population of the village was gone.

Laughter echoed through the dark courtyard of Tucumcari's great palace. Margus Han and his compatriots reclined at the low dining table, enjoying the first of many bottles of wine. A few talked, while others watched with leering appreciation as young slave women danced to the sound of harps in the moonlight near the fountains. Dressed only with strings decorated with small gold sequins, their movements caught the torchlight of the mandarin's dinner party, so that when assembled in a line their collective adornments looked like glittering golden fireflies moving rhythmically to the music.

The men clapped and Margus wordlessly beamed, keenly aware that the impressions he made went beyond reinforcing old friendships. Such lavish, pompous displays were a reinforcement of power and prestige.

Alin watched as well, but always returned to rigidly consume sips of his wine as the suggestive comments of his betters became more lewd. He consoled himself, weakly, that it would all end soon and the decadent elders would retire, no doubt to make fools of themselves with women half their ages. Surely they, old men one and all, wouldn't be able to stay up the entire night?

Worse, he secretly cursed his uncle for the manner and type of his chosen display. Alin was naive to many of his uncle's shortcomings, but he knew his uncle too well to believe the show was for his own entertainment. Margus arranged his best harem girls here tonight to impress the other elders, not for his own degenerate gratification. He was not a man who lingered long to satisfy the base drives of the human body, even with Kseniya, not even when he had the idle time to do so. No, this was all a carefully prepared stage show for the benefit of drunken men who just so happened to hold considerable power in the Clans.

But what made Alin angriest, even a little sick, was the thought of how the men would react when his future bride, Gale, would make her appearance. Driven and aroused by the night's entertainment, they would certainly have no mercy when Gale appeared. Alin drunk bitterly from the cup put before him.

Alin had never seen Gale, and had only heard a brief description of her after bribing a messenger of his clan who had visited Tucumcari months before. But from what little he had heard, he knew he could love this woman. The messenger, delivering news of water production in the distant Arid City, had had the opportunity to meet Margus with Gale at the meeting. He spoke of her as being quite beautiful, of being around Alin's age, and at the same time... sad.

Sad. That word had struck him even when the messenger spoke it. It wasn't a word of much consequence to the men of this day and age; it was generally taken for granted, after all, that women were property and most men knew that such treatment seldom bred happiness. But that emotion, *sadness*, had been so pointed in Gale that the messenger had noticed it first off. And it had impressed him so much that it seemed important enough to mention in his clandestine report.

Perhaps he was delving too deep into idle thought, but deep inside Alin suspected Gale was a lot like him. An individual who, though finding himself/herself at the center of it all, sat outside the goings on of the world. Though he stood to inherit great power and responsibilities, he wanted something else. He wanted to change the world.

Alin snapped out of his ponderings as a deep gong resonated through the garden. The harem girls departed with a flourish, and a train of servants entered. In their midst a young woman in a formal *cheongsam* stepped forward, looking straight ahead, an emotionless expression on her face, holding her chin high, seeming impressively regal despite her obvious youth. The men clapped, a few murmured with a drunken slur that flirted with Alin's smoldering anger, tempting him to make an outburst.

Mandarin Margus Han introduced his ward, Gale, to the others and without a word Gale sat and began to play her elegant wooden *pipa* for the gathering of men. She didn't look at any of them, not out of humility or the respect demanded of her, but simply not wanting to look on their leering faces, as if looking at them would pull her back to the dark and ugly place that the garden of her father had become. She plucked the pear-shaped instrument's strings as she had been taught, but none of the vibrancy of her usual performances shone through; she was a robot, a wind-up toy, going through the motions while praying that time would go by in a whirl.

To Alin, the experience couldn't have been more different. He leaned forward where he sat, hands on his knees, swept away. The messenger had spoken of beauty and sadness, but now the words seemed impossibly understated. Not only *could* he love this woman, he *was* in love. His eyes never moved from her face, as if his vision was constrained to her face alone, and nothing else in the world mattered.

One of the elders whistled at Gale. A few others began to snicker, giggling like fools. As the inevitable began, Mandarin Han's eyes slowly moved from watching their gradual slip into inebriation, which he had most certainly engineered, to Alin.

Stand up for what is yours, boy, his eyes seemed to say.

Alin's heart now raced, not with the embarrassingly awkward fire of adolescent love, but with rage. But these were his elders, these were men who commanded his respect and worship! He wouldn't, couldn't, dare!

He saw Gale close her eyes as she played. She was being humiliated, openly. Alin pounded his fist into his thigh and tried to order the lascivious drunken elders to apologize, but his voice cracked and didn't even break a whisper.

Margus' eyes flared with interest. He was locked on Alin's every move. He understood enough about the boy now that he couldn't restrain a smile. Alin Han was the kind that could easily be molded into whatever Margus wanted him to be. Whether he wanted to make Alin into a beloved king or a hated tyrant, it would begin *here*.

Suddenly Alin found the courage, buried somewhere inside him, but now rushing to the surface. He could do it, he could stand up to them. He had to. This was his future wife!

"Stop!" he thought he yelled... and found that it wasn't his voice that broke the laughter, and Gale's music. It was someone else. Margus Han had snapped the men in place with his commanding voice, not Alin's. One hand in the air, Margus demanded everyone's attention.

Alin looked over at his uncle, breathless and speechless. *Margus Han had stood up for him and the honor of his future bride.*

"That's enough, gentlemen," Margus said. "You've certainly had enough to drink, perhaps too much. Alin, stand. Gale..." Margus stood and brought Gale to Alin, and Alin to Gale.

Water trickled with a quiet chattering noise that echoed throughout the sanctuary of Margus Han and his court. This sanctum was designed with a natural aesthetic in mind; the walls were made from a tangle of intertwined tree trunks and their rope-like roots, their branches extended upwards to join together to form the roof. The delicate vines draped from above caught sleek curves of bluish light reflected off the waters of a large pond dominating the center of the room, around which the entire circular chamber was arranged. The reflected slivers of light danced and whirled across the arched ceiling like dancing dervish-blades locked in an eternal, violent struggle. Like the very walls, wood was used extensively in the decor; unpainted wood in the coiling, serpentine chairs, rough wood for tables and siding, and leafy decorations worked into the rim of the grand pond as if to remind all present that water (and those who controlled it) was the source of life.

Alin Han looked across the ten short steps that separated him from Gale, who seemed utterly out of reach on the far side of his uncle, sitting in a chair at the mandarin's side among many other advisors. He watched her, unaware of how much he was actually staring, searching for any sign in her serene features that she might be regarding him just as fondly.

They had only met last night, and while he had taken her hand with his uncle's introduction, they had been swept away from one another far too quickly. Margus had decisively put out the fire of that uncomfortable situation by segregating the company last evening, and so Gale had slipped from Alin completely. Yes, he had seen her at the gathering, spoken to her briefly, but he hadn't had the chance to pull her aside or even apologize for the behavior of his kin, of which he was even now horrendously ashamed. The elders were sober now, of course, their minds no longer tied up with entertainment but instead bent on business, but he still burned with embarrassment. He wondered furiously and frantically what his next step should be, what he should say, but for the time being he could only wait for an opportunity to get her alone.

The other Clan courtiers chatted excitedly about their anticipated visitors, the chief of the barbarian northerners and his entourage. The chamber was rife with whispered speculation and gossip.

"The *bei man* play an odd game," Elder Hamut said, "where the men arrange themselves in a broad circle. One of them throws a leather ball, which another on the opposing team must hit with a cudgel."

"How does one win?" a woman asked.

"I imagine the further the ball flies, the better off one is."

"Isn't running involved, somehow?" asked yet another.

"Yes, something like that. Running... and spitting prodigious amounts of chewed leaf."

"Disgusting!"

"All things 'barbarian' seem disgusting," Hamut reminded them. "Consider their food; they delight in a dish made from the castoffs of the swine, which they grind down and pack into a length of the beast's very intestines. They boil these, or fry these, and devour them in great quantities." The story elicited moans from the gathered courtiers.

Soon everyone grew silent as the great oaken doors slowly opened, pulled by towering janissary guardsmen, and the sound of puma-hide drums spilled into the great hall. The gathering of Clan advisors, servants and courtiers all looked towards the spectacle as expected, but the elders glanced to Margus to gauge his reaction before acting themselves. Cool and indifferent, he reclined comfortably in his seat, unmoved by the clamor. Taking his lead, the other elders attempted to remain unimpressed.

Eight warriors in skins and wielding sharp spears entered the hall. As tall as the mandarin's janissaries, their bearded faces and deeply-tanned arms were a reminder of the harsh realities, war and brutal survival, that were the order of the day just a few miles from the walls of Tucumcari. The huge warriors lingered for a moment as if unsure what to do in such a serene and comfortable sanctuary, until their leader entered the chamber as well, followed by the two drummers.

The warriors stepped aside as their war chief, the one the tribesmen called "Uncle Sam", lord of the *bei man*, thrust forward from their midst to the head of the pack, his chest puffed out and the veins in his muscled neck bulging. Thick eyebrows came together as he glared menacingly down at the Clean council clad in their light, airy robes of white, so different than the odorous furs that wrapped about his body and the chainmail that protected his chest. A huge broadsword hung in a sheath at his waist, and around his thick wrists were clusters of mangy human scalps and coils of sinew bristling with human teeth taken as war trophies.

A great beard covered the lower half of the man's face and most of his torso, tied into three braids with loops of yellow horn. He wore loose red pants and a regal blue cape fell back over one of his large shoulders, sweeping behind him in a swirl of coarse barbarian fabric, attached loosely around him with a tin broach in the shape of an eagle clasping at arrows. As he exhaled, his breath carried the stench of the pungent pork sausages he had consumed somewhat excessively that very morning.

"MARGUS HAN!" the barbarian shouted, showing the points of his yellow teeth. "I have come here to give you one chance to answer for your crimes!" As he spoke, he placed one giant hand on the hilt of his sword. The eight warriors with him tensed. All eyes moved from the red-faced chief to Margus, who looked at his primitive counterpart for only a moment before speaking in a calm, level tone.

"*Uncle Sam*," Margus started, a disdainful look on his face as he recited the chief's trite and sentimental title, "feral king of the desert rabble, you come into the palace of my people and dirty it with your presence. You dishonor me with your tone and bring armed men into my sanctum." His voice grew impatient and he sighed. "What are these 'crimes' that you accuse me of?"

The barbarian chief scowled at Margus' easy indifference to his rage. He threw his shoulders back defiantly and stepped forward, gripping his sword tighter.

"So lightly does the great Margus Han dismiss the anger and ferocity of the natives of the land surrounding his tiny bubble of *civil-i-za-tion*," Uncle Sam replied, his own voice dripping with sarcasm. He now paced and addressed the men and women

Burning Lands 117

who sat around Margus, his advisors, his servants. "So eager is your great leader to overlook the little men who sustain him."

Margus' eyes narrowed momentarily. *What was this fool doing, speaking past him?* Margus turned his head slightly to Gale, but his eyes remained on the barbarian king, unwilling to give away his secret edge.

Gale looked up and beheld the loud Uncle Sam as he barked and shouted at the assemblage of astonished Clean courtiers. Immediately she liked him, with or without the powers of her acute mind. He was big and boastful, loud and somehow gifted with the obnoxiousness of youth, despite being middle-aged. She noticed gray streaks in his wild, unkempt hair, and wrinkles around the corners of his eyes. It occurred to her that among savages there were likely only a few who survived to his age. He must have been either a good warrior, or a great leader. Similar to the degenerate raiders of the desert, he and his kind had no plan for life short of living fast and free, accustomed to death and sorrow and the short bouts of passion and joy in between each tragedy. So he was a survivor. And his brown eyes burned with something that didn't exist here in the cool, sheltered, security of Trade City, the lust for life.

His anger was real, but she sensed that at other times his face could exhibit goodness and justice, bravery and even compassion. This was a king beloved by his people. His name itself represented a link to their shared heritage as the original inhabitants of this land, an honorary title only bestowed on a handful of *bei man* leaders throughout history. Beloved uncle of the people, *Uncle Sam.*

And well he should be. It was common knowledge that the people of the north did not yield easily to any master, even one of their own blood. So disorganized were they, so obsessed with living free, that it was rare for any man to rise to the challenge of actually *leading* them. The penultimate showman, Uncle Sam was such a man, but even he must take care to address his people as peers, to earn their consent. He was a king, but in the north the people must back a man for him to have any power over them.

Gale focused her mind; it was what Margus expected of her. She liked the warrior-king, but she knew she must do her master's, no, her father's, bidding.

Into his mind her consciousness crept, touching discreetly upon his thoughts like a light hand feeling for a pulse.

The chieftain pointed directly to Margus. "I come here to demand an answer for the murder of my people, the attacks on our tribal lands, the interrogation of my wordbearers, and the enslavement of our captive women!" His thundering voice echoed in the room and the air still trembled long after he spoke.

His pride has been angered by our attacks, but he is not afraid of the Clean and its armies. In fact, he is quite calculating. He is here for mixed reasons, though he hides them well... No, his anger swells. My lord, Margus, your campaign to hunt down every last member of the Scorpions to make them pay has finally upset the people of the wastes, and perhaps you should...

Margus heard Gale's mental voice, but not her counsel. Sensing she might be unable to stop her father's growing anger, she turned her attention to Margus and immediately she detected thoughts boiling with hostility against the savage leader standing before them, sullying the serenity of the sanctuary. His voice shouted in his mind: *Uncle*

Sam, return to the wasteland you crawled out of; find a rock and hide beneath it, for you and all the tribal chiefs can do nothing to stop civilization!

Uncle Sam bared his teeth as he continued to speak. "Your attacks merely whittle away at our weakest settlements, they do nothing to our might, but know that we stand strong, and remain committed to those whom we've vowed to protect! Do your fine janissaries hone their skills at war fighting women and butchering children? Ha! If you seek a war, Margus of the Clean, remember we are *warriors,* not *merchants* who hide behind other men!"

Father, heed his words, this is neither bravado nor simply one proud man speaking. He has the weight of many men behind him, men eager to fight against the suffocating encroachment of civilization, if nothing else.

For the first time Margus shifted, but only slightly. He had heard her. But instead of seeming wary or concerned, his eyes glimmered with the dire gleam of a skillful negotiator.

"Of course we do *not* seek a war, Uncle Sam," Margus said, scaling back the onslaught of words.

"Then what of the villages slaughtered?" Uncle Sam asked angrily.

"There have been no slaughters," Margus replied with a chuckle, "only raids against villages that harbored outlaws."

"NO!" Uncle Sam rebuked him, "A lie! Three encampments in the eastern part of my lands were destroyed in their entirety, their inhabitants slaughtered and dismembered, their remains left for the buzzards. Do you deny you had a hand in this, Margus Han?!"

Margus indeed looked prepared to deny it, but a look of confusion on his face kept him speechless. As he was usually quick with a response, Gale, Alin, and the others looked to him for a reaction, but none was forthcoming.

Gale looked at Uncle Sam; he was not making a bold claim. People had indeed been butchered by some unknown hand. Against all that she had been taught, she shifted back to Margus and looked deep into his mind but there she could detect no guilt for the accusations leveled against him. *The Clean were not responsible for this mysterious atrocity...*

Margus knew nothing of the strange massacres and said so. "I extend my sympathies for the deaths of your people, but know that the Clean had no hand in these events. Uncle Sam, return to me *all* who bear the brand of the Scorpions, and there will be peace. There is an estimated *one hundred* who fled the destruction of Oasis to *your* lands, and found shelter among the tribes of *your* frontier. Until they are dead, or made my slaves, the raids will continue. Do you understand me?"

Uncle Sam looked incredulous, but before he could shout out a retort Margus' voice softened.

"If we can come to an agreement, however... your wordbearers will be released and returned to your lands with a purse of corium apiece to pay for their time in captivity. Be satisfied that they soothed my anger, Uncle Sam, and earned their pay.

"As for the sale of those my generals may or may not have taken in their campaign, you will be compensated with a fair price for each slave you can prove was taken illegally."

Burning Lands

Uncle Sam seemed to consider. There was still the question of the mysterious attacks that left three entire settlements in wreckage, not a single survivor among the ruins. It would be hard for such a man to back down from his anger.

Secretly Gale found herself hoping he wouldn't. People had died, innocents taken into slavery and families broken up to be liquidated for profit. She had seen the corium nugget buy off many things, but would corium dilute and wash away the infamous pride of a northern tribesman?

"The rats live among us?" Uncle Sam asked, as if it was the first time he'd heard of it. He feigned innocence well, managing a genuine look of concern on his face. "If they do, we will find them then. Those who bear the brand of the Scorpions are not welcome among my people. We will deal with them as you ask... And know that if you are lying about the destruction of our settlements, Margus, there will be a reckoning."

Uncle Sam was certainly wary of Margus, but he seemed to see a chance to postpone open war and buy time to gauge his rival, which was always wise. He had given an inch, promising to find the outlaws in his midst (which he didn't want around anyway), and had also clearly delivered Margus a warning that his people would fight should Clean janissaries march onto his tribal lands again.

Alin, eagerly watching from the sidelines, found himself smiling as the war chief spoke. At the brink of war with the savages to the north, his uncle, Margus, had somehow convinced the enemy leader to do his bidding and turn the outlaws over. Face was saved on both sides, but ultimately the will of the *Clean* would be done!

Margus grinned almost as if he hadn't picked up on Uncle Sam's subtle threat, and gestured for water to be poured, taking a beautiful cup formed from hardened tree sap from a servant, and waited until Uncle Sam did the same.

"We have come to an understanding, then," Margus said, taking a drink from the gold-hued flagon. Uncle Sam looked at the water momentarily, wary of anything so precious given so freely, but then realizing his men were watching took a brave and hearty swig, until the entire cup was drained. Water trickled down the curls of his beard, and he sighed pleasantly.

"You have traveled a great distance to see me," Margus said, "but I invite you to stay here in my palace until you are ready to return to your lands. I will send my best men to investigate the attacks on your eastern border. The justice I demand can wait a week or so. Please consider yourself... and your warriors... my guests, Uncle Sam. Please make the palace, indeed the *city*, your home."

Hours after the audience with the barbarian chief, Margus Han paced about calmly, but Gale knew his mind was racing. She had been listening to his thoughts all evening and, all of a sudden, they spilled free from his lips now that they were in the privacy of the garden.

"Gale," he said, addressing her without looking at her, "the barbarian spoke of villages being razed. Did you..."

"Yes, milord," she said, "I reached into his mind and sensed his words were *true*. These events did indeed occur and he is as baffled as you are."

He looked up at the term "baffled" and shook his head at her as if to disagree. "Perhaps it was raiders, some small band in the east of which we're unaware. They rise and fall all the time, burn out and fade away. He's probably using the tragedy as grounds to threaten war, to use as a bargaining chip in the negotiations. Accuse us so that we are put on the defense, puff up his chest so we back down a little. Yes, that's it."

"I'm not so sure," she said demurely. True, she had sensed some deception on the chief's part, perhaps explainable as a diplomat's guile, but Uncle Sam' *anger* was real, his surprise and mystification at the attacks genuine.

Alin entered the garden but stopped when he saw Gale there. Realizing he was just standing about, awkwardly, he stepped down onto the grass in an attempt to join the conversation.

"Alin," Margus offered, "what do you think of all this?"

Alin considered for a moment, his mind jumping from Gale to his uncle to the meeting earlier that day and back again. He closed his eyes to clear his mind and then spoke clearly.

"You managed to convince the *bei man* king to hand over the outlaws, so that justice may be served, Uncle. Soon the mutineers who killed the lord of the Scorpions and murdered our envoy during their coup will be dealt with. The marauders will be punished and we can re-establish relations with Oasis."

"Oh, no," Margus said pointedly, turning to his nephew, "Oasis was decimated. Let none think we, the Clean, will tolerate the murder of so much as *one* of our people." But he considered Alin's words for a moment, then nodded, an eyebrow arched. "But the watering hole there remains a valuable source that shouldn't be left to dry up as summer approaches; we should come up with plans to eventually occupy the ruins of Oasis and set up a trading post there. A good idea, Alin." It's not at all what Alin had suggested, but the young man nodded anyway.

Gale stared at Margus. How conveniently had the murder of his envoy served to benefit the Clans… With his death the Clean could righteously seek revenge, drive off the Scorpions and lay claim to their lands. Hunting down every last Scorpion for the crime seemed excessive, of course, even pointless now that he had achieved what he wanted, but cracking down hard could also serve to provide an exhibition of the Clans' strength to the natives who were no doubt watching their encroachment into the Forbidden Lands with increasing agitation. *Civilization was coming... may as well show them that to stand against the Clean was folly...*

"But that's not what I meant," Margus continued. "What do you make of the chief's claims that villages on the frontier of his lands were destroyed?"

Alin shrugged vaguely. "A lie? An exaggeration?"

Margus didn't agree and it showed. Feeling small, Alin looked at Gale to gauge her reaction, but she wasn't looking his way, she was examining the face of her father.

"He said those villages were in the east," Alin said as he turned back to his uncle, suddenly regaining the strength in his voice. "To the east lies the *Kui Tu Di*, the 'Burning Lands', and no one could dwell there, not raider nor any of *our* armies. Uncle Sam should know this as well as anyone. To send men there, for any length of time, would be suicide. Does he think we would do that?"

"No, he's no fool," Margus agreed quietly.

The region they spoke of, the *Burning Lands,* was a great wasteland that skirted the northern edge of the Far Desert, a white-hot cancer in the heart of the desert. It was a cursed region, broad and vast, covering many miles of broken and blasted terrain, the very sand infused with radioactivity that would last another ten thousand years or more. Here more than anywhere else, fallout from the Final War had settled during the first year-long winters that ravaged the globe, accumulating in a thick layer of death-dealing dust among the flat plains of what used to be Kansas and Nebraska. Hundreds of years later the land itself was now utterly dead, turned into wind-swept barrens where it was said no life could be sustained, and from which trespassers never, ever returned. Packs of wild dogs did sometimes wander there, unaware of the danger, only to come out as *ravening hounds*, the sickly, fleshless, barely-animated beasts that in recent years had become the thing of nightmares. Driven insane with pain and suffering and hurling themselves against the outskirts of settlements and villages even under heavy fire, tirelessly seeking the blood of other beings to cool their fevers (even if they died trying), they were monstrous things. Human life never survived a journey into the Burning Lands, so none could tell its effect on a human being, but considering what happened to *dogs*, fewer and fewer people were eager to find out.

Like a deep and deadly hole in the world, the Burning Lands were avoided, and humanity struggled to survive outside its poisonous borders, turning its back on whatever secrets it might hide.

"So then who did it?" Alin asked. Margus looked focused and said nothing. Gale looked at her father, sensing he knew more than he was letting on.

Margus felt her eyes on him and, to her surprise, openly spoke of it. "Villages are something new..." he said cryptically. "... but these aren't the first reports of vanishings. There have long been stories of scavs and other vagabonds vanishing near the edge of the Burning Lands, going back at least ten years. Hmmm..." They waited in silence as their master pondered.

"I shall dispatch paid men to investigate this, get to the bottom of what's really going on." Margus walked away, his attention consumed completely by his own thoughts. Both Alin and Gale knew to leave him be and let him go.

When he was gone Alin turned to Gale, now that they were alone. The time seemed somehow right. The troubles of Margus and Uncle Sam and the rest of the world weren't here now. Just the two of them, together.

"I..." he said, trying to catch her eye. "I would like to get to know you, Gale..."

"Now is *not* the time," she said quite seriously, only looking at him momentarily with her striking green eyes before walking through a different archway and back into the east wing of the palace.

The large barbarian, Uncle Sam, looked at his elegant surroundings with some unease. Tree trunks held up the clay roof and walls, their larger branches woven together into archways. Soft light came from lanterns whose panes were made from hardened amber-colored tree-sap and in the distance could be heard the fountains of the gardens, flowing freely even at night with no one to enjoy their beauty.

"I wonder where the water goes?" Uncle Sam said to Boren, his right-hand man, who stood nearby as his king reclined on a strange wooden divan. Even now the large chief struggled to figure out just how to sit properly on the thing and the sight of him looking uncomfortable made his bodyguard smirk a little.

"The runoff, I mean. Do you think they just let it wash away?" he continued.

Kseniya, slender and silent, entered the chamber and put down another bowl of fruit for the mandarin's unusual guest, while the rest of the servants departed, heads lowered in respect.

"Look at them," Uncle Sam said, misinterpreting their intention. "They're afraid to look at us. Are we that ugly to them?"

Kseniya stood there, looking at the two men. Boren, always watchful around his master, turned and noticed and stopped chewing his food.

"No, it is far too precious for that," Kseniya said suddenly. "The water goes back underground, to the Water Vaults beneath the mountain."

"What?" Uncle Sam said, turning her way.

"The water. In the garden," she repeated. "It is taken back down through underground channels to the caverns of the Water Vaults, beneath the mountain."

Boren and his master looked to one another, then back at the mandarin's concubine.

"But I've probably said too much," she said, suddenly realizing her place again, and moved to clear some of the serving platters the visiting barbarians had finished off in their gluttony. These northmen ate like animals, and their appetite seemed unending!

"Oh?" Uncle Sam said, suddenly realizing she might be the answer to all his questions about the Clean's strange ways. "And how about these damn seats? How is one expected to sit on them?" The tension lifted and Boren grinned, biting back into the fruit.

Kseniya couldn't help but grin as well. "Not like that, *bei man*, you *recline* on it."

"*Recline?*" Uncle Sam said with a smile of his own. "I'm not familiar with that word."

"No doubt," Kseniya said playfully. "I imagine it's not in your nature to *recline*."

Boren felt more at ease and wandered over to another table and poured some wine for himself. Uncle Sam sat upright in the chair and looked at Kseniya as she worked.

"You're not one of them," he said abruptly. "I don't see an ounce of the yellow man in you at all. Your eyes are normal... in fact, you're very pretty, actually."

Kseniya raised an eyebrow; his comment had been rude, but she was used to dealing with rude men and had learned not to look offended by their offensive ways.

"Where are you from then? You couldn't be a *bei man* woman, could you? And if you are, what tribe did you come from, eh? Who did the Clean take you from?"

"I'm not a *bei man*," she answered. "My people came from across the oceans in the Final War. They were your enemy, too, northman. Only they all but vanished in the years after. There are very few of us left."

"Huh," he said. "Well you look normal. For a Clean woman, that is. That is to say, you seem unhappy..."

Kseniya said nothing as she moved the few remaining bits of food from one plate to another, and picked up the empty platter to take it away.

"*Are* you unhappy?"

"This is my home."

"No, your home is across the seas." There was more than a bit of prejudice in his tone.

Burning Lands

Kseniya smirked again. "I've lived here my entire life, good king. My mother, and her mother and her mother before her all lived in this wasteland, struggling like your own people to survive. This is my home, just as much as it is yours."

Anyone else speaking so defiantly would normally have insulted the king's sense of ancestral pride, but he found himself unable to chastise this woman. He was a guest, she was a servant, there was no need for a clash, no requirement to stand up and defend the validity of his ancestry and cast doubt on hers. Instead he shifted in his seat as if considering her words, then chose to renew the conversation.

"Are you happy here?" he asked.

"I'm happier than most women," she said elusively. The chief smiled.

"Come back with us," he said brashly, and the unexpectedness of the offer took her by surprise. "I'll take you with us, back north, to the lands where women are free. You can live among us. Enjoy what we have..."

"And be your woman, is that it?" she countered, now looking tired.

The chief shook his head. "No, not like that. I already knew the love of *my* life. Her laughter, her happiness, her loyalty. And her spite, jealousy, and rages, too! Ahh... you know, child, I loved every moment of it."

Boren turned and grinned, remembering the chief's colorful wife. Uncle Sam continued.

"When she died these five years past I knew there could be no other. There is a right woman for each man, and the right woman is unique; she changes a man, she fulfills him and leaves him wanting no more, even after she's gone and all that is left is the echo of her voice. Her voice is still inside my head. I'm hers until I pass from this world, too."

Kseniya looked up from her labor and stared at the king.

"No, I don't offer you this for any base reason, child. We *bei man* live a better life than you. That's no bold statement, that's fact. All this finery, all this luxury, it doesn't suit this rough land. The land will buck it off like a bronco bucks a rider. Give it time, you'll see I'm right. So what do you say?"

Kseniya found herself wondering for a moment, imagining the bitter, not better, life of the northern people. She shook her head.

"You've other designs, then?" Uncle Sam said with a gleam in his eye. Afraid that he might actually know something of her plans, Kseniya was taken by surprise, but she expertly hid her expression and said nothing.

"There aren't many places for a woman to go," he said. "On her own." He sighed and got up, and Boren brought him more wine. Kseniya turned to leave.

"The offer still stands," he said, catching her before she left. "If you ever change your mind." Kseniya stood in the doorway, looking back at the two men. She turned and with a whisper-soft rustle of satiny cloth vanished into the corridor.

Rider moved with the purposeful dexterity of a lean, famished coyote over the rocks of the high desert. His hands were so calloused that the sharp edges of every rock no longer cut him, and his knees were like stony knobs so that each stumble and fall didn't even hurt anymore. His hair hung down like oily white ivy, concealing the blisters that were welling up on his burning white cheeks.

He had taken risks out of necessity, traveling by day only to put as many miles as possible between him and the corium mines of Vegas as he could. Now, afforded the privilege of choice, Rider moved only by night, effectively naked as he was to the elements. Without melanin (the photoprotective pigment that colored other men's skin) travel in the daylight risked serious, debilitating injury. The rapid development of skin cancers was the foremost thought that usually occupied his mind, but with a suicidal plan for revenge consuming him, he found he no longer cared. But it was on the first day that he also re-discovered how painful the sun was to him; after spending three years almost exclusively underground, it burned him badly. And his vision was slowly getting worse. In daylight, murky mirages lingered at the edge of his vision at times, and at noon it was not only painful to look, but sometimes impossible. The undeniable agony that arose from exposure, and his own failing vision, had almost crippled him the first day, and so, like a wounded animal, he now skulked about the desert solely by night.

His vision was different at night, though he was at a loss to explain why. Unlike during the day, at night he could see clearly, in the dark his vision was keen, as if Nature was telling him to stay to the shadows, to live as a skulk. He could see better than a normal man in the shadows, in the moonlight; whether he liked it or not, it was his element.

Travel under the stars also proved expedient. Night was the friend of any loner, whether animal or man, especially one that found itself ill-equipped to face the wilds alone. There were other things that lived only at night, usually the weak things that couldn't survive in the daylight world. And here, now, he certainly fit that description. With little more than bare hands and the briefest bit of clothing, he had nothing with which to fight. He was at the mercy of every wild dog, every miserable ravening hound, and certainly any human predator upon which he might stumble.

Rider had been traveling roughly east-southeast, following the sketchy route that connected the industrious mining town of Little Vegas with distant Tucumcari, but giving the actual trail a very wide berth. He didn't want to wander into a caravan of Clean merchants bringing water to that hideous prison-town for fear of being rounded up and shipped back, and though he might want to warn others he might encounter on the trail from getting sucked in, he knew that the starry-eyed wanderers drawn to Little Vegas with each passing month would be so consumed with corium-fever that they wouldn't listen anyway.

At the same time he didn't want to wander too far north either; somewhere off the trail lay the legendary "Caves of Sorrow", a place taboo and forbidden to the people of the wasteland, a series of cliff-side tombs said to house the disintegrating bodies of many Ancient dead.

As Rider staggered over the next rise, he instinctively hunkered down. A white glow sparkled on the horizon, but the rest of the world was pitch black. He strained his eyes to see better.

To Rider, Tucumcari, the Trade City, looked like a hoard of cursed treasures spread out on a black blanket waiting for a temple thief to snatch them in his greedy hands. To others, however, it was a glowing oasis filled with promise, rising like the foam on the sea of hopelessness that was the rest of the world.

It and Little Vegas had much in common.

Burning Lands

Rider crouched on weary legs on a high crest overlooking the rocky, mountainous terrain. The terraced mountain of Tucumcari was brilliant and bright. But out here there were only shadows, in the dark miles of barren wilderness surrounding the trade fortress.

Rider was contemplating a choice; whether to try to slip into the city by night, or wait until morning and approach with the crowds that would inevitably form with the coming of daylight.

Nighttime offered him the cover he would need to scale the city's wall and enter unseen. If he was to be an assassin, he'd need total surprise. But moving by moonlight made him visible to the "creatures" that surrounded Tucumcari like invisible moths attracted to Trade City's flame. He had once used the threat of Tucumcari's "predatory people" to keep that girl Gale from making noise as they traveled to Tucumcari under the stars, and he hadn't been lying.

Out there, living among the maze of crevasses and rocky hills, were dozens, if not hundreds, of what he could only call "creatures". Not monsters in the traditional sense, but bestial, degenerate men who were no less a threat to his life than wolves, or worse. They were true predators, true desert scavs who had surrendered all humanity to prey on passerby and travelers, and even themselves when no one else fell into their traps. These were murderers who lived most comfortably in absolute darkness, stuck to the shadows as if it alone embraced them without passing judgment, and lived for the chance to kill anyone who wandered foolishly into their sight.

Tucumcari was ringed by them. Of course they mostly kept out of sight, as patrols from the Cartel swept the mountains now and again to clean them out. Most merely vanished with daybreak but returned at night to wait and watch.

Moving out in the open would make him prey. Rider didn't know how many might be out there tonight, but he didn't relish the idea of having to find out. But waiting for daybreak meant wasting time. The years in Little Vegas pressed down like a mighty weight upon Rider, squeezing out the lifetime he had spent building up his often ruthless and distant sense of self-preservation. With a quiet curse he broke cover and ran towards the distant city.

Up and down old arroyos, over a rocky shelf and towards one of a sea of dunes, Rider raced and bounded. He felt like a desert hare making a mad dash to escape the hunter's stewpot. Ironically, his haste to get to Tucumcari was just as likely to be fatal as getting caught. He didn't expect to get out of Tucumcari alive, but as long as he accomplished what he came for...

After ten minutes of running, Rider had to stop to catch his breath. He hunkered down low at the top of a sand dune, staring straight ahead at his objective. As he squatted on his knees to rest his shivering feet, letting out three short gasps of breath, there was only a slight sound of shifting grains as something rose from the sand behind him. Though Rider heard the sound and moved to spin about, the assailant, who had buried himself in the dune to take his prey unaware in the fashion of a trapdoor spider, lunged far quicker than Rider could react.

In an instant Rider felt the knife blade cut into his loose garb, bending only slightly as it glanced his bone. A wobbly-bladed skinning knife, the serrated edge tore at his skin. His attacker had a pathetic weapon, but it only showed his desperation. It was then that Rider realized who, or what, his assailant was. While he was exhausted, instantly Rider knew this was a fight for his life. Though his enemy had a knife and he was unarmed, he threw himself back against his surprise attacker, knocking both off balance. Together they tumbled a few feet down the far side of the dune and the purplish shadows grew deeper the further they went.

Gaining his footing Rider got up, and his enemy did the same before Rider could take advantage of knocking him prone. Like lightning the would-be killer leapt to his feet, and the two faced off, giving Rider a chance to get a look at the man.

There, facing off with him, was a rather small creature in a suit of all-concealing cloth, leather and bits of rusted chain. He was so well-covered against the sun, the sand and the wind, that only his pasty yellow fingertips were visible, with cracked, dirt-caked nails. Welder's goggles covered the hunter's eyes, while a cumbersome breath mask concealed the rest of his hungry face, through which came the only sound the ghostly figure made, a gurgling, sucking sound like a partially clogged vacuum cleaner struggling to clear itself.

This was not a fight Rider could afford to lose. This was one of the "creatures" that haunted the outskirts of Tucumcari. The wordless scav lunged forward without even so much as a cry, changing the knife to his other hand with a quick toss in mid-run, forcing Rider to change his defensive posture at the last moment. The move caught Rider unprepared, and the knife slashed over Rider's forearm as he pulled it up to defend his exposed neck.

With a sharp cry that seemed to echo for a mile Rider tumbled back, this time rolling head over heels even further into the darkness created between the towering dunes. Disappointed that his feint hadn't done the trick, the alien scav waited for a moment, goggled eyes trailing Rider's uncontrolled descent. Then, when Rider stopped moving and, stunned, lay sprawled on his back, the hunter lunged down the side of the dune, picking up momentum and holding the blade ahead of him like a harpoon.

Rider regained his senses in time as the sand beneath him shuddered from the scav's heavy footfalls. Literally throwing himself aside, he managed to escape just as the scav reached the bottom of the dune, skidded to one knee and lunged with the knife, bringing it up. If he had been there just a second ago, he would have been cut open from the top of the pelvis to the bottom of the ribcage like a cleanly gutted animal.

Rider snapped to his feet but the scav stayed put. The man's strange goggles prevented him from getting a good view of his surroundings, and his head darted to and fro like a twitching bird as he tried to find his "prey". He didn't see Rider as he came around and leapt on the crouching scav from behind.

In the scuffle Rider's blistered hand tried to strangle the scav's neck; when it proved impossible because of the thick rubbery padding, his hand slowly moved to his enemy's mask, somehow trying against all odds to mangle it against his face or bend his neck back through sheer force of will. Instead his efforts caused the scav's mask to slip back and over his head, flinging it away and into the cool shadows.

Rider had seen a lot, but this scav's face made his eyes narrow and his nostrils flare in disgust. On the Twisted Earth, there were mutants, and then there were *mutants*.

The man, if indeed it were a man after all, had no jaw, only a gaping, mucus-lined hole where a jaw should be and where the feeder tube of his mask had probably just been knocked loose. Even now the scav's throat shuddered and convulsed as if trying to draw in air, like a dying fish struggling to breathe without water.

Rider stumbled back wordlessly, breathing heavily and shivering from an unwholesome feeling that now gripped him, clinging to the newly-acquired knife with his trembling, white-knuckled hand. As the scav thrashed and gagged, he, or it, began to emit a soft series of pathetic wheezes and whines. Hands flared out for the mask, but it had already slipped down the dune and out of sight in the night's darkness. Back arched, feet kicked out weakly to regain its footing, but soon the scav collapsed, unable to breathe.

Rider had no time to see him suffocate. He had to keep moving.

The moon had risen over the desert, illuminating in a cool blue light the walls of Tucumcari, of which Rider now stood at the base. Stucco and stone stretched in both directions and out of sight, and beyond he could hear the distant sounds of people; music, laughter, and barter. But here, outside the city, it was getting cold the later it became, and as time passed he felt further and further isolated from the city on the other side of the wall.

As he studied the wall he realized this was just like escaping Little Vegas, only in reverse. And this time he didn't have a Brotherhood mentalist to help distract the guards from their posts. This was going to be difficult, and for the time being he had no idea how he was going to do it.

More laughter, this time louder. Rider looked up to see a small group of men in leather armor with skins walking along the parapet, swords sheathed at their sides and carrying bottles of the local beer in hand. Tribal warriors, and certainly not janissary guards of the city, they were given a brief nod by a wall sentry as he passed by them and out of sight.

Who would be allowed to walk freely atop the walls of Tucumcari? Rider listened intently, not entirely trusting his failing eyes.

"*And the women!* This city's mandarin has many fine, busty brides! Though I can't say I like the odors they douse themselves with. Give me a good, sweaty woman, with the right smell to her. You know what I mean, a woman should always stink! Then you know she works hard, both to feed her man and please him during the night! There is a woman worth buying and keeping, eh?!"

The men laughed, more than a bit drunk. They spoke with the voice of wild northerners, lacking the underlying Asian accent that marked the speech of the people of the Forbidden Lands and Far Desert. They could probably trace their ancestry back to the original inhabitants of this land, Americans, whose culture had dissolved with the great wars of the past and left only scattered barbarian survivors. Unaware that their empire once spanned many, many lands, from California to the forgotten east, they were now a rarity, those unpolluted by foreign blood, living in primitive camps and warring clan strongholds across the northern plains.

These men were not native to Tucumcari, but were visitors, and because they were allowed access to tour the walls freely, they must be important visitors, not mere rabble. Rider surmised they must constitute the entourage of a traveling tribal chief of some order or another, though who exactly, didn't concern him.

He realized he had very little cover to hide behind just in time for one of the tribal warriors to lean over the wall and point at him.

"Over there," the man hissed, "you see that? *What is that?*"

The men leaned towards the edge of the wall. The largest of the warriors moved to the front; he seemed significantly less drunk than the others.

"Someone's out there…" he said in a low voice, though his voice carried in the night over the open sand.

"A scav?" asked one. "Looks like a *sandman* to me, Boren" said another, motioning to Rider's pale skin. But the large dark-skinned warrior, Boren, didn't answer. Instead he called out.

"You there! Quit trying to hide and come here when I speak to you."

Rider hesitated for a moment, then moved forward. "What?" he asked, making sure they heard him, but instinctively quiet so as not to draw the attention of prowling sentries.

"Sandmen don't speak," Boren said over his shoulder to the other men. He turned and regarded the tiny figure at the base of the wall for a moment before speaking.

"Who are you and what are you doing skulking about at night?" He was amused and also curious. This wasn't *his* city, or *his* people, and so he wasn't as guarded as he would have been atop the walls of his own camp. If the Clean and Cartel guards were foolish enough to leave a stretch of wall unattended, that was their problem.

Rider thought quickly. "A merchant! My caravan got lost in a storm. The group got away from me and I fell behind. I've been tracking it here ever since."

Boren crossed his arms and didn't seem convinced.

"I must return to my master," Rider said, "or else face his wrath. You understand, no? Could you help me? I must be allowed into the city…"

"A likely story!" one of the men snorted. "You want us to toss you a rope so you can get in without paying the tax, that it?"

"No!" Rider called out, his voice strained. "No, I swear it! Toss me down a rope so I can get back to my master's caravan before he knows I'm gone. Have mercy!"

Boren walked away, leading the rest of Uncle Sam's men.

"You'll make good sport for the scavengers out there tonight," one of them laughed. The bearded man beside him said nothing, stared down at Rider, then hurled a long-bladed knife into the sand at his feet.

"At least now you'll have a chance," he said somberly, then joined the others as they walked off.

Rider waited until they were gone, then drew the fine sword from the sand. He moved to the wall and buried the blade into the soft stucco, which chipped and flaked away but allowed the blade to sink deep. He smiled, withdrew the weapon and swung it over his head, digging another divot higher up. Making a crude handhold, he lifted himself up, swung the blade point-first into the stone again, and began to climb. Lifting himself from handhold to handhold he managed to scale almost twenty feet in a minute, and before he knew it, he was hauling himself up on weary arms onto the battlements of the city wall.

Without gasping, he slipped down the wall and dropped to the stone walkway skirting the street on the inside of the wall. Music played somewhere down the street, and rats watched him from the shadows of a nearby window, its curtains closed to the night. His eyes swept the alleyway for any signs of sentries or guards, and in the distance he saw the light of a single corium lantern, swinging from the hand of a watchman headed the other way.

Rider weighed the long-bladed knife in his hand, wondering whether it was better to keep it in hand in the event that he should be discovered, or hide it to remain inconspicuous. But where would he hide it? Unwilling to give it up now that he had it, he held the hilt tightly and instead kept to the shadows where there was less chance he would be seen.

As he had learned in other towns, Rider knew how to move unseen and crept along with great patience, taking his time. He passed groups of shady men walking through the streets, as well as peddlers moving their carts or herdsmen pushing their livestock along to the sound of weird pipe music. He passed pens for the shaggy *bawthoks*, and slipped through the cool darkness surrounding the city forges, where smiths worked well into the night hammering at salvaged steel to create musket barrels and sleek scimitar blades. Lamps burned in the open windows of boarding houses and inns all over town, where merchants traveling to the great Trade City enjoyed a princely diet of fine food, wine, and comfort. Twice he almost stumbled onto the path of inebriated off-duty Cartel soldiers, drunken and crude and wearing their drab sackcloth uniforms, spilling from various taverns and wandering off, singing and laughing into the night.

He avoided all of these, unwilling to risk the chance of being discovered. At least not until he could find garb that would make him look less like a slave and more like someone who belonged walking freely on the streets of Tucumcari.

Turning a corner he finally came into a small cobblestone square on the second tier of the city. Large buildings loomed up on all sides of the square, creating deep shadows, and only a sliver of the vivid cerulean moon could be seen in the starry sky overhead. Pitch black windows faced out onto the backstreet courtyard, in any of which could be unseen observers, but he nonetheless felt safer than on the streets.

Rider stayed in the shadows and observed the uninhabited square. A sinuous web of ropes ran back and forth overhead, each laden with huge sheets of dyed fabric left to dry in the calm night air. More of the woven fabric hung from open windows, gently moving and swaying with their own slight rhythm.

Eyes ever alert, he reached up and pulled a green sheet of fabric from the line, pulling it around him like a cloak. He spun the trailing end around his head and neck, covering the lower half of his face, when all of a sudden a soft voice spoke to him.

"Excuse me, can I help you?"

Rider turned, ready to pull the blade, but found it was well hidden beneath the stolen robe. In this light his eyes were as sharp as ever; in front of him stood an old woman, keeping herself straight with the help of a gnarled wooden staff. Long locks of wooly hair fell about her head and neck in a mess of tight curls. Her expression was soft and hospitable. A venerable crone, she seemed utterly harmless.

"Not unless you have a weapon, or armor," he said grimly, turning back to fix a passable imitation of a hood over his head.

"Ah," she said, "the greatest armor of all."

Rider turned and looked at her, expecting her to elaborate.

"*Hope*," she explained simply. Rider frowned, fixing the hood so that only his eyes could be seen. They looked solid gray and utterly inhuman in the dark shadows of the courtyard. She walked past him, hobbling along with the aid of her walking stick, until she came to a set of stone steps leading to a large wooden door on the other side of the square. She looked back with a slight smile, then entered into the building beyond.

Rider gripped the knife hilt, remembering his mission. But he looked over one shoulder at the doorway. What was the woman up to? Did *every* dark town have a sinister secret? He moved over to the doorway and could already hear voices within. Dozens, and the pounding of a gavel. He felt the slippery metal latch and pulled. He stepped inside the dark textile mill.

Rider came into a large, low-ceilinged room where dozens of men, young and old, were gathered by the light of torches, fitting into every space they could, sitting on heaps of well-bound textiles and wooden work benches abandoned by the mill's workers at the end of the day. He wondered if the mill's operators knew that their factory served as the impromptu meeting place of a mysterious clandestine society, or if in fact, he was merely dreaming what he was seeing.

There were a few uncomfortable coughs and some quiet chatter as people settled in and even more arrived, until at last silence fell over the gathering. There were workers from all over the city, men from various sweatshops, porters, rickshaw haulers, laborers of all sorts, and even beggars. People clad in simple brown and gray clothing, with at least one article of green; a scarf, a sash or a cloak to identify them as members of the cell. Some greeted one another, others stayed to the shadows or the loft above, waiting quietly.

The old woman climbed some narrow steps to stand beside a somewhat younger man with blond hair and a face creased with lines who was now ready to address the small crowd. Rider seemed to recognize him from somewhere and lifted his head to examine the man's features more clearly.

"Alright then, let's begin," the man said, and his voice seemed very familiar. Rider knitted his eyebrows in an attempt to remember where he had seen this man before. "The time draws nearer when we will be ready to act. It's clear now that the evil lies not just in Margus, the Deceiver, but pollutes all among the merchant clans who descend from the ancient Enemy and hope to build their false 'culture' over the ruins of ours. Power has consumed them all, and these tyrants look at the world around them like cruel kings surveying their subjects. But Margus and his ilk forget they rule by no mandate except their own.

"Today Margus claims his decree to send soldiers against the lands of the tribal chief, Uncle Sam, is done in an effort to eradicate the menace of raiders being sheltered by the barbarians. But it is just a ruse to force his vision, the Clean and Cartel's vision, of civilization upon the wastelanders. In fact, upon *all* of us.

"Here in Tucumcari we know what 'civilization' looks like: brothels, slave markets, children inhaling glue on every corner, scavs and raiders welcomed onto our streets so that the merchant houses can pry every last bit of corium from their hands. And who pays the price for Margus allowing killers and rapists among us? We do. Just this week a girl in the Factory area was raped and left for dead. And three men were killed

Burning Lands

by a Cartel truck when it rolled, out of control, down the street! What solace do their families receive? Empty apologies?

"Now Margus' thugs drag our people off the podium, calling us 'disruptive to trade'. The teachings of the past, of our shared heritage as *free men*, do not conform to their vision of 'civilization' either!" There were murmurings in the crowd.

"They try to tell us that the war of the past is over, that we are all brothers now, natives of the same land, but their ways are too foreign. We want nothing of it. It's time to make a stand!" A few began to shout in agreement, but the speaker, whom Rider now recognized as the speaker he and Gale and Tank had seen in the Tucumcari square three years before, seemed eager to calm the angriest among them.

"Quiet, quiet. You are all here because you believe in something better. Creating your own destinies, without some heavy hand to force you down one path or another. You are not alone. In the time of the Ancients all men were united; tribes of the wilderness and of the cities all worked together for the common good, rose in rebellion against foreign enemies. That time can be had again. No, it won't be the same, but it *will* be better. We must be ready to pay, in blood and butchery if we must, to see that day come."

Tribes of the wilderness and of the cities, working together? What was he talking about? Rider wondered.

"Our friends across the Wei Shan have sent agents to help us. They have returned once more, and they say the time is right..." Suddenly a deep, stuttering voice spoke from behind Rider.

"I kn-now this man!"

Rider spun around to see a lumbering, ogrish man standing behind him, clad in a poorly-fitted green tunic and sackcloth pants. He recognized the small head and glassy, featureless eyes, though they had changed since he'd last seen them. The years had diminished the ogre physically; he seemed older, the lines of his tested and tortured face now deep and irreversible. His *microcephaly* was also more pronounced than it had been three years ago; his brow was gradually sloping to give him a Neanderthal's profile, his large ears stood out to the sides, and he had the vacant look of a child as his face spread into a broad open grin of recognition.

"*Tank*," Rider said, astonished. But he could instantly sense something was amiss; the old bounty hunter who saved his life in the desert years ago was no more, and little, if anything of the past, lingered in his memory, except for that vague familiarity that, to a simple mind, could be mistaken for... friendship.

"R-Rider!" Tank said, clasping one large hand on Rider's shoulder as if he was embracing a long lost brother. The assemblage of would-be revolutionaries turned around to see the source of the commotion. Some may have been readying weapons beneath their cloaks and robes, prepared to defend their identities against discovery by a stranger in their midst, but their fair-haired leader held up a wrinkled hand to call them off. He looked across the room at Rider and Tank, and smiled a warm, humble grin, full of strong white teeth.

"It's alright, Tank. *Rider*, you say? We've heard a lot about you over the years, Rider. My name is Karos, and I lead these people. How did you escape the corium mines? And did you bring with you the attention of the mandarin?"

"I came unexpected and unseen," Rider said in an effort to appease them. There were more murmurings; not everyone believed the strange albino, but Rider was prepared for that. What mattered was their leader. Karos considered for a moment, then motioned for one of his followers, a man named Gaius, to take over the meeting. He gestured for Rider, Tank, and the old woman to join him in a connecting chamber away from the gathering.

When the heavy metal door closed behind them and torchlight filled the small, plain room, Rider spoke again. "How did I escape the corium mines? With a little Brotherhood help." Karos, the old woman, and Tank looked to each other for a moment, astonished. Rider stared straight at them, his eyes seemingly glowing pink from within, though it was only a trick of the light.

"You w-work for the B-brotherhood too?" Tank asked. Karos help up a hand to silence Tank but it was too late.

"So you work for the Brotherhood? Well, I work for no one," Rider said defensively. "They helped me escape, and I'm sure I'll be expected to pay back the favor someday... but right now I've got my own plans."

Karos stared at Rider, wondering why on earth the Brotherhood had found it necessary to aid him. He had once been a part of this, he'd been the one who'd sold the girl to Margus Han, but what could he do to help the cause now? Karos realized he wouldn't fully understand their reasons until he met with the Brotherhood's agents again, face-to-face. Damn, why couldn't they be here now and explain things!

"I don't care what plans you people have for this city or the wasteland, but I have plans for Margus Han," Rider said. "It sounds like you do, too. If you can give me a decent weapon, maybe we can help each other."

"You plan on *killing* Margus Han?" Karos asked in surprise.

Tank looked concerned for his old traveling companion and once again put his hand on Rider's shoulder, struggling to speak. "You, you can't go in there, you'll, you'll die! There are guards everywhere, n-not just Clean janissaries but, but Cartel as well. It's impossible, anyone in t-town will tell you that place's a f-fortress! You'll never get out alive."

This man was dangerous. If he failed, he stood to put every one of Karos' followers in jeopardy. The Clean and Cartel would crack down hard on the city, and root them out. Exile, if not execution, would follow. The Brotherhood would be exposed, and the cause of unity and freedom would be defeated before it ever had a chance to take flight!

Rider regarded Tank for a moment with pitying eyes but said nothing. Karos, eager to dissuade the albino, detected the wavering emotion and saw his chance.

"Tank spoke well of you, Rider, at least until his memory began to fail and his mind diminished. He was, and is, a good man. Truly... *good*. We will always take care of him, just as we take care of others like him, here and in small villages up and down the trade routes. We have many cells; our aims appeal to many, near and far. We would do the same for you, if you could change your ways and turn to a more benevolent path. Just put away your anger, let's talk this over..."

Rider looked over at Tank, who, suddenly distracted, fetched a flashlight from the canvas web belt his side and flicked it on and off.

"See! N-now I've g-got one of my *own!*" he said excitedly.

Karos looked on Tank as a man might look on a stunted child, but returned to renew his line of reasoning with Rider. "You cannot go it alone, not forever. Everyone needs friends. We work with the Brotherhood, yes, but we also strive to help the people of the Far Desert. With the Brotherhood's help we will bring peace and unity to this land. No matter your affliction, white skin, pinheadedness, there is a place for you among us."

Karos saw he was having no effect on Rider and so decided to change tactics. "Look, I've seen 'white skin' and what happens to those who have it. They almost always go blind eventually, you know. And how long can a blind bounty hunter survive on his own?"

Karos let the suggestion hang there, let Rider have a moment to consider. It was true; like Tank, the last three years had taken an irreversible toll on him. Just like Tank the defects of Rider's own body, genetic errors he had been burdened with since birth, were inevitably catching up to him, making themselves known again, as if his bad genes had waited patiently all this time and were now making every effort to take over and destroy the cursed life form that carried them. And he had only the Ancients and their great weapons to thank for that. Weapons that not only killed, but cursed the survivors for generations afterwards to short and miserable lives filled with deformity and disability.

"Tank is right, the palace *is* a fortress," the old woman said, breaking the silence with her strained voice. But she was trying to reason with a very unreasonable man.

"That's just it," Rider said, turning to her as if she could somehow understand his desperation and give him her blessing. "Places like that are designed to keep sane men out, men whose plans always involve getting back alive. But I don't plan to come out alive. Just so long as I take him with me."

Karos thought of the girl; if Rider managed to get into the palace, might he be putting the girl in danger?

"You can't go..." Karos started, but Tank cut him off.

"Stay with us, instead," the giant stammered. "W-we have a plan, we have a str- strategy. When the time is right..."

Karos stopped Tank short with a glance and looked right at Rider. His face normally seemed so peaceful, a slight smile on his lips, but now he seemed almost menacing. "I can't let you go there, Rider," he said softly. "You go in there, and make an attempt on the mandarin's life, it puts so much at risk. There is more going on than you know. And whether you succeed or fail you will draw unnecessary attention. Now listen to me, we are building our strength and I will soon be leaving to gather allies to our side. Going now risks everything. Don't jeopardize our cause simply for your petty revenge."

"There's a much bigger picture to consider," Karos continued, suddenly regaining his warmth. "Stay here; we have food and water and warm clothing. Vestra here can take care of those blisters and cool your fever," he said, motioning to the old woman. "Just give us the time we need!"

Rider made a move to push past Karos, but the lean, sandy-haired speaker pushed Rider against the adobe wall with unexpected strength, winding him. Tank blinked with surprise but moved to Karos' side and helped pin Rider with one large, mitt-like hand. The old woman looked sad that it had come to this and opened her mouth to protest, but ultimately did nothing, instead shutting her eyes and shaking her head slowly from side to side.

Rider glared at Tank for his betrayal, but seeing that the man he once knew was firmly under Karos' spell, turned to look directly at the cell's leader, his white brows arching and his pink eyes narrowing on the soft-spoken speaker. "Let me go, windbag, and I'll let you keep your hand. You've got *one* chance." His voice was shaking with anger.

Tank instinctively went for Rider's weapon, which he knew must be under his robe somewhere, but Rider was quick and had it out in a flash, the bright orange torchlight glimmering off the metal blade like liquid rivulets of fire. Karos' mouth hung open with surprise as, with a sudden swing, Rider brought the blade down and sliced off Karos' hand cleanly at the wrist. Vestra shrieked and stumbled away, and as Karos fell back into Tank, Rider made a mad dash after the old woman, pushing Vestra to the side and bounding towards the rear doorway out. The door crashed open as he hit it full tilt, stumbling into the street. He could already hear the rest of the cell's followers coming for him, as he ran full speed out into the moonlit night. High above the streets loomed the lofty third tier of Tucumcari, and the brilliantly-lit palace of mandarin Margus Han and his household.

Tank moved to give chase but an injured Karos stopped him.

"No, let him go. We've got to clear out, now. Head into the desert. We have more important things to take care of. *Remember the cause!*"

In a courtyard high up on the palace terrace of the city Alin Han walked among fragrant flowerbeds, his mind lost in thought. The slight chocolaty smell of a bed of lyreleaf greeneyes did nothing to distract his attention from the skyline spread out before him. He could understand why, in ancient times, this mountain had been chosen as a lookout; first by the long-extinct Comanche whose braves might have stood watch here on cold nights under the stars, and later by caretakers of the boundless wilderness keeping an eye out for the distant glow of wildfires. He walked over to the low wall skirting the edge of the garden and looked out over the rest of the city as it lay below; this city was large and it teemed with life even at this hour. He saw the immense *caravanserai* of the Cartel not too far away, bustling with activity as Cartel workers scrambled to make room for a new caravan of dusty trucks as it pulled in through the gates. The enormous behemoths of rusting steel groaned and thundered as they pulled into the dry yard of the tight Cartel compound, their wheels pulling dust up behind them until they came to a stop at the foot of three humongous fuel reservoirs. This late at night all that could be seen were the running lights that adorned the ancient rigs, but even from this height he could still hear the sound of idling engines and deep-voiced Cartel teamsters shouting orders to begin the tedious process of unloading.

While the structures, caravans and indeed the *art* of the Clean seemed "organic" in comparison, the Cartel had no pretensions of elegance and their house virtually embodied the darker side of the alliance, the dirtier aspect of the rise of civilization. Forges, smoke, soot, oil and trucks were their hallmarks, not gardens or buildings made from living trees. Simply put, their cousins, the Cartel, were grimy and dirty. They obsessed over profits and control, and their work teams, convoys and prospectors crisscrossed the desert and chipped away at the ruins ringing wrecked cities like industrious swarms of ants, busily scrounging materials for the construction of a great hive. But their "hive" was not a physical structure, but rather an empire of dirty, sooty and greasy looting. It was as if they were carrying on the mission of their invading ancestors, tearing apart the ruins of America as if the country's carcass was itself a war prize and its contents theirs to pillage.

How they had ever become allies, Alin could only wonder. Sure, they were brothers of a sort, descended in part from the same foreign invaders of this land, and they shared the same ideology to rebuild now that the Final War was just a savage memory. But in style, in sophistication, there could be no stranger bedfellows.

But Alin also wondered what wares the Cartel trucks were carrying tonight; a few precious gallons of thick and impure oil scavenged from the bottoms of gummed-up fuel tanks at old gas stations, or in rusting pipelines left idle by the ages, or taken from lost depots scattered across the southwest. Maybe they carried shiny bits of bottle glass picked out of a sea of sand by the patient, searching hands of scavengers, and bartered for a few drops of water at some far-flung Cartel outpost, only to be brought here to be sold at ten times the rate as fixtures in jewelry meant for the forehead of someone like Gale. Or perhaps the trucks contained simpler, more practical things, like the sturdy hand-manufactured goods bought from the skilled tribesmen living in the isolated deserts of the west, which served any number of functions once they arrived here and found their way into the markets of the city. One day a lampshade would be sold for the purpose intended, but once the fad for lampshades had faded, it might be passed off as the cover for a cooking fire, or even a hat "in the bizarre barbarian fashion". These rigs connected Tucumcari to the distant Cartel settlements in the west and brought goods straight to Trade City itself, where the demand for things of all kinds, any kind, was ravenous.

There was a commotion in the Cartel caravanserai, but Alin couldn't hear exactly what was going on, and in the half-light provided only by the headlights of the trucks, could only see figures scrambling frantically about. Had the Cartel truckers run into trouble on the way here; did they bring word of even more dire events up north? Alin gripped the wall tightly and sighed; if there was important news, he would no doubt hear about it tomorrow when his uncle did. Yes, he knew now that his uncle was taking him under his wing, preparing him for something greater. Though he hadn't said as much, it seemed to Alin that Margus was getting him ready to become much more than a young *talib*, and that one day, perhaps soon, his uncle would groom him to be the city's future mandarin.

Alin turned from the view as he heard the familiar footfalls of another Han relative, his elder, Hamut, approaching. He turned and in the light provided by the few spherical lanterns arranged in the garden, could see Hamut's strong angular cheekbones and the short, trim beard of gray hair that ran the length of his sharp chin. The old crow was smiling and as he came up he unsheathed a polished scimitar from its scabbard and swung it once to get a feel for its weight. Even at his age the fine weapon seemed natural in his hand, as familiar to him as any flesh and blood part of his body. Like all members of the vast, extended clan known as the Han, Hamut's ancestors had been warriors simply to survive in the anarchic years after the Fall, and though their descendants would come to rely on trade and manipulation to struggle their way to power, there were some in the clan who never turned their back on martial pursuits.

There were also those who remembered too keenly the decades of living in fear as the hunted, instead of the hunters. The ancient terror of the great raider armies, of the massive proto-road gangs who ran lawless in the post-nuclear wasteland attempting to build their own nations (before they trimmed themselves down to the levels of today through internecine warfare) were still remembered by some. Hamut was a living book, a master of the lore of those times. He had secretly nurtured the knowledge of weapons and defense both out of a love of the artistry of combat and with the lingering belief that he, and his kin, should always be prepared to defend what they had built.

For a moment Hamut's blade caught the moonlight and sparkled brilliantly before it came to rest peacefully at his side. He smiled warmly at Alin before speaking.

"Are you done staring off into space, or should I come back later?" he mused.

Alin smiled, but seemed tired. "I'm ready," he said.

Hamut raised his sword, ready to test Alin once more with the blade. Alin gestured respectfully and Hamut stepped aside, allowing Alin to find more room out on the stony terrace overlooking the night-lit city. He drew his own falchion from his side, found comfortable footing several paces away, and turned to face Hamut before bowing an inch.

Hamut brought the weapon forward but continued to speak, though he was clearly concentrating for the coming practice. "Your uncle Margus believes diplomacy will solve all of the problems that face the clans now and in the future. But the Clean haven't always been so prosperous and fortunate, Alin, and long ago we had to fight to carve out our little niche. Many of the old dangers are pacified now, but the world is still a treacherous place, and we may have to fight again to survive."

Alin readied his sword; Hamut continued.

"In the time after the Fall many men sought to rebuild the world in the image of what came before, but like blind men assembling a fractured puzzle they had neither the tools nor the vision to make it complete. Petty empires rose and fell, each just a pathetic semblance of the past that tore itself apart or simply fell in on itself, unable to stand. Former armies, once marching under varied flags, dissolved and joined with the natives of this land to make children of their own. Gangs and bandits, unleashed from ancient prisons or simply spawned from the ruins of the great cities like hornets made angry by fire and smoke, roamed the highways and the deserts extorting the peaceful survivors for their fuel, their food and their water. Our American ancestors, who had been virtuous merchants even before the Fall, suffered at those hands the most. We cherished our water, the 'Clean' brand, but in those terrible times we gave it where it was needed, to quell fevers and give life. We cared not for ancestry, nor ethnicity. But the native gangs poisoned the minds of the native people and, one and all, they turned against us. We only managed to survive by *fighting* for what was ours, losing many lives but *earning* our place at the top in this violent world. The skill to win wars we can only attribute to our foreign ancestors, who taught their children to *fight*. Only once we became strong did the depravations cease and only then did the killers and thugs begin coming to us as the beggars you see clustered at the city gates each day. It's only now, in this age, that water is a 'business', but never forget it is *them...*" he was, in a sweeping gesture, referring to everyone outside the walls of the Clean's sanctuary, "... who made things this way."

Burning Lands

Alin watched with interest, but Hamut wasn't sure his history lesson was getting through. He simplified things. "Don't let your uncle, Margus, fool you into thinking words alone can win wars; it takes strength, courage and a cold heart."

Alin's eyes were locked on Hamut's; now, unlike ever before, he seemed firmly ensconced in his element, not off admiring his silver-tongued uncle or blushing embarrassingly over some girl who might or might not become his future wife. It was plainly obvious that sword-wielding was second-nature to Alin, and though over the past few years he had become a true master swordsman, it never ceased to amaze Hamut - the distinctions in the two very different personalities that made up the young princeling. On many an occasion he was foolish and foolhardy, hopeful and even naive, but his attention and degree of focus were unmatched by any student he had ever taught. Alin had been an eager *talib* as a boy, and while his elders sometimes dissuaded him from swordsmanship to study the tradecraft or languages, Alin had returned time and again to Hamut's tutelage with sword and more importantly, the determination to learn how to use it.

After a few brief minutes, their swords biting through the air, clanging off one another, and slashing just short of trailing sleeves and pant legs, Hamut came to realize he had reached the end of what he could teach Alin. It had been clear weeks ago, back in their home far to the southeast, that the boy knew everything he knew, but now he could no longer prolong the inevitable. What was most remarkable to Hamut was the fact that the boy's eyes still burned with an insatiable thirst for more knowledge, for an even greater mastery, but what could he do? Hamut, swordmaster of the Clean, could help him no more.

"Well done," Hamut said simply, thinly veiling the fatigue brought on by the acrobatic swordplay they had played out on the terrace. Alin smiled broadly as Hamut lowered his sword and confessed the student had reached the limits of his aging teacher's knowledge. As Hamut took his arm and charged Alin with perfecting his skills alone, the boy's mind was already wandering back to the view of the broad open deserts beyond the city and at the deep, dark expanse of a world that waited just beyond the city walls.

Rider's breathing wasn't heavy or strained when he stared out across the shadowy plaza towards the enormous wooden doors leading into the palace of the mandarin. He knew what he had done earlier had probably set a number of armed men on his trail, not only because of what he did to their leader, but also because he had seen their meeting place and many of their faces. But if they were following him, he had apparently managed to get to the gate well before them. With only a quick glance he surveyed the darkness behind him for any sign of his imaginary pursuers, before he slipped through the shadows to move closer to the walls that enclosed the mandarin's compound.

Three janissaries in supple horse leather armor guarded the portal, with white capes drawn about their shoulders and necks to keep away the cold. Each of the Clean's slave-soldiers carried an ornate musket and like hawks, kept a sharp watch on the approaches to this, the top terrace of the city.

Rider scrutinized the men for several minutes with remarkable patience, but they never wandered far from the door and never walked out of sight of one another.

Passing through this gate wasn't going to be a realistic option; not without firearms and not by himself. His eyes wandered from the great door to the walls and he noted they were, after all, made from the same white stucco that plastered the outer walls facing the desert. It occurred to him that the same method he used to chip away at the outer wall and scale it could be used here as well; he only needed to find a bare stretch of wall out of view.

That wasn't going to be easy. Guards with corium lanterns walked the streets every few minutes and even if he managed to remain unseen through expert timing, he would still have to scale the wall itself, leaving himself completely exposed for the agonizingly long time it would take to reach the top. Clean musketeers weren't renowned for their quick shot due to the crude nature of their firearms, but it would only take one successful hit to shoot him off the wall; even if by some miracle he survived being shot, the fall would certainly kill him. Just like that he could be unceremoniously killed as he climbed, helpless, like a fly swatted against a wall.

Rider shook himself when he realized the cold steel nerve that had brought him dozens of miles across the desert in little more than rags to see the death of Margus Han accomplished, was slowly slipping from him. He forced himself to stare ahead at the imposing battlements before him and go through with his suicidal plan.

As the last patrol passed by one of several small alleys between buildings crowded at the wall's edge, he broke from cover only momentarily to cross the distance from one side of the street to another. As he reached the other side he threw himself against the wall of one of the alleyways and, fully expecting the cry of alarmed voices or even the thundering shot of a sentry's musket, found the alley to be deafeningly silent. He breathed once or twice, then calmed himself, and moved to the buttressed bottom of the mighty palace wall, readying the sword like a mountain climber preparing his piton.

In the nearby compound of the Cartel the engines of a fleet of trucks suddenly began to turn over. *What luck!* The streets were flooded with the sounds of the vehicles warming up; surely exhausted laborers all over town were roused from their sleep, fat merchants in boarding houses cursed the hour and most importantly, guardsmen went deaf to the sounds of an assassin in their midst...

After two full minutes the throttling engines continued uninterrupted, and by now Rider was almost two-thirds the way up the wall. The star-speckled sky was pitch black. From this height he could see not only the dimly-lit streets of the city below, but also out into the desert which was not only illuminated in starlight but whose dunes and mesas were clearly visible even to his bleary eyes. He saw, from a height, into the yard of the Cartel, where a caravan of trucks was getting ready to leave again, their engines choking on bad fuel as the mechanics put them through their last warm-up before the whole fleet headed out. He could see men moving about, their long shadows made more dramatic by floodlights around the compound, but from up here they seemed so tiny. It was this sight that suddenly tore him back into the real world, back to the realization of just how high up he was and how lethal any fall would now be.

His heart sank as, looking down to confirm the height he had achieved, he saw a trio of sentries move into the square just below. He was sure they couldn't hear him, but if one of them so much as looked up, they were sure to see him climbing there, slow and awkward and unable to get away, and...

He felt his foot slip from the foothold he had clumsily made with the sword and bits of stucco flaked away and dropped to the street below.

He was sure someone had noticed, but just as the sentries began to turn to look, a group of men in long swishing robes entered the square via one of the side streets in a long, curious procession. The guards turned to watch as the Brotherhood entourage passed by, murmuring strange, whispered litanies that echoed through the streets and alleys. They were men, one and all, made uniform by their purple robes, but underneath the cloth some seemed crumpled and hunched-over like lepers, while others walked with strange limps, not from missing limbs but from the unseen presence of extra legs and feet. All of their faces were masked which must have been a mercy, for the mutants of the Brotherhood were only rarely human, and more often than not nauseatingly disfigured. Leading the hooded procession was the sole member of the congregation to go unmasked, and his bald head resembled that of a small, under-developed child with enormous protrusions from his forehead like massive "lumps", and two mouths, one over the other. This unique deformity allowed him to sing his prayers in a strangely hypnotic dual tone, a weird drone, that seemed to rivet the Clean sentries to him and his flock as they wandered by.

Rider realized a distraction had been presented to him, whether by chance or through some continued complicity on the part of the Brotherhood; for some unknowable agenda. Although the uncanny appearance of the procession at this precise time seemed too coincidental for his comfort, he recognized that the distraction (intentional or not) would not last long and he'd best make use of it before it was too late.

Inside the palace several house guards were already eating at the table in the guardroom, snatching up meat and bread served up by the timid servants who had already retreated to the kitchens below. Some of them played at a game of *mah-jongg* as they ate, but the rest remained in silence, focused on their meals.

At the head of the table was the master of the palace armory, with the rest of the men arranged around him and down the table in descending order of importance, with the newest recruits waiting for the scraps that their betters passed down to them. Tonight there was plenty for all, however, and before long all of the soldiers were eating and drinking heartily.

After he had taken his fill of roasted pig, the armory-master moved to one of the small windows from which he heard the sound of Hamut and Alin practicing their sword fighting. He spoke to his men:

"Another Cartel convoy has come under attack by raiders," he said. "Now General Rhylor is personally leading his Cartel men into the deserts to track the scum down."

There was a low chuckle from his men, who weren't at all unhappy to have the city to themselves. The armory-master looked outside with a grin on his own face, passively watching the practice match as if it pleased him to see the masters of the house bearing arms.

"The young prince fights well," he said over his shoulder to the rest of the feasting men sitting at the table. "This one's a warrior, not a negotiator. Maybe he will lead us to glory someday." He raised his cup to his lips and drank, considering what the future might hold should this youngster come to lead the Clean merchant house.

Suddenly one of his men began to cough, grasping at his throat and pushing his plate away from himself until it tipped and spilled its contents on the man across from him. The other soldiers pushed back from the table, but already a few of them felt the effects of the fast-acting poison and were choking also.

The armory-master spun around in surprise, watching the ten house guards flounder about the room, falling off their chairs to the floor or attempting to run for the door but collapsing before they made it. Like fish left out of water they struggled to breathe, their neck muscles and temples straining and sweating, while their eyes became bloodshot and red-rimmed from desperate exertion.

He reached for his sword instinctively, but as he pulled it free from its scabbard, felt his vision suddenly split and blur and his throat lock closed almost instantly... as if a hangman's noose had been drawn right around his neck, cutting off all oxygen. He lashed his tongue at the air, mouth gaping, stumbling with one hand out to find a wall to brace himself as he lost his equilibrium. One by one his men stopped moving, bodies wracked in pain, faces frozen in fear, as the potent toxin laced into their meal finished them off.

In that moment the master of the armory realized what was happening and found an unexpected inner reserve of strength, pushing with all his might against the wall to start himself stumbling towards the door out of the room, where the pull-alarm waited on the other side, just out in the narrow corridor. With the momentum behind him he shuffled toward the spinning portal, stumbling once or twice to avoid the bodies of his men, until, just out of arm's reach of the door, his foot caught under the arm of one of the dead guards and he fell, face-first, into the hard stone floor.

The door opened with a slight creak and a half-dozen delicate figures moved into the room, led by Kseniya, who entered first to make sure the poison had done its work. Most of the men lay lifeless, faces tinged pink and tongues swollen grotesquely, their eyes still red-rimmed and bulging. Lying at her feet was the flush-faced master of the armory, whose clouded eyes stared blindly upwards as he rolled onto his back, reaching one weak arm out to her for aid. He released his sword as he reached for her, but she moved away for a moment, then returned, putting a long dagger to his neck and cutting it cleanly open with a firm stroke.

Kseniya remained in the doorway as the guardsman sputtered his last bloody croaks, keeping the other household servants back until she was sure he was dead. She watched him flop about, her own breath stolen not by poison but with horror at the act she had just committed. *She hadn't wanted it to be this way, she had done everything to avoid this, but he had made it this way... and now he was dead.*

Still strong though his life was draining fast, the beast of a man rolled slightly to one side in an effort to get up, but blood spurted out in a torrent over the floor as the last of the vital essence flowed free, and he fell unconscious. In only a few seconds he was dead altogether, his strained muscles relaxing and his body shivering one last time before falling completely still.

Once he stopped moving, Kseniya managed a choked gasp, tears threatening to spill from her eyes, but she knew there wasn't time for that. Killing a man had proven to be surprisingly, *shockingly,* easy; her hands had done the work, her body had made the motions on its own, leaving her mind to catch up. Her eyes stared down at the man whose throat she had slashed, the man she had killed, even as her feet moved her body aside to let the others into the room. Then, realizing the others were waiting for her guidance, her mind snapped to attention and she motioned them to take the soldiers' weapons, before kneeling herself, to take the key that dangled from around the armory-master's waist.

Standing, Kseniya patted down her skirt and nervously pulled one long bang back around her ear, closing her hooded eyelids for a moment to take a reinforcing breath so that the others couldn't see how shaken she really was. When she opened her eyes she saw Sarah and the other servants waiting, terrified but clutching the scimitars and daggers of the house guards in their hands. Kseniya managed what she thought was a reasonably stern look, which seemed to carry, as the others seemed momentarily heartened.

"We have the key," she whispered. "Follow me to the armory."

Rider came over the top of the wall and descended into the garden at the center of the compound, which was mostly dark except for a few pools of weak light from oil lamps placed here and there along the meandering pathways like dim islands in the night. This place did not seem familiar; it wasn't the grand garden in which the mandarin had given him an audience when he had first come to Tucumcari, and as such he took a moment to look around and get the lay of the place. Strange trees and plants that he didn't recognize, lichen-draped flora and tall flowery fronds that would have been more at home in the jungles of Southeast Asia decorated this garden.

It seemed quiet enough, so eventually he moved from his spot by the wall and crossed the garden to one of the many paths. He turned to the left to start towards the main archway leading inside, when all of a sudden someone shouted "*Qin ru ze!*" He couldn't see from where the voice had come, and so leapt to the side and started running through the garden, hoping to avoid any ensuing gunfire.

Instead of gunshots someone sounded the alarm; a guardsman somewhere pulled on a lever that activated the scavenged air raid siren that immediately came to life and wailed out across the top tier of the city.

Rider kept running, feeling thick fern leaves bend around him as he moved forward and snap back to lash him as he crashed through the underbrush. He kept running until the alarm sounded far away, on the other side of the palace. Breathing heavily he stumbled out the other side, dashed across a covered path that split the gardens in two, then returned to race up the path towards the giant portal that led towards the main building. Before he could pick up much speed he came to a sudden halt. Standing just a few dozen feet from him was a large number of men.

Boren, leader and most capable of Uncle Sam's personal guards, instantly lost his smile as he and his half-drunk compatriots walked down the path on their way to the palace's guest quarters, sequestered in another building. There, on the path in front of them, was a cloaked man with a short sword in one hand, creeping through the darkness. The laughter of his men trailed off as they also spotted the intruder, and as one they realized they had seen this man before!

Seeing their hesitation Rider instantly bolted, running off the path and into the trees, vanishing from sight. In their stunned silence, Boren and the others were now able to hear the palace alarm, which in their drunkenness they hadn't heard before.

"*Was that...*" is all Boren could muster, as he drew his sharp blade to the accompanying hiss of his half-dozen companions doing the same. He turned to look back at his men, two of whom stood ready, warily looking into the night, but the rest joined him in turning to look at the one bearded warrior who stood without a weapon.

Boren frowned angrily at his fellow northman. "You *had* to give the man a blade!"

"He's gotten away!" said one of the others, looking into the heavy foliage in the direction Rider had gone. "Who do you suppose he is?" asked another.

"We could be in a lot of trouble," Boren said, voicing his suspicion that this was no coincidence and that they may have, in fact, let an assassin into the city and even more foolishly, given him the means with which to accomplish his mission!

"Back to Uncle Sam's quarters!" Boren commanded. "Blood may be spilled tonight!" As a group, the armed northerners made haste to return to their sanctuary.

Gale came out of her quarters in the west wing of the palace as the alarm sounded in the distance. The hallway was dark and empty and she moved along close to the wall, feeling out with one hand until she came to a window pane of solid glass-like tree sap, peering out at the dark courtyard and the starry sky.

Out of the darkness of the hallway came Kseniya, Sarah, and several of the household's handmaids and servants. Gale was relieved and turned from the window to come over to Kseniya and Sarah, but stopped short when she saw the scimitars in their hands, as well as the blades held by the others.

"Kseniya! Sarah!" Gale whispered. "What's going on? There are guards in the courtyard!" A few of the women moved to the small window and crowded there, just out of sight among the shadows, keeping their weapons low lest they shine in the starlight, and looked out at the guards converging in the main yard.

"Gale!" Sarah whispered desperately, "You've got to get out of here! Go back to your room!"

Kseniya seemed oblivious to the other menials and her face lost all expression as she touched Gale's cheek, as if to reassure her, but as she opened her mouth to speak Sarah inadvertently cut her off.

"They're marshalling towards the *east* wing, away from us!" she said, and for a moment Gale thought she detected joyous relief in her friend's voice. Indeed, some kind of tension relaxed in the household servants, though they said nothing and instead, gave each other hopeful looks.

Satisfied that they were unnoticed, Sarah moved without a sound, and started leading the way down the corridor towards the palace armory. Kseniya took Gale by the arm forcefully and began to pull her along with them. "Gale, we have to get moving. You must come with us!"

Sarah looked exasperated. "Mother," she said, using the affectionate nickname all the menials had for Kseniya, "shouldn't she stay?"

"I can't just leave her! We *must* take her with us!" Kseniya cried.

"She's better off here! Where we're going..." Sarah argued enigmatically, letting her voice trail off. But Gale caught on; a strange feeling seeped into her like icy fingertips along her back, and she realized something was wrong with Kseniya, Sarah, and the others.

"No..." Gale said suddenly, halting the argument. "Where is Margus? And why are you all holding swords?"

"Never mind that," Kseniya insisted, ultimately shrugging off Sarah's well-meaning objections. "We have to go. You always wanted to leave this place, and now you have the chance." She could tell Gale would resist as long as she was forced. After a moment's hesitation she released Gale's arm and took a step away, in the direction of the others who were beginning to vanish out of sight down the hall. She stood beside Sarah, and looked back. "Are you coming?"

Sarah stared at Kseniya, then at Gale. "Come on, Gale," she relented. "Come with us!"

Gale bit her lip, powerfully aware of great danger in the air and all around her; unsure why Kseniya wanted her to come so badly but suddenly realizing that this was the right thing to do. She had plotted her own escape over the course of several weeks, a plan full of uncertainties and risks that she had dreaded facing alone, but now, all of a sudden, it was a reality being placed into her lap, and she wouldn't be doing it by herself. Everything came crashing down on her at the same time; the cold longing to leave this life, the everyday fear of change and the unknown, and the thought of losing her adopted sister who now seemed so much larger and mysterious than ever before. With no further protest she nodded to Kseniya and Sarah, ready to follow.

One close call after another, Rider thought. It gave him a new appreciation for the art of assassination, and that strange, reviled class of men hired by the great desert factions to do away with annoyingly stubborn tribal leaders. Or those stalking individuals who might risk death to open the gates of an otherwise secure citadel so that it might be laid to waste. He thought of those nameless men, insignificant and unknown in the grand scheme of things, but whose perilous actions over the course of a single night, could change the face of the wasteland forever. Most did it for corium, but he was doing it purely for hate's sake. In that moment he wondered how many others like him had turned their hands to murder to avenge wrongs done against them, and then he suddenly found himself wondering why there weren't *more* assassins in the world, considering how foul and cruel its inhabitants had become.

He dismissed these wandering thoughts and searched for a window through which to peer. He came to a narrow opening and looked inside, seeing a torch-lit hallway on the other side. Looking back to make sure no one was close behind, he pulled himself up and through the window into the hall beyond.

Entering the corridor through the narrow window seemed to transport him into another world, into a dark hollow winding through a living organism, the passage's walls made of conjoined tree trunks that still flowered and bloomed. These were *Onam* trees, a curious strain that bled a phosphorescent violet sap from tuber-like protrusions up and down its length, the sticky stuff shedding a dim radiance that softly illuminated the entire hall. An adaptation of nature (the glow of the syrup would draw insects, which would become stuck and absorbed for nutrients) the Clean cultivated these trees as natural, living light sources.

Waiting for his weak eyes to adjust in the purple light, Rider turned and saw a well-lit room down the hall. Here the glowing tree sap made plentiful shadows, so he remained in the dark, listening.

He could hear excited voices and the sound of armed and armored men from the large chamber down the hall. As he prepared to head the other way and avoid having to fight, he heard a singularly familiar voice that caused his head to spin right back around and his fingers to grasp the hilt of his weapon with a terrible determination.

"If it is an assassin, the first place he will head for will be the throne room," he heard Margus Han say. "We must move to another, more secure place immediately. Hamut has already left to secure the palace gates; Alin, you come with me."

Whoever was with him must have concurred, for they said nothing and in a moment, Rider sensed a group of men coming his way. He looked around for somewhere to hide and leapt across the hall to dive into a shallow arch, his back against the rough back of an *Onam* tree, trusting in his friends, the shadows, to hide him.

Not a second later Margus Han came around the corner, leading a group of musket-wielding janissaries from the front. His long white sleeves billowed behind him as he walked sternly at the head, holding a large automatic pistol in one hand and using the other to feed it an extended clip. *Hypocrite*, Rider thought. Close beside him was another man who immediately stood out among the janissaries, a youthful individual in the airy robes of a Clean *talib*, holding a mastercraft scimitar at his side. It was this boy who first caught sight of Rider concealed slightly in his niche, and his eyes flared wide with stunned surprise as Rider lunged outwards like a moray striking from a deep, dark coral bed.

Rider's best hope was to get in close so that the musketeers wouldn't be able to bring their guns to bear; they would be ineffective until they managed to free their scimitars for a melee. By then he would be upon Margus and the boy, but the latter was of no concern, and he believed he could take Margus down with just one swing. That's all he would have, after all, before they struck him dead.

With only a few quick steps, Rider found himself among the astonished guardsmen, barreling into their long muskets with the force of a man driven by revenge, causing them to fire off and down the hallway in churning wisps of smoke. Two of the guards stumbled on coiling roots underfoot and fell on their faces, while the remainder moved back uniformly to draw their scimitars and defend their liege.

But with the momentum of the charge still with him, Rider pushed through the more competent janissaries, relying on his weight and speed to knock them aside.

Margus spun around and his pistol turned with him, and he fired a deafening shot that missed Rider by just an inch and exploded into hot lead fragments as it struck the wall behind him. Rider's sword came down in a fierce arc, with all his might and strength behind it, straight towards Margus' defiant face.

An instantaneous flash of sparks lit the hallway as Rider's blade came to a sudden halt, just inches from Margus Han's head. Another sword had come up in that brief fraction of a second to block the blow and save his life.

Alin stood at his uncle's side, his arms brought together to hold the sword firmly and parry Rider's attack. Alin glared at the would-be assassin, his nostrils flaring with exertion, as he managed to not only lock the enemy's weapon with his own, but pushed back and successfully unbalanced Rider and knocked him away.

Though he was thrown off balance, Rider managed to keep his weapon though only just. It was then that his finely-honed survival instinct, which he had deliberately buried for the past three years under a mountain of hatred, took over, bursting free from within and instantly changing him back into the skulking survivor that he really was. Rider quickly pulled back, hunkered over to present a low profile, in the same way a rat might retreat to a drainpipe before turning to scamper off, only momentarily baring its teeth to dissuade pursuers. Across the few short steps between them, his eerie eyes glared back at Alin, and with the weird pinkish color that resulted from the curious play of light in the hall, made Alin and even the janissaries stay their ground just for a moment, terrified of what kind of creature they might be facing.

Sensing their sudden apprehension, Rider turned and imparted the same look to Margus, who had retreated behind his men. He could have fired but he didn't; either he was afraid like the others, or maybe his mind was racing to recognize the vaguely familiar man before him. Maybe he was simply stunned by how suddenly the attempt on his life had come, just moments after he had voiced his suspicions.

Rider felt the need for vengeance succumb to his survival instinct and he took off down the hall with a swirl of his cloak. Margus fell back against the wall, gripping at his chest as pain, a minor heart tremor, overcame him, while two of his men struggled to help him remain standing. Alin immediately discarded his own cape and chased after the albino, straining every muscle to catch up and finish the fight. As he gained his senses, Margus followed as well, leading the guards with him.

Uncle Sam was furious, any of his warriors could see that plainly. The barbarian giant paced back and forth across the room, his face bright red, his eyes wide and fierce. The sound of the palace alarm was dulled here to little more than a methodic throb, and his men stood in the uncomfortable silence, their countenances exhibiting an awkward mix of shame, embarrassment and concern.

"I brought a bunch of idiots with me," he finally said, breaking the silence. The words were spoken harshly but not nearly as harsh as they could have been. While he was angry it was clear, to Boren at least, that Uncle Sam was, deep down, mildly *amused* by what had happened. The others would not get off without a rebuke, but Boren knew, having been the leader of the chief's guards going on ten years, how the chief really felt, and he was intrigued.

"Out," the chief said gravely, and the seriousness of his tone only made Boren more fascinated. While the others filed out one by one with their warlord's admonishment weighing heavily on them, Boren knew something was up.

"Stay," Uncle Sam said to Boren, but the younger warrior had already been expecting it and didn't seem surprised. Uncle Sam gave him a slight grin, but when one of the men turned back he expertly hid it behind a scornful, angry stare that sent the soldier running.

Once they were all gone, Uncle Sam's bearded face broke into a large, toothy smile. He slapped his knee.

"If only the assassin *was* able to complete his mission!" he joked. Boren found himself a little shocked by such a suggestion being made so casually, but Uncle Sam merely laughed a stifled guffaw before reaching a hand out to lean against some nearby furniture. Boren felt comfortable in his master's presence, but such talk, even in private, seemed inappropriate; especially when the deed might actually occur!

None of the northerners had any love for the Clean, especially Margus Han, but few of the current generation of young warriors had known a world without him. It was a dichotomy; in olden times the tribal people of his homeland, the Forbidden Lands, had scrounged and foraged for their water, eking out a desperate and fragile life among the wastelands between the world's glowing, ruined cities. Life was harsh; there was no denying it, and virtuous, good people, God-fearing people, were as subject to wholesale slaughter, starvation and famine as much as anyone.

In his time, Boren, considered old at twenty-eight, had seen that slowly change. The enemy invaders had learned to adapt, abandoning their sequestered ways to become the world's great merchant clans, rising from the ashes to begin peddling water and an easier way of life to whoever would listen. Or more accurately, trading with whoever had the scavenged junk or bits of hot blue corium to pay for them. They bargained water to quench the thirst, to alleviate the sick, cool the fever, water the crops and wash away the dirt and grime of their savage existence out on the plains. Good, well-meaning folk, his neighbors and clansmen, had traded in lives of honest hardship and day-to-day survival for regular contact and trade with these foreigners, these people of muddled blood. The water merchants and their ilk found many inhabitants of the wasteland willing to buy into their vision of a "better way", and made them slaves to their demands. But enough escaped their treachery, sensible enough to see the Clean's efforts as a sacrilegious encroachment on their age-old way of life; and many on the fringes of the wasteland whispered of rising up...

Margus Han and the Clean, with their smart, snapping banners of white, were the juggernaut behind the onslaught against the wild freedom of the wasteland's scattered peoples. More poetically, the Clean and their Cartel allies were Hell's legions; Margus Han was Lucifer himself, leading from behind their formidable ranks, directing with one wrinkled hand the rape and domestication of their desert world. With silver tongue and wicked lies he in particular pitted one tribe against another, secured trade agreements with raiders and secret alliances to wage war on other trade houses, elevating his people to the status that they now enjoyed. But their subjects, the lowly "savages", were the ones propping him up, feeding his coffers with their goods and the garbage they scoured from the desert floor to acquire the water he controlled.

And while they were bitter, they weren't stupid. Margus represented power and stability, and with his alliance with the Cartel traffickers and truckers, he seemed invincible... at least from the eyes of a simple chief's guard.

Boren couldn't fathom what the world would be like without Margus Han, but the glee his master got from the thought made him wonder. It seemed foolish to flirt with such a thing, the breaching of a dam that would let chaos free across the wasteland. Would the world turn over on its head? Would people live free, or would another tyrant just come along and pick up Margus' mantle and carry on? But what if people learned, truly learned, and turned away from that path? What if by his death Margus' evil would be suddenly and magically revealed to the world, and from that point on the words "culture" and "civilization" gave men a foul taste in their mouths. *What if?*

They only needed someone to stand and lead them...

Uncle Sam joked, but only half-heartedly. "We'd better prepare to head out; the palace and the city aren't going to be too hospitable to us for much longer. Margus will live, fate isn't kind enough to let him die. So we'd better go while we're still outsiders to this affair, before Margus points the finger in our direction. Margus will cool down; the sword with our name on it will be forgotten. We'll return to our lands and find the one hundred men he demands and turn them over... buy us time. We conserve ourselves, we protect our young... and with what we've learned from being here in the city, in this palace, we prepare for *tomorrow's* war."

The last of the menials ran quietly out of the armory carrying as many weapons as she could in a bundle thrown over her back, leaving Kseniya and Sarah to finish wrapping up bundles of Ancient-era firearms. Kseniya pulled an old Springfield rifle from the wall and laid it at the center of the cloth, then retrieved a stockless Kalashnikov and prepared it as well. She bundled several banana clips in a knot of cloth and tucked it into her belt, then returned to the wall for more rifles which she grasped with each hand.

Gale paced around one of the rooms of the armory, listening to Kseniya pack her own bundle, but keeping an ear out to make sure they weren't discovered. But feeling useless there, she tore herself away and entered a nearby vault, joining Sarah by taking weapons down and readying them to be carried. *Who would carry them? Would she be carrying them? Why would they need so many weapons? Were they needed wherever they were going? And where were they going anyway?*

"Just move quickly, we don't have much time," Kseniya said to them from the other room. She seemed to know what Gale was thinking even though she couldn't read minds and wasn't even looking her way. "We have friends in the desert who require an offering in exchange for security. You understand? It's vital that we bring these with us."

Kseniya's voice quivered, and Gale wasn't sure if Kseniya was afraid of these mysterious 'friends' she spoke of, or if it just now occurred to her the danger they were all in and was shuddering from the realization.

Sarah finished packing her things, then turned to Gale. "I'm going. Stay with Mother, understood?"

Gale lifted her hand, showing Sarah the ring on her finger. Seeing it Sarah smiled broadly, lifting her own hand to show the ring Gale had given her. She then departed, leaving Gale to pack whatever she could carry.

After Sarah left, Gale hurried. The weapons all seemed the same to her. She touched a rifle, and a pistol, and placed them side by side on her blanket. At last she picked up a small, dusty, Micro-Uzi lying on a shelf and examined the ancient firearm. It seemed very familiar to her, this weapon, and she wanted to keep it, but she suddenly realized Kseniya was readying to leave and was headed towards the back exit, which the other conspirators had left open. She didn't want to be left behind, so she put the gun down and returned to kneel at her own bundle, preparing to tie it tight with cord.

Rider hurried down the hallway, breathing heavily, his sensitive eyes acutely aware of the contours of the strange organic passages. Here and there patches of luminous fungus and oozing Onam sap gave a little bit of light, but not enough for him to get any idea of where he was, or how close he might be to an exit from this place. By chance he felt compelled to stop to catch his breath and realized some light spilled from a nearby corridor, at the end of which was a large door. He returned to the corner and peered cautiously around, noticing that the door stood open. He heard hasty footfalls echoing through the tunnels; the boy was almost upon him.

Rider's weak eyes narrowed on the writing carved into the face of the door, a blend of Arabic and Chinese characters that denoted the Trade tongue. He stepped forward, oblivious to the danger that was getting nearer, as his mind raced to decipher the word with his limited understanding of the language.

"*Armory...*" he muttered, finally recognizing the writing. He immediately ran forward and into the first, outer chamber, his head darting from side to side as he searched the walls, all of which were empty. Several small passages extended from the room, and all were well-lit with the vivid blue glow of corium lanterns. Drawn deeper, he moved down one hallway and passed several small vaults, spotting racks of medieval pole arms and swords, as well as dusty cases of precious pre-Fall weapons. He handled a few, scraped away the grime and dust on others, but most were in terrible shape, broken or missing components. It seemed to Rider that the Clean had taken great pains to scavenge every last weapon they could find, whether or not they could use them, to keep them out of the hands of the people of the desert. There were weapons and just *pieces* of weapons; the walnut stock from a hunting rifle, the upper receiver from an M16, disembodied barrels from assorted shotguns and military sniper rifles, and the rusted and pitted cylinders of police and civilian revolvers stacked one on top of the other. There were other weapons as well, artifacts from the twilight years of the Ancients, the things that no one remembered how to work anymore; the sleek chromium rod from a laser weapon, the bent magnetic rail of a man-portable mass-driver, and the cracked outer casing, damaged and de-fused, of a battlefield neutron grenade. This last he let his hand pass over and caress with the lightest of touches, knowing that it was weapons like these (albeit far larger ones) that had made the world what it was today, and had given birth to the mutations that now ran rampant through the tattered remnants of the human gene pool.

This was no simple armory, it's location beneath the palace no mere coincidence. It was a vault designed by the Clean to bury the weapons of the past, to erase the fact that they ever existed. These things were brought here to be forgotten.

He passed kevlar helmets of the Great Enemies who landed on American shores centuries past, emblazoned with the symbols of long-forgotten nations. He saw gas masks from three world wars, and a gallery of old dusty radiation suits once earmarked for the cleanup and reconstruction crews that would sweep away the mess of the nuclear conflict and rebuild. These heavy plastic suits sat idle; the crews never came, the Ancients never rebuilt.

Mesmerized by the hodge-podge mix of weapons and junk, Rider at last found one that made him grin, a simple automatic pistol, a well-balanced Swiss gun which he picked up and weighed gently in his hand. Apparently satisfied, he looked around for a clip to feed into the empty grip, his eyes sweeping the shelves and boxes until they came to rest on something that made him put the pistol down and his eyes widen in surprise.

Stepping over to the low shelf he reached out and picked the Micro-Uzi up, recognizing it instantly despite the years of dust that had accumulated on its surface. Nearby sat two pistols in a leather holster, which he immediately grabbed with a growing grin. This was *his* stuff, taken from him years ago and which Margus Han had simply put here to forget rather than figure out how to use. Reaching out, Rider found some suitable nine-millimeter clips and checked them for dust and dirt, before stuffing them into the sash around his waist. He put his old holster on with a snap and replaced the pistols to their respective cases, once more getting accustomed to their considerable weight at his side. But as he went to grab the Uzi again and turn to leave, he was surprised as a young woman in a white robe entered the room from another short tunnel, carrying a bundle on her back.

Though he knew he had to move quickly, the unexpected sight of this strange woman's soft face, sharp green eyes, and curly fair hair, standing in such close proximity to him, almost made him stammer. At the same time Kseniya re-entered the room via the back exit and cried out in shock when she saw Gale and Rider standing there, the latter with a gun.

"You! What are *you* doing here?!?" she hissed.

Rider scowled and grabbed the younger of the two; though she seemed to anticipate his move, Gale was unable to make herself dodge aside as he took her arm and spun her around, pulling her so that her back was flat against his chest and his arm held her tight, rising up to grip her neck in a wordless threat of strangulation. Kseniya took a single step forward to stop him but halted herself.

"You should be dead," she said, inching her way closer, as if somehow she could snatch Gale away from him if she got near enough.

"Let me go!" Gale tried to gasp, but Rider only held her tighter, cutting off her breath.

"Let me handle this," Kseniya said to her, struggling to contain her exasperation, struggling to soften her voice. "Let her go."

Rider ignored her.

"Let her go and you can take *me*." She was desperate, but she looked into Rider's eyes for a long moment before calming herself and continuing. "I remember the way you looked at me, scavenger."

She let the suggestion lie for a moment, but Rider said nothing.

"Do you still want me like that?" Her voice was throaty and soft at the same time, a tigress' purr. All of a sudden the three of them heard more people entering the armory complex, this time from the front entrance. Rider had almost forgotten he was being chased!

Gale felt powerless as Rider grasped her, as helpless as a rag doll with no strength to fight back. *He's taking me hostage*, she thought. *Why am I letting him?!*

The footsteps grew louder, and a moment later Alin came running into the room, his sword readied for the attack even before he saw Gale in the assassin's arms. Guards poured in behind him, but when he realized that she was in peril his face turned from a look of surprise to a mask of seething anger.

"Don't move!" he called to Gale. *Alin, you idiot! I have no intention of moving!*

Rider held the short barrel of the Micro-Uzi to the girl's temple but he looked at the men gathered in front of him. The threat was enough to make them draw back a few steps.

Alin's face, up until now fixed with the single-minded desire to slay the assassin, was now contorted in desperation for the well-being of Gale.

"Let her go!" he commanded impotently. Rider seemed unmoved. "If it's a hostage you want, take me instead. You'll get a far larger ransom..."

Alin's gesture was cut short by his uncle Margus, who pushed forward. "Move aside!" he shouted. He looked shocked when he saw Alin attempting to negotiate with the assassin, and his eyes widened when he realized his priceless Gale was also in danger.

"*You!*" Margus sneered, as he now realized who the "assassin" was.

Rider found no little pleasure in that. He hadn't been able to deal the man a killing strike, but he had dealt a blow nonetheless; a blow to his pride, to his sense of security and to his family... whoever this girl was.

Rider glanced over one shoulder quickly and saw Kseniya had retreated to the shadows, out of sight of the others, but still looked at him with steady eyes. She stepped backwards towards the rear exit through which the other menials had escaped, only breaking her stare once she vanished through the doorway.

It was his only chance. He turned back to the men and leveled the gun at the mandarin and his nephew, but kept his grip on the girl. Their bodyguards moved forward to shield them.

"You've made a mistake, bounty-hunter," Margus said, "You should have been thankful for the corium mines. At least there you were alive. Now you're a dead man."

"No one moves..." Rider said defiantly, trying hard to ignore the mandarin's threat. Somehow he found it a hard contest, shrugging off Margus' booming voice, as the very words brought back a flood of awful memories of that living hell and the agony he had languished in for three full years. Rider slowly began to back up, and the girl with him, though she looked astonished and kept trying to speak, despite the hand gripping her around the neck.

"You follow and I kill her... *zhidao?!*" he shouted.

A few moments later they had escaped through the rear exit to the armory, where Kseniya and the other women waited, ready to bar the door.

As they entered the passage, Sarah seemed poised to strike Rider from the other side of the doorway but Kseniya maneuvered her body in the way; there would be no chances taken so long as Gale was still in danger.

Rider stared at the wide-eyed group of female menials, young and old, his own look betraying his detachment from their gender.

"The way out?" he asked immediately.

"The eastern passage," Kseniya explained with a slight gesture down the corridor. "It leads below the guard complex and to the palace stables. If you want to get out alive you'd better come with us, we've some horses waiting".

"No thanks," Rider replied, already pushing Gale along in front of him. Sarah tried to grab his arm but he waved the gun vaguely in her direction and she and the others backed off instinctively. "I can make my own way out of here. I'll take what I need and send the rest of the horses running. Wouldn't want you following me, would I? For the time being I'll just hold on to this little piece of furniture, until we're free and clear, alright?"

As he stated his intentions the women began to panic and started to protest.

"You can't!" one cried.

"Without those horses we'll never get away!" Sarah snapped. "We'll be trapped here!"

"Don't," Kseniya pleaded, almost stepping forward but staying her ground as he now waved the gun her way, "Let her and the others go, take me as your hostage, you can do to me whatever you want..."

"Yes, let her go!" Sarah insisted angrily, her eyes darting from Rider to Gale and back again.

Rider ignored the younger woman and looked past her to Kseniya. The stirrings Rider had once had for Kseniya had clearly faded with his time in the corium mines, she could see that in his cold eyes.

"Everyone wants to be my hostage today," Rider said flatly, speaking in Gale's ear. "But at least you stay still. I guess I'll keep you."

Spurned, realizing he was intent on abandoning them to the mercy of Margus Han, Kseniya's face turned to scorn. "We will find you," she said, her voice smoldering. "We will find you, only when we *do* there will be no mercy for you. Not now."

He grimaced before speaking again, this time with a little bit of amusement to his tone.

"*If* you find me."

CHAPTER 3

One hundred and fifty miles to the north lay the ruins of a crumbling metropolis, blasted and wrecked by the long-forgotten wars of the past. Lying at the foot of the Rocky Mountains which spread out behind the cityscape as a sea of bare earthy peaks, the sweeping, ancient city, once a monument to man's eager effort to leave a lasting mark on the land, had gradually been humbled by the fierce and unrelenting forces of nature. The lingering death that came to all things from the scars of radiation killed the plant life in the upper reaches of the mountains, scouring grass and trees alike from the slopes, so that each year seasonal winds drove earth and dust from the high peaks, lashing at the bony ruins with fierce sandstorms that broke and ground the remnants to dust in an unrelenting tide.

Even then some man-made things still stood, though in time they too would succumb. Crumbling, devastated wrecks that used to be tall buildings of steel and concrete still resisted the elements, but they were shrunken and dwarfed by the erosion of the wind and the unusual toxic rains that swept the city every decade or so. Old crumpled street signs proclaiming the distance between one city or another, or the approaches of a certain exit, traffic lights with shattered lenses, dilapidated water and utility pipes, looming highway overpasses, railroad bridges, and *maglev* monorails, and even the tattered remains of a labyrinthine network of overhead power lines were covered in thick layers of rust in the same way that undersea wrecks are gradually consumed by oxidization. Entire districts of the dismal ruins were painted in broad swaths of a uniform, ugly brown-gray color, particularly in areas that were once centers of Ancient-era industry... with which this city had bristled.

The streets and highways were completely choked with the husks of thousands of rusted automobiles, from cars to trucks to buses and emergency vehicles. Every

Burning Lands

roadway seemed to be jammed tight with these wrecks, ordered roughly bumper-to-bumper away from the heart of the city and towards the desert as if frozen in a desperate race to escape. The glass was missing from every window, the paint burned and evaporated from every car body and the rubber of the tires fused to the blistered asphalt. Tens of thousands must have perished in the paralyzed city traffic when the bombs first detonated over the metropolis, killing them instantly in a sudden white-hot flash. Charred skeletal remains could still be seen inside many of the metal wrecks, which had become death-traps for their occupants, some still stuck in the same pose they held when the mushroom clouds burst into the sky, shielding their eyes or grasping at their loved ones sitting beside them. All of them were victims of the same nuclear nightmare that had rendered people into complex structures of delicate ash, which only vaguely resembled the human beings they once were.

Towards the center of the city, things were just as lifeless, though not as reposed and peaceful; here it was clear weapons of great violence were the agents behind the city's instantaneous destruction. Here colossal skyscrapers stood out against the raging red sky, though the tops of these megalithic structures had been shorn off, leaving burnt and fused stubs where massive structural supports had once stood mightily. Galleries of gleaming window panes and the crystalline siding that sheathed these great, once-futuristic high-rises had been completely obliterated by the concussive force of the multi-megaton warheads that blasted the city hundreds of years ago. Towards the outskirts of town, trillions of tiny fragments of glistening glass carpeted every inch of the broad streets and avenues, littering the tops of old rusted car wrecks and the toppled hulks of city buses, so that at mid-day the sunlight on the streets became brilliant and blinding. But towards the heart of the city, the heat had been so intense that these whirling clouds of glass shards had vaporized in mid-air, only to solidify as horizontal stalactites or quartz-like icicles clinging to lopsided telephone poles or the few standing signs. Defying gravity to create a prickly maze of dizzying green crystalline structures that resembled a deadly alien landscape, in places some of this slag (an ambiguous green-gray substance related to "trinitite") cooled into radioactive pools both minute and grand, creating weirdly-distorted mirror images of the tortured skyline in their glassy, solid, reflective surfaces.

The city was by and large avoided by the sane inhabitants of the desert, many of whose ancestors fled from places like this during the time of the Fall and passed down a vague knowledge of the lingering death that slept there, waiting for new victims. Superstition aside, where the bombs had fallen, towards the heart of the city, they had indeed ripped deep craters in the earth that still burned fiercely with the invisible fire of that most feared hazard of the wasteland: *radiation*. This poisonous heat still made any journey to the inner reaches of the ruins a foolish and fatal endeavor and was also the source of an eerie red corona that floated above the cityscape night and day (though at night, in particular, it lent a sinister and hellish brightness). Moreover, the windstorms that ravaged the Rocky Mountains churned up lingering fallout in distant, isolated places among the mountains where it had been allowed to accumulate over the years, so that now and then a curiously warm snowfall fell over the city, spreading the lethal stuff (evaporated radioactive elements) for miles and miles, with no one place being safer than another.

This was the ruined city of Pueblo, Colorado.

Delicate gray flakes drifted down from the deep red atmosphere above the city, like tiny flecks of ash slowly falling from the churning, volcanic cauldron that seemed to be the Pueblo sky. Because the wind had died down to an unnatural stillness, already the unusual snowfall was beginning to accumulate atop ruined buildings, sagging overhangs, crumbling stone monuments, the tops of car wrecks, and on the cracked and buckled sidewalks. Old bits of Ancient garbage left in the streets were slowly being buried in the warm and radiant stuff: a dented-in post office mailbox on a street corner; a collection of toppled garbage cans; heaps of petrified newspaper and discarded magazines clogging street drains where the acid rains had swept them, their headlines still screaming "WAR!"; a bicycle left on its side and abandoned outside of a downtown shop.

A crisp silence filled the air as it snowed, for the first time in years, over the ruins of Pueblo, suffocating the sound any footfall might make. It dulled the noises that sometimes sounded out in this desolate landscape, the low moan of the wind winding through the corridors made by streets and surrounding buildings, a sudden groan and crash as some ancient structure finally gave up to the pressures of time and collapsed, or the hideous, disembodied shriek of some unknowable creature making its home in a distant corner of this lonely necropolis.

The young tracker knelt down on one knee to examine the tracks in front of him even as they began to vanish under the fine dusting of fallout that carpeted the ruins. With a soft whir he extended one metallic hand, from which he got his name, *Shubazang* (the invaders' word for "metal hands"), to the warm earth as if to touch the lingering trace before it disappeared completely, forever, but kept his clunky cybernetic fingers just short of the fine, ash-like snow.

Like most scavengers who dared to venture into the ancient cities to loot, the boy wore something to shield his eyes from the gleaming glass and from clouds of dust swept up by the wind, though what he wore was obviously not the cheap apparatus used by the majority of desperate scroungers. His eyewear, reminiscent of foundry goggles, were quite black, but small glowing green characters moved swiftly across their perfectly circular lenses like the letters of a Times Square marquee, constantly in motion. Rubber-coated wires connected the polycarbon frame of the goggles to a complex pack on his shoulder and continuously fed information about his surroundings to a pin-sized projector which in turn cast the information, in legible form, onto the inside surface of his lenses. Information including the time, current temperature, wind direction and speed; and most importantly, the general level of radiation, "high", "medium" or "low", in the vicinity.

Shubazang was surprisingly young for someone with his acclaimed reputation, with light skin and only the faintest of Asian features. He was fairly handsome, with no facial deformities other than the lingering disfigurement that comes from healed injuries to the face; signs of once having had his jaw broken, his cheekbone fractured in a fight and re-set clumsily. Small scars marked his face here and there as if to remind onlookers that this boy was, in fact, a fighting man. His chin was clean-shaven, only adding to his youthful good looks, and he sported black hair that draped down over his brow, unkempt and messy.

Burning Lands

The boy wore an ancient Chinese army greatcoat that was far too big for him, long and of a faded olive color, its collar trimmed in thick black fur. He wore it not out of some lingering sense of allegiance to the foreign invaders who once conquered this land; it was merely a good, warm coat. It still had most of its shiny brass buttons sewn in place and it bulged in spots, giving away the presence of hidden gear and gadgets underneath, so many that the boy looked bigger and heavier than he truly was. Shubazang was still quite tall for his age, just nineteen years old, but other than his slightly malnourished frame, he looked in fine condition and ready for a fight. Beneath his deceptively bulky greatcoat he wore handmade overalls of shoddy brown sackcloth, and beneath these the ratty and worn remnants of some unidentifiable uniform, no doubt snatched from a corpse left on a forgotten battlefield dating to the time of the Fall.

Around one thigh the boy wore a leg holster for one small device or another; around his shin was a sheath containing a huge bowie knife, with a compass ball for a hilt that spun wildly from the magnetic interference in the atmosphere over the city. Slung from his shoulder as he crouched, was a long rifle of some indeterminate kind, with a tapering barrel and a cluster of power cords that hooked into the solitary grip and extended back to a small cylindrical pack strapped around his waist.

Shubazang exhaled, nostrils flaring slightly, looking up from the faint tracks and to the barren, wintry streets ahead of him.

"This just doesn't seem right," he said after come consideration. "The pieces don't fit."

For a moment it seemed like he was talking to himself, but another figure stepped quietly up behind him now, having given him space to do his work. The latter was just as tall and wore an all-concealing cloak of a faded color, gray, with a hood drawn about its head to conceal its face. This individual said nothing and simply stood silently as he continued speaking.

Shubazang gritted his teeth, then sighed. Even at his age he was already an accomplished survivalist and his skills and endurance had brought them this far safely, but for the first time he allowed his fatigue, and his weariness of an unexpectedly prolonged chase, show.

"I don't get it," he said. "We've been up and down the Tucumcari-Midway trade route and stopped at every little village, oasis and hellhole along the way. Spoke with every damn merchant and scav and come up with two dozen different clues and leads. There *has* to be an answer somewhere. This *has* to be it."

He didn't sound convinced even as he said it, he knew he didn't believe it and when the quiet one just bowed its head, he realized his silent companion knew as well.

Without a word the robed one stepped past him and trampled the fading trail, returning to its place at the head of the duo, already walking steadily off down the street with a swish of heavy cloth as the man strained to get to his feet. He swore he could sense amusement in its sprightly step, but he wasn't sure.

As his companion went ahead, the boy took a moment to fish out a piece of potassium iodide gum from a pouch at his side, bringing the bright red stick to his mouth so he could begin chewing. He would need to continue chewing so long as he remained here, as the chemicals in the gum would be absorbed by his thyroid and would prevent him from accumulating a harmful dose of radiation while wandering among these blasted ruins.

Together the boy and his silent companion continued on, following the last impressions of the tracks they'd been pursuing for days, even though now they were almost imperceptible under the ash-like snowfall. The young man trusted the one in robes to lead, allowing his gaze to turn from the trail to sweep over the empty buildings and shattered skyscrapers that loomed up around them. He observed the thousands of signs and advertisements plastered on degenerating billboards, disintegrating walls and the sides of rusted buses; tri-color posters, monochrome flyers and photo-quality ads proclaiming the next generation in shaving cream, fuel-efficient transit systems, cellular technology or shoe inserts. Broken words and fading pictures screamed silently at him from every flat stretch of wall and from every sign, a dizzying and frantic parade of images and sights preserved on blistered, rotting paper and warped poster board.

One could spend a year looking at these pictures and catalogue them meticulously and still come up with a grossly incorrect idea of what Ancient life was like, what was important to them, what constituted "culture" in those bygone years. What had ranked higher in the minds of those busy, long-dead people? Newspapers in their uniform black and white print, boring to look at and even more tedious to read? Or colorful tabloids and slick-cover magazines with gigantic letters screaming for the attention, and alarm, of passerby? Were the Ancients really more interested in crop circles, UFO sightings and the freakish face of Bat-Boy than in stories of a war spiraling out of control overseas? What could a modern-day reader believe, anyway? If one story was true, weren't they all? Or if some were make-believe, how could you tell what was true and what wasn't? Was it all entertainment, or all fact and news? Where did the Ancients draw the line; certainly no one today could tell. Either keep them all and believe in a very wild and fascinating past, or discard them, one and all, and consign Ancient history to the heap.

The images themselves didn't give any answers; the survivors who lived on after the Ancients were gone were left to come up with their own conclusions. Each visitor to the city, any city, could come up with a dozen ideas of what the Ancients were like on their own, and none of them were ever even *close* to being accurate.

The boy with metal hands wasn't looking for those answers, he was keeping an eye out for the signs and symbols the Ancients used to denote things that, in their time were mundane and routine, but which were now a goldmine for survivors and scavengers. Gun shops. Pawn shops. Army surplus stores. Police stations. Or, for someone like him, electronics stores, computer outlets, TV repair shops.

They passed by several storefronts facing the snowy street, and the cloaked figure in the lead deliberately walked close to them, turning its hooded head to look into each window as they walked past. Most were too grimy and dusty to see through; others were smashed open and looted.

After a while the robed one stopped and looked into one broken-open storefront, where a mannequin lay slumped and lifeless, its flesh-colored plastic faded in spots, one of its arms missing and whatever clothes it had been wearing disintegrated long ago. The head was partially shattered, leaving only the right half of the face.

Burning Lands 157

Shubazang noticed the long stare and moved over to the patch of broken glass surrounding the storefront, bending over to examine the mannequin.

"No good," he said aloud, "Too much damage." He leaned closer still.

"And it's a *guy*."

The robed one picked up the broken head and wordlessly looked at it, then brought it to its chest and began stroking the plastic face in a manner not unlike a child clasping a favorite doll.

"*No*," Shubazang repeated firmly, "I don't want *that*."

He continued walking, waiting for his robed companion to return to its place in the lead. For a moment the cloaked figure retained its hold on the life-like plastic head, then lifted it up and placed it over its own face like a mask.

The boy looked back, startled for a moment to see his companion's features replaced by the smooth, off-white, waxy face of the mannequin. It might have been meant as a joke but he wasn't amused.

"Put that down and get up here on point," he insisted.

They continued walking, the robed one returning to the lead, moving its head back and forth from side to side as it watched the streets ahead of them for signs of their quarry. Shubazang seemed less concerned with danger with his companion back in front of him, and so tore his eyes from their surroundings to continue glancing for unclaimed finds.

Bingo. He stopped and pointed to the left, and immediately the hooded one turned to regard the building he was indicating. A small storefront in an otherwise crowded downtown street, its front windows covered in dust and plastered with debris swept by the hot winds of the nuclear blast and sealed by that heat against the glass. A large sign, once neon and bright, hung lopsided over the automatic doorway, depicting the universal symbol for the disabled, a stylized man in a wheelchair.

"Wait a minute," he said, already moving ahead and to the darkened doorway. "Just hold up. Give me five minutes."

He went into the building alone, unslinging his laser rifle but fairly confident the place was empty. The layer of dust was thick and there were no prints anywhere; cobwebs hung here and there but even these had been abandoned long ago by their tiny arachnid builders, leaving a few fat, desiccated cocoons which held the ancient remains of petrified moths or other prey.

It took a moment for his eyes to adjust. Green letters flickered across the lenses of his goggles informing him that the temperature was cooler here and that dust levels, while irritating, were not hazardous. Around him old rusted racks held dozens of artificial limbs, and folding wheelchairs were stacked against one wall. He passed by a case displaying dozens of amazingly life-like faces, each a thin mask made from a sheet of artificial memory-shaped synthetic skin, once intended to cover the deformities caused by horrific burns or in catastrophic car accidents. They were of men, women and children too, white, black, and various shades in between. A normal person might look at these and come to tears thinking of the poor victims who needed such things to feel "human" again, to rebuild their lives to some level of normalcy, but his examination was cold like someone casually looking for parts in a tool box. After a few moments he seemed dissatisfied with the selection and turned away.

Several large, glass tubes filled with a still liquid caught his eye and he moved over to peer into them, his own reflection distorted by the curvature of the glass. Inside one was what appeared to be the skin off the front of a man's chest, free of any blemish and formed with a complete set of well-toned musculature. In the next floated another, this one more trim and clearly intended for a young female, with plump, life-like breasts off of which the dim light of the room seemed to scintillate playfully. He recognized these two disembodied torsos as *synthiskin* grafts, probably meant to cover full-body burns or extreme surgical scarification. Each a testament to the medical miracles once commonplace in the time of the Ancients.

The boy knocked his knuckle against the latter tube and called out over one shoulder. "Check this out. *Tits!*"

A service counter drew his attention and he approached, stepping over a prosthetic leg lying on the ground, but only after giving it a momentary once-over. Without putting anything down, he looked over the counter to the shelves behind it, cluttered with boxes filled with parts. He lifted his goggles and, with murky yellow eyes discolored by jaundice, scrutinized the faded writing used to label each. Something caught his attention and he came around the counter, broken glass crunching beneath the hard soles of his boots.

A shadow swept over the room and he turned to see his voiceless companion enter, taking a moment itself to scan the place. The boy grinned slightly at his friend's apparent curiosity and went back to searching through the boxes, giving each a quick look, fingering through their contents, and if nothing caught his eye, dropping them to the ground and adding to the mess underfoot.

The robed one looked through the glass, staring at one face in particular, that of a finely-featured woman with icy white flesh. It extended a finger and prodded the glass.

"Nah..." Shubazang said. "I don't like any of those. The artificial pigment has faded. It's freaky."

The robed one poked the glass more firmly, determined. Shubazang looked over his shoulder.

"I said *no*."

The quiet one deferred. The young man continued to look around. Looking behind the counter he was quickly distracted by something else and pulled a small cardboard box out to get a better look inside. He worked at something in the box, trying to pull it out, then reached down and retrieved a small screwdriver, using it to pry the small device out. A small metal chip, with the dimensions of a saltine cracker, sheathed in a coating of buff-colored plastic with copper contact points in five different places.

"A voice modulator. We can definitely use this," Shubazang said, without explaining what exactly he had found. The robed figure turned from its continuing examination of the room to regard the small chip that he held, bringing its hands up and clasping them firmly together as if pretending to be overjoyed.

Shubazang seemed amused and smiled. "Considering where we found it it's probably badly damaged, but give me a while and I might be able to repair it."

Hours passed before they heard the first sounds of the men they were following, men who were now not far ahead of them. Echoing through the ruined city they heard the noisy engines of their quarry's hotwired vehicles, and unidentifiable crashes, bangs and booms that thundered from whatever mysterious activity they were undertaking deeper in the city.

The two trackers sat in silence, listening. At this point Shubazang's veiled companion didn't seem too interested; instead its gaze was fixed on a large statue nearby, its head reduced to a melted, deformed stub by the acid chemicals in the city's seasonal rains. Through posture alone he could tell his comrade was fascinated by the statue's face, whose stony visage had been eaten away at, the features fused together in an inhuman mass.

He looked away from his curious companion and back ahead of them, from where the sound had come. His ears strained to hear something more, and though for a moment there was silence, he soon heard a repeat of the strange sounds - the beeping of a horn, followed moments later by a loud bang and then the choking sputter of an engine.

He knew by now what they were doing; they had found fresh tracks in the snow that told the whole story. There were seventeen or eighteen men riding in five internal combustion vehicles, getting out every now and again at select stores and shops. They had so far hit every gun shop and police station in the outskirts of the city, working their way dangerously close to the heavily-radiated zones towards the heart of the crumbling ruins. They were desperate for weapons and ammunition, *but why?*

To find out was only a matter of sneaking up on them, which wouldn't be a problem because of all the noise they were making with their vehicles, starting and stopping, yelling orders out to one another as they split up to search separate buildings on a given street. Their quarry wouldn't hear them coming.

The boy motioned with his hand to get his companion's attention, then both set out with hastened footsteps to bridge the distance.

Snow fell lazily down onto the flat, bare earth of an old urban park, flanked on all sides by cracked streets and large warehouse-like buildings and old businesses. After two hours the odd warm snow now covered everything, as if a giant's brush had swept over the city and painted everything a uniform white. A few desiccated, stunted husks that were once trees sat in dead clusters at the four corners of the park, covered in a fine dusting of the odd powder, while a graffiti-decorated skateboard course depressed into the earth dominated the rest. An old automobile wreck hung part-way down into the shallow concrete gulch, where youngsters once played, its tremendous weight easily picked up and tossed by the devastating force of the nuclear blasts of the Fall.

This place had been ravaged by the ancient war, but now, with a fine layer of snow, the scars of its violence appeared to be smoothed away. It seemed peaceful, serene.

In this part of the city the virgin snow was broken only by the tracks of vehicles that had recently passed this way. Across the street and on the far side of the park sat the small convoy of automobiles, arranged in a row outside of what appeared to be a large warehouse. Barely visible on the building's plain gray exterior, just above a sagging fiberglass overhang weighed heavily by the radiated snow, were the words: "Army/Navy Surplus". The five vehicles idled noisily, filling the park and the nearby streets with the guttural gasp of their ramshackle engines, which at the moment was the only sound that could be heard for miles.

The autos were typical post-Fall "revived" vehicles, each based on the chassis of some salvaged wreck found among the city ruins or out on the barren highways of the desert. Partly rebuilt with sheet metal and scavenged parts, with the end result of looking like working piles of junk, they were adorned with rusted, riveted, armor plate and shuttered slats through which the driver and crew could see. Most of them were homogenous hulks of garbage, no longer recognizable as the vehicles they once were. Only three stood distinct from the rest.

The lead vehicle had clearly been an off-road pickup at one time, with heavy-duty tires covered in mud and wheels caked with soil, and a sharply-pointed ram plate fixed to the front that was clearing the way for the convoy through the accumulated snow. Bent and rusted wire mesh protected the cluster of lights and searchlights on its front end, on a swivel mount by the driver's window and on the roof, all of which glowed brightly to stave off the encroaching dusk. In the truck's bed sat snow-dusted crates of ammunition and bundles of canvas sheet that probably concealed a variety of weapons.

Another vehicle seemed out of place, a late 1970s Lincoln Continental with armored wheel guards, fully-plated windows and a series of chipped and jagged scythe blades running along its exterior so that it resembled a sleek whaling harpoon from above. Such a vehicle was often referred to by raiders as a "blockade runner", a bullet-fast ride that would tear through enemy lines using its body blades to cut, often cleanly in half, those poor fools who stood in its way.

The last vehicle of note had enough of its original body remaining that it clearly resembled an old military Hummer, though welded armor plate sheathed the windows and covered the wheel wells. Sticking out to man the top ring mount (which bore a heavy, belt-fed machinegun) sat the only visible crewman in the small convoy, a single raider sentry who kept watch over the park and the nearby streets.

From behind distant cover Shubazang pulled his laser rifle out and peered through the scope, passing it to his cloaked companion so it too could see. From here the two silent trackers could observe the crewman clearly, without being seen.

The raider was abnormally large and fit, wearing a bulky kevlar vest over the sleeveless tatters of a fatigue tunic that barely fit him. His head was protected by an army helmet with a frayed kevlar cover, the chin strap dangling loose. His strong, sun-burned face was partly concealed by the translucent plastic of a cancer patient's oxygen mask, its rubber tubes leading around his shoulder to a hand-made breathing device saddled on his back. Mirrored swimmer's goggles covered his eyes, but behind the bulging, reflective lenses he was certainly sweeping the area for any sign of movement. On the one bare arm that faced their direction they could see a large tattoo of a sergeant's chevron, his rank in the raider gang artfully drawn into his flesh with faded blue-black ink. He wore three metal wrist watches on each arm, perhaps an odd affectation for telling time? Most importantly, however, his big heavy hands held the handles on the machinegun, his large thumbs resting against the twin triggers, ready to fire at a moment's notice.

It was obvious from a glance that this man, and probably his companions too, weren't typical desert raiders. Most of their kind, living in the deserts and mounting raids only when easy opportunities presented themselves, looked lean and famished with the cowardly posture belonging to mangy, sick dogs or rats. But this one was clearly healthy, well fed on the abundant spoils taken from their victims, and seemed unafraid of his current surroundings. With such confidence exhibited in a lowly grunt it was safe to bet he and his comrades came from one of the wasteland's larger, more dangerous gangs, not some two-bit, oasis-bound pack of dune bandits.

Considering this, Shubazang took the rifle back and peered through the scope to confirm his first impression. Yes, these raiders were clearly members of a large, powerful, and successful raider army. There, on the hood of each of the vehicles, was emblazoned in crimson spray-paint the multi-armed insignia of the "Ravagers", one of the premiere gangs of the Forbidden Lands. Actually, "gang" didn't do the Ravagers justice, for in fact they were an *army*, three full regiments of tough, disciplined killers who rode out of their mountain stronghold every few months to wrench tribute from the hands of weaker survivors... and lay waste to those few foolish communities who dared to defy them. Many legends circulated through the squatter camps of the Forbidden Lands concerning the Ravagers; some believed the thugs and rapists that made up their ranks were forged into a coherent battle force by a single man with great charisma and military skill, a modern-day Guderian. But such wild stories were common around the campfires of merchants who had a need to explain the effectiveness of such raider armies against their own house troops, and few took them seriously. Others explained their martial bent by linking together patchwork fragments of local history. Some believed they were in fact descended from an army unit known to be stationed in the area during the Final War, but which some claimed deserted during the conflict, fleeing to the wilderness of the high mountains to avoid being consumed in the nuclear holocaust. Keeping alive their discipline and organization, they managed to stay one step ahead of the savages of the surrounding lands, and avoided the entropy of the dismal years following the Fall. But as times grew lean, it was often believed, they eventually came down from the mountains and turned their guns to the conducting of murderous raids, exacting cruel depravations on those too weak to resist. Cannibals in a sense, feeding off of their fellow survivors, they were no better than the other mindless monsters that infested the wasteland... and considering that they were once guardians of this land, it quite possibly made them *worse*.

From inside the building came two more Ravagers in attire closely resembling the machine gunner's, burdened by a large black munitions crate that they struggled to carry between them. Each of these men also carried an old-style automatic rifle in his free hand, with bandoliers of bullets and web belts with extra clips clustered around their chests and hips. With a quick heave they hurled the heavy crate into the bed of the pickup. A fourth raider passed them on their way back, this one cradling a cardboard crate filled with boxes of shotgun shells, pistol ammunition and an odd collection of submachine gun and rifle clips, which he put into the back seat of the Lincoln through an open window.

They were certainly looting, and certainly in a hurry.

Shubazang and his voiceless comrade waited patiently for a full hour, watching as the raiders loaded up the truck until it could hold no more, then stuffed the other ramshackle vehicles with boxes of ammunition and Space Age preserved foods; the kind of freeze dried, induction sealed and vacuum packaged packets of algae-based meals that replaced "real" food well before the Fall. By now the sun was beginning to set, the snow was dwindling and as it began to grow dark, the raider soldiers showed the first signs of fatigue.

Through his partially-cracked scope Shubazang watched the machine gunner as he checked one of his many wristwatches, then appeared to call out to his men. A moment later they started to come out of the building, assembling in a ragged line outside, a loose interpretation of standing at "attention". He gestured and said something that Shubazang couldn't hear, and after a few moments the men began to disperse.

Shubazang continued to watch as the raiders began to unpack two of the cars and began setting up a few lean-tos and tents; several more of the raiders went inside the warehouse itself. Within minutes the warm glow of a campfire could be seen flickering somewhere within.

He continued to watch the machine gunner. The nameless raider looked out into the night, slowly, scanning all directions. The city was dark. After a long pause, the raider seemed satisfied that the city was empty and he slipped down into the Hummer. After a few moments inside, he came out the side door, leaving the machinegun up top unattended. After smoking part of a cigarette and observing his men setting up their shelters outside, he went into the warehouse and disappeared out of sight.

Shubazang and his companion, Euryale, had been tracking this small band of Ravagers for over a week now, following them from east of Midway to the heart of Pueblo over miles and miles of open desert. Long-time "adventurers", the two companions had a history of working well with the water merchants of the Clean clans (in no small part because of his ancestry), and had been hired in Midway by a representative of that merchant house to investigate some recent trouble in the Forbidden Lands. People had gone missing, villages mysteriously wiped off the map and accusations were being thrown around between the Clean and the affected natives, accusations that threatened *war*. Despite being young, Shubazang had no delusions; he knew other trackers and hunters had been hired as well but he believed that he and Euryale were the best of the best in this particular line of work. It wasn't just youthful arrogance, it was quite possibly true. Professional troubleshooters, extra eyes and ears, scouts and trackers, hired guns, name them what you will. They were good at their jobs, they had to be, especially in a world where they had to compete against much more experienced men.

Shubazang thrived not so much on the corium (though it helped keep him at a level of comfort he enjoyed) but on the acceptance and patronage of the established houses, which meant he, at least, always had work available as well as the gratitude and flattery of his patrons. These were good things, but deep down there was more; the excitement and danger of it all, and the reputation, knowing that his name was recognized in far corners of the wasteland. The only downside was that he was more often than not greeted with disbelief by those who expected an older, more seasoned man, but he was always quick to exhibit his capabilities and prove the stories true.

Unfortunately they had about as much trouble finding clues and leads as any of the other scouts hired by the Clean. Making base camp in one of the frontier villages of Uncle Sam's tribal lands, where wild rumors were rife among the local populace, they tried to learn as much as they could but found no clear information, nothing more than speculation. Stories abounded of scavs and tribal hunting parties vanishing, never to

Burning Lands

return; local legends spoke of strange thunder and eerie, high-pitched screams heard every few years or so on the eastern horizon, dubious reports stretching back for at least a decade. Gaining an earful of stories but no credible ground to begin their investigations, they thus had to strike out into the desert to look for themselves. They had visited one of the recently-destroyed villages, and it was here that they found signs that he recognized as pointing to weapons *predating* the Fall.

Of all the hired men sent on this mission, it had been a revelation that only he could bring, for he had always been more close to machines and gadgets than his fellow man, and knew to a great extent the types and variations of gizmos of the ancient world. As a child he had been a prodigy, a tinker and an inventor, amusing his people with creations that either made their lives easier or simply made them laugh. In his childhood he had grand ambitions to revive the technological wonders of the past world, to single-handedly be the hero that would rebuild "America" from the ashes, but he quickly learned that one man can't do it alone. Few people shared his fascination for the Ancients, turning their backs on the past and cursing their mistakes, vowing never to return to the way things were. It was different for him, however. In every spare part, machine bit, coil of wiring and whirligig that the scavs sold to his father, a trader, he saw a million possibilities, a million keys to unlock the truth of the past. He spent much of his childhood imagining what the world had been like, with only these fragments of technology to provide sustenance for his voracious imagination. He envisioned a world of beautiful cars, graceful rocketships, shuttles that raced across the desert on rails, robots made as companions or toys, of huge sprawling cities lit up against the cold night with a warm and hospitable glow, visible even from space; hand-held devices capable of communicating over hundreds of miles, electric viewing-boxes that never ceased to entertain people night after night; electricity conveyed across the countryside in cables; power created, held and stored for future use. He saw limitless wonders coming from these broken pieces and components, and inside his mind he had built and rebuilt the ancient world over and over again until he could imagine a thousand variations.

As a child his imagination had been allowed to run free, but as he grew older he found the elders no longer approved of his foolhardy ambitions and unlikely crafting projects. They warned him time and again to cease dreaming and put his skills to use in practical affairs, but he could never fully tear himself away; technology had become his one true obsession. Granted he consumed great resources in the trial-and-error of invention, but hadn't it been worth it to try? No, it hadn't, or at least *they* didn't think so, and that discovery eventually changed his life forever. With a crystal clear mind he could remember the very day, the very hour, that his grim-faced father presented him to a band of visiting slavers and promptly exchanged him for a heavy sack of corium nuggets. "You've wasted enough of your life," his father had said, as he himself stood there in disbelief. "Wasted enough of our supplies with your foolish tinkering. Gentlemen, he's a smart boy but we can't afford to keep him any longer."

His world changed in an instant. Taken from his community he was made a slave, marched off into the desert with strangers who spoke a lexicon of bizarre languages and dialects, from all walks of life. They were the weaker ones, those whose own people couldn't support them and thus sold them to ease the strain on their resources... and make some cash in the bargain.

Dispersed like grains of sand in a strong wind, they were sold off as human cargo to the highest bidders in one of many nameless, temporary trading towns that came and went in the Forbidden Lands. The settlement was no longer there, its tent stakes and corrals replaced by sand long ago, but he remembered the festive night when the slavers set up shop to sell their stock to crowds of travelers and tribesmen attracted to the market from miles around. A gang of reasonably successful raiders was among the patrons there that night, come to sell off some near-dead women of which they had taken and now grown tired. They were rich and wealthy from the sales, but what they desired was something they didn't have, a slave with technical skills who could improve their chances in the deadly day-to-day game of raiding in the wasteland.

The raiders had been drunk on their own ambitions, to become the next greatest scourge of the Forbidden Lands, but they proved to be no better than any other gang. They eagerly bought the boy, purely for the purpose of repairing a cache of weaponry they had found in the wastes, and after branding him as a "member" of their gang set him to work immediately once they returned to their hideout in the desert. He was starved for many days, left alone in a cold, dark cave to complete his work.

The raiders had acquired some astonishing finds in their short, ferocious time: pre-Fall weapons, energy rifles, an infantryman's magnetic defense screen from the time of the Fall, and a cache of priceless portable power sources like chemical energy clips and thermionic power packs. It was no wonder they wanted to repair this 'tech and put it to use against their enemies, replacing muskets and swords with lasers and pulse rifles! But their cache also included other objects not related to war and life-taking; there were things in the heap of artifacts that they simply *assumed* were weapons but were in fact something entirely different. Electronic tablets with entire books recorded in their memory, videos describing the robotic, bionic, and cybernetic advances of the pre-Fall world, a catalog of domestic androids once available to private buyers, and pieces ranging from documentaries on the space program to modern marvels such as military weapons systems and vast civil engineering projects. Among these bits of arcanum sat broken and twisted engine parts, light fixtures, recording equipment, the shapely legs of some bodiless android, severed at the hip... all of them ensconced in the heap with every other bit of refuse like them littering the cave.

Up until then Shubazang had feared for his life, but here in the cave, even as they starved him and kept him with only a small light to work by, he found he was at home. He spent days exploring the sand-crusted devices, taking them apart, cleaning them, and rebuilding them, examining components and minute electrical work, memorizing each weapon's structure and making a mental schematic of it that his mind just naturally absorbed into memory. This small motherlode of technology provided him with days and nights worth of entertainment and discovery, re-kindling the wonder of his childhood, until after a month he had completed his labors and emerged to present his work to his masters.

His reward came quickly. The raiders were indeed overjoyed by the newly-revived weapons, as well as being instructed on how to use and maintain them, but they were not nearly as long-sighted as he had foolishly assumed. After only a few test shots with their lasers to see them in action, they boisterously assumed they were ready to take on the world. *He* was no longer needed.

Burning Lands

The petty raiders wanted to be overlords of the desert's people, but didn't want another mouth to feed; they wanted to reign uncontested, and feared anyone else brandishing weapons like theirs. But their leader was especially cruel, and instead of killing the boy he ordered his men to hold Shubazang down and, drawing an old-style sword, the raider set about severing both of the boy's hands at the wrist. To prevent him, their leader said, from ever using his hands to revive technology again. They laughed as Shubazang bled furiously, until he was too weak to stand, before they looted the remaining weapons from the cave and left in a fading swirl of dust.

Shubazang somehow survived. With a heretofore untapped inner resolve he dragged himself into the cave, and set about binding the stumps that were his hands, forcing himself to utilize his feet to tear and attach bandages. For days he languished in the cool cave's depths, fighting off fever and starvation, licking at moisture on the rocks and only eventually finding a foul-tasting lichen to eat. Somehow he lived, somehow he beat the odds, and he regained his strength. He found ancient medicines among the discarded "junk" of the cache, that had saved his life.

Motivated by instinct he rose again over the next few months, and with only the aid of his increasingly agile feet and stray beams of sunlight coming into the cave, he set about rebuilding his hands out of spare parts left in the jumble at the cave's bottom.

That particular part of his past was only four or five years away now, but they had become distant memories, and he in fact regarded them almost fondly, without bitterness; after all, those events had shaped him and made him what he was today, a better and ultimately more useful human being. He had become a *man* over the span of those short years. True he had gradually given up on trying to piece together the past and bring back the Ancients' ways, but he had never lost his zest for life and in fact found a new source of exhilaration flirting with the dangers of the wasteland. He still carried in his heart an obsession and fascination with old technology, and over time had hand-built many of the unique devices that he now employed in his trade; his electrical eye goggles, for instance, a working device he built using spare parts after examining a similar one years ago in the raiders' cave. His bags and packs were filled with all manner of half-finished doo-dads and contraptions, little things that kept him busy and which he used to occupy his mind when he was restless. With some of these he had practical uses in mind, but others were simply Rube Goldberg inventions, pointlessly-complex creations that whirled and clicked impressively, but served no function.

He wasn't just a tinker, however, he was also a killer, and to be sure he now took a certain pleasure in slaughtering raiders and others who preyed just as mercilessly on the people of the wasteland. Feelings of revenge were gone now (he was a "professional", after all) but from his experiences he knew raiders intimately and knew just what a cancer they really were on the face of the world. They were the boy's antithesis; to him the *building* of something was an achievement, not the *destroying*. Unemotionally he had decided that they, he and raiders, were ideological opposites and he felt no remorse whatsoever in eradicating their kind from the earth.

Shubazang looked over at his veiled comrade, Euryale, and motioned it to proceed as planned, while he stood up, dusted off his pants and slung his long rifle over his shoulder. In a moment Euryale was gone.

With a huff Shubazang stepped over some rubble and headed down towards the park where the Ravager convoy was camping for the night.

As he walked Shubazang tried to put the pieces together in his mind. The villages in the outlying part of Uncle Sam's lands had been destroyed by the bearers of some form of advanced technological weaponry. In the Forbidden Lands there were only two groups that had weaponry even close to that sophistication, the Doomriders and the Ravagers. The Doomriders, an enigmatic death cult, restricted themselves to the lands far north of here. Thankfully. That left the Ravagers, who were in fact known to scour the desert far and wide in their raids. It wasn't impossible that they struck the settlements along the edge of the Burning Lands but, Shubazang wondered, *why?* Why not attack closer prey, the small trade towns nestled in the shadow of the Wei Shan, or the Cartel trade routes to Midway? It was a nagging doubt that had been with him ever since he and Euryale started off towards Pueblo.

Along the way they had heard rumors that the Ravagers were active again; rumors and gossip in the nomad camps of savages spoke of seeing Ravager war parties riding out to the edge of the Burning Lands, recently, for no known reason. These parties returned soon after, and seemed in a hurry to get back to the mountains from where they came. Their actions in the area *seemed* to confirm the theory that the Ravagers might have accomplished the raids, but Shubazang still couldn't fathom *why* they had done it. Certainly not for spoils; tribal villages were seldom rich enough to attract anyone, let alone powerful raiders from the other side of the desert.

But then, if the Ravagers weren't out raiding, what *were* they up to? *There was only one way to find out.*

Inside the warehouse-like structure the more experienced raiders had made a temporary camp, occupying the dusty old rooms to stay warm while their lower-ranking comrades were forced to sleep in tents outside. It had stopped snowing, so as long as they remained bodily removed from the eerie white dust outside the risk of accumulating *rems* was no more than a night camping during one of the desert's typical sandstorms. They had set up their mats and blankets here and there for the night, and three or four campfires set up in various rooms kept them warm and provided a modicum of light by which to see. A sentry patrolled the second floor, accessible by a crumbling stone staircase, looking out the windows now and then while he himself remained in the dark.

On the ground level a few of the men were playing a game using a deck of ratty, worn-out cards, but they were for the most part quiet, the game itself nothing more than a means to pass the time. None of the men looked at each other; few words other than quiet whispers passed between them as cards were laid down and rough stones pushed back and forth between players. Guns were propped up against the cracked stone wall of one room, where the most men congregated, each weapon within easy reach of its owner.

One of the men was busy tearing open the heavy rubber cover of a *ready-meal*, one of the few pre-Fall wonders that men of this dark age could enjoy as it was meant to be. A pre-packaged dinner, ready-meals were the product of years of space-age technological development bent towards the creation of preserved edibles usable in a wide variety of households, even environments. In the time of the Ancients such meals were commonplace in supermarkets and widely popular on family dinner tables. Cheap, easy to stack and store, and simple to prepare, they represented a vital convenience in the lifestyle of the Ancients, who were often too busy indulging in their hedonistic pastimes to cook real meals and thus delighted in the time saved by these "meal packs". A quick pull of a tab to open the pack, a moment to remove the plastic spork, wait two seconds for a chemical reaction in the contents to heat the sludge-like slurry within, and enjoy.

The grim soldier looked completely consumed by his task, his heavy brows knit as he worked to tear the package and get at the food inside. When the packaging ripped suddenly and the plastic spork dropped onto the wooden counter with a soft clatter, it was the loudest sound in the building and everyone turned with a startled look.

His men were tense, the machine gunner, a *sergeant*, could see that clearly. But he said nothing, and simply went back to the methodic ritual of stripping his sidearm down and cleaning it as swiftly as he could. It was a custom of his particular brotherhood of killers, disciplined men who claimed to descend from actual soldiers and warriors, and it soothed him. He had always assumed it soothed his men as well, but looking up he noticed none of them following his lead. As he removed the barrel of his pistol to swab it, he cast a hard glance at a few of the men idly smoking cigarettes, who caught his angry glare and abruptly set to work doing the same.

Content that he still had their fear if not their respect, the sergeant continued to clean his gun, though his mind wandered. These men were well-trained, the best of the best, and he knew they wouldn't crack, not while on a mission mandated directly by the supreme leader of the Ravager army. To fail here was to face certain death back at home, and while they had already risked their lives by going to the edge of the Burning Lands on this insane mission, they had survived to make it this far and were eager to get home. Alive.

He was confident his men weren't cowards; true, a few had spoken of desertion when the order came and the mission was explained to them, but he had dealt with the dissenters before they had ever reached the edge of the Burning Lands. The only men that remained were seasoned veterans, grizzled fighters who had faced death before and were unshaken by its prospect. But they were tired, and the looming unknown of what they had heard and seen was taking a heavy toll on them. Even the best of the best could be worn down under this kind of stress.

The sentry upstairs saw movement at the edge of the weak light coming from the building, a dark shape moving across the snow. He brought his rifle up to his shoulder and hissed a warning out the blasted-open window to the men camping in tents below.

One of the men heard the call and immediately crawled out of his tiny one-man tent, gripping his rifle in hand. On his feet he stood an imposing seven feet tall, and while he couldn't see anything in the darkness, he brought his weapon in a high-ready position anyway, waiting for his eyes to adjust to the night but ready to blast away at a moment's notice.

Out of the blackness came a boy in an old army greatcoat with a rifle held in one gleaming, silver hand, ready to be brought up to defend himself but not held aggressively. He wore strange circular goggles in which the sentry could see a stream of tiny green letters pass, though they were too small for him to make out clearly.

The stranger stopped when he realized he could be seen, and observed, clearly. He stood still, not giving any ground but not advancing any further either. His face was serene and still, his mouth a thin, flat line. He looked unafraid.

A few of the raider's comrades had stirred and were now arming themselves as well, standing and moving slightly forward in a loose semi-circle, weapons ready. They observed the newcomer, but they didn't seem too concerned by his presence, perhaps because he looked so young. They seem relieved at what they saw, as if they expected something far worse to emerge from the gloom of the dead city.

The tall raider thrust his weapon slightly forward as if he was jabbing a spear at the stranger. "Okay, kid. The weapon. Lose it."

Shubazang stood his ground. He kept his rifle where it was, in hand and ready. The other raiders watched, expecting the young man to cave, and when he didn't they looked first insulted, then unsure of what to do next. Shubazang sensed his opportunity.

"Stand down, private," Shubazang stated, removing his goggles to show the terrible scar near one eye, where once long ago a brand had been placed against his skin, close enough to the right eye to permanently blind it, and hot enough to leave a brutal, telling scar. Such brands were a common identifying mark of raiders and criminals. Merchants and community lawmen were quick to brand thieves, killers and rapists before casting them out into exile, and ironically, raiders themselves frequently adopted the brutal practice (perhaps to laugh in the face of authority) as a part of the ritual initiating new members into their ranks. Almost all of the Ravagers had one, and it clearly marked Shubazang as having once been a member of a gang.

The tall raider seemed to look at the boy in a new light, his confrontational stare softened by a sort of familiarity, and after a moment of silence, he cautiously gestured Shubazang to follow. He eyed the rifle warily but said nothing, lulled into a false sense of security by Shubazang's youth and the scar that marked him as a fellow raider. The other guards kept their guns trained on the boy, but their anxiousness ebbed and a few relaxed enough to mill about and start pulling out their cigarettes.

"Sergeant," the tall raider said, entering the back office of the surplus store, "Found this kid outside, says he's a raider."

The sergeant finished cleaning his pistol and slapped a clip into it. He looked up with an arched eyebrow as Shubazang entered from the shadowy corridor, his boots clicking on the bare concrete floor.

"Why didn't you strip him down?" the sergeant asked in surprise. "Do you recognize this *fuck?*" The gigantic raider, who now looked very foolish, floundered for a response.

Shubazang lifted his rifle and slung it over his shoulder in an effort to dispel their suspicions. "I came to talk. *But if the gun intimidates you...*"

The sergeant's eyebrows flattened out and he frowned, obviously irritated by such a suggestion coming from someone so young.

"Look, you punk," the sergeant retorted, "you must be one dumb son-of-a-bitch."

He rose from his seat, but Shubazang raised his other hand, palm forward, to show he wasn't looking for trouble.

Burning Lands

The sergeant stared at his metallic hand. "Nice chrome," he said. "What's stopping us from taking those little hands of yours, eh? I imagine they might be worth some corium to someone somewhere..."

"Look, I came here to join," the boy said quickly, hoping he didn't sound too eager. And that they'd believe him.

The sergeant looked at the other raiders in the room with an amused grin, and they all chuckled heartily. Most didn't even look up from what they were doing, eating messy foods or reloading bullet bandoliers with fresh rounds, but Shubazang could sense they were still *watching. He was in a den of thieves, the hideout of a gang of murderers, and his presence wasn't wanted.*

"Okay, kid. What gang did you serve under?" the sergeant asked suspiciously, reaching for a stick of potassium iodide gum on the table and popping it into his mouth. He was humoring the kid, but for how long?

"*Death Machines*," Shubazang replied. The others looked to one another; no one seemed to recognize the name of that now-extinct gang, the one that had been famous, momentarily, for acquiring a lost horde of technology, before going out in a blaze of glory trying to sack the Cartel enclave at Midway.

But the sergeant did, or at least it seemed like he did, by the way his posture shifted as this unexpected revelation sunk in. Rumor had it that all of the *Death Machines* had died on the walls of Midway, killed to the last greed-possessed man.

"You're too young to have been a *Death Machine* grunt. Now who the fuck are you, punk?"

"Too young to be a grunt, but I was their *tinker*. Weaponsmith. Still got the know-how, if you need it..."

The sergeant looked at him for a moment, trying to gauge if he was telling the truth. But he simply snorted. "Well we're not looking for recruits right now," he said, but the man sounded unsure.

"Well... then what *are* you looking for?" Shubazang countered slyly.

Outside another figure moved through the darkness around the building. The sentry at the second floor window saw it and pointed, leaning to whisper out the window that "another" was coming.

A thin slice of elegantly-shaped steel, colder and more tangible than any fleeting snowflake, entered the soft flesh of his throat before he could manage even a sharp cry of surprise. The *kunai's* diamond-shaped throwing blade, propelled by a tremendous force, carried through his jugular vein and severed his spine cleanly, cutting straight through his neck and shooting out the other side without making even the slightest noise.

A shadow passed momentarily over the canvas of one of the raider tents outside. One of the soldiers was awake and spotted it, and rolled over to get to his feet, crouching. Grabbing his rifle and fumbling for a clip, he stepped out the tent flap to emerged into the night, ready to investigate.

"Where the fuck are you going?" asked his groggy bunkmate, who struggled to force himself awake. His hand groped for his own firearm, which fell over as he clumsily flailed around.

"Just a sec..." the first raider said, stepping fully into the cold night air.

Chock. As quick as that, a mastercraft carbon-fiber blade came down on his head from above and split it in two, embedding itself in the thick coils of muscle that tensed up around his neck. His arms shuddered uncontrollably and he dropped his rifle to the ground, losing his senses instantly and falling, lifeless, to the ground.

The raider inside the tent saw his companion drop, and by the way he fell (like a sack of potatoes) knew he was in danger. The last numbing effects of sleep were instantly leeched out of him and suddenly replaced by the cold tendrils of heart-gripping fear. He grabbed his rifle, moving instinctively towards the middle of the small tent, crouched, and began to feed the clip into the weapon despite not being able to see a thing.

Whunk-whunk. In the last instant he managed to look straight up as two long tent stakes came down through the fabric of the tent, swung downwards with the strength of some invisible colossus, right through the thin material and straight into his forehead and astonished mouth; the former stake cracked through the bone of his skull and the latter impaled the lower half of his face.

Two more raiders, returning from a smoke around the side of the building, stopped dead in their tracks as they approached the small tent camp at the front of the warehouse. They were shocked to see one of their comrades lying dead outside a tent, his head split perfectly in half, and even more so by the silent robed figure crouched over him, in the process of wrenching its finely-crafted *dadao*, a curved sword, from where it had embedded the blade in the ruins of his neck.

"What the fu..." one stammered, while the other simply backed away, horrified by the sight, fumbling for his gun but dropping it as he lost control and panicked.

Euryale detected it had been seen and whirled to confront them. With a grotesque pop it tugged the sword free, and with a flourish, spun around in one fluid motion, casting its cumbersome robes aside in preparation of the inevitable melee.

There, in front of the two raiders, stood two beautiful feminine legs, perfectly sleek and supple with only the slightest dimples around its knees. But where the meticulously sculpted legs met the waist there was no more skin, no more beauty, no more confusion as to who or *what* they were looking at. From that point up, above the shapely smooth pelvis and vaginal mound, were the beginnings of a grotesque body, a machine nightmare of blue-black metal rods, shafts, silently whirring clockwork spools, and bundles of silver-gray musculature that vaguely mimicked what lies beneath a real human being's skin. Euryale... it, she... stared at them with featureless silver orbs for eyes, each burnished bright by constant exposure to the elements, so that they gleamed dully. Euryale's face was just a steel mask, crafted to appear angelic, feminine and fair, but it lacked flesh and animating life; only sleek bare metal in the shape of a beautiful woman, framed by a head of hand-spun hair of white plastic strands fashioned by Shubazang, the boy-genius, himself. It was a platinum-haired construct, his creation, a Pygmalion's artificial woman come partly to life to please its demented inventor... and when not working on her back, to perform a very deadly function as his teammate.

As the men stared, Euryale wordlessly struck a momentary pose, bringing one crude robotic claw to its flesh-and-blood hip as if mimicking some saucy, sultry stance it had seen somewhere in a perverse magazine its creator had once owned. The men stumbled backwards as the voiceless "thing" came forward, their minds still trying

Burning Lands 171

to comprehend what exactly was attacking them and why. Prowling with an almost comically-sinuous stride and the practiced, deliberate come-hither glide of a harlot, the two legs seemed utterly unnatural attached to the ghastly upper torso, that unnaturally human-looking hulk of steel and myo-carbon weave.

Their human eyes and minds didn't work fast enough for them to respond, because by the time they realized they faced a living machine, a *killing* machine, Euryale had brought the dadao back around and began whirling it in a pattern to slice the helpless soldiers to bloody pieces.

"I don't have time for you, punk," the sergeant said, looking a little more irritated now than before. Shubazang chose his words carefully, but managed to sound calm and even slightly aloof.

"You're in an awful big hurry to get back to the mountains," Shubazang suggested. "Why is that? Doing something you don't want noticed on the radar? Found something you don't want anyone else to see?"

His eyes narrowed on the tattooed raider sergeant, now hoping to gauge *his* reaction. The sergeant's eyelids widened slightly at that last part, but there was no acknowledgement. Something didn't seem right. He hit on something but that wasn't it exactly.

"Running... from something?" he offered.

Until that moment he hadn't noticed how pale the sergeant's face had become, and how silent the other men had fallen. The men stirred, suddenly uncomfortable at being here in this room, in this building, in this dead, empty city. They said nothing but their body language agitated for getting the hell out of here now, tonight, *this minute*.

"What did you fools find in the desert? What are you running from?" Shubazang said firmly, his voice switching back to the disparaging tones of the cold-blooded raider-hunter.

Just then there was a loud *thud*, a sound that attracted everyone's attention. There was a crash as the front door came down, and the first automatic gunshots pealed out, echoing and thundering off of the surplus warehouses' looming ceiling more than thirty feet overhead.

Some unknown terror gripped the raiders, and they were coiled tight like a spring. The sergeant ignored Shubazang and roared with a spray of spit for his men to pour out of the back room and hold off the "attackers".

Gunfire shook the building as the raiders opened fire on the front doors, but the death machine cleaved its way through them, closing the gap between itself and the first line of defenders. Slashing steel cut through the men, opening up chests and abdomens and precisely severing heads from their necks; there was more strength in each of Euryale's swings than ten men could produce in tandem. It danced gracefully on slender legs through their midst, its mechanical body erupting in blinding sparks each time a bullet struck and glanced off its sleek metal stomach, off its clearly-defined myo-carbon breasts.

As his men fell, the sergeant stumbled back into the office, past Shubazang, firing off his last rounds out the darkened doorway.

Shubazang rushed to the door to get a look at the attacker, only to see Euryale finishing off the last of the raiders. Their anticipation of whatever terror they feared stalked them was contagious, because for a moment he had been expecting to see monsters, phantoms, pouring through the front door to kill them all. Instead it was the familiar shape of his beloved creation.

The battle was already over. Euryale looked slightly ashamed, hanging its head low, as it struggled to pull the dadao blade from another corpse it had embedded itself in.

"Euryale, what are you doing?!" Shubazang called out in disappointment. "We were just about to get to the bottom of this!" Euryale pulled the blade free with a wet sound and sheathed it at its side. It turned around and walked away, its hips swaying side to side as it went back out into the night.

Shubazang found himself aroused by the sight of Euryale's body in motion; not just his confused hormones but even more so his ego, at perfecting her walk and duplicating the hypnotic sway of a real woman. Not an easy task. He'd like to see someone else try it. The boy turned around and looked at the one surviving raider.

The sergeant could see an undercurrent of dementia in the kid's eyes. This was no ordinary teenager, this was a future Dr. Frankenstein. The raider choked down a throat full of dry air.

"Looks like you're in luck," Shubazang said, crossing his arms over his chest and releasing a deep, satisfied sigh. "Now tell me, what have you Ravagers been up to?"

The smell of blood, sweat, and urine from his dead men assaulted the senior raider's nose. He regained his composure, managing to look strong and defiant, but spoke.

"Shit's going down. I don't know what, I'm just a sergeant in this here army."

"You must know something..." Shubazang suggested.

The sergeant looked reluctant but finally spoke. "A few weeks back we hear rumors that our scouts are vanishing in the Forbidden Lands, near the territory of the *bei man*. Living near the eastern fringe. So we send out a sortie of raiders to kick the fear of God back into the primitive fucks."

He let that statement sit for a moment, realizing Shubazang was staring at him. He felt he needed to explain, so he did. "It's our... policy... to curb lawless activity in the Policed Zone."

Shubazang surmised that by "lawless" he must have meant "acting without permission" and by "Policed Zone", he was really saying "Ravager territory". How quaint - raider colloquialisms.

Apparently satisfied that his explanation was understood, the raider continued. "Only they don't come back either. So the higher-ups get real interested, get their backs up. So we ride out and set up camps, waiting for this 'invisible enemy' to show his fucking face. We know it ain't the locals; they're a bunch of musket-wielding fags, scared as fuck. But whoever this enemy is, he doesn't show. And one by one the camps are snuffed out, I mean overnight, just 'snuffed out'. Ain't no one left, no sign of nothin'. It's like they were *taken by fuckin' ghosts...*"

"Someone saw something, somewhere," the sergeant said, "I... I don't know who saw it, or what he saw, but the rest of us, we get a coded order to pull out, *pronto*. Smells like something bad. Stinks like *fear*. And Ravagers don't fear *nothin'* on this earth. We get word that the high command is pulling the entire army back into the mountains, out of the desert. That shit ain't *ever* happened before. So we're taking this shit seriously. Everyone's got orders to loot what they can; food and water and medicine, and guns and ammo especially like there's a goddamn war comin'; and get their asses back to the hills."

The sergeant went quiet, his jaw moving from side to side as he considered his next words carefully. Shubazang notched his head slightly in interest.

"Look, kid, we just stopped here to get stuff to weather the storm and... I don't know shit, but it sounds like it's going to be the storm of the century. You let me go, you can take the other vehicles, take whatever you can carry. What do you say?"

"I'll think about it," Shubazang said, and in the same breath drew a pistol from his hip holster and shot the raider through the forehead.

By a small campfire, next to the hulk of the Lincoln Continental that they had taken from the raiders, Shubazang worried away at the voice modulator they'd found earlier that day. He sat, cross-legged, working to open the small chip and examine its interior components. His spirits seemed to lift with this busy work, and soon it was as if the combat and killing that afternoon had been an insignificant side endeavor.

He sat quite close to the crackling fire as he worked, needing the warmth to counter the bitter cold that chilled the metal of his bionic hands and the myoelectric connectors that fused them to his stunted wrists. Loops of hideous scars ringed the ends of his forearms where his real hands had been severed violently in the past. The familiar sound of a pot of boiling water provided a steady rhythm for him to work by; it was also a necessary process, boiling his drinking water, considering that with the imbalance of bilirubin in his body, his liver functioned inadequately to detoxify the substances in his surroundings.

For some time he continued contented in this crude laboratory-like environment, with water boiling in the background and his hands working on the artificial voice box like a mad scientist, until he shifted, got up and left his work behind. He paced over to a nearby rock, unzipped his pants, and began to urinate. The stream of brightly-glowing fluid, a side-effect of the radiation-cleansing potassium iodide gum, splattered a nearby rock.

With a sigh of relief the boy returned, sitting back down and taking the chip and tweezers. As he held the small device he returned to his prying, opening it and giving the fine web of wires and processors inside a quick look over. Seemingly content, he reached out with one prehensile leg and, using his toes to grip, retrieved a small screwdriver that he used to close it back up.

"Take off your robe," he said, finally finishing a few minutes later. He knelt, looking up at Euryale like an errant knight presenting a gift to his queen.

Euryale bent its head with a swish of colorless hair, regarding her "knight" for a moment, then playfully slipped the cloak off its sleek metal shoulders, at first revealing its silvery chest, then its narrow waist. The motions were sensuous, a perfect imitation of how a real woman might slowly seduce a man, but there was nothing there but a casing for its internal wiring and aging servomotors. The machine-woman stared down into Shubazang's eyes, its angelic face bearing the same, unchanging smile on its face.

The boy sat up and began to work at Euryale's throat, opening the machine up and laboriously installing the tiny bit of hardware. Retrieving the small tool from his leg holster (an electro-binder) he began to feverishly work, using it to fuse the chip's wiring to Euryale's severed connections. When he finished, Shubazang backed away, momentarily gazing at Euryale's nakedness.

Euryale turned its head shyly as the boy stared, casting him a sideways glance, before delicately touching its throat, exploring the new piece of hardware that he had just added. It looked eager to speak.

There was a loud, grating buzz from the android's mouth, a sizzling crackle, and then in an instant a spark sputtered from Euryale's mouth, followed by a momentary puff of smoke.

"Damn it," Shubazang cursed. "Bad chip!"

In a rage Shubazang kicked his tools across the campsite, cursed and spat, but the eerie android just watched him, unmoving except for the slow rotation of its head.

He eventually calmed down, and sat with a tired sigh beside his robotic friend.

"Don't worry, I'll find you a voice. Someday, I promise. But for now," he said, "get some sleep. We've got a long drive ahead of us."

The artificial woman didn't need to sleep, so it merely nodded as he bedded down for the night.

Hoof beats rumbled across the open plains, sweeping up dust through the large tribal encampment. Over one hundred tents of hide, stretched over bone and wicker frames, dominated the graceful bend of a great dry arroyo, creating one of the largest nomadic settlements in the Forbidden Lands. Horse riders arrived every few hours, carrying word back and forth between the isolated communities of Uncle Sam's tribal kingdom.

This was just one of the many villages of Uncle Sam's lands, a bustling settlement where clansmen and their families ate, drank, and lived, where scavengers came to camp for a brief night before plunging back into the wastes to scrounge for more junk, and where weary adventurers rested their heads between legs of their exhausting journeys.

Foreigners were not normally welcome here; it was not the custom of the land's natives to accept or trust outsiders, especially those who looked "southern", those with the most obvious Asian traits. But today the camp was extremely crowded nonetheless, more so than Shubazang had ever seen. Not with outsiders, but with refugees; villagers from outlying settlements to the east had recently begun abandoning their homesteads, bringing livestock, small children, and steeds burdened with all their worldly goods with them to the imagined safety of this larger town. Each day more families arrived at the outskirts of town, adding their number to the growing gypsy camp that had sprung up virtually overnight on the village's eastern edge. With such an influx of new people there was a great deal of excitement in town, as newcomers struggled to find space to camp among the established tents and temporary structures that already stood here. Tensions simmered since water and food was already scarce, but more than this, talk about town centered squarely on the anticipation of *war* with the Clean.

Shubazang and others like him had used the village as a base while investigating the mysterious vanishings in recent weeks, and a few of his adventurer-peers had grown uncomfortable with the recent turn of events, now that peaceful coexistence seemed to be slipping out of sight. They were clearly outsiders, all of them, and were known to be here on behalf of Margus Han, master of the "southern devils" and the very leader

Burning Lands 175

of the people who seemed likely to be their future enemy. Few of the parties originally hired by Margus Han were brave enough to remain in camp, and most of those who'd been paid a goodly sum of corium to search for an answer to the butchery had since abandoned the cause.

Shubazang and Euryale stayed, however, either ignorant of the stares and whispers of the villagers who watched them, or simply not caring. They had business to take care of before moving on. But Shubazang was an observer as well, and as much as the locals liked to stare at him he liked to stare back. Theirs were strange ways, these "American natives", men and women who descended directly from the ill-fated defenders of this broken land, whose blood was unpolluted by those who had conquered them. They were ragged and degenerate, their noble heritage almost forgotten, but here and there were signs that "America" was alive in some fashion in their hearts and deeds.

Here and there about camp people were preparing meals with what they could muster, cooking large sides of meat over an open fire, serving not only to feed but also a chance for family groups to come together, converse, socialize. Like neighbors at a barbeque, they congregated together, sharing food, while at the same time cleaning lice from each other's hair, beards, and blankets like the most primitive of primates. Many of the older men smoked the butts of scrounged Marlboros, but wearing beards so heavy as to engulf their cigarettes, it almost seemed as if they breathed smoke. A few malnourished, pot-bellied youngsters played the ancient game of *marbles* with their elders in a sandy patch of ground; nearby women cleaned pots and pans with sand (as water was too rare to waste on washing) gossiping and chatting as they worked. The warriors of the camp clustered around large bonfires, letting the smoke burn away the cantankerous reek that pervaded them and their clothing, all while imbibing enormous quantities of beer. An abundance of dogs wandered through the entire village like unchecked vagabonds; here, as was the case in many tribal camps of the north, dogs were cherished as pets; *eating* one was grounds for whipping and expulsion, though more because the northerners believed it smacked of the distasteful adoption of an Asian stereotype, than for any real love of the canine itself.

So this was freedom? This was what America had become? Shubazang wanted no part of it. Neutral politically, he was nonetheless aware of the inevitabilities of this world, namely that man would eventually rebuild something, if not the past that everyone thought they remembered. For him it was a simple choice: he would rather be *with* the tide of civilization when it came, rather than *against* it.

Euryale sat motionless, watching the arrival of more mounted messengers, while Shubazang bartered with a local trader in an effort to sell off the raider "blockade runner" they had taken from the ruins of Pueblo. Its gas tank was bone dry, but certainly some tribal smith or armorer would have some use for the motherlode of metal that it represented, just waiting to be torn apart and re-forged as dozens of swords and axes.

A few crude nuggets of corium changed hands, but it was in limited supply here in the impoverished frontier, and so he had to make do with a few bits of fresh food and some small hand tools, things he always collected for his incessant mechanical tinkering.

As the deal came to a conclusion, another rider approached, singling Shubazang and his companion out of the throng of newly-arrived refugees. The man on horseback was lean like a fencepost, with grayish-tan robes that covered him from neck to toe. His face was narrow, his head topped with short black hair. Wrinkles and cracks crowded around his eyes, but he was all wiry muscle, and the long-barreled rifle around his back may have looked primitive, but it was in fact an Ancient-era laser rifle covered in tight cloth wrappings just to keep the dust out. This man was a fellow adventurer, a hired gun paid by the Clean to operate in the barbarian-infested Forbidden Lands as a tracker, hunter, outrider and sometimes killer.

Shubazang knew him; *Ambrose* was a humorless ghost of a man, whose entire life had been consumed by his work for the Clean. He was also quite good at his job, and like Shubazang he had been hired to scour the land looking for any sign, any clue, of the invisible "raiders" (for that's what they had been instructed to assume was behind the mysterious attacks). They were co-workers of a sort, professional peers, and although they didn't work together, they sometimes corresponded in the course of a shared job so that they could cover more territory, or work more effectively to get a task done.

After a curt greeting, the outrider, Ambrose, spoke.

"Boy! Listen! There is news, your mission has changed."

Shubazang shifted his goggles from his eyes to his forehead, then stared at the man with his one good eye. The boy looked alarmed, but said nothing.

"Four days ago there was an assassination attempt on the mandarin of Tucumcari, though he escaped the blade of his would-be killer... and managed to get a good description of the thug in the bargain. They want your services in tracking him down."

"What about the source behind all these disappearances?" Shubazang asked. "There's some weird stuff going on in this desert, and I think I'm getting close to finding out what. You should have heard the raiders we trailed; the Ravagers are terrified enough of this invisible enemy that they've tucked tail and run for the hills."

The outrider didn't seem impressed by this new information, which secretly frustrated Shubazang.

"Is getting revenge more important to the Clean than protecting the peace in this region?" Shubazang said, but he instantly smirked, well aware of the answer.

"Marius, in Midway, has been given the authority to offer you a substantial amount to travel to Trade City and pick up the trail," Ambrose stated plainly. "You'd be a fool not to take it."

"Does it even *matter* to the Clean that they made a promise to Uncle Sam to find out who was responsible for these raids?"

Again the outrider just stared forward, unconcerned, though he seemed curious about Shubazang's reaction to the news.

"Margus Han seems to have a vendetta against this man," the outrider continued, "and is willing to pay fifty pounds of corium to have him killed."

"That's a lot for just one man," Shubazang said, finally giving up.

"There's more. The assassin took a hostage during his escape, and the mandarin wants that hostage returned alive."

"Hostage?"

"A young woman."

"A *woman?*"

Burning Lands   177

"Apparently a valuable one, at that. But it is imperative that she be alive and *unharmed* when she is returned. That is the mandarin's condition. And he will put the same price on the head of anyone who harms her in the process of bringing her back to him."

The boy rubbed his eyes in frustration, but finally relented and shrugged. "So he wants me to just drop what I'm doing and come to Tucumcari? Shit... Well, they've paid for my services for another three months," he said with a sigh, patting his dusty pants, "so I guess I still work for them. I can either tramp all around this desert looking for signs of mysterious killers I might never find, or I can travel south and track one man who happened to piss off a mandarin."

He looked over at Ambrose, but the stoic outrider didn't seem to pick up on Shubazang's exasperation. So he sighed again. "I guess it really doesn't matter to me."

Shubazang looked over at the hooded Euryale, which just nodded as if to say "I'm ready."

A small army of tribal warriors was gathering in town as Shubazang and Euryale prepared to hit the trail, packing their things and coordinating with a small trading entity that was also headed south towards Tucumcari. It would be a tough sell (the merchant was dubious of the boy's abilities, even after he dropped his name), but eventually Shubazang negotiated a small fee for his services in "escorting" the caravan on the trail. He also kept an eye out, knowing that what he saw here in the lands of the *bei man* might be worth some coin back in Trade City.

Several hundred tribal warriors lingered near the village center, each attired in handmade leather armor or studded breastplates, wearing the colorful sashes and horse-hair helmets their wives and sons had made for them. Crude axes, swords, and spears glittered in the midday sun; pennants dyed red, white, and blue flapped and billowed overhead. These were veteran soldiers, skilled warriors, and their presence suggested that someone of great import was passing through town.

Shubazang stood and looked over to where, just a few dozen paces away, a burly bearded warrior sat firmly in the saddle of his mount, surveying his handsome company of troops. He was flanked on both sides by his best warriors, clad in chainmail, each holding a long pole topped by the bronze icon of an eagle, a sign that marked them as guards of a great northern chief.

The soldiers milled about as a large band of men was marched through the crowds, pushed and prodded by armed guards until they reached the presence of the mighty king on his silently stirring mount.

Uncle Sam leaned slightly forward, his leathers creaking, as he surveyed the motley collection of one hundred men brought before him. Killers, rapists, thugs and thieves. Vagrants and diseased beggars. One hundred unwanted men snatched from all over his lands and assembled here to be given as appeasement to the mighty Margus Han.

He looked at the faces of the men in the front ranks - old men, bald men, wiry men, stocky men. Some few did indeed bear the brand of captured raiders, but only a handful. The rest were simply ne'er-do-wells that had run astray of his harsh code of laws and found themselves in prison in one village or another. Quite unfortunate for them, since there was a desperate need to round up one hundred souls to send Margus' way to keep war from erupting.

These men were scapegoats, to be sure, but they were also criminals and vagabonds who wouldn't be missed.

Uncle Sam snorted; his right-hand man, Boren, could see he wasn't too happy with what they were about to do. It had been the chief's idea initially, but now, staring into the eyes of the men he was condemning to death and slavery (some for comparatively mild transgressions), he seemed to waiver, his conscience nagging him over this most unsavory of deceptions. But the warlord kept the moral crisis to himself. When all were accounted for he finally spoke.

"That's one hundred?" he asked. Boren looked to a nearby tally-man who nodded quickly in his direction. Boren turned and nodded more solemnly to his liege.

Uncle Sam took the reigns of his horse and turned it slowly away. *"Then begin,"* he said over one shoulder, trotting off in the other direction.

One by one the criminals were led, pleading pathetically or cursing defiantly, to a post where they would be branded with the sign of the Scorpions. Whether or not they had ever served that defunct raider gang, or even taken a life, they were now to be branded as killers for the masquerade.

Shubazang chuckled to himself and continued packing his last goods. Euryale stood, walked to his side, and placed its hands on its hips as if imitating curiosity, quietly watching the gruesome spectacle.

"That's right, Euryale," Shubazang shouted over the cries and screams, "witness an atrocity committed in the name of 'peace'!"

Uncle Sam and Boren rode over to the merchant who was busy assembling his caravan for the coming journey south. Shubazang watched from afar as the merchant bowed respectfully, no, *fearfully*, and listened as the imposing warlord instructed him to take the one-hundred prisoners with him on the journey to Tucumcari. It was an hour before every man in the train was assembled and shackled, and two hours before the caravan was even remotely ready to head out. Uncle Sam charged the merchant with keeping his slaves safe at all costs, and as he spoke, a few barbarian tribesmen brought forward two large sacks of corium pieces that they loaded directly into the merchant's treasure wagon, not even giving him a chance to decline Uncle Sam's "offer".

Eventually the caravan headed out, with Shubazang and Euryale accompanying it, and Uncle Sam watched quietly from a distance. As it vanished into the heat mirage on the horizon the large warrior-king turned to his right-hand man.

"What *have* we done?"

Days passed as the caravan sluggishly wormed its way south from the edge of Uncle Sam's territory and through the heart of the Forbidden Lands. The methodic creak and groan of old wooden wagons was matched by the repetitive lash of the slavers' whip, as the hundred-strong slave train marched relentlessly behind the merchant caravan.

One hundred men walked through the ankle-deep sand, some with barely any shoes at all, some entirely barefoot. By day they burned under the glowing sun, and by night they froze by the meager campfires set up by the merchant and his guards. They came from varied walks of life; thieves, dispossessed vagrants, men made poor by misfortune. Killers, rapists, men accused of buggery (apparently a crime in Uncle Sam's lands), youngsters sold into slavery by their families to make ends meet. A few cried the night through, others busied themselves caring for their injuries, while still more begged for food and water from passing guardsmen, who on occasion threw them a morsel with Uncle Sam's command, to keep them safe at all costs, still lingering in their minds.

A hand scrabbled for a greasy piece of meat that fell on the sand, but its desperate groping was cut short when another darted swiftly in and snatched the meat from its grasp. The hungry fool could have pursued, lunged at the man who stole it, but seeing the gray-brown eyes peering from the dark he simply whimpered, pitifully, and skulked away.

Valero stared the coward down as he crawled off into the night. Only once he was sure the wastrel was gone did he bring the meat to his mouth, sinking his sharp teeth into it and devouring it messily. Other slaves looked in his direction, but none said a word, quickly moving away to avoid attracting his attention.

Once the leader of a great gang, Valero still commanded respect and fear from those around him, even reduced as he was to one of Uncle Sam's uniformly decrepit slaves. He looked different now, having grown his hair out in an effort to blend in with the people of the north, a full head of long dark hair with a premature grayness that made it look like a tangle of steel, and a beard to match. He wore stitched fleece breeches on his legs, and simple shoes like a Berber's *amazigh* made from leather straps, its sole cut from the rubber of an old car tire.

He knew his ultimate fate would be dealt to him in the next few days, either at the end of a noose or before a firing squad, for his role in the death of a Clean diplomat years ago. But he didn't feel sorry, didn't resent what he had done. For a brief moment he had challenged the onslaught of civilization, and had tasted real freedom. He had risen to command some of the desert's most notorious raiders, and while his rule was brief, he had reveled in it. When the Clean army came and laid waste to Oasis he had fought like a maniac; only the dire wound to his leg, which bled profusely and caused him to pass out, had prevented him from fighting to the very end.

He had awoken the next day as his few loyal followers carried his injured body off into the wastes. They had fled the wrath of the Clean, and had spirited their leader into the lands of the tribal savages, where they would recuperate and figure out what to do next. For several months they waited for Valero to be able to walk again, living off the land and, eventually, the cautious generosity of their tribal hosts. Afraid of angering the dangerous, hunted men who had wandered into their midst, the tribesmen accommodated Valero and his small group of followers and allowed them to live in their small village for over a year. Valero had come to take a wife in that short time, a local woman whose rowdy personality was a perfect match for his own; something he had never expected could happen in his lifetime. A few of his men had also taken brides and settled down in the span of that one long year, and slowly he had seen their fire diminish, as they settled into new lives as husbands and herders.

Things could have been different, they could have made for themselves a new life with every day spent seeking redemption, but karma has a way of catching up to men of his ilk. Murder and rape were acts that could not be forgotten, or forgiven. Slowly, over time, word had spread that wanted men were living among the villagers in the outlands, and in time agents of the Warlord came to visit them... and smoke them out. Over the course of a year they were all uprooted, driven into the wilds and eventually taken captive, rounded up like livestock, and marched off as prisoners. Valero's fiery-tempered wife had resisted Uncle Sam's soldiers when they came, taking an axe and striking one of them down, an act that brought her to a swift finish at the end of a cavalryman's pike.

It had ended there for Valero, any attempt to change his ways. He remembered then, and would never forget, that he was a raider first, and a man and human being second. Like any wounded mortal he washed away the pain with wine and beer, and also by preying on his fellows, raising himself above the misery by keeping others down.

While he was here, squatting among slaves, he was boss again. Even among slaves he was a leader. Unlike most of those who shared his company (against their will), he was actually guilty of being a killer and raider; he wore the brand of the Scorpions unashamed on his flesh. They were afraid of him, these petty burglars and bread-snatchers, and he could use that to his advantage. They listened to him, they cowered in his presence, and they would do as he said.

If only he had the opportunity...

He stirred in the darkness as the other slaves began to nod off, the merchant retired to his wagon-tent, and most of the other house guards bedded down for the night. A few guards patrolled the perimeter, scanning the blue-black desert plains and the low hills surrounding them. A few other guards retired in two- or three-man groups by small fires, warming their hands and feet before rising to keep watch again.

Valero listened as three guards squatted by a fire not far from him, one of them producing three dice for a game of *sic bo*. These he revealed to the surprised smiles of his comrades; they were generally forbidden to take along such Asian affectations while traveling in the north. With conspiratorial smiles they sat down and began setting up for a few rounds.

Valero watched through half-closed eyes, feigning sleep, his arms crossed over his chest. Each man carried a spear with a broad iron head, while one had a musket fitted with an old, pre-Fall bayonet, its blade no longer holding any luster. They wore "armor" made from leather hides, onto which were sewn horizontal slats of wood, brightly painted. One had a large iron ring at his belt, from which dangled keys to the slaves' chains.

The men chatted and laughed quietly, but soon their conversation turned to whispered ghost stories, all for their amusement. Valero listened, but in the increasing darkness began to move, slithering slowly towards them, crouched and supine, sneaking over their way.

"... these very hills, I tell you! There is a legend among the savages that speaks of an ancient cave where 'hungry things' dwell. It's said that long ago it was the custom for freakish children to be taken from their homes and, as their grieving mothers looked on, thrown down into a deep, dark cavern hidden among the cliffs. Most died from the fall into darkness, but some hardy freaks lived. In time they grew into monstrous things, and to this day mill about at the bottom of the deep pit, awaiting their regular feeding."

"I heard that tale as well," said another, nodding his head vigorously, "It's said that the superstitious would travel for dozens of miles to find the cave and drop toys and baubles into the pit, a sacrifice intended to ensure that their own children would be born normal."

"In these hills?" one whispered, staring out towards the jagged crags to the west.

"*These very hills...*" one replied dramatically, drinking from his small cup.

As the men drank, Valero, having crawled right up behind his target, used deft fingers to slip the metal loop off the guardsman's belt, taking it quickly in hand to smother any sound of its chime-like tinkling. He rolled back into shadow, closing his eyes and breathing quietly. The men continued to talk, oblivious that he had even been there.

"Surely they must have died off by now," one countered, incredulous.

"Oh?" asked the storyteller, playfully raising an eyebrow. "What makes you so sure?"

"Because... well, what would prevent them from starving?"

"They feed off the carcasses of those children that don't survive, those that die broken on the rocks. And, over time, small animals, rabbits, rats, dogs, *anything* that mistakenly fall into the pit, providing a rare treat..." The men went quiet, and the storyteller returned to his drinking. The others looked out into the night.

"Oh, don't wet yourselves," he teased, suddenly slicing through the tension he had so expertly built up. "It's just a myth..."

Shubazang woke up the next morning to the sound of activity, and the feeling of the sun warming his flesh. Coming towards him in a hurry was the merchant caravan boss, his sweeping red cloak billowing over his shoulder as he stumbled over the sand, buffeted by the easterly wind. A few embarrassed-looking guardsmen followed close behind, careful not to trip and fall.

The merchant stared at Shubazang, who seemed to be lying still against a rock, arms folded over his chest and hands buried in his armpits. The boy-mercenary wore his reflective goggles even in his sleep, and he wasn't sure if the kid was asleep or awake.

The merchant bit his lip, not sure how Shubazang would react. But he was desperate.

"You there!" the merchant shouted. "That's right, you! You said you were a tracker, boy, is that true?"

Shubazang slowly removed his ice-cold metal hands from beneath his arm-pits, the place where he always warmed them to prevent the contact points with his muscles and tendons from freezing during the night. He wriggled his stubby mechanical fingers for a moment to make sure they still functioned correctly, then stood up and began brushing off the sand that had built up on his body overnight.

The men stopped as they came into Shubazang's small camp, set apart as it was from the rest. Euryale rose up from the blankets, extending its long arms over its head, exposing its metal nakedness as it arched its back in imitation of an exhausted stretch. Curling its long feminine legs underneath it, its hip slightly bent, it began fishing for its robe. It moved with the grace of a living woman, but its face, a poor steely impersonation, was too emotionless and still to be real. Its long hair was nothing more than a complex weave of fine, colorless, plastic strands. Cheap artificial android-hair that had lost its color long ago, bleaching the thing as pale as a ghost. Euryale turned to regard them with hooded silver eyes, and notched its head to the side as if to say "can I help you?".

"That's right," Shubazang replied to the merchant, ignoring their reaction to his hand-built companion.

"Well..." the caravan master started, turning from staring at the tinker's clockwork mistress and back to him. "It seems last night a few of the Warlord's slaves escaped. We can't strike camp until they're found. Why, the Warlord will demand *I* take their place! I need someone to track the slaves and bring them back, *immediately*. I've got other goods on this caravan and we've got to get to Trade City by week's end or there will be all sorts of complications!" Shubazang looked at him, saying nothing.

"Don't toy with me, boy! Will you do it?!" the man asked, exasperated.

Shubazang considered for a moment, then looked back at Euryale. His companion was already up, quickly tying its cloak about itself with a narrow sash, but leaving it open enough in the front to reveal the shape of its breasts. *It was beginning to develop an awareness of its body*, he thought, *and it seemed proud to exhibit it openly*.

Shubazang smirked. Euryale's developing personality wasn't at all what he had planned, even though he had programmed it from the very beginning. Its electrical brain, composed of intricate biosynthetic parts scavenged from all over the wasteland and pieced together with scattered diagrams from before the Fall, was still a mystery to him. He knew how it functioned, physically, but the psychology of this hand-made artificial intelligence had outgrown even its creator.

Though Euryale had originally started as a clean slate, over just a few short years he had poured his heart and soul into it, perhaps too much. He had originally intended to build a simple traveling companion, someone to help battle the things of the desert, but soon his very human, very mortal weaknesses overcame him and, in the dead of night, he began molding Euryale with feminine traits. In the beginning he merely sought something with which to engage in conversation, but when its voice modulator burned out and Euryale went silent, his slip into dementia started to accelerate. Too many years in the desert, too many months on the trail, with no other voice to keep him sane, the already unstable boy slipped into a quiet kind of madness. When he did come to town, to mingle among other human beings much older than he, Shubazang stopped looking to the diseased women and foul-mouthed harlots of the trade towns for his pleasure, seeing a better answer right at his side. He yearned for something soft and receptive, something that would understand him, and so he *created* it.

But something had gone wrong somewhere. He had shared too much with Euryale, put too much of his own soul into building and programming its behavior patterns, and had lewdly partaken of its lifelike parts too frequently. He had fallen for his own creation, and with its single-minded purity of purpose, Euryale had responded to his affections, in an effort to continue pleasing him, by becoming more and more sexual, deviant, and debauched to match his degenerating tastes. It was a woman, but a wicked one, a grotesque and intimately revealing reflection of just how debased the boy's true nature had become.

He turned back to the merchant, his goggles coldly reflecting the man's desperate look. "Alright, but just make sure you're still here when we get back. Understood?"

Burning Lands 183

Valero scrambled over the bare sandstone rocks, throwing a cautious glance over his shoulder every few minutes in the direction from which they had fled. Behind him were three other men; two of them were surviving Scorpions, the third a conspirator from among the innocents rounded up by Uncle Sam. The four of them moved quickly through the crags, gaining a surprising amount of elevation for so short a time.

The slave caravan was well behind them now. Up here they could only hear the buffeting wind, the sound of small rocks crumbling underfoot and their own quiet cursing as they skinned their knees, shins and hands as they climbed and crawled up the mountainside.

"Do you think they'll forget us, just move on?" the innocent asked. Valero ignored him, as if speaking one way or another would ensure they came after them.

Pretty soon Valero discovered a crude rocky trail, which seemed to ascend further into the bare stone heights. As he stepped onto the path he stood tall, taking a moment to breathe while also look back again for signs of pursuers.

There would be pursuers, he had to consider that. They might be lucky, the merchant might be in a hurry to get to Trade City, but more likely the slavers would send someone to hunt them down and bring them back. He had to figure that in his plans; and he *had*. Right now his contingency plan was simple. The other three would tie the hunter down, or serve as bait, while he would come around and strike. With the hunter dead they (he and any survivors) would have a weapon, and their chances of surviving would increase exponentially.

Once his followers stumbled onto the trail with him they continued up, breaking into a sloppy run. Valero continued to scan down the slope, then turned and joined them.

An hour later his men were slowing down. The two former raiders, loyal to him for many years, tried not to show their fatigue, but he could see it in their eyes, their heavy sweat. The other slave moaned pitifully, clutching desperately to a rock to avoid falling over. His head was spinning from the exertion and the elevation.

The sun was almost directly overhead; they had nothing to take cover under to shield from its glare.

"O-o-ver th-there," one of the panting raiders said, pointing down the stony path. They all turned and looked.

A small mound of broken boulders stood out from the rest of the rocky mountainside. A cool shadowy cave, tucked under a bulbous overhang of stone, beckoned to them.

"No good," Valero said, wiping his own sweat from his brow. "If their tracker comes up this trail we'll be bottled in."

"You've got to be kidding," gasped their slave companion, but his men stared down the trail at the cave entrance, wondering if Valero was right. Wrong or right, they dared not disobey him, but they couldn't hide their exhaustion any longer.

Seeing this, Valero looked back down the trail, then scratched his neck. "Okay, into the cave, for a while. I'll stay out here and hide among the rocks. If I see the tracker coming, I'll come and get you and we can slip out before he knows we're here."

His men nodded in agreement, even as the slave had already started running towards the cave. Valero split from the group and disappeared into the alien landscape of rough boulders and rolling crags.

Twenty minutes later Valero still waited in silence, hidden behind some rocks, listening intently. He had intended to get moving ten minutes ago, but he found he too, was tired and thirsty and he'd convinced himself to stay put just a little bit longer, at least until his muscles no longer ached. *I must be getting old*, he said to himself.

He had done this many times in the past, usually in the company of many armed warriors, waiting for heavily-laden merchant caravans to ambush. In the desert, among dunes, among canyons, or in crags just like these. He felt confident that he would hear anyone approaching and be able to get away before he was seen, so he allowed himself the luxury of a few more minutes of rest.

Suddenly there was a small flash just a few inches over his head, as a beam of laser light struck the boulder he was taking cover behind, scorching the rock face with a small white halo. Sparks sprinkled down onto his back, singing his skin, and immediately he bolted off and away.

I guess I've lost my touch, he said sarcastically to himself, dodging about before sliding through the sand to a spot underneath a boulder thirty feet from where he had just been. He listened.

The power pack around Shubazang's waist whined softly, indicating the rifle was ready for another shot.

"That oughta be warning enough," Shubazang said to Euryale, who crouched behind him.

"Listen up!" he yelled, giving his voice a moment to echo and bounce back and forth off of the maze of stones. "You must be tired. I don't want to kill you, so don't make me! This is an *M-13 Crusader*, your basic laser rifle. The Ancients used weapons like these. One hit will sever your leg cleanly. Now we can either play this game all day, you running and me trying to slice off your legs, or you can come down now and surrender!"

He strained his ears to listen, but there was no response.

"My friend and I can either drag you back, legless, or you can come down now on your own power! What's it gonna be?"

Even as the tracker shouted Valero hunkered down and broke cover, trusting that the rifleman was probably not looking out from cover while he called out.

He was wrong. Another laser blast shot past, just two feet from his knee, cleanly boring a hole into and through a TV-sized rock on the side of the path.

Valero avoided being hit, however, and kept running, head down, until he saw the cave mouth ahead. He had to get to the others and get them moving; at the very least if they started scattering it would mean more targets for the hunter to track, giving him a better chance of getting away.

He charged into the small cave, expecting to see his men crouched and cowering, but instead he saw only a sandy cave floor sharply declining to the east. Too late to stop himself he plunged into the pit, the same way his men had when they first entered the cave, falling head over heels down a deep, dark shaft into the belly of the earth.

Valero woke to a reeling sensation, and the pain of having fallen some thirty feet to the cavern below. It was utterly dark here except for a gloomy stream of vague, indistinct light from the surface cave above. After a few moments he found it was just enough to barely make out his surroundings.

The first sight to confront him was the broken body of one of his fellow escapees, and more tragically, one of the raiders he had escaped the destruction of Oasis with years ago. A faithful soldier who had evaded certain death with him, carried his body and nursed it to health, and married a tribal woman in the small village they had come to call home. He had wrecked his head upon some rocks, and now lay dead and lifeless within arm's reach, his glassy eyes peering upwards to the unattainable hole in the cavern roof.

The second thing he saw was what had saved his life; he had landed on a heap of shifting sand, its slopes bristling with rocks, and only by chance avoided breaking his neck or cracking his skull by landing in between them. He wasn't one for thanking the gods (or good fortune) and merely jumped up, taking a defensive posture, until he could be more clear of his surroundings.

Strange noises echoed in the darkness; the cave must have been rather large and irregularly shaped. The sound of crumbling bits of rock skittering off into the depths, of the tell-tale trickle of water falling off the surrounding bedrock into tepid pools somewhere in a measureless network of tunnels below.

He moved down the small mountain of sand, almost losing his footing as his feet sunk into the sifting dust, stepping over a dead tree branch, crushing a dry puff of sagebrush underfoot, until he reached the bottom. He prepared to move forward, to feel out for the contours of the cave to better understand his predicament, but he tripped on something and fell to the hard stony ground with a clatter.

Reaching out blindly, he felt something near his foot and fumbled to pick it up, to feel its shape and ascertain what it was. His hands wandered over it for a second until he had explored its entire shape, but he remained confused. *A toy truck? With crude wooden wheels?*

He released the thing, seemingly out of place here in the dark, and pulled himself up. Not realizing how badly he had injured his leg in the slip, he stumbled up against the wet cavern wall. He panted, straining to prop himself upright in a manner that wouldn't put any more undue strain on his weak appendage, and listened.

He heard a slight shuffling from somewhere to the east, someone coming steadily up a tunnel that he himself did not see. He felt defenseless, being so blind, and so simply remained still and silent, trusting in his senses to detect the danger before it was upon him.

"*Boss*..." came a familiar voice, and he immediately recognized it as the last surviving member of his gang. He wasn't alone; the other escaped slave, the bread-stealer, was also with him. Valero couldn't see either of them, but he could hear relief in his man's voice.

"Just let your eyes adjust. You should be able to see okay in here. But it's much darker down the tunnels."

"How many tunnels?" Valero asked.

"We found two. We tried to find a way out down one of them but the stone was wet and slippery and the smell was awful. It was pitch black, and seemed like it was going deeper into the ground. So we turned around and slowly crawled back here."

Valero looked back at the hole in the roof. It could be hours before the hunter that stalked them gathered the courage to explore the cave they had all disappeared into. He might fall in as they did, in which case they could grab his gun, but then again he might not, he might start tossing down grenades instead. If they wanted to get away they had to get moving.

"Which one did you try?" Valero asked, now vaguely able to make out his two disheveled followers in the deep shadows.

"That one," the ex-raider said, indicating the rough passage to the south.

"Alright, let's try the other."

Valero led the way, feeling around with his hands. His men were right; once they plunged into the passage they were swallowed up wholly by the subterranean shadows. Though unaccustomed to it, he let his hands become his eyes, and felt his way, inch by inch, along the tunnel wall. He wasn't sure but it seemed that they were going deeper, which gave rise to a nagging doubt that they might never get out.

But they had to try. He continued leading the men, stopping only every so often to make sure they were right behind him. Shuffling feet on bare stone echoed down the tunnels in all directions, which was soon overwhelmed by the increased breathing of Valero and his followers.

The passage became more rocky, signs of a recent cave-in. Even as they proceeded at a more careful pace, one of his men hit something with his foot which made a loud "clang" as it skittered away.

"Shit!" the raider cursed, and the others fell immediately silent. They had no reason to think anything lived down here, but their continued discovery of discarded things, the refuse of the cave's past victims, gave them reason to wonder...

Valero's intuition guided him to the unseen object; it was metal, after all, and might be a weapon he could use. While the others strained to listen fruitlessly at the deafening silence, he grasped it and scrutinized it with his fingertips. He announced his find the moment he recognized what it was.

"A lantern."

He shook it gently, and felt the sway of oil in its small reservoir. "Quick, feel around to see if you can find a match!"

Invigorated by hope the other two immediately dropped to the tunnel floor and felt around. Their hands darted between jagged stones, lifted smaller rocks, and combed through the gravelly residue left by the recent cave-in.

Maybe this was some kind of *mine*, Valero thought.

"Found something!" said the slave. Valero reached out to grasp his shoulder; he took the object from the slave and felt, in his hand, a small tattered matchbox. For a few minutes Valero struggled, striking one match after another. Dull, short-lived flares lit the darkness, but none lasted long enough to allow them to see for more than a moment.

"Fuck!" he cursed quietly. The other men waited breathlessly, gathered around their leader, praying at least one would catch.

Suddenly the darkness was burned away by a flickering light; Valero held a single lit match in his strong hand. He quickly moved it beneath the dusty glass of the lantern, igniting the kerosene inside.

A dim but welcome orange light was cast by the old rusted lantern, illuminating a very sweaty and dirty Valero, and the wide-eyed, dirt-covered faces of the two other escaped slaves.

Valero looked deeper down the tunnel. For some reason he felt his sense of smell sharpen now that there was light to see by, and a ghoulish odor drifted his way. He recoiled momentarily, but stood firm while the others gagged and spat up.

"Dead animals," he explained softly, "probably trapped in here when they fell down the shaft. Let's keep moving." After a time they came to a branch. The other two squatted, silent, waiting for Valero to pick a path. He looked over the two tunnels, and picked the one that seemed to move away from the awful odor.

They continued down this low passage until it began to slowly taper, forcing them to crouch. At one point the lantern flame flickered and sputtered, eliciting fearful glances from the others, but Valero pressed on.

Eventually they came to a dead end, a rough nub that bluntly put an end to any further exploration. Valero's raider comrade rubbed his eyes in fatigue and began to turn back, but Valero held up a hand that made him stop. He knelt down, reaching into a pile of loose dirt and retrieving what proved to be a badly-rusted shovel, its spade pitted and partly dented as if someone had whaled it wildly against hard rock.

"Someone tried digging here..." Valero guessed aloud. He brought the lantern closer to the end of the passage. All three men gaped.

There on the wall were frantic markings left by some desperate soul, four vertical marks left as a result of frantic digging with a human hand. *Had some poor digger given up on his shovel in a vain attempt to burrow free with his bare hands?*

But what Valero's lantern revealed, embedded in two of the vertical scratches, caused a sudden panic. There, stuck in the rock face, were two entire human fingernails, caked in earth and dried blood. This man hadn't been digging, he had been trying to hold on for dear life while something pulled and yanked at him, eventually wrenching him free and dragging him off with such force that it left his fingernails in place.

It was then that they realized they were not *alone*.

"Get a hold of yourselves," Valero snapped. He had no patience for cowards. Their innocent companion was gasping and babbling incoherently, as if all of a sudden he had developed claustrophobia and all of the mountain weighed down on him with unbearable pressure. He had to get out. He had to flee. There had to be a way out.

To Valero he was useless. The ex-raider, on the other hand, was quick to follow Valero's command, only momentarily burying his head in his dirty, black hands in an effort to regain his composure. When he looked up his eyes were still wide with terror, but they locked onto Valero with the desperate hope that he would somehow get them out.

Valero snarled. "What are we afraid of? We've got a weapon." He held the dented shovel in hand. He didn't seem afraid.

Valero led the way, retracing their steps back to the intersection. Only now he proceeded more carefully, aware that every footstep might bring the attention of whatever creature, or *creatures*, lived down here. A few paces past the intersection he almost stepped on an old rubber beach ball, and what looked like a primitive baby rattle lying next to it. These strange bits of garbage were both covered in a fine layer of dust and dirt. But with only a moment's hesitation he nudged the ball out of the way and kept going.

He looked left and right; deeper into the subterranean dark, or back to the cave entrance? He sneered at the idea of going back; the hunter might be there, and he was never going back to being a slave, not without a fight at least.

"This way!" Valero commanded, and started down the steep slope eastwards. The others gagged as the stench of rotten meat grew more pervasive, but they wouldn't let Valero out of their sights and followed swiftly after him.

Rocks skittered past as they built momentum. Valero felt his balance slipping, so he passed the lantern back to his raider comrade, leaving one hand free to brace himself against the curved tunnel wall. But he kept the shovel in hand. The raider seemed comforted by the lantern; in an emergency he could swing it like a bludgeon, after all. The slave trailed a little further back, the expression on his face clearly revealing his doubtfulness about going deeper.

"Let's go back," the slave blurted, his voice echoing off of the hard rock and down the tunnel in both directions. "I - I don't want to go any further. I'd rather be a slave than die down here."

"When you get to Trade City they're going to kill you anyway," Valero's ex-raider companion reminded him.

It wasn't necessarily true, Valero realized; sure Margus Han would execute the weak slaves to make a public spectacle and get the blood his sense of justice demanded, but he would probably sell the stronger ones to the corium miners of Little Vegas, to make some money out of the whole affair. But he didn't say anything.

Their short conversation ended when the tunnel leveled out and Valero entered what appeared to be a small natural cavern, its floor covered in moist sand. Valero grew momentarily cautious as they entered the place, at least until his raider comrade brought enough light to bear on the room, until he felt he perceived all of its niches and hiding places.

Flies swarmed in the air, but there was no other movement. Valero stepped forward, allowing the others to enter. The ceiling was low, and stony slivers of rock, angled sharply downwards, made them feel like they were walking into the very maw of the mountain.

It seemed like another dead end. Though they clustered together for a few minutes, eventually Valero moved forward and began examining the room. Moments later the ex-raider followed, walking along the walls with his lantern held high to make sure no small passage remained concealed by shadows.

Valero swatted at the cloud of swirling flies but shied from the center of the room where they swarmed around the bones of some desert beast. He recognized the partly-devoured skull of a panther, wormy and rotten; as he had guessed, the unfortunate thing had probably taken cover in the cave above and fallen into the chute, to be trapped down here. He could only guess, but he assumed it had perished either of starvation or from injuries suffered from the vertical drop to the floor of the entrance cave. Not much of it remained.

"Something over here," the light-equipped raider muttered. Valero turned from the carcass and moved to the other man's side, where he crouched against the cavern wall.

Close to the ground, perhaps where a child could reach, the wall was gaily decorated with crude figures drawn by clumsy hands. These images depicted strange legless creatures, hopping along on their hands. Each seemed to have an oversized head painted with a large, happy smile, somewhat reminiscent of the kind of crayon art one might see on a kindergarten wall.

But what these figures were doing in the pictures made the men recoil. The happy little demons were cornering a human-shaped stick figure, and in another picture, tearing it limb from limb and devouring the pieces - arms, legs, and head.

"We need to get out of here," Valero said with an unexpected urgency that rattled the others.

As he turned to start out of the cave there was a chilling sound like the moving of sand and the clacking of claws. The raider by the wall spun around and aimed his lantern towards the center of the room, just in time to see the carcass of the panther pushed aside by something burrowing up from *underneath* it. The cloud of flies dispersed instantly as a creature pulled itself from the sandy cavern floor, a grotesque abomination that made the raider scream and drop his light source.

The thing resembled a human child, but only so far. It had the grossly underdeveloped body of an infant, but overgrown to colossal size, while still lacking any legs whatsoever. Instead all sorts of wet and twisted viscera trailed back behind it, including a rotting umbilical several yards long that dragged limply in its wake.

Its arms had grown strong and each hand, tipped by grossly-fused digits, ended with sharp, broken claws caked with gore and embedded with minute fragments of human and animal bone.

Its head was most monstrous of all, a massively deformed skull that would be proportionate only on a fetus, a *hydroencephalic* mass that loomed atop a thin, precarious neck. And like a fetus its features were fused and undefined; its "eyes" were deep red globs that trailed off with spidery veins, its nose non-existent, its mouth a gaping, gasping apparatus more suited for a fish. But behind its wriggling, sucking, hungry lips was a bear-trap of jagged and nonsensical tooth-like fragments, which gnashed and chomped at the air in front of it.

The innocent slave that had followed them here tried to scream, but the thing snatched him up in its terrible arm and drew him close, almost like a child grabbing for a toy. Instead it gripped his skull and yanked his head back until his spine broke and his neck tore open, spraying blood in a geyser all over the other two, until finally his head came completely off and fell among the shadows.

Pleased by its kill, the creature lifted its heavy head and wailed in victory. But the sound that rattled and chortled free from its blasphemous head sounded nothing like a monstrous roar, but rather the shrill cry of an anguished human *infant*.

How could you defeat something that Nature herself couldn't kill? Such things were once human, deformed babies born to mutant mothers, flushed from the corrupted womb and tossed into the desert (or in a deep, dark pit) like garbage. Too badly mutated to live among men, they were forsaken things, stunted mentally and physically and more often than not psychotic and cannibalistic. Most were murdered at birth to prevent their stain from living on, but some people, too weak to do what needed to be done, gave them up to the wilderness to give them a chance at life. Such misplaced mercy was always a mistake, Valero knew, and the good intentions of others had just cost an innocent man his life.

The thing dragged itself from its hiding place, the concealed entrance to another near-vertical shaft slipping away to even deeper caverns of the complex, and rolled wetly over the decapitated slave towards the raider with the lantern, that bright lamp that burned its vaguely translucent skin with its light. The frozen raider screamed as the iron-hard nails ripped through his chest and stomach, gutting him in one quick swipe and toppling him over in a twitching heap.

Valero turned and ran, dispensing with any pretense of battling this thing. As he broke away from the slaughter, he heard the thing wail out again, but this time it was joined by many more, these more distant, sounding like a great cry from Hell's nursery, issuing up from the undiscovered passages and lightless caverns that wormed through the rock just below his feet.

Euryale lifted a hand to get Shubazang's attention as its audio sensors detected a slight sound. The android was perched at the edge of the dark hole leading underground, feeding a rope into the pitch black abyss like a sailor taking a sounding of the ocean depths. Shubazang moved over, laser rifle at the ready, aiming into the pit.

They heard someone coming, *racing*. Euryale brought up a flashlight and snapped it on, aiming the beam downwards.

Clambering up the sandy mound directly below them, thirty feet down the shaft, they saw one of the escaped slaves. As he began to lose his footing on the sandy slope, he cast aside his rusty shovel and began climbing with his hands. He apparently saw the light, because he reached out for it and shouted up the shaft.

"Get me out of here! Hurry up! There's something down here with me! Get me out!"

Valero looked up and saw the shadowed face of a 'woman' looking down at him. To him the strange-looking Euryale seemed to have a completely relaxed look on her face, as if totally at peace with watching him die at the hands of the things that lived below.

"Get me *out!*" he shouted one last time, not realizing the 'woman' he was speaking to actually had no concept of mercy or compassion, no conscience to worry it at night over letting another human being die. This thing had no nightmares, it had no tears. It *was* curious, watching him plead for his life, but only momentarily fascinated by his frantic body language and the panic in his voice, with an expression that suggested it might grow bored any moment now and, just to see him squirm, slowly pull the rope back up, inch by inch. It was as if a third-grader was staring down at him, he the bug slowly writhing beneath a magnifying lens in some sadistic classroom experiment.

Shubazang let Euryale play for a moment, then motioned for the android to begin feeding the rope into the shaft. At that Euryale immediately released its grip and the rope fell well within Valero's grasp. Without a moment to lose he started up it, holding his breath for the moment he emerged into the murky light of the upper caves.

As Valero neared the top, Euryale yanked him up and into the cave, tossing him aside like a toy before coiling the rope back up. He gasped and wheezed, stunned by being thrown so casually, but also relieved to have escaped the horrible things that lived in the cave of lost children.

Valero opened his eyes to see a boy crouched over him, putting the barrel of the laser rifle right under his chin.

"Just a kid?!" Valero sneered.

"A kid with a *gun*," Shubazang replied. "Now, I take it by the blood on your pants that the other slaves were eaten by whatever lives down this hole? That's fine. But you're coming back with us, *zhidao?*"

Shubazang, Euryale, and the remaining prisoners continued on south in the company of the worried trader and his men, until, two days out from Trade City, they joined up with a vast Clean caravan heading towards their shared destination. Huge and sprawling, it was a welcome sight.

The Clean caravan was a fleet of wooden and wicker wagons, vehicles made from reeds like old Egyptian barques preserved on the crumbling remains of papyrus scrolls. They were pulled by the seamless, cooperative efforts of animals and shackled slaves, flanked on both sides by columns of ordered, white-clad janissaries. Each wagon was an ornate work of art, crafted by skilled artisans to celebrate the greatness of their most prestigious of trade houses. Hulking, weighty things mounted on huge rolling wheels, their precious goods were concealed beneath pristine white canvas drawn tight over a domed frame of wooden ribs, resembling giant bony beasts creeping slowly across the desert.

At long last, Trade City... It glowed like a city of jacinth walls and towers as the sun began to settle in among the mountaintops to the west. Great herds migrated towards the city in a steady stream, long lines of men seeking shelter for the night, traders weary of the long trail, and livestock driven by herdsmen from the surrounding wasteland.

After parting company with the merchant caravan at the gates, Shubazang and Euryale had collected their meager pay and were swallowed up by the commotion in the city markets. As they walked through the crowds of traders and peddlers, they passed colorful stalls and shops, locals selling fresh barbecued food and rare fruits, the pavilions of foreign merchants selling refurbished junk found among the dunes of the desert. They passed a rail-thin man selling smoky sticks of odorous meat simmering on skewers, another with bad rosacea on his arms and face selling large vegetables harvested from among the tribal communities of the Wei Shan. They walked along through the covered stalls of vendors selling trinkets and other luxurious things; a woolen blanket on which weird wares were exhibited, such as a fine collection of over one thousand pre-Fall rings, including simple wedding bands, restored engagement rings, plastic rings, decoder rings, plastic-wrapped ring suckers, and even things that only barely passed as "rings" - circular beer can tabs, hoop earrings, the hollow copper coin of some long-forgotten Asian nation. All of them considered lucky, since they once brought happiness to the Ancients, and thus (if the gods were willing) might still bring good things to their buyers.

Another merchant displayed a menagerie of odd and oily car parts, some unrecognizable by the amount of grime built-up on their rusted surfaces, others in admirable condition. Suspension springs, fuel injectors, spark plugs, a radiator, a tire iron; an engine hand-crank from the first decade of the 20th century, side by side with a hover car's VTOL gyroscope, the latter in bad condition.

Raider-types clustered here, their interest in such things obvious, edging out all but the most stubborn parties from the bartering going on. Shubazang simply stole a look, but seeing nothing that really interested him, moved on.

They passed the set-up of an unusually enterprising peddler, a "scavenger" of another sort entirely, a crusted and diseased looking man in the advanced stages of what they called "Methuselah syndrome", his face shriveled and his downy white hair falling out in handfuls. He called out "*Ni ke ma!*" to draw their attention, a suggestive call that would cause all but the most wealthy traveler to at least take a look.

The man offered the use of his "miracle machine", a complex contraption of brass bowls, steel tubes, rubber hoses, and plastic whirligigs spinning and sucking and draining with obscene, life-like noises. Shubazang smirked in disbelief, so the man offered to show its efficacy, pulling down his pants and urinating in the funnel at one end. As they watched (Euryale with an especially steel-gutted curiosity) the urine was passed through filters both physical and chemical, strained and sponged, until all that came out in the beaker at the end was pure, potable water.

Euryale seemed intrigued but Shubazang silently waved his hand in disinterest and just moved on. But it was an act to cover his bitterness; in fact he had thought it a remarkable little invention. He was secretly cursing Nature itself, a failed mother who produced faulty children like the man, whose genius would die with him in a relatively short span of time, and himself, whose own encyclopedia of ideas would likewise pass into oblivion when his body failed him and he died well before his time. His particular curse was seemingly minor, almost invisible, only exhibited by the yellow tinge to the whites of his eyes. An imbalance in bilirubin but like any other deviation from the human norm, it was a problem that would almost certainly result in an early death.

While he wandered away from the fellow tinker, just like Euryale he could not hide his fascination with the other sights and sounds of the city, an eye-opening change from the dry open desert and the endless monotony of dunes and mesas, brightened up only by the odd appearance of a dry riverbed or the cornerstone of some ancient building that hadn't yet crumbled into dust. This city was filled with all manner of things that interested him, from the markets and their assorted junk wares to the very people themselves, a mulatto mix of the races whose ancestors once fought over this land. He felt at once both assured and isolated here; he felt embraced by the civilization espoused here (in contrast to the wild ways of the tribesmen who lived in the trackless miles outside the city's walls), but he also felt alone, a young man who would never fit in among the mundane: the merchants, beggars and domestic inhabitants of Tucumcari.

He would spend his corium here quickly, on things he wanted and needed, spare parts and supplies, things to tinker with, anything that caught his "gearhead" fancy. But he would then move on and return to the desert beyond the walls, regardless of whether or not he stayed in the employ of the mandarin of the Clean and continued to do their dirty work.

Shubazang reclined, cross-legged, on a soft cushion on the floor of mandarin Margus Han's audience chamber as the last beams of daylight poured into the hall. He felt distinctly out of place here, this young man who was part metal and who had spent most of his life toying with or trying to revive the technology of the past. He had been forced to forsake almost all of his valuable equipment upon entering the palace of Tucumcari, including his laser rifle and "toys", as these were of course considered distasteful by his Clean patrons. Euryale wasn't here; he hadn't bothered to bring the 'droid with him, knowing full well how they would react to such a "machine-abomination" being present in their sanctum.

He was confident Euryale could handle itself and so tried to relax somewhat, waiting to receive his new instructions from whatever go-between the Clean mandarin would send. Ironically, merchants (and especially the leaders of the Clean) seldom liked to "dirty" themselves with talk of death, even when they were hiring its dispenser, and frequently sent lackeys to discuss it for them.

Thus he waited, uncomfortably naked without his shiny, jingling, clockwork things, awaiting the arrival of some forgettable Clean agent to fill him in on the details of his new mission.

He was quite taken by surprise when the grand doors opened and in stepped Alin Han, his face austere and serious. Behind him came Margus Han himself, his regal countenance showing slight traces of the ignoble injury recently inflicted on his pride. He looked angry as he went, his robes flowing behind him, as he walked past the reclining adventurer and took a seat on a broad wooden couch on a small stone dais at the room's far end. A few guards trailed behind, but they remained discreet, standing nearby but out of sight.

Margus looked at Shubazang and seemed surprised. "You... are Shubazang?"

Shubazang grit his teeth, but nodded. "Yes, master Han."

Despite his politeness Margus didn't seem to believe him, and was forced to look over at his chamberlain, who confirmed with a nod. Margus looked back at Shubazang's face, then down to his metal hands, the one thing of metal on him they couldn't take. His eyes lingered only for a moment, his frown of disapproval quickly replaced by a forced smile.

Margus opened his arms momentarily to gesture his customary welcome. "I hope my money has been spent well? I trust things are going along speedily in the north?"

Shubazang saw an opportunity. "Actually no, master Margus, the leads are *very* few and far between. My comrade and I spent several *weeks* tracking down rumors and stories of 'phantom raiders', with little to show for it. Only when we tracked a Ravager scouting party to the ruins of an old city in the northwest did we get even the briefest hint of progress."

He let his statement hang there, expecting the mandarin to show interest, but Margus seemed preoccupied. Out of politeness he raised an eyebrow and listened, but to Shubazang's chagrin he could tell the merchant-lord wasn't going to be as concerned as he should by his tale.

"It seems the Ravagers encountered *something* out there, along the edge of the Burning Desert, and have themselves begun to retreat, pulling their war parties from the Forbidden Lands completely. A raider 'exodus' of a sort. They were looting everything they could find, food, water, ammunition, weapons, and were headed back into the western mountains to wait out the storm."

"I see," Margus said vaguely. A few days ago he would have been extremely interested in Shubazang's testimony, but Rider's attempt on his life had apparently shifted Margus' priorities, closing his mind to anything but *revenge*.

Frustrated by the mandarin's disinterest, Shubazang wondered if he should mention what he had seen in the village of Uncle Sam (the forced branding of innocent men to pass them off as raider captives) but then decided it was none of his affair. And it would serve the mandarin right for being so obtuse!

"Well, we shall have to put some more men on that right away," Margus said dismissively, finding his own opportunity as Shubazang fell silent. "But you, Shubazang, your reputation precedes you and your expert services are required elsewhere. At least for the time being."

What could be more important than keeping the peace when war with the savages seemed so imminent?

"As I am sure you have been told," he continued, "a recent attempt was made on my life by an assassin, who during the course of his infiltration of this palace abducted my charge, a youngster, Gale Han. The assassin had numerous accomplices whom he either bribed or enticed into aiding his flight, including some of my own household staff..."

Margus' eyes narrowed as he said this; he was deeply injured by the betrayal by Kseniya and the other slaves he had treated so well, and who now languished in some dark dungeon in the city, ready to be executed for their role in murdering the armory master and his guards. Margus shook those thoughts from his mind and returned to filling Shubazang in about that alarming night.

"The assassin managed to take a horse and escaped into the night. Before word could reach the outer gates of what had occurred, he and his hostage had slipped out into the desert. That night I sent men into the surrounding wilderness to track them, and by dawn assembled a large hunting expedition, but none of them have availed to bring back anything other than a belief that they headed *east*.

"You, Shubazang, have served me in the past, and according to your handlers, you've *never failed*." He wagged his finger as if to illustrate his point. "It was you who dealt decisively with the Steel Blades at the ruins of Salida, tracked and rooted out the Gang of Six living in the mountains west of Trinidad and brought an end to their pillaging. You've fought the Ravagers and Wastelords on three separate occasions in defense of Clean caravans, and delivered from danger all our agents to whom you've been assigned as protector. But now I ask you to work not simply for the good of the Clan, but for me and my household *personally*."

The boy blinked and crouched slightly forward, listening.

"The would-be assassin is a man they call 'Rider'. A one-time wasteland wanderer of no significance other than the hunting of a few bounties for the fledgling communities of the Forbidden Lands, making his living off of whatever coin or water he could get for his cold-blooded killings."

"The albino? *That* Rider?" Shubazang asked. He'd heard of the name before, though he'd never met the man, a skilled marksman who had vanished a few years ago. He'd assumed he was dead.

"A *useless* albino. A pathetic wretch. This same man spurned my generosity once before; guilty of associating with a band of killers who murdered a Clean emissary traveling under the flag of truce, I granted him clemency by staying his execution, instead giving him a life of servitude for his crime. But he somehow escaped, and I imagine came here to avenge some perceived 'injustice'.

Burning Lands

"I don't care why or how he came to infiltrate this palace, but what he took was precious to me and invaluable to the Clans. Gale is possessed with gifts... rare gifts *of the mind* only periodically seen among those born outside the Brotherhood. She must be protected and brought back to me. That is imperative, do you understand?"

Shubazang nodded cautiously. Bringing someone back alive wasn't his usual line of work. He imagined hunting and trapping someone with psychic gifts would be even more difficult.

"The typical indulgence of corium will be offered by the Clan for this task, plus I will add my own reward, a small fortune, if you succeed swiftly."

"Can we *then* return to looking into the vanishings up north? I really hate to leave a job undone," Shubazang said, only half-joking.

Margus smiled thinly. "Yes, of course, my boy. But for now..."

"*Ting dong le*, master Han," Shubazang said almost impatiently, "I'll take the job."

Shubazang waited impatiently outside. During the meeting Euryale had vanished and now none of the guards who were with the android knew where the silent construct had gone. In the meantime Shubazang had arranged for transportation and supplies from the palace quartermaster, but without his companion he suddenly felt alone and, remarkably, insufficiently prepared for their latest adventure.

Waiting in the vestibule, checking the slowly-ticking fob watch dangling from his pocket, he was surprised when some of the guards gasped and turned, motioning towards the individual that now entered the room with them. Shubazang turned and for a moment didn't recognize his own creation, clad as it was in such entirely different attire.

Catching its master's eye, the android struck a seductive pose, hand poised on one angled hip, the other resting on the hilt of its sword. Euryale's flesh-and-blood legs were now clad in black five-inch heeled platform boots, with shiny, buckled straps and a row of spikes down the tongue. The perfectly-sculpted legs were otherwise bare, as was the android's entire body except for a black leather jacket that hovered just above its bare bottom. The creature wore what appeared to be a perverse fetish harness underneath, kept together only by straps and large silver rings, serving as little more than a frame to display its sleek metal body. But for the jacket, it revealed its nakedness openly, brazenly exhibiting it was no living creature, but a mangled creation of steel and silicon. The metal rods and knobs and motors that linked each of its limbs to its slim and slender body robbed it of any appeal to all but its creator.

Nonetheless Shubazang looked it over from head to toe, admiring its intriguing choice of clothing and the new hairstyle it had picked for itself, its off-white hair cut in severe straight lines like a Bettie Page pinup. Euryale notched its head to the side as he did so, as if the robotic thing could "feel" not only his eyes wandering its vaguely feminine shape, but also sense the obsessive love that its creator felt for it.

"A... a... *machine* of some sort?" one of the other men blurted out, breaking the silence. The others began circling the android, guns held firmly in hand.

"Parts of it flesh... the rest *metal? Ke pa!*" The others seemed just as offended by its presence, but Euryale simply stood there smiling as if mistaking their curiosity (and disgust) for adoration.

One of the guards turned to Shubazang, staring at the boy in the way a pitying orderly might look into the eyes of an asylum patient. "Kid... you *built* this... *thing?*"

"Does the mandarin know he hires a lunatic?" another asked his fellows.

Oblivious, Shubazang shouldered his laser rifle and walked past Euryale. Of course they didn't understand. No one did. That's why they were better off alone, out there, just the two of them. As he walked away, he called back to Euryale over his shoulder.

"Come on. We have work to do."

Elsewhere in the city came the sound of quiet mourning, the whispered grieving of hopeless men waiting for almost certain death. Hundreds of criminals languished in the dark, sweltering confines of the city's primitive prison, a featureless and functional structure of gray stone that, purely coincidentally, resembled an African slave fortress of the colonial era. Already overcrowded with countless malnourished miscreants (men who had committed some crime or otherwise run afoul of the Clean and Cartel) the prison was a dilapidated monstrosity that seemed on the verge of collapsing. Menacing guards walked the corridors, the bare stone hallways echoing with pitiful sounds of pain and futile cries for mercy. Cells with thirty, forty, fifty or more prisoners at a time looked like crab pots crammed with a human catch, their arms extended through the bars not to beg for release, but because there was simply no other room.

Into one dark dungeon a full ninety-eight men were marched, the lucky waiting for the brand of the slavemaster, and the rest preparing for a swift public execution. Some were consigned to their fates, exhausted from the long march that brought them to the city, but some still wondered how their deaths could possibly be for the benefit of the wasteland, for the good of all. They were to be "an example for all others to see"... but the hollow nobility their Clean captors assigned to their deaths held no appeal at this hour.

Valero, edged in on all sides by other prisoners, looked up as it came to be his turn to enter the cell. He looked at the iron gate for a moment, sensing a yawning abyss, then wordlessly stepped in, joining the huge crowd that was already filling the place. Existing occupants of the cell shoved violently to hold onto what space they had been accustomed to, but at long last they were overcome by the surge of new bodies until their protests were lost among the lamentation.

With a natural aura of command, Valero pushed through the throng until he came to one of the clammy brick walls, its white paint peeling and its cracks interlaced with spots of moist, odorous algae. Rusty stains streaked the walls near the anchoring points of the single barred grate covering the only window into the cell. A few men followed behind him, silently yearning for leadership, but Valero remained silent so they simply lingered just out of sight.

As he stood, adjusting to his new surroundings, Valero noticed next to him several unusual captives congregating together at the edges of the thin stream of moonlight coming through the barred window. Here, so far from the cell door, only a few slaves now sat, mostly the weakest or the sickest of the pack. After all, when their captors came to feed them and tossed their muck and gruel through the cage doors, there wouldn't be much to go around. Thus most of the slaves crowded there, at the front of the their cage, waiting for the inevitable battle that would ensue when the Clean guards eventually made their circuit through the dungeon corridors.

The cloistered captives were only partly visible in this light, but he immediately recognized the willowy figures of *women*. He had to take a step closer to be sure, and when he did two of the women turned to confront him with silent stares. They had no weapons, but seemed unusually prepared to fight him, bare-handed if need be.

The other women remained seated, whispering to each other, but these two looked ready to defend whatever secret the others were discussing.

Sensing trouble Kseniya cut her instructions to the others short and looked over at the broad-shouldered ex-raider who now stood within earshot. The other women, those former household servants who had gone along with Kseniya's attempt at escape, glanced over as well, but were distracted by the soft moans of one of their own, and returned to tend to her.

"Leave us be," Kseniya said quietly to the stranger, "we have no water or food. And there are enough corners for everyone to brood in."

Valero just stared for a moment, then leaned over Kseniya and with one hand tested the iron bars of the window. He seemed satisfied that it was beyond his capabilities to remove, then moved on and found a place nearby where he could put his back to the wall and wait.

Two met squatted in the shadows near Valero, their eyes following his to the women. One of them spoke:

"They were the mandarin's servants," he explained. "The dark-haired one, she was his own mistress. They betrayed his highness, sought to loot the palace armory and escape into the desert. They're guilty of murdering guards of the merchant house."

Valero listened but didn't acknowledge the man. Instead he looked back at the woman, Kseniya, and her fellow menials. Apparently they were as condemned as he was.

Hours passed, and most of the prisoners slowly fell asleep, until the entire cell floor was covered in a carpet of sleeping men, their bodies intertwined and burying one another. A few whimpers arose here and there as some prisoner struggled in a fitful dream; distant snoring echoed from another cell down the pitch black corridor outside.

Valero watched from the shadows as Kseniya fought to save the life of one of the young menials, whom he presumed had been taken by the guards the night before and used for "sport". Even hours later the young servant was still in shock, pale, and looked on the verge of fading away. Kseniya stayed at her side throughout the entire night, held the girl's hand and comforted her, but ultimately it wasn't enough to keep her alive.

Around midnight the serving girl passed away. Kseniya closed her eyes, while the other menials wept quietly or merely sobbed.

As he got to his knees Valero was reminded of how tired he was, and how little food he had consumed since they had left the tribal lands of the north. He slowly came over.

Kseniya sensed movement and turned, seeing the large ex-raider lingering in the darkness. She muttered something to her sister menials and they all readied for a fight.

"Stay away..." Kseniya warned, but Valero lifted up one large hand and held it, palm-first, to show he meant no harm. The rest of his arm was covered with tattoos and a large brand sat on his shoulder.

Now recognizing the significance of Valero's brand, marking him as a raider and killer, she sneered. "Get out of here, scum!"

"Woman," he insisted, ignoring her disgust, "What would you do to get out of here?"

Kseniya and the others looked at Valero as he, and a few simpering men drawn to him by his boldness, emerged like shadows out of the darkness. His eyes were dangerous and he looked almost feral with his injuries, bruises, and fighter's frame, poised for action. The men behind him looked like a pack of rats, just waiting for the charismatic man to give the command to surge forward.

He spoke of escape, this large man, but he was as impotent as she was here in this dungeon.

"I'd give anything," she said with daring.

Valero smiled, and for a moment she felt disgusted, but the gleam in his eyes looked right past her body and into her eyes. If he could in fact deliver them from this hell-hole, it was clear he wanted something besides her company in return.

"I don't know what you thought you could achieve by betraying the city's mandarin, and I don't care, but working together we can escape," he said. "All of us."

Other prisoners were beginning to wake, but immediately there was a contagious realization of what was going on, that an escape attempt was beginning to take shape. Dirty faces looked their way; gangly bodies and sickly survivors scrambled over towards the window. Valero's "followers" grew into a shuffling, murmuring, whispering crowd.

"No!" Kseniya said. "Go away! Go back to sleep!" She spoke to the others as much as to Valero, hoping to dispel the miserable army of prisoners that was beginning to gather.

Valero ignored her and moved to the window, grasping the metal bars as if appraising them again. "These bars are solid, but I have strength enough to break them."

He turned back to her. "You had a plan, didn't you? You wouldn't have betrayed the mandarin and raided the armory if you hadn't had a place in mind to go to. Now where is it?"

Kseniya said nothing. It should have been a warning, but Valero was desperate, and he kept going:

"You know this city... can you lead us to safety?"

Kseniya looked dubious that he could perform a feat such as bending solid iron bars. But she found herself humoring him. "There are trucks, in the Cartel caravanserai. At this hour they would be unattended. We could get away..."

The other menials gathered around their mistress.

"We could get away and take you somewhere safe," Kseniya said, offering a promise.

Valero wrapped his hands around the formidable bars and continued. "What are the guns for, eh?"

Kseniya had no need to tell him, but she found herself talking. "To arm our friends in the wilderness," she said. "To bring battle to those who would hunt us!"

"Battle, eh? You? A bunch of *women*? Who are you going to fight?"

"The Clean, of course," she whispered testily. "And the Cartel."

"The Clean?" he inquired slyly. "Tell me you've got a better plan than just stealing guns and running amok in the desert!" He knew she did; he was trying to tease it out of her.

"I'll say nothing more to *you*," she said angrily, "And we *don't* need your help, scum. We're *ready* to die!"

He hadn't planned any of this, but as a lifelong opportunist he could sense now was his chance. It was time to make his move, and he played on the current desperation of everyone present. He had a captive audience...

"Listen, sister," he said with a patronizing grin, "you want to fight a *war?* How about you do it with some *men* on your side, eh?" He looked over his shoulder as he spoke, and the gathering multitudes of slaves, killers, and thieves began to understand what he was saying. Some smiled, some simply nodded, others rose defiantly to their feet, a spark of hope and ferocity in their eyes. Ninety-eight sets of wide eyes gleamed with the thin slivers of moonlight that reached through the window into the great oubliette.

"Right now you'd be better off out *there*, then in *here,* suicidal gallantry be damned. Look, we can work together. I can get us out of here, but these slaves and I've got nowhere to go. You say you've got friends in the wilderness? Then take us there! We'll join you... and we'll even fight for your cause. Against the Clean? We wouldn't even ask for pay! What do you say, sister?"

The women looked at one another, eyes wide. Apparently the man didn't quite understand, but before any of the menials could say anything, Kseniya held up a hand for silence. She looked back at Valero, this man who had somehow brought the entire gathering of slaves together and now offered her a tantalizing (if dubious) offer. She whispered again:

"You think we can escape with over a *hundred* slaves? We'd be caught for sure!"

"Not with me leading them," Valero insinuated. The slaves looked to him and back to her, and many nodded.

"You can lead these men?" she asked skeptically.

"I can," he affirmed, "and I *will*. Just give us freedom and the arms to fight, and we will bring the Han dynasty crashing down to its knees!"

His well-chosen words enflamed the spirits of the doomed prisoners, who now looked not only hopeful, but eager. He sensed the shift, visible even in the faces of the guarded women, and lunged ahead. He would have to be creative, deceptive, play to their hopes and passions. *Oh, it would be easy.*

"The mandarin will fall! And the people of this city will be free! We'll tear off the shackles and break the chains, make them pay for all they've done, make them taste the wrath of the downtrodden, and in the smoking aftermath we'll rebuild something new!"

Her good sense warned her that this was foolish; she had no reason to trust this total stranger (let alone one who wore the mark of a raider), but Valero's dark charisma was infectious and she found herself believing he could very well do what he was now promising. Bring the house of the Clean to its knees? Slay the mandarin? Free the people? Rebuild something new?

She couldn't speak for those who lived in the wilderness, but she was swept away by the idea of it. She agreed at that moment to take Valero to them, petition them for protection and shelter, and then see how they felt about such a dizzying plan.

Valero smiled evilly; though she said nothing, to preserve her pride, the leader of the women had clearly been swayed by his bravado.

Assuming victory in the war of words, he turned to the bars. "Concentrate!" he said to himself, as he seized the bars and began to struggle. In that moment his face twisted into a veiny mask of pure exertion, sweat beading on his forehead and gathering at his temples. Eyes closed tight, he concentrated and summoned every last ounce of physical strength in his body, reluctantly tapping a hidden reservoir deep within himself. It was his invisible edge over the many dangers of this world, the one useful legacy that his mutant forebears had given him through generations of freakish births and short lives. With an exhausted, violent gasp, he triggered a flood of hyper-developed androgens from his oversized adrenal glands, and in an instant his was a body possessed. Muscles visibly rippled, purple-blue veins bulged from his swarthy skin, and moments later the bars bent, tore from their stony frame, and the entire barred window came free and dropped quietly to the floor.

Valero seemed staggered by the phenomenal exertion, but the entire gathering was astonished by the amazing feat of strength he had just performed.

Whether impressed or not Kseniya wouldn't show, as she immediately began motioning for her female followers to begin escaping through the narrow window. As Valero leaned against the wall, fighting to stay calm and slow his dangerously-racing heart rate, she prepared to leave as well. She was surprised when his voice cut weakly through the darkness. "Hey, sister... Don't forget about *us*."

Kseniya led the way, though she moved without the aid of any light, keeping herself, her menials and the army of gangly slaves and ex-raiders tattooed by the lash to the confines of the shadows. With Valero's help the women and other escapees were shepherded along, a long sinuous snake composed of over one hundred lean and unhealthy bodies. They were outside in the moonlight, moving along the inner wall of the courtyard towards the yawning black entrance to the "tunnel of no return", a legendary passage here in the city of Tucumcari that channeled slaves down into the caravanserai of the Cartel below, where human cargo would be thrown into awaiting trucks for transport across the desert.

A few of the slaves hesitated on seeing the looming dark passage, some of them vaguely aware of those who had preceded them along this route, nameless men and women who had been herded this way like cattle to the slaughterhouse. It seemed counter-intuitive to go on, but Valero moved through the stalled mass, tall and sure of himself, and his confidence gave those staying behind the courage to continue.

Kseniya descended, followed by the women, then Valero and the others, keeping an eye out to make sure they had not been detected.

"This is foolish," whispered Sarah, walking among the menials. She pulled a few strands of her long black hair behind her ears. "There are too many of us. We're sure to be spotted."

No one answered. The plain dirt floor of the tunnel angled downwards at a steep angle, its curved walls and ceiling made of crudely-painted white mud. The moonlight shining down on the upper tier behind them filtered down into this passage and lent the chalky walls a cool blue glow and illuminated the enormous black iron portal at the end.

As they came to the bottom, Kseniya listened gently at the door, while Valero and the others stopped and waited. The slaves continued moving, until the crowd at the passage's bottom began to grow. Bodies pushed into bodies, men pressed against women, all of them stifling any expression of discomfort. Kseniya looked to Valero to keep his men under control, and he swept his eyes over the mass of prisoners, issuing a silent threat to anyone who might endanger them through some foolish outcry.

The door was, surprisingly unlocked. Kseniya lifted the heavy iron handle and slowly opened it. Beyond sat the wide open yard of the Cartel caravanserai. A nearby guard shack overlooking the "tunnel of no return" sat dark and empty; this late at night no one was expected to be here in the yard, so the usual garrison of sentries was fortunately absent.

In the darkness they saw the vague shapes of over a dozen large trucks, some tankers, some transports and others freight haulers. An armada of the Cartel's priceless trade vessels waited in the open. Some still groaned as their massive weight settled in the sand; most of the rusted metal titans had arrived that very night from some distant trading post; their engines might even still be hot. A blessing... they wouldn't have to wait to warm them up, but soon, in the icy desert night air, the old machines would cool over, making a quick escape impossible.

Kseniya wondered where their keys were; certainly not in their cabs, but quite possibly in a nearby building?

Valero must have been thinking the same thing, because his eyes were already scanning the edges of the courtyard, onto the faces of buildings where the faint moonlight played. He saw a generator house, a well house, a covered bay with a corrugated iron roof where two 1950s-era gas pumps sat idly, three enormous oil reservoirs with rusted ladders winding up their sheer sides, uniform bungalows for housing convoy crewmen and drivers; another guard shack with an oil lamp flickering inside and a block of three identical warehouse buildings, each of them cracked and slightly sagging.

"Over there," he whispered, motioning to the small guard shack across the yard, its dirty glass window lit by a wavering orange light. "That's where we'll find the keys for the others." He looked over at Kseniya for a second, anticipating at least some form of hesitation, but she simply nodded. She was braver than he imagined. He grinned and both of them took off quietly to cross the distance between the tunnel exit and the shack.

Sarah didn't waste time, even as Valero and Kseniya ran off. The girl rushed to the Cartel rig and, as she came closer, marveled at its size. This was no pre-Fall truck, but a huge conglomeration of truck, car, and motorcycle parts lashed together with wire, metal coils, and crude solder. The thing was a juggernaut of rust and iron, covered in angular armor plate, its doors and wheels bristling with spikes made from broken sword blades, *gront* tusks, and *mutagon* teeth. She couldn't see inside, because the enormous cab was completely buttoned up like a tank. Pipes of soot-stained brass rose up from the back of the cab like lop-sided chimneys, and a hatch up top seemed to be the only way in; it was also where a crewman would pop out to make quick flag signals to other trucks in the convoy, should it encounter trouble while the "road train" was in motion. The troop bed was made from wooden planks and steel joints and attached to the bare metal chassis with coils of rope and old lengths of barbed wire, the latter to dissuade raiders who might try to board the truck on the open road.

She had no time to appraise it further, and ran behind the vehicle to pull back the canvas flap, peering cautiously inside. The interior was wide, tall, and spacious, like the back of a gargantuan Conestoga wagon. But it was relatively empty; it held only a broken crate of empty beer bottles, a pair of shovels, and an overturned, empty jerry can. The powerful odor of old fuel swirled in the confined space in the back. A small door led into the cab from the bed, but it was closed.

"Quickly," Sarah commanded to her fellow menials, "Get in."

Once Sarah was sure all of her charges were onboard, she left the stronger women to fend off the men trying to climb into the back, then moved to the small door leading to the cab. She had to get this thing running soon, before they were overwhelmed by the rest of the escaping prisoners.

Sarah turned the stiff handle and with a groan the hatch opened. It was dark inside and the "tunnel" that faced her looked like a corrugated iron tube leading towards the front of the cab. Taking a deep breath she crawled down the tunnel, passing a small hatch overhead that led up to the top of the cab, or perhaps to one of the weapon cupolas on either side of the vehicle. She continued on, slithering on her stomach, until she emerged on the other side in the cramped interior of the driver's station.

The dim light of the moon made its way through the narrow view slits in the armor, casting scattered beams over a horse-hide chair, strange mechanical levers and spin wheels, and an exaggerated tangle of two-foot long gearshifts. No one was present in the cab, but it still smelled like sweat, urine and spilled beer.

She pulled herself into the driver's seat and felt around for the ignition, only finding it after chipping and tearing away a good part of a fingernail on some thorny part of the steering column. Looking up she saw the truckers' traditional charm dangling overhead, a pair of fuzzy dice, and kissed her fingers before putting their tips to the talisman in a plea for luck on the coming voyage.

Valero led the way to the shack, aware that he and the woman were exposed for the full sixty seconds it took to cross the yard. It was a miracle that no one saw them as they came up alongside the single door leading into the shack, the moonlight illuminating them clearly.

The two of them listened. Inside they heard the crackle of an old cassette player and the eerily-distorted sound of "Wolverton Mountain", its jangling guitar accompanied by some faceless, jaunty country singer. The music was cut short, there was a clatter, and the sound of slurred, apish laughter.

Valero leaned closer. *Two* men. He raised two fingers to Kseniya, who saw them but said nothing.

Valero looked back and saw that the youthful concubine, Sarah, had loaded all of the menials into the first truck. The other slaves were gathering at the truck but it was clear they couldn't all fit. It was only a matter of time before there was noise enough to wake the sleeping guardsmen in the nearby barracks.

"Now..." he whispered to Kseniya, and went for the door.

Burning Lands

The interior of the small shack was lit by a single oil lamp on a small folding TV dinner table in the center of the room, sitting on an extensively-stained Navajo-patterned rug. An old arm chair sat partly on this rug, beside a few other chairs and stools arranged around an old rotting pool table, its felt stripped in places like a green-brown zebra hide. Sitting on the table was a dented football helmet, a Winchester rifle, a baseball bat, and some scattered beer bottles; obviously junk. Next to these were over a dozen colorful credit cards covered in unintelligible words and numbers, a small heap of magnetic tapes, and a large dual-cassette player. Two Cartel truckers were busy playing with the cassette player, listening to each scavenged tape for a few moments before laughing, yanking it out and discarding it on the floor underfoot.

One of the noticeably deformed truckers took a deep drink from an old beer bottle, while the other popped in another tape and listened. Each of the men was rather small and spidery, a race of hunchback dwarves selected specifically over the past few generations by the Cartel to man and operate their truck convoys. These "haulers" were diminutive, like midget jockeys, their small size allowing them to move easily in the hot, confined spaces of an armored Cartel truck. They were exceptionally dexterous, so that they could not only negotiate the tunnels and weapon stations inside the cab, but also climb out onto the exterior of the vehicle and perform external repairs without it having to come to a stop. They were fearless of heights and of motion, with good eyes and sharp ears for spotting the signs of raiders far away; hardy and courageous little men, who had more in common with the brave sailors and submariners of the past than anything else.

Valero and Kseniya slithered into the room unseen as the tape crackled to life. For several moments there was no sound, no smash hit from the Ancient era. Looking disappointed, the trucker turned the volume all the way up to maximum, filling the small shack with the sound of white noise; crackles, pops and ghostly whirring.

Suddenly a solitary note blared from the tape, loud enough to shake the glass pane of the window. It was some old Chinese cultural performance, a group of *sihu* players recorded long ago for anthropological posterity.

The music appeared to please the small men, as its soothing sound was more familiar to them than the rattling guitar of the previous recording.

Kseniya started to creep towards one of the men, while Valero stepped silently to the table and reached for the Winchester.

At that moment one of the small men turned and saw them both, his jaw dropping in surprise. Though taken off-guard, he immediately lunged for the rifle, his swift hand darting with lightning reflexes.

Valero was too slow to beat him to it, and so jumped behind the pool table and crouched, expecting a gunshot to rip into the wood just inches over his head. Instead the dwarf cried a garbled cry of alarm and came round the table, brandishing the old rifle by its barrel, apparently intending to use its stock as a *club*.

Kseniya lunged out in an attempt to gouge the eyes of her startled foe, but he dodged aside, dropping his bottle to the floor and causing it to spray sudsy beer in a wide arc. Slow to regain her footing, Kseniya stumbled past her target, unable to make a second go of it before the dwarf slipped away.

As Valero crouched under cover, the wooden stock of the lever-action rifle came whirling around the corner of the table, slamming against the side and cracking fragments off the edge. The trucker howled angrily and advanced, but Valero instinctively kept his distance, his eyes locked on the gun.

He has no ammo, Valero reassured himself. With that he mustered the courage and, as the trucker came around again for another swing, lunged out and tackled the small mutant, bringing him to the ground.

While the other two struggled, the trucker facing Kseniya picked up the baseball bat from the table, and donned the dented football helmet. Through the grilled mask he smiled at her, his face a leering grin.

Kseniya backed away, looking furtively for a weapon of her own. The trucker followed cautiously, crouched and predatory, angling his bat outwards like a sword. With a giggle the trucker swung it at her, causing her to drop to the floor with a stifled scream to avoid being struck. The bat went wide, accidentally smashing the cassette player and sending it flying into the oil lamp, in turn knocking it onto the ground where it shattered. Immediately the Navajo rug under their feet caught on fire, as the oil spilled wildly, fueling the start of a dangerous conflagration.

The tape player hit the ground upside-down, landing on its buttons. The cassette containing the *sihu* recording popped out, while the tape in the second slot suddenly began to play. As the old tape crackled to life, a strange, deep voice seemed to beckon through the mists of time from a bygone era:

"Love... is a burning thing... and it makes... a fiery ring..."

Valero realized their plan, if they could even call it that, was quickly unraveling. But right now there wasn't time to come up with something better; he continued fighting with his own opponent, grappling and struggling to hold him down and choke the life out of him. He saw Kseniya drop and, turning his head instinctively, saw the fire spreading outwards from the shattered lamp. In the hot orange light of the fire he spotted the other trucker moving around the table, eager to get at the panicking woman.

"Bound... by wild desire... I fell in to a ring of fire..."

Kseniya reached blindly outwards with one hand, hoping to grasp something, anything, that might be used as a weapon. Her fingers groped at the rug until it touched something metal, a rusted fireplace poker lying discarded at the foot of the table. Fire fueled by the spilled oil licked all around it, and she had to move quickly to snatch it up before the flames consumed it completely.

"I fell in to a burning ring of fire..."

The helmeted trucker saw her grab the weapon but was immediately upon her, eyes glowing in the firelight. He swung the bat again, and as Kseniya moved to parry it, the bat hit the poker directly on its spike. It embedded itself in the wood of the bat and was instantly yanked from Kseniya's hand.

Kseniya let out a shriek, and rolled away just as the trucker pulled the poker free. He now had two weapons, and boldly risked the fire to give chase.

"I went down, down, down... and the flames went higher..."

Valero continued to wrestle his foe, who proved to be a stubborn, slippery opponent. Each time he tried to get the trucker in a lock, to strangle him, the midget fought back with frenzied attacks, gouging at Valero's eyes or even biting at his flailing hands. In desperation Valero once more called on his reserve of inhuman willpower, tapping his mutant adrenal glands to flood him with just enough strength to do what he needed.

Burning Lands

His face turned bright red as blood flushed his cheeks and forehead, and his temples bulged. He let out an agonized grunt as his arms clutched around the struggling dwarf beneath him, and all at once bent him into an unnatural angle, snapping his spine with a gut-wrenching "crack".

Hurling himself to his feet as fire crackled around him, Valero spun to face the other trucker, who was just now standing over a terrified Kseniya, cornered against the wall. The Cartel-hired crewman, armed with a bat in one hand and a poker in the other, was taken completely by surprise as Valero descended on him from behind. Valero's muscles seemed to spasm like a puppet possessed by an evil spirit, as he sank his fingers into the trucker's throat until blood sprayed from the points where his fingertips tore through. The trucker choked and gasped, eyes wide and fluttering, but a moment later he dropped, lifeless, like a bag of bricks.

Smoke was beginning to fill the air. Kseniya got up and saw, in the wavering orange light, the tough raider slowly slump against the pool table. His fingers groped weakly at the rim, until he lost his grip and fell with a thud to the floor, plunging into unconsciousness. She rushed over to check for injuries but found none, only an exhausted man whose ribcage rose and sank at incredible speed while his body struggled to wind itself down.

Time was of the essence. The fire was burning out of control, and sooner or later someone would notice, smell smoke, and raise the alarm.

Looking around quickly the woman saw walls covered in yellowed bits of paper, and old postcards tacked to frames and beams. Some were beginning to burn, while others flapped in the swirling, hot air. She scanned the lewd graffiti, and the racks containing scores of bottles, cups, and jugs. Then she saw it. She stepped over Valero's collapsed form and over to the blistered wall, where a corkboard pierced with rusted nails held over a dozen ignition keys.

Quickly Kseniya took the tiny keys in hand, careful not to make a tangle, peering every now and then at the dead bodies of the men Valero had killed with his bare hands, aware that the fire was consuming the building around her. Through the smoke she moved over to Valero, looking down at him. Even unconscious he looked formidable, as if any moment he might spring up and take a swing with a concealed knife. *Why am I taking him along?* she wondered, but before she realized what she was doing she found herself helping the scarred raider to his feet, and with his heavy weight burdening her, stumbled out the door.

From outside it seemed like a bright orange light filled the windows of the small shack, and though the fire had yet to burn through the roof, Sarah knew it was on fire. She worried for her mistress, but was relieved when she saw the door to the guard hut open and Kseniya emerge, with Valero struggling to stay upright close behind, both of them trailing smoke.

Sarah put her fingers through the view slit and wiggled them to get their attention. Though choking, Kseniya noticed and ran over, standing on her toes to slip the right key through the armored slat and into Sarah's hand. With it now in her possession, Sarah inserted the key into the steering column and the truck engine began to shiver, rattle and rumble. In a moment a thick cloud of black smoke erupted out of the brass pipes high overhead, and the entire rig began to shake and vibrate.

Once the sound of vehicle engines reached his ears, Valero regained his senses quickly. He followed Kseniya and took the remaining keys from her, and began throwing them to men he surmised were once raiders; those men would know how to drive, after all. Eagerly the vagabonds accepted their assignments and took the keys from their "leader", before running off in groups of ten or fifteen to the nearest truck.

Soon the yard began to clear as men ran to and fro looking for a ride to climb onto, and just in time, as lights in the Cartel buildings down the street began to come on. A watchman on a distant stretch of wall woke when he heard the truck engines roar, and on turning saw the escaped army of slaves scrambling all over, and the glow of the fire slowly consuming the guard shack. The alarm was suddenly raised, blaring out across the yard.

But it was too late to stop the momentum of the escape. Kseniya got into Sarah's truck along with the other women, and vanished into the back. Valero looked to the remaining men and led them to another rig, climbing the rungs on its armored exterior to slide down the top hatch into the driver's seat.

Gunshots sprinkled across the dirt, bounced and flared brightly off the heavy armor plate of the trucks. Valero put the enormous truck in gear and started driving, already gaining speed, towards the gates to the caravanserai. Sarah released the brake and followed close behind, struggling to maintain a hold on the huge wheel, her cry of surprise at the vehicle's power lost in the thunder of engines. Two, three, four other trucks rumbled into line behind them, forming a small convoy of its own.

Valero's face was a gleaming grin as his truck plowed through the wooden gates, sending splinters in all directions. There was a violent bump, the rig rattled from side to side, but it cleared the compound and began racing down the street. Peddlers and other street people panicked and raced to leap aside, but whether they got out of the way or not didn't matter; there was no stopping them now.

Sarah held on for dear life to make the first sharp turn, angling her truck down as it descended from the Cartel's tier to the lower level of the city, following the sound of Valero's lead truck. She choked on the bitter exhaust that came through her view slit and filled the cabin, but she dared not let go of the wheel to cough. Soon they would be free!

Valero saw the city gates ahead. Fifteen or twenty Cartel and Clean guards were being hastily assembled in a line and were preparing their muskets for a volley. His grin grew bigger as he pushed down on the accelerator and his rig leapt forward with a guttering throb.

"Get out of the way!" someone cried and a few of the armed men blocking the gate came to their senses, running to the side at the last moment. The others remained to let off a few futile shots, their lead slugs ricocheting off of the armored cab of the lead vehicle, until they were rolled over and crushed in a cloud of dust.

The front gates buckled and instantly came crashing open, and the trucks of the hijacked convoy roared off into the wasteland. Lights flickered on all over the city, on the walls and in the towers, and even up in the palace of the mandarin. But they had already escaped.

Tucumcari was many miles away now, and around them rolled the dunes of the deep desert, their captors left far behind. Hours and hours had passed, and the road west had vanished into a sandy trail. A few trucks foundered, requiring the escapees to consolidate their numbers on a few of the lighter rigs, but in time these were abandoned as well. As one, the mass of escaped prisoners abandoned their rides and faced the desert on foot, gradually turning away from the trail and striking out to the north.

The sun was beginning to rise now, sluggishly painting the desert in a pre-dawn bluish light. The desert began to change; sand was replaced by the beginnings of weird stone formations.

Strange rocks sprouted from the desert, eerily-contoured monoliths in whose features an imaginative person might see the shape of human faces, wracked with pain. Their shadows were dark, cool and long, providing a convenient hiding place for small, cowardly creatures dreading the coming of day.

Up ahead could be seen a great wall of stone, the edge of a rocky plateau stretching off in both directions. Sheer cliffs faced the oncoming party, leaving Valero to wonder how on earth would they scale the plateau to reach the top.

Kseniya, who had been silent up until now, extended a hand and pointed to something at the base of the cliffs, which were now just a mile away.

"The Caves of Sorrow," she said softly.

Made deceptively small because of the distance, an enormous cave was visible even from this far, its mouth black and ominous. But it was only one of several, a multitude of gargantuan caves, their entrances three stories tall or more, that riddled the base of the plateau. They seemed dead and dark to Valero, like the mouths of giant corpses awaiting the return of life. His mind wandered to the legends of this place, of the Ancients who came here to die in the cool darkness of the caves, and of the taboo they were violating by coming here. Even raiders sometimes respected old tales and legends, shunning the final resting places of the Ancient dead. It was more than a superstition, a primitive belief that their ghosts might rise again to bestow a curse... it was the subconscious fear of discovering what Ancient man really looked like, and finding out by comparison how wretched the rest of humanity had become.

The other men wordlessly followed Valero, but the unusual silence that fell over them spoke volumes. They, too, were afraid and aware of the legends, and it was only his presence that kept them from deserting, from leaving this foolish expedition now that they were free, and running off into the gloomy gray desert.

It was Kseniya's look of determination that made Valero stay, however; after all, though she seemed cautious, she was clearly not turning back. It was enough to pique his curiosity... and he certainly wouldn't run while a woman stood firm.

"This is where your 'friends' are?" he asked.

A few of the women looked afraid at the mention of the word 'friends', but Kseniya silenced them. "Yes," is all she said.

The wind began to pick up. The men marched on. The women gave each other strange, doubtful looks but they followed their own leader, Kseniya, despite their misgivings. Sarah came up beside Kseniya, looking to make sure no one heard them. "Mother, without the weapons from the armory we have no bribe; there is no guarantee they will let us join them. We're taking a very big chance..." Kseniya knew she was right but chose to ignore her.

The cave entrance soared overhead as the gang of men and women neared the great cliff face. Valero marveled at how accurate his first impression had been; ridges on its dark ceiling made it look like the interior of a titan's maw, yet silent and empty. It dwarfed him in scale, this portal into the earth, and for the first time in a long time he felt... insignificant.

The men shifted uncomfortably at the entrance, hesitating to go any further. At Kseniya's urging, the menials crouched wordlessly by the cold remnants of some ancient campfire ring just inside the cave. She looked out into the depths of the cave. For the first time Valero saw a look of worry in her eyes, in the way she wrung her hands nervously. But she stood tall, as if expecting someone to emerge from the underworld to greet them.

Moments later there came a sound from the darkness: the skittering of rocks across the pebbly cave floor. Footsteps.

Valero had seen his share of dark caves, so remained by the entrance with his men, but turned to see who might be coming their way, ready if need be, to defend himself.

He was surprised as a large group of women emerged from the tunnel. They were lean, muscular and fit, survivors of the wasteland and warriors one and all. Each woman wore some form of body armor, from leather coverings to striped animal hides, scavenged football armor and pieces of chromed metal pounded into the shape of breastplates and arm greaves. They were still women, with their own affectations; some wore colorful earrings of copper or steel, others decorated their wild hair with feathers and colorful beads of turquoise and bloodstone. Some wore war paint, a solid black line across their eyes, while others tinted their faces with chalk and painted "teeth" over their lips so that they appeared more grim and skull-like. Here stood a woman in a highway patrol motorcycle helmet, her steely eyes staring out at him; over there another wore her blond hair in long ropy dreadlocks, partly obscuring her eyes like the branches of a willow tree. Others wore more fierce masks to completely disguise who they were; a hockey mask, a gas mask, an old samurai face plate with tusks and flaring nostrils. Each proudly, defiantly, exhibited signs of past battles won in the name of freedom, in the form of clearly-visible scars on arms, hands and cheeks. They also wore symbols of their former captivity as slaves to the men of the world; each had a scar both emotional and physical. A woman nearby was missing a finger or two, taken as punitive punishment from a cruel master long ago; another was missing an entire breast, lobbed off by raiders once they had tired of her. More than a few had been completely scalped (a common punishment for concubines who committed adultery behind their owner's back), and most had that "thousand-yard stare" of someone who's seen too much suffering in her time.

At once Kseniya, Sarah, Valero, his men and the menials were surrounded by spears and swords. Valero stood firm; his eyes gleamed with fascination at this most unusual of encounters, but he showed no fear.

Through the crowd of armed women came a short female with wiry muscles and jet black hair worn swept straight back from her face and braided into sweeping cornrows. She had rich olive skin, high cheekbones and eyebrows so thin they were seemingly penciled on.

"Who are you to walk right to the gates of the Sisters of the Desert?" the woman asked. "Who are you to bring *men* into this camp? Speak quickly before we kill you all."

Was it a wild boast, Valero wondered, or were there really enough armed warriors in the tunnels, or even in the desert outside, to overwhelm the hundred men at their doorstep?

Kseniya stepped from Sarah and Valero's side and came forward. She looked at the amazonian leader, a woman possessed of physical power, whose strength was a match for many men and whose every feature spoke of toil and suffering in the lifelong quest to live free. Awed and afraid, Kseniya bowed her head respectfully.

"I am Kseniya," she said pleadingly, "and I have come to join the legendary Daughters of Ridaya, the desert sisters." The dusky-skinned woman seemed suspicious of Kseniya and looked at her sideways. But Kseniya continued.

"The stories of her sisterhood are known all over the desert. In Trade City, the servants in all the households of great men chatter about the outlaw heroine who leads her warriors in defiance of their former masters."

"You come without an offering? We're not looking for extra mouths to feed." the short woman replied.

One of the desert sisters came over to her and whispered in her ear. "I recognize her, she is the mistress of Margus Han."

The shorter woman looked back at Kseniya and her eyes narrowed. She looked displeased, insulted by Kseniya's very presence.

"The *whore* of Margus Han?" she stepped forward, arms thrown back, head held high in disdain. "We should drive you out right now."

Kseniya looked shocked and afraid. The other menials gasped and gathered around her. *Had she made a mistake bringing them here? Had she brought them all here for nothing?*

"Who are you to come here, you who have long spread her legs for the wicked mandarin and sold out her own gender? How many women have you delivered into his hands, and the hands of his 'guests', for their pleasure? You are as much a slaver as he is. No, you are worse, you have betrayed your own kind in exchange for a pampered life as a tyrant's plaything."

The menials pulled at Kseniya, hoping to surround her and protect her. Sarah came to Kseniya's side, ready to defend her, but Kseniya stayed and listened to the amazon's withering appraisal.

"Look at you, so pretty, so fine..." the shorter woman taunted, walking on muscled legs as she paced around Kseniya. Her leather armor creaked; bits of chain jingled softly. "You wouldn't last a week. Or a month. You've got nothing to offer us at all. You're a waste of time."

"Let Ridaya decide," Kseniya demanded.

"I *am* Ridaya," the short woman declared, punctuating this with a widening of her eyes. At that the other warrior-women began to laugh.

Just then there was a flicker of light from the tunnel, and out of the darkness on swift-moving feet came the heavy frame of a large man, wearing a long green cloak. He almost stumbled for a moment on the uneven floor of the cave, but he came to a stop a dozen or so paces away when he saw the gathering, then approached slowly.

"I-Is there trouble?" he asked.

Valero looked from the shadows and immediately recognized the man. It was the mutant bounty hunter, *Tank*. It had been years, and he looked corrupted by his deformities, but it was the same giant he'd met prior to the fall of Oasis. *What was he doing here, in the company of a tribe of escaped women?*

Ridaya looked over her shoulder at Tank. "No trouble. We're just dispensing with trespassers."

Tank looked at Kseniya, the menials, and the men. "I t-think I should g-get Karos..." he said.

Ridaya raised her spear at him. "Yes, go get your master. He can have a look before we kill them." A few armed women moved to push Kseniya along, when Valero stepped out from among the pack of men. It was enough to cause Tank to stop and look back down the tunnel.

"I go with her," Valero demanded. Ridaya turned, eyes burning with interest. She looked at Kseniya, then back to Valero, and smiled. She walked over to him and put a hand on her hip.

"So the mandarin's harlot has picked up a new man along the way," she said teasingly, her eyes sweeping over Valero's face, chest and arms. "And a *raider*, no less! How fun! Tell me, does he please *you?* Or do you please *him?*" Valero felt women moving in on either side of him. He didn't move.

"No," Kseniya said, "he and these other men were prisoners in the dungeons of Trade City. *He*," she said, motioning to Valero, "made our escape possible. He gave me his arm and he pledged his life to the fight to destroy the Clean."

"Don't you know? There are no men allowed among the Daughters of Ridaya," the amazon leader countered, and the others began to laugh cruelly.

"He wants to fight the Clean. Don't you?" Kseniya protested.

Ridaya stared off at Kseniya. "*Why* does he want to fight the Clean?" she asked. Valero shifted his weight. The women's leader noticed and raised her chin, looking directly at him. He could tell immediately by her posture and demeanor that throwing lies at her would be like throwing droplets of water at a raging fire.

He uttered a single word. "Freedom." The short, vengeful matriarch seemed to follow, and listened intently.

"Margus Han... the embodiment of all that is wrong in this world? A chance to strike at him? A plan, even a dumb plan with no chance of success, is better than living in the shadow of his 'civilization'."

"You're brave," the women's leader said with a dubious arch of her eyebrow, "and you speak well, but I still don't trust you."

"Oh?" Valero asked. "I've had plenty of opportunities since leaving Trade City to abandon these women and strike out by myself. So have these men..." for the first time acknowledging the motley regiment that had followed them. "But we've stayed, *they've* stayed, to see justice done."

"*Justice?*" one of the sisters asked, almost laughing, stepping forward. "A raider speaks of 'justice'? Listen, Ridaya, shouldn't we just kill him now? For blasphemy?" Valero crossed his arms leisurely across his broad chest.

"D-don't do it!" Tank called out from the tunnel. "R-remember our a-agreement, Rid-daya!" Without further explanation he immediately turned and began scrambling up the tunnel and into the dark.

Ridaya watched Tank go. "It isn't up to us," she said over her shoulder to the others, turning to follow Tank. "This isn't just *our* choice alone."

Burning Lands 211

While the men and servants waited below, Valero and Kseniya followed Ridaya and a few of her sisters higher into the cave complex. It was a maze of passage and tunnels, all of them showing signs of current habitation. Side tunnels appeared to be stockpiled with foodstuffs and the salted carcasses of animals, and here and there were niches clogged with dozens of clay jars containing enough drinking water for what seemed like hundreds of warriors. They passed small caves with open roofs high overhead, in which diminutive campfires burned allowing the savage sisters to cook their morning meal and stay warm.

Valero looked to the side as an infant's cry echoed down a side tunnel. He heard song down another. They continued on, this time ascending up a tunnel that rose higher into the cliffs that gave the plateau its sheer face.

After ten minutes they stopped at a natural cave that opened onto the cliff wall itself, gazing out into the sky; they were almost fifty feet up and could see the cool blue desert clearly as the sun slowly began to rise. Ridaya motioned to one of her female companions.

"Signal that it's okay to turn their lights back on," she said.

The companion moved to the precarious edge of the cave mouth and began fluttering colored flags, signaling the other caves, each situated a half mile apart, up and down the great cliff face.

Valero and Kseniya as, one by one, lights could be seen glowing in the entrances of the other caves, dozens of caves, sprinkled all across the base of the plateau.

Ridaya pressed on without comment, and they were urged to follow at the point of spears. Eventually they all came to a large cool cave, well lit by oily torches, the air only slightly stained with the odor of sweat and the continuous occupation by humans. Valero's eyes narrowed as he saw women of all ages, young and old, training with spears, javelins and swords alongside one another. Girls as young as eight were being taught to swing a sword, hurl an axe and engage an *atlatl* to cast a javelin with the strength of a grown man.

There was laughter and camaraderie, strength in numbers, and far more to these caves than he had first imagined.

Ridaya led the others up to a raised area of natural stone, where a few larger campfires burned, their fires crackling as good air fed them. A number of wooden tables sat here and there, some with weapons on them, others cluttered with metal helmets, a plate with picked-at food, and numerous, odorous rolls of animal hide bound with twine. The stone walls behind these tables were decorated with hand-painted *maps*, almost like cave paintings of old, depicting the wasteland surrounding the great city of Tucumcari, the trade routes and the position of Cartel trading posts, as well as the layout of Trade City, streets and all, and even the palace of the mandarin with its many towers and guard rooms!

Perhaps for the first time in his life Valero seemed amazed at something, bending his head back to take it all in. Whoever these women were working with, they had been planning this attack on the Clean for a long, long time!

Valero saw Tank there, standing by a man with sandy-colored hair, who turned from poring over a map to regard him, Ridaya, and Kseniya. The man had a freshly wounded arm, his wrist reduced to a stump, wrapped in blood-soaked bandages. He was lean, but he looked like he was regaining his strength from the various poultices and jars of theriacs scattered about the table.

"Ridaya," Karos said. "Tank says you have visitors?"

Ridaya smirked as she came forward, a feminine sway to her proud walk. She stopped midway between Karos and the group of captives. "Yes, Karos, and you'll never guess who. A raider, a small army of escaped prisoners, and the mandarin's mistress herself."

Karos looked from Valero to Kseniya.

"I expect you'll do as you please to the raider," Karos said, "but if I might, I'd like a word with Kseniya."

Kseniya was surprised that this strange man knew her name.

"Oh, I know you," Karos reassured her. "I've had my eyes on the palace of Margus Han for a long time now. I've long wanted to meet you, or someone like you. Someone with inside knowledge of the palace, its workings, its passages."

Kseniya saw her opportunity to save her own life. She was about to speak when Valero cut her off.

"Who *are* you?" Valero asked.

Karos turned and smiled at him as evenly as he had smiled at the fair Kseniya. "My name is Karos. You?"

"Valero," he replied, finding himself playing along.

Tank suddenly looked up from his master's side, a spark of recognition in his eyes. "V-Valero? I-I know you! You once commanded t-the Scorpions!" Karos looked at Tank for a moment, then back at Valero.

"Good to meet you, Valero. A former raider, hmm? Well I'm no one significant, just a traveler trying to make friends. But it seems you've made the same mistake I did, wandering into the territory of the desert sisters. But unlike myself, you don't seem to have a bargaining chip to secure your safety."

Valero looked at the man. "Bargaining chip? What did you offer these women to stay their blades?"

Ridaya walked over to Valero and put her short spear to his neck. "Another word, raider, and it's your head."

"Ridaya, please," Karos said, stepping down from the elevated tier, with Tank close behind. "I beg you, show some courtesy. He only wants to talk."

Ridaya considered, then stepped away. "Karos," she said, a hint of warning in her tone, "remember whose home this is."

Karos nodded in appeasement, then returned to Valero. "Bargaining chip, you ask? How about a mutual enemy? I lead a group of people from Trade City who have worked for the past few years to build a coalition against Margus Han and his Cartel allies. We have agents in the city, and connections with many of the tribes along the trade routes of the Jia Lang. We have slowly been building our strength, getting others to join us, and preparing for *war*."

As a warrior of many years, Valero should have smelled the rank odor of war brewing on the horizon. He shook his head slowly.

"A warrior with no sword hand?" Valero looked incredulous.

Burning Lands

Karos smiled weakly, regarding his devastated wrist. *"The price I paid for foolishly getting in the way of destiny..."* he said cryptically. "But I don't need a sword, I have the strength of my followers."

"I doubt that. You're a prisoner here too, aren't you?"

Karos smiled. "Ridaya did indeed capture my followers and I as we traveled too near these caves, but she has proven to be a reasonable captor. She and her sisters have longed for an opportunity to strike at the Clean and the Cartel, to whom many of her kind once belonged. When she realized who I was and why I had come, she recognized her chance to move against the Clean was finally here. Together we have formed an alliance, her desert sisters and my people, the hungry souls of the city, the barrios, the villages of the wasteland. All those yearning for change."

Ridaya moved to Karos' side, bringing the hafted end of her spear down on the rock with a solemn "thud".

"What you see before you, in this cave and in the other caves here at the base of the plateau, is an alliance of people ready to bring war to the doorstep of Margus Han," she said.

Valero chuckled. "What I see before me is an alliance of slaves and escaped, undomesticated women. Poorly-trained peasants and wild amazons? Hiding in the desert, waiting for an opportunity to strike?"

"Like *scorpions*," Karos said cleverly, staring at Valero's brand.

"Not what I expected when I signed on," Valero stated grimly, ignoring Karos' coyness and looking at Kseniya.

"We can help," she said eagerly.

"I know *you* can," Karos said to her, and by inflection indicated that Valero was of no use to him. "Tell us of the tunnels beneath the mountain, the passages that lead up into the top tier of the city..."

"He brings with him a hundred men," Kseniya said, continuing right over Karos. "A hundred escaped slaves with the same burning need for revenge that you have. Don't squander the opportunity."

It was enough to make Karos pause. The one-handed man looked at Ridaya, whose pride seemed to simmer down somewhat. She also seemed to recognize the value of the situation, the rarity of the opportunity that had just presented itself. An additional one hundred warriors was not an insignificant thing, even an untrained mass. She returned Karos' glance with a hard look of her own. *It's up to you.*

"We'll see," Karos said noncommittally. Kseniya sighed, knowing the others would be pleased to know they were going to be allowed to live a little longer.

Valero stared straight ahead, at the maps painted on the cavern walls and the symbols that indicated the troops being assembled for the war. "Even with my hundred men you're still going to need more," he muttered. "Much more..."

"I agree," Karos replied, to Valero's surprise. "That's why I will be heading north into the lands of the *bei man,* to sway them to our side. With them as our allies the odds will be in our favor."

"They will never join," the ex-raider said grimly. "Their king just sent these hundred men to their deaths to buy peace with Margus Han. He's not going to risk everything by joining your alliance."

"We'll just have to see," Karos said with a resolute stare.

Kseniya considered for a moment, remembering her meeting with Uncle Sam in the palace of Tucumcari, and the rapport, however brief, she had with him. "Let me go with you," she said to Karos suddenly, stepping forward. "I've met the lord of the *bei man*; he'll recognize me, and he'll speak with me. Your chances of success will be much greater if you take me along."

Ridaya crossed her arms like she didn't like the idea, but Karos looked at Kseniya for a long moment and finally nodded his approval.

"C-can I go too?" Tank asked.

"No," Karos said, much to everyone's surprise, including Ridaya. "Our 'friends' have other plans for you, Tank." Tank looked stunned, having expected to join the coming war as a footman in the front ranks, to spend the last months of his miserable life in defense of a greater ideal before he became too stupid and too slow to contribute anything more than a childish grin to the cause. Now his leader, Karos, hinted at some other role he might play, and he could only wonder what that might be.

"And take the raider with you," Karos said with a slight smile. "Maybe he *can* be of some use."

Valero was confused and looked to Ridaya, whom he'd assumed was running this show, but the woman silently deferred to Karos. These "friends" he spoke of must be very influential indeed.

"Who are these 'friends?'" Valero asked, voicing his suspicions.

"You'll see soon enough..." Karos said enigmatically.

Karos and a small group of his men prepared for their journey into the wasteland, and an extra horse was outfitted for Kseniya, who would be accompanying them. They would be avoiding the trade route north, instead going cross-country to the lands of the *bei man* to avoid any chance of being seen by agents of the Clean or Cartel. There was only a brief farewell as he, Kseniya, and their small entourage hastily set out for the north as the sun began to rise.

In his absence, Karos left it to Ridaya to show Valero and Tank the mysterious "friends" of whom he had spoken. Only an hour after he had left, Ridaya solemnly returned to the cave where the two men waited, alone. Standing at the entrance to a separate, darker passage, she put two torches to a brazier to ignite them, one in each hand, then turned quietly to Valero and Tank and motioned for them to follow.

For some time Ridaya wordlessly led Valero and Tank higher up into the mountain, through rough natural tunnels into the deep darkness underground. There were no loose rocks here, no soil or sand, only bare bedrock carved from subterranean water that had dried up long ago. The hydrological history of the cave left the tunnel smooth in places and weirdly shaped in others, as if they were passing through the stony intestines of Mother Earth herself. At some point Ridaya passed the second torch to Valero, and together they lit the way as they walked, their flames quietly lapping at the still air.

Tank walked close to Valero, and though for a while they said nothing to each other, Tank finally broke the silence.

"I t-thought y-you were dead," he whispered to Valero.

"I guess not," Valero responded. Tank went quiet, as if he imagined it unlucky or even dangerous to speak further. So this time Valero spoke.

"Never thought I'd see you again," Valero said, with only casual interest. "I'm surprised to see you're still alive, too."

He was referring to Tank's progressive deformities, of course, and Tank knew it. The large mutant looked momentarily saddened, and almost ashamed at his physical degeneration, but at that moment, in his mind, he remembered the words of Karos. The kind-hearted, soft-spoken leader who had told him to accept the way he was and rejoice in the time that he had on this Earth. Tank struggled to remember his voice, his friendship, and with that lifted his head and revealed the stony look of determination on his face to Valero's light.

"I know," he replied. "I s-suppose I just refuse to die." Valero regarded him silently for a moment, then nodded a respectful nod.

"You're falling behind," Ridaya interrupted, with some annoyance. Valero and Tank looked ahead to her and renewed their pace.

"Where are you taking us?" Valero said to Ridaya, as they entered a new passage.

"To see Karos' friends. Our *allies*. No more questions."

Valero ignored her command and continued. "Friends? Allies? Maybe you should explain."

Ridaya seemed uncomfortable with words, and for a moment she simply kept walking, leading them along. Just when Valero thought she would ignore the question altogether she began to speak.

"Karos brought them here. *He* summoned them from across the Wei Shan. They are strange to me, I know very little of them, only that Karos trusts them implicitly. I think he may be working for them, but they are shy of being seen, and so they speak through Karos when they need to be heard. It doesn't matter to me, so long as they don't stand in our way."

"I k-know," Tank said from the back. "K-Karos spoke of them often, in m-m-mysterious terms, and sometimes met with them in s-secret. But I never a-actually saw them."

"Who are they?" Valero asked. Tank could not say.

"I don't know for sure," Ridaya said, sounding impatient with a line of questioning that made her look ignorant. "But they have offered us great gifts, gifts that will aid us in the coming war. They promise the fall of the Clean and the destruction of their alliance with the Cartel; they foresee a new era in the lands of the Jia Lang."

Ridaya bent over to clear a low passage, and the other two followed.

"So this is all about unraveling the Clean's efforts to re-introduce order to the desert?" Valero asked.

Ridaya hesitated when Valero put it like that. "But look whose 'order' is being forced upon us. We, Karos and I, both believe each person is free to determine what is best for them. In this age, in this time, there is no one law, no one code of ethics, that can govern us all. With the destruction of the Clean and Cartel we will be free to live our lives as we will, with the understanding that any other way, as well meaning as it might seem, is folly."

It was quiet again as the trio continued through the caves. Valero was now distracted by Ridaya, whose own mysterious story piqued his curiosity. "What of you, and your tribe?"

Ridaya found it easier to speak about herself and her fellow women. "My sisters and I have always been hunted by the men of this desert. Most of us came from the degenerate cities and towns of the Clean or the Cartel, slave women and captives of their harems..."

Valero looked at Ridaya's shape, draped in armor and wielding a barbed spear, and for a moment found it impossible to imagine her dressed and perfumed as a concubine.

"... while others came from small villages whose people traded them away to the merchant houses for food and water. Our masters have invariably been cruel and callous men, and we being traded back and forth like currency, forced to surrender ourselves to whatever new man owns us, and bear children as the need demands.

"Almost all of the women you see here is a mother," Ridaya continued. "Some with one, two, even a dozen children who don't even know her name, or remember her face. You see, in the lands of the foreigners, sons are taken away to be raised as good princes, sheltered among men, while girls are groomed to take their turn in the harem when they come of age.

"Many try to escape. Those who do would rather face death in the desert than submit any longer to humiliation and control. We call ourselves 'sisters of the desert' because we are all united by a bond, a shared lust for freedom that only life in the desert can bring. I brought them here, where it is safe, where men no longer go."

"I've heard of the legends of these caverns," Valero said. "What of them?"

Ridaya smiled cleverly. "The legends keep men away, and the taboos ward off looters and the curious. That's why I brought my people here."

"And the stories?" Valero asked.

"Long ago some Ancients *did* come here to die after the Fall," she said, considering. "But of the skeletons I have seen, I have encountered no magic, no great revelations of the past. Only junk and refuse. The caves are empty now, and there are no secrets here. Other than our presence."

As Ridaya spoke, they passed through an old cave. She continued on, seemingly oblivious to the bone fragments on either side of the path, lying on the floor encased in dust, or in small niches here and there that might have once served as beds for the infirm. Some of the skeletal remains showed signs of limestone growth, being partly ensconced in the slick wet rock itself, so that these human bones had become a part of the caves themselves. Any shred of ancient clothing or usable tool was gone, having rotted or disintegrated decades ago.

Tank, who'd never been this deep in the caves, looked at the skeletons as they passed through, those skulls and bones of the beautiful Ancients. How uniform they must have looked in life, standing tall and handsome... unlike the grotesque "zoo" of deformed men and women the world had since become. Now there were a thousand different races of man, with mixed blood and damaged genes, broken faces and shambling bodies, most of whom would be considered nauseating monstrosities by the Ancients, who were angels in comparison.

Ridaya led them into another grand chamber, where Valero and Tank recognized the broken remains of ancient weapons; bent rifles, smashed pistols, a laser dismantled and its chromium rod fractured into a thousand pieces. Rust covered every metal surface, fusing the weapons into heaps of useless slag that could never be revived for their original purpose. An entire pit, almost thirty feet across, was filled with them.

Burning Lands 217

"Here is all that they brought," Ridaya said, motioning in a grand arc towards the cache, "the 'treasures' of the Caves of Sorrow. Their great weapons reduced to *rust*."

Valero noticed something above, on the cavern wall, and raised his torch up to read it. The words were hard to recognize.

"I've seen that before, but I cannot read the Ancient tongue," Ridaya explained.

"I can," Valero said, to everyone's surprise. He moved closer to the wall and examined the writing, reading aloud:

As we come here with our dying brothers and sisters,
Our hair falling out and our stillborn infants in hand,
Let us say one last prayer:
That this atrocity we call War be banished forever from this earth;
May our survivors in the aftermath finally know peace.

All three stood speechless; Tank in wonderment, Ridaya uncomfortable by the message's insinuation, and Valero realizing the irony.

"They destroyed their treasures deliberately," Valero surmised aloud.

Ridaya walked away quietly, and Tank followed. Valero gave the fragmented skulls and bones one last look and continued with them.

They pressed on in uncomfortable silence for several more minutes, up and down passages and through tiny caves. Valero wondered why these "friends" chose to dwell separately from the rest of the alliance, why such isolation was required. Ridaya seemed unable to explain, and said nothing until reaching a fork in the passage. She stopped and raised her torch to illuminate the twisting tunnels.

"They wait in one of these, I think," she said simply. "There's one more thing I should tell you. Karos' friends may promise us many things, but they have demanded a price in return. That price has yet to be paid, and from what Karos has told me, they've waited a long time to collect."

She looked at Tank. "They spoke of their desire to see you, specifically, "she said. "And you, raider, I imagine Karos thinks you should go to help Tank in his mission."

She looked down the passage. "I suppose they will explain further..."

Valero, torch in hand, looked at Tank. Tank seemed just as ignorant as he, uncertain of what was to come.

Although he was afraid, Tank trusted Karos' judgment in all this, and so he took a courageous step forward. He looked down each of the passages, shrugged, and chose the left tunnel. Valero, without any reason to choose one over another, casually followed behind him.

After a while they entered a large domed cave, its roof dripping with spear-like, rocky growths, angled downwards.

One cave was as good as any other, Tank guessed, and apparently the mysterious "friends" of his master, Karos, agreed. From dark niches came a dozen crippled and decrepit figures in shoddy purple robes, some shambling weakly, others hop-hopping on covered appendages too ghastly to be revealed to the eye. Some were obscenely tall, slightly bent from the weight of their own bodies coming down on their stilt-like legs; others were inhumanly short and stunted, but not like goblins or dwarves which might seem comical and harmless, but rather only half-formed, partly-developed things that one was thankful remained cloaked. Pulling back a hood or veil one might be confronted by a terrifying sight, a glimpse of how badly Nature can go wrong. Twisted faces, multitudes of blind, blinking eyes, fangs hanging in extra mouths, fingers and thumbs sprouting from cheeks like clay bits stuck to an unfinished bust, permanent grins pulled tight across their deformed skulls like grinning idiots.

The Brotherhood is here, Valero realized. *What on Earth has brought them to this far-away land?*

Tank recoiled in terror from the glimpses of what he saw beneath their hoods, backing right up against Valero.

"W-what w-w-would you have of u-us?" Tank sputtered, fear in his voice.

Unafraid, Valero raised his torch in an attempt to see what Tank had seen, but the Brotherhood monks and nuns now pulled their hoods and cloaks tight, so that their terrible deformities would hereafter remain hidden from view.

"Here come the ones who will deliver..." spoke a hissing congregation of mutant mouths and misshapen snouts, a susurrus of ungodly voices that spoke both aloud, and in the *mind*.

"Here come the ones who can find *her*..." they spoke again.

After a moment of silence the crowd resumed speaking, as one. "We lend our far-sight to the alliance, the ability of prophecy, snatch glimpses of the future from the web of time, and offer them as pearls to those who care to see... Karos and Ridaya are but two of many. We do this so they might succeed, accomplish what they could not accomplish alone... but we do so for a price..."

"That price?" Valero asked defensively, somehow fearing he and Tank had been sent here as sacrificial lambs to the slaughter.

"The girl... the child... the young one... the oblate of Margus Han... must be rescued and... brought to us. She alone can give us what we require..."

"*Who?*" Valero asked. Tank's blank eyes fluttered wide as he suddenly realized who they were referring to.

"Gale Han..." the voices whispered, "You must find her and bring her to us, to the alliance... She is the one who will put an end to that which *really* threatens the land... and its future..."

How could that small child, from so many years ago, have a part in all this? Tank wondered.

"What do you require?" Valero asked suspiciously, returning to their previous demands.

"To unlock her memories... to show her the *truth*."

"I don't understand," Valero muttered.

What did it matter? Tank thought. He was willing to do whatever he had to for the alliance, he had long ago committed himself to Karos and the movement, and if realizing victory meant doing the Brotherhood's bidding, what difference did it make whether they fought in battle or spent their time searching for a small girl?

"You want us to attack the palace of Margus Han?" Valero asked.

"No... Another has already taken her... someone whom we vastly misjudged..."

"Then h-how can we find her?" Tank asked.

Burning Lands 219

"You once traveled with the man who took her..." the voices explained, and he suddenly felt their attention directly upon him. "You know his mind... you will find him... you will find her with him... you will convince them to return."

"If you have the gift of 'far-sight', then surely you know where they are," Valero countered, prepared to provide an argument dispelling their claims of prophecy as a hoax, but the voices returned and silenced him.

"They are in constant motion... among the deserts, among the dunes... heading east... with speed... soon with others... You will catch up to them *in the city that still stands...*"

Minutes later Ridaya looked down the passage as Valero appeared, coming her way. Tank was right behind. She turned to lead them back the way they had come, speaking over her shoulder:

"Karos has left for the north, and I must ready my sisters for the coming battle," she said. "If things go as planned, and Uncle Sam can be won over, Karos will bring his armies south towards Trade City without delay. The battle will begin whether you've brought the girl back or not. For now I've been instructed to provide you with horses for your mission."

"They told us the 'price'," Valero said solemnly. "A *girl*..."

Ridaya looked over her shoulder in surprise, back in the direction of the dark passage where the Brotherhood's seers awaited in darkness. She suddenly looked very suspicious, her lips tightly drawn, and her eyes flaring.

"Oh?" she asked.

"N-not to harm her," Tank reassured her, though even he knew very little. He was going on trust alone, trust in Karos and his benevolence. "F-for information. They want us to r-rescue her."

Ridaya momentarily looked ill at ease with this deal, and the feeling of not being in control seemed to annoy her.

Valero picked up on her wavering trust, finding an opportunity to ask a question. "What aid *have* they given?"

She was quiet, then stopped and turned to face the ex-raider, finding herself defending their mysterious benefactors. "They have seen things, given us information, information that can turn the tide in our favor."

"Like what?"

"They predicted the great Cartel general, Rhylor, would leave to fight raiders in the east; he left only a few weeks ago, just as they said. They have given us information on how the guards of the city operate, so that we can infiltrate the tunnels beneath Tucumcari and seize key parts of the city..."

This bit Ridaya left vague, but she continued. "And they have predicted the coming of a great *sandstorm*, one which will hide our army, allowing us to march right up to the walls of Trade City unseen. Karos believes it will come to pass, just as they say. With the power of prophecy on our side, how can we lose?"

"Do *you* believe it will come to pass?" Valero asked slyly.

Ridaya looked angry at his indifference to all this, indifference that did nothing but chip away at her confidence in Karos and the "plan". She said nothing to Valero and turned to lead the two men out.

Both Valero and Tank were quiet as they followed. Valero stopped to look back down the dark passage and in the direction of the cave where those monstrous mind-masters awaited their return.

"You remember the bounty hunter I used to work with? *Rider?*" Tank asked over his shoulder, sensing Valero lingering behind.

Valero looked surprised. Tank kept walking. "He's the man we're looking for."

CHAPTER 4

The sun was low on the horizon, turning the flat open expanse of the desert a miserable red and pink. Here, in the lands many miles east of Trade City, the desert was hard-packed sand and cracked mud, and every now and then could be seen the crumbling remains of rocks and boulders. There were no mountains to be seen anywhere, no large hills, just broad open spaces left naked to the sun.

A single horse walked weakly along the remnants of an old trail that, to any but the most skilled tracker, would seem invisible. From a distance the horse looked sickly; its head hung low as it walked along, with one of its two riders slumped against the other as they went.

Rider held the reigns and stared out at the desolate expanse from beneath his hood. Gale clung to him, not out of affection, but because she had fallen asleep and didn't want to be left behind. The horse was weak, Rider could tell, even more than they were, and wouldn't last for much longer.

They had ridden many miles from Tucumcari in only a handful of days, a tremendous feat that few men could boast of accomplishing. He had pushed their stolen steed mercilessly, drawing from it every ounce of endurance and strength, to put as much distance as possible between them and the vengeful Margus Han. No other man could coax such loyalty from a steed, and Gale wondered if this man had some power over horses that she was unaware of.

They had left the great eastern trade route and gone cross-country over some of the desert's worst terrain, including mesas, cliffs and ravine country, and now plunged headfirst into a featureless expanse that offered no tantalizing promise of ending any time soon.

Gale came back to her senses as a few sand particles got caught in her long eyelashes, her hand coming up to wipe them free. She had forgotten the stinging feeling of sand from her years with the Clean, and the flood of sensations of desert life were quickly returning.

Suddenly realizing she was holding onto Rider she quickly let go, and in doing so alerted Rider to the fact that she was awake again.

"Where are we going?" she asked in a guarded tone.

Rider spoke without looking back. "Not sure."

"You're not sure?" she asked, brushing strands of hair from her face. Her captor was silent.

"Do you even remember me?" she asked.

Rider was quiet for a moment, then turned slowly to look into her eyes. He saw only an attractive, pampered servant of the mandarin; if he had looked harder he would have seen her determination and defiance, qualities that would have immediately stood out and made him look deeper. Instead he merely said "no."

The horse stepped through deep sand and almost stumbled. Gale held onto Rider again.

"You killed my only friend," she said softly, staring out into the desert. "Then you handed me over to a gang of raiders. You sold me to Margus Han for a *horse*."

He looked at her again. "I've never met you," he protested.

"I was a child then," she explained soberly.

He turned in the saddle and took a longer look at her. "You're that old ghoul's plaything?"

"He was no 'ghoul', he was my friend." Rider said nothing. He looked forward again.

"Let me go, Rider," she said, "you don't need me anymore, you've already escaped."

"No," he replied, "I think I'll keep you with me for a while."

"At least tell me where you're taking me."

"Home."

A dark speck appeared on the horizon, and without any other destinations to choose from, Rider directed their horse towards it.

Three hours later that "speck" was now a discernable structure, a low, squat building providing the only shade for a hundred miles. The building was made of red stone, its four corners held up by pillars styled to look like cairns of rough red brick. An overhang shaded the front entry, under which stood two ancient gas pumps, still coated in a brilliant fire engine red paint, as vivid as the day they were installed.

Rider dismounted, followed by Gale, and both listened. They only heard the sound of the horse's hooves as it walked over to the shadow of the overhang. Rider followed and retrieved a canteen from its saddle, even though he doubted they'd find any water here.

While Rider approached the building, Gale stayed outside. The fact that Rider didn't bother to tie her up reminded her that there was nowhere to go even if she did try to escape.

Burning Lands

She walked a few paces from the building and, holding her hand at her brow, stared out at the blinding desert surrounding them for miles. If Margus had actually sent men after them, they were nowhere to be seen, possibly hours, even days, behind.

For some reason the thought didn't worry her like she imagined it should. She felt right with Rider, despite what he had done to Johnny and the effect he had had on shaping her life, and found her heart easily forgiving him. *Why?* She consciously wondered. He had always been cold, callous, and selfish, a survivor first and a human being second (if at all). But he was also the closest thing she had to a brother, a strong male figure from her past who, though he never seemed to care for her, had somehow earned her affection.

Why was that? Had she known something all along? As a child, had she been able to sense, unconsciously when her powers were just developing, that he was merely a wreck of a man, torn up by a failed life, a man who only had enough heart left to keep on living, even after all other reasons were gone? As a young girl had she been *that* perceptive and not even realized it?

It seemed so clear now, as she looked at him. Granted her mind was sharper now after years of mental training with the Mothers of Fate, but looking at him she could "feel" his pain, a lethal scar on his psyche that had killed his old self and created the new. Of course, the "new" was just a build-up of psychological scar tissue, a self-made facade of detachment that only hid the corpse of what lay beneath.

If she wanted she could probably tear into his mind and find out the truth; what had happened to him as a young man to end up as this hollow shell? But she sensed that someday soon he would relent and tell her, in his own words. For some reason she was willing to hold off and let him keep his dignity... even if he *did* handle her rudely at times.

She turned back from gazing at the wasteland and followed as Rider went to enter the old building. He cautiously approached the door, Micro-Uzi at the ready. The glass was cracked and coated in dust, and a "CLOSED" sign hung on one broken chain on the other side, just barely legible. Rubbing a clear spot on the glass he peered in, allowing his unusually sensitive lowlight vision to give him an idea of what waited in the unlit interior.

His daytime eyesight might be weakening but in the dark his vision was generally unmatched. It was a reminder that with his albinism Nature was trying to tell him to live underground, out of the sun and away from the rest of the human race. He realized now it was Nature's peculiar way of taking care of him, cursing him with light sensitivity but giving him the nocturnal sight needed to lead a troglodilian life where a creature his size would be at the *top* of the food chain.

Of course he had no desire to emulate *sandmen* and other subterranean dwellers who feared the sun, and got a smug kind of enjoyment using Nature's gift to help him get along just fine on the surface.

He saw rows of shelving filled with old foodstuffs and trinkets, souvenirs and baubles. The fossil of some prehistoric marine creature dangled from the roof with maps to other local attractions. A large sign hung over the interior of the small store reading: "Cool stuff to remember your trip, Souvenirs and More". Beneath were racks of dusty clothing, funky hats, cowboy boots, and cheap mirrors for the passing motorist to admire him- or herself in, before growing embarrassed and leaving without buying anything.

"Seems clear..." Rider muttered as he wrapped his cloak around his fist, suddenly smashing the glass and reaching through to release the rusted lock.

Inside it was at least twenty degrees cooler, and with the door open enough light filtered in for Gale's eyes to see by.

As Rider went to check that the interior was clear, Gale wandered, looking at the veritable storehouse of cheap consumer goods preserved on the shelves: gaudy sunglasses, key chains, disposable lighters, coffee mugs, lucky rabbit's feet, binaca spray dispensers, candies and breath mints for the long drive, gimmicky toothbrushes with a state icon worked into the handle, and a dazzling assortment of awfully-flashy earrings, spangles, and plastic finger rings set with faceted, colored glass.

It didn't disturb the two searchers when their horse joined them, lowering its head to come through the doorway and into the cool interior, where it waited just inside the door.

Rider looked back only momentarily before sighing, finally content that the three of them were alone. Putting the Uzi down on top of a stack of candy bar boxes, he turned to the display of embarrassing faux-Western clothes on the racks - arrow-collared long-sleeved shirts, blue jeans with overly fancy stitching, and rawhide jackets in all sizes and styles.

"Look for something to wear," he said to Gale. "I don't want anyone recognizing you." This last bit had a hint of menace, but she realized she wasn't afraid.

"Those clothes aren't going to withstand a long journey," he continued, and gestured to her fanciful *cheongsam*, which was already showing signs of wear. The two of them began searching the racks until, after a full fifteen minutes, Rider gave up and went deeper into the building.

Beyond the front area stood a veritable clothing store, with racks of garments and trinkets pandering to the long-vanished biker gangs that once roamed the highways of the American land. Beneath an enormous black flag depicting a Gothic and ornate Maltese cross sat racks of black leather coats and obscene pants, shirts emblazoned with swastikas and the emblems of various death metal bands, as well as displays of leather boots, bracelets, collars and more.

Rider wandered among these, quickly finding among the racks a long charcoal duster (still in a plastic coat wrapper) that fit him. As he put it on he let his ratty cloak fall to the floor. He prepared to move on but stopped at the display of musty boots, collars and biker hats. After snaring some combat boots from the shelf his eyes wandered over the hats for a moment. He seemed ready to go, but at the last moment he reached out and took the one at the very top of the pyramid display, an old black fedora, donning it with a slick and fluid flourish.

Rider kept the black hat and coat, moving down the aisle deeper into the shadows, when he stopped and turned. He reached into a wire basket that held some twenty or more cheap sunglasses, rummaging through them clumsily with one hand. He finally settled on two identical pairs, putting one in his pocket and putting the other on.

As Rider searched, Gale lifted a rabbit's foot charm and put it to her left earlobe, mistaking the fetish for some kind of jewelry. Fearing Rider might spot her, she maneuvered so that the tall rack of trinkets stood between them, before looking at herself in the dirty mirror. After a moment of looking at herself she put the trinket down, instead turning to wander among the racks of clothing that had seemingly swallowed Rider whole.

While she wandered she looked at the dark and gloomy fashions of ages past, and tried to envision the chaos and anarchy that once gripped these roads. Not unlike today, she imagined. The first great biker gangs had been made up not only of the typical criminal miscreants, but also the dispossessed masses expelled from the cities by virtue of their poverty and the severe laws of an increasingly-Orwellian government. Barred from the cities, which were being rebuilt into model communities in their absence (and sealed off from the environmentally-ravaged wilderness outside by walls and sealed domes) they had come to create their own nomadic, lawless culture that had eventually given rise to the "raider" bands that now haunted the wasteland.

Gale began going through the racks of clothing, her eyes noting the strangely insubstantial nature of most of the attire designed for her gender. It boggled her mind. She flipped past racy bustier and slinky tank tops, in that moment imagining how poorly the women of the ancient world must have been regarded by their male counterparts. But she had very little choice.

Gale looked up and noted that Rider was well out of sight. After a moment's hesitation, she reached forward and undid the buttons of her frayed *cheongsam*, pulling the sweat-soaked garment free and tossing it aside quietly. Still aware that he was somewhere nearby, she searched for something that might fit her. She eventually took the most conservative thing she could find, a black basque corset, slipping it from its hangar and pulling it around her torso, struggling to fasten it in the front. She patted the slippery material down, sucked in her gut until she managed to fit the last button into its loop, then finally exhaled.

Rider noticed the sound and turned. She heard him coming in her direction and hurriedly pulled some leather pants from among the racks, taking a moment to slip them on. As the sound of Rider's new boots came closer she leaned over and picked up some footwear for herself, settling on a pair of suede, fur-lined boots to replace her sandals.

Rider came around the corner of the clothing racks and stopped to look at the girl. Gale stood up, facing him, lifting her chin to look straight into his eyes. He looked over her just once, and without saying so much as a single word he continued past.

Rider walked fifteen feet to the cash register, which sat open. He took a lighter from a box of lighters waiting on the counter and a knife from a souvenir rack, then looked inside the register and felt around for some coins. He took some, putting them into his pocket. Not only did he like the feeling of change in his pocket, but every now and then a scavenger like him might find a working vending machine that only accepted coins. They could be useful.

Gale was still pulling on her other boot when Rider called to her. "Come on," he said, sounding short-tempered, "there's no water here. We're going."

Days passed, but without water the two travelers inevitably began to grow weary. Even Rider, a survivalist by nature, could find no trace of water out here in this, the most desolate part of the Far Desert. Gale slumped against Rider as they rode, reserving her dwindling willpower just to hold on. Rider's eyesight became more and more blurred as the daylight seemed to burn brighter, and his own strength began to leave him.

Their mount never failed them, however, a testament to Rider's uncanny affinity with the race of horses, from whom he could coax unearthly feats of endurance and loyalty. The poor creature had become lean and bony, its ribcage showing through its brown hide, but it continued on faithfully in an unflinching effort to issue its rider wherever he chose to lead it.

Just then Rider spotted something... the circling of buzzards in the sky. It looked like a dozen or more in the air, but when he narrowed his eyes the blurry black forms seemed to come together and merge; there were really only four or five. Still, with renewed interest he pulled the reigns to direct the horse in that direction.

Gale woke up as the horse came to a stop. The two of them looked at what lay before them.

Rider and Gale saw several men and women lying spread eagle on the desert sand, clothed only in shadows cast by the scavenger birds soaring overhead. They sensed no movement except for the circling of buzzards, and the flutter of one or two of the big black birds next to the bodies.

Corpses.

Keeping a cautious distance for several minutes, Rider waited until he was quite confident the corpses were left to rot. This was no ambush, but the remains of a one-sided slaughter. Eventually he guided the horse towards the bodies. He was surprised by what he saw.

The bodies were reasonably fresh, perhaps only a few days old. Their injuries were unlike any Rider had ever seen before; the three men and two of the women had pencil-thin holes in their bodies and skulls, these ringed by white blistered skin as if instantaneously flash-burned. They all showed signs of having been mutilated, but the last, a woman, had been staggeringly brutalized.

They were all mostly naked, except around their wrists and ankles, where shreds of a sleeve or socks still remained, as if their clothing had been surgically removed by someone keen on examining the primitive fabric in some distant laboratory. One, an old woman, had had her guts cleanly sliced open, and even now an exceptionally bold vulture stood on her, sinking its head down low (with one menacing eye on Rider) to put its head inside and peck at her exposed innards.

Rider was unnerved by that large black-feathered beast, for he knew he looked on the verge of collapse himself, and the sight of it feasting, with its eyes on him, seemed like a preview of things to come. He shuddered and edged the horse towards a body a little further away.

A small family group of desert scavengers, Rider guessed, but who had done this to them? On closer inspection their bodies were subtly mutilated, mangled not just out of the sadistic glee that was pitiably common these days, but with cold, clinical precision. Someone had defaced these bodies, only leaving them for the carrion birds once they were finished taking trophies; a strip of one's cancerous skin, a yellow-tinted eyeball, another's teeth. The last, a young woman only a few years older than Gale had been tortured, true, but also humiliated. With her legs splayed open like that she had most likely been violated, and perhaps something had been taken from within.

That last bit struck Gale as chillingly important, but she couldn't reason why.

Burning Lands

Rider wasn't a compassionate man, but he found himself thoroughly disgusted, on levels he never knew existed. No quip about women being property, no callous disregard for human dignity slipped his lips this time. He was made silent by this gruesome atrocity.

Just then, a croaking whisper rasped out. The horse jumped, expecting an attack from the oversized, hungry-eyed vultures. But the weak voice came from the woman they stood next to.

"C-c-loser..." the dying girl murmured, head lying to the side and staring at Gale. Her eyes were wide, unblinking. It was like talking to a corpse come briefly back to life. Gale felt herself compelled to move closer. She jumped off the horse and landed nearby.

The young woman's eyes were glazed over. She wouldn't be alive for much longer. But she could see well enough that she jerked her head up to curse Gale.

"Go back... *demon!*"

Rider dismounted to be at Gale's side.

The girl's head hovered there, for a moment, staring straight at Gale, her eyes only slightly off the mark. She clearly thought Gale was someone else; surely she looked nothing like the ones who had done this! She was clearly delusional... but for some reason Gale suddenly felt... *guilty. Why?*

The girl's eyes rolled back; her chest heaved one last time, her ribs poked through her skin, and she sunk back down never to rise again.

Gale tried to reach out to revive her, but found herself unable to touch the corpse.

Rider sensed Gale's grief but said nothing. Instead he turned and looked at the nearby vulture, which just now raised its gnarled head in interest as the young woman passed away.

He shouted and charged the overgrown bird, and suddenly the winged bully-beast took to the air with a clumsy "whoosh" of fluttering feathers, cawing in a surprised and terrified croak as it vanished with the other birds back into the sky.

Once the vultures were gone Rider returned to her side. "Who did this?"

Gale was speechless, but he could tell her mind was racing. *Did she know something he didn't?*

He paced around for a few minutes more, but there were no more answers here, only questions. As he turned back towards Gale, Rider heard a rumble on the horizon, the desert air pierced by the sound of a truck horn. He turned and ran over to the other side of the horse, and looked out into the desert.

At the extreme edge of his vision he saw a thin gray line... and movement. The remnants of an old highway, running west to east. He couldn't make them out, but in the distance a convoy of four or five Cartel trucks raced down the road, headed east, laden with wares and troops. Exhaust plumes burst from their pipes and hovered in the sky before being dispersed by the wind and vanishing completely, but he had seen them.

"The east-west trade route..." he said, his dry voice only barely audible to Gale. "We must be near the outskirts of Amarillo. Let's go. This horse has done all it can for us, and we can find new transportation there. The scrap merchants in Amarillo are friendly, and the Far Traders sometimes pass through there on their migrations. If we're lucky we might be able to convince them to take us with them."

Gale's mind was still reeling as she and Rider reached the outskirts of Amarillo that evening, where just as he had hoped one of the mammoth fleets of the Far Traders was moving through, having passed the fort of the local scrap traders only to send men out to replenish their "crawling city's" supplies. After an hour avoiding the Cartel in town (he had reason to believe Margus had them out looking for him as well) Rider managed to make friendly contact with men from the neutral Far Trader convoy, hesitantly exchanging his weak horse to secure passage for him and Gale on one of their great wagons. By dawn the next day they would set sail across the desert sea towards wherever their nomadic hosts would take them.

Over a hundred miles away a small group of riders on horseback made their way north through the desert of the Bei Jin Zhi. Karos, Kseniya and a trio of hand-selected men rode steadily onwards despite the changing terrain. Karos was surprisingly not very world-wise, ill-equipped for the desert, a man born of the city and who had made its warrens, back streets and slums his home. And Kseniya was certainly no better, having spent her whole adult life as a mandarin's mistress in the high comfort of the palace. The three men, Gaius, Ryo and Ardor, were from the industrial works of Trade City, workers who'd pledged their loyalty to Karos in the cause to overthrow the Clean but none of them was any more competent at wilderness travel.

Karos seemed driven purely on determination, and dedication to the vision of his allies that spoke of the Clean and Cartel invariably being undone. He knew more than most but at the same time was still unsure as to how exactly the prophecy would come to pass. He seemed eager and unafraid to play his part, knowing that his life was a vehicle through which lasting changes would be wrought.

The others were determined as well, but their faith began to dwindle as the terrain became more unfamiliar, water ran low, and they became surrounded by this strange new wilderness on all sides. The men stayed loyal, and Kseniya remained mostly quiet, swallowing her uncertainty, but there was a definite realization among them that Karos was leading them on the power of faith alone.

As the land became more and more rugged, turning into crags and rocky outlands cut by swaths of ravines and deep gulches, the sandy wasteland gave way to a new kind of desert, a desert of rust and steel. The five riders had entered an old and almost forgotten part of the Forbidden Lands, a great rolling lowland that stretched as far as the eye could see - the *Valley of Tin*.

The valley was a pathetic reminder of how massive and voracious the Ancients' world had been, for the few barren miles of the valley were taken up entirely by a vast junkyard, a colossal dumping place for every imaginable bit of refuse cast off by the industry and consumer-crazy inhabitants of the pre-Fall world. It was an unsightly orange, brown and gleaming metallic desert, comprised of rolling dunes of rusted debris and mountains of twisted, broken scrap. There were cars, cars and more cars, the dented, smashed and wind-stripped remnants of at least ten thousand automobiles of all shapes and sizes. Enormous magnetic cranes towered over the landscape, huge machines once used to arrange crushed and compacted cars block by block into long walls made of one-ton chrome and steel squares. Beneath these towers were literal *seas* of junk; rolling, frozen waves of tin cans, aluminum cans and rubber tires. Billions and billions of colorful plastic bags created a swishing, crinkling underbrush and were blown along like artificial tumbleweed on the moaning winds. Toys, dolls and balls sat partly buried here and there, beside rot-blackened cardboard boxes looking like rows of miniature houses. Pieces of furniture, stripped to their rusted frames, sat out in the narrow gulleys between garbage heaps, upright or toppled on a side. Here and there one saw smashed computer screens, the hulk of wound-down mechanical apparatus, and appliances such as entire washers and dryers, simply sitting out in the open and succumbing to rust. Engine parts lay about in an oily heap, and jerry cans and oil drums stood or squatted in the open like cancerous growths sprouting from a diseased countryside.

Various containers, large and small, leaked chemicals, gasoline, oil and detergents into this lifeless environment. Gravel made from nuts, bolts and washers crunched under the hooves of the intruders' horses. Puddles of water, twinkling with minute globules of mercury, and ponds made yellow and gray with arsenic (too deadly for even the hardiest bacteria), provided some of the only breaks to the rolling monotony. Tiny streams bordered by orange shores of rust wandered through the artificial wasteland, their waters tainted with so much oil that they reflected with all the colors of the rainbow, each a pulsing, ever-changing liquid ribbon of wild hues threading its way through the valley's alien landscape.

A toxic, chemical stink hovered over the Valley of Tin, an acrid, alkaline odor that was punctuated here and there by momentary breezes carrying the reek of rotten garbage. Between the mountains of sifting metal were desolate glades of rust, and above these were those same cranes, those monumental constructions of steel looming five, ten, fifteen stories overhead.

"Oh, the smell!" Ardor exclaimed, drawing his hand over his face to shield from the stench. Karos and Kseniya did the same, while forward-thinking Ryo lifted his kerchief so that it would cover his nose and mouth for the rest of the journey. Gaius merely frowned and wore a look of disgust on his face.

"I think we've wandered too far from the trail," Gaius said cautiously. "This valley is not indicated on the maps. We'd best turn back."

"What do you suppose this is?" Karos asked, appearing to be fascinated by their surroundings.

Gaius looked around as Ryo dismounted and sifted through some nearby junk. Ardor watched on, while Kseniya remained in the saddle of her own steed, listening to the men converse.

"I'm not sure, master," Gaius said. "But it is certainly an unnatural place. I, for one, don't like it."

"How long will it take to go around?" Karos asked again. Once more Gaius looked at their surroundings but could not give an adequate answer.

"Then let's continue through. Be wary, my friends, and keep your muskets and sabers close. Kseniya, ride next to me. And all of you, keep your eyes peeled for anything unusual."

Whether they agreed with Karos or not, the men once more prepared to follow. As they readied themselves, Karos looked over at Kseniya, a serious look on his face. "Can you use a blade?"

Kseniya thought of the armory-master she had killed with a knife. She remembered how easy, *surprisingly* easy, it had been. She nodded. Karos handed her a scimitar in a rawhide sheath, which she put at her side.

Karos led the way, Gaius close to his side, with Kseniya on the other. Ryo trotted a little further out, his steely eyes watching for signs of danger. Ardor merely followed, trailing behind on his own mount, taking in the sights of this strange new countryside.

An hour passed, and by then they had slowly grown used to the unnatural smells that pervaded the gray air of the Valley. Nothing emerged from the rusty wasteland and its maze of hills and mounds, and so Karos gave Ryo permission to ride ahead and scout a path through the Valley's meandering canyons and gulleys. Every ten minutes or so he would return with word of a safer path for their party to take, before riding off again once more. Ryo had just departed once more when Kseniya spoke for the first time in hours.

"How do you plan on getting the *bei man* to join your cause?" she asked.

Karos looked over at her, then ahead, considering her question. "The *bei man* live free now, but they stand to lose everything if the Clean and the Cartel aren't stopped. Uncle Sam has to realize this, he's no fool. He must know that he is only delaying the inevitable through his appeasement of Margus Han."

"And if he doesn't?"

"Then I'll make sure he does," Karos said with a smile. Kseniya was quiet for a few moments, then continued her questions.

"What brought you here? I mean, to become the leader of a movement, this 'revolution' of yours?"

Karos sighed. "For a long time I saw the people of Tucumcari enslaved by the Clean and their Cartel lackeys. My people live their lives in miserable work houses, providing endless labor for the Clean and Cartel industries, melting down scrap to make armor and weapons for the Clean's janissaries, or purifying old oil by hand so that it runs in Cartel engines. In exchange they are permitted to live within the walls of the city, safe from the predators that haunt the desert outside, or in small villages up and down the trade routes that the Cartel pledges to protect from attack. Robots, destined to be nothing more than consumers for the Clean's water.

"You may not realize this, but most of those same people were first drawn to Trade City by *hope*, hope for a better life than the one that exists out in the wasteland, among the raiders and scavs. What they got was a typical Clean-brokered deal, a trade - freedom for security.

"Ours wasn't the worst lot, by far. Ridaya and her sisters were all slaves of the Clean or Cartel at one time, women taken as servants and concubines and treated far more brutally. Those women that escape, if they're lucky, sometimes fall in with Ridaya's tribe, a secret sisterhood of the desert. Ridaya has kept them safe for years from hunters and raiders who'd love nothing more than to re-capture them. She and her kind have more reason to hate the merchant houses than anyone else.

"For years my people tried to preach to the population of Tucumcari and other settlements to rise above the Clean way of life, to look back at the past for guidance, but the world doesn't really want the past. They want a *future*.

"I didn't truly understand that concept until, about three years ago, I met some unusual men and women from a ruined city across the Wei Shan. Mentalists, moving unseen and unnoticed among the crowds of Trade City, they had listened to my message and had understood the change I was driving at. They contacted me, and explained their own mission in these lands."

"What mission?" Kseniya asked.

"To watch, to witness," he explained vaguely. "There is a prophecy among their people that speaks of 'Eden', the birth of a new and bountiful country at the heart of the eastern wasteland. They've come to see if the Far Desert and its peoples are ready for its genesis."

"Eden?"

"They say it will be a place from which fantastic new life will be born. It will be the heart of a new religion, the capital of an empire for all mutantkind, for all the survivors of the Fall."

"So your 'friends', whoever they are, have come here just to *watch?*"

"No," Karos said urgently. "They shared with me their vision and I shared mine with them. I told them of the suffering, of the desperation, of the tyranny. They have agreed to help, to lend their far-sight to aid in the fight against the Clean and the Cartel."

"*Far-sight?*" Kseniya asked, suddenly realizing who Karos had entered into service with. "You're talking about the *Brotherhood*, aren't you?"

Karos said nothing, but his eyes were filled with excitement.

"You think Uncle Sam will really join you?" Kseniya asked, this time brushing the hair from her face as the wind picked up in strength.

Karos looked back at her, considered for a moment his response. He grinned. "Nothing is ever certain."

Gaius looked over his shoulder and interrupted. "Ryo has been gone for some time. I'm worried..." Ardor seemed concerned as well and trotted up to join the others.

Karos looked around, realizing that Ryo *had* been gone for an unusual amount of time. He should certainly have come back to report by now, but he and his horse were nowhere to be seen.

"Maybe he's found something of interest, a clear path out, and is simply scouting ahead?" Karos offered, but Gaius seemed unconvinced.

"No," Gaius replied, "I think he would have come back either way. He could be in danger. He could be injured..."

"No, I don't think so," Karos said calmly. "This place seems dead. We've seen no life so far...

"*Ryo!*" he called out, shouting over the wind. His voice carried, echoing through the Valley and among the sagging heaps of garbage and metallic refuse. But there was no response.

"What should we do?" Ardor asked.

"*Ryo!*" Karos called out once more, followed by Gaius. Again, no response.

"Alright, he can't have gone too far. Let's listen for him..."

As if to answer them a strange sound echoed from somewhere in the land of junk, carried by its sighing, noxious wind. It was the sound of a voice, unfamiliar, but unmistakably human, and not too far away:

"*Look at all this junk... for the taking!*"

Karos looked at the others, and sure enough they'd heard it too. "There are others here," Gaius stated.

"Maybe they can help us," Ardor offered hopefully. "Maybe they've seen Ryo."

Karos led them around the bend into a gulley created by heaps of garbage on both sides. They expected to see someone there, or perhaps even a group of men, scavengers or junk collectors wandering this bizarre place with sacks of rusted loot over their shoulders. Instead they saw only another empty gulley, a tunnel created by walls of junk on both sides, empty and quiet.

"I could have sworn I heard something!" Gaius insisted aloud, despite knowing that everyone with him agreed. They *had* heard a voice, from this direction, only no one was there now...

From somewhere behind, in the distance, they heard another voice call out over the wind:

"*Who's there?*"

Followed moments later by:

"*What is that thing?*"

Ardor looked behind them, turning his skittish mount to get a better look. "Did you hear that? From back that way?"

"But there's no one there," Gaius said, struggling to maintain control of his own steed, which began to grow nervous. "We just came from that direction!"

Karos looked back as well, only this time he drew his blade with his one good hand. "Arm yourselves," he said cautiously. Kseniya and the others sensed his apprehension, and one by one drew their weapons as well.

They were unsure if they faced an enemy, or just phantoms of their own mind. Bodiless voices floating through the maze of junk, carried by the winds of the valley, could neither be seen nor fought. Their weapons were of little comfort.

"*Tao zou!*" someone yelled, his voice shrill and indistinct. It caused everyone to look immediately towards a nearby crest, where the wreck of a paint-stripped car sat, without wheels or windows. But there was no one there.

"*Wan jiu!*" another voice called out, just moments later, from over another hill.

"Trade tongue..." Karos said excitedly, recognizing the sound of the words. "Anyone know what it means?"

Kseniya held her horse's reigns tight. "I do," she said. "I think it's someone calling for help!"

"Let's go then," Karos said resolutely, and dug his spurs into his horse and led them in that direction.

The horse riders came over the hill, and as they reached its summit, were confronted by an unexpected scene, a large open vale in which the hulks of over a dozen gigantic trucks lay forgotten and rusting under the sun. Enormous scrap movers, each three stories high with wheels as broad as a small house, requiring ladders to reach their drivers' pits from the ground. These huge trucks were tremendously ancient, and had probably been abandoned here since at least the time of the Fall.

"No one here!" shouted Ardor, but Karos led them down among the trucks nonetheless.

Shadows fell over Karos, Kseniya and the two remaining men as they wandered through the wreckage of the deserted heavy movers.

Karos saw something ahead that caught his eye. He got off his horse for a moment to investigate, and in that instant his steed bolted and fled, racing past Kseniya's own panicking mount, almost knocking her off as it went.

For no clear reason, all at once the horses began to strain at their reigns, whinnying in panic. Sensing the woman was in danger, Karos ran over and helped Kseniya from the saddle just as her riding beast began to rear. Once she was clear the beast ran off after his own, kicking up dust as it galloped away. Ardor's horse attempted to bolt as well, and the youth cried out as he fell completely from his saddle to the hard-packed gravel below.

Gaius continued to struggle to keep his mount under control despite its violent protests. "Let the horses go!" Karos cried, but Gaius was stubborn and gripped his mount tighter, cursing aloud. It gave up trying to buck him, and instead simply turned and ran, carrying the shouting man with it and out of sight.

"Gaius!" Ardor cried after him, pulling himself to his feet out of the oily puddle he'd fallen in. "Gaius! Come back!"

Karos watched Gaius vanish, but there was nothing he could do. Instead he regained his weapon and started towards the thing that had drawn his attention in the first place.

There, lying on his back in the shadow of one of the huge trucks, was Ryo. Only he had been mauled by some creature, the flesh of his neck slashed open as if his throat had been deliberately ripped apart. Blood still oozed from the fatal injury, but the man was surely dead.

Kseniya felt nauseous but kept her composure, and walked over to the dead man. His sword was several feet away, unbloodied, as was one of his packs, which had been torn open and its meager contents scattered haphazardly about. His horse was nowhere to be seen.

A voice, this time more distant, echoed through the maze of trucks from somewhere in the direction of where Gaius had fled. Remarkably, it sounded just like Ardor:

"*No one here!*"

Gaius' horse scrambled to get away, fleeing through the dusty corridors of the junkyard, walled in on some sides by abandoned cars and trucks, and in others by the giant heaps of trash that decorated most of the valley. His horse screeched in panic as it galloped at full tilt, and he feared for his life.

As they turned another bend Gaius finally lost his grip and fell from his mount, rolling away into the rubble. The beast kept going, leaving him behind.

Getting to his feet, breathing hard, he managed to look around, nursing a painfully broken arm. He walked a few steps, then noticed, just a few feet away, a collection of bones hidden cleverly in the shade beneath a sheet of scrap metal.

Gaius went forward to get a better look, and sure enough he saw the broken skeleton of some past victim of this haunted valley. From its rags and the bulging pack still bound around it in a leathery tangle he could tell this poor fool had once been a scav, an opportunistic looter who had likely found this place long ago... and had paid the ultimate price for desecrating the Valley's slumbering relics.

"*Look at all this junk... for the taking!*" came a strange voice from behind, echoing off walls of crumpled steel and rusted heaps of trash. Gaius spun around, drawing his sword, but it was already too late.

From above something dropped on him, knocking him over and immediately lunging for his throat. He didn't even have a chance to scream.

"There's no one here for us to help," Karos said grimly. "So who was it that we heard? Are you sure someone was calling for *help?*" he asked Kseniya.

Kseniya nodded. She didn't know the Trade tongue fluently, it was rarely spoken in the harem (where business was deliberately left outside), but she knew enough that she was sure. *Wan jiu...* "Help".

"That was *my* voice, just then," Ardor said, wide-eyed and fearful. "I swear that sounded just like me!"

Karos looked away in the direction that Gaius had fled. He knew Ardor was right, but he said nothing to avoid shaking the boy up even further.

"Just a trick of this maze..." he started, but a new voice called out, from an entirely different direction, cutting him short.

"*Just what manner of beast do you think it is?*" the voice said. It was getting closer.

"I think we should go," Ardor said, his own voice breaking. "I think we should go *now!*"

"No!" Kseniya shouted, but it was too late. Ardor began to run, kicking up dust as he plodded off through the labyrinth of enormous trucks. Karos and Kseniya started after him, but there was fear in the air and they couldn't prevent Ardor's fate.

From around the corner of one lopsided truck a large creature burst, barreling into Ardor and knocking him, stunned, to the ground. As he brought his arms up instinctively to defend his face, the *thing's* head lunged downwards and completely engulfed his neck in its mouth, shredding his jugular and crushing his windpipe with a single, powerful bite.

Ardor continued flailing about, shocked and terrified, but the beast held him firmly, reducing him to little more than a rag doll thrashing in its grip. It waited patiently for his life to bleed away, for his breath to fade, until he passed away.

Karos and Kseniya stopped in their tracks when they saw it. An abnormally large feline beast, hugely muscled with a mangy, spotted coat, black with the vague traces of grayish stripes around its chest and slender flanks. It walked on strangely human paws, with long and slender fingers instead of claws, its digits grasping at the rocks underfoot. It had a long, sinuous tail that writhed behind it, coiling and uncoiling as it waited for Ardor to die, its eyes locked on Karos and Kseniya.

Its head was nothing like the rest of its body; instead of a panther's face, it had a strangely-shaped mask of bare flesh, with angular cheekbones over a death-trap of interlocking fangs. It relinquished Ardor, now dead, and gazed in Karos' and Kseniya's direction. From the side it looked suitably feline enough, but as it turned to stare down the others its features took on an almost human appearance - bare skin, flat nose and a grinning maw open wide so its wet tongue, freshly coated in gore, could repeatedly slip out and taste the air. Its eyes, set in the front of its face, were dull orbs of crimson, lacking pupils whatsoever, and ringed by wrinkles from a lifetime spent enjoying the terror and fitful spasms of its prey.

As they stood, not knowing whether to run or attack, the thing's tongue retracted with a wet "slosh" into its mouth, and with its jaws frozen open Ardor's voice, seemingly disembodied, issued from its throat and through the stillness:

"*I think we should go,*" it said. "*I think we should go now!*"

Karos gaped. "Ardor's voice! It has Ardor's *voice!*"

Even as it mimicked its most recent victim, snaring the boy's voice and perfectly recreating its timber in its fantastically-complex throat, the creature almost seemed to smile, and began to move towards them.

Karos readied his sword, but the creature sensed the danger he now posed and instantly leapt on him, using its great weight to take him to the ground. As Karos struggled, it swiped a misshapen claw across his chest, only just cutting his skin with its dull and broken nails. It hissed at him, its face transforming into a smile that showed needle-sharp teeth, before bounding off and up the nearby hillock.

Kseniya now held her weapon out, prepared to fight for her life. The thing saw this and circled, pacing back and forth, its tail winding and unwinding as it considered its next move. It watched her, its red eyes locked upon her, its mouth dangling now and its tongue flipping to and fro in front of it.

"*Just what manner of beast do you think it is?*" the creature said again, perfectly mimicking some curious victim from the past.

Karos stumbled to get up, looking weak and frail. Kseniya noticed and called for him to run, ready to stand in the way if it went after him.

"No!" Karos called back, rising to his feet and finding the strength to regain his blade.

The thing darted when Karos stood back up, coming quickly down the slope and attacking him from behind. It bit his shoulder blade, sinking its teeth into his flesh, but Karos fell down again and avoided a more deadly follow-up. This time, instead of retreating to survey the situation, the strange creature unexpectedly turned and lashed out at Kseniya, slashing her right forearm with its powerful paw and leaving deep gouges where its dirty, filth-caked nails raked across her arm.

As her skin broke and blood streamed from the grievous wound, Kseniya cried out in shock and clumsily dropped her weapon. The creature sensed her paralysis and came after her, immediately standing up on its hind legs and coming down on her, paws to her shoulders, so that they both fell to the ground together.

Kseniya struggled to get free but she was pinned by it. The menacing thing looked down at her, a throaty, feline purr building in its throat, and a great monstrous grin sweeping over its hideous face. It prepared to lower its head to her soft, exposed neck, when all of a sudden the whistle of *arrows* sang out through the air.

Two arrows flew out from the bows of a group of tribal archers, striking the creature directly in its flanks. A third hit it in the neck, causing it to shriek in pain and leap from Kseniya and start off towards the top of a nearby hill.

Karos got up, bleeding profusely from his back wound, and stumbled over to Kseniya, who was grasping her arm but staring off towards their unexpected saviors.

There, on a nearby crest, were four tribal warriors armed with bows and spears. They were immediately recognizable as *bei men*, wearing dirty breeches and leathery shirts, with wild curly beards and unkempt heads of dirty hair. Despite their ragged appearance the natives exhibited great skill with their weapons, as the archers let off another volley, hitting the creature several more times. As the last arrow impacted the horribly mutated thing it collapsed, and as its head rolled skywards, all at once it released the many voices it had "captured" in its years of killing.

"Who's there! What is that thing? Ryo! Tao Zou! No one here! Help me! It's playing with us! You killed my son! It looks wounded, finish it off! Wan jiu! Look at all this junk... for the taking!"

With that last final thrash of defiance the beast was dead.

Kseniya stared at the lifeless animal, and for a moment found herself wondering how such a thing could come to exist, a monstrous mutation that had somehow come to adopt human traits, including the ability to perfectly mimic the voices it heard, to become among the wasteland's most clever predators.

Though weak and injured, Karos hid Kseniya behind him, aware that there were still tribal warriors to deal with. Two of the men descended the hill, but ran past Karos and Kseniya to check that the creature was dead, drawing machetes as they went. The final two warriors, each tall and broad, stood back for a time, watching the others hack the thing's head from its corpse, and only then did they came forward.

The one in the lead came over and looked at Karos. His blue eyes narrowed as he saw him crumpled there, covered in dust and grime and his clothing shredded. He drew a broadsword from a leather sheath at his side and held it up, ready to kill.

"You there, scavengers! You're in the lands of Uncle Sam, lord of the northern freemen. You take from our scrapyard, you pay the price!"

The huge warrior lifted the broadsword, ready to cut off Karos' head as easily as he'd been prepared to decapitate the beast, when the other man behind him overruled him.

"No. The woman is familiar..."

Kseniya looked up and saw *Boren*, Uncle Sam's right-hand man, standing with the sword-wielding tribesman. Boren's blue cloak flapped in the wind, the chain links of his armor gleamed, and his muscled, hard face seemed to beam with amusement.

The armed tribesman looked back at Boren and, realizing he meant business, put his sword away and stepped aside. Boren crossed his arms over his chest and looked at Kseniya as she slowly got to her feet.

"You're a long way from home, milady," he said with a smile. "This is *our* junkyard, where we mine the metal for our weapons and armor. This is no place for you. How on earth did you get here?"

Kseniya looked at him, her eyes expressing great relief. "What was that *thing?*"

Boren grimaced and looked over at the other men, who were now holding up the creature's severed head and smiling.

"They prey on our workers, ambush our work teams, but most often just kill the weak, the stragglers. This one must have been desperate to attack an armed party. We usually kill them on sight. You're lucky we came when we did..."

"Indeed," Karos said, stepping forward.

Boren acknowledged him with a nod. "Who are you?"

Karos was about to introduce himself when Kseniya stepped in. "His name is Karos, a friend from the south. He is on an important mission, and must be taken to your king right away."

Boren looked suspicious for a moment, but looking at Kseniya's pleading eyes concluded she was telling the truth. He brought his big hands back to his sides and spoke.

"Well alright. I'm sure he'll be happy to see you," he said to Kseniya, a smile once more forming on his face. "Up here among the lands of the *barbarians*."

They ventured some ways north and west, joining with the rest of a work team from Boren's tribe returning to the camp of Uncle Sam with loads of metal and scrap from the Valley of Tin, destined for the forges of the *bei man* king's master smiths. Boren explained that despite his promises, Margus Han seemed unable to find those responsible for the mysterious attacks on the eastern frontier, and Uncle Sam was beginning to take things into his own hands. For several weeks they had begun frantically crafting crude arms and armor for their people, preparing to equip a sizable portion of the tribe's male population for war.

Karos' eyes glittered with excitement when he heard this, but he and Kseniya remained silent. They waited and followed as Boren led them into Uncle Sam's large, sprawling camp, through a small city of tents, huts and teepees to the lodge where the great northern king made his court. Here they were fed and their wounds tended to before they were brought into Uncle Sam's hall.

Uncle Sam sat in a throne room walled on all sides by hanging furs and tapestries of rare beast hides. The floor was scattered with similar skins, on which sat a handful of his relatives, armed nephews and cousins smoking foul-smelling cigars or sharing meat fresh from the fire. Guards lingered not too far away at the various entrances to the chamber, with two standing straight and at attention on either side of the platform that bore the chief's throne.

Uncle Sam himself reclined on a lofty leather chair, a huge seat that almost seemed to engulf him in its warm comfort. It was a worn, tattered thing from the ancient world but it seemed perfectly suited for him. At its side sat another chair, a smaller wooden throne with an embroidered seat cushion, but this one sat empty; a thin wooden crown sat on the seat, a reminder of the queen that once sat at his side.

When Boren led Kseniya and Karos into the throne room, Uncle Sam's face noticeably brightened. A few of the other warriors turned to regard Kseniya's rumpled and ripped *cheongsam* with something close to suspicion, but the great king rose as she came forward, a gleam of recognition in his eyes.

"Kseniya," he said warmly. "Welcome at last to my lands. And while I never expected you to actually take me up on my offer, I am glad you did."

Karos looked at Kseniya, finding himself thankful once more for agreeing to bring her along. She hadn't lied, she had met the chieftain before, and he did seem fond of her in a fatherly fashion. Kseniya kept her eyes away from Uncle Sam for a moment, but then remembered why she was there. She looked up, bringing her stare to meet his.

"Great king," she said, "I cannot lie to you. I did not risk my life to come here for my own sake, despite your offer of hospitality. But I have since met this man, an important man, and I have accompanied him here so that he might make a request of you."

Uncle Sam shifted his weight, listening to her. For once his eyes moved to Karos, the sandy-haired demagogue who stood at her side. He said nothing, but he seemed prepared to listen.

Karos stepped past Kseniya and came forward. "*Bei man* king," he said. "I come at the behest of the people of Trade City, and of the villages and towns that lie under the shadow of Margus Han and his alliance with the Cartel. I come in the name of those who yearn for a better life free of the great merchant houses, unshackled by their brutal laws and unforgiving ways. I come on behalf of the people of this ancient land."

Uncle Sam listened, but seemed wary. He sat back down on his throne, holding his chin and unconsciously stroking his beard.

"Uncle Sam, you and your people have lived free of the Clean for a long time, but we both know the Clean are insidious. Their offer of clean water for cheap prices has lured many to their walls, and their ideas of 'civilization' pollute whatever settlements they come to visit. Your people, of all the tribes of the desert, have resisted this encroachment on their culture; but the Clean and Cartel are strong and their ways mysterious. For years you have sat paralyzed, unwilling to act, because of the fear of their gun-toting armies..."

"We are not afraid," Uncle Sam interrupted. He seemed mildly insulted by the insinuation.

Karos chose his words carefully. "But you are certainly no *fool*," he continued. "You know the Clean have many janissary warriors, and their Cartel allies are industrious workers as well. I understand your hesitation. You've tried ignoring them and you've tried co-existence, but now the Clean have come to make impossible demands. I have long wished that the legendary *bei man* king would hear me out; I *pray* that you will now see the righteousness of our cause."

Uncle Sam's eyes twinkled. "What 'cause', eh?"

Karos lifted his head, his eyes alight. "To overthrow Margus Han, the Clean, and the Cartel."

There were excited murmurings among the men and women gathered in the chamber, and even Uncle Sam's solemn guardsmen turned to look at this bold man who spoke so openly of treason against the mandarin of his own city. But Karos did not let their stares affect him, he stood resolutely.

Uncle Sam surprised them all by laughing, a deep, hearty bellow. "Overthrow Margus Han? You? With the peasants of that wretched little city? Oh, and maybe a few villages, too? You tell a good joke, master Karos! But it will require more than angry slaves to take on the Clean and the Cartel!"

"Not just slaves," Karos said softly, "but visionaries as well. Seers, from across the Wei Shan. Agents of the Brotherhood are here, among us, offering us their assistance, the power of their minds. Uncle Sam, I have seen their vision for the future of this land, and it is a future without the banners of the Clean and the Cartel over our heads." The assembly quieted at the mention of the mysterious Brotherhood.

"Vision?" Uncle Sam asked.

Karos closed his eyes. "Once, long ago, they graced me with a chance to see their vision, to share in a glimpse of the future. I am not psychic, and my mind was unable

Burning Lands

to truly understand what I saw, but as I joined with their... consciousness... I think I saw for the first time a new land, a hopeful future."

He was speaking vaguely, cryptically, remembering an incident long ago when the Brotherhood first recruited him. That one glimpse, from momentary, direct contact with those potent mentalists, had left him reeling, but it had seared an image into his mind. Even then he hadn't been able to fully grasp it, or wrap his mind around what he saw, and so now struggled to put it to words.

"I saw a land, our own dark land, over which a silver sun rose. Shedding the light of a new day. I saw the ruins of a wrecked city, a devastated pyramid... a symbol of the past? And new light springing from it, washing away the old. I believe it was a prophetic vision, great king, a glimpse of a world for all the survivors of the Fall, for everyone."

Uncle Sam and his *bei man* court seemed impressed, as evidenced by their awed silence. But the king at least was a realist. After a moment of quiet, he reminded Karos once again: "Still, without an army behind you you're only left with 'visions'. And while visions may *see* the future, they cannot *change* it."

Karos listened to him, but continued unabated; his faith was strong. "I've rallied many men to the cause, great chief. Two hundred eager volunteers from the city itself, and another two hundred men and women from the assorted tribes and villages that strain under the Clean's bitter rule. The will to fight for a new way of life is much more widespread than you think. We're not alone in risking our lives. There are others as well. Ridaya, and the Sisters of the Desert, have pledged their swords to the cause, one and all. That's another one-hundred and fifty women-warriors and their trained war beasts, a force to contend with on any battlefield."

Uncle Sam looked ready to laugh off this last as a wild boast, but Kseniya stared at him and nodded, backing up Karos' words.

"Five hundred-and-fifty men? And women?" Uncle Sam chortled instead. "*That's* your army?"

"With your people we could more than *double* that," Karos answered quickly, eagerly.

Uncle Sam looked playful for a moment, as if he considered spouting another amusing question, but at that moment his smile subsided and he leaned forward, looking serious.

"And what do we get in return for our aid, hmm?"

Karos looked at him. "What do you want?"

Uncle Sam considered for a long moment. "We have more reason than most to want this thing that you suggest. 'War with the Clean'. They sell us their civil-i-za-tion like a vendor peddles a jeweled necklace. Sure it's pretty, sure we all want something like it... but to us a jeweled necklace is still just another yoke. This land was once *our* nation," Uncle Sam continued, "not theirs, and yes, long ago we did lose our unity and nobility, we lost the war to keep the enemy at bay, but we will still defend our way of life against the forces of change. No matter the cost.

"Now they raid my people. They respect nothing, not even the sovereignty of a native king. They search for raiders in our midst and are willing to butcher my villages to get what they want. They seem hell-bent on war...

"You ask me what the *bei man* tribes want?" Uncle Sam said, returning to the question at hand. "My people want to be *free*. Like they once were. Without the influence of outsiders. Without being manipulated and controlled. We want to return to the life of our forefathers before we grow corrupt like the Clean, like all that they stand for. Can you give us freedom?"

Karos' face seemed full of the power to make the king's dream a reality. There was a silence in the chamber that was deafening. Karos drew in a short breath of air, then spoke his reply.

"Yes."

The men in the great hall stirred and whispered. The younger men glanced to each other, then sat up, the air of excitement brought on by Karos' promise drawing their full attention. The obstinate looks of older warriors softened and they murmured quietly to one another, debating the likelihood of success. Through it all Uncle Sam sat quietly, scrutinizing Karos' face for any sign of trickery. But what he saw instead was stoic, unshakable determination.

"How soon would we march?" Uncle Sam asked.

Karos took another step forward. "As soon as you can muster your men. The mystics have seen the coming of a great sandstorm that will sweep the deserts around Tucumcari. If we march now, we can join up with Ridaya and my own forces near the Caves of Sorrow. Together we will use the sandstorm to screen our advance on the city."

"And once we get there, prepare for a siege?" the *bei man* king asked in short order.

"No," Karos said, his eyes gleaming. "No siege. When we get there, *the gates will already be open.*"

Uncle Sam didn't know what magic the Brotherhood had to make such a thing happen, but at that moment he was ready to believe. He stood straight up, and cast off his cloak, revealing the armor and weapons that he always wore underneath, that all *bei man* leaders wore to show their readiness for war. He looked at his man, Boren, and shouted a command:

"Send the call for every man who can bear arms! Assemble the army! Assemble the cavalry! *We leave at dawn!*"

Amid the rolling desert dunes of the Jia Lang, Shubazang looked through his rifle scope at the two men standing out in the open, just a few yards from their horses. From almost a mile away he could make the two riders out clearly; one a giant wearing a weathered cape over a tunic of rusted and tattered chainmail, the other a tall muscled man bearing the brand of a raider. They were walking among the remains of four or five corpses left out in the sun, each of them now more than a week old. Buzzards had rendered the corpses unrecognizable, but the larger of the two men seemed to see something among the carnage and pointed off to the southeast.

"Looks like we're not the only ones on this assassin's trail," Shubazang said softly, slightly grinning.

He stopped smiling and looked closer at the smaller of the two men. "Euryale," he said quietly, "where have I seen that guy before?"

Euryale took the rifle and peered through the lens for itself. Shubazang could hear the whirring rotation of its mechanical optic lens as it focused on the distant individual, but it of course said nothing, it simply stared.

"Looks a lot like the slave we plucked from the depths of that desert cave up north. What the hell is he doing here? And who's that with him?"

He spotted movement and took the rifle back. He watched through the scope as Tank and Valero mounted their desert horses and began riding off to the southeast, following what was left of Rider's tracks towards distant Amarillo.

After half an hour they had disappeared into the swirling vapor of the desert horizon's heat mirage.

"They're gone," Shubazang said. "Let's go."

The boy got up and eventually wandered over to the spot where Tank and Valero had been, among the collection of corpses, curious to see for himself what they had been looking at. Euryale followed close behind, leading the horses by their reigns.

The bodies of three men and two women lay scattered about; a scene of carnage and massacre. Buzzards had done a fair job over the past few days of removing the flesh from most of the bodies, and had opened the bloated stomachs with their beaks to gobble down the soft, delectable innards. Desert beetles had eaten away the eyes, but despite this their faces were relatively intact.

Shubazang saw the trail the two riders had left and the vague impressions of another horseman, probably Rider, whose tracks he and the other party were almost certainly shadowing.

Convinced they were still on the trail, he relaxed and returned to examine the dead. He went over to one of the men, and, taking his lead, Euryale walked over to one of the women, playfully mimicking his scrutinizing interest.

Shubazang looked at the stripped, rotting cadaver, completely unmoved by the mites eating away at the flaps of skin around the burst stomach. Instead he narrowed in on the pencil-thin hole in the man's skull.

Tiny green letters appeared on the lenses of his reflective goggles.

"This was done by a *laser?*" he said vaguely over his shoulder, in Euryale's direction. "No, that can't be right..."

He looked at another one of the corpses to check to be sure, and remarkably the signs were the same. Whoever had killed this family of desert scavengers had used powerful Ancient weaponry to do it. Decay, and the effort of the desert's animals, had almost erased the evidence, but enough was still visible to confirm what he now knew to be true.

"This *definitely* couldn't have been the Ravagers," he said. "We're *way* out of their territory. This had to be someone else..."

Euryale stood up, now wearing the face of one of the dead women, which the android had carefully removed from the cadaver with a blade. It turned to Shubazang and gestured to its new skin, cocking its head to the side as if to ask "what do you think?"

Shubazang ignored the pesky android and stood, facing north. Miles of sand and desolation stretched as far as the eye could see, but he knew that beyond the horizon lay the edge of the Burning Lands. The rest of this terrain was bleak and empty; what invisible enemy could be waiting out there? Who was it, and why were they exacting such a terrible toll on the insignificant inhabitants of the land? He could understand raids on merchant caravans, and even attacks on the diplomats of the Clean and Cartel (there were enough angry natives out there willing to nab a southerner just for bragging rights), but the senseless butchery of scavs?

The young man drew the fur collar of his greatcoat around him as the sun began to dip low. Night was setting in, and they had to get moving again.

East-northeast of Amarillo the desert was a boundless landscape of flat, dry, cracked earth, the evening sun boring down on it without clouds to obscure its blinding radiance. Dust devils rose up here and there where the wind touched the ground; heat mirages rippled and distorted the far edges of the horizon, hiding whatever might lie beyond, isolating the great convoy of the Far Traders, their "crawling city", to a few square miles of barren, unbroken terrain.

The "city" itself was one grand caravan, an entire bustling frontier town on wheels; always on the move, always following their own invisible trails, highways of sand, never stopping until they reached where they were going. Skyscrapers of dust followed behind this armada of makeshift vehicles, rising miles into the crystal clear sky almost like a bold proclamation that the Far Traders were traveling through.

The "buildings" of this moving city were a mismatched collection of odd and truly unique post-Fall vehicles; trucks, buses and cars, as well as weird mechanical structures thrown together so crudely that they lacked a definable shape. Three wheels, five wheels, six wheels, ten wheels, lumbering giants of rusted, scavenged steel, arches of wood rising up like ribs of an eternally landlocked sailing ship, the yellowed tusks of monstrous beasts worked into each rolling ark's majestic framework. Much more than the humble howdahs of nomads, each huge vehicle was a rolling *keep*, with two, three families living in its cramped interior or in the rickety tower of wood rising above it, the dirty faces of children peering out tiny windows to stare at neighboring "buildings" as they passed by. Armored slats hung over each portal; every thundering, diesel-fueled vehicle capable of buttoning up to fend off attackers, of defending its own, until reinforcements arrived. Like the great bomber fleets of a forgotten, ancient war, some of them could be damaged and slowed by determined attackers and might fall behind, sucked into the permanent sandstorm that trailed the city on its continuous migrations. Those that did, vanished and were surely lost, for there was no turning back, and the city never stopped between its far-flung destinations.

Thankfully there were no attackers today, and life in the crawling city continued as normal, if that word could ever be used to describe a typical day for the fleet. Gale stood on a rickety wooden platform on the side of one of the great rolling wagons, staring out in wonder at the moving city, her hair whipped by the wind and her eyes struggling to stay open despite the dust and sand kicked up by its progress. She was high up (almost three stories above ground) and from here she could see other wagons, some larger and others smaller. She could see people walking on other platforms like hers, and musicians playing weird pipes under a brown tarp atop another. In between the lumbering behemoths of steel, the stripped-down and souped-up dune buggies of Far Trader scouts weaved in and out, racing behind and ahead of the city, alert for whatever unseen dangers might lie in their city's path.

Rider climbed up the narrow stairs and took a moment to take the sight and sounds in as they assaulted him from all around. Gale stood by the edge, at a dangerous-looking rail, but she seemed happy, a wide smile on her face. He struggled to keep his hat on but moved over beside her.

"We'll get off twenty miles ahead," he shouted, his voice barely audible over the din of the great moving city. "The rest of the way we travel by foot."

Gale turned and looked at him, holding a hand up to shield her eyes from the sun. With the sun to his back she could only see the dark outline of him, his silhouette - a ghostly cowboy at her side. She felt comforted.

But where are you taking me? And why? she thought, knowing somehow that it was right to follow and not intrude too deeply into his thoughts. Normally she could easily tear into a man with the aid of her gifts, but now, with Rider, found herself utterly unable and unwilling to do so.

Their host, a Far Trader patriarch named Theo, ascended the stairs and joined them, smiling as he saw her look of wonder. The city was indeed a sight to see, and sometimes he forgot how impressive it was for outsiders. He walked over to the railing and stared as well.

"In your travels... where have you been?" Gale asked him curiously.

"All across the desert, young one, and even to lands more fruitful. Our people have traveled to the distant ends of the Far Desert, visiting the tiny settlements and villages of the wasteland's tribal folk, and seen all manner of things. Our men have found rare treasures in the hands of savages, and taken beautiful wives from deep desert tribes living days from the established trade routes of this land. We've been to the shores of the Dune Seas, and seen from a distance the mighty, wrecked shells of ancient metropolises scattered across the Graveyard of Domed Cities. We've been to Free Water, that storied trade town where water seems endless, and let me tell you, it is not at all as the tales suggest. We've skirted the fringes of the Grassland Empire and encountered the vast herds there, done business with the nomadic plains people, and passed through the lonely Forests of Iron and their haunted spires."

Gale looked out at the horizon as he spoke, imagining these distant places, far corners of a new world she was only now beginning to see. She thought of Johnny, and others like him, spending their entire lives in some tiny, five-mile area, soothed by its familiarity, never leaving because they were too afraid of what lay over the next hill. But how much larger the world was! How much more there was to see!

"We've traveled up and down these trade routes, to the white walls of Tucumcari and through raider-infested lands to the west; through Trader Gap ringed on both sides by the towering ramparts of ancient mountains, their peaks encased in ice. Through storms of sand and snow we've crossed the treacherous passes to the legendary city of Styx, and come to the very edge of the Grand Canyon and seen its wonders. Through the mountains we have slogged on, never stopping, to break bread in the company of primitive peoples forgotten and disregarded by the civilization of the Clean and their Cartel allies. There are so many wonderful things in this world, woman... would you like to see them?"

Gale looked at him with a pleasant, questioning look.

"With *me?*" he offered.

He was not entirely unattractive, but nearing fifty the offer seemed... unusual to her. He had warm, kind eyes, and she dreaded insulting their gracious host, but the suddenness (and the circumstances) made her uncomfortable. She unconsciously extended a hand in the other direction and took Rider's arm.

The Far Trader noticed and smiled, then turned to address Rider in a most honorable tone.

"You have a fine-looking companion, sir. I wonder what price you are asking for her hand."

Rider looked at him with an arched eyebrow, then to Gale, suddenly realizing she had taken his hand. He quietly pried her fingers loose from his sleeve, then spoke.

"She's not for sale, Master Theo. She travels freely."

Gale looked at Rider suddenly. *Freely? Hadn't she been a captive, a hostage, up until yesterday?*

Theo smiled and apologized, but no offense had been taken by his question, as Rider assured him. The older man nodded humbly and stepped away, leaving the two of them alone.

Later on, Rider found a table among the other rowdy patrons of the Far Trader city, relegated as they were to one of the larger wagons, a gigantic rolling building set aside for the carrying of unaffiliated passengers. This particular wagon in which they rode, featured a theatre house, and patrons were already drinking heavily in anticipation of the coming show. From the rafters high up limber men and women sang bawdy songs, swaying with the movement of the wagon, threatening to spill beer on those sitting at tables and crowding for room below. With so much drink, music and laughter swirling around them, it was easy to drown out the creaking of the enormous wagon and to forget the dizzying sensation of constant motion, even though the lanterns overhead jostled with each bump of the road.

Rider nudged Gale slightly into her seat, looking around to make sure no one was watching. He then sat next to her, ordering two drinks which at first neither of them touched.

Several elderly men in rags, their faces weathered and brown and their eyes closed in delight, worked through the crowd, playing *paixiao* pipes whose synchronous harmony seemed playful and fickle. As they passed among the revelers they took deliberate, arched steps, directing their way with pointed toes, making their way like satyrs weaving through a forest of drunkards, lending their flighty score to the Bacchic revelry being played out around them.

The music continued for some time until, at last, the musicians departed and all that was left was the chatter of the crowd, the sound of mugs clinking and some muffled conversation and arguments in dark corners of the theatre.

Gale looked poised to ask Rider a question when, at that moment, the curtains on stage came open and a curious creature emerged from backstage. It was a tall, *dicephaloid* mutant in a sweeping black costume, long and lanky of limb, bearing two separate human heads on its shoulders. They were not fully formed faces, either of them, but rather stunningly misshapen as was often the case with such mutants. Each face resembled the other, of course, but their noses lacked definition, their heads were grossly egg-shaped and each had only a few swirls of dark hair atop them.

When the mutant appeared before them, a few sober onlookers in the crowd began to clap, which was always the custom before a theatrical event. Despite the weak applause the dual-headed performer bowed, with surprising grace for something so deformed. Then one of its heads opened its small mouth and spoke.

"Donations and contributions may be given at any time during the show." Its second head, speaking with a different voice, chimed in. "Your continued support helps keep this theatre alive."

A few crumpled pieces of paper, nutshells, and garbage flew through the air. From above came a shower of bottle caps and a few stray gobbets of spit. Another two-headed mutant, identical to the one on stage, moved through the crowds with a collection bowl, seemingly impervious to the insults and bullying of the more inebriated patrons. It managed a simpering smile on each of its two faces as it passed by Rider and Gale's table, extending its bowl for a donation, but Rider shooed the creature away.

Attention soon returned to the stage. "Tonight," spoke the performer still standing there in its embroidered black *shenyi*, "we shall put on our acclaimed production of 'The Fall', a tragic tale of the madness of Ancient man and the loss of What-Once-Was."

The lights dimmed, and there was movement as scenes changed, but the stage was otherwise still, except for a few bits of garbage and swill landing there from the patrons seated among the rafters. During the performer's absence Gale noticed Rider taking more interest in his drink, putting his hand around the glass but refusing to drink. He ignored what was going on around him and stared at the golden liquid sitting in the dirty glass.

Ten minutes later, as the two-headed mutant was now well into its bizarre, one-man show, Gale looked back as Rider took the glass in hand and stole a sip. A minute later he drank the rest down, and soon poured himself another. He stared into the glass as he refilled it, as if it was a crystal ball, a gypsy's divining tool, seeing in its crystal face something that had to be forgotten. He downed the glass and refilled again, but whatever he saw, whatever haunted him, was still there. So he drank again and again and again...

On stage the two-headed actor was wearing a rubbery Halloween mask on each face, the one on the left depicting some square-chinned American hero from the past, John Wayne (complete with cowboy hat) and the other the great leader, Mao Tse Tung, with an enormous, exaggerated wart on its chin. Apparently nothing was sacred to the performer, because the mutant played both roles with equal disdain. In two separate voices the heads bickered with one another, throwing comical insults and accusations back and forth.

John Wayne: "You put up the iron curtain, now open its doors!"

Mao: "I've got a million missiles, so I say 'up yours!'"

Behind them stood two Ancient-era posters; the first depicted a great city seemingly torn from the imagination of Fritz Lang, with mile-high skyscrapers, elegant walkways and bridges connecting them hundreds of feet above the streets, and multitudes of flying cars weaving between them. A faded pronouncement read: "Denver - Come See The Future!"

The other was in the Heroic Realism style, a three-tone poster probably manufactured in some Third World propaganda factory long ago. It showed broken men in chains begging at the feet of a tall, sinister-looking man in ridiculous red, white and blue clothes, a top hat crowning the white mess of hair on his head. This central figure had red skin, horns and a forked tail, and a wicked gleam in his eye as he dispensed food from a bucket held in one hand. The image had no words to go with it, but seemed to be an indictment of the entangled reliance of the pre-Fall Third World on the First.

The crowd laughed and laughed, both because the tale was degenerating into idiocy as well as the fact that the majority of the spectators were now getting terribly drunk on the cheap whiskey flowing freely from the Far Traders' casks. But while the crowds were busy making a discordant orchestra of noise, John Wayne continued to sing nonetheless.

"You want a war, we'll give it to you! One million missiles, and bomber fleets too! We are high and mighty, you are low and dumb, if you wanna fight, well, come and get some!"

More laughter roared through the throng. There might have been a story here, some illuminating grain of truth as to what really led to the Fall, from the perspective of those who survived (passed down through the years by oral tradition) but in this atmosphere Gale could barely hear the dialogue, even as dumbed-down as it had become. Instead of paying attention she found herself drawn back to Rider, over and over again.

Rider finished a sixth, then a seventh drink, and before he knew it was slapping down his thirteenth and fourteenth shots.

Gale watched him with wide eyes, partly in fear of him, and partly afraid *for* him. He looked up as the crowd laughed again, and caught her stare, his white eyebrows angling sharply upwards in simmering anger.

"Don't look at me like that," he said bitterly.

Gale said nothing, afraid to anger him and set him off, but he insisted on getting up on wobbly legs. She considered slipping away, but Rider took her by the hand and, giving her a stern look despite his weirdly-dilated eyes, pushed her ahead of him and out of the theatre.

It was night. Rider slept near the exit of their room, his body preventing Gale from escaping. She stared at him for two straight hours but said nothing while he drifted off into a drunken slumber. Nor did she move. Their long trip together had drained her, and besides, for some reason she felt safer here than anywhere else.

Though she embraced sleep after their many days together, Gale slept fitfully that night, her mind dipping deep into her subconscious again and again, providing her with fleeting images of things she had seen recently, as well as long ago. In her mind's eye she saw, vividly, the corpses of the desert scavengers from days ago, their bodies mutilated and left for the buzzards. She thought of the dying woman, remembered unerringly the wild dementia in her eyes, and her weak voice called out through her dream as clearly as if she were there beside her, lying still on the mat not two feet away.

"... *demon!*"

Gale's mind flashed; she saw the dead bodies, one missing a rectangular strip of skin, another missing an entire eye, another missing teeth; the woman's reproductive organs removed from inside her, leaving her an open, gaping, bloody shell.

Suddenly she was awash in a sea of blinding white light. So bright, that there was no point of reference to judge scale by, until at last her vision narrowed on a pair of big green eyes, ringed by soft blond eyelashes.

Burning Lands 247

Her memories were only half-formed, but she recognized the eyes as her own. As she struggled in her sleep to keep hold of her vision, she now saw herself, sitting cross-legged while staring into a large mirror on one wall of a pristine white room. She looked so young; she couldn't have been more than five years old, and she wore a high-necked overall of a spotless white fabric, her small hands at her sides. Everything was silent. Her youthful self blinked once, then twice, and then everything began to come into focus.

An older man wearing small glasses and carrying a transparent plastic clipboard walked among many children her age, of which she was only one in a line. *A kindergarten class?* He wore an identical overall to hers, so white that it was hard to look at, and his head had only a few curly tufts of white hair at his ears. He was talking, but his voice sounded as if he was speaking in another room at the end of a long hallway.

Unable to hear what he was saying, Gale looked back at her young self. *This was an event from her past.* The child Gale looked up and their gazes, young and old, met.

Suddenly Gale could hear everything through her child-self's ears.

"Now take a look." the man said, and all at once the children got up, herself included and ran over to a large mirror that slowly faded black, then became completely transparent, so that the assembled children could see into the next room.

There, lying on the brushed steel surface of a sterile operating table, was a dead man. He was no human, but a mutation, clad in the dusty remnants of a desert scavenger's rag clothing, complete with boots and frayed gloves. His faded brown shirt had been cut with surgical shears and pinned back, in exactly the same neat and orderly fashion as the very skin of his chest, which had likewise been sliced open and peeled back to reveal his internal organs.

A dissection. *Of a man.*

The children crowding in beside her pressed their faces almost up against the glass, their eyes wide with curiosity. Gale felt horrified when she realized she, too, stood on the tips of her toes to get a look at the dead stranger left inhumanely out for display in the next room.

Through her own young eyes, the older Gale struggled to understand what she was seeing. The man had the classic physical manifestations of a mongoloid, along with large tumors on his deformed chin and the left side of his forehead, and the beginnings of what appeared to be *gills* at his neck. The latter appeared to have been the source of great curiosity by whoever had dissected this man, because gleaming silver scissors still held two of the gills open, revealing soft tissue underneath.

"As you can see," the teacher explained, "our distant surface relative is a monstrous thing to behold. Children, notice the predominant evidence of Down's syndrome, the presence of skin and bone cancers, and the immature development of gills, which in this specimen were found to be non-functional. Considering its desert environment, under normal circumstances this mutant would probably not live long with these handicaps, but notice the clothing it has acquired, and the evidence of its age, which we estimate at twenty years. Somehow it has managed to survive.

"The creature was found with various tools, including an old axe or hatchet blade, a rusted knife and even a primitive device we surmise served as binoculars, constructed with scavenged lenses. In a pouch, made from rat skins, we found meat from a native strain of gopher, several scalps of indeterminate origin, as well as a collection of humanoid teeth that it was apparently *collecting*."

The children looked terrified at this, their eyes moving from the corpse to their teacher, then back again. They were now quite thankful for the presence of the glass partition.

"It is quite clear that the creatures that survived us on the surface, creatures like this one, are anything but human. Though they appear to have a rudimentary understanding of tools and their use, the presence of advanced mental retardation and physical deformity almost certainly guarantees an inability to speak, grasp advanced concepts, or reason..."

The voice drifted off as young Gale stared through the window at the dead mutant. Whoever he had been, a simpleton born with such physical and mental handicaps that he had survived this long solely by the grace of God, he had crossed paths with something beyond his comprehension, and even God couldn't save him from the cold-blooded curiosity of her people.

"The future looks grim, children. We have yet to find a single healthy, unaltered specimen, and evidence suggests we probably never will. We have a tremendous task ahead of us..."

He had been someone's son. Maybe his mother abandoned him, or maybe she tried to raise him the best she could so that he could rely on himself, so that he wouldn't have to suffer as a village idiot or some merchant's whipping boy. He once had simple hopes and fears, and maybe even knew love from another mutant with similar crippling deformities, a female Frankenstein's monster...

"Our current project involves monitoring the desert in the hopes that we will find a mature female specimen, preferably one that is pregnant, because we believe we can learn a tremendous amount from the genetic information locked up in the placental tissues..."

With those words Gale felt her body grow icy and cold, and she awoke with a nauseated croak at Rider's side. She hadn't been able to muster more than a gasp, and Rider slept soundly through it.

The room was dark. The memory of her dream faded until it was only a shadow lingering at the edge of her mind, but though it teetered there, she *remembered*.

Horses thundered as they rode past, their armored riders taking up positions as colored flags signaled their arrival. Uncle Sam's own massive steed stirred, but the great warrior-king held the reigns firmly and it obeyed his command.

His own mount was a well-muscled *desert horse* that had taken him into battle many times before. A new breed of horse, evolved from the wild mustangs of the pre-Fall world, such creatures only resembled their distant cousins from afar; up close the evolutionary differences were more noticeable. A desert horse lacked hooves and instead had broad pads for feet, distributing the beast's considerable weight over a wider area, allowing it to race swiftly across even the most unsure footing (like the sifting sand of the desert's dunes). Its hide had thicker hair to better capture sweat, cooling it during the hottest times of the day... and giving the desert horse its legendary stench. Its narrow eyes had unusually thick layers of eyelashes that caught stray particles of sand and kept them from the creature's eyes, so that it could see even in the worst sandstorms.

Uncle Sam sat on his fancifully-embroidered saddle atop the great stallion, at the head of the army, with Boren at his side and five of his best hand-picked horsemen, each of them armed with long pikes to protect the warlord from approaching footmen in the coming battle. They also carried steel maces and flintlock pistols in the event their master dismounted and they were required to join him on foot.

The seven huge warriors, mounted on their majestic desert steeds, were just a small part of the massive army that was slowly assembling in the early morning dust storm, their movements concealed by the haze of gray, biting dust.

Uncle Sam looked at his fine men, clad in long leather coats sewn with metal rivets, stiffened hide shields hanging from their shoulders to catch stray arrows and musket balls. Each man was outfitted with a WWI-era small box respirator to allow the cavalrymen to breath despite the dust kicked up by their mounts. These respirators were little more than rubberized face masks with murky glass eye pieces, connected by a thick rubber hose to a box filter worn on the chest and covered by canvas. Each cavalryman had to ride light so their armor was minimal, but their arms were sheathed in metal greaves forged from the steel of old highway dividers, hammered to fit each warrior's distinctive weapon arm.

Uncle Sam raised his own gauntleted hand to signal the flag bearer among his riders to raise the war banner. A tribal footman standing nearby brought an ancient flag forward, an old bundle of cloth religiously preserved since before the Fall, and helped the last horseman fix it to the tip of his pike. For several quiet moments they worked, until at long last the banner bearer lifted his spear to the sky, letting the wind catch the flag's tattered edges and unfurl it for all to see.

As the ancient American flag appeared over the gathering cavalry, more soldiers moved forward, emerging from the swirling dust clouds and descending into the shallow depression where Karos' great army was assembling.

Over one hundred armored warriors marched in a line over the crest of the hill, shields draped with exotic skins and leather helmets topped by horse-hair plumes making them look like a wall of advancing animals. *Desert sisters.* Spears tipped by sharpened beast tusks, *maquahuitl*-like cudgels adorned with vicious flint shards and animal teeth, and a few steel crescent axes gleamed (despite the dust kicked up by the growing wind) along the line's advancing edge. Some of these masked women led trained animals on long chain leashes; emaciated mountain lions kept hungry for flesh and bristling *carnage* hounds slavering for the first drops of gore to be spilled.

Ridaya, leader of her great tribe of ex-slaves, pulled ahead of her impressive company of battle sisters, atop a war chariot made from the front half of the chassis of a pre-Fall roadster, skidding along on dusty rubber tires and pulled by two enormous male lions tethered by their spiked collars and harnesses. She held a Clean musket in hand and wore a black breastplate, her slender limbs protected by *ad hoc* arm and shin greaves made from cuirboilli and dyed as black as night. Atop her head she had a conical black helm with a narrow nose guard, a chainmail veil hanging down to cover her long hair and neck, an armored drape she could draw up to cover her entire face, leaving only her eyes unprotected. Her helmet was topped by a tall, stiff frill of striking white horse hair, so that all of the women-warriors could see their leader wherever the tide of battle swept her.

Less impressive to see than their comrades-in-arms, but carrying the momentum of hope and fury in their hearts came the many regiments of Karos' followers, a chaotic hodge-podge of former slaves freed by the demagogue's mischief up and down the trade routes, a handful of professional mercenaries drawn by the promise of loot and plunder in the aftermath of the Clean's fall, and dozens of workers and craftsmen from Trade City who'd managed to flee the city under the cover of night and join up just days before. This sprawling mass of men walked irregularly forward, each man armed with whatever he could bring to the fight - a bludgeon, an axe, a hammer, a blade, and rarely, a musket or black powder pistol. They came with a great clamor of voices, many different languages, some on foot, others in *howdahs* atop *bawthoks* or riding flighty *fraxx steeds*, fighting one another for the honor to lead from the front.

Karos walked with them, wearing a suit of quilted armor with a long cape flapping behind him. He wore no helmet so that his men could always see his face and hear his voice, and wore a gauntlet over the stump of his arm, concealing his injury from view. With the large pistol he held in the other hand, he exhibited to his people that he was prepared to fight to defend his words.

Currently at the head of the army marched the core of Valero's brigade of a hundred blackguards, branded criminals and ex-raiders consumed by a lust for vengeance against the self-styled masters of the wasteland, the Clean, all of them armed with an assortment of antiquated but equally-murderous weaponry: heavy iron quadrelles, broad-bladed falchions, javelins and windlass crossbows. Some wore leather jacks or scavenged bits of chainmail; only a few had managed to secure plate armor at all, so that together the ragged bunch resembled nothing less than an army of escaped gladiators. Some lucky few wore tight-fitting goggles, the rest had to make do with simple, slatted arctic shades to protect their eyes from the dust kicked up by the army's movements.

Many of these last men ran ahead of the rest of the army, eager as they were to get to battle and strike at the Clean, even though the fight had yet to start, giving their regiment the appearance of one enormous, uncoordinated mob. They stayed clear of Uncle Sam's legions, rightfully despising the king that had branded them and traded them away like cattle, but they remained loyal to Karos, Ridaya, and the cause.

As the great army came to a stop, Uncle Sam edged his horse out in front of the assembled battalions. Ridaya rode up with her chariot and came to a stop beside him, and the two waited and watched as Karos finally caught up.

"Fine day for a battle," Ridaya said, looking to the sky.

"Just as your Brotherhood prophets said," Uncle Sam shouted, "a dust storm to conceal us as we approach the city!"

"We must keep moving with the winds," Karos warned. "Unless we fall behind, we will be at the city walls when the storm breaks."

"Let's hope your people in the city are able to accomplish their objectives," Ridaya said to Karos.

"They will," Karos affirmed.

Ridaya nodded agreeably. "*Heeyah!*" she shouted, and rode off back to her troops.

Burning Lands 251

Now that they stood alone, Uncle Sam looked at Karos. "This is *your* army, Karos. Do you want to speak to them?"

Karos looked over his shoulder at the one thousand men and women who had come together for this battle. They were his to command, eyes and ears eagerly looking to him for guidance and leadership. Regiments of men and women, waiting in the storm, sustained by hope and in awe of the supernatural ability of their Brotherhood allies to deliver such a convenient cloud to cover their advance. The same thought gripped them all. *With such prophetic power on their side, how could they fail?*

"No grand speeches, no big words," Karos shouted, his voice carrying despite the groaning wind. "Today we come to fight, because we desire to. We face an enemy in his fortress, an invader who brings with him wicked ideas and a poisoned way of living. He would make us all slaves and remove 'freedom' from our language. He attacks the frontier of our ally, and butchers the *bei man* people. So I say march with me! Let this storm be a blessing, and lead us to the walls where our enemy waits, sleeping!"

A great roar rose from the army, muffled as the winds grew stronger, and with that Karos turned and began leading the great alliance of rebels into the storm and towards distant Trade City.

The small fort at Amarillo had not suited Shubazang well at all, and he was glad to be gone from there. After only a few hours they had tracked down a merchant who had dealings with Rider, and who'd overheard that he and his "companion" were looking to sign on with the Far Traders. Shubazang had no doubt they were onboard one wagon or another in their "crawling city", continuing their flight eastwards.

He wasn't sure what happened to the escaped slave and the giant, but since they were on the same trail he was fairly confident they'd run into each other soon enough.

Shubazang and his machine-woman had managed to convince the small Cartel garrison at Amarillo that they were on a special mission for the mandarin of Trade City, and in doing so, secured a ride on one of the Cartel's truck convoys headed out towards a desert encampment in the vicinity of the ruins known to wastelanders as "The Scab" (the Clean and Cartel had an equally simple name, "Can Hai", or the "Wreck"). Carrying supplies for a protracted campaign against a raider gang known quixotically as the "Knights of Route 66", the convoy was loaded with ammunition, water and fresh foodstuffs for a small army under the command of the Cartel's infamous General Rhylor himself, waiting in the desert south of the ruins. Shubazang planned on riding the whole way, as far east as possible before getting out and striking north on foot. If they were lucky they'd intercept the Far Traders' "roving city" and maybe even catch Rider asleep.

But riding in the cabin of the Cartel truck was an experience he wouldn't soon forget. Oily, rusted, dark and smelling of sweat and bad breath, it was far too confined for his tastes. Diminutive Cartel haulers operated the enormous rig; one reclined in an exaggerated position at the "helm", casually holding the large circular wheel while his other hand insisted on wandering over to Euryale's leg, getting dangerously close to touching the android's knee. He laughed as he spoke, like a seaman of the ancient world; boasting of past journeys across the wasteland, telling stories of daring convoy runs through tribal blockades, or of outrunning raider armadas in this particularly souped-up "ship" of his.

Their aloof driver seemed to have little regard for the road, even as the titanic rust-bucket of a vehicle shook, rattled and vibrated violently as it hit rock after rock, pothole after pothole. He kept only one gnarled hand on the wheel, and only two fingers gripped it. The suspension on this thing was crude at best, and every jolt and jostle had them shaking in their seats, but the driver simply laid back and chuckled, only returning his gaze forward every few seconds to make sure he didn't ram into the truck ahead of them.

Euryale ignored the driver as his hand touched its knee, the dwarf finally feeling welcome enough by Euryale's passiveness to let it remain there. Euryale looked away disinterestedly, turning its head and instead looking out the narrow window at the desert sweeping by in a blur, up and down. The android lifted a hand and knocked slightly on the glass, making a sound that drew Shubazang's attention. He looked out over Euryale's shoulder and saw what looked like a few desperate vagabonds by the roadside, extending their arms towards the trucks as if begging for them to stop.

The driver shook his head and grinned, then pointed straight ahead, finally changing his posture and sitting up straight. The truck ahead of them drove up onto the shoulder but kept its speed, and as it moved over he, Shubazang, and Euryale could see why - sitting in the middle of the road, perhaps a quarter of a mile ahead, was a squalid little infant in soiled swaddling clothes, waving its arms in the air as it cried.

"Bandits," the driver explained, smiling as he shifted to a higher gear. "Put children in the middle of the road, hoping you'll stop. Then they come out and swarm all over you, drag you out and hack you to death, take everything you have. Suckers'll strip a truck down in ten minutes flat, leave nothin' behind..."

Shubazang had seen a lot of death in his short lifespan but he felt his throat tighten. He sat up to confirm if what he was seeing was real, but by the time he made it to the viewslits the truck hit the slight bump... and kept going.

Shubazang sank back, thankful he hadn't witnessed what just occurred. He suddenly felt encapsulated in the small cabin, as if claustrophobia had just now reared its ugly head, and he felt trapped. He checked his watch, then looked back at one of his maps, suddenly overwhelmed with impatience to leave the Cartel truckers' company. Euryale turned its head to the side to examine the expression on its master's face. It had the same eerie smile, its thick lips full and gleaming.

"Gonna have to clean that off the underbody when we get to where we're goin'," the driver said, unaware of the boy's nausea. Shubazang ignored the comment, while Euryale returned to staring out the window.

An hour later Shubazang sat up with renewed interest. There, crossing the great highway at an angle, were the tracks of the Far Traders' "crawling city", the meanderings of a hundred or more bizarre house-sized vehicles that turned and headed north-northeast away from the road. The Scab was still miles away.

"Stop," he shouted over the roaring engine. "Let us off here."

The Cartel convoy of trucks and guide cars came to a halt and with the help of some Cartel laborers onboard their truck, Shubazang unpacked their gear from the bed. When he was finished and the laborers returned to their vehicles he waved to the truckers, and in moments the giant rigs were off and rolling again. They wouldn't be by this way again for days, leaving the young hunter and his mechanical lemans to their own devices for at least a week.

But, Shubazang wasn't concerned. Instead he turned to the tracks left by the passing of the "crawling city" and examined them momentarily. The wind had yet to erase the deep ruts left by the colossal machines, giving them a clear path to follow into the open desert.

North and east, into the wastes. As Euryale started walking, Shubazang reached into his coat and retrieved an old road atlas he had carried for years. He examined it, estimating their current position and tracing one metal finger northwards. Before the Fall this area had been the border between the kingdoms of Texas and Oklahoma. What lay out there, in all that desolation? He searched for sites of interest along the route north and east, now erased by the desert, and anything that might be Rider's ultimate destination.

He put his pack on his back and held his rifle at the ready. They would follow the trail of the Far Traders and hopefully catch up to the slow-moving city at some point, or else find out where Rider and Gale disembarked and follow their tracks. Either way it woudn't be long before they caught up.

Rider and Gale parted company with their Far Trader hosts ten miles north of the ruins of Can Hai, the Wreck, the Scab. As the early dawn light spread out across the desert, he seemed to spot something in the unbroken tracts of sand and gestured to the driver of their great motorized wagon to let them off.

Some time later, as the Far Trader city vanished in a miles-wide thundercloud of dust, Gale looked around at their surroundings. Nothing. Just flat open desert extending in all directions as far as they could see.

Rider donned his hat and knelt to pick up one of the packs for which he'd traded his knife, each of them containing some small amount of food and water. He looked back over one shoulder in Gale's direction. Gale stared at him, her hair whipping fiercely in the wind. His black sunglasses hid his eyes completely, making it hard for her to read his thoughts without consciously reaching into his mind to find them.

Whether or not he realized what she was thinking, Rider turned abruptly and started walking east, each heavy footfall leaving a cloud of dust that hovered there for a moment before clinging to the legs of his dark pants. As the wind picked up in force he leaned forward to make the going easier, looking like a lost man trudging through a snowstorm.

Gale looked back in the direction of the "crawling city" but it was gone now, no longer visible thanks to the great smokescreen of sand it left with its passing, though they could still hear the distant rumble of the hundred-plus engines that kept its wagons and buildings on the move. Soon even that sound would fade, though, and they would be utterly alone out here in this nameless desert.

Gale picked up the other pack and took a sip of water, then reluctantly followed in Rider's footsteps as he led them into the unknown.

They passed through the flat desert, in this area skirted on either side by the old disintegrating wrecks of Ancient weapons of war; the half-buried hulks of tanks, painted orange by rust and pierced with holes or missing entire turrets, blown clear by the powerful cannon used in the Final War. They passed lines of overturned armored personnel carriers, fitted with hover skirts and bristling cupola, and the silent behemoths that were once the Great Enemy's main battle tanks, their barrels still pointing ahead of them towards some long-gone foe.

Gale wanted to stop and explore, but Rider pushed past, almost as if his vigor had been renewed on discovering this nameless landmark.

Tank held the bridle of his horse as he spoke with the little man standing patiently in front of him and Valero. The desert tribesman was incredibly dark, his richly-tanned skin gleaming under the bright sun. Despite a preponderance of wrinkles, beneath his sagging skin were strong and wiry muscles that were capable of more difficult labor than most men half his age. His face was cleanly shaved but the man had a long mane of gray hair streaked with white and eyes that barely opened more than a slit. With those eyes he passively regarded the two traveling trackers who'd come more than two miles across the flat terrain to speak to him and his family.

An old woman waddled behind the man, carrying a young boy on her back, while two other youths, probably his sons, continued walking, eyes to the ground, their bodies laden with so many pots, gourds, water skins, pouches, machetes, knives and tools that they looked comically overburdened. Neither boy complained or said a word, instead trudging on through the deep dust of the desert in the direction their patriarch had been leading them.

Valero watched them go, wondering where on earth they had come from... and where the *hell* they thought they were going.

The woman seemed worried, staring at Tank and Valero, but Valero readily dismissed the look, assuming it was simply the precaution of all women to be afraid of men in the wasteland.

"H-have you seen a m-man, and a w-woman traveling to-together?" Tank asked the old man, speaking slowly to make sure his words came out as clearly as possible. "Th-the man you'd remember, w-with w-white skin and hair, yes?"

The old man shook his head and mumbled something, pointing to the west. Valero could not understand the language, it pre-dated the Fall; it was the tongue of the land's ancient natives.

Tank seemed to be having trouble as well. "No... I understand y-you're heading w-west, that's not what I'm asking. I'm asking... have y-you seen a w-w-woman and a w-white-haired man traveling in this area? It is important we find them. W-we will pay you if you tell us."

The struggling giant pulled some corium pieces from a sack and held them in the palm of his hand for the old man to see.

The old man's face split into a smile, showing jagged yellow teeth, but he only shook his head and chuckled.

"They rode with the F-Far Traders. Did they pass along this w-way?"

The old man shook his head slowly from side to side. His wife touched his arm and began walking away, saying something unintelligible over her shoulder. He turned, still shaking his head, and followed.

"That didn't help at all," Valero said, watching them go for a moment before getting back up on his horse.

"It d-doesn't matter," Tank said. "They're around here s-somewhere. The F-Far Traders passed this way, I-I'm sure of it, only Rider probably got off somewhere a-along the way."

"So we've a thousand miles of desert to search?"

Tank nodded grimly and mounted his own steed.

"If we keep an eye out for the signs of an old road... look, Tank, if there's anything out here in these wastes, its likely *some* road exists leading to it. So that's what we need to do, keep an eye out for road signs."

The old man looked back and shouted something at Tank and Valero, but the two men couldn't understand. The old man pointed north, then shook his head as if to say "don't *go* that way, you fools". The two men watched as he started shaking his head again, before giving up and returning to his trek westwards, not to look back again.

Tank shrugged when Valero looked to him for an explanation. The two men refreshed themselves with water before moving out, continuing roughly east-northeast into the featureless desert landscape.

Gale opened the cap of her water bottle but knew there was nothing left. For two straight days and nights they had walked relentlessly northeast, through the most isolated stretch of sand she had ever traveled. For two full days they had seen nothing but a great empty space, and now they had run completely out of water.

Gale was not one to complain, but Rider sensed her hesitation to follow him further without either water or a reasonable explanation to sustain her. Without looking back he broke the day-long silence with a single promise: "We're almost there."

At dawn the next day Gale felt her legs weakening, but she followed Rider unquestioningly. If he was leading them to their deaths, then at least they'd die together. She and the only family she had left, the silent albino cowboy who walked just a few paces ahead of her.

Rider stopped as the sun's first rays came over the horizon, flooding the desert with fiery orange and bright yellow colors. It touched on everything, the sand, the dust and the rocks... and the distant outline of a city nestled among hills not more than ten miles away.

"We're here," Rider said dryly.

For the better part of the day they walked through the outskirts of the ancient city, following the broad, sun-baked highways that laced the abandoned metropolis. Both were silent as they walked, Rider ahead and Gale only a few steps behind, the former concentrating on where they were going and the latter speechless by what she saw.

The city was remarkably intact, its buildings mostly unbroken and its streets clear of traffic. There were signs of looting in the small strip malls and storefronts visible from the highway overpasses; in a deserted parking lot she could see a plasma TV just lying out in the open, or a rotted leather chair or overturned sofa dropped where thieves left them in their haste to get away. Elsewhere she saw a fire truck and several ambulances parked by a sprawling convention center, from the top of which was a handmade banner emblazoned with a crude red cross.

"I wonder what went on *there*..." Gale pondered aloud, her mouth growing drier as she spoke. Rider didn't reply.

"We need water, Rider," she said, but Rider kept going.

Rider kept them to the highway and prevented Gale from exploring on her own. He was leading her somewhere, and seemed sure of where they were going.

Elsewhere she saw evidence of past fires; appliances and businesses left unattended after the Fall had led to the beginnings of large conflagrations, infernos that had consumed many neighborhoods, leaving a checkerboard of city blocks burned to the ground. But beyond these periodic islands of ruin, the city was eerily untouched, a fact that made it only that much more mysterious.

It was around noon when Gale first laid eyes on the giant statue that rose over the surrounding neighborhoods, a colossal representation of a muscled man wearing an oilman's helmet, plated in what appeared to be *gold*. At first she thought she was imagining things, a delusion brought on by her burning thirst, but on seeing this same statue Rider finally changed course, taking one of the many exits off the highway and leading Gale towards it through the maze of abandoned, silent streets.

Half an hour later Rider and Gale walked past the foot of the giant man, which faced out across a broad street edged in by burned-out buildings on either side. Up close it didn't seem nearly as gigantic as before, but it still towered over them, casting a long cool shadow over the sun-scorched macadam of the avenue. The monument's height reminded her of the great statue that once stood over Oasis, but unlike that vaguely-humanoid megalith from her childhood, this wasn't a statue of the foreign invaders' god, this was surely the image of an all-American deity.

The wind sighed past them as they stood there. Rider kept walking, but Gale stopped to look up at the huge figure, shielding her eyes from the bright sun overhead.

"You're looking at their God," came an eerie, rasping voice from out of nowhere. Gale looked and saw only abandoned, rusted cars, piles of burnt junk, stacks of old tires, a sooty oil drum and a small toy robot, partly buried in the rubble of a burned-out building.

Had the *robot* been the one speaking? No, impossible, she was forced to convince herself. *A toy couldn't speak! Could it?!* She needed water, and soon, or she'd go crazy.

"No, really," the croaking voice returned, "that there is what the Fall was all about. That's also why this city isn't a heap of glowing wreckage."

Rider appeared at the edge of the ruins, sunglasses off, his pink eyes wide and alert. By that look she could tell he'd heard the voice too, but unlike her, he wasn't questioning his sanity; he had his gun at the ready. She remained silent, in case the voice spoke again, so that Rider would hear it clearly and be able to determine from where it was really coming.

"No need for that," the invisible caller said, "don't you think these ruins have seen enough of that already?"

It was almost mirthful, the voice, and as she and Rider wandered, looking for its source, she felt their efforts amused it. She half expected they'd turn a corner and come across a grinning Cheshire cat reclining on some rubble, or perhaps it would simply phase into existence right behind them, taking them both by surprise. Instead they came into a rubble-strewn intersection where a crouched figure in a filthy brick-red robe sat atop a rusted car wreck, a wooden staff held in one gnarled hand.

Burning Lands

Rider raised his gun, and the hooded individual nodded its head in respectful recognition of its lethal power. The mysterious speaker raised a spotted, bistered hand to show it meant no harm.

"My name... is *Ludd*," the old man said from beneath his hood.

Rider stepped around some rubble but kept his gun at the ready. The old man sat alone, with a bedroll, a few cowhide water skins, some pouches, but no weapons other than a long trench knife at his side and the staff in hand.

Rider watched him for a moment, then, recognizing the stranger as too feeble to really threaten them, turned away to search the nearby streets. The old man watched Rider turn away, and seemed content. He looked back to Gale.

"I bet you're wondering why the city seems intact, but no one's here?"

"Who are you?" Gale asked, ignoring his question.

"I believe I already introduced myself," he said, placing his clawed hand flat against his chest. "*Ludd.*"

"No, I mean... what are you doing here?"

"Some men call my kind 'sandwalkers'. Travelers, you could say. Wanderers. The insatiably curious. A rare breed of men who, once they start walking, never stop. Well, except perhaps to rest awhile..." he mused, gesturing to his curious choice of seating.

"Sand walker?"

"Mmm-hmm. Chronicler. 'Bard', if you will. Witness to the world's ever-changing condition and surveyor of all that remains of this twisted Earth."

She saw a grin creep over the lower half of the old man's swarthy face, revealing broken, brown teeth and a lolling, grayish tongue.

"Sage of the world, past and present. The *future...*" he said, "... is beyond my purview."

"You know about the past?" she asked, the desperation to piece together her own memories to make sense of her past suddenly overcoming her ingrained caution of dealing with strange robed men dwelling alone in haunted cities.

"Oh yes. Want to know about the Ancients? Ask me, I know all about them! Their wicked ways. Soldiers, sluts, politicians, patriots and pornographers all. Conceited and obsessed with possessing the best the world had to offer, being better than their neighbors. Gods of violence, greed, conceit, and complacency they were, oh yes. Great, fat lizards who wanted too much, spent too much, squandered too much, and cared too little that their own end was coming."

"How do you know that?" she asked.

"You are looking at a walking encyclopedia of the Ancients, young madam. My particular *forte* being the cataloguing of the songs and music of the Ancient world. What better way to know the Ancients than to study what they themselves venerated, in song and celebration?"

Gale looked doubtful.

"Ahem. Shall I *quote*?"

She crossed her arms but listened.

"Violence. 'They're only going to change this place by killing everybody in the human race. They would kill me for a cigarette, but I don't even want to die just yet.' Or conceit. 'We are the champions, no time for losers, we are the champions of the world'. That song was sung all across the land, in the great stadiums that celebrated the Ancient's decadent way of life. Greed? 'Everyone knows who they are, they need no address. They get rich while we get poor, and the country's in a mess. They say buy that land, start that war, keep those people poor!' Or how about this: 'It seems to me that the powers that be, keep themselves in splendor and security. Armored cars for our mega-stars. No streets, no bars, your wealth is ours'...

"And of course, 'Everybody wants to rule the world...'" he hummed.

"You say they knew the end was coming?" Gale interrupted. "How could they have known?"

"Ah, the complacency of which I spoke: 'Crying parents tell their children, if you survive don't do as we did. Son exclaims there'll be nothing to do to; daughter says she'll be dead with you. While foreign affairs are screwing us rotten; line morale has hit rock bottom. Dying embers stand forgotten, talks of peace were being trodden.' Or 'The day will come, you cannot run, white hot clouds fill the sky. See the red flare, blasting hot air, there's no place left to hide. Blinding our eyes as the sun turns to black, a world full of hatred and fear. All are committed, there's no turning back, there'll be no one left to hear...'"

Gale was quiet. She was impressed, but she wasn't sure if she believed his particularly-skewed vision of the long-dead Ancients, or if he had embellished some of the ancient lyrics. And anyway, they were just *songs*... Were the songs and fantasies of their ancestors being used to judge them, did he consult old record sleeves like a gauge measuring their crimes and consciences?

"Why are you here?" she asked, changing the subject.

"Well, this 'lost city' has become a legend among sandwalkers. Few know it exists, but it is said the greatest of sages have come here for ages, risking its dangers, to read the books that still sit in old stores, on dusty shelves, to learn of the past. One-point-seven million volumes in twenty-five separate libraries. Now that I'm here, I plan on living out the rest of my days reading... That's why *I'm* here."

She wasn't exactly sure why *she* was there, so she dodged his obvious follow-up by asking another question. "You were telling me about the city?"

"Ah, yes. Just *why* the city is intact, unlike any other in the wasteland?" He gave a moment's pause for dramatic effect.

"It's because of that big golden idol, that sacrilegious icon of the Ancient god..."

"What the hell are you talking about?" Gale asked.

"I'll *tell* you what the hell I'm talking about," the old man continued, annoyed by her lack of respect for his storytelling. "Oil. Gasoline. Go-juice. The stuff the Ancient world ran on. Its industry. Its cars. Its cities. All the lights that lit up the world's great metropolis, each a constellation, so that it was never truly dark on this earth. All of them powered by that lowly black sludge that bleeds up from the bowels of the Earth."

The old man spoke like an old-time preacher. "Insidious, the Devil's semen, humbly born from the ancient earth, but giving birth to greed, jealousy and war.

"The Ancients were voracious consumers, self-righteous locusts. They raped other lands, sucked them dry, until they alone held what little was left. What did the Ancients expect the world to do? Bow and beg for a few drops to sustain them? Watch as *this* land beamed brightly as their own cities grew dim and dark?

"The Great Enemy came here to acquire all that was left. This city once made oil, it streamed from every building, every hole in the ground, and so it was spared the fire of the atom. It was too valuable to destroy, in fact, it was one of the *prizes* the Enemy fought to capture. But it suffered it's own cleansing nonetheless."

"*Cleansing?*" Gale asked curiously. Rider said nothing and continued examining the rubble as if looking for something.

"Ah," Ludd grinned, raising a branch-like finger, tipped with a gray-black nail, "the most malevolent weapon of the Ancients' arsenal. Oh yes, they had weapons that spewed evil magic on the land, great arrows that didn't explode in a bright, fiery cataclysm, but rather released wholesale destruction in invisible clouds and unseen vapors. Human wickedness taken form as gas, bottled up in mighty rockets, and hurled across the ancient seas with as much forethought as bickering children throwing harsh words at each other in a schoolyard scrap."

"It killed them all, the unsuspecting people who lived here, spreading as the plague does until no man or beast was left. All that remained were the industries and the great machines that extracted the Devil's seed, dead but for the hand of a new operator. They eagerly laid waste the people of this place, but made sure the precious oil would be there when their armies arrived on these shores."

"So what happened? Where are they?" Gale asked.

"Gone, too," Ludd replied. "Who knows, really? We only know they came here and waged a legendary war, and none came out sane or whole again." Gale thought of the ghostly battlefield she and Rider has passed through on their way here.

"Was no place spared? I mean, some kind of destruction, of one sort or another?" she asked desperately.

Ludd hummed to himself for a moment, then grinned again. "Why actually, yes. Or so the stories go. In the times after the Fall the survivors of the Final War fled west to the imagined shelter of the Rocky Mountains, what your people call the 'Wei Shan'. Most died, of course, from disease and radiation; others gave up and settled these lands, but legends speak of a kingdom in a sheltered valley among the snow-covered peaks founded by those who made it, after years and years of searching. They say the kingdom, isolated from this dark and ugly wasteland among the mountains, is a place of peace and generosity. Anyone who can make it there, beyond the wastelands and through the mountains, is welcome to stay and make it their home."

"Just a legend..." Rider muttered. Whether it was true or not, Ludd chose not to say.

Gale wondered, but her mind returned to their current surroundings. "So this place has been empty since the time of the Ancients?" she asked.

"*No*..." Rider said unexpectedly, locating a faded line of chalk on the sidewalk forming an arrow that pointed down a dark side street. Ludd looked surprised and immediately struggled to get to his feet. Gale wanted to help the old man, but suddenly aware of disease she feared touching this filthy stranger.

"That's *not* how the story goes," he called after Rider angrily. Rider ignored him and looked around the alleyway, at one point using his hand to clean a sickly, stringy lichen from the wall of a building on one side of the street, revealing a rusted sign underneath. He put his machine pistol away and went to the center of the street and crouched at one of two manhole covers.

Gale watched, dumbfounded, as Rider worked to uncap the manhole lid. Ludd shuffled over to the sign and pulled back part of his hood so his own red, cat-like eye could pop forth to read what was written there. The sound that came from the manhole's removal reminded Gale of a sarcophagus lid sliding off a stony mausoleum. The odor that came from below seemed to confirm it.

Rider looked down the hole, then, without warning, began to climb the rusted iron rungs into the earth's musty interior. He seemed too familiar with this place, too incautious. *Why?*

Gale moved to peer down the shaft after Rider, but Ludd quickly hobbled over and held her back, a look of warning on his face. The sound of Rider climbing faded until it was quiet. No gunfire, no screams.

Ludd's exaggerated look of concern quickly transformed into one of curiosity. Even as he held Gale back, as much by his odor as his holding out his outstretched arms, he glanced over one shoulder and down the dark hole. Summoning courage, Gale darted under Ludd's arm, pushing past his long shoddy sleeve, her nostrils filling with his smell - body odor, sweat, urine, and the sweet odor of too much tribal kriek. She leapt at the ladder and began to climb down after Rider.

"Not wise," Ludd warned, but no one was listening. He stared at the hole for a few seconds, then looked about for a moment at the empty ruins. He clutched his staff and soon joined the others in their descent underground.

It took Gale a moment to spot Rider, who'd lit a battery-operated lantern waiting on a sewer wall, and was now looking at the garbage around his feet. In the weak orange light he blended in with the walls and sagging rusted pipes, all of which were the same gloomy amber color. Rider drew his gun in one hand and took the lantern in the other, and began to head north down the sewer tunnel.

Gale wondered where he was going, until she saw, on the wall where he'd found the lantern, another chalk arrow pointing the way.

Rider was getting ahead of them. Ludd kept hissing at Gale to slow down, pretending to be worried for her, but clearly he was more afraid of this place than her. Or maybe he knew something they didn't? After all, he'd been dwelling in these ruins longer than they had... No, Gale felt no danger, she felt strangely at ease here, at least underground. Gale came around a turn, following Rider's fading light as quickly as her legs would carry her.

Small bits of stone and dust trickled down from above. Rider paused and looked back. "Be careful, these tunnels are falling apart..." He eventually led them to a doorway. A metal portal in a ramshackle "wall" of corrugated steel sheets, chicken wire reinforcement and parts of old street signs; a makeshift barricade sealing off the passage completely. Water pooled at the foot of the door; sickly lichen hung from the cracks between broken bricks in the ceiling. The door's hinges were rusted shut.

Gale could sense this place was dead, there were no monsters waiting to jump out at them, but Rider continued with all the care of a man walking respectfully through a graveyard. Suddenly Gale felt an overwhelming sadness, an eruption of buried emotion that gripped her so unexpectedly that she was paralyzed by it.

Rider pushed against the door until it creaked open, its stubborn hinges finally giving way. Gale felt crushed, a weight of sorrow pressing in on her. Ludd pushed past her,

Burning Lands 261

oblivious to her empathic trance, led solely by his curiosity. He was no longer afraid, but rather eager to see what Rider was discovering up ahead.

As the door opened, sunlight lit up the other side. Rider stepped cautiously inside, looking upwards to the huge hole in the tunnel roof, where the street above had collapsed. He winced at the sun as its rays found their way down here through the collapsed gap. He hadn't expected such a large hole here, but he didn't seem surprised by it. He said nothing and simply continued over the rubble to whatever lay on the other side.

Ludd entered and looked up at the sky above, then around the collapsed room, head darting from side to side as if searching for treasure he could snatch before Rider took it all. But there was nothing there that interested him, only junk from a long time ago.

Gale entered too, but saw something entirely different. A dining room that once mimicked the parlor of a pre-Fall home, now a shambles beneath tons of broken stone. An old collapsed table; half a dozen plates, once delicately whisked from the surface and brought underground, now shattered into a million pieces. Busted picture frames still dangling from rusted nails on the walls, with images of peaceful surface scenes - green fields, sunlit farmland, majestic mountains, as if whoever lived down here had desperately needed to believe they lived a normal life despite the circumstances.

Rider pushed through a small doorway, allowing rubble to follow him as he slid down into a connecting room. They were underground again.

Not only did she sense sadness, but guilt as well. This place conjured up choking emotions, phantom feelings coming from someone nearby. Gale looked at Ludd, but his childlike eagerness to loot caused her look past him to... *Rider?*

Rider looked at the dimly-lit chamber he now stood in, but his face was once again unreadable. He stared long and hard at the small beds in the room, all of them having rotted down to their rusted bedsprings.

"Some people did return." Rider's voice was clear and calm as he explained their surroundings. "This here... this was someone's *home*..." he said sharply, turning to regard Ludd who was rudely going through a child's toy box and its cheap costume jewelry, a strand of plastic pearls in his hand. Ludd cocked his head to the side, listening to the uncharacteristic edge in Rider's voice. He let the necklace slip, bead by bead, back into the overturned coffer.

"People came here, tried to make a home for themselves. Start something new." Rider turned and took a step, but there was a "crack" beneath his feet. He sighed, looking down at the framed photograph he'd unwittingly stood on, fracturing the glass. He crouched and picked it up, carefully removing the shards.

"Years ago there was a community of people who used to live out in the wasteland west of here. Herders, nomads. Rode horses and migrated with their livestock across miles and miles of desert. They were a good people, all things considered, living outside the affairs of the rest of the 'civilized' world. They were holdovers from the past, they believed in the old Christian god, and lived their lives the best they could. They were generous and giving but also shrewd and insular..."

As Rider spoke, Gale looked at Ludd for a moment, then back again. Rider wasn't one to engage in sudden, unexpected storytelling for no reason, and she felt a need to remain quiet and let him explain whatever it was he felt he had to say.

"... so it was surprising when, one day, they accepted a young wanderer into their midst."

Rider sighed. "He was a bit hard to live with at first, a little rough, and more than a bit wary of accepting their god and parroting the prayers they said in His name. He was too much the loner to participate in the community, always volunteering for guard duty or night watch to avoid the larger gatherings. When they came together for evening prayers he would be gone, at the edge of camp, or out in the night, but he would always linger nearby, never too far away."

Rider put the picture upright on a gaily-painted nightstand by one of the beds. Gale looked over at Ludd again; was he making sense of this? Rider didn't seem to notice and so continued.

"At sixteen he was *always* getting into trouble," Rider said, smiling like a man remembering his own happy past. "On more than one occasion he did something foolish or selfish that would normally warrant being expelled, but no matter how hard he seemed to try they refused to give up on him. He would never come to fully understand and adopt their strange ways, but despite this he gradually became a part of the fabric of their people.

"From the beginning one of the clan fathers decided to take a chance and took the boy in, introducing him to his own family and making it his personal crusade to get through to the kid. He soon found the boy had a surprising willingness to learn to *read*, and so he used books to get through to him. The old man gave the boy books whenever he came across them, and it wasn't long before the kid was always carrying one with him. He might have a dog-eared book under one arm as he went to feed the animals, or an old novel at his side when he slept by the campfire after a day spent on the trail. He loved the tales of knights, and especially stories of cowboys who always seemed to ride off into the sunset at the story's end."

Rider's wistful tone changed. "Of course he found it harder and harder to find time to read as he got older, as his responsibilities to the community changed. As a young man without the obligations of marriage he was expected to stand watch, carry a gun, and spend most of his time on the back of a horse, shepherding the animals and keeping an eye out for the aberrations that preyed on them. He soon began to show an uncanny aptitude with horses, both in riding them and in breaking them in. He quickly became one of the clan's best outriders. With his adopted family he began to build a new life. His adopted family were good people, all of whom treated him well..." Rider touched the photo, his voice momentarily trailing off.

"... and in no time at all he found himself falling in love with the old man's eldest daughter, a strong, smart, willful, cocky girl."

He was quiet for a long moment; Rider's mind was obviously somewhere else now. "The family didn't approve, of course. Oh sure, he was shaping up to be a good man, becoming a solid part of the community, but his white skin and pink eyes were considered a threat to the family blood, a danger to the precious genes of the clan. Taking a wife meant risking the chance of passing his curse on to the next generation. At first his adopted father tried to dissuade him from seeing his daughter, Yolanda, but when that failed to keep them apart they were forbidden to see each other altogether. To drive his point home, the old man sent the young man on the summer cattle drive hoping time... and distance... would cause their love to diminish and fade.

"For weeks he traveled away from home, taking the herd from the dry plains to the edge of the grasslands of the south. It was long, tedious work, with entire days spent under the killing sun and nights slept alone under the cold, unchanging stars. Somewhere on the way back, however, the young man and his fellow herders passed in the shadow of a great, nameless city. He was fascinated by it, but the others warned him against going there, reminding him of the legends of radiation and strange lurking diseases that polluted all ruins. They were simple people, you see, content with their simple, nomadic life, but he wasn't like them. His curiosity compelled him to see it for himself."

"Just before dawn, as his fellow herders lay sleeping, he rode off to see the city with his own eyes."

Rider took a deep breath. "By noon he made it to the city and was surprised by what he found. This was no dismal place. Seen from far away it looked like a gray blotch, but here, among the actual streets, the sun was bright, its rays streaming through the spaces between the rows of ancient buildings. He heard the soft sighing wind, but no sounds of life. It was peaceful. It was beautiful."

"He'd heard the stories, had read books, but he had never actually *seen* a city before. Towering skyscrapers surrounded him on all sides; the cracked streets were bare except for bits of trash and overgrown vegetation. Flowers grew everywhere, white, pink and blue, from the mossy patches carpeting the streets to the ivy that slinked its way up five, six stories on every building. Stone statues in a grand city park stood ahead of him; in the distance he saw the golden idol of the Oilman, still standing proudly over the ancient necropolis."

"He had only intended to sneak a peek of the city, to catch a quick glimpse, but he spent two entire days wandering and exploring. He was wary of imaginary monsters, but what he found were just empty streets and storefronts, skyscrapers and bridges. The city was almost completely *intact*, only its inhabitants missing. He spent hours looking at the mannequins in old display windows, and exploring old stores, wandering the aisles and discovering what the Ancients had left behind. In one small shop he found hundreds of toys, dolls, balls, airplanes, and trains. A mile away he found a great vaulted structure, where row upon row of shelves, some twenty feet high and stacked with building materials, seemed to be just waiting for someone to find them and put them to use. In another place he found stores filled with all sorts of strange clothing and apparel, and on the upper level, dark arcades and dead gardens. He saw the rusted remains of automobiles on every street, and took in the sight of great billboards and signs everywhere, some of which stood taller than houses. On one block he found a lot filled with the sleeping hulks of over five hundred abandoned cars; on the next he found an old bank, its vault still full of stacks of old money, rotten bills and sacks of tarnished coins."

"The ruins of an ancient civilization were his to walk through," Rider explained, "to see firsthand, to explore. I guess it was a wonder that he remembered to return at all. When he did go back to the others, he found them anxiously waiting, having worried when he'd gone missing. But when they asked him where he'd gone, he kept it to himself. It was still all too much to put to words, it had to be seen firsthand to believed, and there was only one person he could think of bringing here to share it with him."

Rider paused and shifted his weight. "They eventually returned, and though Yolanda's father had hoped she would have forgotten about the young man while he was gone, they reunited like long-lost loves." Rider's smile flattened out as he voiced that sentimental idea. But he continued. "Only a few weeks after he came back, the young fools married in secret. But living in the fear of being 'found out' was impossible for him. For some reason he couldn't just be happy with having Yolanda's love, even if it meant concealing it. Stubbornly he wanted more, and so he convinced her to run away with him, to leave the nomadic life behind and start anew in the ruins of that ancient city."

"Though they dreamed in secret it wasn't long before others, too, heard him speaking of the marvelous city, and soon they wondered if they could also make a go of it. Childhood friends came forward and asked if they could come as well, start a settlement of their own, a colony, leaving the stifling life of their forefathers behind."

"He soon found he had been thrust into the role of guide and *leader*. He should have known better, he should have called it all off, but he was swept up by the idea and believed it could work. So, one night, he and about two dozen others left the camp under the cover of darkness, turning their backs on their old lives. They came here..." Rider said quietly, looking around him. "... and over the years built homes, their own fragile community. They figured out how to survive, and in time even had children of their own."

He stared at the picture, but the others couldn't see what held his attention so unshakably. "Yolanda gave him four beautiful girls. *White as mice...*" Gale left Ludd's side, and crept around trying to see what exactly was captured in the photograph.

"Because their children inherited the same albinism as their father, the man led his people into inhabiting the tunnels underground. Not only for his sake and the sake of his children, but also because they would go unnoticed there, should unwanted outsiders ever visit the city. And the tunnels were defensible. After clearing out the probing, waddling things that lived in the depths, they made their homes in the sewers, and built an elaborate web of passages to connect the maze of newly-secured tunnels."

A grin spread over Rider's face. "Yolanda was a real sport," he said, "She always joked that if she followed me... if she followed *him*... she was sure she'd end up living in a 'shit-hole'." Gale and Ludd both found themselves blinking, but Rider plowed on, unwilling to let them interrupt his tale.

"They found the trails of game surviving in the ruins, and learned to grow small amounts of crops in old parks and gardens. They foraged for food, and found precious sources of good, clean water. They discovered old books washed up on the shores of the sewers, or in the basements of buildings their digging led them to. *Books*. The city seemed full of them. He enjoyed sitting and reading with his girls. Ellie and Manda shared his passion for horses, and the same stories that he himself had enjoyed as a youngster. Britt was a tomboy, and her father's shadow, learning to ride and track game by the age of seven. Carrie... the littlest one... believed in *unicorns*..."

Rider noticeably hesitated, and once again his tone stiffened. "It was a good life, but one that became increasingly more difficult as the summers gradually grew hotter and dryer. As time went on the men were forced to go further and further to find game, spending days away from home looking for sustenance for their families. But resources were slim, the times lean. Water all across the city began to dry up. Thirst set in. As the wife of the colony's 'leader', Yolanda was soon bombarded with demands by of the female colonists, mothers and wives worried for their children. They wanted to give up on the city, to return to their people out in the plains. They were sure the nomads would accept them back, that all would be forgotten."

He sighed. "But the man, for one, wasn't ready to give up. He wanted to stay, to make it work; he stubbornly resisted going back, refused to admit failure. So the colonists argued, and they fought. In response to their growing concerns, as their leader, the man came forward and addressed the colony. To quell their fears he announced his plan. He would go and find water. He vowed he and his own family wouldn't consume a drop until he found and brought back enough for the entire community."

"The next day he gathered up a large posse of men and set about putting everyone's fears to rest. Yolanda was left to deal with the women and the children, while he led the men out on their life-saving mission."

"They spent days searching the ruins, through the most wicked summer dry spell the colony had ever seen. Finally reaching their wit's end, the expedition at long last came across a lake, a large circular body of water at the center of the city ringed by damaged and disintegrating buildings. But the water was crystalline and clear, and his men eagerly drank from its waters before filling their skins, canteens and empty jugs for the journey back." For some reason Ludd seemed interested in this turn of events, and leaned in close. Rider continued his story.

"They came back with full skins, to the amazement of the rest of the colony, and the water was distributed eagerly. Children and nursing mothers were nourished first, then the crops, then the remaining women and the men..."

Once again Rider fell into a telling silence, his eyes glimmering wetly. "Even before they had finished distributing the water, people began to fall sick. One by one children, women, and men grew ill. Some held on, but others succumbed quickly, bleeding from their eyes and nostrils and every pore, expiring after days of unimaginable pain. There was a panic, and a realization that the water they had taken from the lake was poisoned, diseased. Illness floated invisibly in the water, a remnant of the last war waiting centuries to find one last group of innocent people to lay waste to."

Rider sounded bitter, angry. "While his own wife and children seemed healthy, the man realized what he had to do, for the sake of his people, the people he had led here. He had brought this catastrophe on them, and he believed he alone should be responsible for finding their salvation. So he packed a horse, said his farewells, and rode off with the desperate hope that he might find some people, somewhere, who knew of a cure and could be persuaded to part with it."

He was there now, remembering the moment vividly. It had been so many years ago, but it still managed to stun him, a single moment in time that froze him. Before he left, Yolanda looked directly into his eyes, held his face so he couldn't look away, making sure he remembered her face. She muttered... "I love you, I love you," over and over again, so that he would never forget her voice, so that he would always remember *that* as the last thing she said. His four girls crowded around, they held onto his pants and jacket, they begged him to stay no matter what.

"So what happened?" Ludd asked, breaking Rider's trance.

"He traveled for weeks looking for the signs of passing traders," Rider explained with a dry, rasping voice, "but because of the drought the trade routes were empty. So he gave up and made his way to the nearest village. And then the next. But when he spoke of plague, of searching for a cure, he was driven out by the fearful inhabitants of virtually every place he went. He continued on regardless, he and his horse, but soon weeks became a month, months became a year..."

Rider put on his hat, regaining his composure. "When he finally did return he found the city empty. The colony was gone."

"Gone?" Gale asked, surprised.

"*Gone*," Rider replied, nodding methodically. "Just... gone. Everyone gone."

The sensation of sadness was overcome by a wave of guilt emanating from Rider that made Gale shudder. "It wasn't your fault, Rider," she said. "You know that, don't you?"

"Oh, it *was*, kid," Rider said, having convinced himself long ago of his guilt. He spoke as if it was fact, without a hint of self-pity. "I'm the one who brought the sickness to them and killed them all. They trusted me, they looked up to me. I brought Death right in through the front door." Gale was quiet.

"What happened to your family, then?" Ludd asked.

"I imagine the bacteria got them. All of them, every last one..." Rider said this as he looked at the photograph of the four young children smiling with toothy grins around him, and at the two-dimensional face of his long-dead wife. They were beautiful, all six of them; a young Rider with an uncharacteristic, loving face, his arms around a beautiful, dark-haired, green-eyed woman in front of him, and the four albino girls dressed in what could once be described as their Sunday finest.

He stopped there, momentarily. He could see Yolanda's face now, remembered her smile and her uplifting sense of humor, could hear her voice and remembered its strength and optimism. In that one instant all his memories of that one woman came together; laughter, excited eyes, a deep love of God. Belief in her husband, the courage and faith to follow him as he led her from her people to start a new life. Years spent among the ruins of the city, like pioneers building a life from scratch. He remembered days filled with hardships, working together to build a home, struggling to gather food, and nights of lovemaking. He remembered his worry when she first went into labor, and the joy of bringing their first child into the world despite being surrounded by adversity. He remembered Yolanda's smile on seeing the face of her firstborn, albino like her father, and the pride in her eyes despite knowing then that their children weren't going to have it easy. She wouldn't abandon him just for that, she was with him for the long-haul. It was love, true and strong.

She was gone now, all her goodness and bravery erased from the world, a brilliant, bright candle that stood out in the darkness but had been snuffed suddenly from the world by the lingering curse of an ancient, forgotten war. There would never be anyone like her, ever and her death had essentially killed him as well.

Closing his eyes tight he tried to fight the memories of the four small children that he once called his own, but he was unable to keep them at bay. To someone else they might have all seemed identical, with their fair skin, white hair, and pink eyes, but he remembered each unique voice, each freckle, each missing tooth. They had died so young that he was almost grateful they weren't here to live in this decrepit wasteland, almost thankful they had been taken away from this life of inevitable suffering.

He hadn't been there when it happened, so his mind was free to imagine what their last moments were like, each of them, as they succumbed to the bacteria. As their people died around them, as the community fell apart, until no one was left. It consoled him to think they died together, that none of them outlasted the others, so that none of them had to be alone in these tunnels surrounded by the dead.

"I brought them here, Gale, to this city. I led them to their deaths. It was my idea to try to start a new life here. They trusted me. Yolanda trusted me. I convinced her to come, I sold the idea to her, I tricked her into thinking I could protect her and we'd be safe... I killed our *babies*, Gale."

Everyone was silent. Then, gradually, Rider thought of Valero's words from long, long ago and, taking a breath, recited them. "But I take comfort from knowing that others suffer more than I do."

"No..." Gale muttered, finding herself compelled to come over to him and kneel at his side. "No, you won't. You'll take comfort knowing that you've survived, against tremendous odds and the cruelty of Nature, and you'll go on surviving. What happened here, to your people, to your family, it wasn't your fault. Rider, you did what you did because you believed you were *saving* your community. You tried to give them a new life, you tried to find them water, you left the ones you loved behind to find a cure. You did it all for *them*."

"Maybe it was in God's plan," Ludd chimed in. "Maybe your people were meant to die, to finally know peace, not having to live like rats on this blasted earth anymore. Maybe He granted them the dignity to finally die as humans and end their lives of misery, bring them back to His kingdom. If only the rest of us were so lucky, to be snatched away so quickly to join Him in Paradise! And you know what? Maybe your selfless desire to provide, your *intention*, is what saved you, in His eyes. Maybe He let you live, to spread this tale to inspire others... God knows we could use a little more humanity, bravery and self-sacrifice in this world. Why, you just might be the last true hero on the planet Earth!"

Ludd mused, but Rider looked away, appalled to be called a "hero". He thought of all that he had done to Gale, and to others like her. He didn't tell the old man to his face, but he knew he was no hero, he was nothing more than a survivor like the nameless scum that infested every other degenerate corner of the desert. Everyone had a tragic tale, everyone had started good and turned bad; everyone had been ground down by the harsh realities of life and survival and come out like this.

Rider turned and now looked at Gale, kneeling at his side. He had no tears, which didn't surprise her. He wasn't the kind of man to cry, or voice his admission of defeat.

Gale looked at him. "Your people are at rest now, Rider. You don't have to just *survive* anymore. You can live again. And while we still have strength, and air to breathe, we can change things. *Together* we can change the way things are, for the better."

He stared into her, to her very soul. For the past ten years he had never believed in grand causes, or even the prospect of change. Gale spoke of toppling an established order, death and misery, that had existed for generations. She spoke in broad terms, she had no plan, but somehow her optimism, her *hope*, touched him in a place he long thought dead. In that instant he was no longer an impassionate bounty hunter, a raging assassin, a callous captor. He was a man, frail of spirit and flawed at heart, another orphan of this violent land, just like her.

In his eyes she could see he was willing to listen, and follow. "We've got to go back now," she said, getting to her feet. "Hotwire an old car, head for the trade route. We'll be alright. We're free to start over." Rider joined her, but Ludd was slow to rise.

"Come on," she said to the old man, "we can go together. All of us. We'll head for the mountains, the Wei Shan, we'll find that 'kingdom' among the peaks..."

"It's not going to be as easy as that," Ludd said.

"Why not?" Rider asked.

"Because there are *others* living in the city now. I've seen them, heard their insane calls. We'd best wait until dark. And we'll have to be quiet..."

Gale and Rider looked at each other. "Who lives here?" Gale asked the old man.

"Why, *hermavs*, of course..."

"What'd I tell you," Valero said over his shoulder to Tank. "Old raider trick... *always* follow the road signs. They always lead somewhere interesting, a crossroads, a small town, or, in this case..."

Night was beginning to fall over the desert, leaving only two distinct features to the wasteland, the black of the desert floor and the deep blue of the broad night sky.

"... a *city*."

They were already approaching the outskirts of an old metropolis, a city seemingly forgotten by the people of the outside world, its mighty towers visible in the distance, its outer neighborhoods sleeping quietly under the stars.

For the first hour they traveled in total silence, both men wary of their new surroundings and on edge. Valero feared radiation and kept a keen eye out for a sure sign of its presence, the carcasses of animals that died of a wasting sickness, only slowly rotting away due to the absence of insects or scavengers to feast on their remains. But he found none. He listened instead for strange noises, but only the sound of their horses walking on cracked asphalt issued out into the night.

Tank stared at the empty complexes of industrial parks, the large, dark office buildings that rose here and there and the distant outline of solid skyscrapers, all of them seemingly intact, unbroken, undamaged. It was as if they had found an entire city that had just been shut down and "switched off", patiently awaiting the return of its long-vanished inhabitants.

"*You will c-catch up to them in the c-city that still s-stands...*" he said quietly, remembering the prophetic words of their Brotherhood mind-guides.

Valero suddenly remembered as well, and took another look at their surroundings. It was relatively intact this place, remarkably preserved despite periodic swaths of destruction. At first he tried to deny it, but the more he saw the more he realized the true clarity of their Brotherhood "allies'" far-sight. If it *were* true, that the psychics had seen this place and known Rider would come here, then there were more important things to worry about than being awed by their mysterious capabilities. This place might *seem* still and quiet, but somewhere out their Rider was most certainly hiding, with his hostage, and being no fool, would be aware that someone was coming to hunt them down.

Valero remembered Rider's reputation as a crack marksman and remained alert for the shrill sound of a sniper's shot to ring out through the slowly-enveloping night. They were surrounded on all sides by tall buildings, each of them faced with dozens, if not hundreds of pitch black windows, each of them capable of hiding the ghost-faced rifleman in their shadowy recesses. Wherever Rider was, there was a good chance he would see them before they even knew he was there.

Valero didn't need to remind Tank but he did anyway: "No lights, no sounds whatsoever..."

They continued on for another quarter mile before Valero and Tank came across faint signs in the sand, blown in from the desert, that showed Rider and Gale had passed this way earlier that day. After a short discussion the men agreed to dismount and leave their horses in a nearby underground parking garage, laden with their packs and heavier equipment, and proceed the rest of the way by foot.

In the dead of night Tank led the way, his small eyes struggling to find the trail. Valero let him take the front, while he kept a watch on the city around them, holding the old Garand rifle given him by Ridaya. He knew he hadn't been trusted, made clear by the fact that she had given him only a single strip-clip to see him through this little "mission". She'd given him protection consisting of a cuirboilli breastplate and leather armor, but he'd discarded all but the sleeveless jack and leggings to move unimpeded. Like most raiders, he preferred speed over durability, the ability to get out of a fight as quickly as he got into it.

The night was all around them, but at the edge of his vision Valero spotted what appeared to be the dim glow of a firelight. He immediately tapped Tank's shoulder with his knuckle, and wordlessly pointed in that direction. Both men moved for cover, and after a moment, looked back out into the abandoned ruins. In the dim starlight both men saw that they were near the banks of a dried up river. Almost a mile away, on the far side of the wide open riverbed, was a line of riverfront buildings, their dark shapes facing out across the dry waterway like stark sentinels. In one of these they saw a distant glow, perhaps a campfire burning inside the shell of one of the larger structures.

"*Trap...*" Valero insisted, but Tank simply stared.

"M-maybe," he stuttered. "But what choice have w-we g-got?"

Staying to the shadows both men moved to the edge of the street, where the asphalt had crumbled away into a slide of broken gray rocks that sunk deep towards the dry, sandy riverbed. The half-mile width of the ancient waterway seemed a daunting distance to cover with only the cover of night to hide them.

Disregarding the absence of cover, Tank immediately began to descend the slope to the bottom, sliding on the oval-shaped stones and porous sand until he had come to a stop. He looked back to Valero, who slung the heavy, antiquated rifle on his back and prepared to follow. But Valero suddenly stopped, and instead extended his hand.

"Give me more ammo," he whispered.

Tank considered his demand. Ridaya had been suspicious of the ex-raider, but now that they were alone here, together, he felt he *had* to trust him. Tank hesitantly reached into his pack and threw up another two clips, one after the other. Only once Valero had stashed them in his belt pouch did he descend.

Hunkering down and scattering a few paces apart, the two men started running across the wide open river. Despite the small pebbles underfoot, the ground was remarkably level, the evenness only broken here and there by an old rubber tire, an empty plastic milk jug, bundles of cable and wiring that once crisscrossed the river bottom, a toppled river buoy, and the rotted remains of a small motor launch, all of them partly embedded in the earth and draped with traces of calcified vegetation.

Sitting in the middle of the dried-up riverbed was the wreck of a large, rusted river barge, its mighty bulk having been stranded when the waters receded long ago. Both men made a direct line for it, only stopping their unwavering race across the sandy river floor once they reached safety in the shadow of its groaning metal hull. Tank stopped to catch his breath, but Valero skirted along the hull until he came to the front end, peeking around. They had crossed more than half the distance. From here he could see the buildings looming not far away. There were more lights now glowing in the shattered windows of that one particular building, but still no sign of movement.

"What do you make of that?" he asked Tank casually, as the giant quietly come up beside Valero to get a look for himself.

Tank said nothing, and instead checked his own rifle to make sure it was loaded and ready. He then stepped out into the starlight again and started jogging towards the far embankment no less than a few hundred yards away. With no other choice, Valero went along with him. They reached the far bank minutes later, taking cover among large rocks and boulders that had once been the riverfront street but which had collapsed, piecemeal, over time, so that now large chunks of pavement littered the river floor. Hundreds of multi-colored brown and green beer bottles littered the sandy bottom here, remnants of a past age tossed carelessly into the river long before it dried up.

Tank started to climb, heaving his mighty weight upwards and upwards, until he reached the top and pulled himself over. Valero did the same, until both men were at ground level. A huge building soared above them, flanked on either side by other dark, city buildings. Sleek stone pillars fronted the place, creating numerous shadows for them to hide in so long as they moved from one to the other without being seen.

Orange light burned in the ground floor; the enormous wooden double doors that looked out onto the street were open, one lying flat in front of the structure, the other still bound by its verdigris-draped brass hinges to the stony frame. Valero tried to sneak a look inside but only saw stony rubble from a structural collapse, lit by the flames of a fire burning in a large oil drum in the center of the building's grand antechamber. Tank scuttled from pillar to pillar until he was right outside the entrance. He unshouldered his gun and looked back at Valero.

Valero felt ill at ease. Looking up he saw the broad arch over the entrance, part of the masonry chipped and fallen away, though the one word remaining was still legible: "LIBRARY".

It meant nothing to him. He readied his own rifle and traced Tank's footsteps until he joined the giant mutant just outside the entrance.

It was quiet inside, except for the methodic crackling of the flames burning in the open oil drum. There was very little smoke, only the crisp smell of charred leather and scorched paper. Tiny fireflies of glowing ash rose up from the oil drum, swirling crazily about in the air before winking out of existence in the darkness above.

Tank almost jumped as an unexpected crackle and pop exploded from the fire, but it was only the sound of a heap of old books burning in the recesses of the drum. He looked around for any sign of Rider, or the girl.

The room was a shambles, rubble-strewn and stripped bare, with wild graffiti decorating the walls in dizzying circles and whorls. The tiled marble ceiling was partly caved-in on one side of the grand antechamber, and the light from the fire barely illuminated what little could be seen of the level above, more rubble and dusty, collapsed support beams.

Tank went towards the bottom of a grand flight of stairs that ascended to the level above, each end flanked by a life-sized statue of the *Thinker*. These, too, had been defaced by spray paint, so that each solemn, stony face now wore a clown's vivid red smile.

Tank detected the faint sounds of wild laughter just as Valero approached the fire, momentarily looking at the stack of old musty books that had been piled there to provide its fuel. He could read a little of the Ancient language, of course, but he didn't recognize any of the strange authors. *Didache, Eusebius, Tertullian, Chrysostom...*

He heard the laughter too; a single voice just barely carrying down from above, before it completely vanished.

Valero came over and began scaling the stairs, head cocked upwards to make sure nothing waited for them in the darkness of the second level. As the stairwell curled around both sides, they passed more wild graffiti and strange symbols of which neither man took much notice. They were instead riveted on the shadowy void ahead of them.

At the top of the grand staircase they faced a cold dark hallway, lined on both sides by statues of classical Romanesque figurines, some broken and toppled, others still standing in place. Another fiery light came from an open doorway on the right-hand side of the hall, just thirty feet down the marble corridor, bathing the wide passage in a warm, amber glow.

As they started down the passage, suddenly both men heard the screech of sneakers on marble echoing from the level below. They instinctively turned to look in the direction of the descending stairwell, only to spin around again when they heard more laughter, this time three or four voices, from somewhere on the levels above.

Valero moved away from the stairs and Tank followed close behind. More noises from above. And below. Valero looked at Tank, his eyes conveying a simple question: *stay, or go?* Tank made the decision and proceeded down the corridor, until they came to the entrance to the well-lit room.

The huge chamber they entered was quite impressive, even though its dark, shadowy corners were barely visible in the weak light provided by the few burning fires. A few oil drums like the one below sat about the room, each a beacon to provide some illumination over the massive, echoing interior. Marble pillars buttressed the walls and rose into the darkness overhead, while between these columns ran shelf after shelf of dusty books, dozens per shelf, hundreds per column. Chunks of masonry from the ceiling littered the floor and formed sharp, rocky piles here and there, and chalky white dust covered the cracked, rose-colored tiles that decorated the floor.

Valero stopped suddenly when he realized they were not alone. One of *them* stood by a nearby chair. Another hung, ape-like, from the rungs of a ladder once intended to allow patrons to reach books high overhead. Another squatted atop one of the broad wooden tables, sifting through piles of books stacked there, picking them up one by one and letting them drop to the floor.

These were not human, these things. They were skeletal shapes, their bodies riddled with all sorts of unmentionable diseases, each a carrier of crippling syphilis, of painful gonorrhea, their bodies sickly and emaciated. They were strangely androgynous, willowy men with slight arms and legs, wearing their hair either too long or too short, their ears and noses and lips pierced with metal rings, their eyes crudely decorated with eyeliner and their lips clumsily painted with the most lurid red or shining silver lipstick. Moles sprinkled their exposed, white flesh, and scabrous lesions swarmed about their mouths and nostrils, and pockmarked their bare backs. Some wore metal gauntlets, others cocktail-length leather gloves; those that showed their hands had carefully painted their nails a rainbow of pastel colors. Each of these "men" was clearly not normal, however, for they exhibited feminine traits as well; beyond slightly upturned noses and small mouths, dainty frames and slender fingers, they also had pronounced breasts and, as their lack of modesty showed, wickedly-circumcised penises behind which hung the loose openings of deformed vaginas.

Each of these eerily-quiet hermaphrodites wore body armor scavenged from the city, old fetish gear adopted first for fun, then later added to for real protection. Steel studs and rivets mixed with glittery rings and meaningless symbols that were merely intended to catch the eye; ankhs, upside-down crosses, pentacles and even buttons with cute catchphrases on them, admired more for their color than any witty slogan they might advertise. Along with these they wore bits of chainmail and plate made from scavenged scrap metal, formed into exaggerated arm-guards that resembled hulking football armor, so that each one looked so top heavy that it might topple over at any second. One wore the scalps of past victims woven into its attire, while from the broad hips of another hung a belt of human hair, from which dangled a collection of human teeth.

Valero noticed the guns. Each of the half-dozen hermavs carried some form of firearm; one had a "grease gun", two carried MAC 10s, relics of the gang wars that once swept the ancient cities, and the rest had weapons and rifles he didn't even recognize. The hermavs remained silent, watching the newcomers with steady but relaxed gazes. For some reason they weren't attacking.

Across the room from the two men, standing inhumanly tall behind one of the burning oil drums, was a singularly massive hermaphrodite whose very appearance made both men recoil in horror. This was something that should never have survived birth, this perversity of mutation, and seemed only to live to perpetuate the ghost-story image its race had among the survivors of this earth.

Almost eight feet tall by virtue of its ridiculous stiletto-heeled boots, the creature that loomed before them was hard to look at without triggering stirrings of unease. A horrific Siamese twin, the leader of this band of hermaphroditic killers was an impossible combination of both male and female; one half of its body was male, the other female, the head partly split to give it a vague heart shape. On each lobe of this wide, grotesque head sat half of a separate face, man on one, woman on the other, their four separate eyes looking off in weird directions, their movements independent of each other.

The mistress of these thugs wore tall shoulders of overlapping metal plates, giving the menace a dramatic, gothic flair, and from these shoulder plates hung curtains of black chainmail. Its chest was completely bare, revealing a single but noticeable breast crowned by a brown nipple, while its navel, exposed in its well-muscled abdomen, held a faceted red gemstone that swirled in the firelight. The creature looked up momentarily at the men who'd stumbled into its lair, its four black-lined eyes regarding them with a cold, alien stare before returning to their work.

Valero and Tank watched as the hermav leader reached down with elegant fingers, tipped by six-inch black nails as sharp as knives, and picked up another old book, opened it over the fire, and began reading by the flickering orange light:

"A woman who takes up devilish ways and plays a male role in coupling with another woman is most vile in my sight..." The sentence elicited a few chuckles from the otherwise silent and still hermav gang.

Valero itched to fire his weapon, or at the very least retreat. He shifted his weight to take a step back, but with that slightest of movements three of the hermavs reacted, standing up from where they had recently been sitting. They hadn't even raised their guns, but their sudden motion had succeeded in getting their message across. He stayed put.

The leader's black lips curled into an amused smile, as if the ancient words held no more weight than a child's rambling book report. It released the book and it fell into the crackling fire.

"Another!" came a cry from one of the hermavs deeper in the cavernous chamber. In response the leader picked up another book and opened it, wetting one finger with its long, gray tongue to flip the pages to a particular spot.

"Nothing can be more worthless than a man who has pandered himself. For not the soul only, but the body also of one who hath been so treated, is disgraced, and deserves to be driven out everywhere."

Crude laughter as one another patted themselves on the back, embraced and kissed wetly in the darkness. The leader grinned at its followers' actions, revealing a mess of black, glistening teeth. That book, too, was fed to the hungry fire. In silence they watched it burn away; even the hermavs that had been eyeing the two stunned newcomers turned to stare into the flames.

"*This* one..." one of its underlings said softly, coming forward with a large, leather-bound tome. Their leader took it and examined the cover, gently touching the gold gilt title on its face, its long nails clacking against the cover with a sound like raindrops against a window.

"Now *this* has some of the *best* ones..." it said with a grin. It opened the book and began paging through, its eyes widening with fervor to find its "favorite" passages. It decided to start with the best, the one they all knew.

"Thou shalt not lie with a man as with a woman!" it shouted, its voice filling the chamber with echoes, and with that the rest of the amused hermavs chimed in: *"It is an abomination!"*

Their leader looked to its followers, one by one, then to the two men who'd intruded on their readings. Its eyes sparkled. But it would deal with them soon enough; right now it wasn't finished. More flipping of pages.

"Do you not know that wrongdoers will not inherit the kingdom of God?" Smug smiles.

"Aww..." a voice teased from the recesses of the room, pretending to be disappointed. "He can keep it..." said another, calling out from the other side of the chamber. Despite their playful banter, their leader continued.

"Do not be deceived. Neither the sexually immoral nor adulterers... nor homosexuals... shall inherit the kingdom of God."

All fell silent. The creature ran its hand over the page and closed its eyes. It brought its clawed fingers together, crumpled the page in hand, tearing it from the dusty binding and dropped the paper ball into the fire. Wisps of ash blew upwards like glowing red moths. Moments later, the creature let the entire Bible drop from its hand and into the flames to be consumed. The fire raged hotter.

The hermav leader opened its eyes and looked across the fire at Valero, then Tank.

"Our given name is Taba," it said, "the name our people gave us before they drove us out. You will soon know why..."

With that the hermavs descended from their perches, from their seats, from the shadows and the surrounding darkness. They began cocking their guns.

Every man dies, but not like this! Valero screamed in his head, then found his hands responding. He lifted the wooden stock of his Garand to his shoulder and immediately opened fire. *Crack-crack-crack* came the shots, as one bullet struck the gangly hermav leader in the arm, causing him (or her, or *it*) to recoil back beyond the glow of the fire and out of sight. The other two rounds shot off into the dark, one vanishing into the shadows while the other struck another androgynous thug nearby in its chest, exploding in a shower of blood.

Tank was much slower and when he brought his gun up to fire, one of the hermavs had already moved within striking distance, bringing its weapon up to knock the gun over and out of his hands. The rifle let out a flaring burst that went wild, striking stone and sending sharp shards of masonry skittering through the darkness. Like a nest of angry bees the hermavs descended, a chaotic mess of machete-armed and firearm-wielding freaks intent on slaying the interlopers who had injured their monstrous leader.

As his gun dropped to the ground Tank formed a fist and hurled it towards his attacker, striking it in its belly and sending it flying into a heap of books. But two more hermavs rushed in, one brandishing a large Bowie knife, the other an M16 that it prepared to fire. A shot struck out and sunk into Tank's chest, but the mammoth mutant simply roared with fury and barreled into his two assailants. The one with the rifle fell over, while the other was crushed under his weight as he tripped and fell, pinning it against the ground.

Valero fell back, reloading his rifle, as gunfire erupted all around him, breaking off bits of stone and tearing holes in the old wooden doors that hung idly in the doorframe.

Amazed he hadn't been hit he fired blindly into the confused mass of surging enemies, watching one after another get hit, spout blood in a crimson fountain and collapse beneath the feet of even more killers emerging from all around.

"Tank!" Valero shouted. "Tank! Pull out, now!" He ran back to the doorway and out into the shadowy corridor just as more bullets from a Korean War-era grease gun tore into the doorframe, reducing what was left to splinters and causing the heavy doors to fall to the ground like discarded kindling. Tank rose just as another hermav ran up and hacked his exposed stomach with its machete, the blade tearing his chainmail and slicing through his flesh. He staggered back and grabbed another of the wicked mutants that dared to come near, picking the thing up and tossing it into a line of others to keep them at bay.

Valero had retreated out the door. Tank would follow, plowing through the enemy if need be, but he momentarily stopped to retrieve his rifle. As he bent down, he felt an almost insignificant prick as two tiny metal darts impacted his shoulder and back, each of them leading an ultra-fine conducting wire, their barbs clinging to his thick skin. He shot up with a confused start and turned to follow where the wires trailed off to, and saw, at the edge of the wavering fire light, the tall and willowy Taba holding a taser in one bloody, outstretched arm.

"*Sing for me!*" the hideous, wounded abomination hissed, its four eyes flickering insanely as it pulled the trigger. Tank felt his skin numb, then sizzle, then burn with fire. His muscles spasmed, his arms flailed uncontrollably, he lost the contents of his bowels as they emptied in his pants. He shrieked in a pitch he never thought imaginable, saw explosions of stars in his eyes, then fell over and hit the ground with a powerful "thud".

Valero heard the cry and turned to look around the corner, seeing Tank fall to the earth and shiver and shake. Taba strode forward among its mass of gangers, repeatedly hitting the trigger to continue electrocuting the helpless giant, smiling wider and more savagely as Tank's body shook and danced on the stone floor. Valero raised his gun to shoot but another burst of gunfire kept him suppressed, forcing him back into the hallway.

They were coming. He heard more of them descending the steps from levels higher up, and they were swarming towards the door, enveloping Tank in their midst. With a shot backwards to buy some time he heard the strip eject and clatter somewhere in the darkness, then began running as fast as he could towards the grand stairs. As Valero ran his old leg injury awoke, sending pain swirling through his bones, but he kept up his speed. At the top of the stairs he stopped for a fraction of a second to fish out his last clip, just as more shots cut into the marble railing tearing stone shrapnel free. Arrowhead-sized slivers tore into his back, slicing through his leathers as cleanly as cloth, but instead of incapacitating him the pain gave him the impetus to start running again.

Down the stairwell Valero ran, slid and fell, leaving streaks of blood on the marble steps. Enough blood that when he tried to get to his feet his rubber-soled sandals slipped from under him, preventing him from rising.

Down on the bottom floor, an unusually muscular hermav wearing a black latex fetish mask ran through the open front doorway to the great library, its long red hair bobbing up and down behind it as it leapt over the collapsed door. Only its flaring, insane eyes (one gray, the other blinded by a cataract) showed, the mouth concealed behind a metal vent. The beast turned and saw Valero lying there at the foot of the steps and pulled the string of the rusted, oil-caked *chainsaw* held in its hand.

With a sputter the venerable chainsaw struggled to come to life, suddenly spewing oily smoke from a rusted grille on one side. The hermaphrodite came charging forward, carrying with it a strange, nauseating perfume of latex, leather, sweat, and gasoline. Valero kicked his leg out as it lunged at him, catching the hermav in the center of the chest and knocking it over, winding it and cracking a rib. The chainsaw skittered away as the hermav lost its grip, but as soon as it came to a stop, began crawling across the floor, dragged along by its titanium saw-tooth blades.

Valero got up, pain and blood be damned, and started for the doorway, dodging past the burning oil barrel and smashing broken stone and scattering discarded books underfoot. The works of Clement of Alexandria and Hildegard of Bingen were trampled and ruined. But the hermav hadn't given up, it got up just as quickly and ran to the 'saw, pulling the heavy logging tool from the ground and held it ahead of itself like a spear.

Valero heard the motor roar as the operator fed it more gas, and turned to see the masked, red-haired hermav coming after him, tracing his steps through the obstacle course of oil drum, stone rubble and books. With a determined stare and swift reflexes the ex-raider brought his rifle up, took aim and shot. The bullet exited the barrel and impacted the hermav's forehead, crumpling whatever malformed face was concealed behind the mask and ejecting the contents of its skull out the back in a gory explosion of bone and soft tissue.

Valero almost fell as the pain in his back increased, but he made it to the doorway and stumbled out into the night. Without a moment's hesitation he began to run.

Rider, Gale, and Ludd were moving along quietly through the darkness near the river. Ludd had led them across the groaning expanse of a precarious metal highway bridge that connected the east side of the city with the west, when all of a sudden the night sky erupted with distant crackles and pops. *Gunfire.*

"You said you'd be able to get us out of here without trouble," Rider sneered, trying to maintain his calm. He took cover in the shadows of a bridge support; Gale and Ludd followed.

"No," Ludd replied, "I said if we were *lucky* we'd get out..."

More gunfire. Rider searched the night and saw in the distance the glow of fires in some far away building on the side they were running from.

"Celebration?" Ludd suggested. Rider listened for a moment but said nothing, then continued across the bridge, quickening his pace. *When you're unsure about something, it's best to keep moving.* Gale and Ludd followed, but after only a few steps Gale stopped and looked back. A strange feeling touched upon her subconscious. She felt...

"A friend is in danger..." she blurted aloud. Ludd kept moving but Rider stopped and looked back at her.

"A friend... I think..." she muttered, seeming unsure.

"Foolish girl!" Ludd called. "Keep moving! Do you know what those things do to 'breeders' like you?"

"We have to go back, Rider. Tank is there... he needs our help." Rider's head snapped back from looking out at the night when she said that name.

"Tank? *Tank?*" he said, recalling when he'd last seen Tank, in the company of a man whose arm he'd severed with a sword. "He's no friend, now, Gale. He's one of the enemy!"

"No," Gale said, looking even more confused than him, as if she was listening to voices that no one else could hear and was only partly conscious of Rider and Ludd standing nearby.

"No, I don't know why, but we *must* go back and help him!" she insisted. Rider drew his gun but seemed hesitant to go. Gale looked into his eyes as if attempting to appeal to his conscience.

"Tank's family, remember? The three of us, in the desert? He saved our lives! We can't leave him now..."

Though he didn't answer, Gale turned and started running, full tilt and with no apparent regard for what might be out there, heading directly towards the sounds of the distant gunfight.

"Come on, Rider!"

Valero kept running, but the pain only increased. He felt warm waves sweep his back and buttocks and realized he was once more bleeding profusely from his wounds. His running started to slow, he felt his lungs on fire from the exertion and he began to feel dizzy, until at last he stumbled, wobbled and collapsed against an alley wall.

The hermavs were not too far away, he heard their footfalls, their maniacal laughter and their eager, hyena-like giggling as the night's entertainment began. But it would be a short game of cat-and-mouse; he was out breath and out of strength. He had nothing left to go on. He held his rifle close, crouched down in agony, and prepared to go out fighting.

Gale neared the end of an alley and almost walked out into the moonlit street, but Rider grabbed her arm and hauled her back, throwing her against the alley wall. Ludd was somewhere far behind, but for some reason Rider felt they couldn't wait for him.

Shadows darted down the street, and they heard strange, husky laughter distorted by the maze of alleys. Rider stepped out, Micro-Uzi held out ahead of him, and immediately opened fire.

At a distance of thirty paces the two hermavs running down the street in their direction were taken completely by surprise. They expected a wounded rifleman with only a bullet or two left, not a killer with a machine pistol. The bullets tore into their leather-clad bodies, making each creature jiggle and dance in place for a brief moment before they collapsed, dead, on the pavement.

Gale came around the corner once the shooting ceased, seeing Rider as he began walking across the street. Careful not to stray too far, and looking towards the dead bodies that were still smoking some distance away, she felt useless. She wanted to approach and see what these "things" really looked like, but she was afraid to leave Rider's side.

"Go grab a gun," he whispered to her, returning his vigilant gaze to the street from where the nameless mutants came. Without a moment to lose she broke from Rider and went to the two dead hermavs, kneeling at the first. She hesitated as she saw it, this diseased heap of wickedness, lying in a pool of its own tainted blood. She picked up the grease gun, finding it unexpectedly heavy, and struggled to flip the wire stock down for support. Her eye spotted a clip pouch at the thing's side and she opened it, taking out the black rectangular boxes and putting them, side-by-side, in her own sash.

Just then she looked up and saw the weak eyes of Valero, staring at her from the shadows of a nearby side street. He looked malnourished and injured, his gray-black hair hung over his face, but she sensed he wasn't an enemy, and possibly a key to finding Tank. Valero stared back, wondering at the mirage before his eyes. He raised his gun, ready to fire... then passed out from blood loss.

"Over here!" Gale whispered, and Rider came swiftly over. The two darted into the alley and knelt at Valero's crumpled body.

Rider didn't seem to recognize him, but trusted Gale's judgment, and turned away to keep an eye out for Ludd... or approaching enemies. Gale felt for a pulse, then noticed the blood seeping from the injuries in Valero's back. She took his rifle, propped it up against the wall, and started peeling off his leather coverings. The skin was sliced open, the wounds were pretty deep, and blood was still gushing. Putting down her submachine gun she tore off some of the fabric from Valero's shirt, then wadded the cloth and bound the injuries the best she could.

"Ludd's coming..." Rider said, and sure enough the old man came hobbling from the far alley, across the street and over to them, gasping breathlessly as he limped after his new 'friends'.

"Kill any?" Ludd asked excitedly. Rider motioned with his gun towards the dead bodies down the street.

"This one of them?" he asked again.

"No," Gale said. "We've got to revive this one." Ludd crouched with the sound of popping bones and cartilage until he rested almost eye-to-eye with Valero.

"Eh, you sure, young woman? This one wears the brands of a *raider*."

Rider looked down and noticed, as Ludd drew back Valero's jack, revealing the dark brown branding mark, shaped like a scorpion, on the man's bulging arm. Rider immediately crouched and pulled back Valero's hair, recognizing the face despite the years since their encounter at Oasis.

"Gale, he's a cold-blooded killer. A *maniac*. Let him die, or let me kill him, but *don't* save his life!"

"No!" she insisted, "He can help us. Now help me wake him up!"

Ludd grinned eagerly and leaned close. "Back away. I know something of medicine." Surprised at this Gale picked up her gun, moved aside, and let Ludd work.

"Mmm, yes, I see..." the old robed man mumbled, comically adopting the tone of a physician. At first he sounded curious, then gravely serious, and finally he let out an "ah-ha!" as if he'd had an epiphany about the "patient's" condition. After all the drama, Ludd simply pulled his hand away and quickly brought it back, slapping Valero across the face twice in quick succession.

"What are you doing?!" Gale gasped, but by the time she had a hand free to wrestle Ludd away, Valero's eyes were fluttering open and he began to breath more normally.

"Where's Tank?" Rider asked, looking down at Valero.

Valero looked back up, his eyes narrowing. "*Rider...*"

"Tank?" Rider asked again, pointing his gun directly at Valero's face.

"You've got nothing to fear from me, Rider, I'm only here to find the girl," Valero said, regaining enough strength to start to rise. Once he stood he matched Rider's cold stare, as if everything they'd just done to save his life meant nothing to him.

Finally he spoke, a single utterance that showed his gratitude by acknowledging their question. "Tank's back in the library..."

Tank slowly began to wake up as his body was heaved into place. It was no easy task raising the giant into a standing position, but through the use of rope and pulleys the savage hermavs had managed to secure their prisoner in their favored position.

"Ugly thing, isn't he, Taba?" one of the hermavs asked.

From the shadows came the tall, lanky Taba, its arm still trickling blood from the slight bullet injury. The beast brought its hand up to the wound and played with the strings of torn flesh, enjoying as much as agonizing over the pain it caused.

"From behind they all look the same," Taba said in a deep, throaty chuckle. The others laughed, then began to undo Tank's breeches and pull them off the ungainly giant. Taba watched, pacing, its many eyes wandering over Tank's bloodied body. It leaned forward and smelled his neck, sweaty and dirty. It came around the other side and did the same thing again, this time closing all of its blinking eyes.

"You've wandered into my domain, you poor thing," Taba taunted. "This city, you see, is mine. And those who do not pay proper respect will be made to receive me. You understand?" Tank's eyes blinked wildly and he struggled vainly to escape.

"This city is no longer a place for *normals*. We taught that lesson to those that we found when we first came here, a plague-ridden people living in miserable holes in the ground. An infestation of *little... white... mice...* Such a sweet game it was, the hiding, the chasing. The screaming. The whimpering. How we miss the hunt!" The others chattered excitedly.

"I can see your terror isn't going to be as sweet as those freakish albinos, but you'll do. Though I dare say it seems wrong to defile something with such diminished capacities..." Taba said playfully. "Unable to truly understand what is happening to it... Poor creature..."

Tank was awake, aware of the rope binding his wrists and his feet. His heart started to pound, and he struggled to break free, but there wasn't enough give to either snap the rope or yank his bindings free from the pulleys overhead.

"You know," Taba continued, returning to his side, "I almost hate to do this; you're like a brother. No fault of your own, you were *born* to be like this. Fucked up genes, brother, fucked up genes. Just like us, two people in one body. We can't help being what we are." He wasn't sure if Taba was speaking solely of itself, or of all hermavs in general.

Taba vanished behind him, as two more hermavs knelt and began to undo their leader's leggings, unbuckling belts and pulling the slippery fabric from around its waist.

Naked, Taba mockingly parroted the words of the Ancient law-givers:

"A man who sins with another man as with a woman, sins bitterly against God...

"*Poieo Adelphos!*"

With hateful desire in his eyes Taba took a step towards Tank's bound body just as Rider came into the room, his long duster sweeping in a swirl behind him. The albino stared off with the other accursed errors of Mother Nature that were gathered in the room, mercilessly prepared to erase them from the earth.

Gunfire cracked from the barrel of his Micro-Uzi and a round tore into Taba's chest, while two more stitched its uninjured arm and stomach. Black blood spurted out ahead of it as it stumbled back, flailing its arms in a vain effort to stem the tide of fluid gushing from its gaping wounds.

Valero stood at Rider's side and fired the last two rounds of his rifle, one shot striking an unsuspecting hermav in the back, severing the spine, the other hitting another's leg, reducing the knee to a mess of broken bone and sweeping the beastly creature to the floor.

Gale came in too, and held her submachine gun far out in front of her as if she was afraid it would explode, pulling the trigger only once she'd extended it as far as she could from her face. With a metallic roar the gun leapt upwards in her hands, sending a hail of automatic fire into the ranks of more hermavs, cutting down three and going on to spray the far wall with over a dozen rounds of white-hot lead.

The hermavs shrugged off the loss of their leader, and pounced like a pack of angry lions towards the unexpected intruders. Gunfire popped around the three gunfighters, only ceasing as the blade-wielders among the gang closed into melee range. Swirling swords whipped at Valero, who held his empty rifle in both hands to deflect and parry their blows in the fashion of a martial artist's quarterstaff. One slash after another he blocked or deflected, catching one's hooked knife-blade in the trigger guard and using that as leverage to attempt to disarm his opponent. With a heave he pulled his rifle back, but instead of relinquishing its weapon the hermav allowed itself to be picked off the ground and tossed, bodily, aside. Such was the determination of their enemy to remain armed!

Gale turned and instinctively opened fire on the stunned (and still armed) hermav, stitching its prone body with bullets until it stopped shaking and moving.

Rider exhausted his clip but, instead of reloading, kicked out and broke the jaw of a machete-brandishing attacker, sending it spiraling into another and forcing them to the ground. With his free hand he swiftly drew a pistol from his side, and shot twice into another hermav coming at him from the side, taking off a finger as it raised an arm to shield its face. The second round hit a spot right above its left eye, taking a large chunk out of its head and sending bits of its shattered skull backwards into the ranks of the oncoming gangers.

Valero moved forward, bringing the heavy rifle butt into the face of another masked assailant, crushing its nose, then whirling the weapon around and grasping it just in time to use it to block another attacker's blow. Rider saw Valero struggling and fired into his opponent, the bullets blowing straight through the freak's naked ribcage and out the other side. Gale fired on the remaining hermavs, cutting them down with various hits to their torsos, abdomens and necks before her last clip ran completely dry.

As quickly as it had begun it was over. Smoke filled the air, along with the smell of carnage. But Rider didn't celebrate their small victory, he immediately began to reload his submachine gun. Gale dropped her weapon and stepped over the line of dead bodies, and immediately ran to Tank's side to try and undo his tethers.

"Tank!" she shouted, trying to meet his eyes with her own. "Tank, are you alright?"

Tank looked up weakly, then his little white eyes fluttered in recognition. Before him was an angel; despite the years he recognized what Rider hadn't, her face, her voice, her eyes. He seemed surprised to see Gale standing right before him, and in his joy found himself blubbering like a fool. "G-Gale! Y-you... you little g-grub!"

Ludd stepped into the room now that the fighting was over and looked around. He crouched and, without regard for the dead, began picking through their more colorful belongings like some sort of scavenging magpie. Then, with an astonished "ah!", he headed for the books that lay scattered all about.

Valero watched Gale and Tank for a moment, then looked around for a better weapon now that his was exhausted. And there were many weapons to choose from. He finally decided on a Type 56 automatic rifle with a camouflaged barrel sheath and scope, and immediately set about looking for spare ammunition among the still-warm corpses, moving quickly as if additional danger might catch up to them at any moment.

Despite all he'd gone through, despite what he'd just narrowly avoided, Tank took in a breath and wiped the smile from his face. He looked from Gale and over to Rider, determined to explain what needed to be done. "W-we have t-to take Gale b-back to t-the Caves of S-sorrow a-as soon a-as possible."

Valero now came over to help Gale with Tank, since he was still too weak from the electrical torture he'd underwent to stand on his own. Rider listened to Tank for a moment, then turned away and reloaded his pistol. With cool detachment he walked away from them, and went wordlessly from dead hermav to dead hermav. With a startling *pop* that filled the immense chamber with thunder he put a bullet in each and every one of them, with the cold monotony of some kind of executioner's ritual. Turning back to the task at hand, the others assisted Tank in getting back on his feet. They'd seen enough killing for one night.

Rider continued on his unpleasant errand. At last he came to the malformed shape of that hideous monster, Taba, which lay sprawled on the floor in a pool of blood, chest rising and falling weakly, unable to rise from unconsciousness. He looked at the creature passively, until he caught sight of a small silvery tag dangling about its neck, one of a collection of charms it had taken from the ruins, trophies from countless past victims.

The charm was a simple, hand-wrought tangle of metal in the shape of a *unicorn*.

Rider stood still for a moment, his reaction unnoticed by the others. Then, face going flat and expressionless, he lifted his pistol and aimed it right at Taba's head. Rider pulled the trigger once, then twice, and didn't stop firing until the last bullet completely obliterated its skull, spilling the hermav leader's brains out onto the grimy tiled floor... ensuring it would never rise again.

By late the next day the five travelers, Rider, Gale, Tank, Valero and Ludd, had reached a point far south of the city where the metropolis and its golden Oilman were no longer visible. It was brilliant out among the white sands and a gentle breeze blew the light sand off of the top of the hard-packed earth, creating short-lived dust devils that rose up suddenly, swirled in the sky overhead, then vanished altogether as a new wind swept them away.

Tank held the reigns to his mount as Gale sat high in the saddle, while Valero, wounded, rested atop the other horse. Rider and Ludd walked on foot, leading the small party through the desert.

Now that daylight fully illuminated the landscape, Gale sat high in the saddle and struggled to recognize some sign, some landmark, to gain her bearings, but she didn't seem to recall passing any of the flat rocks or descending any of the sandy depressions that pockmarked this part of the desert.

"We didn't come this way," she called out to Rider, who was a full thirty feet ahead. When she broke the silence, Ludd assumed it was safe to stop to rest.

"I know," Rider called back. "But this way will take us to where the Far Traders will be passing, and if we're lucky we can hitch a ride with them all the way back to Amarillo. From there we can get horses to take us the rest of the way..."

"*Wherever* we're going."

She liked it when he said "we" instead of "you". They *were* becoming family. And he said the rest in a curious tone that seemed to hint to Gale that, if she changed her mind about this at any moment, he was more than willing to help her run off to some far corner of the world to escape what was coming. They could send another thousand bounty hunters after them and Rider would still stay with her and defend her until his last ounce of strength was gone. But she knew she had to go. Something compelled her.

"The Caves of Sorrow," Tank stated again. "T-that's w-where we have t-to go."

"There are agents of the Brotherhood there," Valero said from behind, and Rider looked surprised. "... working with the alliance of tribesmen and sisters who've gathered to attack Trade City. They want you, woman. They specifically wanted *you*."

Rider looked suspiciously at Gale for a second, then back to Valero.

"Why her?"

"S-she k-knows s-something..." Tank offered.

Valero stared at Gale for a moment. She felt him looking her up and down as if searching for some physical reason as to why she was so important. He raised an eyebrow.

"They say they can use their mind-powers to unlock your memories. Something in that head of yours concerns them," he said, leaning forward in his saddle with a creak of tight leathers.

Gale felt scrutinized by all of them; Valero accusingly, Tank sympathetically, Ludd curiously, and Rider... concerned for her well being, not only because of the idea of delivering her to the mysterious Brotherhood, but also because of what might happen when they released the flood of cryptic memories locked up in her mind.

Rider sensed she felt most uncomfortable by his invasive stare and as a result looked away.

"But I'm not sure if 'working *with*' is an accurate description..." Valero continued, "Something doesn't feel right. That wide-eyed fool and his cocky amazon crony think the Brotherhood is *helping* them with their war. But I'll bet there's something else going on, some other reason that's got those freaks dispensing their wisdom so glibly."

"Karos t-trusts them," Tank reminded Valero.

"Karos?" Rider said. "So the peasants finally got up the courage to *do* something about Margus Han?"

"Y-yes!" Tank countered. "*R-rev... Revolution!*"

For the first time in a long time Gale noticed a smile on Rider's face. "Well, kid, I kind of wish we hadn't left. Would've been nice to have been there for the fireworks."

"Ah, yes, *war*," Ludd said with a grandiose flourish, "If nothing else, his thirst for war, his need to be perpetually miserable, will be the one genetic trait Nature cannot change or remove from Man, no matter how hard she tries to re-invent him."

"Survival of the fittest," Valero shot back at the old hunched-over wanderer. "This is Darwin's world. No one got anywhere by shaking hands politely, that's just talk cults like Karos' preach. The freedom just to survive on this bleak rock is won by taking, not by asking."

"And you say you fight *for* Karos?" Rider asked sarcastically.

"That's just it, Rider," Valero said, looking off into the desert. "That's the beauty of this plan. We *all* win. We're not looking for unity, or to bring back some 'golden era' that never really existed in the first place. We're fighting to be free... of each other. Each man his own path. Each people their own destiny. Give peace a chance if you want. Or kill yourselves. As long as you let other people do the same."

They all continued walking in silence, poring over Valero's surprisingly philosophical speech.

It was growing dark, and night was setting in. But Valero seemed to spy something on the far horizon.

"*I see smoke,*" he said, pointing some ten miles or so away in the direction they were already traveling.

Devastation. An entire city reduced to smoking, burning wreckage. It was only a small reflection of the destruction the Ancients had once wrought across the world, but it was still staggering.

Gale sat atop Tank's horse, white-faced and ashen, staring at the heart-wrenching sight spread out over an entire mile of open desert: the roving city of the Far Traders was no more, its fabulous wheeled houses, giant wagons, motorized structures and towering tracked "keeps" completely destroyed. Great columns of churning black smoke boiled from the burning wrecks and fires still raged within the wooden hulls of some, eating away at their shattered interiors. The odor of burning rubber bit at their eyes and nostrils, the smell of oil and gasoline mixing with the choking stench of burning bodies everywhere.

In the cobalt blue light of twilight they saw only what the stars and the scattered fires illuminated - a city in flames, a people exterminated. Valero kept his horse steady as he rode ahead, gun in hand, to look over the destruction. He swept his eyes over two, three dozen dead men and women who seemed to have spilled from their enormous wooden carriage in an effort to escape whatever force had attacked the city, victims of an unknown enemy. Their bodies were burned, their flesh and skin reduced in places to black crumbling bone and glowing ash.

Tank and Rider spread out, running no more than fifty yards in opposite directions to investigate other nearby wrecks. Minutes later they returned, each giving a hand signal or gesture that suggested that the interior of the other Far Trader wagons concealed evidence of an even more widespread massacre.

The grand archways of rolling arcades, the wooden beams and curved bow supports of massive wagons and the hulks of great wheeled vehicles lay broken and burning everywhere. Fire consumed sundered wooden vehicles of all shapes and sizes, while ugly black smoke belched from the fatal wounds suffered by the ornate metal vehicles that formerly stood tall over this once-majestic city. The great theatre-vessel Rider and Gale had ridden on sat on only five of its ten wheels, the entire structure now leaning precariously to one side, its upper works groaning noisily in a manner not unlike a sinking ship's death rattle. Fires gutted its interior, crackling madly as curtains of flame exploded from the theatre's many windows and reached for the sky.

The wind began to pick up; the unprecedented high pressure front sweeping the Far Desert, creating dust storms up and down the length of the land, was now fueling the creation of an intense, localized sandstorm. In the face of the growing tempest, Ludd held the reigns of Tank's mount and led Gale along. As the wind pulled at them, they saw dead goats, chickens and other livestock commonly seen among the Far Traders meticulously disassembled, and dead children treated with the same calculated precision, quartered like sides of meat at a butcher's shop. There was no distinction between the humans and the beasts that lay mutilated in neat clusters between the burning buildings. Horse, man, bawthok, woman, goat, child. Over and over again, the same victims, only in different combinations.

Valero got off his horse and jogged over to a body that he thought seemed alive, then stopped short, realizing it was just a trick of the light. He gripped his gun and whirled around slowly, staring at dozens of dead, pale faces. He beheld the still faces of Far Traders, young and old, as well as hundreds of unwitting passengers and patrons who'd paid for the "safety" of traveling in the grand vessels of the mobile city, only to die in a terrible, one-sided battle.

"Who would do this?" Gale asked no one in particular.

"*Why* would someone do this?" Ludd asked soon after, calling out so his voice could be heard over the intensifying wind. "I know these people, the Far Traders. They are neutral to the goings on of others. They count many friends among the desert people. They have no enemies!"

"It was the C-Clean!" Tank shouted impulsively, then stumbled on a woman's corpse and toppled over.

"The Clean?" Valero replied dubiously. "Are you joking? You *really* think the Clean could do all this?!" Gale listened to them argue, but a familiar feeling slowly gripped her, distracting her from what was being said.

The wind blew dust all around, folding in the edges of the night around the remains of the burning city. The sky became hazy, the ceiling dropped to only a dozen feet or so, and sand carried by the wind bit at her unprotected eyes. She ignored the storm; something else had her undivided attention. She felt the stirrings of an ancient dread, more than just the precognitive eye that always circled her, alerting her to danger, but a hauntingly-familiar sensation that conjured up the terrors of her forgotten childhood.

Huntsmen. Many of them. *And close by...*

Burning Lands

She turned to cry out a warning just as an explosion echoed out in the night, drowning out her voice; a fuel tank burning somewhere finally burst, detonating with a deafening blast. A plume of bright red flame licked upwards to a height of fifty feet, casting a momentary orange glow in the dust storm and spreading its weak light out over the ruins of the Far Trader "city".

As the light pierced the darkness with the brilliance of a starshell, it was Rider who was the first to see *them*. Expecting the light to reveal only more charred, dissected bodies, his eyes widened as the fading light caught the edges of strange armor, silhouetting towering giants who stood at the very edge of the dust storm.

For a moment Rider just blinked, as if he had spotted a mirage in the storm, but sensing something terrible, Gale ran to his side to see what was going on. Valero followed close behind, wondering what Rider was seeing. When they realized they were standing right out in the open Rider immediately grabbed Gale and pulled her towards nearby cover; Valero quickly joined them.

Another, secondary explosion sounded out through the night, and the light began to fade, the storm began to intensify. In a moment they would be gone, but in that short time Rider, Gale and Valero saw *them*.

They looked human in shape, but their skin was uniformly pale and sandy colored, ideal for moving unseen among the sands of the wastes, especially in the twilight hours to which they confined their appearances. Each had a body elegantly muscled like the nude physique of a Greek statue, vaguely definable as men and even women, though gigantic and exaggerated in form. They were each at least seven and a half feet tall and were unbelievably broad at the shoulders, yet they walked with all the predatory grace of a pack of panthers on the hunt.

On second glance these creatures didn't resemble actual humans at all, even though from a distance they had looked like naked giants. Now, watching closer, the three could see that the sandy white "flesh" they had first seen was actually made up of bundles of a strange muscular apparatus that only mimicked, or perhaps enhanced, a human's musculature, each artificial tendon and ligament ending at a minute nexus of plated bundles of wire and circuitry. Similarly-camouflaged tubes connected the electrically-assisted joints of the arms and legs, running the length of each limb to vanish into the slight hump that stood out on each creature's upper back.

The heads of these whisper-silent shadow-warriors were most startling; each a featureless phantom face that looked like a ghostly mask of muscle and skin, without either a mouth or a nose to give it some sort of familiar, human characteristic. Weird hoses, squid-like and rubbery, swept from a place at their chins and underneath their arms to connect to that same hump on their backs. They did have eyes, but these were perfectly-round goggles set into the artificial musculature of each creature's face, whose lenses constantly shifted and rotated, angling up and down and to the side in varied directions with the barely-perceptible whir of miniaturized mechanical motors, either narrowing to bright pinpoints, or flaring wide like shuttered camera lenses. Each time they shifted, narrowed or widened, each glass orb flooded with a bright blue glow that swept ahead of them and could be seen clearly in the dark.

Gale sensed the rich psychic aroma of untold antiquity emanating from these creatures, detected the unbroken purity of living, human history beneath their armor, but at the same time the feelers of her mind danced harmlessly off their weird carapaces of wire and myoelectric bundles. These strange fallen angels, these cursed "Nephilim", evaded every attempt to steal a glimpse into their hollow souls.

Gawking, the three saw them, over a dozen sets of cold, glowing, blue eyes, lighting up the darkness at the distant edge of the ruined city. Whatever they were, they were now walking away, plodding heavily off and into the storm. All of them carried strange, complex rifles, but a few also hauled the dissected bodies of men and women slaughtered in the night attack on their backs like sides of fresh meat, or carried larger ones between them. They walked steadily off, leaving the scene of their work, until the raging storm swallowed them back up again.

Moments later the sky thundered with an ear-piercing sound, louder even than the storm, a noise that caused Rider, Gale and the others to wince in pain. A shrill, high-pitched shriek emanated from somewhere in the storm, in the direction the strangers had gone, a sound of powerful engines and turbines that almost deafened them. But after only a few seconds the alien noise faded into the sky. Whatever machine had issued the strangers here, had taken them back to wherever they had come from.

Ludd ran over, having picked out the shrieking noise from the roar of the dust storm, but none were able to voice the dozens of questions that were now running through their minds.

Drawn by the sound of the detonating fuel tanks that lit up the destroyed remains of the Far Trader city, Shubazang raced through the storm to get a better look. Finding cover he peered out through his rifle's scope, watching for any sign of his prey.

He saw figures scattered about among the wrecks of the great Far Trader caravan, and in that instant he recognized the large mutant, Tank. He immediately opened fire, the beam of his laser cutting through the storm and hitting the ground near where Tank was trying to get to his feet. The brilliant ray exploded in a fountain of blinding sparks and a whiff of white smoke. The giant flailed his hands ahead of him to shield his eyes, but stumbled back again over another body and tripped.

Rider and Valero both ran, looking for cover. Not seeing any nearby, Gale and Ludd instead dropped to the sandy ground. The horses reared and bolted, galloping off into the storm.

"We want the girl alive!" came Shubazang's voice from somewhere in the night. "And the albino, too! Give them to me and there'll be no trouble."

The boy stared through his scope, his one good eye awash in a luminous green light. With it he could see almost perfectly in the darkness and the storm. The huge mutant was pinned down, two unidentified armed men had run for cover in a nearby wreck, and two more were lying prone, just hoping to remain unseen, staying as still as possible. One of those was the girl. A moment passed as his quarry waited.

"I see you..." he called out again, his voice piercing the raging storm. To show he meant business he pulled the trigger again, and his laser rifle shot once more. This time the beam burrowed into the scrap metal framework just inches above Valero's head, forcing him and Rider to split up and run for separate hiding places.

"I know you came a long way for this guy," Shubazang shouted, vaguely addressing Valero and Tank. "But this is *my* bounty now. I'll be taking them back *alone*. If you know what's good for you, you'll realize I'm giving you the opportunity to get away clean. Now take it."

"Who the fuck is that?" Valero called out, vaguely remembering the voice but unable to put a face to it.

"Seriously, guys," Shubazang continued, and now he sounded nearby. "There are other bounties out there. Go now while you've still got the chance." Valero looked off towards Tank, but he knew the idiot would never leave Gale now that he'd hiked halfway across the world to find her.

"Who are you?" Gale shouted off into the ruins.

"Doesn't matter who I am," Shubazang's voice replied. "Just that I'm here to bring *you* back to Margus Han."

"Didn't you just see those 'things'?!" she called out in exasperation. "Didn't you hear that *noise?*"

"What 'things' are you talking about?" he asked. "What noise?" He hadn't seen or heard anything, not over the raging storm.

"Fuck this!" Valero yelled, emerging from cover ready to fire his rifle blindly in a show of defiance. But as soon as he broke from the collapsed metal wall he'd been hiding behind, their unseen observer's laser shot out and struck the rifle, blowing it right out of Valero's hands. Valero jumped away and fell back behind another bit of rubble, cursing as he fell to one knee.

Tank saw the point from where the laser fired. Without a moment to lose he got up and started charging towards it, a spot in the darkness. Shubazang reacted quickly, bringing his rifle about and letting loose another shot, this one hitting the tip of Tank's right boot, burning a hole straight through and into his foot. Tank stumbled and fell once again, this time reaching out to grasp the smoking remains of his thick rubber footgear.

"Stop it!" Gale desperately cried, watching Tank collapse helplessly.

Shubazang stopped firing but, crouching, ran some yards distant to take up a new firing position. With so much sand whirling about them no one saw where he went.

Rider's eyes searched the storm, but with clouds of sand sweeping over them and so many fires burning all around, it confused his nightvision. He gritted his teeth in frustration, but remained low and out of sight.

"Look... How much is my father paying you?" Gale shouted.

Shubazang chuckled, but decided to humor her. "Fifty pounds of corium. Another fifty for the albino assassin's head."

"I'll pay you fifty pounds when we get back to Tucumcari if you let Rider live," she called back.

Though no one noticed, he shook his head and lost his grin. "Grown attached to your kidnapper, is that it?" he shouted. If she had, getting her to come back wouldn't be easy...

Gale continued to attempt to negotiate, unabated. "Do we have a deal?"

It was quiet. Just when she realized it was *too* quiet, Gale heard footsteps over the thundering wind. Before she could react, Ludd cried out as a strong metal hand grabbed him from behind and hauled him over onto his back. The old man tried to defend himself with his staff, but his assailant was quick and strong. Euryale, the voiceless android, stood above him, the glow of the fires of the burning city captured perfectly in the smooth contours of its naked, metallic skin, and reflecting off of its mirror-like eyes.

Ludd was confused by the friendly smile apparent on the android's face, and was thus shocked when Euryale slid the long steel spike of one its numerous blade-like implements through a non-vital part of his abdomen, pinning him to the ground in the same way a collector might pin an insect in a museum display.

Gale gasped in surprise, then began crawling away instinctively as Euryale turned to face her. Gale was aghast by what she saw, the outline of a sleek metal woman framed against the burning structure of some colossal Far Trader wagon. A predatory thing with only minimal human characteristics standing on a pair of flesh-and-blood legs, attached to a pivoting waist that because of its great age, only barely resembled a real human's.

Ludd was alive, but if he moved just an inch he would inflict serious injury on himself. Terrified, he simply lay there, gasping for air and grasping at the long prong that impaled him, feeling for the first traces of blood seeping from his wound, but finding nothing. The android had found an almost perfect spot to incapacitate him without risking killing him.

Euryale drew another kunai and walked towards Gale as the young woman rose to her feet.

"Wait!" Gale cried, repeating her offer again, this time her voice sounding desperate. "I promise you, I'll go peacefully! I'll pay you fifty pounds of corium to let Rider go free. And you'll get whatever my father gives you for returning me!"

The thing before her had no mind, it had no soul, it was a machine acting on complex, pre-programmed impulses. She could no more read its thoughts than she could a computerized car. A black void to her extra-sensory vision, it came at her without any fear of her capabilities. Rider saw the android approaching Gale, and despite knowing a sniper with a laser rifle waited somewhere out there in the dark, he opened up on it. His bullets cracked out of the snub-nosed barrel; only two hit, and much to his surprise these reflected off the machine-woman's blue-black metal skin with a high-pitched ricochet, leaving only tiny dents. Euryale disregarded Rider's feeble attack and continued after Gale, who ran off and out of sight.

While Euryale gave chase to Gale, Shubazang reacted to the attack on his metal lover by shooting at where the flash of Rider's submachine gun had pierced the darkness. He'd expected to strike the old bounty hunter down with that first shot, but when the laser beam shrieked outwards the ghostly albino was already gone.

"Ah..." Shubazang said with a growing grin. "So I get a chance to fight the legendary *Rider!* And it looks like you're still as slippery as they said you were..."

Gale had run off and Rider had no idea where. The others were scattered all around, and the old man was injured. More importantly, however, there was someone out there who'd been sent to kill him and get the girl, someone who sounded like he was itching to bring an old gunfighter down just for the thrill.

While he sat under cover Rider calmly topped off his clip. Even his jacketed rounds had been unable to crack the armor casing of their stalker's android helper, but unless their unseen hunter was made of metal too, there was still a chance of getting out of this alive.

"Rider!" he heard Shubazang call out, from somewhere in the storm. "Rider! Margus wants you dead! Come out and we'll finish this quickly!"

Burning Lands

To "motivate" him, Shubazang fired at a spot not three feet from where Rider sat. A blinding burst of sparks exploded from the spot, but Rider simply slipped from cover and opened fire in Shubazang's direction.

The *crack-crack-crack* of Rider's burst was almost lost in the din, though the bullets peppered the ground all around where Shubazang lay in waiting. Shubazang twitched slightly, then grinned even wider when one of the bullets passed through the fur-lined collar just inches from his face.

"Good shot! Now my turn!" he shouted eagerly, and squeezed the trigger. The elegant laser rifle hummed, its barrel filled with compressed neodymium, and its beam pierced through the darkness. Rider ducked and rolled away just in time.

Rider looked around. Tank was making for Ludd, it seemed, but Valero was nowhere to be seen. He was probably hunkered down somewhere, waiting it out, but considering Valero's rifle had been shot right out of his hand, Rider realized he'd probably be playing it safe as well. He also realized that it meant he was alone.

Rider looked out from cover, expecting a shot. Instead it was quiet and still. Looking over to the next patch of cover (a slouching, smoldering ruin of a grand wagon) he started to run when Shubazang fired again. This time the beam crossed right in front of Rider, striking past to burn a hole in a heap of burnt iron not ten paces away. Rider stumbled in surprise, sliding the last few yards like a baseball player trying to make it home.

"You got lucky!" Shubazang laughed. Now Rider grit his teeth, silently surrendering to the fact that their enemy, whoever he was, was just as slippery as he had been in his prime.

With no small amount of exasperation Rider decided to stay low and under cover, to stop running around chasing an invisible target. He listened for the sound of the unseen sniper, hoped for a mistake on their hunter's part... and at the same time secretly worried for Gale.

Gale ran for a full thirty seconds before finding cover inside the wreck of an enormous collapsed wagon. The metallic woman was somewhere behind her, not far away, but she was getting tired and had to rest.

The interior of the wreck was dark and hollow, providing a reasonable shelter from the lashing, relentless winds. Gale looked around for a way out, a hatch or a door or simply a rend in the vehicle's exterior, but saw none. She lingered at the entrance, breathing heavily, thinking what to do.

A minute passed, giving her time to catch her breath, but she feared going out there again. That "thing" was out there, looking for her, hunting her, and she was afraid of it. But she was also desperate, and considered risking calling out. Whoever controlled the thing, the android, had to be reasonable. Her father had hired this man, and surely Margus wanted her back in one piece?

She found herself shunning the idea of falling back on her relationship to Margus to ensure her safety. She had to try something else. She moved over to the sole opening to the wreck and called out.

"Look around you, you fool! Do you think *we* did this? This wasn't the work of raiders! Who do you think did this?"

It was quiet again, and no one responded. But she wasn't about to give up.

"We don't have time for this! We have to go back before it's too late!" Gale shouted hoarsely. "They were just here! Things wielding technology as old as the Fall, not men of *this* age!"

"They were just here! Things wielding technology as old as the Fall, not men of this age!"

Though he was enjoying keeping the once-famous Rider pinned down with his laser rifle, Shubazang found himself distracted, listening. Had he heard the girl right? *Technology as old as the Fall?*

Gale's voice, though almost drowned out by the storm, called out again. "We have to go back and warn the people! You have to let us go!"

Shubazang looked back through his scope, and saw that Rider was still hiding behind cover, and not about to leave any time soon. He tapped his finger gently on the trigger, contemplating.

Shubazang' common sense urged him to ignore her, but deep down her words tugged at his better judgment. After all, this scene of carnage was not too dissimilar to the slaughtered villages of Uncle Sam' tribal lands... replete with wanton death and bizarre mutilation. *If the girl really had seen something, he had to know what. This could all lead to the answer he'd been searching for...*

Gale expected to be ignored again, but at that moment Euryale emerged from the sandstorm not twenty feet away from the wagon's entrance. Gale stifled a cry of surprise as the gleaming silver android regarded her with its unchanging smile, then began walking straight towards her with a sway in its saucy, human-mimicking gait.

Gale retreated back into the interior of the wagon, while the android pulled out another kunai, its diamond-like cross-section promising to leave a stigmata-like hole wherever it impaled her. Euryale prepared to strike Gale in a manner similar to Ludd; not enough to kill, only to incapacitate.

Gale ran, but tripped on the debris underfoot, and as she struggled to get up Euryale was immediately upon her. With amazing strength the artificial woman grabbed Gale's leg and dragged her back, ready to draw the kunai across the girl's Achilles' tendon to sever it with the razor edge of its murderous blade. Seeing it gleam in the weak firelight, Gale screamed.

"Alright!" Shubazang suddenly called out, freezing Euryale in its place. Then, a moment later, "Let's hear what you have to say..."

"Everyone, come out!" Gale shouted, emerging from the storm with Euryale not far behind, the android walking casually and calmly as if they were all now friends. Tank came forward, cautiously, and came to Gale's side, then looked around for Valero and Rider.

"Let the old man go," came a voice from not far away and from the darkness Valero appeared, facing off with the android.

Euryale stared at him for a second, then walked over to where Ludd lay, wheezing, and pulled out the implement that impaled him. Ludd gasped as the creature came at him, afraid it would hurt him further, but instead found he was free. He reached down to the point of injury and realized there was only a very small amount of blood and that he could now move freely.

The others watched the robot as it moved, noting the strange effort its master had made to mold it to perfectly resemble a human woman of exaggerated charms. Gale noted the android's legs, waist, and crotch, the only parts that seemed "real", and imagined why they alone were made of "flesh". She felt slightly nauseated and more than a little afraid of the demented inventor who had pieced the creature together that way.

"Rider, too!" Shubazang shouted from the darkness. He wasn't going to reveal himself until Rider joined them in the open.

Gale looked around for a moment, until Rider finally came into view, Micro-Uzi in his hand. He looked at her, then to the robot. Euryale turned and regarded him curiously, then started walking towards him.

"Drop the gun..." Shubazang called. As Euryale approached, kunai in hand, Rider hesitated, then remembered how ineffective his gun had been against the thing. He relinquished it.

Euryale picked the gun up, then stepped away, looking into the storm.

Everyone turned when Shubazang came into view. A young, strange-looking man in a dramatically-sweeping greatcoat, holding a long, spindly laser rifle in both of his oversized metal hands, with strange black goggles covering his eyes. Little green letters appeared on their lenses, then swept to the side to be replaced by yet others. They couldn't read the characters that appeared and quickly vanished in his eyes, but they partly wondered if he, too, was some form of robotic creation.

"You've all met Euryale," Shubazang said, almost pleasantly, "now meet me. The name's Shubazang. Friends call me 'Shuba'."

What an odd thing to say, Gale thought. She realized this man had no friends at all, no one to use that affectionate nickname. Just he and his mute companion.

Tank noted the metallic hands and stared at them. "Metal hands?"

"Perfect imitations," Shubazang replied proudly. "Just like Euryale." The boy turned his head in Rider's direction, keeping his eye (and his gun) on the dangerous albino.

"You're my prisoners, now," Shubazang explained, "so give Euryale your guns." A minute later Euryale had collected their weapons, removed their clips and chambered rounds, taken their spare ammo from them, and given it all to Shubazang. Once he was satisfied he motioned Euryale to give them back their now-impotent weapons.

"That's great," Shubazang stated. "Let's make this as friendly as possible." He turned now to Gale, though he kept his gun on Rider. "You'd better make this good."

"I'm good for my word," she said. "You'll get your fifty pounds of corium for both Rider and I, I swear it. Only you've got to let me warn my father about what's going on, what's happening in the desert."

"What is it?" Shubazang asked.

Gale tried to clear her mind. She was already trying to piece things together, to understand, to remember.

"N-no!" Tank insisted, coming forward despite the threat of Shubazang's rifle. "W-we must go t-to the Caves of S-Sorrow! W-we h-have to go there f-first!"

"Why?" Shubazang asked. Gale wondered as well, but found herself drawn to the idea. She didn't know why.

"The B-Brotherhood, that's w-why! They sent us t-to find Gale, to bring her to them!"

"The Brotherhood?" Shubazang asked. "How are they involved in all of this?"

"We're not entirely sure," Valero said honestly. "She could be some kind of *prophet*..." he ventured.

Shubazang looked at her more discerningly, but despite what he'd been told about her powers she seemed harmless to him. "Well, I'm not going to let them take her," he insisted. "She's mine, at least until I hand her over to Margus."

Tank looked at Valero, conveying his desperation. Valero realized Tank might make a move to attack Shubazang, a move that would ultimately be suicidal.

Valero was about to stop Tank when Gale stopped them both. "Listen, *Shuba*," she said softly, "We go to the Caves first, then Trade City. You have my word I will go with you when you demand it. Rider, too."

She and Shubazang both looked at Rider. He said nothing, but his silence was enough for Shubazang.

"Alright then," the boy replied cautiously. "But I have your word on this?"

Gale nodded. "You have my word."

CHAPTER 5

The great dust storm swept the land for many miles. It had raged for days on end, and now the winds grew with increased intensity, until the swirling mass of rolling sands roared and raged against the stony black cliffs of the Caves of Sorrow.

Tank and Valero led their party through the storm, thankful for the strange rock formations that littered the desert for miles around the legendary escarpment, using them as navigation points to find their way. Half an hour later the sight of the great cliff face revealed itself to them, emerging from the storm, vaguely visible in the distance with its many black, yawning caves.

"I'm finished," Ludd called out weakly over the wind. "Just leave me here to die. Let the sand make me a grave and bury me!"

Valero ignored him and shouted to Tank. "We've made it!"

The giant gave Valero a broad grin despite the dust and sand hitting their faces. He looked back at Rider, Gale, Shubazang and Euryale, and pointed towards the caves.

Some time later the deafening sounds of the storm subsided as they passed under the dark roof of one of the entrance caves. Valero stopped to pound the dust from his body, shake the sand particles that infested his hair like fleas. Tank went a little deeper, looked around and produced the flashlight from a loop on his belt to push back the enveloping darkness.

"This w-way," he said.

Gale's eyes traced the lines of stone illuminated by Tank's light, trying to get an idea of the true size of this cave and its antiquity. Ludd followed close behind, his own red, staring eyes riveted to the darkness ahead of them, his curiosity once again renewing his ability to continue on.

Shubazang held a hand up for Euryale to stop and nervously gripped his laser rifle. "I don't like this. If this is a trick..."

"What are you afraid of, *xiu ba zhang?*" Rider asked patronizingly.

"I wasn't talking to you, *fen hong se yan!*" Shubazang snapped.

Valero kept walking. Tank, already ahead, turned back and swept his light over his companions.

"N-no trick, boy. Keep your g-gun if you want, but t-those who dwell here are f-friends."

Shubazang looked hesitant to trust Tank and Valero, and even less the bounties he'd been paid to hunt. He seemed unwilling to go any further into the depths of the unknown cave system.

"Then stay here," Gale said bravely, turning to follow Tank.

"Not likely," he shot back, and went after her, making sure she and Rider stayed where he could see them. They continued into the dark, ascending dry tunnels and up hollow, sloped fissures that wormed their way through the rock. The cavern system seemed empty.

"Where is everyone?" Valero asked, producing his own light and letting it wash over the hollow caves through which they passed. In the darkness, without the torches and lamps that once populated the walls, the complex seemed alien and unfamiliar.

"Off f-fighting. Ridaya said t-they were m-marching for Trade C-City, remember?"

"I don't think this is the right cave," Valero said.

Tank seemed sure of where he was and ignored Valero, leading the way down another natural passage. He felt his way as they came to another empty cave, then kept going.

"Does your guide even know where he's going?" Shubazang chided. "Let's head back. We had a deal!" Shubazang's voice went silent as they entered the cave filled with hundreds of ancient weapons, discarded here as if ritually buried by their makers hundreds of years ago. Rider looked as well, and most of the newcomers came over to at least steal a glimpse.

"Gads!" Ludd gasped, coming to Valero's side as the ex-raider used his beam to explore the pit of junk. Sensing Ludd's curiosity he handed the flashlight off to the old man, then continued after Tank.

Gale seemed less interested than she should be. "Are you coming?" she asked the others, but Ludd, for one, shook his head.

"No, child, I'll be here. Come get me when you need me." Euryale watched Ludd, seeming amused, then looked into the pit, unmoved by the sight of so many weapons. Instead the android looked up at the wall and to the faded writing there, and pointed to it so Ludd could see.

"Do you really want to head back?" Gale asked Shubazang over her shoulder. He wanted to stay and sift through the discarded artifacts as well, but he wasn't about to let Gale and Rider get away from him. He followed the girl, leaving Euryale and Ludd behind.

Dark passages spiraled off in different directions. Tank waved his light from left to right.

"Which w-way, Valero?" he asked.

Valero came up behind him. "This way. It was *this* way."

Gale felt drawn to the cave to which Valero was headed. She walked away from Rider, who felt ill at ease down here and waited for confirmation before proceeding, and went over to Valero's side. She stared into the darkness with determined eyes, then looked at Valero.

Valero stared at her. How she had grown, this grub. He remembered those eyes, that once quivered in fear before him. They now looked at him with more understanding of what was going on than he did. His stare narrowed, and he pulled out a two-foot long glow rod from his pack, snapping the plastic sheath and shaking it vigorously. In moments chemicals within the lightweight wand mixed and began to fluoresce, casting a bright orange glow over the rock of the tight tunnel and lighting the way.

He looked at Gale, who took a step ahead of them towards the black cave ahead. He stopped her by taking her arm lightly and placed the glow rod in her hand. He let go of her. Gale took a deep breath and stared ahead. Rider came up beside her and nodded to confirm he was right with her.

Tank watched, then flicked off his light; there was enough illumination from the glow rod for all to see, so there was no need to waste his precious batteries.

"Are we moving ahead, or what?" Shubazang asked from the rear. They all looked back at him, eagerly holding his rifle at the ready, staring at them through his curious black goggles.

Gale led the way, drawn by her senses. She descended a tunnel, using her hand to maintain her balance as the floor became more and more uneven. Rider followed right behind, then Tank and Valero. Shubazang maintained a distance of a few steps, but wasn't about to be forgotten. His boots echoed on the stone as he kept pace. They entered a pitch black cavern, the walls invisible to the radiance emitted by the cavers' rod. But there were others here with them.

Out of the deep darkness came the robed men and women of the Brotherhood, the mentalists who'd hidden here while the alliance bravely marched to wreak the natives' vengeance on the great city of the Clean and Cartel. Silently they had watched, their minds envisioning that place miles and miles away. Now the mentalists simply observed what unfolded, silent and detached witnesses to the catastrophe occurring in the city.

"It will begin soon," they said passively, a chorus of garbled whispers rising from the shadows. "The battle's outcome cannot be seen, our hand can no longer guide them. What happens now will be the result of their own choices."

Tank looked worried for his comrades; he thought of Ridaya, Uncle Sam and Karos, the man who embodied their hope that the day could be won, that the people of the wasteland could be free if they only rose and fought for it. He wished he could be there, among those great figures, part of molding the new future of the wasteland.

Gale courageously stepped forward, holding the light like a torch in front of her, letting it illuminate her for all to see. The hooded beasts shifted and turned as one to face her, taking a few menacing steps closer. Tank closed in near her, and Rider came to her other side, hand idling just inches from his knife. Regardless of what she intimated, he was ready to fight to defend them all.

But something in the voices seemed familiar to Rider and gave him reason to pause. One voice in particular sang out from the chorus. He'd heard that voice before, not too long ago. Clever, and planning. He strained to listen, to hear them speak again so that he might pick it out from the rest and put a face to it.

"So she comes at last..." they whispered quietly, a rolling wave of many voices speaking as one.

Just then he recognized it. *Torak*. Rider turned and spun about, searching the small army of cloaked monsters for Torak's familiar face... but saw only demented, child-like smiles and tumor-bristling extremities where ratty robes failed to cover flesh.

"I am here..." the voice came again, suddenly addressing his confusion, and now he realized the truth. That there was no Torak, no single entity, but a community of minds linked over unimaginable distances, each mutant's body nothing more than a drone once it had surrendered to following this new world cult.

Torak, or the body in Little Vegas he had assumed was "Torak", was nothing but a puppet, a living sensor through which clairvoyant minds miles distant could see and manipulate events far beyond the boundaries of their Glowing City.

What was the voice, then? Not one being, but a conclave of minds only *directed* by singular entities, the fabled "Illuminated" said to direct the Brotherhood from hiding across the mountains, who wove together the potent mental energy of their followers - the senseless meanderings of madmen, the gibbering of idiots, and the pointless plotting of paranoids into one cooperative thread of determined thought. Using the mind energy of its willing subjects, of such anguished and elated minds, the Illuminated projected their telepathy over many miles, powering it like living batteries, each subject boosting the range of their unified psychic "signal" by miles. They could see and hear through the eyes and ears of their followers in a form of blasphemous "union", and could watch, from safety over and across the Rocky Mountains, all that occurred in these war-ravaged lands.

"Be quick with it!" Rider shouted, uncomfortable with his revelation and the idea that Gale was about to submit to the probing of these unseen, inhuman masters. His sharp tone elicited a simultaneous, child-like smile from each of the monsters assembled in the shadows.

"Death walks along the fringes of the Burning Lands, it wipes out all that it touches and takes the dead to be examined in ancient vaults beneath the earth. This is no Hades, but a real place. We all face the same threat, an age-old remnant that has grown evil and demented over time. Once they slept peacefully, and then they merely watched patiently, for years, but their genius has since slipped into insanity. They will stop at nothing until we are all destroyed.

"*She* knows this danger. She comes from its *womb*. She has the tools necessary to go back and end the pain of the writhing, agonizing thing that lives there, calling out with its mind for its miserable light to be extinguished."

Gale felt the voices overwhelm her, felt many minds make contact with hers like attackers swarming all around her. She instinctively tried to resist but these beings were far more adept at an assault of the mind than she was, and she succumbed.

Her memories exploded. Like a single strip of film that played in a dark room far away, the soundtrack dulled and the image too small to see clearly, it was suddenly

Burning Lands   **297**

thrust to the forefront of her mind, until she was seeing the past re-played right before her eyes in full reverse.

The past crystallized before her eyes, playing *backwards* in a rush of fragmented scenes.

She remembered Johnny staring at her, extending his warped and calloused hand. She remembered taking it.

She remembered the Huntsmen wandering off, searching for her vainly in the night, their eerie blue eyes winking out two by two in the darkness until she sat alone with the corpses of her family.

She remembered the deafening wind, and being told by her father to run and hide in the void of the great metal towers to avoid being seen.

She remembered her parents and others running as fast as they could for cover among the towers. She remembered breathing heavily in the radiation suit, terrified that she couldn't tell which among the adults was her mother and father, afraid she would lose them in the chaos of the night.

She remembered the adults shouting in panic. The Huntsmen were after them.

They ran, they raced, a panicked exodus to put as much distance as possible between them and the place from where they had come. She remembered the methodic ticking of Geiger counters for days on end, and stern commands from her father reminding her to keep her suit and helmet on, no matter what happened.

She remembered miles of rugged, burning wasteland, of strange white lightning and a black storm brewing on the horizon as far as the eye could see. Raging winds and lonely lifelessness everywhere she looked.

Her father reassured them all, if they kept going, they'd find an end to the devastation and a world whose air was safe to breath, lands still untouched by the war. They only had to keep going!

She remembered emerging onto the surface for the first time in her life and wincing from the murky light that came weakly through the boiling clouds above. She remembered the adults leading the way, marveling at the destruction around them - a world blasted into a nightmare landscape of shattered plains and molten cities, a desolation they no longer recognized as home.

She remembered their silent, terrified ascent through deep dark caverns, the roar of a dozen great chthonian waterfalls, a calm, misty lake deep underground at the center of which loomed, through the fog, a colossal *island* ringed by beaches of rust and surmounted by a mountain of steel. She remembered their fear of being seen, of being discovered, as they made their daring escape across a great causeway over a tenebrous black sea.

She remembered fleeing for their lives.

They knew her. Now she had to know *them*. She fought back against the intrusion into her mind. With all her might she pushed, launching her own offensive into the thoughts of the Brotherhood's distant mind-controller, far over the mountains. Through its zombie-like nodes here in the chamber, she invaded its alien mind and unlocked their own terrifying secrets.

In that instant she was made privilege to the Brotherhood's vision of what the world would soon come to be - a momentary glimpse of their prophesized "Eden", the future they envisioned for all of mankind's mutated descendants. It was a symbolic vision, of something that had not yet come to be, colored by her own inability to grasp things yet unseen, so that her mind raced to portray what it sensed in visual imagery that her conscious self could comprehend.

What she saw was a changed land, blooming from the banks of a quicksilver river at the very heart of the Burning Lands, where radiation and strange forces brought into being new and wonderful forms of life to seed the Twisted Earth. A weird white sun ringed by silver halos of light rose on the horizon, bringing the light of a new day to the desert... and the promise of hope. Beneath this sun rose a broken pyramid; power and energy pulsed from within its depths, lighting up the ruins of a blasted cityscape that ringed the pyramid for miles.

It was the same vision that had inspired Karos to greatness, given him the will to lead an army to war and unite the people, but at that moment Gale realized this was no mere prophecy of the future, but an actual, physical place that existed far away in the Burning Lands. It was here that the Brotherhood would send her, to do what had to be done.

With that last glimpse Gale collapsed to the ground, eyelids fluttering and eyes rolling back into her head. Rider dropped to one knee at her side to make sure she was alright, then looked up at the shambling creatures in their all-concealing robes.

"Tell us what we face!" he demanded.

"What you face, what we all face, is really just One, though it is served by many. There's nothing left of its former greatness... and though it will fight and struggle, it must be brought to heel."

"That didn't make any sense to me," Valero said.

"Was it meant to?" Shubazang asked.

"To clarify," the monks said, "Only one of you needs to know, to understand. Only one of you needs to be clear on what must be done, what she alone needs to do when she gets there..."

While the other remained baffled, distrusting the monks' wisdom, Gale awoke. She had heard their words, and began to understand what they wanted her to do.

Gale walked out of the cave and down the tunnel with renewed purpose. She stared ahead of her as she passed Euryale and Ludd, leaving the two to wonder what had happened.

Rider, Valero, and Tank followed, calling out to her to break what seemed to be a trance gripping her and leading her outside. Shubazang rushed close behind, throwing his head over his shoulder now and then in the direction of the dark cave and the strange robed people with whom they had just met. His mind raced, contemplating what was said.

"Where are you going?" Rider shouted as Gale left the cave and into the warm orange light of early dawn. At last his voice got through to her, because she stopped, turned, brushed the curls blown across her face by the wind and addressed him, Valero, Tank and Shubazang as they followed her:

"Rider, where did you find me, when I was younger?" Rider stared at her, wondering what this had to do with anything.

"Where did you find me?" she repeated.

"Some ways northeast of Oasis. Living with a..."

"Northeast of Oasis. How many miles?"

He couldn't see where this was going. "I don't know! Ten, twelve miles?"

"What's twelve miles from Oasis?"

"Nothing!" he shouted. "There's nothing out there until you reach the edge of the Burning Lands." Shubazang looked interested by where this might be going.

"When I was with my adopted father, in Tucumcari, Uncle Sam of the northern barbarians came to us with grievances. Villages had been attacked. Burned to the ground. Their inhabitants slaughtered. The mysterious attacks *occurred near the edge of the Burning Lands*."

"The Far Traders," she continued. "Where did we stumble upon the ruins of their roving city?"

"Quite a few miles northeast of The Scab," Valero confirmed.

"Not too far from the edge of the Burning Lands," she reminded them.

"What are you saying, grub?" Ludd asked, finally emerging from the cave with the aid of his long staff.

"I'm saying I've got to go back," she said, picking up her pack where she'd left it when they first arrived. "To the Burning Lands."

"Why the Burning Lands?" he asked.

"That's where I came from. That's where *they* came from. That's where they still live." Rider looked at her, searching the depths of her eerie green eyes for answers to his own questions. But he stayed quiet.

"But they're not truly alive anymore..." she whispered, confused. The others looked at one another, before Shubazang spoke.

"You came from the Burning Lands? I thought you were Margus Han's daughter..." he said.

"They've been watching you for years," she said, ignoring him. "Waiting and abducting those who came too close, those who wouldn't be missed. But now they've grown bold, attacking entire villages and taking the dead to further their understanding of you and your people. Only when they're done, when they know enough about the people of the desert, who knows what they'll do. Maybe... the beginnings of a new genocide..."

"You mean to say there are people living out there, in the Burning Lands?" Valero asked. "And that you're one of them? And that those creatures we saw were *them?*"

"My people are responsible for these deaths..." she continued, almost oblivious to the others, vividly remembering Theo and the Far Traders, thinking of the villagers of Uncle Sam's kingdom, remembering the poor, gilled mutant lying open on the operating table when she was a child. Everyone was quiet.

"You can't go now," Shubazang reminded her. "You made a promise. Trade City, first."

"Don't you think this is larger than all that?" she asked.

"No, not at all. Hell, if what you say is true, we can get to Tucumcari and stop the war before it's too late. Each side thinks the other is responsible for these massacres and disappearances. You can tell them the truth! Maybe we can come up with a coalition, band together to fight the *real* enemy."

"It's too late for that, boy," Valero said quietly. "The war's already started. It's not going to stop, not for Gale, not for anyone. The clash between Uncle Sam and the Han goes beyond the destruction of a few villages; you're talking about a war of *ideologies*."

"I think we should try anyway," Shubazang said resolutely.

Valero questioned Shubazang's motives. "Look, kid, going back to Tucumcari won't help you get your bounty," he argued. "It's under siege."

"That's *not* why I'm suggesting you go back," Shubazang responded defensively.

"Either way, it *will* help us with Gale's mission," Rider suddenly interjected, breaking his long silence. The others looked at him for an explanation.

"A thousand square miles of radiated desert, the Burning Lands. Gale, I know you mean to go, but you wouldn't last long without something to protect you."

For a moment, Gale remembered the suit Johnny had found her in long ago. Suits like that had protected her and the adults who took her from her home while they escaped from the heart of the Burning Lands. She couldn't exactly remember why they had done it, but she remembered they had taken great care to protect themselves on their desperate flight.

For a brief moment Shubazang thought of his potassium iodide gum, but not only was there not enough to go around, even that wouldn't be enough to protect from the five hundred-plus *rems* that were common in the sands of the Burning Lands.

Rider continued. "But I remember, in the armory vaults of the mandarin's palace, what looked like protective suits. They were old, they were covered in dust, but they might still work. If we can get there, get into the city and get them... you wouldn't have to go *alone*." Gale looked at him and saw that Rider understood. There was somewhere she had to go and he wouldn't stop her. But he sure wasn't letting her go and commit suicide either.

"Then we'd better go right away," Valero said. "If we head out now we can be there by tomorrow."

The fine horses of Alin Han's expedition reared as a large pack of *bawthoks* crossed their path, carrying woven baskets, colorful blankets and over two dozen sets of pots and pans between them. Two dark-skinned boys led the herd of pack animals by the sound of their clicking tongues, waving sticks in the air ready to give each shaggy beast a sharp whack if it wandered out of line.

Alin Han shouted angrily at the boys, while his own men struggled to calm their mounts until the *bawthok* caravan moved on. Royal horses in their finery frightened by odorous *bawthoks?* The sight made nearby merchants and vendors break out in laughter.

They were gathering at the front gates to the city despite the protests of his uncle, Margus, who had forbade Alin from going after Gale on his own. But how could he stand by when she was in peril? No, he had to go, and gathering his own personal guards had formed an expedition to go out to find her, and avenge his family's honor by putting an end to the albino thug who had taken her. He would return a man, with a wife.

One of his men came over and saluted, shouting over the dust storm that had lashed against the city walls for a day. "Sir, we have the water and provisions secured. We are prepared to go. Are you sure you want to leave in this?"

"Yes," Alin said simply, getting ready to mount his horse. As he put one foot in the stirrup he noticed something strange out of the corner of his eye.

Moving on either side of the marketplace, in rows, were some two dozen men and women in shoddy clothes and tunics, each wearing a strip of cloth or a cape with the color green worked into its design. *Curious...* They walked with their cloaks drawn tight, their arms and bodies concealed, in a clumsy attempt to move as subtly as possible through the throng. Remarkably, most of the vendors, peddlers and teamsters arranged in the square in the shadow of the grand gatehouse didn't notice, busy as they were with their own affairs or fighting off the beggars that ringed them, or trying to stay clear of the *bawthoks* of yet another caravan that rested lazily despite the storm.

Alin took his foot from the stirrup and watched as the two columns of men, one on the left side of the street and the other on the right, ran right past them and to the small wooden doorways leading into the towers of the gatehouse.

"*What...*" he stammered, as the first man in each column crashed through his respective door, bull rushing the guard on the other side and knocking him flat. As the first men pushed inside, the rest of the peasants in line threw back their cloaks and drew swords, scimitars, axes, spiked clubs and javelins. They began to storm the gatehouse!

"Over there!" Alin shouted, alerting his men and the guards at the foot of the great gate to the danger. They were taken completely by surprise, and watched dumbfounded as Karos' clandestine followers began battling for the bastion.

Alin drew his finely-balanced scimitar, its blade making a song-like shriek as it slipped out of its sheath, and used it to point the way, commanding his men to follow him. Abandoning their steeds they raced over to the left tower, immediately engaging the peasants standing there waiting their turn to get into the bulwark. Swords and spears clashed in a spectacle of whirling steel, and after only a few moments, many lay dead and Alin was pushing into the tower after the rest of the would-be revolutionaries.

Karos' men heard the sounds of combat on the floor below and realized they had lost the element of surprise. Drawing back her hood, the old woman, Vestra, looked at her men with a charged gleam in her eyes.

"Open those cases! Get out the guns! Hold them off here! We command the grand portal from these towers! The rest of you, come with me!"

Her men brought forth the axes and smashed the wooden lockers containing the garrison's muskets, allowing them to spill out onto the floor. Other hands readily snatched them up, loading the crude rifles as quickly as possible before moving into place at the firing loops in the clay walls. One of the men stared out a slatted peephole, spotting Clean reinforcements already rushing down the street, a thundering wave of men in long white tabards worn over their leather armor, drawn to the city gates by the sounds of battle.

"FIRE!" he shouted excitedly, almost stumbling over the word, and the men and women with him pushed the barrels of their guns through the loops and eagerly opened fire. Dirty smoke erupted outwards; hot, red sparks flew out in showers and lead shot scattered all over the streets. Advancing city guardsmen, stunned merchants and unsuspecting animals alike took stray hits; some were struck dead immediately, some were rendered incapacitated by terrible injuries, while the rest panicked and began to withdraw back up the street and deeper into the city.

Using her walking staff to keep herself upright, Vestra led the rest of her men up the sloping spiral stairs, circling back and forth as they climbed, finally emerging onto the wide open tower top, buffeted by the wind. There were none older than she among the rebels, but she led from the front with a sprightly energy in her step.

A Clean janissary braving the storm to keep watch on the approaches to the city turned immediately, only just alerted by the sound behind him. He was surprised to see the wrinkled old woman facing off against him, her cottony hair blown wild by the gale. Without a moment's hesitation she lunged forward with her staff held in both hands ahead of her, using it to unbalance the much larger warrior and push him from the tower top to his death below.

A gunshot pealed out from the other tower; the watchman over there saw Vestra and her men and shot his musket in their direction, but the bullet hit the battlements, tearing off only slivers of clay from the wall. She immediately dropped for cover behind a large chunk of stone, just as her men surged forward to the crenellations to return fire.

Gunfire popped and cracked up and down the towers; black smoke was swirling wildly in the groaning breeze. On the lower level, Alin cut down another one of Karos' men with a powerful overhand stroke, but even as he drew back his blade, another rebel pushed forward in his place. This one, a terrified boy maybe a year his junior, held a primitive matchlock pistol in front of himself and immediately pulled the trigger, the hammer cracking and the barrel exploding in a puff of churning black smoke. The crude lead bullet left the barrel at a relatively low velocity and only just penetrated Alin's shoulder, embedding itself close to the bone. The boy was brought down by one of Alin's men, but it was too late to prevent the injury.

Alin fell back from the unexpected blow, and fearing he had fallen, the rest of his men began to withdraw behind a wall of flashing steel blades. Two of his personal guardsmen stayed behind to pick him up, refusing to abandon the young prince and dragging him off with them. In moments they had escaped the tower, running for cover inside a bullet-ridden building just down the street. Here more Clean janissaries were gathering, taking opportunistic fire at the gatehouse windows and its narrow firing loops. They were making no headway whatsoever, but at least here they were safe from the frenzied fire of the rebels.

On top of the tower the old woman peeked from behind cover and saw more of her men overcome the watchman on the other tower top, before one of them rose up and waved his rifle at her, signaling that the right tower had finally been taken.

"Bring it here!" she commanded, and a young girl emerged from the stairwell with a colorful cloth bundle. Even as she tried to unfurl it Vestra grabbed the staff it was attached to, and with an exasperated groan that tested all of her ancient muscles she held it aloft.

Alin's head spun but he fought to keep his eyes open, even as his men worked to pry the bullet from his arm and bind it in with cloth dressings. He looked down the street, dusted in fresh desert sand, and saw the aftermath of the carnage - dead men, children and animals all over the sandy square, and the twin towers of the gatehouse taken by the enemy.

Over the left-hand tower a hand-made flag was raised into position, a shoddy thing with alternating red and white stripes and a bright blue patch stitched onto one corner. Flapping smartly in the wind, even as smoke from the gunfight and dust from the storm outside billowed past, it signaled the start of the war for Trade City.

On the second tier of the city there was a series of deafening explosions, each followed swiftly by another. One of the huge gasoline reservoirs of the Cartel caravanserai exploded, the result of some malicious mischief, gushing liquid fire that incinerated screaming workers caught unsuspecting in the yard. Choking, oily black smoke began to rise into the sky, blotting out the few rays of sun that managed to peek through the dusty miasma of the storm. Wherever the fiery gobs of fuel landed, more fires spread, taking to the rooftops of the Cartel compound, so that in moments it seemed everything was on fire. Cartel soldiers began pouring from their barracks to begin fighting the conflagration, but their disorganized bucket-brigades seemed ineffective against the overwhelming onslaught of flame. Cartel truckers began running for their fuel-laden rigs, each a ticking time bomb in this inferno, hurrying to start them up and slowly moving them towards the gate to remove them from the threat of fire.

Despite this another explosion tore through the Cartel compound, this time at the base of the wooden water tower near the gate to the caravanserai. In an instant the dozen or so men ferrying water down to feed the bucket brigades were disintegrated in the blast. With a tell-tale groan the huge tower toppled, its stilt-like legs shivering and cracking apart as it came down, crashing into the ground. With a "boom" the water tower fractured into a thousand splinters, sending a flood of water across the dusty ground right inside the gate, sweeping men off their feet. The first truck heading for the exit was tipped over and onto its side by the force of the rushing flood; the next vehicle in line immediately sunk into the mud created by the waters, grinding its wheels to a spinning halt. The vehicles were trapped!

"Those 'thunder-sticks' did as you said, and more!" a young member of Karos' movement shouted out to Sarah, crouching along with a handful of Ridaya's sisters who had snuck into the city prior to the battle to wreak havoc from within. She gave the boy a brief grin, then lifted binoculars to her eyes, staring at the nearby prison. Clean and Cartel guards were abandoning the walls and were pouring out of the entry portal to the complex, headed to help fight the fires down in the oil yard.

"Wait for it," Sarah said excitedly, watching patiently for the last group of enemy soldiers to leave the prison, "wait for it... okay, let's go!"

Soldiers ran haphazardly all over the palace, and Margus rushed with them towards the gates to the third and uppermost tier, staring out at the city as it came under attack. Servants trailed behind him attempting to put his ceremonial armor on him as he walked, or strap a sword to his side, but by the look in his wide brown eyes it was clear he had to see this himself.

While the storm raged just northwest of the city, dirty black gun smoke rose in all quarters of town. Clouds of deadly, toxic oil smoke from raging fires were consuming the Cartel's caravanserai. Tucumcari, the ancient trade city, seemed to be in peril.

More janissaries ran past to take up pre-arranged positions on the palace walls and in the towers. They were out of range of the fighting in the city, but their presence, entrenched here in the palace's defenses, would make an assault on the top tier of the city a difficult prospect for even a well-organized rebel force.

Hamut stood nearby as well, also surveying the damage that was being done to the city.

"Not the getaway you expected, eh?" Margus mused to his grim-faced relative, before changing his tone.

"Report!" he yelled angrily in the direction of his stunned advisors. One of his commanders, wearing fanciful lacquered armor similar to his own and holding a plumed helmet under one arm, came forward with his estimations.

"It seems to be an uprising of some sort. Rebels among the working caste have taken the gatehouse of the Trade Gate and are holding it despite repeated counterattacks."

"Why have we failed to take them?" Margus asked impatiently.

"Because we don't have the means to root them out without doing serious damage to the gatehouse," he replied.

"What about the Cartel? Get the general's men into action!"

"It seems rebel saboteurs detonated one of the caravanserai's oil tanks and their water tower. The Cartel's men have been tied down trying to keep the fires under control, before they spread and burn down everything in the city."

"The rebels have tied the entire Cartel garrison down with a few simple explosives?" Hamut gently criticized, discreetly hiding his admiration for the rebels' cleverness.

A tertiary plume of fire erupted over the city as the capsized tanker truck at the main caravanserai entrance exploded.

"Should we send reinforcements to the front gate?" the commander asked, poised to go.

Hamut looked at Margus but said nothing, wondering how his great cousin would handle this messy affair.

"No," Margus said dismissively. "Let's wait. I want some of General Rhylor's men to bleed for this little alliance of ours. Let's not have the Clean do all the fighting today."

"Rhylor is still off hunting raiders," one of his men reminded him.

"Then send for his second-in-command: Colonel Shin."

"I'm sure we'll have these rebels wrapped up soon," Hamut reassured him, as the messenger ran off. "They can't hold onto the gatehouse forever; they can't last if we just wait them out."

Margus considered for a moment. "I agree. Commander," he said, turning to the awaiting officer, "Pull our men back into the city, out of musket range of the gatehouse. If anyone tries to leave the towers, under any circumstances, give the order to move in and take them."

"I'm going down there," Hamut said, looking to Margus for approval. Margus looked at his cousin for a moment then smiled as if this was all just for sport.

"See that things go smoothly," he said.

Minutes later, Hamut rode up to the defensive position where the Clean soldiers had been taking cover and dismounted, just as the officer in charge of the disorganized troops by the gate started giving the order for his men to pull back.

Hamut saw many wounded men, bones broken by musket balls or eyes plucked from their heads by shrapnel. He had seen this kind of bloodshed in campaigns before and was unmoved by the grotesqueness of the wanton maiming, but when he saw Alin holding his bleeding shoulder and in terrible pain, he immediately came over with a look of concern on his face.

"Alin!" Hamut called, shaking Alin awake from his trance. "What has happened to you, boy? You've been hit; you should be back at the palace!"

Hamut motioned for a horse to be brought forward. But as the men around him began to mobilize, making it clear they would be pulling back, Alin tore himself from Hamut's side and moved weakly over to the outer wall, peering out despite the swirling sand biting at his eyes.

The city was smudged black and gray from numerous fires in the Cartel part of town, and only now the dust storm was beginning to clear, lifting from the city to reveal sandy streets and a fine layer of dust on the bodies of the men and animals sprinkled, dead, near the gates.

Through it all he saw the enemy flag still flying. The gatehouse remained in rebel hands. As he gulped a dry gasp, Alin noticed that the mighty front gate of the bastion was slowly opening, exposing the city to the deserts outside; *the rebels were opening the Trade Gate!*

The wall of sand from the storm lashing the northwest side of the city was thinning. Through the dwindling haze of the retreating dust storm outside Alin saw a sight that made his eyes flare in surprise.

Approaching the city from a mile away was a great column of soldiers, tribal cavalry armed with pikes and vividly-colored war banners, huntresses leading weird desert beasts, and rank after rank of disheveled peasant infantry and freed slaves, clad in cloth armor (or completely naked) and flying the makeshift flag of the rebels' lawless cause. Marching through the storm, using the swirling clouds of dust to conceal their movements until now, it was too late to muster a force to meet them on the open field.

"Come back!" Alin shouted back to the retreating janissaries. "We have to counterattack now! An *army* is coming! The gates are wide open for them! If we don't attack now the enemy will gain a foothold in the city!"

At first Hamut looked incredulous at Alin's claims but he soon rushed over to see for himself. His eyes widened as he saw the approaching army, appearing out of the dust storm like a phantom legion suddenly winking into existence within musket range.

"Assemble!" the old soldier cried out, quickly getting to his feet. "Commanders, prepare your men for an assault!"

"Sir, the order seems to have been confused. Our men are assaulting the gatehouse again."

"Hamut, what are you doing?!" Margus cursed, following his commander to the top of the palace wall to get a better view of what was going on down in the city. Sure enough a sea of white-clad soldiers, channeled by the narrow streets of the lower quarters, flooded the market in an attempt to reach the gatehouse and assault it *en masse*.

"Over there!" a watchman cried, his hand darting out like a lightning bolt towards the desert as it became visible again through the dwindling storm.

Margus looked surprised when he, too, saw the army, one thousand man strong, quickly approaching the outer walls, a sweeping wedge of men and beasts shaped like a spearhead pointed directly at the yawning portal that was the open Trade Gate. As the last winds of the storm subsided and the dust cleared, the entire rebel army was revealed in its entirety, less than a mile from the city gates!

This was no disorganized uprising; this was a concerted attack on the city itself!

"This is no game, you old fool," he chastised himself. "Signal the troops in the city to take that gatehouse at all costs! It *must* be held!" He shouted to a signalman on a nearby tower, who immediately began waving blue and gray flags in the air.

There was a commotion from a nearby doorway as a ruddy-skinned Cartel officer in a meticulously groomed uniform, along with several rifle-armed soldiers, came to meet with Margus.

"Colonel Shin," Margus greeted him curtly. "What news do you have for me?"

Shin, a career soldier in the Cartel's military arm, looked out over the city, a grim look on his badly freckled face. "General Rhylor took over one-hundred and fifty men with him to fight raiders operating east of Amarillo. The garrison here still has three hundred armed men, but most of these are tied down fighting the fires. I've started pulling men together to counter reports of sporadic uprisings in various parts of the city..."

"Mostly in and around Cartel interests, of course," Margus offered cynically.

The Colonel was quiet, and looked only slightly amused. "Maybe if you held onto more Ancient weapons than you destroyed, the sight of a thousand tribal warriors at our gates wouldn't be such an issue."

Margus ignored the snide comment that attacked his religious convictions and turned to look back at the fighting. "We've sworn a blood oath, you and I. Our houses may not have been born on the same day, but their fortunes will wax and wane together, to their ultimate success... or undoing. We've got to come together, ally, if we're going to restore order..."

Shin said nothing.

"Mobilize as many men as you can spare, Colonel," Margus said.

"For the sake of civilization," Shin replied, his strange tone reminding Margus that the Cartel was fighting for a shared ideal, *not* for the survival of the Clean.

"*For civilization*," Margus agreed, only now taking a fanciful leather helmet from a nearby servant and donning it, hastily adjusting the chin strap for a tight fit.

Alin accepted a poultice for his injured arm but got to his feet with the rest of the Clean soldiers readying to advance on the gatehouse. Hamut looked surprised, but his shock at Alin's resilience soon turned to pride in the young prince; his presence at the side of their men noticeably filled the soldiers with courage and gave Hamut reason to regain his old fighting determination, a steely reserve that would be needed for the coming task.

"Advance!" Hamut yelled, pointing the way with his scimitar.

As the battle raged the rebels seemed to be getting better with their weapons, because as soon as the line of Clean warriors moved from cover a wall of coordinated musket-fire erupted from the twin towers on either side of the Trade Gate, their heavy lead shot hitting various men and tearing through their mediocre armor. Men began to drop, but it was too late, the assault was on.

Running at full speed through the smoky marketplace, scimitar-wielding Clean swordsmen raced towards the looming bastion, while their musket-bearing comrades behind them ran, took momentary cover, opened fire and were up again and following close behind. As their own fire began to bear down on the gate fortifications, the defenders inside the gatehouse began to button up its windows and firing ports, reducing their own fire by a full third.

It was still too intense, however, and Alin and Hamut saw and heard men being hit and killed all around them. They were only halfway to the gatehouse, and already there were so many bodies on the ground that running in a straight line became an impossibility. Alin, Hamut and the handfuls of brave men who followed them, had to dodge collapsed animals, leap over corpses and zigzag towards the bastion under a relentless rain of murderous gunfire.

Suddenly Hamut fell, brought down by the impact of a rebel's bullet. He cried out in pain as his body crumpled beneath him, while several footmen fell behind to see if he could be saved.

Alin was alone now. He wasn't so sure they would get to the bastion in time, and even if they did, would there be enough of them to root the rebels out of the towers? They had to do it, they had to succeed; *his uncle was watching, as were all of the Clans, and with so much at stake, Trade City could not fall!*

Hamut's angry shouts faded behind the brave soldiers as they raced towards their daunting objective. Alin slid, breathless, against the dusty carcass of a lice-infested *bawthok* killed early in the fighting, taking cover behind the massive shaggy beast while bullets popped all around him. More men caught up, also taking cover behind the dead beast, until at least a dozen of them waited, swords at the ready, their long white tunics stained with blood, sweat and desert dust.

Alin thought of Gale, of how terrified she must be, so far from home. He worried for her, even in this desperate time when his own life was in danger. He could only see her face when he closed his eyes. His men waited. When this was over he would find her. He would ride out and track her and nothing could stop him.

"For Tucumcari!" Alin screamed, tears welling in his eyes. "For our people!"

The hearts of his bedraggled men swelled as Alin's tears streamed down his cheeks, as he leapt over the dead beast, as he led the charge towards the bastion, now just a few dozen paces away. The men roared Alin's ferocious battle-cry and ran with him; for a moment it seemed like a small group of such determined men could topple even the mighty bastion with their unshakable spirit.

Margus sat atop a handsome horse, as white and perfect as a marble statue, riding alongside Colonel Shin and a long column of disciplined Clean janissaries in their white robes and leather armor, Cartel soldiers wearing hodge-podge body armor. They swept down from the upper tiers of the city, heading to join the battle at the city gates, with Margus at the lead.

There was a surprised cry when, from a side street, over two hundred men came streaming, running in a mass towards Margus' regiment.

Slaves, released from the city prison by clandestine agents of the rebel alliance and worked into a frenzy, were now swarming through the streets without any plan or direction, running amok and destroying everything in their path. Street vendors fled in every direction as their businesses were torn apart, as the escapees looted and pillaged while they advanced down the street. Theirs was a cry of angry rage, which preceded the horde as it surged from the prison district in the direction of Margus, Shin and their column of reinforcements.

"Look out," Colonel Shin calmly warned, as one of the escapees broke from the pack and ran directly at Margus, holding a stolen scimitar in both hands, his wild eyes burning with a desire for revenge. Shin smoothly lifted an old VP70Z machine pistol from its leather shoulder holster at his side and opened fire, a crack-cracking burst, cutting the naked man down in a splash of vivid red color.

"Continue on!" Margus commanded his men, even though his soldiers were now disorganized and were openly battling the escaped slaves, opening fire on the desperate prisoners and cutting them down with swords. "Ignore them! We must keep moving!"

Another prisoner ran up, and Margus was forced to slay him with a quick slash from his scimitar. More pressed in around their horses and soon they were swallowed in a swirling, confused melee.

"We can't let them get to the front gates! We have to buy the army more time!" Sarah cried to her sisters, who were hiding in the doorways and nooks of nearby buildings, watching the prisoners' battle with Margus unfold. She brandished an iron mace, its heavy head shaped like a fist, and held it up like a lightning rod to galvanize their courage, then drew the mask of her chain coif across her face in the manner of a veil.

"*Charge!*" she cried, as she and the desert sisters spilled from their hiding places along the street to join the chaotic fray from all sides.

"What is going on?" Margus bellowed, his commanding voice almost drowned out by the crackle-pop of muskets from the Cartel soldiers and automatic gunfire from Shin's compact machine pistol.

"Just hold your own, my lord mandarin!" Shin shouted heartily, struggling to reign in his steed which now became skittish from the deafening noise of battle.

Already weighed down by gore Margus relinquished his sword, instead pulling out his own sidearm and firing at another prisoner who dared come near him. The powerful .45 caliber round caught the man below the jaw and nearly took his head clean off. Margus' horse turned around and about, desperately looking for a way to escape the fighting all around it, to get away from the angry report of the high-powered pistol that thundered away just inches from its ears.

"Hold, boy!" Margus shouted, trying to ease the beast, but it began to fitfully rear, trying to buck its rider.

As they ran to join the fighting, one of the amazon fighters dropped to her knees and tucked her head down, turning herself into an *ad hoc* platform. Sarah saw her and ran up, leapt onto her back, and with her sister's aid flung herself up and over the line of distracted Cartel riflemen to land on top of Colonel Shin, using her weight to drag him from his saddle and to the ground in a cloud of dust.

"*Yaagh!*" Shin shouted in surprise, gritting his teeth as he impacted hard on the soil below, losing his breath (and his helmet) from the shock. The woman who had leapt on him scrambled to get up and bring her weapon to bear, but he struggled with her, refusing to allow her to lift her heavy mace, clinging to it with his free hand.

Margus saw Shin go down through the eyeholes in his ornate helmet and was shocked by the sight of General Rhylor's second-in-command being brought to the ground, but he could tarry no longer. He raised his pistol to the sky and shouted to his men: "To the gate!" Another volley erupted in the street, as Clean musketeers formed a line near their mandarin and cut down an entire rank of prisoners.

Though younger by many years, Sarah fought with the bloodied Shin, biting his neck and drawing more blood from the surprisingly competent Cartel officer. She tore the mace away from his fluttering hand and lifted the mace over her head, the gleaming iron fist looming above like a symbol of her people's defiance.

Crack-crack-crack came the sound of the antique German machine pistol he held at his side, and Sarah's body shook violently from the three direct hits that tore into her stomach and pierced her chest. Without so much as a cry she instantly slumped over him, and with a shove Shin pushed the young woman's lifeless corpse aside as if it had all been a mere inconvenience.

"Come on, then!" he shouted impatiently to the Cartel men around him, getting swiftly to his feet. "Let's clear this rabble out and get moving!"

Men ran to and fro through the low-lying smoke as it draped the city in a sulfurous fog; wounded guardsmen appeared from the din, limping away from the fight, bandaged and bloody; terrified merchants and panicked peddlers with goods on their backs fled past and deeper into the city, vanishing once more out of sight. Margus rode through the smoky haze and past these small groups of worried stragglers, leading his company of footmen as they came around the last bend and into the marketplace lying just inside the Trade Gate.

Margus saw Hamut being carried away by several grimy janissaries, and called for them to stop. As they came over, the old swordsman regained consciousness momentarily, just long enough to look up at Margus with a look of worry in his eyes. "*Alin's charged the gates...*"

Margus looked to the largest of the men struggling to carry Hamut. "Take him back to the palace and see to his wounds." With that order Hamut stopped struggling to regain his feet and let the men take him off into the haze.

"Into the market," Margus said to his men, beginning to lead them forward again.

Margus pulled back the reigns of his charger as the scene at the Trade Gate came into view, just fifty yards away. Through the smoke he could see the bastion still stood, battered and bullet-ridden. Over it flew the dirty, ragged flag of the rebels. The gatehouse was ringed by the dozens of brave men killed in the day's fighting, cut down in various failed attempts to retake it. Trampling over these corpses, *over Alin's corpse,* came over two hundred rebel footmen, with another fifty barbarian horsemen at their lead carrying the colored standard of Uncle Sam and the banner of the rebellion he had chosen to support.

They were too late.

"Betrayer!" Margus hissed through gritted teeth, at once realizing how much of a fool he had been to let the barbarian into his city, to hear his grievances, to make him a guest in his own palace. Seeing the enemy army already well inside the gates, too many to fight back with the paltry forces at hand, his plan to drive the enemy from the gatehouse and seal the gate faltered... and crumbled.

The men all around him sensed their master's hesitation and began to retreat slowly.

"Pull back!" Margus shouted, hatred for the enemy and disappointment in himself clearly audible in his voice. "We fight these curs from a more tenable position! Back to the palace!"

But it would not be as orderly as that. Seeing the mandarin himself, atop a white horse at the head of his troops, some few eager gunmen among the ranks of Valero's escaped prisoners opened fire with their muskets and crossbows, their deadly projectiles landing among Margus' troops. Horsemen at the lead of the enemy army sensed the excitement of their comrades and lifted their pikes to begin riding forward, already building speed as they rode ahead in a race to be the first to slay the city's infamous mandarin.

Two crossbow bolts struck Margus' desert horse on the neck and flank, bringing the fine stallion down with a high-pitched whinny. Margus cried out as the heavy beast collapsed onto its side, pinning him under it and in so doing crushing his leg instantly. He waved his pistol angrily in one hand, but grew so weak from his condition that he soon dropped the weapon and lost it among his troops.

A band of courageous Clean musketeers stepped forward to shield their lord, while others worked to free him from his agonizing entrapment. A team of men abandoned their weapons to lift the creature's corpse, and with a heave pulled him painfully from underneath. At this point Margus lost consciousness, but his men swiftly issued him away. Because of his armor it required three men to carry him, but enough stayed behind to buy them time that they were able to take the fallen mandarin back to the white-walled palace atop the city's uppermost tier.

Margus woke to the distant sounds of war. He pulled himself up but winced in pain as he realized how badly his leg had been broken. A humble healer withdrew himself and his medicines from the mandarin's presence, while the commander of the house guard, now battered and injured himself, came into the tower room with a bandaged Hamut at his side, bearing news of the battle.

"They've set fire to the eastern part of town," the commander said, "and we've too few men to put them out. Our forces in the lower tier are concentrating on battling the enemy, not fires."

With the help of several men under each arm, Margus, still wearing his wooden breastplate, stood upright with a groan.

"Our forces are dug in all over the city. We're making a good fight of it. But the enemy is already rallying men to scale the walls and bypass the first tier. And I fear they've infiltrated the secret passages beneath the city," the commander continued.

"We have men fighting desperately to keep the rebels in the passages tied down," Colonel Shin interrupted, coming forward. "All is not lost, my good mandarin. We still have some tricks left up our sleeve. We only need to buy time for General Rhylor to arrive."

"*Your nephew is dead*," Hamut said softly, suddenly dispelling the optimism of the officers.

Margus fought the knot in his throat. His choice for an "heir", someone to inherit all that he had built, was dead; the future of all the Clean Clans was now uncertain. Even if they won this battle, without a strong man to lead them through the dark times ahead they would become prey again, as they had been in the early years after the Fall. The uncontested rule of the Clean over the people of the wasteland would be a thing of the past.

Colonel Shin sensed something was amiss and seemed interested. Perhaps he realized the repercussions of Alin's death; perhaps he saw an opportunity here for the Cartel to shine, to come through with their military might and snatch victory from the jaws of defeat. A *coup* of sorts, in which their roles would become reversed, with the Cartel now coming to wrest control of the throne of civilization, and the Clean, humbled, becoming the weaker partner from this point onwards. Whatever he was thinking, Colonel Shin changed the subject.

"Milord mandarin, you are badly injured and you cannot contribute any more to this fight. I would suggest you retreat into the Water Vaults beneath the palace tier where it is safe, while the battle unfolds. We will continue resisting the rebels, and keep you updated."

Margus suspected Shin of some kind of trickery but realized the Cartel officer was right. There was no more he could do here, and his morale was shaken.

"Perhaps you are right, Colonel. My vision is clouded by my tolerance for these people. Perhaps this problem requires a firmer hand. Very well. Colonel, I hand over command of the garrison to you."

"Steward," he called to an awaiting servant, "gather up all the things in my apartments and send ten men to start moving the contents of the treasury to the Water Vaults beneath the palace. *Immediately.*"

"We're really going underground, then?" Hamut asked.

Margus nodded unhappily. "Shin is right. There's enough water there to last us several months if need be. It's the water that the rebels will need if they plan on holding the city. We'll fight to keep it out of their hands; up here and in the caves below if we have to. With the water under our control we can easily hold out until General Rhylor arrives with his army and lays siege to the rebels."

After Margus, Hamut, and their men left, Shin turned to his own subordinates as they stood in the silent chamber, ready to hear his orders. For a moment he said nothing, only checking to make sure his sidearm was reloaded. He then spoke, in a quiet but clear tone.

"Are the fires in the caravanserai under control? Excellent. Assemble the engineers. And call out the recoilless team. It's time we start fighting this battle *our* way, the sensible way..."

"Let's light some fires of our own."

A half hour later Margus, Hamut, the mandarin's medicine man, and several Cartel soldiers graciously assigned to them by Colonel Shin, descended a flight of natural stone steps into the interior of Tucumcari mountain, a massive recess created by tectonic activity less than a century before. Ahead of them struggled a dozen servants porting chests filled with corium pieces, various valuables and documents, as well as food and bottles and jars of medical supplies stockpiled in the palace for an emergency such as this.

With his injury Margus needed help down the stairs and was assisted by a handful of Clean janissaries, but Hamut lingered for a moment to admire this rarely-seen haven beneath the mountain. He had never known of Trade City's little secret, this place, and marveled at its raw, natural beauty, even in this desperate time.

The Water Vaults were comprised of a series of jagged caves transformed by an earthquake under the mountain, a violent upheaval that had created caverns as the earth was uplifted and forced in opposite directions. The great hollow caves echoed with the quiet sounds of small subterranean waterfalls; eerie light from quartz rocks reflected off dark, still water at the Vaults' deep bottom, where several large pools had gathered at the base of these young cascades. Purple, indigo, and pale green threads of light cast by large quartz formations danced off of the wet, glistening rocks all around.

Winding its way down through the rock from the Hydro Station above were surprisingly primitive wooden wheels and other apparatus that had been constructed long ago to draw water from these caves up to the surface. The machines were now switched off; until this siege was over the fresh water in the caves, the city's *greatest* treasure, would remain locked securely underground and out of rebel hands.

"If things develop poorly, we can abandon the city, return east to the Arid City and to the camps of our cousins." Hamut suggested. "We can rebuild our strength. The fate of the Clean does not need to be decided here. We will live on and we will prevail through other battles."

"No," Margus said. "I built this city into what it is. Any failure now will only weaken our cause wherever we go... and the Cartel will be more than happy to fill the void if we flee. We can't run, Hamut, can't you see that? The savages want to see this land seeded with chaos and death. They fight the idea of law and order with tooth and nail, and if they have it their way this land, this *world,* will never rise from the ashes. We are fighting the good fight, Hamut, for the benefit of all. *Zhidao?*"

Hamut stared at Margus, not knowing if it was his injured pride, of losing a city he had almost single-handedly built into the most profitable trading hub in the Far Desert, or if what he said was really true, that the stakes were really that high. Now, as they retreated underground like rats fleeing a fire, even the noble cause of the Clean to re-establish civilization in this violent, unprepared land seemed foolish, echoing the naivety of Nimrod's effort to build a tower high enough to touch God.

Tribal warriors celebrated raucously in the smoky Trade Market of Tucumcari, pouring into the damaged buildings surrounding the marketplace and dragging out cowering women, jugs of wine, sacks of fungus bread and all manner of valuables. Here two warriors struggled to tear the clothes from a screaming teenager, while over there men hacked open cloth sacks to fetch the corn within and toss it carelessly into the air like golden rain. A huge warrior, his body still caked in blood from the day's slaughter, lifted a silver cup full of wine to his lips, drank thirstily, then poured the remainder over a companion's head, all to the sound of laughter and strange musical instruments.

The scene was being repeated up and down the streets in this part of town, as the Clean forces seemed to have just vanished from the buildings and alleys in a general retreat deeper into the city. There was no one to defend the poor, unsuspecting inhabitants of the quarter. Some brave few came out to greet their "liberators", while others feared their drunken cries and hunched in hiding in their homes, praying to primitive gods that they would go unnoticed and unravaged.

Uncle Sam raised his own flagon, a wonderful piece of goldwork taken from some dead craftsman's shop, to toast their success. A few men of his personal guard stayed close by, vigilantly eyeing the horde that was his barbarian host, but with only a small amount or urging they too were soon smiling, at this, a most unexpected victory over the Clean.

Uncle Sam's horse reared, raising him high above the crowds; the northerners' chieftain laughed heartily while his people called his name in a rising and ebbing war chant.

"Sam! Sam! Sam!"

The barbarian lord lifted his flagon in one hand and his axe in another, shouting at the top of his lungs to be heard:

"Two days' plunder, my lads! Make them count! Gold and wine and jewels for all!"

The men cheered once again, a deafening roar that drowned out the small islands of brutality playing out amidst their numbers. Boren struggled to stay on his own horse, but as men began tearing apart a cloth merchant's stall the huge warrior dismounted and ran over to prevent them from ruining the fine bolts with their drunken violence.

Entering almost unnoticed at the far end of the crowded square came a small band of armed women, led by Kseniya. She carried with her a report of the fighting in the eastern part of town intended for Uncle Sam's ears, but as the sisters entered the scene they stopped dead in their tracks. Men pushed in around them, fumbling about as they celebrated, and the women were forced to use their shields to create a wall around themselves to prevent from being overrun.

Kseniya stood as high as she could to see over the heads of the hundreds of warriors clustered in the square, looking for someone, anyone, in authority. Over the spears, pikes, and muskets of the masses of looting soldiers she barely spotted Uncle Sam atop his grand desert horse, his presence only given away by the tall banners of his personal lancers.

"Uncle Sam!" she shouted angrily. "*Uncle Sam!*"

The warlord reached down and clasped hands with a cousin, and both laughed. He was oblivious.

Determined, Kseniya marched forward, her own guards shoving their way bodily through the throng until they came to Uncle Sam's horse. The warlord continued to laugh, turned to see Kseniya, and raised a curious eyebrow, his laughter thinning to a tired chuckle.

"Uncle Sam, you old fool!" Kseniya shouted. "Call off these dogs you call 'warriors'! We came here to save the city, not destroy it!"

Some of Kseniya's women were already moving among the men and began physically removing the unwilling captives among them, wrenching wailing, half-naked women free from their giddy captors and leading them back to the relative safety of Kseniya and her sword-sisters.

Uncle Sam saw the venom in Kseniya's eyes and it froze his smile, stole his laughter. He looked around and realized to what she was referring.

"Ah... yes..." he said diplomatically, in his mind quickly weighing the impact of one woman's words against the morale of his army. He found a vague compromise. "Listen up, lads! The woman's right! No plunder! The day's not won yet! Captains! Gather your men! The fight's this way!"

He drunk his wine in one swig, threw away the goblet and pointed the way with his axe. A great rollicking army, the hundreds of tribesmen in the market began moving out, burdened by bladders of wine, golden trinkets, necklaces of coins and fresh food stolen from nearby shops.

"Animals!" Kseniya remarked in disgust.

Face covered in soot, her forehead injured and bleeding, the old woman Vestra looked down from the bastion and at the hundreds of barbarians moving through the open gate. They were looting and pillaging as they went; terrified civilians were abandoning their homes ahead of them, running off like frightened lemmings in the other direction, deeper into the smoking city.

"This is madness," she said, wide-eyed. The men and women with her, holding the tower tops of the gatehouse, seemed just as frightened of the criminals and savages they'd let into their city.

This wasn't how it was supposed to be. The alliance came to free the citizens, not decimate them; it came to bring hope, not violate them further. It was one lawless mass; the army swept through the city, scouring it of its valuables and fixtures like a swarm of locusts.

Vestra began looking into the crowds for someone, and when he didn't appear, looked off to other parts of town where more of the alliance's soldiers were scaling the outer walls. Now that the defenders were withdrawing from the edge of town it seemed the city was falling fast.

"*Where is Karos!?*"

There was a barely-perceptible "thud" from somewhere in the city; a heartbeat later, one of the large clay-walled buildings that occupied the corner of the Trade Market exploded in a cloud of brown dust. Hundreds of shards of broken clay blew outwards from the blast, sweeping some men off their feet and burying others in an avalanche of collapsed stone. With a rumbling crash the rest of the building collapsed a moment later, and a choking dust cloud swept through the ranks of stunned barbarians being herded by their leader towards the heart of town.

Men ran to and fro screaming and shouting; warriors and escaping civilians were trampled underfoot as war beasts panicked, bucking their riders from them and plowing through ranks of surprised footmen.

Another "thud" thundered over the city as an ancient 105mm recoilless rifle round, over two centuries old, erupted in a concussive wave from its rusted and corroded barrel, soared across the rooftops with a thin whistle, and impacted another random building in the marketplace. The high explosive shell detonated among the panicking ranks of Uncle Sam's warriors, disintegrating three men in the fiery burst and sending over a dozen more skywards, only to land dead among those who were blown prone.

A *bawthok* with a howdah atop it collapsed from terrible shrapnel wounds, spilling its bloodied occupants and crushing six of Uncle Sam's men, too burdened by wine and water vessels taken in the looting to get out of the way in time.

Uncle Sam heard the explosions and was taken completely by surprise. "Take cover!" he commanded. As one his army began to break, fleeing in every direction away from the square where the cannon's rounds were being directed. The streets were flooded with warriors, who dropped their ill-gotten gains as they went, searching desperately for cover down the numerous winding side streets.

Kseniya led her sisters and those they had rescued from the hands of the tribal army down a separate alley, keeping her cool surprisingly well despite the high explosives bursting all around them.

"Get down!" Vestra yelled to her young rebels, most of them unable to see or hear what was going on. Obediently following her orders they began to crouch behind the shattered battlements of the gatehouse and covered their heads, their eyes flaring in fear.

Thud. A second later another round struck the tower somewhere beneath Vestra's feet, some two stories down. The blast exploded through the interior of the gatehouse, tearing out the far side and shredding the huge wooden beams that kept the building aloft. Bricks cracked, crumbled and broke; with a monstrous groan the tower came crashing to the ground, killing everyone within it and atop it. As it came down the gatehouse's structural integrity came crumbling apart, and as its stones fell it dragged the other tower with it, so that in moments the entire barbican that was once the legendary Trade Gate of Tucumcari was no more.

"*Direct hit!*" yelled the artillery spotter, still staring through his binoculars.

Colonel Shin lifted his own set of spyglasses and saw the results of their preliminary bombardment. From the palace tier of the city they had been able to bring their great gun, a Vietnam-war era M27A1 recoilless rifle, to bear on the unsuspecting rebels. Foolishly congregated near the gates, where they'd gained their foothold inside the defenses, they had made themselves extremely vulnerable to the weapon's powerful, high explosive rounds. Dozens were now dead from the blasts, and many more maimed. The remainder were fleeing, a great body of disorganized rabble.

"The rebel strongpoint has been destroyed," the spotter confirmed. The gatehouse that the rebels had held, and hung their flag proudly from, had been completely leveled. A huge cloud of orange-gray dust rose into the sky where it had formerly stood.

"Excellent," Shin said, commending the gunner. He then shouted to a signaler nearby holding two colored flags.

"Signaler, give the order for the *engineers* to move in!" Flags whipped about in the air.

"Sir," asked a Cartel subordinate, "are you sure we want to risk this much damage to the city?"

"Yes, Captain," Shin said menacingly. "I plan on doing more than just pinning the enemy until General Rhylor gets here. The wilderness natives need to be taught a little lesson about the power of civilization. Now... let the streets burn!"

Boren fell off his dying horse, himself injured by hot metal fragments that riddled his legs. One fell limp and useless, and he only barely dragged himself along using the other.

Ahead of his men, Uncle Sam turned his horse around to see more stones falling as a building face nearby crumbled and fell into ruin. Many of his clansmen were buried alive; a handful of Karos' volunteers came stumbling blindly through the clouds of dust, stunned by what was happening.

Uncle Sam spotted Boren struggling to escape the chaos, and began to ride over. Twenty more men passed by, barely keeping out of the way of his horse, hoping to flee back the way the warlord had come and deeper into the city.

All of a sudden there was a strange "pop" and "hiss" sound, like a gas range igniting. Moments later the dust clouds swirling down the street were impregnated with a hellish red glow. Men screamed, shrieking in ear-piercing octaves of hideous pain. The glow faded as suddenly as it had appeared, but from the dust cloud came stumbling a half-dozen men, their bodies completely engulfed in fire.

Marching boots stamped a martial rhythm. Following their screaming, burning victims came six Cartel soldiers clad in long, embroidered crimson greatcoats and wearing armored vests, with gas masks and pitted army helmets concealing their faces. Each had a heavy metal cylinder on his back, connected to the rifle in his hands by a long, segmented metal hose. A flickering blue pilot light burned at the tip of each. *Flamethrowers!*

"*Dragon warriors!*" Uncle Sam cried. "Pull back!"

Another gusher of flame poured down the street, incinerating a few of Valero's slave soldiers who had run ahead looking for a safe place to hide. Behind them came some of Karos' peasant warriors, who'd had no choice but to follow their comrades now that the army was beginning to unravel amidst pitched street fighting.

"Run!" someone shouted, and as the burning, screaming convicts shambled about before collapsing, the rest of the men darted to the imagined safety of a nearby building, taking up positions by the windows and peering out with muskets at the ready.

Two Cartel engineers came marching down the street, their flamethrowers still drooling red-hot globs of murderous fluid. They looked formidable, these "dragon warriors", clad in their hammered steel breastplates and armor, with shapeless gas masks fitted with small slatted lenses making them appear as unrelenting, animate statues.

"Fire!" someone sensible commanded, rallying his men for a volley at these new players in the war for control of the streets. Musket balls popped off from the windows of the building, white cottony smoke vented outwards, and they waited for the air to clear to see what good they'd done.

Clang, twang, zzzip! Low-velocity lead shot hit and bounced off the advancing, armored, "dragon warriors", leaving them unharmed.

One of the Cartel engineers calmly fetched a grenade from his back, pulled out the ring, and tossed the explosive underhand so that it soared through the window into the building's interior. Few of the defenders saw it in the confused, smoky conditions inside the building. Some spotted it, but didn't recognize the danger the small metal capsule posed. Those that did just barely escaped in time as the grenade went off, killing everyone left inside in a shower of molten fragments, only to run right out into the sweeping, scorching rays of the other engineers waiting for them to emerge.

The alliance's early gains, the element of surprise, their control of the Trade Gate, their sabotage of the Cartel compound and their foothold in the city, were now slipping away as the ruthless Cartel garrison came together to sweep the rebels from the streets and pin them where they could be contained.

Kseniya walked through the din of battle, stunned by the violence unfolding all over the city. Through streets embattled by warriors on both sides of the conflict she led the other desert sisters, searching for their leader, Ridaya, and some island of sanity amid all the madness. They heard fighting up ahead, the sounds of a pitched melee, steel against steel, the clang and clash of metal. Kseniya rushed with her sisters into a small intersection of streets where they stumbled upon a scene of unexpected carnage.

Ridaya, clad in blood-streaked black armor, swirled a spiked flail over her head and screamed angrily as she battled over a dozen sword-wielding foes. Behind her crowded a group of civilians, pressed hard against the walls of an alley, trapped along with the amazonian woman by a mass of soldiers.

Dead sisters lay all around, having fallen at Ridaya's side to defend the screaming, defenseless inhabitants of the city. Ridaya stood with just two remaining women, all of them badly injured and fighting mercilessly against their foes.

Their attackers were men from Valero's band of prisoners, and bearded rabble from the northern tribes, Uncle Sam's men, deserters who had given up on fighting the Clean in the streets to plunder what they could before fleeing. Apparently Ridaya had found them besetting a group of women and children attempting to escape the destruction, and had abandoned the battle to fight the curs to the last.

"Ridaya!" Kseniya cried, and immediately broke into a run, leading the other enraged sisters into the rear ranks of the mob. A few of the gangly prisoners broke on seeing the ferocious sisters coming at them, dropping their weapons and fleeing. But not all of them. A few of the northerners turned, lascivious leers in their eyes, and turned to add Kseniya and the other women to their plunder.

Kseniya fought hard, bringing her curved sword down and to the side to slash it across the necks and bodies of the men standing against her, cutting through their hard leather gorgets and breastplates and into their flesh. The wounded men jabbed with their spears but she managed to deflect them, as did the women at her side, deftly outmaneuvering their more heavily-armored opponents and bringing their weapons back around to spill more blood.

Ridaya continued to fight, emboldened by the appearance of reinforcements, but she had grown tired. The ferocious leader of the desert sisters screamed in anger as another man came forward with an axe, using his shield to deflect and entangle her flail, but she refused to let go. Instead she brought her foot up, kicking the man in his groin with all her might, toppling the giant over and into another rank of attackers.

The civilians screamed as one of Ridaya's warriors was taken down by a powerful axe blow to the shoulder, cutting cleanly into her torso in a spray of gore. Ridaya turned as blood splashed her and whipped out a long dagger from her side, plunging the weapon into the man's throat to punish him for his victory.

But there were too many. By the time Kseniya and the others had shown the men it was foolish to stay and fight, eventually sending the survivors running, Ridaya and her two sisters had fallen.

As the last of them fled, Kseniya let out a gasp of pent-up breath and ran over to Ridaya, who leaned against the body of one of the sisters who had died at her side. The white horse hair of her helmet was stained red with blood, her armor was crumpled and gory, and she bled from numerous wounds on her torso, face and arms. A finger from her left hand had been taken in the battle, but she didn't even seem to notice. She looked out at Kseniya with glazed eyes, blood already welling at her lips, a look of pain and anger freezing her features into a bitter, disappointed frown.

"Ridaya," Kseniya pleaded, but Ridaya merely grunted, trying in vain to undo the buckle of her cuirboilli breastplate to aid her shallow breathing. She was too weak to even unfasten it, and instead gave up, letting her arm hang limply at her side. Kseniya went to help, but it was clear it was of no use.

"No... Ridaya..." the other women whispered, coming over to Kseniya's side, reaching but recoiling when they saw just how wounded their queen really was. The desperation to see Ridaya rise once more from a pitched fight was clear, but it wasn't to be.

Ridaya looked at the others, one by one, then her eyes gravitated to Kseniya. Both women, survivors from two different worlds entirely, locked eyes for a moment. Kseniya stifled her tears; Ridaya gurgled blood. She lifted her arm with a tremendous expenditure of effort, and clasped Kseniya's shoulder.

"You're still here?" she muttered weakly. "I thought you'd be cowering somewhere..."

She tried to sound tough, but Ridaya's eyes reflected her sorrow, and soon tears followed. "But here you are... and you're going to live longer than me..."

"No," Kseniya said impotently, beginning to weep with the others. "You're going to *live*..."

"Listen to me," Ridaya said sharply, regaining her spirited strength if only briefly. "Don't be stupid. Get them out of here. The people... do what you can. Rally the sisters and take them into the mountains. Away from all this. I want you to do this... promise me?"

Kseniya couldn't speak, she could only shake her head. She couldn't do it... she didn't have the strength!

"*Promise me!*" Ridaya demanded, her grip weakening. She stared at Kseniya, her gaze transforming slowly from anger and frustration to worry and fear; fear for what lay beyond, in the afterlife and for the future of the women she was leaving behind.

In a moment, Ridaya faded away. Her head slumped back, she no longer drew breath; the legendary partisan queen was no more.

Burning Lands   **319**

Though she and the surviving sisters shook and shuddered at the sudden, unimaginable loss, there was no time to grieve. Already the women and children they had fought to save agitated to leave, to run while they still had time, before more men came and decided to renew the fight. Kseniya found herself rising on weak legs, and led them to find some means of escaping the city.

Colonel Shin watched the battle in the streets through his binoculars, his face knit in fascination. Through the lenses he was able to keep the burning murder at a distance. Up here he wasn't forced to smell the stench of gunpowder, or the distinct odor of seared human flesh and hair. Up here the war was sanitary, at arm's length.

Not that he wouldn't want to be down there, among the fighting. He was a fighting man and hated the treacherous tribal savages of the wasteland now more than ever. The *bei man* had dared to attack Tucumcari, to use trickery to get in the city. They must be made to pay not only for their arrogance, but for their foolish belief that what they were doing was in the interests of humanity. Theirs was the cause of absurdity - division, disunity and a retreat into the post-apocalyptic Stone Age out of which humanity had only just recently begun to pull itself. This was a fight that could not be lost.

Swirls of orange, red and yellow fire ballooned in the curved lenses of his binoculars. The engineers were systematically advancing through the streets towards the under-armed and under-equipped enemy, an enemy who had expected only Clean muskets and scimitars, not Cartel inventiveness and resurrected technology. They were slowly being bottled up where the Colonel wanted them. The fire was ingenious, it played on the undisciplined fears of the savages, and they were breaking.

"Over there," came the resolute call of a watchman, pointing into the desert to the east. Colonel Shin turned his glasses to take in the great trade road and its eastern approaches.

Just a few miles from the city they spotted the dust plumes and black, rusted cabs of a Cartel convoy steaming for the city. Glistening wetly with oil even from this distance, they looked like a train of gleaming black scarabs inching their way towards the lofty city across an unending sea of sand. By the distinct orange flags flapping wildly from each cab he recognized it as the body of the 5th Cartel Brigade, General Rhylor's elite unit of raider-hunters, returning early (and quite fortuitously at that) from their campaign in the east. Colonel Shin grinned.

Shin wasn't the only one to spot them; horsemen from Uncle Sam's alliance, still lingering outside the city walls, noticed the newcomers too and began to assemble. Some of Uncle Sam's barbarians, having deserted the war effort after getting what they wanted from the city, were also outside, laden with goods stolen from the homes of people killed in the early fighting. These miscreants were loathe to give up their ill-gotten gains, and instead, on seeing Rhylor's mighty army closing in, turned and began fleeing in the opposite direction, the "cause" be damned.

Lookouts among the convoy must have seen the smoke over the city. Spotting enemies outside the walls as well as inside, the trucks of Rhylor's army came to a grinding halt, preparing for action.

Shin knew Rhylor, his superior officer. It would take some time for the General to survey the situation and realize what exactly was occurring, but once he did, he would set up his forces for an engagement and at dawn the next day, systematically lay siege, prepared to blast what was left of the tribal resistance from the city.

From this distance Shin could only see the fighting as it played out far, far away. The horsemen left outside the city walls as a rear guard for the rebel alliance rallied quickly, hurling themselves at the trucks of the convoy as they began to spread out and take up positions. The trucks immediately began disgorging troops, and small wheeled infantry guns were unhitched from their prime movers and pushed into firing range. The swords and spears of the primitive cavalry whirled around them, but in short order these skirmishers would be destroyed or driven off, and the General would then be prepared to come to the garrison's aid.

Tomorrow, the wrath of the Cartel would be directed at whoever still stood against them.

General Rhylor was a tall man with a dour face filled with creases and lines, a boxer's nose, and a head of thin white hair that he combed neatly with a part on the side. Unlike Margus Han, his closest counterpart in the Clean, he didn't seem extraordinarily healthy or fit, but what he lacked in physical endurance he more than made up for with a broad chest, big arms and a hard and inflexible demeanor. His American lineage was obvious, but he was no tribal sympathizer; he was a pragmatic believer in the cause of civilizing the wasteland. He looked through his own binoculars, surveying the battle which had raged throughout the night from his spot several yards from his command truck. It was a scene of stark violence, but the general was a veteran of many battles, of many campaigns, and the death, suffering, and wanton destruction consuming the city hardly phased him at all.

The Cartel caravanserai still burned, the flames churning out thick, dark smoke that enveloped a large part of the city and stained the sky black for miles, even as the first rays of sunlight began to light the desert. The famed Trade Gate, once seen as a symbol of civilization in this lawless land and a destination for thousands of merchants, wastelanders and pilgrims from all over the Far Desert, was now gone, replaced by a gaping wound in the city walls from which more smoke poured. Other fires lit up the city, its clay and wooden buildings going up like torches wherever the battle raged. Even from this distance he could hear the soft "pop-pop" of sporadic gunfire, intermixed with the vague sounds of barbarian horns and drums attempting to coordinate troop movements as the war raged chaotically inside the walls.

Stragglers escaped the city. Scavs, raiders and merchants fled from whatever openings the barbarians left in the walls. The people of Trade City were slowly fleeing the sack of Tucumcari, like blood seeping from a cold carcass.

The new dawn had not brought hope, it had brought devastation and fear.

Rhylor shifted his attention to the palace of the mandarin, which rose on the third and final tier of the city over the other damaged quarters, its elegant white walls once considered the most beautiful in the world. Now it sat at the center of a moat of carnage, the city itself a ring of sporadic fires, while the palace walls were besieged by clouds of black smoke that threatened to erase it from view. But atop the walls, he saw janissaries holding firm. From the northern casemate he saw men firing the recoilless rifle down onto the barbarian hordes swarming at their feet and from the towers he saw that the smart white flag of the Clean still flew.

He returned his gaze to the caravanserai, where one of the great Cartel oil reservoirs burned, while the other two still stood firm, being washed down with water pumped from a salvaged fire truck, keeping them from exploding. The situation was tenuous, but not lost.

"Is there enough light?" he called out, in an unshaken voice, to one of his signalmen. A nod confirmed that there was enough dawn light to begin sending signals with their flags, enough light to be sure the beleaguered defenders still holding out would receive their message.

"Alert the palace that we are preparing to attack," he said simply. With a flutter of flags the message was sent.

For the next half hour Shubazang and the others watched the Cartel army setting up positions around the city. As dawn turned to morning, flags were waved and General Rhylor's greasy black trucks began to move in an encircling maneuver, ready to completely surround the city and bombard it from different directions. Their guns were relatively small by the standards of the world's pre-Fall armies, but even small infantry "thud guns", for a prolonged period, had the potential to reduce Tucumcari to embers.

Shubazang reluctantly passed his scoped laser rifle to Rider who also took a long look. Valero and Tank lay nearby, on the other side of a dune, watching the battle a mile away with mixed thoughts and feelings. Ludd, Gale and Euryale waited out of sight, listening to the others talk.

"Looks bad," Valero started. "They're trapped between the Clean... *and* the Cartel."

Tank squinted as he looked. "We've g-got to get in there and, and, and h-help!"

"Are you insane?" Valero shouted, gesturing to the smoke and flames visible over the walls. "What's the point in going in there now?"

"They n-need me! " Tank said desperately.

"Why do you want to fight so badly?" Shubazang asked suddenly, trying to reason with Tank as if the dumb giant spoke for the entire population of the wasteland. "Why does everyone want to destroy the Clean and Cartel? Their oil burns in a thousand villages. The glow of the corium they buy from the miners of Vegas is what holds back the night, and keeps the monsters in it at bay. Who'll light the desert when they're gone? Civilization is just a thing, a tool and not in and of itself evil. Why not try change from within, or hell, just embrace what's coming?"

It was quiet for a moment, as they watched trucks rumble past a few hundred yards away, each of them hunkering down to remain unseen.

Despite what Shubazang said, Tank thought of Karos, Ridaya, Kseniya, Uncle Sam, the others. If they were going to die, he wanted to die with them. Anything but see the flags of the Clean and Cartel still standing when tomorrow's dawn came to the wasteland. To everyone's surprise Tank got up and began to run, almost slipping down the dune as his clumsy body moved.

"What are you doing?" Valero called after him.

"Where's he going?" Shubazang snapped, grabbing his rifle back. Rider went to chase, but stopped.

"*Tank, you idiot!*"

Tank kept running, kicking up dust as he sprinted straight towards a gap in the damaged city walls. A troop truck trailing an artillery piece raced by a hundred yards away, but none of the soldiers on board seemed to notice, so intent were they on getting to their designated position for the coming bombardment.

Gale saw this and stood up suddenly. Euryale watched curiously as Gale darted off over the dune and after Tank. Ludd reached to stop her but fell on his face. A moment later Gale had slipped out after the giant, and was now only a dozen yards behind him.

"Shit!" Rider cursed, and got up and followed after her.

Valero shook his head but felt drawn by the momentum. *War*, it always returned to war. Live by war, grow strong by it, and soon you find you can never turn away from it. Try, and it will only hound you, until it has caught up to you and dragged you (kicking and screaming if it must) back into its fold. If his lot was to always be a warrior and a killer, never to know peace, then the only choice he had in the matter was *which* war to fight. After all this time killing and surviving, evading the inevitable truth of his existence, here was finally a war worth fighting. Redemption. This was his chance. Valero ran after them as well.

Shubazang rose and looked at Ludd, feeble and weak, then back at Euryale. "Stay here with the old man. I'm going." He grabbed the satchel that contained everyone's ammunition, taking it with him.

The five of them raced across no-man's land towards the city. Another truck drove past, so near to Gale and Tank that the helmeted Cartel men on board turned and watched them as they rumbled on, seeming disinterested in just two stragglers.

Gale kept running, closing the distance between herself and Tank as her sprightly feet carried her. She knew the others were following close behind - so far there hadn't been any trouble.

Suddenly someone opened fire. Automatic gunfire cracked from someone on the last truck, some infantryman taking pot-shots at what he assumed were fleeing "rebels". Puffs of sand shot up into the air as bullets landed all around Tank's feet, but like a juggernaut he continued on, unable and unwilling to stop.

More gunfire, just a little more distant, as unidentified combatants on the city walls took opportunistic fire at her and the others, not knowing if they were friend or foe. Gale heard shots whiz over her head, sounding like angry hornets dive-bombing her. She instinctively sunk low, but she continued running as fast as she could.

Tank felt his temples pounding, his blood racing. The city walls were close, great white ramparts that spread in both directions; he had almost cleared the full mile between where they'd lain in hiding and the looming walls. There was a hole in the clay rampart near the base where a recoilless rifle round had strayed and blown a gap. Rubble littered the sand just outside the hole. He had to get there before the gunfire finally found its mark.

Shubazang caught up with Gale and the others and went through the hole in the wall, just as another Cartel truck drove dangerously close, its soldiers openly firing off the side of the truck in his direction. He heard the bullets impact the wall around the hole, heard them ricochet off the hard clay, loosing an avalanche of thick clay dust. Rider

Burning Lands

and Gale coughed as it swirled in the air, but Tank pushed on, emerging from the other side of the hole and into the battle zone that was the city beyond.

Bodies lay everywhere, flipped to and fro by the recoilless rifle's high explosive rounds. Fires burned, and what animals were left alive now, wandered aimlessly through the streets; chickens scattered, a goat ran past, and a cow aimlessly lingered near an abandoned shed, not knowing what to do.

Tank looked and listened. He heard gunfire and shouts echoing through the streets in one direction. He immediately ran that way, leaving a winded Gale, Rider, Valero and Shubazang behind.

"Tank!" Valero and Gale called.

"No, let him go!" Rider said, taking Gale's arm. "If he wants to join his comrades, let him." He thought of Tank, his retardation, his short life. Maybe this was best. "We've got to get to the palace, right?"

Valero must have been thinking the same things, but instead of staying with them he got up and ran after Tank.

Gale almost seemed surprised as Valero took off into the smoke, but said nothing. Now there were only three of them.

Shubazang kept his eye on them both. "Alright, I'm with you two. To the palace?"

Rider ground his teeth, looking from Gale to Shubazang, then back again. They were both so young. He didn't feel particularly confident with them at his side, even though by now he should know better.

"Okay," he sighed, "let's go."

"Wait," Shubazang interrupted. "You're going to need this." He reached into his pack and started handing Gale ammo for their guns. Gale looked at him, then smiled, passing clips on to Rider before reloading her own weapon.

Artillery fire crashed down on the building tops like explosive rain. Fragments of hot steel and broken stone showered the spaces between buildings, cutting down anyone out in the open. Dead bodies, of rebels, city guardsmen and innocent civilians and animals, cluttered the streets. The smell of burned flesh was a pall lingering through the smoky air.

Karos hadn't counted on the ruthlessness of the Cartel, their willingness to render the city into ruin to rout the rebels from their doorstep. He'd imagined the battle would be hard fought but, on taking the city, the enemy would realize they had lost and retreat, writing Tucumcari off. Had it gone as planned, they would have celebrated their freedom on the first night.

Now his naivety felt like foolishness. He was horrified by the idea of so many men and women listening to him, believing him, only to be brought here to their deaths. Their blood, and the blood of the citizens of the city who had died in the crossfire, was on his hands.

Another shell exploded nearby. Rocks broken in two fell from up high, smashing into dozens of shards, sending chalky dust billowing around him. Bits of fire licked his face and back, but he felt no burns. A fragment of glowing red shrapnel bit him in the elbow but it felt like a pin-prick. The deafening blast was muffled as his mind retreated into a shell-shocked hole.

"*Ridaya is dead!*" came the booming voice of Uncle Sam, running over to the stunned Karos who stood, senseless, even as the men and women with him ran for cover or to the aid of their wounded comrades. There were several dozen of them, congregating around Karos, terrified, not knowing if they would die this day or if they would ever see the noble vision of "freedom for all" come to be.

Uncle Sam saw Karos, saw his eyes, saw him bleeding. He was injured himself, but the blood shed for this fight actually invigorated him. He was followed by a wounded and limping Boren, two other members of his personal guard, on foot and some thirty ragged barbarians and tribesmen who still had some fight left in them.

The words sunk in. Karos turned and looked at Uncle Sam and blinked. "Dead? And her sisters?"

"Kseniya has risen to lead the rest. Last I heard they were fighting to get people out of the city, but their numbers are thinning."

Another ear-piercing whistle shrieked in the sky. Some of the barbarians looked up momentarily, wondering from where the sound came. An explosion engulfed part of the street, creating a small crater and drilling the witless men with thorny bits of twisted, hot steel. Bodies were holed; others torn apart.

Karos' men and Uncle Sam's warriors scrambled for cover but soon there wouldn't be much rubble left in this quarter to hide behind. Nearby alleys lit up with a glow; Cartel engineers were coming, sweeping the streets with liquid fire.

Uncle Sam's eyes were wild with excitement, the thrill of a good fight. The odds were against them, things had gone horribly wrong and the enemy had turned the momentum entirely around. But as long as he still had one good arm he could fight, and until there was no fight left, the cause would not be lost.

"Continue the attack, my boys!" he shouted over the din of raining artillery. "I don't know how the enemy got so many guns, but we've got swords a-plenty for 'em and we'll answer every one of theirs with one of ours!"

The ensuing hurrah from his men was genuine, but the sound of their voices was weak. There weren't too many men left to be swept up by the example of Uncle Sam's steadfast courage, but the great chief seemed confident they could carry on through hell or high water on spirits alone.

Two men in heavy rusted armor turned the corner, just forty feet away, two Cartel engineers with rubber gas masks and flamethrowers. One spotted the gathering of rebels but, instead of pointing them out, simply aimed his nozzle in their direction and began hosing the enemy warriors with a jet of napalm, the legendary "dragon's breath".

Uncle Sam lifted his weapon and began to charge up the alley, screaming as he went. His men ran with him, past the burning dead. Sheer weight of numbers would carry them through the sheets of flame being poured down the street; the two "dragon warriors", as formidable as they were, could be overcome.

Karos' men got up and began charging as well, brandishing their pathetic hodge-podge of axes, clubs, spears and muskets, using the latter as bludgeons now that they had exhausted their supply of black powder ammunition. Karos watched them go, then his feet began moving on their own, until he realized he too was being swept down the street and into close-pitched, hand-to-hand combat with the enemy.

Burning Lands

Rider led the way through the abandoned streets. They had to find a way up to the palace tier, while at the same time avoid the Cartel soldiers that would almost certainly be descending from the top level of the city now that the rebel army was in chaos. High-explosive rounds were dropping in from above at complete random, making the crossing of every street a potentially fateful decision.

Smoke obscured all and the hellish glow from the fires turned everything in the lower part of the city red, or at least gave it a touch of orange color to remind one that the fires weren't far away. The streets were swept by a quiet gloom; everyone was either dead or had fled, leaving only the sounds of distant fighting, the crackle of flames and the hiss of smoke billowing up off of charred rooftops.

"The Brotherhood is up to something here," Rider said quietly, revealing to Gale that he'd been pondering about it the whole time they'd been in the city. "They're up to something in Little Vegas, and they're up to something here."

She said nothing to hint she believed him or not, but he felt compelled to explain his hunch anyway.

"I thought maybe at first it was all the corium underground, the radiation in the rock, that they wanted to get at. But maybe their little operation in Little Vegas was a cover for something else. A watch post. An observation station. To watch what's going on in the wasteland, the deserts east of the mountains. But what... what're they watching *for?* A *sign?*"

Gale thought of the stormy barrens of the Burning Lands, a churning, bubbling cauldron filled with unseen mysteries. It held the key to her past, but also to the Brotherhood's future.

"I don't trust them, Gale," Rider continued. "They're not here to see Karos liberate these people from tyranny. I think they want the wasteland weak for when it comes time for them to reveal themselves." Rider might be onto something there, she thought, but even with her senses she wasn't sure.

"We've got to watch out," he said quietly again, "We've got to be careful. When this is all over, we'd better be ready to fend for ourselves, Gale..."

Despite being psychic she found herself taken by surprise with Rider's choice of words. He *assumed* she'd go with him. Would she? But the fact that being together seemed "right" to *him* startled her. Pleasantly.

"This land won't ever be the same..." he finished, just as Shubazang caught up to them.

Rider could be right. But she knew something malevolent *did* dwell in the Burning Lands, as the Brotherhood said, something inseparably tied to her origins, something for which she felt partly responsible, and drawn to confront. The Brotherhood might indeed have designs on the Far Desert once the power of the foreign invaders crumbled, but whatever it was, it would wait at least for her to travel there and come face-to-face with the remnants of her past.

Rider peeked around the corner, oblivious to her thoughts. Shubazang approached, glass shards crumbling under his heavy boots. He looked at Gale for a moment then, passing by her, went over to Rider.

The two of them peered out and saw a smoky square, many dead bodies, a fog of smoke and a steady snowfall of red embers and ash raining down from other districts. Shubazang saw among the bodies and debris the remains of a small machine of tubes, filters and pipes. By the twisted black wreck he saw the corpse of the withered inventor, his features (aged beyond their years) now still and unmoving. No salesman's pitch came from his blood-stained lips; the creator of the "miracle machine" was now dead, and with him his ideas and genius were gone from this world.

War would erase everything that man created; like sand castles built up and then swept away by the tide, man was destined to think, create, and imagine better things, but his own destructive nature was fated to return to wash all the progress away. All that would be left each time would be the misery of knowing what he had lost, forever lamenting as a result of his unshakable addiction to violence.

Shubazang kept his thoughts to himself; instead he decided to comment on what he'd overheard between Rider and Gale.

"So you think the Brotherhood is scheming to use your little alliance, then do away with it once it has what it wants?"

Shubazang had never worked with, for, or against the Brotherhood in his short "career" as a mercenary, but like any seasoned traveler he had heard the tales, knew the rumors. The "cult that controlled the deadlands across the mountains", the legendary New Church of the wasteland, the beacon of hope for all mutantkind. He'd heard the stories. But if they were to be the saviors of the dying human race, where were they now, why hadn't they unleashed their powers to *help* this land? Generations had lived and died in squalor, without hope. Who were they to promise it now, in this dark age?

Or was it simply a matter of timing? Were they like all religions that had come before, obsessed with the magic of numbers, waiting for a specific date, some apocalyptic time predicted long ago, in which to reveal themselves? And if so, would he be so fortunate to be alive in the decade they chose to visit their vision on the rest of the miserable species?

The idea that the Brotherhood harbored a secret evil, some dark design for the wasteland, suited his pessimistic view better. He was more comfortable imagining their "vision" was a smokescreen for conquest; he was wary of any notion that someone, anyone, could ever change the way things were for the better.

"No, kid," said Rider. "I didn't say that." But Rider himself didn't seem too convinced either. Like Shubazang, he was a man who had no faith in religions, cults nor the promises of preachers, no matter how zealous. Mistrust of the Brotherhood loomed in the back of his mind.

"We'll just have to find out," Gale started, "because once this war is settled I'm afraid there's not going to be a whole lot left to stop them either way."

Rider just turned away, readied his gun and began leading them eastwards, past burning bodies and buildings towards the vague shape of the mandarin's palace on the topmost tier of the city.

Ludd stared at his silent companion, looking Euryale up and down before finally giving a dissatisfied snort. Choosing to ignore the only *vaguely* human-like contraption, he tore into his pack to retrieve a delicate pink parasol and extended the shade to its full width to protect his head from the bright sun. With his free hand he put his pack down on the ground, kicked it once or twice to soften it up, and then sat his aging bones down upon it.

"I guess we wait then," he said with a prolonged, tired groan.

Euryale watched the little man with interest, but as always said nothing. Instead the android turned back to the sounds of fighting in the distance.

Ludd pulled out a wrinkled bit of newspaper from his sack and unfolded it, turning to his reading. "Says here," he read aloud, "that bioengineering giant 'Zoogenic Corp' successfully spliced the genes of a human and an animal last week... And here it says a new dome city just opened up in the state of Missouri. A city of the future, with the capacity for a hundred thousand households. Fully protected from the elements, with UV dome shielding, one-hundred percent guaranteed to keep out those harmful rays..."

"... and here, in the gossip section, it says the president's daughter has been kidnapped by punk-rockers! Can you imagine that?"

Though the sounds of war were clearly in the background, the old man went back to his paper as if nothing was amiss.

Covered in blood and the oily soot that came off the charred bodies of his followers, Uncle Sam nonetheless continued to fight, swirling his axe around and breaking it off the armor of one of the Cartel engineers. Though his weapon was shattered, without hesitating he grappled the surprised soldier in the long gray trench coat, drew the long dagger from its sheath at the man's side, and plunged it up under his breastplate, into his guts, twisting the blade once it reached its limit inside the man.

Aware that the other engineer would turn and torch him as soon as he finished with Karos and his men, Uncle Sam tried to keep the engineers' body against him, as if to create a shield. But as he turned to face the fiery blast of another "dragon warrior", he was suddenly faced with an empty street; empty except for the few surviving men of Karos' cell, Karos himself and a handful of his own brave fighters. The dragon warriors were dead.

"Ah ha! They *can* be killed!" Uncle Sam laughed, holding up the dagger as it dripped, awash with blood.

As he held the weapon up, the surviving men gathered, weary but alive. Karos looked exhausted, his face smudged with ash and sweat, but he looked revived by the small victory they had just won. And others were gathering as well, drawn by the sounds of combat and by Uncle Sam's rumbling voice, meek faces from the darkness and the smoke, more survivors of their shattered army. He saw boys and girls of Karos' movement, tribesmen and even a few of Ridaya's desert sisters. From a smoky side street came Tank, who grinned when he saw Karos was still alive. Behind him came the ex-raider Valero, whose unexpected presence there began to gather the remaining miscreants who had escaped the city prisons with him.

Uncle Sam looked as some fifty men came together in the street, looking once more to their general for guidance.

Drifts of black smoke blew past the citadel atop the uppermost tier. The recoilless rifle pummeled away at other rebel forces in the city, sounding like a master smith's hammer beating out steel.

A clever gleam sparkled in Uncle Sam's eye.

"Come, my boys!" he shouted, having lost none of his voice. "To the top tier of this blasted city! We'll assault their walls, create a human ladder if we have to, and take that damned hell-cannon for ourselves!" The men cheered, and like a boy swept up onto the shoulders of his schoolyard friends, Uncle Sam led the way with a carefree laugh.

A half dozen men and women in long green cloaks lay dead on the tunnel floor or slumped against its walls. These were Karos' agents, who had attempted to infiltrate the tunnels beneath the palace in the early stages of the attack. They had apparently been repulsed; many of them were horribly burned and scorched, suggesting they must have come across "dragon warriors" in the dark passages beneath the citadel. The horror they must have faced on seeing the pressing darkness light up with gushers of flame, enveloping their comrades before them, with nowhere to go...

Kseniya looked into the yawning tunnel entrance and hesitated. A few other women were at her side, all of them dusted with soot and bleeding from two or three minor injuries. The fighting had been intense all day, but now it seemed the enemy would simply pulverize the city to get rid of the rebels. They had almost toppled the Clean; but now the Cartel had taken over and was forming a ring around the city; there was no escape.

Kseniya knew that this tunnel and others like it riddled the rock beneath Tucumcari's top tier, each a secret passage or sally port that led higher up into the mountain. Karos and the rebels had expected to use them to seize the palace and mandarin Han early in the rebellion, but the fighting had been too intense. Even with mystics on their side chance still had its part to play, and they had lost the gamble.

In a small, selfish way she was thankful she didn't know these men, whose bodies were now shriveled up and black, covered in enormous welts and oozing burns. The tragedy was only blunted by her inability to put names to these faces.

"We need to link up with others," Kseniya said, but the other sisters seemed too shaken to move. She looked back, and seeing their faces, understood.

Ridaya was dead, and with her the strength and direction of the desert sisterhood was broken. How could they face the new world alone, without her to guide them? To all of the sisters there had always been Ridaya, her face and her voice, leading them, nurturing them, chastising them, teaching them to rise above their hatred and believe in themselves. From now on her voice would no longer be there, whether admonishing them to fight for themselves or shouting at them in anger, and it was sorely missed. Kseniya could see that in the eyes of the other women, in their tightly-drawn lips, in the contagious silence that infected all of them. Everything now seemed unpredictable, the only thing certain being that they would now have to find their own way through the dark future without her.

Kseniya looked at the tunnel again. "We have to continue what we came here for. The mandarin is holed up in the palace; if we can find him, take him, the enemy may falter."

The idea of attacking the citadel, just the handful of them, seemed daunting, impossible. But they said nothing, and prepared to follow her.

As Kseniya moved to enter the dark gap that marked the entrance to the tunnel, her sisters heard a noise from the street behind them and as one they turned. They immediately readied their weapons as a small party of three appeared on the street behind them; Shubazang, Rider and Gale emerged from the shadows and into sight.

Burning Lands 329

Kseniya looked back and instantly recognized Gale despite her new attire... and the man standing beside her. Like her sisters, she drew her scimitar and moved forward to make her intentions clear.

"No!" Gale shouted, moving in front of Rider while holding her hands up in front of her. "Stop, Kseniya! *Stop!*"

Shubazang and Rider stood defensively, ready to fight if need be. Rider stared off at Kseniya, wind tugging at his flapping duster. He lowered his weapon.

But Kseniya's eyes burned with anger. "Step away from him, Gale!"

"No, Kseniya, he's here to help."

A small artillery round exploded not a hundred feet away. The blast caused everyone to scurry for cover, but soon Kseniya was ready to renew the attack.

"That scav took you from us, he left us for the Clean! He left us to be tortured, Gale! A sister died because of him!"

Gale called out from hiding. "The past can't be changed, Kseniya. We've got to mind the future now. He's here to help us!"

"Stand aside, Gale, I vowed to make him pay!" Rider tensed, but trusted in Gale. He remained still.

"We can't afford to waste time with this," Gale said firmly, emerging from cover just as the women did. "There's something more important we have to tend to, and the tools we need are in Margus' palace. You can help us..."

"Why would I help *him?*" Kseniya said with a sneer, and to all it seemed her face was entirely unsuited for such hatred.

Gale was quiet for a moment. "Because I forgive him for taking me. I forgive him for all that he has done to my life."

An incoming round detonated fifty feet away, a few streets down. Another building collapsed in a cloud of dust.

"Sister," Gale said. "Time is short. Join us and help us." Kseniya's hard stare slowly softened, but she couldn't even regard the man now standing at Gale's side. "You trust him?" she asked, implying that whatever he might do would hereafter be Gale's responsibility.

Gale nodded. "Yes."

Kseniya lingered for a long moment, then walked forward. She was sweaty, bloodied and exhausted. Ignoring Rider, she walked right up to Gale, looking her in the eye. She extended hand out and opened it.

Gale looked at Kseniya's open hand and in her bloody palm she saw the ring she had once exchanged with her young friend, Sarah.

Kseniya had already cried too much this day, so she simply stared with red, dry eyes. She put the ring in Gale's hand and closed the girl's fingers around it. Realizing what it meant to have it returned to her, Gale suddenly found herself speechless.

"If we're going to do this, then we have to go this way," Kseniya said, gathering her composure and motioning to the tunnel. "One of these passages will lead into the palace itself."

"It's sure to be guarded..." Shubazang warned.

"Of course," Kseniya said to the unfamiliar rifleman. "Did you think attacking the palace would be easy?"

Kseniya didn't give Shubazang a chance to voice his disapproval of this entire affair, and instead took a step towards the tunnel. Just then another artillery round from General Rhylor's siege army struck the side of the mountain, this time battering the rock fiercely enough to tear a large chunk free. Those below ran for cover as the rock face plummeted to the earth, kicking up choking clouds of dust as it impacted the street, burying a nearby building in the ensuing rock fall. When the dust cleared everyone was scattered; the tunnel beneath the mountain was completely sealed under tons of broken stone.

Through the dust only coughs answered the crash. "Now what do we do?" Kseniya asked, though few could see her.

"We find another way!" Rider shouted back. "But we'd better go quick, that Cartel general won't stop until he levels the entire city!"

Rider noticed Shubazang under a heap of shattered bricks; he wasn't moving. As he came closer he noticed the boy's shin was pierced with bits of shrapnel, his pant leg torn in places and his boot cut open by twisted bits of metal. Showing a deep wound on his head, Shubazang nonetheless stirred and awoke.

He looked up at Rider and, despite the intense pain in his leg and forehead, forced a grin. "To hell with what I said about the Clean and the Cartel. Fuck oil, fuck corium and fuck civilization! Let's get the sons-of-bitches!"

Rider looked past the wounded youngster to the city skyline, as clouds of dust and smoke drifted past. From here he saw the two remaining oil towers standing over the Cartel caravanserai, each silo gleaming silver as stray beams of sunlight touched their surfaces.

Oil, gasoline, the lifeblood of the Cartel. Their trucks carry it across the desert, they sell it to the same road bandits that prey on other merchant houses, it's their one great commodity. Their armies move across the desert with it fueling their vehicles.

"I think I have an idea," Rider said, getting to his feet. Shubazang pulled himself up and leaned against some rubble, looking to where Rider had been staring.

Rider started off towards the Cartel compound. With her telepathy Gale seemed to understand but didn't have time to explain. She just closed her eyes for a moment, rubbed the tears from her face with her gloves, then ran after him. Without any other plan Kseniya gathered her sisters and followed, too. Shubazang, hobbling along with them, was close behind.

With the momentum of a speeding train Uncle Sam had gathered to his side at least a hundred men from the remnants of his dwindling army. Together they charged through the streets, heading towards the narrowing alleys that led up to the palace walls. A great gatehouse loomed ahead, and already gunmen at the loops were starting to open fire at the rebels as they swept up the street.

"No going back, boys!" Uncle Sam shouted, carried along with the masses. "It's do or die this time!"

Bullets landed amidst the company of men, but those that fell were quickly replaced by others close behind. A monumental portal of reinforced wood confronted them at the end of the street, through which they would have to pass to take the palace. Already musketeers protected within the towers of this new barbican laid down heavy fire on the approaching mob, but by now their blood frenzy would carry them through the gauntlet and into the maw of Hell itself.

Uncle Sam ordered men to revive a machine lying abandoned at the side of the street, a merchant's rickety milk truck covered in a patina of rust, its bed hung like a gypsy's wagon with scores of shiny hubcaps, coils of rope and baskets of unknown goods. A small cage swung from a hook in the cab, in which a canary fluttered helplessly as Karos and another man climbed aboard.

"Open that panel!" Karos shouted to his driver. "Yes, that one! Twist those wires together!"

As they struggled to get the vehicle moving, Karos' mind went back to his Brotherhood friends, the seers who were no doubt watching the battle, watching *him*, from far away. Waiting for success, or at the very least, *waiting for a definitive outcome...*

Pop-pop-pop, as more fire came down the street in waves so regular they could be timed. The men kept rushing forward but now they were backed up by a jittering old milk truck that swerved ahead of them. Uncle Sam leapt onto the back of it with several cheering men. As bullets shot past them, they cried a furious rebel yell while the truck narrowed the distance to the wall.

Karos pointed the way through the smoke as they rumbled ahead. But at that instant he felt a chilling sensation, felt the emotionless clairvoyance of his Brotherhood allies directed specifically at *him*. In that fraction of a second he realized they were watching him not out of concern, but merely with passing fancy, like a curious master peeking in to witness the death of a servant whose usefulness had passed. He realized he had merely been a pawn in their mysterious game, a servant and a tool whose time had now come to an end...

Gunshots pierced the fractured glass of the front window, striking both Karos and his driver in their chests. Blood spray from the fatal injuries plastered the window, but not in time to stop the truck from crashing through the great wooden gate, splintering one door and causing the other to be torn from its hinges and knocked flat. The truck spiraled onto its side, coming to a shuddering halt, spilling the men onboard out into the yard.

An injured Uncle Sam raced to get to his feet, aware that the enemy was all around, but as he stood, dozens of his own men poured through the hole their daring move had made, engaging the defenders on the other side with axes, swords, machetes and empty muskets. It was a brutal melee.

Surveying the scene from safety behind his men, Uncle Sam turned and saw Boren, fighting to get to his feet, already embroiled in the melee. Uncle Sam couldn't get to him, so instead moved to the door to the cab. Tearing the door open and causing it to fall off with a loud "clang", he looked inside to see Karos and his driver, one slumped against the other, lying still and dead. On seeing this, the old warlord gritted his teeth, bringing his dagger up to the level of his heart to salute Karos' lifeless corpse.

"Pull back!" someone among the enemy shouted, and with that order the Cartel soldiers and their few remaining Clean allies began a fighting withdrawal towards a series of archways leading into the palace from the courtyard.

Uncle Sam's eyes were bloodshot and hateful. He turned from Karos, whose gentle face seemed calm and serene even in death, and barked his anger at the retreating enemy.

"Listen, my lads! Let this be the last battle of that great war that wiped out our forefathers!" He glared at the Clean and Cartel soldiers, those mixed-blooded foreigners, and urged his men onwards. "Fight until you can fight no more! No mercy! Kill them all!"

His men were eager to oblige; the battle at the gate had already turned into a vicious slug-fest, his primitive warriors carried by their fury into attacking, rushing and even hurling themselves at their hated enemy. The defenders were appalled by their savagery and retreated in orderly fashion, discharging volleys of musket fire into their ranks before pulling back behind the cover of a wall of scimitars and bayonets.

As the fighting spilled out into another yard beyond the archways, Uncle Sam saw the recoilless rifle at the battlements, its barrel angled down towards the burning city below. Colonel Shin and his men continued to fire the rifle into the lower districts, targeting other pockets of rebel resistance.

From up here, where the wind blew strongly against the ramparts, Uncle Sam could see the city in its entirety, as well as the desert that ringed it on all sides. He saw General Rhylor's army, like a thin black noose encircling Tucumcari, and could see from a great distance the cannons belching smoke as they propelled rounds upwards into the crystal blue sky and back down into the ruins of the city.

"*Heeyah!*" Uncle Sam cried, and barreled into the battle. A surprised Clean guardsman fell to a sweep of his blade, and before the poor fool could hit the ground Uncle Sam had the man's scimitar in hand. Whirling about he threw himself into the enemy, using the scimitar to slash the throat of another and take the arm of yet another. Blood washed him, but the great warrior-chief was in his element.

"Retreat to the inner courtyard!" came another cry, only this time the remaining Cartel and Clean defenders began to run, signaling a disorganized collapse of morale and order. Men ran in every direction, most fleeing to the next line of arches leading to the famous Tucumcari gardens, while others fled for the nearest doorway or even to the walls in an effort to get away from their pursuers. Screaming men were cut down or picked up and thrown from the palace walls to die on the rocks a hundred feet below.

Colonel Shin saw the battle being fought behind him and immediately gave the order for the cannon crew to destroy the recoilless to prevent it from falling into enemy hands. To buy them time, he turned and drew his machine pistol, killing two of Karos' volunteers instantly with a fortuitous burst. A third came running at him with an old wooden baseball bat pierced with railroad spikes; this last menace he eradicated with a shot solidly aimed at the man's chest.

Shin's face was a mask of concentration as he found his targets and quickly dispatched them with a gunfighter's lightning reflexes, but there were just too many of the enemy and too few guardsmen left to defend the cannon's secure little nest high on the palace wall. Before he could fetch a demolition charge, the gunner of the recoilless screamed a short cry as some nameless savage buried a hatchet in the back of his head. An instant later one of the gun crew pulled out a musket and bayoneted the tribesman in the back. It was a tangled melee in which men were wrestling with one another, blades slashed back and forth, and warriors on both sides began to drop like flies.

Forgetting the cannon now that the enemy was all around his position, Shin climbed up out of the sandbagged ring surrounding the gun and looked into the enemy ranks.

He saw no flag, no war banner, only a mob. One of Uncle Sam's men, having killed a Cartel gunman, tore his foe's rifle free and fired it into the air to celebrate his victory. Shin saw the primitive tribesman carrying the weapon and shot him dead.

Tank and Valero reeled around as gunfire once more exploded in the fight for the palace walls. They saw Shin standing there, casually finding his marks and erasing them with cold precision. Angry, Tank tore from the throng of combatants and ran right towards the Colonel, leaving Valero to fend off a trio of Cartel men armed with bayonets.

Shin snapped around and saw Tank coming at him, but it was too late. The giant's sword tore through his stomach and spilled his innards out in a cascade of warm entrails. Shin fell forward and onto his face, sputtering some senseless statement of surprise. But Tank wouldn't even let him have that; with an anguished roar the mutant lifted the blade up, brought it back down again, and took the Colonel's head clean off.

The defenders had fled, leaving the recoilless rifle in place, but the battle was still raging, both here and in the city below. There was no time to lose.

Seeing the recoilless undefended, Uncle Sam shouted "Man that cannon!", directing Valero to take up this ancient device of which none had any knowledge. Valero came over quickly, hastily examining the tools and implements in the firing pit, and then lifted a large round and clumsily slid it into the breech. Uncle Sam watched as Valero struggled for a moment to figure it out, before he turned and gave the warlord a thumbs up sign.

"Now aim that thing at those guns beyond the walls!"

It took him a moment, but Valero found the flywheel and, using it, elevated the barrel so that the rifle bore straight down on General Rhylor's guns out in the surrounding desert.

"Fire it, goddamn you!"

Rider stopped only when he reached the entrance to the Cartel compound, a part of the second tier of the city that was still draped in ugly black smoke. Fires burned in the yard, as sparse crews of Cartel personnel struggled to extinguish the fires of the burning oil trucks that lay capsized near the gate. Only a few gunmen remained, as the rest had fled to other parts of the quarter in the citywide effort to crush the uprising.

"What does he have us doing now?" Kseniya whispered angrily as she and an injured Shubazang caught up to Rider and Gale.

Rider didn't explain, he only gave orders. "When Gale and I go, you follow. You and your warriors tie down the workers in the yard long enough for us to do our work. Boy, you lay down suppressive fire with that ray gun, okay?"

Finishing tying off a makeshift tourniquet, Shubazang nodded once to Rider. Despite his injuries he stumbled over to a nearby abandoned watchtower, grabbing the bars of its rickety ladder to begin the climb to the top.

Rider waited and watched; at his side Gale also scanned for an opportunity.

A small explosion detonated as one of the burning trucks' gas supply caught fire. Men ran from the shadow of the oil reserves to help contain the fire. There was no one in the way.

"Now..." Rider muttered. He and Gale ran through the open gate and into the yard. For a moment they went unnoticed due to the fires, the noise and the shouting of the

Cartel workers in the compound, but as they neared the foot of the huge reservoirs, someone somewhere noticed and gunfire began to erupt across the caravanserai.

From his perch Shubazang saw the gunman immediately, a guard who'd seen Rider and Gale run past and, after shouting vainly for them to stop, finally fired on them. Before he could fire off a second shot, Shubazang pulled the trigger on his laser rifle, hitting the man directly in the center of his chest, boring a hole through his body.

Chaos erupted in the compound as Kseniya and her women charged out, straight into the workers who began to flee as the women warriors closed the distance. The few remaining guards turned their guns on the desert sisters, letting off an uncoordinated volley that hit one of the women and left many more bullets to stray among the metal shacks and barrack houses.

As he and Gale darted among the buildings, Rider saw the large rusted pipes at the foot of each reservoir ahead of him, and at their side the oily pump valve where trucks and scout cars alike would hook their rubber hoses to be refueled. A single Cartel laborer stood there with a fire axe and fireman's helmet on, distracted by the sudden appearance of the desert sisters at their gate.

Rider didn't stop running, he simply lifted his Micro-Uzi and shot the poor soul dead. Gale winced as the surprised worker fell lifeless to the ground, but she knew what she had to do. Ignoring the bloody corpse she ran over to the fuel valve and tried to unlock the cap to release the flow.

Rider kept watch as she worked, his eyes scanning for more guards coming their way. Sure enough some armed men came running towards them, alarmed by the unexpected sight of more saboteurs in the yard, but he was quicker than they. With two brief squeezes of the trigger, in close succession, all four of the enemy were cut down in a flash of fire from the machine pistol's chattering barrel.

"I... can't get it." Gale said angrily, unable to get the rusty fuel cap off the refueling pipe.

"Stand back," Rider said, throwing her the Micro-Uzi before taking up the dead laborer's fire axe. With a mighty swing he brought the axe blade down on the cap from above, breaking it cleanly off the pipe's end.

Clear golden liquid streamed from the pipe and almost engulfed Rider as it went. The vapors stung his eyes and made Gale's nostrils close instinctively.

Gale saw another group of Cartel men coming and, moving cautiously away from the gushing fuel, opened fire. The gun kicked upwards in her hands but by now she was getting used to the tools of war. One of the men dropped dead while the others, sensibly, ran for cover.

Rider moved away quickly as the fuel bled from the enormous reservoir, creating a stinking puddle that was swiftly growing with each passing second. He took back his gun and with Gale at his side, they began to run back towards the gate, firing off sporadic shots to keep the enemy pinned down or to prod them into fleeing their path.

Once they were thirty feet away, Rider looked back and saw the pool of spilled fuel had turned into a river, an oily waterway that began to flow down through the ruts in the earth towards the collapsed tanker trucks. The men fighting the fires were unaware as the fuel made contact with the flames and ignited. Tongues of fire leapt upwards and shot back up the rivers of gasoline, and in a moment the reservoirs themselves were burning.

A moment later there was a deafening explosion powerful enough to rupture the entire reservoir along its welded seam, sending huge sheets of corrugated metal flying in all directions and even arching into the sky. Fragments of what were once steel rivets blew outwards like buckshot, killing those unfortunates standing nearby. But the fire from the explosion was even more catastrophic, riding outwards on an expanding, concussive wave that first dented the neighboring reservoir, then tore it open, causing it to explode as well in a double detonation that could be heard for miles out into the desert.

Men raced for cover as an unexpected blast struck the earth not thirty paces from where General Rhylor stood. One of the artillery pieces brought back from his attacks on the raiders of the east was hit and damaged; it suddenly careened and fell over. The crew abandoned it, fleeing in the opposite direction with cries of surprise.

General Rhylor stood his ground and calmly stared through his binoculars, indifferent to the changing tide of the battle. Black oil smoke filled the sky, but the breeze was strong enough that at times he could see, through gaps in the miasma, momentary glimpses of Trade City in flames.

Even from this distance he could see plainly what was now occurring in the city. The palace was swarming with rebels. They had taken the recoilless rifle and were now turning it on his artillery pieces. The rebels' fire was clumsy and inaccurate, but it was evidence enough that the palace had fallen into enemy hands. Even now the white flags of the Clean were being brought down. He could vaguely see the surrendering defenders being methodically thrown, kicking and screaming, from the walls by the vengeful rebels.

Looking passively through his binoculars, General Rhylor adjusted the lenses and took another look. This time he swept his gaze northwards, to the Cartel caravanserai. It was a smoldering ruin. Through the smoke he could see that *all three* reservoirs of fuel, his merchant house's priceless treasure (which they had been willing to devastate the city to protect) had been destroyed by the ransacking barbarians.

Another recoilless rifle round found its mark by slamming into the side of one of Rhylor's trucks, less than fifty feet away. As it exploded the truck sent out showers of sparks and bits of burning machine parts, which rained down all around the General and his grim-faced staff. None of them budged, despite the hail of fire.

Rhylor took the binoculars away from his eyes as the wind picked up in strength. After a moment he sighed.

"The oil reserve has been destroyed," he said flatly to his officers. "Signal the withdrawal. *This battle is lost.*"

Rhylor's men wordlessly set about their tasks, and soon the Cartel armada would retreat back into the wasteland. To the Cartel, any strategic value this place once held was now gone, now that the fuel cached there was destroyed. They would withdraw to the lands far away from Trade City, to one Cartel-controlled trading hub or another in the west, but now it was high time to write this disastrous venture with the Clean clans off.

Rhylor looked back one last time at the palace. Fires and smoke leapt into the sky. Margus Han was probably dead, and with him the alliance their two people had made for the mutual benefit of each other, for the cause of "civilizing" the wasteland, had come to an ugly but ultimately unsurprising end. The Jia Lang would slip back into savage territory for all he was concerned; let these barbarians destroy all things good, let them burn down what you've built to help them. If they want barbarism, let them have it.

Disgusted, Rhylor walked off and boarded a jeep as it began to pull away, an artillery piece hitched to its back. He, like the rest of the Cartel army, would soon vanish completely in the dust of the unforgiving wasteland.

Euryale's head lifted slightly as the Cartel army began its withdrawal. Ludd woke from his nap as the engines roared and rumbled, and jumped to his feet, folding up his parasol and letting the newspaper get carried away by the wind. He ran up to the top of a nearby dune to get a better look at this historic turn of events.

The city of Tucumcari was burning, but the thunder of the bombardment had stopped. The colors of the Clean and Cartel were stricken from the tops of the mandarin's palace. Instead of harsh law and ruthless order, anarchy reigned. Even now a trickle of refugees fled the city, its former inhabitants escaping the fires and the rampant looting. Looters gorged with goods ran from the wreckage of Tucumcari, vanishing into the wild barrens that surrounded the trade town for miles in every direction.

"Looks as if the rebels have won..." Ludd said with a tone of disbelief. "What a day for freedom! What a day for chaos! What a day for lawlessness and disorder! *Oh, Belshazzar! Belshazzar! Thy glory is past! For vengeance, long slumbering, Overtakes thee at last! Dire slaughter and havoc around thee await! And the hand of the foeman is hard on thy gate!*"

Euryale looked at him, with that same smile, though it now seemed almost quizzical. It was intrigued by the old man's words, which seemed to celebrate the day but almost sounded as if lamenting what had just occurred. Euryale could not comprehend the complexities of the situation.

"Come here, you bucket of bolts!" Ludd shouted with a grandiose sweep of his arm. "And witness the fall of Babylon!"

Euryale walked up and stood at his side, surveying the destruction. Its cold steel eyes looked out upon the scene as an alien witness to the violent obsession that would forever grip the human race.

Ludd laughed an anguished laugh, as if to say "I can't believe they actually did this, the fools!" He slapped one withered hand against his wrinkled brow and shook his head, laughing, closing his eyes and shaking off his astonishment.

Dust fell from the roof of the cavern where Margus, Hamut and a small core of soldiers and household servants waited. Moments later there was another distant thud, and a few loose pieces of stone skittered free from a ledge far up, fell some distance, and landed in one of the freshwater ponds at the bottom of the underground gorge.

The servants cowered, secretly afraid the cavern would collapse all around them. The soldiers waited, listening with great concentration to the sounds of the bombardment. Margus and Hamut listened, too.

Burning Lands 337

The rumble of artillery faded. The rock walls of their chosen tomb were still and quiet. They all stood for minutes, ears finely tuned for any sign of the ongoing battle; but only natural sounds, of the cave and the waters, came to their ears.

"The enemy has surrendered!" someone dared to offer. The others listened more intently. "General Rhylor must have retaken the city!"

Hamut went to the bottom of the great stairs and looked up, but only saw darkness. He heard celebration. Margus, too, heard the muffled clamor and motioned for his bearers to lift him and take him to Hamut's side by the stairs.

"Our garrison cheers!" he said, a smile breaking across his face. "Come on, let's return to the surface and see what we can see."

No gate barred Rider from entering the palace grounds. Behind him came Gale, and with the help of her two remaining sisters, Kseniya assisted Shubazang as the young man limped along.

The fighting continued, it seemed, though the Cartel army had retreated. Tertiary explosions from their sabotage of the caravanserai still rose into the sky as midday approached. The rebels had been here, they had taken the palace and either slaughtered the defenders to the last man, or thrown them from the walls to die on the streets below.

Rider led the way through the eerily empty palace. In the distance they could hear cheers and chanting, the rebel army's primitive survivors celebrating the destruction of the Clean and Cartel alliance, and the sack of the city. They passed countless dead bodies, of uniformed Cartel soldiers, white-clad janissaries and nameless masses of Uncle Sam's followers in a gruesome tangle of flesh, steel and blood. Flies buzzed noisily in the air, settling on deep wounds and open mouths; a palace dog nibbled at a corpse and ran away as they approached.

For Gale it was like walking through a hazy version of reality, passing through this great castle that had been her home (and her prison) these past few years. She recognized the soaring walls, the crystal and glass domes, the corridors of interwoven trees, the meticulously cared-for gardens. But the carnage, the damage wrought by the siege, and the emptiness left by the massacre of its inhabitants, made it seem like an utterly alien place.

From the courtyard and into the palace they went, Kseniya and her sisters keeping an eye out for trouble, while Rider led the way. He didn't know the palace as well as Kseniya or Gale, but he remembered the contents of the armory and with dogged determination would find his way through the maze of passages to his destination.

At each intersection Rider looked cautiously for others; washed in the amber light of its weird windows, there could be ambushers anywhere, soldiers and guardsmen hiding out in isolation in the palace for fear of encountering the rampaging rebels. But his caution went unrewarded, as there was simply no one left to engage them, friend or foe.

Rider sensed that the rebels had gathered *en masse* in the great garden on the other side of the palace, the fabulous jungle of trees, flowers and fountains that surrounded the palace's Hydro Station. They were celebrating something, with wild abandon, but what he couldn't readily tell.

It made for a good distraction however, and Rider knew enough to make use of an opportunity when it came along. So they continued deeper into the palace, remaining quiet, staying vigilant, the sound of their movements masked by the cheering, shouting and song coming from the north side of the complex.

Finally Rider came to the armory, its familiar door still closed. *How different this battle might have been,* he thought to himself, *if only the fools had tapped this great treasure, instead of keeping it buried.*

"The door is locked," Kseniya reminded everyone. "The key is gone."

Gale walked over and touched the metal door.

"Anyone have explosives?" Rider asked.

"Something just as effective," Shubazang said, coming forward. He lifted his rifle, adjusted the dial on the side of its neodymium gas tank, and raised it directly at the door.

"Stand back."

Gale went over to Rider and Kseniya as the boy pulled the trigger and a brilliant beam of red laser light shot from his rifle into the door. Everyone present shielded their eyes from the blinding glow, which bathed the dark hallway in a neon red flash. Instantly a wisp of smoke puffed out from the contact point, and slowly, with a steady hand, Shubazang began to trace a shape on the door, a circle, roughly man-sized. As it swept in this gradual pattern the laser beam sliced cleanly through the metal of the great portal, leaving only a thin glowing line of molten steel behind it wherever it went.

When Shubazang brought the beam back around and completed the circle, the large portion of the door inside the traced circle simply fell out, falling inwards and clanging noisily on the other side. While everyone else stood, staring in wide-eyed awe and wonder at this, an actually-functioning weapon of the Ancients, Shubazang nonchalantly switched the knob off. A great weapon indeed, but its power was his to control.

"Get what you need," he prodded the others.

Gale was the first to move, going to the hole and carefully slipping through. Rider looked at Shubazang and the rifle for a moment, then joined her as well. Kseniya and the others remained, looking down the hall to make sure no one surprised them.

Moments later Rider returned, bundles of plastic and rubber in his arms. He began feeding them through, letting them fall to the ground on the other side.

"Four suits," Rider explained. "And this..." he pushed a small steel box through the hole in the door, a device that had been attached to one of the suits.

"A Geiger counter," Shubazang said, examining the device. "A better one than what I've got. This will definitely be useful."

Tank and Valero stumbled along the edge of the courtyard, past the bodies of fallen comrades and enemies. Both men were silent, surveying the death all around them.

The battle was over. Margus Han was probably dead; he and a small cadre of survivors had been captured as they emerged from hiding, and one by one they were being beheaded by angry savages in the great garden outside the Hydro Station. Even now they heard the ecstatic cheers of the crowds of vengeful, bloodthirsty rebels.

Burning Lands 339

They should also feel overjoyed. The reign of the Clean and the Cartel over the wasteland was at an end. A battle, fought hard and won, left them the victors. Instead Tank felt sullied, dirty. Much blood was on his hands, and despite the righteousness of his own particular cause, to free the enslaved people of Tucumcari, after the deed was done, it felt as if the blood could never be washed away.

As they approached the palace gates Tank looked at the capsized vehicle that had smashed its way through the grand portal. He walked over and, peering through the shattered windscreen, stared into the hollow eyes of Karos' corpse. Flies clustered around his nostrils and eyes. His face was yellowish and pale; blood was beginning to pool where gravity drew it, so that his hands and the lowest part of his face looked bruised and swollen.

Valero watched Tank walk through the devastation like an aimless orphan. He himself should have felt some kind of satisfaction now that the Clean were humbled; these men that had chased him and his kind from Oasis and forced them to live as outcasts for years. Instead he felt simply exhausted, with no sense of heroics nor justice to console him. He only felt weak, drained, his arms tired from the day's butchery.

Both men sensed what was coming. In a matter of hours the dissolving rebel army would tear the city apart for anything that was left, before returning once more to the wild desert, never to return. Already the poor folk who had lived in Trade City under the shelter of the Clean and Cartel had fled, leaving their homes abandoned. They, too, might never return, and even if they did, without a powerful patron they would live in perpetual fear of raiders and others come to claim the carcass of Trade City.

For those who fled, the next few months would see the desert's wild inhabitants preying upon them, until they gradually dispersed to the winds, carrying with them the tragic story of their once-great city and how it fell to barbarians.

Karos' cause seemed lost. But Ridaya, who had died at the hands of her own allies, might know some victory as the remnants of her sisterhood, perhaps led by Kseniya now, would return to the desert and create a life for themselves.

Uncle Sam would have glory for his part, and his people would indeed live free. They had shaken themselves free from the tyranny and oppression of the great merchant houses, but in doing so had also ended any hope of their ever rebuilding from the ashes.

With no coalition left to reconstruct a new world and a new way of life, it came to each man to fend for himself. Today Tank and Valero walked as comrades, but tomorrow... who's to say what different roads they would take?

Shubazang hobbled into view, coming up against an abandoned cart and resting his weight there. He was burdened by a pair of Ancient-era rifles, in addition to his own, which he methodically slung from his shoulders and into the cart with a tired groan.

Valero walked over. "You taking your bounty, kid?"

Shubazang looked momentarily surprised to see Valero there, but grinned weakly. "I figure they owe me. I did bring the girl back as promised. But somehow I don't think the mandarin's good for the money anymore."

Rider, Gale, Kseniya and the others soon appeared as well, carrying the bundled-up suits, Plexiglas helmets and a smattering of their own looted arms.

Rider threw ammunition of the right type to Valero, who gratefully replenished his rifle. Rider handed Tank another Chinese-made automatic rifle, then unslung the last weapon, an enormous TAC-50 rifle, for himself.

"Did you get what you needed?" Valero asked.

"The armory had everything," Rider said, "and more. More than we could hope to carry. More than enough for an army. Whoever finds it will have quite a bit of hardware now that the Clean are gone."

For a moment those present imagined what power they would have with such an arsenal in their hands. Valero thought of arming the survivors and carving his own little kingdom among the sands; after all, life (such as it was) would carry on even if the Clean were now driven from the Far Desert. Tank dreamed of giving the weapons to the people who survived the destruction of the city, so they might defend against the depravations that were sure to follow now that Tucumcari's defenses were destroyed. Surely raiders would come, but with weapons they might fend off the tide of looting and pillaging. Kseniya, for her part, envisioned arming her sisters so they might finally be safe wherever they went, high into the mountains or deep into the southern deserts.

But no one said anything. In the end, one gun apiece seemed enough for now.

"Then I guess you'll be heading out?" Valero asked, implying Gale would have to go without him. Gale looked at him, and of course she saw something different.

They heard faint cheering again.

"*My father...*" Gale muttered suddenly, her eyebrows knit in concentration. She slung the submachine gun over her shoulder and began to run towards the gardens.

"Don't go there, mink!" shouted Valero. "Those are crazed men!"

"Gale!" cried Kseniya.

Tank and Rider immediately took off after her. The others soon followed.

Gale was the first to arrive at the scene being played out in the gardens ringing the Hydro Station; a jungle of painstakingly cared-for trees from the far corners of the globe, nurtured from small seeds brought to these shores by the foreign invaders during the Final War. Rare plants from Arabic deserts, the mountains of China, the barren wastelands of drought-stricken Africa. A botanical collage, a Noah's Ark of preserved flora, now being trampled and decimated by the hundreds of feet in Uncle Sam's celebrating army. History itself was being danced on, and ground into ruin.

Uncle Sam sat in the lap of the great Buddha, using the fountain at the center of the great garden as his throne now that the power of the Clean had been torn down. His men were drunk with wine taken from the stores of the palace, as well as their own foul mash which they'd lugged from their desert homes. Small fires crackled as delicate tapestries depicting the colors of the Clean were burnt in bonfires among the gardens; others jokingly donned the blood-stained armor and helmets of the former defenders, now slain, mocking one another on how they looked in their "uni-forms". A pair of men fought over Gale's wooden *pipa*, until the argument broke down into a slugging match, the *pipa* quickly forgotten, broken and discarded.

Uncle Sam laughed, lifting his flagon up to salute his raucous men. The old warlord was covered in small wounds, but he beamed, his eyes twinkling with joy over the hard-won victory they had wrested from the jaws of certain defeat that day.

Burning Lands

At Uncle Sam's feet lay the bodies of a half dozen Cartel and Clean soldiers bound by their wrists with twine. Each man had been decapitated, his head placed on one of two pikes standing on either side of the warlord's makeshift throne. A bloody and bandaged Boren stood wordlessly at his master's side, proudly holding aloft the trophies for all to see. He was still except for the waving of his hand every few moments to drive away the flies that were gathering about the dead.

The crowd roared and began to part as more captives were brought to the warlord's feet.

Gale drew in a sudden breath as she spotted Margus at the head of these captives, bound and pushed along like the rest, limping along with the aid of a crutch. She immediately bullied her way into the throng of cheering warriors, pushing through men almost twice as broad as she, moving towards the front of the mass. Rider and Tank followed, adding their considerable weight and strength, attempting to clear a path.

Uncle Sam took a sloppy drink from his flagon, then regarded the new captives. He immediately recognized Margus, despite the wounds and the dirt staining his aged face. While his men bowed their heads in fear, Margus kept his head high despite the slurs and abuses thrown his way; he stared straight ahead and into the eyes of the tribal king who'd only just defeated him.

"So the destruction of your clan is complete," Uncle Sam said with a satisfied grin. "Here you are, oh mighty mandarin, brought before me... humbled."

"Our house still stands," said an enraged Hamut, muscling over to Margus' side. *"The scorpion is still dangerous despite having no claws!"*

"You mean the chicken still *panics* despite having no *head!*" Uncle Sam replied with a smile, evoking deafening laughter from his men.

With that there was a cheer as the assembled warriors surged forward. The defiant Hamut was grappled and brought, kicking and struggling, to his knees. Margus attempted to pull him free but was held firmly in place despite his protests. Hamut cried out as someone took him by his curly hair and stretched his neck out. Others had to hold him down as he screamed and panicked. The executioner muscled his way in, but had difficulty. It took three chops to take Hamut's head.

The crowd roared as the gushing remains of Hamut's head were held high above them in the executioner's hand. Margus looked upwards at his friend's dead eyes, sneered, then brought his gaze back to Uncle Sam.

Uncle Sam looked at Margus, attempting to match his level stare. The fierce warlord sat in the throne of Tucumcari, he had an army with him; his nemesis was unarmed and in chains. But Uncle Sam couldn't keep Margus' stare, and looked away.

"Kill him quickly," Uncle Sam said softly, dismissively waving his hand as if he hoped it would dispel Margus, and those others who shared his dream of pacifying the wasteland, forever from the world.

"NO!" came a single cry, and Gale finally pushed through the masses and to the edge. Men with arms moved to stop her, but she pointed her weapon directly at the warlord, causing them to pause.

The goodness she remembered in this king was still there, but now it was polluted by greed and the lingering adrenaline that followed any pitched battle. He wasn't thinking clearly, but she had to get through to him.

Rider was at her side, his rifle sweeping to Boren and the other warriors standing near the fountain. Tank came over as well, but instead of brandishing his weapon he looked to the assembly with tired eyes.

"Let these men be," she demanded of Uncle Sam, gathering together the sum of her inner resolve.

Despite conjuring up all her strength, the bearded chief balked. "Who is this wench that makes demands of a king?" he laughed. His men laughed too. But her eyes were fierce, and those nearby, those who could see them, found themselves stepping out of her way.

"Gale Han," she said, "and you *will* listen to my words." Her tone, her commands, were nothing short of insulting. The host fell silent.

Margus had been staring at her this whole time, ever since she emerged from the crowd close to his side. He suddenly felt weak. Ashamed and emasculated. For years this girl had been his tool, a thing to be manipulated and programmed for his advantage. When she'd gone missing he'd sent men to find her and collect her, like an object stolen from him, nothing more. Yet now she spoke on his behalf... what reason did she have to return to him like this, and save his life? Gale saw Margus watching her but said nothing.

Uncle Sam's nostrils flared, and he looked down at Gale. "Stand back, girl, there's men's work that needs to be done. I will guarantee your safety, as a princess of royal blood, but your father must pay for all that he has done."

For some reason there was only a low whisper among his men, not the ribald cheer he'd expected. Sensing the growing apprehension of the tribesmen, Gale took another step forward, looking even more defiant. To her relief, Kseniya emerged from the crowd and stood at her side, leveling her own angry stare at the barbarian chief.

"His crimes are many," Uncle Sam explained, as much to the two women as his own men. "He would destroy our way of life! Subjugate us! Erase the legacy of our forefathers and re-write history."

"He can do that no longer," Kseniya said solemnly.

"You've seen to that," Gale added, "by toppling these walls and sacking this city. The Clean are shattered, and the Cartel has fled, abandoning their alliance. Margus is just a man, now. Let him be, let him return to the verge of the grasslands and to his people. The Clean aren't a threat to you, your kin or this land anymore."

Uncle Sam considered Gale's words for a moment but leaned forward and continued.

"It's not as easy as that, child. There is blood to be avenged. Margus murdered my people."

"No," she said, "He did not."

A murmur carried through the crowd, of disbelief, shock and sudden curiosity. *Who then?* they seemed to ask. In the still silence it seemed even the statue of the Buddha was listening for her next words.

"But we've seen who *did*," she continued.

Uncle Sam looked at her, lips drawn tight. He didn't seem dubious, he saw the power in her eyes, he wisely recognized she might know more than he. "Who then?"

Gale exhaled deeply and looked to Rider, just to know he was there. He looked back, stared into her eyes, then nodded. *I am here, no matter what.*

"The Remnant. *My* people."

"*Your* people? Are you not the child of Margus Han?" Uncle Sam countered.

"No, I was an orphan, found by these men in the deserts not far from Oasis," she said, gesturing to Rider and Tank. Kseniya nodded to confirm what she said was true.

"The Remnant is the *real* danger to your people and your way of life. Not like the Han, who work to rebuild a civilization, even a flawed one. Not the encroachment of their ways, which only hope to bring peace and unity, even if they are misguided. My people will kill all of you, they won't stop. I don't remember now, it has been so long, but they are filled with a cold, alien drive to retake the land and cleanse it. You are animals to them, a virus in a dish, nothing more. And this earth, they believe, is theirs to reclaim."

"I've seen them, too," Valero called, approaching through the crowds. Men moved out of his way, warriors admiring his wounds and brands and sensing a cold-hearted killer in their midst. "Giants in armor, eyes like cold blue stars, bearing the weapons of the Ancients. We saw them destroy an entire city of the Far Traders and drag away the dead like butchers hauling meat."

The revelation that one of the legendary Far Trader "cities" had been destroyed caused men all over the assembly to gasp and others to whisper. Uncle Sam sat back and glared at Valero, wondering where his loyalties truly were. Why should *he* be trusted?

"I don't believe you..." Uncle Sam said simply.

"Believe it," Gale replied impatiently. "Heed our warning. I come on a mission for the Brotherhood, those to whom even Karos swore allegiance. Why won't you listen?"

Now, more than ever, the young woman played the role of sibyl expertly. The barbarian king looked... nervous. He gripped his beard, and with some agitation ran his fingers through its wild curls. Then he spoke again.

"If what you say is true," he said cautiously, "if you are to be believed... What then, can be done?"

"Return to your people, and prepare for the storm that is brewing just beyond the horizon. The Remnant has only just now awakened after another long sleep; soon they will return to finish what they've begun."

Stirred by her words, there was some bickering and arguing among the tribesmen.

"No," Uncle Sam said. "Karos said nothing of an enemy from the Burning Lands! Surely he would have known; he had the Brotherhood's ear!"

"The Brotherhood's designs on this wasteland aren't clear to anyone," Gale countered. "But what I know is this: I have always been at the center of their plans. They freed this albino from captivity knowing he would return to Trade City for revenge against the Han. They let Rider into this palace knowing he would stumble into me and try to take me. And when the time came they sent men after us to bring me back to them. It is me, and whatever dwells in the Burning Lands, that they care about. They do not support your war, or your cause. In fact they have very little interest in it."

"They gave us the power to win this war," Uncle Sam reminded her.

"They did nothing," Gale said, almost wanting to laugh. "They directed Karos and Ridaya, two people of great ambition, knowing that they would do anything to see their people free. They saw a sandstorm, and led you to it. They guided you here, into direct confrontation with the Clean and the Cartel, so that battle would be inevitable."

Margus looked at her, his "daughter", his mind already racing ahead to the ultimate question - *why?* She saw him staring and looked directly into his eyes.

"The Burning Lands lie at the center of their prophecies, their vision that from the ashes will spring a new world with their mutant hierarchy reigning over the survivors. I am some kind of 'key' to making that prophecy come true; I'm linked, somehow, to whatever lives there. I'm just a tool to them, bait to bring out whatever vile tenant currently dwells in that place, some violent thing that needs to be pacified. You... you were meant to wipe one another out, just like you have. The Clean are gone. The Cartel has fled. And you, Uncle Sam, have only a hundred or so left of your great army. The slate has been cleared. The desert is ready for new masters."

Uncle Sam rose suddenly, knocking his flagon over. He looked angry, his fierce face turning red, his lips sneering. He turned to Boren and his guards and gave them the signal to fetch their horses.

"No, we leave now, we prepare for their coming. We've bled today, and we'll bleed again if we have to. Send men to the Caves of Sorrow and strike those accursed seers down. We'll avenge this trickery!"

A great commotion arose as the chieftain gave his orders, as men picked up the weapons they had put down for their celebration, as they headed out to spill blood once more.

"No," Gale said over the clamor. "Don't do it! Don't you see? There's an even greater danger out there and we've got to be ready to fight it!"

"And the Brotherhood?" Uncle Sam shot back.

Gale stared at him, herself wondering what the future might bring. But even she couldn't see that far ahead. "We'll just have to wait and see if their religion brings more good than evil... or if they shuffle off to become just another disappointment in the long line of human history."

People were listening now. They didn't see a woman, or a girl, they saw a prophetess.

"But right now there is a battle still to be won," she reminded them, "against a people I haven't seen in years, against an entity they say is waiting for *me*. I must go to meet them. If victory against them can be achieved, I will achieve it. For now I say return to your people, Uncle Sam, and get ready in case I fail. Either way, we all stand at the dawn of a new age."

The dreams and aspirations of humanity's survivors had proven corruptible and fallible; Tucumcari was in ruins, and with the fall of its walls and the collapse of its towers the idea of a secular civilization ever returning seemed to vanish with it. There was only one hope left, and it lay ahead. In the Burning Lands. To Gale, at least, it was time to surrender to the power of prophecy. Something malevolent stirred there, but if the Brotherhood was to be trusted (and what choice had they now?) then the hope for peace and coexistence in the future meant going there and confronting the dark demons of her past.

Burning Lands

Over the course of several days, a great exodus had taken place after the fall of Trade City, with Uncle Sam leading the survivors of his tribal army back north to wilder lands, to prepare in the event that she and her companions should fail.

The people of Trade City gradually left the smoldering ruins of their city; in a great Diaspora, they fled to the far corners of the known world. Kseniya had left, too, after a tearful farewell, rounding up those sisters who remained alive and those refugees who trusted in them, to see them to safety. As Ridaya had done to those who sought shelter, taking them in and protecting them, so too did Kseniya extend her hand to any survivors of the fall of Trade City, allowing them to join her. Hundreds had left in the company of only a few sisters, striking out northwest towards the looming shape of the Rocky Mountains.

In their absence the ruins of Tucumcari were lonely and silent; hundreds of crows and buzzards floated in the sky, weaving in and out of the smoke that still rose from the charred remains of the city's clay walls and damaged structures. The human element was gone; the crowds that once filled the markets had vanished, leaving empty streets. The lines of scavs and miscreants gathered at the gates were absent, leaving behind their footprints and those of their strange beasts of burden.

On the outskirts of town Gale faced off with Margus, the man who was once her father. Margus stood, humbled and injured, but his face was at peace. He returned her unflinching, owl-like gaze, and with it she could sense the slow dismantling of his pride and the beginnings of an appreciation that the world was not a controllable, conquerable thing. Not in this age, not in *any* age.

"You're going now to stop the evil that's always been there," he stated.

Shubazang, who was standing nearby, shifted his weight. Margus looked at him.

"I suppose I was right to hire you after all, young man. In the end you've recovered Gale *and* uncovered who was behind the attacks in the north."

Whether it had been an attempt at humor or not, Gale and Shubazang could only stare. Margus turned, the wind blowing against his weathered face, as he sighed in defeat.

"I just hope that it's not too late, for everyone's sake. You know we... we're not that much different. You see different features in our faces, you hear differences in our voices, but we are as much natives of this land as you are. If what you say is true, if this thing, this 'Remnant', cannot be quelled, we will suffer alongside Uncle Sam's people, our death meted out just as equally."

Gale recognized this was true; Margus didn't need to convince her. All of the people of this twisted Earth were in danger, not just the tribal folk who had seen their brothers and kin vanish near the edge of the Burning Lands.

Margus continued, shaking his head. "The Brotherhood... I never imagined those passive creatures living among us had such grand aims. While we busied ourselves building our civilization they've waited, knowing it would crumble..."

"Let that be a lesson..." he started, but stopped, realizing he was taking on a preaching air.

"You've saved my life," Margus said solemnly to Gale, changing the subject. "For that I am grateful, child. You were not born from my blood, but you will always be my daughter..."

He looked at her, but she was silent. She could feel his agony at having lost his nephew, Alin. He was not a humane man, and his loss was colored by the fact that he always saw Alin as a tool, not a real "heir", but it was, to Margus, a tragedy nonetheless, and it scarred him just as badly as a loving father having lost a son.

"... if you want."

Gale stepped forward and looked up into the old man's eyes. He was as broken and humiliated as a callous man like him could be. She couldn't smile at him, or bring herself to say a kind word, but she nonetheless nodded.

Margus accepted that gesture as sincere and turned to regard Shubazang one last time, before joining the few surviving Clean janissaries Uncle Sam had spared. With their help he was able to get onto his horse, and after looking back one more time at the ruins of their once-great city, they departed to the southeast. As they trotted off, Margus Han nevertheless managed to still seem regal and great, despite his dirty robes and injuries, head held high like a captured monarch being marched off to his royal cell.

The mandarin had been spared, and with the handful of house guards left he would return to the borderlands of the grassy plains of Texas, where other families of the Clean Water Clans still thrived. With the collapse of their alliance, and the desertion of General Rhylor, the influence of the invaders was removed from the Far Desert, though for how long was uncertain, but one thing had been made clear - they were never again welcome in these rough-and-tumble wastelands.

As Margus and the remaining Clean rode off and out of sight, Rider busied himself packing their own horses for the coming expedition. Enough men had died in the sack of Trade City that there were plenty of idle mounts lingering at the edge of the city and he had easily coaxed the skittish beasts together. He secured the four radiation suits as delicately as he could, while also personally gathering provisions from the abandoned and deserted shops along the Trade Market for their journey, such as beans, pemmican and nuts. He also brought along water skins, canteens and even a few milk bottles filled with a speckled gallon of water or two. He collected halazone tablets to purify water, batteries for their lights and Geiger counter, and packed extra ammunition wherever there was room. He considered bringing a separate mule for such things, but ultimately recognized the need for speed. Last came blankets and rope and any other supplies he could think of that they might possibly need where they were going.

Where *were* they going? An unknown pocket of devastation, a hole in the world, where no one went, and from which no one returned.

Tank and Valero, both now armed with rifles and pistols, returned to the site where Gale, Shubazang and Rider waited, carrying the last cartons of ammo for their party's weapons. It had been a long hike from the ruins of the palace, but they were filled with energy. Gale sat down on a rock beside Ludd, not far from where Shubazang also came to rest.

Anxious to kill time until they got going, Gale unconsciously began humming the strange five-note tune she always hummed since she was a child. Ludd sat near her and listened, discreetly, to the sounds she made. It sounded like no tune he had ever studied, nothing past or present; it was neither melodic nor pleasing to hear. Just a jumble of notes strung together. He found it quite odd.

Before he could ask her about it, Valero spoke to Gale:

Burning Lands 347

"So who's going on this little trek?"

Gale looked at him for a moment, an unusually grave expression on her face. Her eyes burrowed into his. It had been a simple question, almost off the cuff, but suddenly he realized that sometime before she had seen him with her precognitive vision. He was part of her story, whether he liked it or not. The realization froze him, because the look in her eyes made it clear that there were dire things in store for him.

"I take it I'm going with you?" he said grimly, as he walked over to one of the horses.

Not understanding, Rider looked surprised when Valero "volunteered". He looked at Gale as if to say "are you crazy?", but she simply watched Valero mount up.

"I'm going as well," Rider said.

"That's two suits," said Ludd. "Three, since Gale is obviously going, too."

"Room for one more," Valero added.

"Count me in," came Shubazang, before anyone could object. "I'm not going to miss a chance at getting my hands on some of that old technology. I can only imagine what else your people have stockpiled all these years...

"... Euryale can go as well," he said casually, getting up and dusting himself off. "If I turn her off, the radiation won't affect her, not like us."

The android turned and crossed its arms, staring back at Gale as if to challenge her to say "no". Instead Gale simply turned and climbed up on one of the horses.

"But I w-want to c-come!" Tank blurted.

"We don't have enough suits," Valero explained.

Rider slid his rifle into a sheath on his mount, then turned to face Tank as well. "We don't even have a suit that would *fit* you." Tank looked devastated that he couldn't join them, but he was at a loss for words.

"Take care of your people," Rider said, clasping him on the arm. "Take a strong horse and catch up to Kseniya. She could use a good gunman where she's going."

Rider looked over at Ludd. "And take the old man with you. He must be good for *something*." Ludd looked up, slightly insulted. Rider got up on his horse.

"N-no," Tank said resolutely. It was enough to make everyone turn. "I... I'm g-going with you."

"But the radiation..." Valero reminded him.

"I-it doesn't m-matter. I-I'm dying a-anyway. L-look at me! Y-you can all s-see it, so don't t-try and pr-pretend any-anymore. M-my face. M-my eyes. T-The way I t-talk. But at least h-here I... I can h-help."

"No," Rider said with surprising firmness. Tank looked at him, his chest rising as he took in a desperate breath. The ogrish mutant seemed ready to fight his old comrade if he had to, if that's what it took to secure a place on the expedition.

Instead, Tank took a less aggressive tone. "T-then l-let us at least g-go with you to t-the edge of t-the B-Burning Lands," he offered. "Y-you might need our h-help... At least until you g-get th-there."

Rider looked at him for a moment, cautiously considering his offer, then looked over at Gale. She seemed to be staring at Tank pensively; her eyes were unblinking as she looked at the giant, her lips drawn so tightly she couldn't speak. When she realized Rider was expecting *her* to make the decision she seemed to snap out of it, then slowly nodded a rigid nod.

Though he had once seen her as little more than a fragile child, Tank suddenly found it hard to be the subject of such a long, uncomfortable stare from Gale. When she finally looked away, closing her eyes to clear her mind, he felt relieved.

"Then we'd better go," Valero said, breaking the silence.

Shubazang and Euryale were already walking off. Shubazang called out over his back. "We'll catch up to you."

CHAPTER 6

Gale had no real plan, other than to re-trace the steps of her life. Here they were, at Trade City - where to go from there but back to Oasis? From there Rider and Tank might be reminded of those years past, and lead her to the "lair" of her long-dead friend, Johnny, whom they had hunted ruthlessly... but from there?

She wasn't sure. The desert was a huge place and the Burning Lands, while only a part of it, were still immense.

Rider, Gale, Tank, Valero and Ludd all rode along the crest of a dune, allowing Rider to get his bearings as he stared out across the boundless wasteland. It had been years since he'd traveled this part of the desert, and since Oasis had been laid to waste by the armies of the Clean, the trails had been left to wither, the sand burying the traces of the raiders that once populated it. Finding it at all would require a stroke of luck.

A mechanical "bang" echoed across the rolling desert landscape, as Shubazang and Euryale came up and over another dune. The vehicle they rode in was just the barely discernable chassis of a 1969 Chevy Townsman, stripped down to its springs and fitted with bizarre wicker seats, loaded with tanks of gas. It looked vaguely reminiscent of a moon buggy, except for the thick, curling tongues of exhaust that belched from the jungle of dilapidated headers and pipes at the rear.

Where the tinker had gotten the car no one seemed to question, but with its appearance some were relieved. As Shubazang pulled up alongside them he let the engine idle, wordlessly inviting the riders to join him and Euryale onboard. As it came to a stop, Ludd was the first to abandon his horse and haul his aging body into the car. Tank and Valero considered, then dismounted and took the opportunity to load their heavier gear into the back, along with excess equipment. Valero put the extra clips for his weapon in a sack and stashed them in back; Tank removed his heavy web belt and stowed it as well.

Rider calmed his horse to the vehicle's vibrant noises but didn't move. He'd packed just enough and not too much, and was content. When the others were ready to return to their horses, he continued to lead the expedition along in a north-northeast direction.

Hours slipped into days, and before long the party found a rhythm. Rider was trusted to guide the way, navigating by the stars at night and the vague impressions of faded signs (and sheer intuition) by day. Shubazang drove ahead, using his swift-moving vehicle to scout out the dunes in front of the group. Each hour they made several circuits, driving north, then east, then south, until he and his passengers completed a full circle around their mounted companions, until by day's end they'd done a dozen circuits over and over again. Every time they saw only dust, unbroken dunes, and not the faintest traces of the old trails that once connected Oasis to the larger world beyond its isolated palm trees.

On the evening of the third day, as the sun set and left the sky to fade into a cerulean shade of blue, with the moon glowing like a bright peephole through the growing night, the mounted adventurers once more heard the sound of Shubazang's Chevy, this time powering down as it swept back in their direction. Fatigue gripped all of them, and as Rider noted aloud, a wind was growing from the northwest, possibly the beginnings of a low-key sand storm.

As the last rays of light began to fade, Shubazang pulled his vehicle up and shouted to Rider over the chortling of its struggling engine.

"A ruined settlement! One, maybe two miles that way! An oasis!" In an instant Shubazang, Euryale and Ludd were gone, the vehicle starting back up and racing off in a swirl of dust.

"That's got to be it," Rider shouted back to Gale and the others. He quickened their pace.

A while later they came to the top of another dune, and looked down into the mile-wide depression beyond. All eyes swept the dark shapes of dead trees, a small lake made turbulent by the growing breeze and a humongous statue of wind-eroded stone. No tents remained standing, only the decayed structures of partly-collapsed mud huts and shacks; it seemed to all to be much tinier then they remembered. The wind was growing in strength, sweeping away the fine layer of dry weeds, sage brush and tumbleweed that covered everything, leaving the old trade town of Oasis bare to the night sky.

"That's it alright..." Valero said quietly, his keen eyes gleaming in the moonlight.

Gale glanced back at him and noticed the look on his face. But they all had reasons to remember this place, it was once the nexus of their lives, the hellhole where they all met years ago. Surely to Valero it was a haunted town, where he had once been captain and later beloved leader, the place where his dreams of reigning over the bandits of the wasteland had been buried under the boots of the vengeful Clean. To her it was nothing but a bad memory, conjuring up the phantoms of violence and fear.

Rider had no sympathetic attachment to these ruins, good or bad. It had been a degenerate place, and he was glad to see it was gone. But now they were returning, and though it seemed dead, he was always on the lookout for surprises.

Burning Lands

Sand, carried by the wind, curled around Shubazang as he and Euryale disembarked from the Townsman near the center of the abandoned settlement. Rider's storm was beginning to reach a steady degree of force, and he worried about the vehicle's engine. He called vainly for Ludd to move his butt and help fasten canvas covers over the cooling intakes on the engine, but the old man seemed reluctant to get out of the relative safety of the vehicle's bed, instead staring out at the storm with luminous red eyes.

"You know you have red eyes?" he asked Ludd. "Worse than that albino. Damned creepiest thing I've ever seen..." Ludd looked at him for a moment, then back into the night.

Shubazang looked out and saw, through the growing haze, the shapes of Rider and the others descending the far crest and heading in their direction. They'd be here in only a few minutes.

Suddenly there was a ghastly, grotesque barking noise. It sounded hoarse from the start, but it shouted out from the darkness not more than a dozen paces away.

Shubazang reached for his rifle and pulled it from the vehicle, turning to face whatever came at them. Euryale drew its dadao, but stayed put at the side of the buggy. Ludd turned and watched, then raised a gnarled finger to point in the direction from where the guttural barking came. Seeing he wasn't alone in hearing the noise, Shubazang walked slowly into the storm, searching for its source.

As he plodded heavily forwards, out of the murky gloom came a partly humanoid shape, which struggled to get to its feet and face off against him. What he saw in that moment made Shubazang stop dead in his tracks.

Tethered by his neck to a heavy wooden stake embedded in the ground was a *man*, or what was left of a man, who looked as if he was little more than an animated corpse. The man's skeleton showed vaguely through his loose, blistered skin, his stomach was gorged with parasites, and he looked flayed and tortured, his body crisscrossed with brutal scabs and ropy scars. He stood on bare feet, his toenails deliberately plucked out, his ankles hobbled, so that walking any distance from his tether would promise pure agony. More startling things were to come as Shubazang's eyes swept upwards, taking in the badly-healed stumps where the man's arms had once been, severed at the shoulders, and his face (oh, his face!) was a clawed and mangled ruin. The man's eyes had been torn from his face, his hair had been scalped, and his teeth had been broken out leaving him to suck on the fatty morsels of meat thrown to him by his unseen captors.

The strange man barked again, a pathetic, dry yelp that sounded more like a seal than a dog. Though terribly weakened, and his voice challenged by the roaring wind, the horrifying man barked out his warning again so that it carried further over the storm.

"What in the name of..." Shubazang gaped. He drew back for a moment, then raised his rifle in the paraplegic's direction, seriously considering ending the poor bastard's misery with one clean shot to the head.

Suddenly the ground beneath Shubazang exploded as gangly yellow arms lunged from beneath the sand. Four clawed hands grappled his legs, sinking jagged gray nails through his pants and into his flesh. The wounds from his injury during the battle for

Trade City were broken open, and with a sharp cry of pain the boy fell backwards until he landed flat on his back.

His rifle skittered away. Even though he was aware of the claws tearing into his flesh, attempting to pull him under the sand with them, he struggled to reach for the rifle that was now only a few inches from his fingers.

As his fingertip touched the barrel of the laser rifle, there was a sucking sound. The rifle slid down into a three foot-wide depression that suddenly formed beneath it. As he stared in horror, Shubazang saw another diseased, yellowish hand emerge from the sucking sinkhole and grasp the rifle, pulling it right under and out of sight.

"My *rifle!*"

The crippled man had been an *alarm*. Some fool had stumbled onto these things, sandmen, and had been captured by them, kept by them as some form of "living alarm". Kept bound by his neck to a tether, they fed him scraps of their cannibalistic gains to keep him just barely alive, while tearing off his arms and crippling his feet so he couldn't escape. Blind beasts of the subterranean world, they tore out his eyes out of pure malice, so that this surface-dweller (whoever he had been) would know the blindness that afflicted all their accursed troglodilian race.

How long had he been here, the wretch? By the looks of him he was only barely alive now, but with regular feedings he might have lived in this nightmare captivity for years!

Euryale, drawn by Shubazang's shouts, emerged from the storm only to be tripped by the hands that reached up out of the earth to grasp it. With a heavy thud the android fell forward into the dirt, and struggled to fight as more hands converged on it to keep it flat on the ground.

Valero and Tank rode up and quickly got down from their horses when they heard Shubazang's cries of pain.

"Where are they?" Valero asked Ludd. Ludd continued to point, but wouldn't move from his spot. He and Tank immediately armed themselves. Gale's horse was still out there, trying to catch up, and Rider was with her, keeping pace.

Tank produced his flashlight and swept its beam through the night. He alone seemed to see something, and without hesitation he plowed ahead. Valero was close behind, taking only a moment to fetch his ammo from the Townsman.

When they came upon the scene, Shubazang was still struggling. The boy's legs were bleeding profusely; whatever held him not only clawed him, but beneath the sand was taking small bites out of his flesh. He stayed remarkably calm despite the methodic torture, drawing a knife and using it to slash at the unprotected hands that held him. A mess of blood, his own and the black essence of the things underground, sprayed all about.

Though Shubazang was still something of a stranger, on seeing him in peril Tank immediately opened fire on one of the hands, striking off two fingers. As the shots rang out Valero ran forward and began using the butt of his rifle to crack the bones of other hands projecting from the earth and send them back underground.

The crippled man on the tether lurched away, fleeing from the fighting, disappearing into the storm.

A dozen yards behind Gale and Rider reached the scene. They heard the sound of battle, and Rider immediately pulled his weapons from his holsters. A terrible, familiar feeling swept through Gale; she nearly choked at the precognitive onslaught, but she held her submachine gun firmly in hand and charged into the storm after her friends.

"*Sandmen!*" someone yelled, and hearing that Rider began firing off shots into the shallow depressions he saw all around them, each a small crater that the burrowing mutants had left behind. Shrill shrieks pierced through the air as his bullets found their mark with invisible targets; puffs of sand, and small explosions of blood tore out of the sandy earth wherever he struck their unseen hunters.

Valero, Tank and Shubazang were somewhere out there. He had to find them.

There seemed to be a lull and with that Tank and Valero ran to Shubazang and pulled the young man, bleeding and groaning, from the hole into which he'd been partially sucked. He was alright, but his wounds were bad, and were likely to become infected, since the nails and teeth of sandmen were breeding grounds for all sorts of deadly bacteria; but at least for now he was alive.

"My rifle!" Shubazang shouted angrily.

"It's gone! There are others in the car!" Valero shouted back.

"No! Not like that one! Damn it!"

Gale came stumbling out of the storm next to Rider, eyes wide and beaming. "Tank! Have you seen Tank?" She then shouted something indistinct as the ground swelled not ten feet from her, then sunk back down. Like creatures "swimming" in a sea of sand, the swiftly-burrowing sandmen left a wake where they went, and as they neared the surface, it swelled into a mound that moved with them.

Rider waited for another to come close to the surface. They could be anywhere, everywhere. There could be a dozen of them, or hundreds of them. The ground quickly swelled again, as one of them came near, perhaps ready to emerge once more and attack. He didn't give it the chance; with a pull of the trigger he shot into the mound, blasting away at the sand until blood and bits of bone blew out in a gory explosion.

Not far away, but still out of sight, Tank fired his automatic rifle at something no one else could see, and followed the shot with a garbled curse that was smothered by the wind. At the same time Valero fell when the ground swelled beneath him, knocking him off his feet. Two gangly yellow arms burst forth and grasped at his legs, but he crawled away quickly, desperately bringing his gun to bear and letting off a few shots of his own before he vanished as the storm momentarily intensified.

Shubazang and Tank were alone; the others were hidden by the storm. Shubazang groaned in pain, but he pulled himself over to Tank, who warily cast an eye about before reaching down and pulling the tinker up at his side.

Their movements seemed to attract the sandmen, as more hands erupted from the earth, latching onto Tank's thick bandy legs like a storm of ropes fitted with wicked, diseased grappling hooks. Long jagged claws tore through his leggings and ripped into his flesh, taking hold. He stood his ground, unwilling to budge, as if resisting their pull would somehow get them to give in, give up. He ignored the agony of the dagger-length nails shredding his skin, cutting through his muscles, scraping his iron-hard, mutant bone; it was a test of wills.

He dropped his weapon and picked Shubazang up, knowing that if he dropped the wounded tinker, the sandmen would be upon Shubazang in a second and drag him below ground. But the hands that held *him* were growing stronger, and he was getting weaker. He realized he hadn't called out for the others, so focused was he on staying up on his feet, until it was too late. He could hold out for hours if he had to, but suddenly the ground itself began to depress, and he began to sink. Before he could mutter so much as an "oh!" of astonishment, somehow the sandmen loosened the sands beneath him and Shubazang, and now he was being swallowed alive by the desert.

Time stood still. Tank thought of Karos, and the other brothers and sisters he had met and cared for, and of the hope they had shared for a better future for Trade City. That was gone now. His dream of seeing that better world, to one day share in the peace and satisfaction known to its architects, had dissipated. It would never be a reality. His mind was small, and he could perceive only the tragedy of what was lost; it consumed him in that instant. He thought of Gale, and of Rider, and of how disappointed he was that he wouldn't be able to help his friends anymore...

Shubazang came to and realized what was happening, and instinctively tore free of Tank, jumping away, falling to the ground and rolling onto his stomach. He immediately tried to get to his feet but fell from his injuries. He looked back, just in time to see Tank pulled down into the ground, first to his waist then, as he drew in breath to cry for help, completely under.

Shubazang struggled for a weapon as Rider, Gale and Valero appeared. Valero moved towards Shubazang, still lying prone. Gale stared at the funnel-shaped hole in the ground, which had already mostly filled itself with sifting sand.

"No!" Gale shrieked terribly, anger and sorrow in her voice. It was too late.

Rider instantly realized what Gale's tone and the funnel-shaped hole meant, and he quickly looked around to take stock of his companions. It was then that the tragedy hit him... they had taken Tank.

"They must have come here after the Clean left!" Valero shouted, to no one in particular. "A lost oasis makes a great lure!"

"He's... gone..." Shubazang confirmed, looking past Valero and to the others.

Valero was stunned into silence when he finally realized what they were talking about.

Rider fired off a few defiant shots into the earth, until he realized he was shooting at nothing. He couldn't help Tank. The sandmen were certain to be gone by now; they had taken Tank with them, deep underground, and by now he had either suffocated or was being taken apart bit by bit for their next meal.

All of them seemed to be having the same awful thought, but it was Shubazang who finally broke the silence, realizing another member of their group was still missing. "Euryale!" he shouted. "*Euryale!* Where are you?"

Minutes later the voiceless android responded by coming into view, its dadao blade dripping rivulets of unwholesome black fluid. Attached to the robot was a severed yellow hand, still clenching insanely to Euryale's leg, while the stump of its wrist continued to leak black blood down to the android's feet. While they had taken Tank, Euryale seemed to have fought her way free before they sucked her under as well.

Shubazang sighed in relief at the sight of her, but the others were still stunned by the suddenness of Tank's death and took little notice. Rider was astonished, his mind stubbornly refusing to believe what had happened; Valero was quiet and Gale simply closed her eyes.

Burning Lands

After a few moments Valero wordlessly abandoned the scene and started back towards the car, towards their horses. Rider stared at the hole which in the storm had all but vanished, having completely filled with earth. In a moment it was entirely gone, so that all evidence of it was erased and the sand here looked like the sand anywhere else.

"We've got to go..." Rider finally muttered aloud to Gale, who still stood motionless.

Gale seemed unable to move. When Rider's voice finally sank in she muttered in anguish, "Rider, no!"

As if responding to her voice, out of the storm came the man on the end of the tether, almost forgotten by all, reappearing like a ghost that haunted this place. The crippled man stumbled forward while making a gruesome noise through his broken teeth and blistered lips.

"*R-r-r-i-d-e-r!*" it hissed inhumanly, as if that word alone meant something to it. It lunged forward and into Rider, knocking the stunned albino to the ground. Rider struggled to get up, to put some distance between him and the ghastly thing that stood over him, but the paraplegic creature fell on top of him, kicking and writhing, bucking its body against him, trying to pin Rider down despite not having arms or even teeth with which to injure him. The brutal mess that had been the man's face came up to Rider's level, and, staring at him with the shattered remains of empty eye sockets, it sneered.

Gale screamed, suddenly regaining her senses. At that instant the thing sat up and turned its attention to her. Its empty eye sockets widened.

"*P-i-g-g-y! P-i-g-g-y!*" It sounded hateful, absolutely *hateful*, that gross whisper that stumbled from its broken teeth and broken mouth.

Shubazang recoiled from the leprous cripple, but Euryale had no such fear. The android walked right over and picked the creature up and off of Rider, tossing it aside. The thing whimpered in agony and tried to roll over helplessly, to regain its footing. But Euryale simply followed as the man wiggled away, raised its sword, and brought it down with such strength that it chopped the cripple's head off. Everyone stared at the poor creature, finally put to rest. Whatever it had been, it was good that the poor man no longer squirmed frantically; it was good that he was dead.

"Let's get out of here!" Shubazang shouted, his voice strained. "Which way, Rider? Gale?"

Rider looked at the dead man, wondering... There had been a familiarity in the dead cripple's voice that he just couldn't shake. But he heard Shubazang calling out to him. It brought him back to the present.

"Come on, I know the way," he said. "The ghoul's camp... we can find it. Tonight. Keep moving!"

Hours later the loss of Tank from their ranks was still sorely felt, leaving a hole in their morale as large as the giant himself. They were exhausted, too, but at least the ruins of Oasis (and the innumerable sandmen who now haunted it) were far behind them. The sandstorm had raged and died, like a fiercely-burning candle that had spent itself, until now a much more reasonable wind wandered across the flat open desert.

The moon was clear and blue in the sky, illuminating a Martian landscape of sand and scattered boulders, laced by the meandering course of an ancient, dry riverbed.

"Yes, I think I remember..." Rider said softly to himself. "Yes, the *riverbed*," he said more resolutely. "It was around here, Gale. It was around here that we... Tank and I... first found you."

Shubazang sat immobilized in the car, replacing Euryale in the passenger seat. He held an old assault rifle in hand, but didn't look at all happy for having lost his precious laser. The android sat in back with Ludd. Valero now drove the crazy car, which he pulled to a dead stop, switching off the ignition. The wind blew across the desert, weaving in and out between the maze of stones and lonely crags.

"Could be anywhere out here..." Rider said. Even his sharp night vision picked up nothing notable out here. He would be surprised if they did; after all, it had been years since they'd been here, and sandstorms, buzzards, and other wandering beasts would have done a fine job erasing the scene they had left.

Gale did not seem convinced. Beyond the riverbed, nothing here seemed familiar at all. She ran to a high point to get a better view. She climbed atop a boulder, standing straight up to look around. Then she moved to another, a little higher up, to get an even better vantage point. Euryale followed, mimicking her, jumping from rock to rock. Ludd stayed in the car, pulling his hood about him and crossing his mottled, swarthy arms over his chest, sneaking a moment's rest. Valero watched Gale, then looked back at Rider, then back at the girl.

"What are we doing out here?" Valero finally asked. "We have no idea where we're going. The Burning Lands? Well that's miles from here. What do we do once we get there?"

Gale ignored him, and stepped over onto another boulder. Tank's death still filled her mind but things were slowly settling back into focus for her. She had to try.

She remembered being a child, playing among these rocks. She remembered Johnny squatting atop one just like these, tanning hides. She sensed a lingering tremor. Her eyes swept to a particular corner of the craggy country, not a hundred yards away.

"*This is it*," she said, and bounded off in that direction.

Euryale stopped momentarily, then looked back at the others. Soon the android was off chasing after her, as if at play.

"I'm staying here," Shubazang said with a pained groan, clenching the blood-soaked bandages looped around his leg. Ludd didn't say a word, though he did turn his head to watch Gale and Euryale prance off. Rider got up and followed.

Gale dropped from a large boulder and onto the sand. The moonlight in the cloudless sky colored everything in a dark blue hue, and wherever beams of its light failed to reach, pitch black shadows arose. But here, among the boulders, she was remembering. She had lived here, for several years. They had been such hard times, but some of the happiest of her life. Now she had returned, but the home her friend had made among the rocks was empty now, his quiet, loving presence was gone, and the simplicity of his gentle way would never return.

She shuddered now. She remembered when Johnny died, how sudden it had been, and how empty she had felt after his loss. Now Tank was gone. Who would be next? How many people would she have to lose? Is that what growing up was about? Becoming tough, hardened to death?

Burning Lands 357

She felt... old. Euryale leapt down beside Gale, and also looked around, its head whirring as it scanned from side to side.

"Looks vaguely familiar," Rider called out, though he wasn't at all sure.

"No, this is it," Gale called out, moving around one last boulder and into a small clearing.

There, almost completely buried in the sand, was a humanoid skeleton, its remains picked over dozens of times by desert beasts and buried, revealed and buried again by the tides of sand. Now the spine was visible as a bright white cluster of bone that extended two feet before vanishing into the dirt. The one visible end ended in an abrupt cut, the very place where the man's dogged hunters had severed his head to bring back to their employer as proof of the successful hunt.

"This is it..." she said softly. That was all that was left of Johnny now.

Rider found her among the rocks and stopped short when he too saw the bones. He felt unable to go any further, and instead stood at Gale's side.

Gale searched around, reaching into the shadows created by the boulders, hoping her fingers would find something hidden in the darkness. Rider took her lead and also began looking for something, anything. When Euryale caught up to them, the android started poking about as well.

The voiceless construct went over to the skeleton and stepped on something. The android's weight was such that it caused the object to sink down on one side, so that the other jutted up from the dirt. Euryale looked down, its steel eyes locked on the object. Without a sound it leaned over, picked the object out of the dirt, and lifted it up.

Rider noticed and nudged Gale. Gale got up and walked over, extending a hand to Euryale. The android looked at the object one last time, then, almost reluctantly, handed the treasure over to Gale.

Gale stared at the android for a moment, unable to hide her fear of the soulless thing. But Euryale merely stood there, watching the young woman with uncanny interest. It unnerved Gale, though she said nothing; instead, she sunk back towards Rider. When Euryale walked off Gale sighed a breath of relief. Feeling more at ease now that the android was gone, she turned to cleaning the sand from the object. It looked like a small metal plaque. She cleared the grime off one side, revealing a *screen* and a cluster of small rubberized buttons. She looked up at Rider.

"What is it?" she asked, putting the eerie android out of her mind.

"You're asking me?" he mused. He took it, examined it and without anything to lose, began pushing the buttons one after another.

Moments later, to their surprise, a weak orange glow lit up the screen, revealing a neat grid work of well-ordered lines. A second later numbers blinked on in the corners and lines traced across the surface as if guided by a ghost's hand, showing in detail the contours of the dry riverbed, the surrounding flats and the high points in elevation for a dozen miles in every direction.

"A map of some kind?" he asked, showing her what he'd found.

"Yes!" Gale said excitedly, remembering. "Now I remember; it was my mother's! But... but I don't know quite how to use it..."

"We'd better get this back to the kid," Rider said, wrapping it up carefully and putting it in his pouch. "He'll know how to figure it out."

Everyone gathered around Shubazang as he sat, weakly, in the passenger seat of the Townsman. Ludd and Euryale perched in the back, looking over his shoulder, while Valero remained in the driver seat, indifferent to the strange device they'd found. Gale and Rider huddled near Shubazang to watch as he worked.

After only a few seconds Shubazang came up with a name for it. "It's a simple *data pad*, an electronic booklet for keeping track of notes, journal entries and even maps. In this case..." he said, opening up the panel on the device's back with a small screwdriver, "... the memory module seems to have been fried by radiation. I'd be doubtful if there's anything left on it."

"There is," Rider stated. "Some kind of map. See?" He leaned over and pressed one of the buttons. The screen came back on, depicting the same diagram composed solely of vivid orange lines.

The luminous contours depicted on the map reflected in Shubazang's goggles. He looked intrigued, and retrieved a stylus from a small cylindrical hole on the data pad's side, something Rider and Gale had missed.

Shubazang tapped the stylus to the screen several times.

"Just a map," he said quietly. "There's no other data on this device."

Rider looked at Gale as if to say "sorry, kid", but Gale didn't give up so easily.

"The map," she said, "does it have any notations? Any at all? Where they were going? Or where they came from?"

Shubazang was quiet again as he tapped away.

"Yes," he said, "there are *waypoints*, a series of 'mile markers' of a sort to mark their journey. No ultimate destination, though; it looks like the 'pad was just recording their progress."

"But with the waypoints, it shows where they came *from?*" Gale asked eagerly.

Shubazang realized what she was getting at. "Yes. If we follow the waypoints in reverse order, they should lead us right back to where they came from."

"Where *I* came from..." she said, looking at herself in Shubazang's highly reflective goggles.

"Then let's go," Rider said, motioning everyone to return to their respective mounts. "Give me the map. I'll guide us. Shubazang, you've got the radiation counter." Shubazang nodded and retrieved the Geiger counter, flicking the switch to the "on" position. Valero started up the car. In moments they headed out.

More hours passed, the broken terrain slipping once more into relentless dunes. A rolling sea which had no features, an isolated plain of sand swept back and forth by the ever-changing winds.

Threads of pre-dawn light scintillated in the sky, hovering about the horizon like a warm halo. Before long this thin corona exploded into many vibrant colors - purple, red, orange, and gold, until the edge of the sky was on fire with the hues of the slowly rising sun. Wherever this light shed, it burned away the darkness, dispelled the shadows and brought its eerie glow to the desert.

From the last corner of the night came a strange bronze glint, a gleam of metal catching the rays of the desert sunrise. Gale was the first to see them; the silence that came over her went completely unnoticed by Rider until he looked up from the

Burning Lands 359

map. When he noticed her staring he looked out into the distance and saw them for himself.

Enormous metal towers rose into the sky, like the spires of some Lovecraftian city submerged in a sea of shadows, only now rising with the coming of dawn. They were humongous, towering things, covered in a myriad of inexplicable pipes, vents, fan ports and rickety scaffolds of rusted steel. These towers were black with soot, stained by the ages, their uppermost reaches scoured by centuries of windstorms and sand so that they gleamed in the light.

Shubazang motioned for Valero to pull the Townsman to a stop close to Rider. As the engine idled noisily Shubazang shouted:

"Refinery! Old, old technology! We still on track?"

Rider looked at the map. "Yes, the last waypoint is dead ahead. We can re-trace the trail from there."

"That's where my parents were *killed*," Gale shouted soberly, looking in the direction of the towers. "That's where I hid from the Huntsmen. That's where Johnny found me. When I was a girl."

Everyone was quiet.

"Where is the next waypoint?" she asked.

Rider regarded the map momentarily. "We continue northeast."

"The Geiger is already ticking," Shubazang shouted. "Not substantial here, but the levels are getting higher."

"We're getting close to the Burning Lands," Rider shouted back.

"Now might be a good time for everyone to suit up," he replied.

Valero switched off the engine. The ex-raider got out and came over to one of the horses, fetching his suit. Rider and Gale both dismounted and began to unfold their gear as well.

"Help me out," Shubazang called back to Ludd. The old man stirred from his rest and got out, moving to help the injured tinker don his rubberized suit.

"If I go back now I can probably still hook up with that sweet little amazon and her sisters, right?" Shubazang joked. "Go with them and make a home in the mountains?" But no one laughed. Euryale even stared at him, looking for all the world *jealous*.

"Just kidding, sweetheart," he said soothingly to the machine.

Shubazang made sure his bandages were swapped out for new ones before pulling on the leggings. His wounds were still weeping, they looked grievous, but he still had a lot of willpower to keep him going.

Gale, Rider and Valero watched him for a moment, then imitated him, pulling on the legs first, then slipping on the sleeves and zipping the suit all the way up to their necks. One by one they snapped the aluminum buttons over the zipper, creating a sturdy seal.

Shubazang felt around inside his helmet. "You know," he said, "these suits are incredibly old. If any of them has a hole, or gets a hole sometime between now and where we're going..." He didn't need to say anymore.

Valero put on his own helmet, snapping it firmly in place. He saw Shubazang and Ludd having trouble and came over to help.

"No, not like that," Shubazang said to him. "Start the air cycler or you'll suffocate in there. And the suit needs to puff up a bit. Let's just hope the cyclers still work!"

He flicked a switch on Valero's chest-mounted cycler. For a moment there was silence, then a soft whir, and seconds later, the limbs of his suit began to puff up and the chest expanded. He looked pot-bellied, his arms and legs swollen. Fresh air swirled around in his helmet, as he breathed in the clean, crisp oxygen. The boy gave him a clumsy thumbs up gesture with one of his metal hands, before donning his own helmet.

Rider discarded his hat and his sunglasses, and prepared to put on his helmet. He stopped when he saw Gale looking at him. She regarded his white hair, his white skin and his pink eyes. He felt scrutinized, but she smiled.

"Your horses won't last long out there," Shubazang called out.

"Give them to Ludd," Gale said. "The rest of us can do this on foot. That's how *we* did it, when we first left."

Rider listened and nodded. He immediately began unpacking their essential gear and the others soon followed suit.

"No, pack it in here," Shubazang said, motioning to the vehicle. "No need to walk when we can ride."

They began moving the heavier supplies, guns and ammunition into the back of the vehicle, until at last the vehicle was burdened with all it could carry. Gale and Rider climbed aboard, finding it difficult to move in the suits, but they found a place for themselves in the back.

Just then Ludd stepped forward. "Make room in there for me," he said. "I'm coming."

"No, you're not," Rider said. "You're staying here. Take care of the horses, damn it!"

Ludd tried to stare Rider down but the albino's eyes only narrowed in determination. The old man chuckled and said nothing more, instead moving to take the reigns of the group's horses. After a moment Rider's hard stare shifted away. "Valero, let's go."

It should have been morning, but the light of the sun was blurred here. Was it just a trick of the light, a freak occurrence of the season, or was this place truly a blight on the earth, a vortex of everything unnatural conceived by the Ancients' twisted minds, and this their resting place?

Ten minutes into the Burning Lands and the Geiger counter was already ticking away madly. Radiation levels had risen rapidly; one hundred, two hundred, two hundred and fifty *rems*. Everyone held on for dear life as Valero continued to push the overburdened vehicle northeast at Rider's direction. The data pad crackled with static. The radiation was interfering with its electronic components, but having made it through years before, it wasn't likely to shut off now.

"Switch Euryale off!" Shubazang called back to Rider. "At the small of her neck, in back, there's a panel and a switch."

"What will happen if we don't?" Rider asked.

"Not sure," the boy admitted. "She's okay with trace radiation, but levels this high? I don't know."

Gale looked over to watch. Rider fidgeted with Euryale, until he found the switch and toggled it. Euryale continued to sit there, but she no longer moved.

"I think that's it," he yelled back.

Shubazang nodded, then turned back to look out at the wasteland around them. He stared out across the open flats, out across the insignificant rise and fall of the terrain. To the northeast, where they were headed, the skies were dark with the beginnings of a great storm. Everywhere else the sky seemed to get greyer and greyer, as if the color itself was being sucked from the world.

Just then the boy sat up with a start, staring off to the south. For a moment he was still, holding onto the dashboard to brace himself, then his hand darted outwards as he pointed in that direction.

Rider turned immediately to see what Shubazang was pointing at. There, at the extreme limit of his vision, he saw a shape following them. A humanoid shape, slowly vanishing as the vehicle outpaced it, but apparently trying to keep up.

"No..." Rider said, then turned to brace Gale. But she was already watching, eyelids partly closed to keep the dust from her eyes. She had no expression on her face.

"Stop!" Rider yelled to Valero. "Stop the car! Turn around!" Valero spun the wheel slowly, the car bounced and shook as it turned around, and they started in the direction of the old man who was doggedly following across the radiated plains. Rider crouched forward as they raced towards the distant shape, as if prepared to leap out when they got there and force him to turn back.

Ludd stopped to take a much-needed rest once he realized the others had spotted him and were coming back. The old man stood his ground, watching the vehicle get nearer and nearer, until he could make out their faces. Valero brought the car to a stop.

"You idiot! Go back!" Rider shouted through his helmet. As he went to dismount, Shubazang grabbed his arm.

"It's already too late," Shubazang said. With that, everyone grew quiet and the only sound that could be heard was the wind... and the steady clicking of the Geiger counter.

Ludd looked at Rider and while his weird red eyes were as hard to read as ever, they somehow seemed apologetic. But he managed a bit of dry humor. "So... do you have any room in there?"

Rider just watched silently as Gale moved forward to make room in the back with Euryale. Ludd climbed onboard.

"What can we expect out here?" Valero asked over his shoulder, his eyes focused ahead of him. They were the first words spoken since the group picked up Ludd, the only one among them who sat unprotected against the withering radiation of their surroundings.

"Does anyone know?" he continued.

"Nothing lives here," Shubazang stated.

"Nothing that we know of," Rider countered.

"The only thing we need to worry about is bumping into Mr. Death," Ludd added jokingly, his voice a dry croak.

The buggy hit a rock, then another and another. The fine sand was giving way to an irregular landscape, a rocky plain of bizarre alien shapes and terrain. Over the course of several hours the familiar desolation of the deserts outside the Burning Lands was replaced by an unfamiliar wastescape that would look more at home on a distant planet than on this, the twisted earth.

They had entered a bleak, wind-swept badlands of bare earth and cracked stone, crisscrossed here and there by black ravines of unimaginable depth, whose jagged shapes were mirrored in the cold white lightning that pierced the roiling gray clouds. Monstrous thunderheads possessed of a lambent fluorescence moved quickly through the dark sky, pushed by the invisible hands of titans, crashing together to the dull sound of distant thunder and swept away again by the raging, deafening winds.

In the relative scale of things, their miniscule vehicle crawled along almost unnoticeably through this weird wasteland of titanic crevasses and rocky badlands, dwarfed by the colossal clouds overhead. Its presence was washed out by the brilliant, dazzling explosions of light created by the unnatural lightning storms that danced silently overhead and in the sky.

They continued on for what seemed like hours. Only gradually did they realize that from this wasteland rose the ruins of another ancient city. Here boiling black clouds, laced with streaks of lightning, converged over the nameless wreckage, a cityscape wrought into rubble. Lances and pikes of solid crystal trinitite stood here and there, thrust up from the ruins at odd angles, scintillating with momentary gleams of green light from the living, breathing storms overhead. Lightning bolts reached down from the smoky black clouds to touch down upon this maze of molten glass and steel - this city reduced to a cooled heap of slag, to dance upon the tallest spires of trinitite that stood like weathervanes. Each burst of contact crackled and lit up the surrounding ruins in a cold and clinical green glow, while electricity coursed down each crystal column and arced from one to the next, a living lightning storm, until the last spark was spent leaving only a lingering aura in the air.

Elsewhere on the Twisted Earth the land seemed dead, forsaken and un-revivable, a wasteland of sand punctuated by dunes shifting eternally at the direction of some pointless plan devised at Nature's whim. But here it seemed alive, struggling to be reborn. Now the liquefied ruins of glass and steel and aluminum didn't seem like a ruin at all, but a fluid cauldron like the primordial ooze of the prehistoric Earth, from which a new world was being born... with great difficulty, but it's birth would prevail nonetheless. A twisted new world was coming into being, its landscape deformed, an ungodly amalgam assuming traits of the broken old and the yet-to-be-seen new.

It became obvious to Gale why the Brotherhood had sent her here. This poisoned land was sacred to them. It was the birthplace of their prophesized New Eden, a black and gray badlands, streaked silver from the congealed rivers that were once cities, its clouds alight with ionizing power, its land shuddering with electrical residue, and all of it bathed and awash in radiation.

What life would spring here would be formidable, the foretold god-gifts to mutantkind that could lead the faithful into a new millennium where radiation would be just the last of five elements, as commonplace as earth, water, wind and fire.

This would be the birthplace of their new world, but they knew something evil dwelled here, an ancient cancer grown lunatic and diseased with age, that would have to be brought to heel to pave the way for their "utopian" future to finally be realized.

The Geiger counter continued to climb as the car was jostled back and forth. Out of morbid curiosity Shubazang shifted to look into the back where Ludd was sitting quietly.

Burning Lands

Wrapped up in his robes and his hood drawn over his face, Shubazang couldn't tell how Ludd was faring. He sat forward and checked the meter. Five hundred *rems* and climbing.

The next hour was passed in sober silence. The buggy chortled weakly along, rolling over sandy ground blasted into greenish shale, so that the sound of tinkling glass seemed to follow them everywhere. Their surroundings comprised a most bizarre alien terrain, but no one was astonished or awed by what they saw. Instead they thought of their lost companion. Rider sensed Gale's anguish and tried to distract her.

"Your people, what do they look like?" he shouted through the glass of his helmet.

Gale was quiet for a few minutes before she finally spoke.

"Like me, I suppose."

Valero chimed in, suddenly interested. "But those we saw, they were giants. Their eyes, inhuman, their skin..."

"Just *skin*," she said, "*Armor*."

"*Powered* armor?" Shubazang offered, suddenly looking excited.

"What?" Gale asked.

"Well, to be more accurate, *dynamic fluid armor*. I've read of it... just becoming operational during the Final War. Your people must have perfected the technology, yes?"

"Dynamic fluid armor?" Rider asked.

"Yes. Heavy suits of armor made with bundles of rubberized ballistic nylon musculature, each artificial tendon and ligament a 'hose' filled with a fluid, like silicon oil, impregnated with metal filaments... barium or titanium, coated in a nitrogen compound. When not charged the suit remains fluid like relaxed muscle, until its advanced motion sensors, a magnetic field surrounding the suit, detects an incoming projectile. Then an electric charge instantly magnifies these filaments so that they lock in place, turning the liquid into a solid, creating a skin harder than steel. Bulletproof, flexible, strong or soft. The same technology allows the suit's limbs to lift far greater weights, creating 'exomuscle' with vastly-superior load-bearing capabilities."

"Meaning?" Rider asked.

"Meaning they are stronger than five, ten men. They can carry heavy weapons like we carry rifles. Each soldier a one-man tank."

Gale seemed unsure.

"No, it makes sense," Shubazang continued. "Your people being war-like and all that..."

"No," she said, "That's just it, my people *weren't* war-like. They were scientists. The 'City' was a long-term research project. They were some of the pre-Fall world's brightest minds. They hoped to survive the war and repopulate the Earth. Rebuild. Theirs was a mission of peace. My father... my *real* father, despised war. That much I remember."

Everyone was quiet for a moment, except for Ludd, who was gently wheezing and gurgling.

"Then who are the 'Huntsmen'?" Shubazang asked, preferring to ignore the sounds.

"I'm not sure," she replied vaguely. "Defenders, I think. Guardians. Soldiers who were put in place to protect the City and its mission. But they were only a small part of what we were."

"Why were they after you?"

"I don't know..." she said, closing her eyes and shaking her head, trying to remember.

"If they're super strong, and bullet proof, what chance have we got?" Rider asked no one in particular.

Valero cut everyone off. "There! Something up ahead!"

As their buggy crept around another bend in the leveled ruins, looming before them came the shape of a vast pyramidal structure, a tiered bunker almost forty feet high made of earth and concrete. Once buried beneath an innocuous hill of soil, the bunker was made bare by the devastation of the war (and nearby nuclear blasts) erosion and the gradual toll time takes on all man-made things. Bundles of jagged metal wire and shorn steel supports jutted from the side of the hill, framing a huge open wound in the mound's side.

Almost thirty feet tall and as many feet wide, this massive wound led into the hollow interior of the pyramidal structure. Valero looked over one shoulder at Gale.

She stared at the opening, unsure, and began to remember. She heard voices. Her father, her mother and others.

"The counter reads levels close to one thousand rems. We've got to keep moving," her father said.

"Put as much distance as we can between us and the City. It could be hours before they notice we're gone," her mother said. The others were in agreement.

"Keep Gale safe!" someone yelled.

At the same time, Gale remembered the vision of the Brotherhood mentalists, and the strange pyramid at the heart of the Burning Lands. *This was it.*

Breaking the trance, Gale nodded once to Valero. He turned back to driving and gently guided the vehicle underneath the yawning entrance.

Rider looked at the data pad. "This is the last, the *first,* waypoint."

Rider and Shubazang armed themselves as a cloak of darkness spread over them, as they entered the gigantic interior of the surface bunker. Shubazang reached down and flicked on the interior lights in his suit, washing his face in white neon light. Wearing his weird black goggles and encased in this bulky protective suit and helmet, he looked like a science-fiction mad scientist preparing to do surgery.

"Each suit has a light," he explained. "We'll need them if we're going underground."

The interior of the great pyramid was a huge empty cavern, nothing more than a staging area of sorts, sheltered from the sand, radiation and storms outside. Macrocarbon support beams circled the interior like webs of heavy metal, an intricate internal support system that shored up the dirt and concrete walls and rose all the way up to the forty-foot ceiling. Spears of rust hung down from these, and more of that contagious orange decay spread to virtually every metal surface inside. This place was *old.*

Burning Lands 365

Valero pulled the buggy to a final stop a few yards or so inside the vaulted cavern, immediately turning off the engine. He slipped out of his seat and went to the back, pulling out a spare rifle and checking to make sure it was loaded.

Sick from the day's travels, Ludd rose wearily to his feet, his lip dripping vomit. Valero seemed surprised and reached to help him down. The old man proved to have tremendous willpower and fortitude, because once he reached solid ground he stood up, braced himself with his staff, and pushed Valero away.

Rider got out with Gale and both looked around. Their eyes swept the darkness, but they saw only an open, hangar-like interior. Rider noticed dormant guide lights on the ground, extending from the outer doorway where the hillside had fallen away, leaving the great open entrance heading into the interior of the massive structure.

While Gale looked back at the entrance, and the dwindling traces of daylight, Rider lifted his gun and went deeper into the cavern until he almost vanished at the edge of the light. He then looked back and signaled to her.

"Gale! Over here!"

Gale and Valero came jogging over, their suits puffing and wheezing. They finally came to a stop at Rider's side.

"Wait a minute... what do you see? Tell me, what do you see?" Shubazang asked, still sitting in the passenger seat because of his injured leg. When he realized they might start exploring without him, he slid out of the car with a groan and tried to regain his footing.

Gale and Valero couldn't see what Rider saw with his sensitive sight, so he pointed at the buttons on Gale's helmet. When she failed to toggle them he reached out and turned on the lights on her helmet, so that their twin beams cut through the shadows ahead of them. The beams illuminated the painted outline of two gigantic elevators, each almost forty feet wide and ringed by orange and black striped lines. The guide lights Rider had noticed before led right up to these. A small hatchway, rusted completely over and fused to the ground, sat almost unnoticed in between these.

"There," Gale said suddenly, pointing to the hatch. "That's our way down."

They moved over to the hatch, sealed shut and covered in rust. Rider tugged on it, though it refused to open. Valero joined him and together they pulled, but it still wouldn't budge.

Shubazang came over, using his rifle as a crutch, but stopped short when he saw their difficulty. "Let me get Euryale!" he called out, before returning to the car.

Moments later Euryale sat up. The android shifted, looked at Shubazang, and extended a hand to caress the glass of his helmet, as if happy to see him again.

"Come on, we need you," Shubazang prodded the machine, and led the way. "Hurry, before the radiation wreaks havoc on your electrical components!"

Euryale and Ludd followed, coming over to where everyone waited. Valero and Rider stepped out of the way. Euryale stared at the hatchway.

"That's it, girl..." Shubazang muttered. Euryale stepped forward, knelt and plunged its hand through the metal hatch as easily as a man might punch through a sheet of Styrofoam. The metal crumpled, and Euryale pulled each bent, jagged flap backwards, just as if it was peeling open a fruit.

Euryale stood and stepped back, placing its hands at its hips triumphantly. Shubazang grinned.

Valero moved over immediately and, toggling his own controls, turned on his helmet lights. He peered down into the shaft, his rifle at the ready, but he saw only a deep black chute and an old rusted ladder, heading underground. Emergency lights along the entire height of the chute remained off, having shorted out long ago.

"Looks clear," he said, slinging his rifle over one shoulder.

"Who wants to go first?" Rider asked, but even as he spoke he shouldered his gun too and began climbing down. Next went Gale, then Valero, then Ludd, Euryale, and finally Shubazang.

As they descended, one by one, the roar of the wind in the cavern overhead was soon replaced by an unidentifiable, thundering rumble from below. So great was the sound that it sent vibrations through the sides of the chute and the bars of the ladder. Moisture clung to the rungs, dripping off drop by drop, and was now beginning to form on their suits. They had to be extra careful as they climbed, for fear of slipping and falling the rest of the way... however deep that might be.

Luckily the chute proved to be only a hundred feet deep or so. But by the time Rider reached the bottom, he could no longer hear the others; the growing rumble was now a continuous roar, and as he, Gale and the others stepped out into this new cavern they soon saw why.

They had come into an enormous circular cavern almost a half mile across, an artificial chasm sunk into the earth. Its purpose evaded even Gale, who from experience should know something of this place, and the others as well, all of whom stood insignificant in this, the bowels of the earth. The air roared with the ear-splitting crash of tens of millions of gallons of muddy gray water coming into the monstrous cavern from innumerable pipes and black side tunnels, some five or six stories tall, channeling dark and noxious waters from the poisoned bedrock for miles around. This unbroken, continuous deluge was channeled over the edge of a great curved precipice, thundering down into a grand gulf that dropped into the echoing emptiness below. A maddeningly complex web of arching power lines and spidery conduits ran from the outer edges of the Niagara-sized cascade. On seeing these did Shubazang surmise aloud that this entire cavern was in fact one titanic power generation facility, drawing subterranean waters from the dead, surrounding wasteland to power some buried city they had yet to see.

Graceful arches of gray, rusted steel spanned the rushing waters and out over the bottomless gulf, reaching to connect with a single pillar-like structure seemingly suspended at the center of the chasm, its cylindrical shape descending into the darkness below. Each of these arched causeways was at least thirty feet wide, but seemed as precarious and fragile as the strands of a spider web when taken against the entirety of the cavern around them.

Dormant lights, with blue-tinted bulbs, ran near the edge of these causeways, similar to the ones above, like guide lights on a runway leading them deeper.

Ludd fell over, not from awe at the sheer size of this place, but from growing fatigue... and cellular disruption. He didn't have much longer to live, perhaps a few hours at most. Rider and Shubazang helped him to his feet, but in an unexpected outburst the old man raved at them.

"No! Deeper we must go! I want to see it *all* before I die!"

Burning Lands

Gale looked at him, frightened by what she assumed was his delirium, then started off down the causeway. The others followed close behind, until after a few long minutes they had spanned the distance, over the rushing waters in which any one of them would be lost had they fallen, and came to the cylindrical "pillar" at the center of the chasm.

Valero moved ahead, letting his lights sweep the base of the structure. There, at the same level as the causeway, was a seamless doorway thirty feet wide and thirty feet high.

"How do we open it?" he asked over one shoulder. Rider looked as well, but saw no handle.

Gale looked around and saw a small panel with buttons, standing at roughly shoulder height not a foot from the doorway. It was draped with dust and encrusted with rust. Would it still operate?

"A keypad," Shubazang said, noticing the small box that had her so riveted. "But we'll need the access code. Without it we could trigger an alarm, or *defenses*..."

He let the suggestion hang there. None of them had any knowledge of what "defenses" this place might have, but considering the technology required to carve such a place from the heart of the earth, it could be anything imaginable. Or worse.

Shubazang considered. "Most access ports allow three tries before locking you out, or raising the alarm. Let me give it a try."

He hobbled over with his crutch and examined the buttons. He looked for signs of recent disturbance, hoping he might see which buttons had been pressed by the absence of dust or dirt on those keys. He angled his helmet to make the most of the lights.

Four keys had been toggled fairly recently. The "2", the "3", the "5" and the "6".

"That's it!" he said. He reached out and pressed them in order. As he touched each key, the access panel made a soft chirping noise, each key triggering its own tone on the musical scale. Just like a telephone.

In a moment of clarity Ludd looked intrigued and stepped forward, but said nothing.

There was a moment of silence, then a flat buzz from the keypad. The doors remained sealed.

"No, that's not right," Ludd said. He raised a finger, even as Shubazang moved to try again. "Wait."

"It wants four digits," Shubazang reminded him.

"How do you know?" Ludd asked.

"Only four keys have been touched."

"*Only four keys have been touched...*" Ludd repeated, thinking to himself. "But it wants *five* digits. The code has five digits. Five tones."

Shubazang looked at Rider and Valero as if searching for someone to explain where the old man came up with this.

"Try them again," Ludd requested. Shubazang hit the buttons again, this time in reverse order. Ludd hummed along as Shubazang pressed the keys. He committed the notes and their associated numbers to his brain.

Again silence, followed by a flat buzz.

"We have only one try left," he reminded Ludd and the others. Valero and Rider got ready.

"Oh, it's not that difficult," Ludd said, surprising everyone. He turned and gestured to Gale. "*She* has the key."

Gale looked at him like he was mad, then back at the others, shaking her head defiantly. "What are you talking about?!"

"Come now, child, you know you do. That little tune you hum. I tried for days to put a name to it. I'm a living library, you know... or I *was*. I know all the songs of the Ancient world. Your little ditty doesn't match a thing."

Then it dawned on her. Her habitual humming. She'd been doing it for years. It wasn't music, some old tune stuck in her head, but a code taught to her by her father, drilled into her brain so she wouldn't forget. She hadn't forgotten. She remembered!

Gale immediately began to hum. Ludd's blood-stained lips curled into a smile as he hummed along.

"Yes, that's the one! Hm, hmm, hmmmmm, hmmmm, hm. Two, three, six, five... *two*..."

"Four keys... five digits!" Shubazang said in astonishment. He returned to the pad and stared at the keys.

"Two, three, six, five, two," Ludd instructed.

Shubazang tapped the code out on the pad, while Valero and Rider stood ready for anything. They hoped the old man was right.

There was a deafening groan as ancient metal wheels began to turn. The gigantic door slowly retracted into the ceiling, revealing a massive vehicle elevator on the other side, taking up all of the cylindrical structure. Another way down. Dim green-white lights flickered on automatically as it came open, illuminating the humongous elevator floor, which stood empty.

Ludd looked weakly at the results, grinning.

Shubazang retrieved the Geiger counter and waved it inside the elevator. The radiation level had died off almost completely.

"We can take off our suits," he said to the others. "It would probably be best if we left them here. We don't want to risk damaging them."

One by one they entered the elevator, cutting the background noise of the great cascades to a minimum. Once inside they began to disrobe, slowly removing the bulky suits with as much care as possible, piling them neatly in the center of the elevator. Shubazang was the first out of his suit, followed by Rider. Gale stood beside Valero as they moved to take off their helmets.

At that moment Gale heard a soft hissing noise, a noise no one had heard before because of the wind raging in the cavern on the surface, echoing in the ladder chute leading below, and over the raging waters rumbling just outside. But here, in the relative quiet of the elevator, it was unmistakable.

Valero noticed too, and looked at her. Both she and Valero began searching their suits, patting down the rubbery fabric looking for tears or openings. Each of them aware that the implications of a suit's failure meant... death.

Valero stopped searching, but Gale continued, growing frantic that her suit might be punctured. Valero grabbed her arm to make her stop. He looked up at her, through the glass of his helmet, then back to three small tears down by his left ankle. Holes small enough to go entirely unnoticed until now.

"It's me, kid," he said resignedly.

Rider came over and checked it out. "It's not that bad," he said. He looked back at Shubazang. "Right?"

The boy said nothing. Green letters flickered across his goggles, but he was silent.

"Forget about it," Valero said, peeling the suit off and getting his gun ready. He didn't look at the girl, who was now staring at him. He couldn't meet her gaze.

"Let's get this piece of junk moving!" Valero shouted.

Shubazang went to an access panel on the interior of the elevator and pressed a button with one of his cold, metal fingers. The door began to close, and rumbled as it sealed shut. The elevator then began to descend.

"This is not how you're going to die," Gale said, breaking the silence, but Valero wanted nothing of it. He looked furious... at himself.

"I don't want to know how I die, sibyl," he snapped back, gripping his gun tighter. Of course he believed her, she was a prophetess after all, but that didn't lighten his spirits in the least. Radiation would slowly kill him, there was no cure. So if that wasn't what was going to kill him, that meant he would die sooner, rather than later. That was not comforting in the least.

"Damn you and your people," Shubazang said quietly, tearing his eyes away from Valero. It took Gale a moment to realize he was referring to her. "All your bombs and radiation and weapons of war. Goddamn the Ancients. Tear our genes to shreds, curse us all, while you remain safe and secure beneath the earth. Goddamn you all."

An *Ancient*. Is that what she was? She was changed, like them, like others. But she knew what he meant. Here, below, her people had never grown to know the outside world, or become a part of it. For them it was a long sleep, disrupted by brief periods of wakefulness, and each journey to the surface just a momentary glimpse at a nightmare world gone awry. They were detached, living in their secret fortress-city underground, believing themselves the inheritors of the past and all its rights and privileges. They believed they carried the standard of the Ancient way of life, and they alone would re-establish "order" when the right time came. Those outside, they were merely "tenants" of the war-ravaged globe, ants and insects fighting their own internecine wars generation after generation, watched by an uncaring race of beings living apart from the suffering. Some day those outside would have to be swept away to make room for humanity's return, and all the chaos of the intervening ages would be forgotten.

Who were they to make such an assumption? Who were they to lay claim to the world, when they hadn't shed a drop of blood to keep it?

"Goddamn us..." she agreed.

Rider heard her but said nothing. He waited by the door as the elevator slowed to a crawl. The lights inside flickered momentarily, the lift came to a shuddering stop and the great door groaned once more.

The elevator door opened onto another causeway of steel and an unimaginably large cavern even greater than the one above. Here, in a flooded basin more than a mile wide, was a small sea of black waters, gently rising and falling against the metal cavern walls some twenty feet below the elevator exit.

The roof of the cavern must have been a thousand feet overhead, punctuated by inverted domes, spindles of steel and wire, and antenna arrays, all of which served some unknowable purpose so far underground. The bright light of cobalt bulbs created a scattering of cold blue stars in the dark void of the great rolling roof, illuminating strange vents, pipes and dormant fan blades as large as carousels.

The thunder of the great gulf above was lost here, but the water cascading down on the level above must certainly have fed this small subterranean ocean, through some indirect means. But instead of creating rapids and breakers, the strange ocean seemed reasonably calm, with only a few rolling waves and a thick, eerily-glowing mist hovering just a few feet above the surface of the black waters.

Through the roiling mist could be seen the vague shape of a titanic island of metal and steel, shaped like a sleek stalactite, coming down from the roof and sinking into the great murky sea, its unseen tip vanishing into the depths. Its sinister shape tugged at the locks on Gale's memory; she *remembered* this place, it was coming back to her, and as it did, she felt a cold terror creep over her.

Sensing Gale's hesitation, Rider led the way, crossing the vast bridge that spanned the deep ocean. It was an enormous metal construction, a causeway built perhaps for titans, so immense that they seemed insignificant atop it, dwarfed by the grandness of its scale, the proportions of its span, and the sweeping, arched supports that held it aloft above the waters.

As the others followed Rider on his trek across the megalithic causeway, their eyes slowly became adjusted to the strange light of this deep, vaulted world. The bridge appeared ancient, but in no danger of crumbling beneath their feet. There were no immediate signs others had passed this way recently but the odd snake-like wire or abandoned pipe swept to the side made it clear the bridge had been prepared for the passage of large vehicles.

They soon saw those very same vehicles, now resting on the broad, crescent-shaped platform on the far side of the causeway, illuminated by the weak blue "starlight" of the cavern's ceiling. They looked like nothing short of odd, insectoid things, two-seat attack craft heavy with bizarre weapon pods mounted under their sleek, stiletto-like wings, each vehicle covered in a patina of centuries-old rust. Enormous squat engines sat at the end of these elegant wings, fitted with huge mouth-like openings at the front filled with rusted and pitted fan-blades. Oil and soot-blackened vectored-thrust ports bristled in the rear. Each of the huge, harrier-like vehicles had an enlarged, bloated hull (perhaps with an interior compartment for carrying a dozen troops or more) that made it look like a great, obese frog squatting on the ground, but as they sat there, as ominous and threatening as they at first seemed, it was clear these strange craft were currently unmanned and unoccupied.

Apparently not to everyone. As they finally reached the far side of the bridge and began to walk among the still hulks of the nameless craft, Ludd moved cautiously over to one, taking small steps, then prodded the metal machine with his staff. He then poked it again, then whaled his staff against it as if it was a sleeping beast, but his efforts did nothing to its armored hull.

Burning Lands 371

While the machines lay dormant, in the back of her mind Gale could vividly remember the shrill ear-piercing shrieks these craft made as they lifted off of the ground and flew through the air.

When Ludd was apparently satisfied that they posed no threat, Valero cracked a glow rod, shook it vigorously, and held the glowing orange stick high overhead. Its bright light danced across the waves of the ocean as he looked back the way they had come. The far side was almost invisible in the darkness, the glow of the great elevator just a pinpoint of dim light. He looked back at the island they stood on, and the mountain of rusted steel that rose up a thousand feet to the ceiling high above. His light illuminated strange lumps, domes and teardrop-shaped bubbles of black glass, but nothing that could be construed as an entrance.

"Look around," he suggested, and the others armed themselves and began to search, but wary of splitting up, stayed close.

Just then Shubazang called out, his voice sounding dull in the darkness. "Over here!" He stood by a portal that slowly began to open, revealing a shadowy bay on the other side, its metal walls covered completely in orange-red rust. Valero moved to bring his light forward, but an ancient bulb in a grilled wall mount came on at that moment, illuminating the passageways that led from this bay and deeper into the artificial "island". The light flickered on and off at irregular intervals but it was enough to see by.

"Who opened that?" Ludd wondered. No one knew, and that realization put them all on edge.

"We're expected?" Rider asked.

Gale nodded to him. They *were* expected. *It* knew she was coming. Somehow, it knew.

Shubazang passed under the doorway into the chamber beyond, which appeared to be a large hangar, perhaps for the same vehicles that now sat on the artificial "beach" outside. The walls were made of steel, ventilation dust of rusted metal loomed overhead, and the wispy trails of broken cobwebs slowly fluttered by like scattered parachutes stirred by an unexpected wind. As they drifted past him, landing in his face and hair, the boy irreverently brushed them off with a sneeze.

"This place could use some repairs," he said.

Euryale followed her boy creator, walking to one of the passages leading from the grand hangar and peering down its length. The others came inside and also began looking around. Eerily-still puddles of oily black water reflected the image of the small party perfectly in their onyx surfaces. Valero's light glowed dimly off of the dull metal surroundings. They saw only dust, rust and ancient cobwebs.

"What's the plan?" Shubazang asked out of the blue.

"Explore," Gale said resolutely. "Find our way. Get our bearings. Some of this is familiar... but I don't remember it being so rundown, so decayed. I guess it's been a long time... It'll come back to me. But for now let's just take it slow."

Rider nodded in agreement and took another glow rod from Valero, cracking it in a similar fashion so that it began to glow with a beam of solid orange light.

"This way?" he asked. Everyone turned and looked. All of the passages looked the same. Gale considered, then nodded back.

For a full hour they explored the upper levels of the strange metallic island, this staggering "facility". Dark metal passages riddled the interior of the great structure, looping nonsensically about one another, doubling back and passing scores of empty black rooms that seemed utterly bare. Huge pipes, power conduits and air ducts wove in and out of these; every surface cloaked in brittle red rust and dripping with moisture. Entire chambers (some as large as auditoriums) were filled with strange, unidentifiable machinery. Other machines' purposes could be guessed at; massive air filtration vents and fans, van-sized power cyclers and burned-out capacitor units, and de-moisturizing sinks once meant to scrub the subterranean air of bad chemicals and toxic carbon dioxide buildup. Spore and mold filters sat dormant on massive metal walls, their slatted vents choked with gray dust and fibrous growths of colorless fungus. Wherever they walked through this quiet jungle of empty passages and deserted rooms, motes of dust and spores of dead fungus were kicked up by their passage, eliciting a few sneezes and coughs as they went.

Gale remembered this place only vaguely, but what she did recall seemed different. It had once been clean, cold and sterile. Now it was a decaying mess. It was clear maintenance of these levels had stopped altogether, stirring up all sorts of questions...

When it seemed they might spend a second hour exploring, and might possibly never find a way down, Rider called out to the others through the maze of passages. He'd found an empty elevator shaft, sinking deep into the metal mountain.

Gale and Valero were the first to catch up, coming up alongside Rider and looking down. Valero noted the lack of an elevator cab, but he immediately moved to find the entrance to a stairwell that should be nearby.

Staring down the darkened chute, Gale sensed something, a palpable evil emanating from below. So sudden, so immense, it staggered her. She stepped back from the black void that was the elevator shaft, mouth hanging open as if choking.

It had sensed *them* earlier, when they first arrived. Now she sensed *it*. It was overwhelming, a sensation of making contact with a hundred minds at once, not unlike being bombarded by the Brotherhood's seers, but far more malevolent and disturbing. For an instant it's eyes were upon her, a menagerie momentarily regarding her with the power of its probing mind. She heard faint voices in her head, stray strands that sounded like the songs of children, the maniacal laughter of men, the horrified screams of women, and the mutterings of the elderly... all a jumble, nonsensical, a thousand thoughts going at once like a whirlpool threatening to drag her down into the depths of insanity.

"No!" she cried out, falling backwards against the wall. Rider ran to her side, and Valero spun around, gun at the ready. But they were alone in the passage.

Shubazang, Euryale and Ludd soon caught up. Shubazang noticed the elevator shaft and checked it out, looking disappointed as well.

"Stairwell?" he asked Rider.

"Still searching. Gale," he said, "you alright, kid?"

Gale looked at Rider for strength. He had no idea what she was experiencing, where her mind had just been, the horror of the sudden, jolting experience, but he saw traces of it in her eyes. He touched her shoulder, squeezed it, and looked at her.

"The stairs..." Gale said, grabbing her gun off the ground where she'd dropped it. "... we can't stop now."

Burning Lands

Valero gave Rider a cautionary look, but the albino ignored him and followed Gale over to a door Shubazang had already opened. The goggled tinker stared down the dark stairwell as it descended out of sight.

At Shubazang's direction Euryale went first, scaling the stairs to the sound of heavy footfalls. He was about to go next when Valero stopped him.

"You sure you want to go next?" Valero asked.

"Oh give me a break," he replied, and shrugged off Valero's hand and went after Euryale.

Gale, Rider, Ludd and Valero soon followed. All eyes swept around them, taking in the darkness, bringing lights to bear to fight off the shadows that seemed to press in from all sides, threatening to snuff their glow rods out and plunge them into lightlessness. The stairs continued down and down, until they finally leveled out inside another in a series of grand subterranean chambers.

"How deep can this go?" Valero wondered aloud, his voice echoing softly through the maze of chambers. *Huge* chambers, fifty feet high and vaulted, with empty, abandoned catwalks at various elevations, riddled with side tunnels large and small. Concrete floors crisscrossed by rubber tubes and hoses, rivers of insulated electrical wiring meandering throughout the caverns with no apparent purpose. Water dripped from the ceilings well above them, and pooled in gray, ugly puddles at their feet.

"Where's the next way down?" Shubazang whispered, hoping his voice wouldn't carry. But the strange acoustics of these caverns caught his voice anyway, scattering it in all directions.

Suddenly Gale turned, eyes darting from side to side. She felt something, a *presence*. She spun around and looked upwards at the rusted catwalk on a wall thirty feet away and forty feet overhead. But at that moment there was no one there; the catwalk was deserted. Rider came up beside her and aimed his rifle where she was staring.

"There's no one there, kid," he said quietly. "Right?"

Gale continued to stare for a long moment, then finally nodded. But she wasn't so sure just a moment ago...

Oblivious to the respect the others gave to Gale's "hunches", Euryale walked a ways ahead, still within sight, then stopped. The android pointed upwards to a spot high on the wall.

Shubazang tore his attention away from Gale and limped over to look. Seeing something, he called back to Valero, "Hey, bring that light."

Words came into view as Valero approached, his light filling the end of the chamber where Euryale stood. Stenciled lettering, partly faded, became visible on the rusted wall: "SUB-COMMUNE GAMMA".

"Does any of this look familiar?" Valero called back to Gale. She tried to remember, but couldn't.

"No," she said, "this, all of this... we didn't see this everyday. This must be some kind of..."

"Support complex," Shubazang interjected, his voice tinged with a hint of growing excitement. "Maintenance, water recycling, air filtration. This is the support complex for something far larger."

"... a hub," she continued, just as if Shubazang hadn't said a word. "This is the entrance to a far larger *city*."

"Really?" Shubazang asked. "Is it really true?"

Gale said nothing but walked over to the passageway beneath the stenciled letters. She felt more familiarity here than anywhere else, even though the corridor was dark, its walls covered in rust and oily stains, and the pipes running overhead seemed to sag dangerously.

Without warning anyone she slipped into the passage and started off. Rider motioned the others to follow and went after her. Shubazang cursed; he'd so hoped to continue examining the antediluvian machinery on this level, but found himself tagging along.

Gale found another stairwell at the end of the long passage and descended, this time only twenty or thirty feet, until poised at the last step, she noticed that this new corridor was partly flooded with gently-lapping gray and brown water. Electricity crackled somewhere down the hall, illuminating part of a side room with a momentary pulse of yellow light. A chipped Styrofoam cup floated by on the water, which by her estimation might be only a foot deep. The sound of dripping water echoed everywhere. Many, many doors and side passages went off in all directions, all of them pitch black.

"This doesn't look good," Valero said, just as Gale took a first step into the murky water, sending ripples in all directions.

As the water lapped around her legs, stirred up by her movements, it frothed and sloshed. An old sock was summoned from underwater and floated to the surface somewhere nearby. A children's book emerged from the murky water, its ancient cover depicting a fair-haired girl in a blue dress kneeling beside a tree stump, peeking around it as a white rabbit vanished down a dark hole and into a fantastical underworld... In a moment the book disappeared once again, vanishing into the translucent grayness of the flooded corridor.

Rider came up behind Gale but hesitated to join her in the water. "Gale..." he whispered, his voice a question, echoing down the partly-flooded corridor.

They saw dark water, stained and eroded concrete walls, rusted, collapsed pipes and air ducts and the periodic flash and pulse of short-circuiting electrical lines somewhere down the tunnel. But at that moment she saw something else:

She remembered a brightly-lit passageway, adults in pure white suits walking down its length, their footsteps dulled by the soft tan carpet. She heard the distinct laughter of children, and from a doorway she and two other kids, a boy and girl, ran out, right into the passing adults, knocking the man over.

There was laughter, and gentle admonishment, that was eventually drowned out by the sound of a soft musical tone that echoed through the halls.

"That's dinner time!" the woman said with a smile, and off Gale and the other children went...

Gale looked in both directions. This was it. This was the place.

"Rider," she asked. "You remember your home?" He didn't answer, he just scanned their surroundings for any danger that might threaten them.

"This was *mine*..." she explained quietly, her voice trembling.

She suddenly began wading through the water, splashing noisily as she went. She seemed unafraid. Before she could slip away from him Rider jumped into the water and followed her. Valero and Ludd were right behind them, each first testing, then hesitantly entering the watery corridor.

Burning Lands

Looking at the dark water below, Shubazang hesitated to follow, remaining at the top of the steps. He and Euryale had significant electronic parts and he didn't want to risk damaging them, and the lure of the chamber they had just passed through so quickly was strong. "We'll be here..." he called out after the others, before tossing a few more packaged light rods to Ludd, who waited at the bottom.

Moments later Gale had traversed the long hall and entered what used to be the community dining complex on this level of the sub-commune. An emergency light flickered on and off, buzzing with sparks as water trickled over its surface. The brief flashes lit the chamber in weak pulses; light shimmered off the surfaces of long elegant tables, whiteboards, huge plasma television screens and the delicate Impressionist pastels on the walls, paintings that attempted to provide the illusion of living above ground.

Rider was stunned. It was just like his home, only on a larger scale, more sophisticated and bright, built for hundreds and hundreds of occupants. He thought of the families that might have once lived here, imagined the laughter of children and the sound of her people's music and chatter. This had been a community once, but like his own (now far behind them) this place was haunting in its emptiness.

Gale saw something else. The water drained away, the light stopped flickering and glowed intensely, from all of the fluorescent bulbs clustered in banks along the ceiling. Faded writing returned to the whiteboards, announcing community events, situational reports and the countdown to the next hibernation period. The echoing trickle of water vanished from her ears and was replaced by a deafening chorus of voices, the sound of chairs screeching on marble tile, of plates and platters and cups clinking during mealtime.

She was suddenly there, years ago. The room was filled with over a hundred people, men, women and elderly. She wasn't supposed to be there, but she peeked from her hiding spot with the other children to listen.

The adults were gathering for a community-wide meeting, a televised conference linking all of the sub-communes in the enormous subterranean complex in one simultaneous "congress".

The television screens came to life, depicting a coterie of scientists in smart white suits somewhere else in the complex, addressing the entire population over the community-conversation system.

"Over the next ten years..." came the voice of the lead scientist, an older man wearing small glasses, his head bald except for a few curls at his ears. It was the man from her earlier dream, the man who'd led her class to examine the dead mutant. Was this before, or after the dissection?

"... we must put into action a plan to begin the improvement of our people so that we may realize the dreams of our ancestors, to return to the surface. As we all now know, the world we came from, the world we hold so dear to our hearts, has long been inhabited by the mongoloid and degenerate descendants of our ancestors' mistakes. Samplings of random survivors found by our scientific teams have led us to the belief that there is little hope, or possibility, of making peaceful contact with these scattered inhabitants of the surface world. Warlike, savage, and in many cases cannibalistic, there appears to be no room for coexistence between us, and them."

There was a sudden exclamation of shock in the room, as men and women alike challenged the commissioner's presumptuous findings. A few shouted, though most merely murmured and gasped.

"Unfortunately we are outnumbered," he continued right over the clamor, "and while we do have a technological superiority, the problem is a matter of mathematics, and time. The cryostasis tanks that sustained us through our long sleep are getting old, so we can no longer count on reverting to dormancy to wait for a more decisive age. This is _our_ time, we must act now and fulfill our mission."

"It is an undeniable reality that our resources, while vast, are dwindling. We need a long-term solution to our problem of not only sustaining ourselves in the violent, hostile climate of the surface, but also to defend our mission, nay, our _obligation_, to rebuild what was destroyed by the Great Enemy in the past, to emerge victorious and claim victory in this war."

Several of the men near the front of the group of adults started booing.

"To this end, the council has formally introduced a proposal before the Community Congress that, as of 1700 hours last evening, was voted into action."

More shouts, this time angrier. A few of the citizens looked afraid, turning to one another and whispering. What dreadful news was coming?

"The community's research division will begin full-scale implementation of the SI drug regimen, as discussed in alpha program 86. Already the Congress has reviewed potential candidates for the first trials of the regimen and selection will begin at 1000 hours tomorrow..."

As the shouting almost became too much, a man stepped to the front of the angry dissenters here in the cafeteria and stood before a glowing white panel in front of the television screen. The room quieted.

"Citizen 2852, James Shea," the man introduced himself through the microphone, interrupting the council on live television. "Speaking from sub-commune Gamma. I'd like to address the respected council if I may." The crowd in the room murmured, apparently being agreeable to this individual speaking on their behalf.

Gale recognized him, even from behind. Standing tall. A strong but passionate voice that gladly revealed his deep concern. He wore his heart on his sleeve. She recognized his curly blond hair, a lot like hers. He was her father.

There was a strange musical tone, which lasted for five full seconds, during which a number appeared in the lower left hand corner of the screen, increasing from 0 to more than 1,500 in seconds. During this the balding scientist conferred with the others on the council for a moment before returning to his microphone, somewhere else in the underground complex. He finally spoke.

"One thousand, five hundred, seventy-one citizens have voted in favor of hearing your petition. Sub-commune Gamma, please speak. Remember, your community is listening."

"Thank you, commissioner," her father replied respectfully, and despite knowing so many people were now hearing his voice he spoke confidently, carried forward by the assurances of those who stood behind him.

"In recent months we, the people of the community, have argued and debated over the needs that consume us. The need for increasing power generation, the need for improving food and water recycling methods, the need for maintaining clean air levels and using our air resources more responsibly. We've also spoken of our long-term need, the very essence of our being, the mission to survive, namely, and also to return to the surface and begin the slow process of rebuilding what was destroyed in the war."

"No one here denies that our ultimate goal will be the healing of the deep wounds suffered not only by our great country, America, but also by the human race as a whole, and even our planet. But there is a general consensus that the approach being taken is, with all due respect, alarming in its implications of violence and cold indifference."

The scientists on the other end seemed surprised and in no small part insulted; they began to murmur amongst themselves in a manner not unlike those here in the cafeteria.

"With all due respect, gentlemen," her father reminded them, "we are *all* scientists here. It's true our entire community was gathered together and put here because of the diversity of our specialties and fields of study, to keep alive what we knew of the past, but let's not overlook that we were also selected to keep alive the very nature of 'humanity' itself. Not just cold hard facts, numbers and scientific data. But also to preserve and, when needed, re-introduce the very real and necessary concepts of truth, justice and compassion to a world still reeling from a nuclear apocalypse."

"What do you propose?" the balding scientist asked rather impatiently.

"*I* propose nothing. What *we* propose is taking more time to review what we've seen and what we've only tasted of the surface world. I fear we are jumping to conclusions about the people who live there..."

"Creatures," the scientist reminded him. "Creatures who show the undeniable traces of overwhelming Asian ethnicity, the ethnicity of the very enemy that invaded our nation and made it what it is. I remind you, good sir, that we are still very much at war with those creatures!"

"People," her father insisted. "They are *people*. And as for the Enemy, it has been two-hundred and fifty years, commissioner. You cannot seriously expect them to harbor the same hostilities and agenda that their forefathers did!"

The commissioner looked embarrassed, and look poised to take the offensive, but he slipped into a more clinical tone. "Politics and ideologies aside, their diminished mental faculties remain reason enough to deny..."

"You know as well as I do that our forefathers charged us with protecting knowledge and dispensing it equally to both the fit and the infirm. We are just the caretakers of these ancient tools, not judges to determine who is worthy and who is not."

The other members of the council conferred discreetly behind the commissioner. He was quiet for a moment, then conceded. "We agree... in spirit. But unfortunately we live in unusual times, and our commune is threatened by these new findings. Emergency measures must be taken..."

"Commissioner..." her father started to interrupt, but was overruled, his voice drowned out and his microphone suddenly frozen to the sound of a flat musical tone heard on the television.

"May I continue? Emergency measures *must* be taken to ensure that our people are capable of surviving on the world above when we finally do choose to reveal ourselves. We have already encountered the very terrifying reality that the deformations of the surface-worlders have led to a new generation of abominations with _psychic_ capabilities, capabilities beyond our original estimations. These, above all else, present the most dire of threats to our security. Why, the very secrecy of our community is at stake here!"

The microphone was off, her father was shut out. He turned around to face the crowd and held his hands up as if to say "what can I do?"

"But there is an answer," the commissioner continued, obviously unaware of the dissent the Congress' decision was stirring in the sub-communes, "and it lies in the development of a drug which appears to unlock latent telepathic, telekinetic and precognitive abilities in a developing human mind. It is our belief, and trials have shown promising results, that continued administration of the drug in a juvenile subject will actually alter the natural development of the cerebral cortex and by extension, unlock capabilities heretofore unknown among the unaltered. We have already seen Mother Nature spawn psychic 'monstrosities' in her crude efforts to advance the deformed species that live like vagrants on the surface world, to allow them to survive in that most hostile of environments. We can do the same here, but under controlled laboratory conditions, where there will be no mistakes, no abortive deformities, no tragic side-effects..."

"But whose children will you take?" someone yelled from the crowd of adults, triggering angry shouts and weeping...

Gale snapped out of it as Rider came to her side. He looked around, wondering what she had seen; but the room was empty now.

Ludd came up from behind, handing off the light rods to Rider. "What did you see?" the old man then asked, his curiosity now also extending to Gale's private thoughts. She closed her eyes but found herself speaking freely.

"My people, their society... they were scientists, all of them, a 'think tank'..."

"A what?" Valero asked.

"A _think tank_," she replied. "A... a group of the brightest minds brought together in one place to get things done. They were assembled during the end times, when the Ancients saw that war was inevitable. This place was built for them. They were installed here with the purpose of re-seeding the planet when the Earth was safe to walk again. They were put in a kind of 'suspended animation' to last the years; most were chosen because they were single, had no families, but some were so valuable to the mission that they were allowed to bring spouses, and up to one child."

Ludd's wide eyes looked alarmed; he could only imagine the horror of those who had had to choose which child to bring...

"Their mission, _our_ mission," she continued, "was to observe and monitor the outside world, the radiation, the development of mutant life. The computers..." she looked up at the ceiling, at no specific point, "... woke us up every ten years so we could check up on things top-side. Sneak outside and take _samples_."

The others were left to imagine just what she meant by "samples".

"For years we believed the survivors, outside, were monsters, degenerate victims of the wars and the mutating effects of radiation. We found only hideous things, full of genetic defects and retardation. But over time we began to see that _your_ people were beginning to develop useful mutations, and the useless, fatal defects were slowly, slowly, disappearing."

Burning Lands

Not completely, Rider thought, thinking of Tank's *microcephaly*, and his own *albinism*. The bestial mine guards of Vegas, the scav he had killed outside Tucumcari, the two-headed performers of the rollicking Far Trader theatre...

Gale went on. "The real threat, they believed, was the undeniable evidence that some of your kind were developing *mind powers*. It terrified them, all of them, because of the threat it posed. Large mutants, *strong* mutants, are one thing, but mutants that can read thoughts, control the mind, and maybe even stumble upon the location of our hidden City was too much to ignore."

"The plan was to develop corresponding abilities in our people, through the use of medical science..." She suddenly stopped speaking and turned away, as if hearing a voice no one else heard, quickly disappearing down another passage.

The young tinker looked down the stairwell and listened. He detected only the dripping of water; the splashes and sounds of the others had faded and were no longer to be heard. He began to get mildly anxious.

"Well they're not coming back," he said to Euryale, who stood there, poised for orders. He looked around, using his own light rod to check that the stairs were indeed intact.

Euryale stepped in front of him to block his view. The android put one hand on its hip for a moment, angling its head as if smiling sweetly at him.

"What? What?" Shubazang asked impatiently, for once unable to guess what his robot was thinking. Euryale slowly pointed to itself, then to him, then back the way they had come.

"No, you oversized jumble of junk! We're not leaving them down here..." He pushed past the robot and looked down the stairs. He sighed.

"Alright, let's go after them. Just be careful."

Euryale hesitated for a moment, then started obediently down the stairs with a sway of its metal hips. It stopped midway, looking back at Shubazang.

"We're not leaving, so cut that out. Just keep going. And don't slip in the water, or your actuators will crap out."

Euryale vanished down the steps; the 'droid would be alright, so long as only its legs were submerged and nothing else. The fake flesh legs, older than the rest of the robot, were of pre-Fall manufacture, the rubbery skin perfectly capable of protecting the metal musculature underneath. The rest of Euryale, the parts he had fashioned, were bare metal and wire and were at risk.

Watching Euryale descend carefully, Shubazang seemed satisfied and prepared to follow, when for a moment he saw movement out of the corner of his eye.

Already alert because of the unusual nature of his surroundings, Shubazang spun quickly and held the light rod above his head. The glow caught on the rims of his goggles and gleamed, but he saw nothing, just the dark passage from which they had all come. He felt an unnerving sensation in that moment, an intuitive alarm that keyed him to the presence of something just outside the edge of his light.

"Who's there?" he asked, bringing his rifle up to his hip.

He was a competent mercenary, a hunter who'd tracked and killed many dangerous men. But this time his voice faltered and cracked as he called out weakly into the darkness.

"I said, *who's there!?*"

Nothing. Silence.

With a sudden jerk of his hand he tossed the glow rod down the hall, hoping to catch a glimpse of whatever might be lurking further down the corridor. The glow rod soared, landed and skittered to a stop against the foot of one wall, casting its eerie golden light over several yards of bare concrete. But there was no one there.

"*Fuck this!*" he whispered, cracking another glow rod as he descended backwards down the stairs, eager to join Euryale at the bottom.

Gale, Rider, Valero and Ludd left the flooded area and passed down dark halls, illuminated only by their vivid orange light rods. They passed dormitory blocks, the individual domiciles of family units (one husband, one wife, and one child each) all neatly arrayed in ordered rows up and down the gridwork of halls. They walked through dormant galleries where ingenious hydroponics had once created islands of lush plant life to break the monotony of living underground, with the added benefit of circulating the unnatural environment's stale air. The dormitory blocks were arranged around these "hydro-gardens", like grand public parks, some more than four stories tall, like the vibrant center of a giant indoor mall. Everything in the complex was designed around the community, and each community was separated from the neighboring one by sealed halls and security doors, connected only by all-day television broadcasts. These measures, from hydroponic parks to completely compartmentalized living, were meant to stave off insanity and, in the event of a disease outbreak or fire, prevent the entire commune from being wiped out in one tragic, catastrophic accident.

But the great galleries were now populated only by dead, shriveled up husks of ferns and flowering bushes, the intricate mechanisms of their hydroponic growers having shut down long, long ago. Each galleria was now just a huge, empty space that echoed every footstep, and collected deep sinister shadows wherever their lights failed to touch. The television systems that once connected the people of one sub-commune to the next were no longer functioning; instead, the wall-sized screens were cold, black and silent. The underground City itself was, in a word, dead.

Ludd leaned weakly against a wall, immediately holding up a hand when Gale turned to goad him on.

"Wherever you're headed, keep going, child," he said. "I'll be here. Just a moment... to catch my breath."

Although he was hesitant to leave anyone behind, even for a moment, when Gale walked off with Valero, Rider went along as well, until the three of them entered a series of softly-decorated rooms. These new chambers appeared to have once served as a communal "daycare" for this particular sub-commune's youngsters; each room was screened from the next by gaily-decorated curtains depicting dancing elephants and circus clowns. Gale lingered in the doorway for a moment, taking in the new sights and smells, moisture, rot and cloying dust, before stepping inside and looking around.

This place was familiar. She remembered it well.

Rider looked at the old crayon drawings pinned to the walls and corkboards, the scattered toys on the floor and piled in plastic laundry baskets arranged along the walls. Valero stared at the banks of video consoles once used for advanced learning, but feeling ill at ease here he returned to the door, looking out and waiting for Ludd to catch up.

"The old man said he'd only be a minute," Valero whispered nervously. "And the boy and his machine? Where did they go?"

"We used to *play* here..." Gale said, ignoring him, her thoughts preoccupied by dredging up her frightful, buried memories. As she spoke her voice seemed louder than it should have been in this dead place, but Gale, at least, seemed unafraid.

As she spoke, Rider went over to the curtains and pulled them back, looking into an adjoining room. More toys, blankets for nap-time, small television monitors. He reached for yet another screening curtain, but when he pulled it back he was surprised by what was hidden on the other side: a discreet setup of medical monitoring equipment.

"You were being monitored," Rider said, turning to Gale. "All the time?"

She didn't answer the question directly. "I remember the scientists doting over my generation. They administered... a special *chemical* to all of us. It was supposed to help our people, give us abilities, unlock powers of the mind we had only once dreamed about. It was supposed to make us 'evolve' into greater beings. They nicknamed it 'Ascendance'."

She looked over at one wall, where a glass partition separated the daycare from another room. Her tone changed.

"Our parents could visit us during the day. I remember my father and mother looking through this glass. Waving hello. They looked on, powerless."

"I remember the scientists were fascinated by what we, the children, were becoming. I remember words like 'psychic', 'telepath' and 'precognitive'."

She looked around at the nursery, finally finding an old, empty IV bottle and its tangle of clear cords. She lifted the needle and stared at it, crusted with a greenish-brown residue. Subconsciously she reached down with her other hand and held the spot on her arm where she had once worn terrible needle scars.

"The drug changed those who took it. Our minds grew in strange ways, enhanced parts of our brains that had always been dormant before. With new pathways opened we began to experience the world differently... we were able to see the immediate future. We could 'hear' other's thoughts, we could feel emotions like you might feel a pulse. Being able to see the future moments ahead we became quicker, our reflexes inhuman. We could sense brain activity, 'see' the energy of a man's thoughts like a beacon in the dark, and we soon had no need for our eyes and ears; we were drawn to other people by our minds."

She looked at herself in one mirrored glass partition.

"Spurred on by our example they advanced the process prematurely, giving Ascendance to everyone. Not just the children. We were just the guinea pigs. Now the adults, the entire general public, were eager to take it. They began administering the drug first to the community's guardians, the military, then amongst the lead scientists themselves. Only a few stubborn citizens declined to take the drug, people like my mother and father. Their warnings fell on deaf ears. Everyone else was ecstatic; they lined up, eager to take part. Too many years sleeping underground; they were ready to take a chance."

Gale looked up again, eyes sweeping over the decaying panels of the ceiling.

"I remember the slogan: *Return topside in our lifetime!*"

Valero looked out, his ears tuned to the passages outside. Ludd emerged from the shadows, with Shubazang and Euryale close behind. He almost fired with his rifle, but the old man held up his wrinkled hand to assure him he was no ghost lingering in this deserted place. Valero gasped in uncharacteristic relief, and pulled his weapon away.

As Valero and the others joined Rider and Gale inside, Gale suddenly looked down a connecting hall, and went that way, as if compelled by a lingering memory to lead them somewhere else... in a hurry. Though they had just caught up, and were becoming increasingly uncertain, the rest of the expedition members followed.

"Find anything?" Shubazang asked Valero, as they brought up the rear.

"Nothing," Valero said, never taking his eyes off the passage ahead, growing wary of Gale's strange behavior. "You?"

"Thought I heard something a ways back... but when I looked I didn't see anything. Still, better keep your guard up..."

Ludd was feverish but he spoke playfully. "Phantoms... *in the dark?*" Valero looked away, choosing not to reveal that this place was beginning to unsettle him too.

After a few minutes passing several intersections, Gale led them by memory to another community center, but this one was different than the one before. This wasn't a cafeteria or mess area, but a recreational facility of some sort, with multiple arcades and inter-connected rooms. But it was the condition of these rooms that alarmed everyone present.

The walls were scratched, and in places gouged with tiny pits. Valero immediately recognized a blood spatter pattern on two of the four walls of the first entryway, each of them violent enough to suggest an explosion of some kind. But there were no signs of pyrotechnic burns, or fire of any kind. Tables and chairs were toppled here and there, and garbage from a bin was strewn all over the floor.

"Not as peaceful as upstairs..." Rider observed aloud, indicating the faded blood spray with his rifle.

"No gunshots, though," Valero said, walking over to the wall and tracing his fingers over the slight gouges in the concrete surface. "Something else? Some advanced weapon? A laser?"

"Mmm, no," Shubazang said, examining them as well. "Looks like shrapnel. Tiny bits of shrapnel?"

"What the hell is *this?*" Shubazang now said, his attention moving to the blood. He lifted his light so everyone could see what had alarmed him. The blood of one spatter had been smeared by a finger, leaving a strange message -

LAL SI LHEL

Ludd came over immediately to read the letters, but seemed as dumbfounded as the rest. He looked at Gale but got only a blank stare. She looked afraid.

More rooms, most empty, all of them showing strange signs of frantic activity. Noticeable gouges in the marble floors where heavy furniture had been dragged to and fro for no known purpose. Then, in one dark and otherwise bare chamber, they found the missing furnishings, comprising a bizarre and alien *sculpture* - a pile of chairs, sofas and couches, all stacked atop one another, in the center of the room. Their presence, and the significance of the "sculpture", escaped them all.

"Curious..." Ludd muttered.

Each of them walked about the room, staring at the sculpture in unnerved silence, from every angle. But it gave up no answers. Eventually they all turned to leave, when suddenly the finely-balanced heap fell apart with a clatter that echoed throughout the miles of passages.

Everyone turned to see Euryale next to the heap, hand extended; it had curiously touched the sculpture and knocked it over.

"*Don't do that again!*" Shubazang snapped at it.

"Give me a heart attack, why don't you!" Ludd wheezed, clasping his chest as he coughed.

The android imitated a look of shame before coming over to Shubazang's side, head hung low.

Rider glared at Shubazang, making it clear he wanted the tinker to keep a tighter leash on his "toy". They then continued on, through other rooms exhibiting dizzying signs of degenerating sanity. Next they passed by a viewing chamber, all of its glass partitions smashed and shattered by thrown furniture. More blood spatters covered the walls and floor, enough gore to suggest a bloodbath. But there were no bodies, not even bones.

They walked through a dark galleria, somewhere near the bottom, with two or three levels above them. Their boots echoed up and down the dark shaft, their lights glinted off of sleek steel railings on the tiers above. Socks, clothing, broken chairs and miscellaneous papers and implements littered the bottom of the galleria as if thrown from the upper levels in some past "riot".

Hanging from one of the upper levels, just visible at the edge of their light rods' glow, was a huge banner made of stitched bed sheets; on it were these nonsensical words -

ADNEMD EW REA

Brazenly splashed across the banner, they were written as if the meaningless words held penultimate significance.

"Gibberish..." Shubazang pointed out. Ludd nodded slowly as if to confirm Shubazang's appraisal.

They passed in front of two idle double doors, one of which still hung open. Rider peered into the dark chamber beyond, his sensitive eyes seeing a grand chamber with hundreds of seats and a great whiteboard on the far side like some huge university auditorium. It was so garbage strewn it looked like a hurricane had passed through.

"Looks like a disaster in here," he said. Curious, the others followed him inside.

Beyond the doors the auditorium resembled a deep dark cavern, except the place was a chaotic shambles, with overturned garbage bins and broken tools and toys everywhere. They beheld a bloodstained carpet, as if buckets of the stuff had been thrown about in a terrible row. More writing covered virtually every stretch of wall, in crayon, marker and swirling pen, depicting indecipherable phrases and words, one over another, until the walls were completely covered in one continuous jumble of wild colors.

"Your people went *insane*," Rider proclaimed.

Gale stared at the blood on the auditorium floor. "My people became gripped by their addiction to Ascendance, and the strange new sensations brought on by the willing deformation of their brains. Some even found it... pleasurable. Mind-altering. *Mind-opening*. They began scrapping other projects, water control, environmental engineering, draining other resources to advance the manufacturing of the chemical in massive quantities."

"Just when it seemed everyone had jumped on board, the first side effects began to appear. A full year after the start of the regimen, the most advanced children began to go insane, uncontrollable. Soon some of the adults and soldiers went mad as well. They became obsessive, crazy over the drug. Any talk against it was considered... *treason*."

"One of the leading researchers, one of those who had first developed Ascendance, was publicly hung when he tried to curtail its production until further studies could be made."

Shubazang looked shocked, the idea of such rash behavior among men of science seemed to rattle him.

"My father, my mother and others were afraid to take the drug. At first they were tolerated, so long as they didn't interfere. But my father was a good man, he believed in doing the right thing, so he began to research a treatment in secret. He had my mother, of course, and other colleagues on his side, and they worked feverishly to find an answer before everything spiraled out of control."

"Did they find a cure?" Shubazang asked.

"My father came up with a *treatment*, which he administered to me. It stunted the process, saved me before I became too far gone. But the scientists, driven mad, thought my father was trying to sabotage their efforts to 'better the species'. They sent military men, our people's guardians, to intimidate my father into denouncing his stand against it."

"That's when my father realized we had to escape. He came up with a plan, he managed to get his hands on radiation suits and supplies, even weapons. He gathered all his notes, put them in a case, and took them with us. But the commission... now just a gang of raving madmen... unleashed the soldiers... who were just as addicted as everyone else... to bring us back. My father hoped we'd get away, find an island of sanity someplace else... but he was wrong. They sent the guardians, now *Huntsmen*, after us. But Ascendance had already changed them, too. Driven to psychosis, they didn't try to capture us alive; they came to kill us and bring back our carcasses."

"We got as far as the refinery towers, just outside the Burning Lands, when they caught up to us. My father and mother hid me when they heard the Huntsmen coming. They tried to resist..."

"You got away..." Valero reminded her. "At least one of you survived." But Gale was quiet.

"What happened to your people, then?" Shubazang asked over his shoulder. "*This* place has fallen apart. Where is everyone?"

"They're *here*," she said. "Waiting."

"Where?" he asked.

"*In the shadows...*"

At that moment Shubazang felt a need to look about, sweeping the darkness with his light, remembering the strange feeling of being watched on the level above. But there was no one there.

"Waiting for what?" Rider asked Gale.

"Waiting for me to return, I think."

"Why?"

"I'm not sure..."

"What have they been up to in the meantime?" Valero asked.

"I suppose they've continued with their 'mission'. They've dissolved into madness, but they still believe it is their duty to reclaim the surface world, and eradicate those who live there. God only knows what will happen if they succeed."

"It's like they're repeating their last directives," Shubazang said, coming back to the conversation. "Like robots?"

Gale didn't answer, unsure.

"So what do we do?" Rider asked, returning to what seemed imperative.

"Someone must still be in charge," she said. "Someone who can still think. I know the rest are automatons, but they must be directed by some higher intelligence."

"How do you know?" Rider asked directly.

"I can sense its presence here," she said, looking straight into his eyes. "And so could the Brotherhood. They knew something still lived in this dismal sepulcher. Something with such a strong psychic signature that they could feel it from hundreds of miles away. And I think they sent me to... destroy it?"

She seemed even more uncertain as she spoke the words.

"What, they're not comfortable with another big, psychic fish in their pond?" Valero joked irreverently.

"What is it?" Shubazang asked, fascinated by the possibilities of what might lie, unseen, on the levels below.

"I don't know. But it is sentient, and it has continued our original mission to a tee. It has taken subjects from the wasteland to be examined and studied. The villages of Uncle Sam's empire, the Far Traders. All of them killed and brought back to be dissected and examined, to give it a fuller understanding of the 'enemy' it will face when it finally chooses to reveal itself."

She looked at everyone.

"We have to find it. I don't know how; maybe guns will work, maybe words, I don't know. But the diseased mind that lives here *must* be dealt with."

They all fell quiet, looking in different directions, suddenly feeling very isolated so far under the earth.

"What if we bump into someone down here? Do we try reasoning with them? Would they listen?" Ludd asked.

"No..." Gale mumbled. "Long ago they were men beneath their armor, but now... Now all I sense is emptiness. They changed, physically, becoming... *monsters*. They became blind to the world around them, hearing and seeing only thoughts and the life-force of living things. It drove them insane. They went mad, groping their way through the dark with only their mind-senses to guide them. And when they found someone in the black void, a man, a woman, *anyone*, they ravaged him, tearing him apart and consuming the energy of his thoughts..."

Gale closed her eyes tightly; it was obvious she had seen someone killed in this inexplicable fashion, and was struggling to bury the horrific memory.

They all looked at one another, but Gale continued.

"Even the smallest child could overcome an un-enhanced adult because they could see where he was going, what he was about to do. Could read his thoughts. They were lightning fast, quick. Ascendance enhances everything mental - thought, speed, senses, emotions."

Rider thought back to their flight from Oasis, years ago, when she had easily avoided the axe of one of Valero's thugs. Now it made sense.

"But it also drives them insane," she continued. Just then she realized everyone was staring at her, and felt compelled to defend herself. "My father found a treatment, he administered it to me... I'm not like that."

"You're a little bit of both," Valero said. "Human... and *inhuman*."

Gale stared at him in response to his comment, but then looked distracted. She pointed down a nearby passage.

"We want to go this way. If you can open the door at the end of this tunnel, I think we'll be close to where we want to be."

They came to a huge metal portal at the end of one of the deeper tunnels, which they guessed would lead them to another, separate "sub-commune" of the City. The metal door was enormous, with half a dozen hydraulic bar locks and several feet of solid metal, something like the massive gate that once kept NORAD secure. Banks of computer screens flanked it on all sides, but these were all dark.

Gale looked at the door and muttered "This is it...". The others brought their weapons to bear.

Shubazang moved forward to examine the door from a distance of a few feet, looking for some kind of access panel.

To their surprise, one of the computer screens came to life. With a crackle it blinked on, bathing the corridor with its grayish glow. Everyone stared at the screen, speechless, as if afraid it might somehow harm them.

Gale was the first to hear it, but then the others too, began to lean in close to hear the strange muffled murmurings coming from the "other side". A pulsing, undulating susurrus that caused each of them to strain their ears to hear it.

Suddenly, from somewhere off-screen, a face slid sideways into view, immediately taking up the entire screen.

It *seemed* normal, but something about the face made the others step backwards, as even their dormant sixth senses were stirred, keenly aware that something entirely unnatural was at work here.

Gale immediately recognized the face - plump cheeks, hanging lower lip, unkempt tufts of white hair at the temples. It was the commissioner.

But something wasn't right. His lips were glossed with spittle, and his mouth hung open. His glasses were missing. His weirdly dilated eyes moved slowly from left to right, then down to some point off camera, as if he didn't even realize where the camera lens was. His head bobbed slowly up and down and tipped first right, then left, as if he was on a raft on a swelling ocean tide. His movements were accompanied by a barely-audible, wet, sloshing noise...

Gale tried to see his neck, his shoulders, but the commissioner seemed to react to her prying by moving closer, until the screen was completely taken up by his face. But, apparently unsatisfied that he was concealing whatever he meant to conceal, the man on the other side abruptly cut the video feed.

The screen went black again. They heard nothing but the momentary crackle of static, then silence.

"What the fuck was that?" Valero asked, the first to break the silence.

"The *commissioner*," Gale explained. "He was our leader, our most senior scientist, the man they elected to make decisions for the community. He's the one that led us to our destruction..."

Like a spirit responding to the speaking of a magical name, the massive door opened with a hiccup of pressurized air, creaking slowly open on massive hinges, its lock mechanisms ticking one by one as they slid back into the wall. Gale, Rider, Valero, Shubazang, Euryale and Ludd all watched with increasing anticipation.

The door stopped as it opened fully.

Valero and Shubazang brought their lights to bear on the yawning opening, barely penetrating the empty blackness beyond.

"Where will this take us?" Rider asked Gale.

"To the deeper laboratories," she said enigmatically, before becoming quiet. Her memories were flowing like water now, and she didn't want to miss a thing. She had to know, even more than they did. She only had to wait for the memories to come.

Rider took in a deep breath, then led the way through the black gate and into the passage beyond. Everyone else came through, one by one, with Shubazang and Ludd at the rear.

Gale eagerly moved ahead of them all. On the other side of the door was a maze of passages, all of them pitch black; on the levels above there had been *some* light, from malfunctioning circuits and crackling wiring, but here it was silent, black, and cold.

Despite not being able to see a thing Gale walked out of the main corridor and into a side passage, immediately choosing the second door on the left and entering, even before the others could see it. Valero had to hurry to keep up; Euryale walked at a more leisurely pace, watching Gale with interest, following them both inside.

Gale knew where she was, but it took a moment for Valero to bring his light forward to get a feel for the place. They were in a clinic. It was dark, the steel surfaces had rusted in places, and ceiling panels had collapsed, letting loose coils of black, snake-like electrical wiring unfurl onto the floor.

Gale began to remember a different time, when this place was well-lit and polished. The scientists were discussing something strange with her father, and whatever it was, began degenerating into an angry debate.

Her father and several other comrades shouted at the huge television screen that hovered over everything in the clinic. The balding commissioner and his gang of scientists were there, in some other sub-commune somewhere else, looking sickly, disheveled. A wild spark danced in the commissioner's eyes.

"We admit we may have made mistakes, but now is not the time to be pointing fingers! We need to put our minds... together... to formulate a solution, not cast blame! We need to bring our ideas and perspectives together if we're going to survive this!"

Her father and the others were baffled to understand what the commissioner meant. They began questioning the commissioner, but the screen grew static and hazy...

She snapped out of it, but the commissioner's voice still echoed hauntingly in her mind: *"We need to put our minds..."*

"... together..."

Rider, Shubazang and Ludd spun around when the giant doorway groaned as it closed behind them, finally settling flush against the wall. Rider ran over and pushed against the massive portal, but it was pointless. Whoever or whatever had opened it for them now wanted it closed.

"Let's stay together," he said, and they immediately followed the others.

They caught up and found Valero and Euryale standing in a large, dark chamber, watching Gale, who seemed to be in a trance. They said nothing, afraid to disturb her.

Shubazang looked around with his light, then moved to a bank of pharmacy cabinets on one side of the clinic, pushed against the wall. He handed his light rod to Euryale, who followed him and now stood motionless like a tree, while the tinker cleared the glass cases of dust so that he could peer through at the bottles of medicine on the other side.

"What are you looking for?" Valero asked, coming over.

"This is a clinic, right?" the young man replied.

"I guess..."

"Ancient medicine," he explained simply. "I've used it before. In a cave, a long time ago, when I lost my hands. It kept me alive. Just barely. Come on, help me find it. Something called 'Polyregenerative Supplement B'".

Valero came over and helped examine the cases. He saw over one hundred bottles, all of them covered in labels crowded with ancient letters. After a minute Shubazang tapped one metal finger against the glass of the right-hand case, pointing at several small glass bottles on the other side that read, *"PolyRegenSuppB"*. He grinned, formed a fist, then punched through the locked door with a startling crash of glass.

"Be careful," Rider warned, "that stuff wasn't meant for our kind."

He meant *mutants*. Ancient medicine was designed centuries ago for a race of unaltered beings, creatures with a uniform set of genetic blueprints; all the same organs, identically-functioning internal systems. Any alteration of this uniform blueprint, visible or otherwise, meant that their drugs might not work as expected. They could even be lethal. A defective heart, malfunctioning kidneys, altered blood cells, organs that produced too much or too little of one hormone or another, and something that was once developed to save lives might instead serve as a fast-acting *poison*.

"I've used it before," Shubazang stated. "Besides, I haven't got much of a choice." He took out one of the bottles, fumbled around for a fresh syringe, and put it through the rubber stopper at one end. As he lifted it up and drew the medicine into the translucent tube, he read the label of the bottle, noted its expiration.

"Thank the Ancients for space-age shelf life..." he chuckled.

When the syringe was full he removed it from the bottle and injected himself close to the wounds on his leg.

Euryale watched as the needle pierced his tattered flesh. The motion of the chemical slowly entering his bloodstream was reflected in Shubazang's goggle lenses, but he didn't even wince in pain.

Finishing up, he removed the syringe and tossed it aside. Rider watched his face for any signs of trouble. Valero looked at the bottle and picked it up.

Shubazang began to break into a sweat. A moment later he paled noticeably. Rider put down his gun and moved in to watch more closely.

"I'm... okay..." Shubazang said in a weak voice. He continued to produce bullets of cold sweat that trickled profusely down his face. He was shivering now.

The men watched in amazement as the wounds on his leg began to heal, the skin regenerating around the open wounds, the deep gouges filling in with a clear fluid that quickly turned opaque, taking on the color and consistency of the surrounding flesh. No scab, no scar, just new skin and muscle that replaced the previously-destroyed tissues.

"Just... a little... *painful*..." Shubazang said haltingly, until at last the drug had done its job. It would take a few weeks for functional hair follicles to form in the new flesh, but the bleeding stopped and the wounds were healed.

"Any cures for radiation sickness?" Valero joked dryly. Shubazang looked back at the bottles in the case, but shook his head.

After regaining his breath, to show that he was alright Shubazang got up on his own power, standing upright on both legs. But as soon as he gained his footing he stumbled, crashing into another of the cabinets.

"Sit back down," Rider commanded, but Shubazang waved him off.

"No, I'm okay... really. Let's go."

Valero looked at Shubazang, then the bottle. He put it down. But while Valero shied away from it, Shubazang was a believer and snatched it up and put it in his pocket, along with a handful of plastic-wrapped syringes. He might need to take that same chance again later.

No one noticed as Gale emerged from her trance. While the others watched Shubazang explore the medical supplies, she moved back to the doorway where Ludd waited, watching the others with amused interest.

Despite his smile the old man's red eyes looked weak and tired; his skin was getting gray and wisps of hair fell from his brow as he sat there. Feeling her eyes on him, he looked up at her.

"Are you alright, child?"

She stopped staring and nodded, then looked back over her shoulder to the others.

"This way."

"There's a way down..." Gale muttered indistinctly, stopping at an intersection. Unlike before, she seemed unsure. It would take her a second to remember.

At that moment there was a distant sound, a rumbling that coursed through the metal walls and floors.

"The door!" Rider said, turning around and looking back down the tunnel.

"It's opening!" Shubazang finished, turning his light that way. The light only went so far, and it illuminated an empty passage. The huge portal they had entered through, and which was now opening to let some mysterious visitor through, was around the corner, out of sight.

"Move!" Gale shouted, with a sudden urgency in her voice that pushed everyone into action.

Gale led the way, running from the sound of the opening portal, turning at another intersection and sprinting down another long, straight passageway. Ludd gasped in agony as he tried to keep up, until Valero grabbed him and carried him alongside him. Rider and Euryale were next, with Shubazang in the rear, the tinker constantly turning his head to look back, holding his light to see whatever he might see while still keeping pace with the others.

They entered a hemispherical chamber that began to glow as they brought their lights in with them. Passages went off in all directions, each of them sealed by a metal door. Gale stopped running as she came to the foot of one large doorway standing opposite the passage from which they had just come. It had no handles, no lock, just a sheet of solid metal that sealed off the passage beyond. A dormant security monitor sat on one side of it.

Gale turned to make sure the others were there. Valero groaned as he released Ludd, and the old man stumbled and fell to the ground in a heap of exhaustion. Wracked by the killing effects of radiation, he was slipping fast, but he struggled to sit upright despite the agony.

The passage they had come from was still dark, a black wall their lights could not penetrate. The sound of the opening portal subsided. But they heard and saw nothing.

Gale turned back to the door. "I think the way down is past one of these," she said. She felt the cold metal of the door in front of her, but it remained in place.

"Get it open," Shubazang said abruptly. "Get it open, now!"

"I can't!" Gale shouted back.

Just then the screen blinked to life again. The commissioner's face floated there, filling it. A speaker crackled weakly with the commissioner's voice. Some trick of the faulty modulator caused an echo, so that as he spoke quiet whispers, many whispers, repeated everything he said.

"Who's... thhherrre?" he asked. The eerie voice coming from the monitor's speaker silenced everyone in the room. Their urgency to flee was replaced by the more terrifying sense that they were being addressed by something *alien*.

While Rider kept guard on the passage, Shubazang, Valero and Ludd all forgot the unseen danger in the tunnels and stared at the face on the screen. Shubazang was the first to speak, a whispered observation - "Have you noticed... he never blinks?"

Whoever (whatever) he really was, he didn't seem to hear Shubazang. The face's eyes continued to shift, up, down, to the corners. It reminded Gale of a ventriloquist's dummy, its eyes moved by unseen hands working behind the scenes.

At that moment Gale felt the onslaught again, the sudden intrusion of hundreds of minds into her own. She was stunned by the sudden, unexpected contact, which felt like slippery, unwelcome feelers probing and prying into the deepest recesses of her mind.

Following this, the face spoke once more:

"Yesss, Alice... welcome baaack... to *Wooonnnderland...*"

With the grinding of metal cogs the door slid upwards into the ceiling, revealing a dank, rusted metal access way on the other side.

Immediately their attention was drawn back to the passage from which they had just emerged. It was still dark and silent, but the hairs on the backs of their necks, one and all, stood on end. *Something* was there. Something was following them, snaking its way through the tunnels and passages and gallerias above after them, unseen. Gale had sensed it before, on the levels above; Shubazang, too. Now they *all* sensed its presence; though it remained unseen, something in the air changed, their bodies felt "aware" of danger and it was only minutes behind them.

"Now, Gale, now!" Rider shouted.

Shubazang led the way, holding his light rod outwards as he might a torch, intending to push back the darkness. Euryale was close behind him.

"Are we going?" he asked.

Hesitating for only a moment, Gale stepped through the doorway with them.

As soon as she crossed the threshold, however, the door immediately dropped from the ceiling like a steel trap, instantly sealing her, Shubazang and Euryale on one side, leaving Rider, Valero and Ludd on the other.

Gale immediately spun around and started hammering on the cold face of the door. "Rider! Rider!" she called.

With this sudden trickery, the sense that they were in danger returned in a flood. Valero turned and watched the dark passage behind them, gun raised and ready, while Rider came over and hit the door with the butt of his weapon. It wouldn't budge.

"Gale! Can you hear me?" he shouted. "*Gale!*"

Gale could hear nothing through the three-inch metal. She continued to hit the thick hatch but her efforts went in vain.

Shubazang came over with urgency. Feeling the door's surface he turned and motioned Euryale to come back, and remembering what the 'droid could do to a metal hatch, Gale stepped out of the android's way.

Euryale seemed to know what to do and immediately punched the door, but the android's metal actuators flattened against the high-resistance polysteel portal. Sparks flew as it whaled against the door again and again, but the metal proved impossible to penetrate, or even dent.

"Shit!" Shubazang cursed.

"Oh no..." Gale whispered.

On the other side of the door it was silent. Valero kept his eyes glued on the passage, while Ludd attempted to get to his feet, only to slip and fall back down. His strength was fading, the radiation was taking its toll.

Rider gave up on the door, cursed to himself, and rejoined the other two.

They noticed a dim light in the passage behind them. An odd bluish glow emanating from something around the corner, weakly illuminating the walls, the pipes, the rusted floor. Something was coming, and its luminous eyes were washing over the corridor as it went, guiding it along.

The sensation that something was close to being upon them now filled the three men with dread. Valero broke from his stand and ran to another nearby passageway.

"Come on, this way!" he shouted. Without any better options, Rider moved to join him.

"Wait... for me..." Ludd said, only now getting up on weak legs. Rider turned back and started towards him, when not one but a *handful* of creatures emerged from the passage and entered the room. Their sudden appearance froze him in place.

Cold blue eyes swept the room, each a glowing lens pivoting wildly on a mechanical servomotor. Their bodies were covered from head to toe in a gigantic suit of intricately-woven kevlar hoses, so fine as to resemble bare human musculature. These bundles of artificial "muscle" came together at a seam that ran the length of each creature, from the top of the head to the crotch, splitting it down the middle. Thick hoses ran from a strange hump on the back of each creature, under its arms, and back up to its face, so that each creature's face seemed oddly squid-like, the dangling hoses swaying back and forth as it moved. From these came a sickly sucking sound, like the life support systems of a dying cancer patient straining to draw vital fluids up and into its mask. Each creature's hand was a gruesome mechanical apparatus, an exoskeletal reproduction of the human appendage almost twice normal size and ending in grossly-powerful claws that gripped strange, complex rifles.

There were four of them, ominous and silent. Their eight eyes scanned the room nonsensically, each moving independently of the other, casting globes of blue light against the walls wherever their beams came to bear. Quickly these lights converged on Ludd, who began to back against the closed doorway. There was no escape.

"Run, Rider!" Ludd cried out, seeing his death before him. With that the first of the Huntsmen moved forward and loomed over the old man. The others gathered around as if eager to watch, as if this was some solemn ceremony, as if each time they fed and snuffed out a life it was a religious experience of unknowable pleasure even to *witness*.

The thing reached up and slowly took off its rubbery mask, its removal accompanied by the hiss of the detached oxygen tubes of its complex breathing apparatus. The glow in its glass eyes faded as the mask came off, and the horror of what had become of Gale's people was revealed at last.

Ludd stared, gaping in terror, at the husk beneath the armor. It only partly resembled what it had once been in life, a human being, and now looked more like the dry, shriveled up remains of an embalmed mummy, its body solely kept alive by the drug, Ascendance, coursing through its very being. Every organ, every system, was saturated by the chemical, its heart and veins pumping and carrying it throughout its body. Its skin had lost its warm color and was now gray, dead and cold; hair no longer grew from its pores; veins bulged and pulsed as the drug coursed through the artificially-animated body. Its face was shrunken, a skull with paper-thin flesh drawn over it, its muscles atrophied now that its electric suit performed every motion and exercise for it. Its eyes were sunken into its sockets, and rolled back blindly now that it had no need for sight, now that it could find its way through detecting life and thoughts nearby.

It leaned ever closer towards Ludd's head. As it came its shriveled lips peeled back to reveal black, rotted teeth and a diminished tongue, preceded by the hideous odor that came from within, the stench of dead and dying organs and putrefying innards kept functioning only by the animating power of Ascendance.

Its mouth fell open with the crack of locked muscles being forced apart, extending to unnatural proportions, until it stood poised to swallow the old man's entire head.

At that moment an ear-piercing shriek, its banshee call, emanated from within the thing. Ludd screamed too, in a pitch so high that it spoke of unimaginable agony and fear. Paralyzed, he could not move, only stare helpless as the thing moved to within a foot of his head and began to devour his life energy.

Burning Lands

Ludd's head shook violently and shrunk up before Rider and Valero's very eyes; it seemed to literally *stretch* out of shape and was drawn towards the monster's open mouth. Ludd's eyes bulged outwards as if being pulled out by its sucking breath, until they popped out of their sockets. Lifeless, his head fell to the side and his body slumped motionless back against the door.

The ghoulish act of devouring Ludd's mind was reflected perfectly off of Rider's wide, horrified eyes. He saw the thing finish feeding and slowly replace its mask; before the headpiece completely concealed it again, he couldn't help but stare at the shriveled head underneath, at the eyes rolled back in the head, knowing that the creature that had done this was no longer a human, or even sentient, but something almost entirely animal in nature. A feeder, a thing motivated solely by its unnatural hungers.

Valero was already gone, having disappeared down the passage, Rider and Ludd be damned. Realizing he was alone, Rider sunk back into the dark corridor. The other creatures began to step forward into the chamber, looking over the old man their comrade had just murdered. Slowly the one kneeling rose to its feet, joining the other gigantic armored creatures until it was indistinguishable among them.

These were once soldiers, professionally trained men and women, but now they were shadows, more mindless predator than anything else, only following the psychically-broadcast orders of something yet unseen. Some lingering compulsion forced them to obey its demented commands, and its command, right now, was to kill everyone but Gale.

Rider knew he faced monsters of unknowable powers. Without a moment to lose he took off after Valero. They had only been momentarily sated, these monstrous predators, and soon they would renew the chase.

Gale, Shubazang and Euryale faced a dark passage of their own. The door wouldn't budge; they heard nothing from the other side. They'd have to continue on alone, and hope that the others found their own way down.

It took Shubazang some prying but he got Gale to give up on the door and follow him and Euryale. The corridor was tighter than expected, perhaps an old maintenance tunnel. It was completely sheathed in metal, metal that was now entirely consumed by heavy red rust. As they walked, led only by the steady glow of Shubazang's light rod, their footfalls made a tinny sound, and disturbed a thick layer of dust on the floor causing small clouds of the choking stuff to explode momentarily at their feet.

The passage continued for some distance, until the sealed doorway behind them began to fade from view. Gale looked back hesitantly. Shubazang noticed, coming to a stop.

"Come on," he said quietly, aware that his voice carried further in these narrow confines. "We can't go back."

She knew he was right and turned, taking a deep breath before nodding. She seemed calm, but inside her heart and mind were racing. She knew Ludd was dead. She sensed Valero and Rider were still alive, but they were fading, leaving the range of her telepathic senses. But at least they were still moving.

As Shubazang had intimated, she realized she would have to let go of Rider and Valero and trust in them to see themselves to safety, to keep themselves alive.

Worrying about their fates wouldn't help her get out of this situation, it would only hinder. She consoled herself knowing that while she had seen Valero's death in her vision, she hadn't been able to see Rider's. What that meant she wasn't entirely sure, but somewhere deep inside she hoped it meant he, at least, was going to survive all this.

They came to a narrow stair, which led to another level of metal passages. Shubazang descended the steps, holding his light rod up to shed as much light as possible in each direction.

"A *maze*..." he muttered. He turned back at Gale. "*You* seem to remember this place, the passages, the twists and turns. Which way do we go?"

She looked both ways, then shook her head. "Not this. I've never been down here before. This level was military-only."

To her surprise Shubazang seemed almost pleased by that. Then she remembered his greed, his desire to get his hands on whatever secrets her people had preserved over the centuries.

"Military, eh?" He looked around with renewed interest, then for no good reason, picked the left-hand passage and started walking.

Gale moved to follow, but Euryale stayed, watching her pass.

Gale felt a brief, chilling sensation, and she turned and looked at the android. It was staring right at her, the same unchanging grin frozen on its face.

Shubazang was almost ten paces away when he too, noticed. He turned back.

"Euryale! Gale! Keep up!"

The android seemed oblivious to his command for a moment, locking its reflective metal eyes with Gale's, but then it turned slowly and began walking, with heavy footsteps, after its master.

Gale couldn't reconcile the strangeness of that sensation; the android didn't "feel", it wasn't truly "alive", it was just a machine programmed to act and behave as its master desired. But for a moment there she felt *something*, almost like a first spark of emotion, before it died out, just as a lone ember might in a dying campfire.

It felt like an eternity before they came to another juncture, and yet another eternity before they came to something even close to a destination. Gale continued to look backwards, now and then, hoping to see Rider and even Valero, but they weren't there. They were alone. She shook her head to clear her thoughts as Shubazang came to a stop.

"These are just maintenance tunnels," he said at last. "We're getting nowhere down here". He sunk back against the wall, retrieved his canteen, and took a drink.

Light scintillated on his goggles, a bright square of white light. It caught Gale's eye, and she moved over to get a better look.

The light wasn't coming from his goggles, it was being *reflected*. She turned to see where the light was coming from, and found herself staring at a ventilation grate on the wall, through which the light could be seen.

She leaned over and peered through the rusted slats, into an otherwise pitch black chamber. A single television screen remained on, but from this far she couldn't see what was on, or anything else in the room.

Burning Lands 395

Shubazang noticed as well and came over. He reached into his belt and pulled out two screwdrivers, giving one to Gale while immediately getting to work unscrewing the bolts that kept the grate secure.

After a few minutes Shubazang pulled the grate into the corridor and laid it down with an unavoidable "clang". Gale moved forward and peered out, but sensing danger she kept her body in the corridor. Her eyes adjusted. The chamber beyond was enormous, and the passage they were in was relatively high up, perhaps forty feet off the floor. Had she stepped through, she would have fallen to her death.

Shubazang came over but she stopped him and motioned for him to bring his light forward. As he did he noticed the same thing; the orangish glow filled the room with a weak radiance, illuminating dozens of dead and dusty computers, each the size of a refrigerator, as well as metal catwalks winding their way through the computer stations like a labyrinth. Dancing shadows flittered everywhere, but these were merely phantoms created when Shubazang moved the light back and forth.

"Good thinking," Shubazang said to Gale. "Saved my life."

He reached to his belt again, this time retrieving a length of plastic-coated climber's rope. He gave one end to Euryale, then began to give himself some slack.

"I'll go first," he said. He looked around to make sure the ground was clear, but being unable to see the bottom he tossed the light rod out of the tunnel. It fell for a moment, landed with a clatter, and illuminated the dusty floor forty feet below in a dome of light.

Nothing stirred. He cracked another light rod, his last, and gave it to Gale to hold.

Securing the rope around his waist he began to descend. Euryale held the rope effortlessly, feeding him slack as he needed it, gently lowering him the distance between their perch and the chamber floor.

Eventually Shubazang reached the bottom. He stepped out of the loop of rope, pulled out his gun, and moved close to the glowing light rod so that the others above could see him clearly. He motioned for Euryale to pull the rope back up.

"Now your turn, Gale!" he called out, his voice echoing in the unfathomable hugeness of the cavernous computer chamber.

Euryale brought the rope up. Gale slipped it around her thin waist, taking a moment to adjust it. She slung her submachine gun over her shoulder, drew back her hair, and took a deep breath before descending.

She dangled in mid-air for several minutes, as Euryale slowly lowered her. But when she was about a third the way down, she came to a shuddering halt.

Gale looked down at Shubazang, who stared back up at her. Realizing she hadn't reached the ground, she looked upwards, her eyes running up the length of rope to the two metallic hands that held it.

Euryale stared out at her from its perch high above, its face illuminated in a sinister light by Gale's glow rod.

Gale felt danger. But Euryale simply looked back at her, observing. Gale felt afraid, and her eyes widened as she met the android's emotionless gaze.

"Euryale!" Shubazang shouted. "Lower her! Lower her! You're next, now come on!"

Euryale held the rope but didn't move, until the last word echoed through the chamber. Then, with a startling resumption of motion, Gale began to descend once more at an even pace.

When she finally touched down on the floor Shubazang was there to grab her and make sure she was alright.

Euryale watched from high above, motionless and still. Gale immediately got out of the makeshift rope harness, as if staying in it would give Euryale another chance to yank her into the air and terrorize her.

"I *really* don't like your robot," Gale said to Shubazang.

"I don't know what's gotten into her..." he said, helping Gale free.

"Okay, Euryale, now your turn!" he called out, taking the glow rod from Gale's hand and holding it so Euryale could see him.

Euryale secured the rope at its end, then slithered slickly down the rope until it, too, reached the bottom. It immediately relinquished the rope.

"Don't play around like that," Shubazang scolded.

Gale looked at the android but sensed nothing. She turned away, picked up the still-glowing glow rod that Shubazang had thrown, and began to look around.

There were computers everywhere, most of them black, gummed-up, and rusted over. Screens were gray, covered in dust, and even a few were cracked or shattered. Above them all was a huge dormant panel fitted with no less than a dozen analog clock faces, each showing a different time somewhere in the world. Above each dusty, dead clock was a brightly-stenciled word - *"ARK 1 Raven Rock, ARK 2 Mt. Weather, ARK 3 Greenbrier, ARK 4 Longyearben, ARK 5 CEGHQ, ARK 6, etc..."*

Shubazang followed Gale as she reached the one glowing monitor in the entire chamber.

On the screen Gale saw an unfamiliar face, a woman, with bulging cheeks, mouth hanging limply open, and unblinking eyes. She vaguely remembered the face (one of the older women who once served on the commissioner's council) but it seemed very different... The face undulated as it spoke.

"Gaaaiiil..."

If the appearance of a woman's face was meant to show some kind of warmth, it failed utterly. Gale rubbed her arms as she felt a noticeable chill.

The face on the other side seemed to realize it wasn't reassuring Gale in the least. It suddenly disappeared, swept away to the right off screen, to be replaced by a more familiar face, that of the commissioner, which scrolled in from the left.

"Did you see that?" Shubazang asked suddenly. "How..."

Gale held up her hand. She'd seen it too, but it baffled her as much as the tinker. *Were they sitting on a rotating stage somewhere? Or did the camera simply turn so swiftly and smoothly that it seemed like they were in motion?*

"Youuu've followed thhhe *whiiite rabbbit* this faaarrr..." the commissioner grinned. "Wwwon't yooou continue?"

The head bobbed momentarily, its eyes moving methodically, but it remained quiet.

"What's he talking about?" Shubazang asked.

"I'm suuure you'll want to meeet the Hunnnters..." it teased.

Gale stared at the screen and bit her lip.

Burning Lands

"I'm suuure you've seeen themmm. Terribly primmmitive, not much leeeft of whaaat used to be there. Shells, reeeally. Such a traaagic waste of irreplaceable rrreeesources. All thaaat training, and whaaat's left? Shaaadows, that's whaaat... Such a disssappointment..."

With that the face on the screen disappeared, being replaced by a black screen and a normal command prompt.

Shubazang waited for a moment, then spoke again. "Creepy... but they left us a computer to toy with."

Gale nodded, taking the submachine gun off her shoulder and holding it at the ready. She would watch while Shubazang went to work.

The boy typed away for a few minutes, attempting to crack codes and decipher the terminology that bombarded him with each success. He scanned through complex diagrams, digitized maps, pages of reports, 3-D molecule models, and a whirlwind of other data. Each of these flashed off the mirrored lenses of his goggles, and Gale was left to wonder how much he was committing to memory.

"Sorry there are no guns," Gale offered quietly.

"That's okay," he replied with a sly grin, tapping his forehead. "Blueprints are just as valuable..."

He continued to scan the archives of ancient information, the projects of her people, their mighty endeavors.

"Your people were developing some odd things..."

She leaned in to get a better look, but to her they were just diagrams and tables, letters and mathematical formulae.

"De-humidifying devices to create potable water from the air," he said. "Interesting..."

She thought of her people's original mission to return to the surface and rebuild; she thought of how the primitive people might have looked upon their "magic", making water out of thin air...

"Nano-scrubbers to detoxify and de-radiate swag snatched from ruined cities. Medicines to fortify the thyroid, to inhibit radiation absorption... Smart!" he continued.

She thought of the prospect of technologies that could clean away the lasting curse of the ancient wars.

"This bit here is odd... A kind of pliant, protoplasmic flesh substitute? For what? To repair wounds? For surgical use?"

Shubazang turned and looked at her as if expecting an answer. But Gale shrugged, unable to say yes or no to any of these ideas. She remembered nothing of the kind.

"A-ha!" he exclaimed, coming to a new screen filled with glowing strings of text. "No more theoretic stuff. This here is the real deal. Those 'Huntsmen' you spoke of..."

He hit a few keys and read what flashed onto the screen.

"Just like I thought - powered kevlar cables, magnetic barium nano-filaments... an internal overpressure system to keep out biochemical agents... fully sealed against radiation... rotating optic sensors giving full 180 degree vision in thermal, infrared and ultraviolet... micro-climate conditioning system... capillary air and temperature circulators... enhanced audio, microwave communications, simulcom networking..."

He looked over at Gale.

"There's no way we can kill these things... not with *these*," he said, tossing his 20th century automatic rifle to the floor with a clatter.

She sensed he was right. But they weren't there to kill the Huntsmen, but rather deal with the thing that controlled them with its psychic commands. There was a controller, and they had to get at it before its minions got to them.

He continued to type, bringing up more images and diagrams. "Lasers... microwave emitters... armor-shredding flechettes... Your people were put down here with quite an assortment of advanced weaponry for their use. We've got to get our hands on some if we're going to have a chance against them!"

After a few more moments he gave up on the computer, getting to his feet.

"There's got to be an armory around here somewhere." He looked back at the computer. "The schematics for this level indicate there's one down access way six... over... *there.*"

Rider wasn't sure where they were, and after a while all of the tunnels looked the same. Valero didn't seem concerned about getting lost, he seemed to have a single-minded drive to put as much distance between them and the Huntsmen as possible, even if it meant winding their way down into the deepest recesses of the earth.

In the distance they heard the sounds of the armored Huntsmen following them. At one point it seemed as if they were nearby, dangerously close, but in the next moment their footsteps sounded far, far away. This was a maze to be sure, and Rider imagined that at times there was only a thin wall of metal between them, and more than that, that the Huntsmen would soon catch them at some intersection somewhere.

But the encounter he feared didn't come to pass, at least not now. They continued wandering for what seemed like a half an hour, and soon the footsteps of the four Huntsmen pursuing them faded out of range.

"Gale said they can 'see' with their minds," Rider ventured to explain. "But maybe their minds have a short range of detection. Maybe we got away."

Valero didn't seem to want to say anything. At that moment he raised a hand, a motion that stopped Rider in his tracks. Valero was listening to the still air of the labyrinth. In the silence they could just barely hear the commissioner's voice; they couldn't make out the words clearly, but the slurred drone was unmistakable. It was coming from a dark passage down the corridor ahead of them, from a tunnel to the right.

Rider looked back the way they came, but it was silent, dark, and still. When he turned back Valero had already started towards the dark passage, led by his curiosity.

Valero sensed Rider's hesitation and looked back. "Come on," he whispered. "He could be talking to Gale and the others."

Rider wasn't so sure, but he didn't want to split up any further so he followed. With just a few short steps he came up behind Valero and readied his TAC-50, then both started into the darkness.

For a few yards the corridor still had some ambient light from the last passageway, but soon it was pitch black, except for the tiny threads of illumination coming through the rusted vents spaced evenly along the walls, which striped the corridor in pencil-thin beams of dim light. They heard the voice again, echoing in some gigantic chamber.

Burning Lands

Valero went to a vent and peered through. He couldn't see much at first, but soon he realized he was looking down into a huge vaulted chamber, lit by sluggishly-fluttering emergency lights. A bank of security monitors near a large doorway provided the strongest light, and on one enormous screen he could see the commissioner's still face, its eyes scanning the darkness.

Rider came up and peered through as well. With his sensitive eyesight, however, he saw not only the chamber and the monitors, but also the still shapes of over fifty Huntsmen congregating beneath the giant screen to hear the commissioner's orders.

"Yesss, myyy liiittle Igors," the voice of the commissioner mused disdainfully, as if speaking to an army of brain-damaged automatons. "It isss tiiime to hunnnt."

To the minds of the soldiers the world seemed frozen in slow motion, each move a long, deliberate, drawn out act. To them a drop of water took an agonizing eternity to fall, and when it hit the ground, the dripping echo thundered for long moments in the stillness. A bullet exploded slowly from a gun, the air rippled noticeably as the projectile displaced it with its passage. If they had eyes to see, the Huntsmen could easily track a bullet with their sight, stepping aside with a minimum of effort. But the ability to see ahead, to step outside the perception of mortal men, didn't come without a cost. They could no longer understand the spoken word, nor the beauty of the human voice, as speech was slurred to the point of being utterly unintelligible. Insanity fell quickly on them, fermenting in their minds in the long dead moments between each tick of the clock; each moment a minute, each minute an hour, each day a torturously empty expanse of hollow time. They no longer lived for interaction or the stimulation of their minds and imaginations. They had long given up on thought itself because long ago they had time to ponder all things two, three times over, so that there was nothing left to think about, so that now they merely stood, vegetative, waiting either for the *hunger* to stir them... or the psychic commands of the commissioner to revive them into activity.

From the large pack of motionless power armor soldiers, came an unusually-large specimen, tall and broad-shouldered, its armor exhibiting the rusted remnants of a gold star above the left breast. It came to the front and stood before the blindingly-bright screen.

The commissioner's face filled the entire panel, looking enormous and monstrous. His manic eyes slowly swept to the side, then back again, then angled downwards to behold the armored soldier that presented itself for his "approval". The commissioner's eyes seemed to linger on the gold star for a moment, conjuring up his own recollections of what that symbol once meant. The commissioner's yellow teeth glistened, his lip hung low, and spittle pooled at the corners of his mouth. He spoke again, both aloud and in their minds:

"Rememmmber, *Major*, you serrrve..."

And all at once, a hundred distorted voices joined in a chorus. "... the *peeeople*."

The towering Huntsman stared straight ahead at the screen. Concealed behind a wall of rubbery armor, the only relief to its uniformly grotesque body being its brilliantly glowing optical lenses, it seemed like a mechanical statue with remotely-controlled spotlight eyes. But a moment later it turned as the telepathic commands sank in, as they registered somewhere in its Ascendance-saturated mind.

The armored assembly was slower to register the orders, the chemical wiring of their ear canals having shorted out long ago, leaving them all utterly deaf. But like the Major, the creatures picked up on the resonating mental energy of the voices on the other end of the monitor, sensed the predatory intent of the commissioner, if not his actual words. As one, the Huntsmen turned to follow their "leader", their long-dead Major, who led them from the chamber to hunt the outsiders who had intruded upon their secret underground City.

The giant doorway opened with a rumble, and red emergency lights began to sweep through the dark. Rider and Valero watched as the army of armored giants began slipping through the yawning portal and into the passages beyond.

"How many?" Valero asked, realizing that Rider saw more than he in the dim light.

"Fifty," Rider said soberly. "At least." Valero said nothing more, but moved from the vent and began hastily looking for another way out.

Shubazang led the way to a door marked "6" and opened its rusted latch. This door wasn't powered, nor at the whim of some cunning sentience located somewhere else. A good old-fashioned, manually-opened hatchway. He liked that. The door swung open, revealing another tight corridor, this one ending in a metal staircase that descended to the level below. But lights flickered in the darkness on the lower level, creating a strange strobe effect on the metal walls of the corridor.

Wordlessly Shubazang, Gale and Euryale descended the stairs, guided by the flickering lights, suddenly aware that the metal walls and the circuits behind them were humming with a flood of unrestrained power.

The lights on the lower level pulsed and shuddered as if responding to a heartbeat that flooded every bit of wiring and circuitry with electricity. It was unmistakable - dark then dim, dark then dim, a methodic throb.

"Like a heartbeat," Shubazang shouted over the noise, putting Gale's thoughts to words.

"Like the lights, the computers, they're responding to its presence. It's powering all this... with its mind," she explained.

"What?" Shubazang asked incredulously. "Are you saying a *creature* is doing this? With its brain?!"

Gale nodded. She was sure of it.

"Imagine the power involved!" he shouted, trying to be heard over the noise of the charged walls and floors. "Whatever it is, its putting out a *tremendous* amount of energy!"

"Mind energy..." she noted.

"Neural impulses are powered by minute amounts of bioelectricity," he confirmed. "This could be the same thing, just on a massive scale. Like a field of static electricity, or magnetism. An 'aura' of thought!

"Is that even possible?" he asked no one in particular.

That's when the last piece of the puzzle fell into place in Gale's mind. This facility was at the heart of the Brotherhood's prophesized Eden, in the center of the Burning Lands, but the diseased *thing* that lived here, now beneath their feet in the mysterious caverns below, was what they were *really* after. Whatever it was, this miserable life form as yet undiscovered, was an organic, living, power source. What designs might they devise with such a monstrosity under their control? She immediately sensed the Brotherhood's cold, inhuman desire to enslave this thing, to power their ambitions and give life to their particularly bizarre brand of mad science, their efforts to terraform the wasteland. It would power their twisted vision of the future!

She had played along, blindly even, *hoping* more than *seeing*. But now their last machination was laid bare. She'd have no part in this, a most perverse form of slavery, in which madmen planned to capture a sick and corrupted beast, enslave it, and force it to do their bidding, like it was some animal to be made to do tricks. It was a sickening thought, and it repelled her. It had to be destroyed, now more than ever!

Acutely aware that a floodgate of sorts had been opened, and a great new menace released into the tunnels with them, Valero and Rider moved hastily through the halls, throwing caution to the wind. It was the two of them, alone, against a veritable army of super-human warriors in a dangerous game of cat-and-mouse. No, this was no game, it was an all-out race to get away. They had no idea where they were going, only that they needed to move as quickly as possible to find a way out of the tunnels, to someplace more secure.

With their footfalls echoing off of the metal grating underfoot, the two men came racing around a corner, just to stop dead in their tracks. Up ahead the metal-walled corridor was washed in a swirling, orange glow coming from a pulsing emergency light on one wall. Beyond lay a wall of darkness, but as they came into the passage so too, did something *else*.

Ahead of them came an enormous Huntsman, clad in the same hulking armor as its lifeless brethren, covered in a thick coating of dust that flaked and trailed from it like dry steam as it plodded inevitably towards them. It already saw them, its blue eyes focusing on the two intruders ahead. With a mechanical whir, it began lifting the enormous cannon held in its arms in their direction.

The huge ornate weapon looked like a bulky, six-foot long rifle, one end tipped by a huge bell-shaped baffle and a small circular port from which a blinding red light emanated; the deafening buzz of pent-up electricity pulsed and crackled within. Power, channeled from the cells within the Huntsman's hunchback suit of armor, charged the massive thing, feeding into a whirring electromagnetic collar that spun at ultra-high speed within the baffle, generating a powerful energy field. There, inside the huge armored weapon, a raging plasma storm was created, building up tremendous explosive energy while contained precariously between opposing magnetic fields.

The Huntsman moved with a sudden jolt, whipping the two-hundred pound weapon up in its myoelectrically-powered arms to level it down the hall. Neither Valero nor Rider had ever seen a weapon such as this, but they knew enough to fear the unknown technology of the Ancients and both scattered immediately.

The rounded firing end of the weapon shook, a brilliant glow spilled from the tiny hole at the tip, and in an instant a caustic vapor of searing plasma energy burst from the end in a narrow stream that swept down the hallway. The plasma stream was kept together by its own magnetism, from a carrier beam of electricity down which it coursed, and slowly dissipated as the stream blew forth from the weapon like the sheets of fire propelled from a flamethrower. Only as the electricity diminished, and the magnetic field weakened, did the pressurized plasma expand and explode.

Luckily Valero and Rider had both leapt aside, as the flash of energy pulsed past them and down the hall, where it detonated. The far wall of the passage buckled and melted away instantaneously, leaving a great gaping hole that revealed the maze of pipes lying between walls. The metal lit up from the intense heat, and an ear-piercing screech filled the tunnel as it reached super-heated temperatures.

"Move!" Rider shouted, but Valero didn't need any prodding. Both men fled back the way they came, just as the Huntsman moved forward, its plasma rifle coming back to full charge.

Shubazang looked around the corner and down a new hall, which was flanked on all sides by steel doors. Rust covered the walls, choking the vents high up on the walls and sheathing the overhead pipes. He looked at the floor before them, and noticed signs of dozens of dirty feet having passed this way, leaving muddy footprints. He looked wary of taking such a well-traveled passage, but looking down the emptier halls he realized there wasn't likely to be anything interesting or significant in the other directions.

As they walked Gale and Euryale stayed close behind, since Shubazang's light was all they had with which to navigate. Following along in the small globe of light surrounding him by virtue of his vividly-luminous light stick, Gale felt as if the darkness was swallowing them whole.

Shubazang turned with a start when, passing one of the ancient doorways, it slid upwards into the ceiling with a sleek hiss. A ghoulish cold seeped from the ominous dark chamber beyond, accompanied by strange chemical smells that sent their senses reeling. Shubazang instinctively turned his light rod to pierce the cloying darkness, and boldly followed the light into this new room. Gale and Euryale stayed in his shadow but accompanied him inside.

After a few moments their eyes adjusted to this new cavernous room. It felt like a gigantic refrigerator, its walls shuddering with a subsonic rumble, its hundreds of pipes and yawning vents hung with an icy "moss" of frozen water crystals. Every surface seemed to collect frost; immediately Shubazang's and Gale's hot breath turned to vapor in the cool, dark air.

Dominating the gigantic chamber were almost fifty stainless steel gurneys and operating tables, though the ones visible in their light apparently bore no patients, living or dead. Curious to see more, Shubazang moved from Gale and prepared to descend the short flight of iron stairs that led into the morgue.

The boy took the first step down the stairs with gritted teeth, aware that his boots made a hollow but noticeable sound on the steel steps, one by one, as he reached the bottom. But no one came at him, nothing emerged from the darkness.

He held up his light rod to get a better look around. Almost forgetting Gale and Euryale he started wandering the rows of operating tables, hoping with morbid curiosity to find someone there.

They passed by several tanks arranged along the walls, enormous glass cylinders filled with a clear, yellowish fluid in which were suspended random flecks of some organic detritus.

Burning Lands

Gale almost gasped when the light of the glow rod lit up the liquid in the first glass cylinder, revealing in its distorted light the body of an entire *cow*, perfectly preserved and floating in a bath of formaldehyde. Shubazang didn't seem disgusted, but rather insatiably curious, and quickly moved to the next tank, in which floated a grotesquely-mutated goat.

"Tribal livestock..." he whispered vaguely, but didn't explain. Shubazang continued on with purpose, and Gale struggled to keep up. They passed more tanks containing typical domesticated animals, until at long last, illuminated in the light, were the first actual *human* bodies.

There, beyond the maze of specimen tanks, sat two naked men, one on each table, their skin cold and white. Both men were rather large and muscular, though their faces were sunken with internal corruption. One had a faded tattoo of a chevron on one thick arm, while the other cadaver was peeled completely open, its innards removed and displaced to a steel basin nearby. Flies landed on the cold rotting flesh in the blood-filled pan, while maggots writhed in the exposed, corrupted organs.

"*Ravagers...*" Shubazang whispered aloud, finding his voice echoing unexpectedly in the dark vault.

Gale came over, but stopped and turned away as she saw the rotting men.

Shubazang looked around and saw many more, at least a dozen of the dead raiders, similarly splayed out on tables, stripped to their skins, almost all of them cut open and their internal organs removed with curious precision.

"These are the raiders that went missing..." Shubazang continued to whisper, explaining more to himself than Gale or Euryale. "... so *this* is where the vanished men went. First just a few, then those who went into the desert to find them too, until entire platoons of men had disappeared..."

"Killed by your people, brought here to be studied..." he continued.

He looked around again, scanning from dead face to dead face. He saw the maggots, the cocoons of other nesting bugs embedded in their rancid flesh. "Looks like your people just leave them here when they're done... to *rot*."

They stared in silence for a moment, until Euryale got their attention by pointing to the darkness to the left. The android put a hand to its ear as if to say "I heard something".

Shubazang listened, and Gale strained to hear as well. They heard, somewhere deeper in the morgue, the sound of an electrical motor whirring softly. Followed by the vague sound of a distorted *voice*. Shubazang gave Gale a cautionary look but headed in that direction.

After a minute of dodging tables and winding through another maze of canopic specimen tanks, Shubazang saw a dim glow in the alcove beyond. He quieted and peeked around the edge of one of the large murky fluid cylinders.

There, in the adjoining part of the chamber, were more operating tables, each bearing the almost completely rotted remains of some poor desert tribesman snatched up in the night. Men, women and even small children, their bodies reduced to skeletons, their flesh stripped by decay... grinning skulls with parchment-dry muscles frozen in place seemed locked in the act of screaming, their bodies splayed out like heaps of meat.

A strange robot of some kind hovered in the air there, several feet off the ground, levitating by the power of quietly-whirring hover fans situated around its base. The machine was just a little taller than Shubazang, vaguely shaped like a bowling pin (with a tapering middle), and bristling with small red lenses and acute optical sensors atop its bulbous head. Arms of folding steel rods adorned the thing in two rings near its top and bottom, and with these clicking and clacking appendages it was apparently working to dissect the corpse of another dead victim.

The cadaver currently being explored by the medical robot was thin and dusky skinned, a somewhat older wastelander with a wrinkled face and a crop of short black hair. His head was bent slightly backwards, his mouth hung open, as if he exhaled his last breath in a horrific scream of terror. The shreds of gray-brown robes lay torn open around him like wrappings savagely ripped from his body. But what was worse, his entire torso was being cut open with the trio of laser scalpels produced by the robot's surgical extensions, opening him from the groin to about mid-chest. Maggots wormed in every exposed thread of ripped flesh, but the robot seemed completely oblivious to the advanced decay.

Gale put a hand to her mouth when she saw the ruin that had been a man, stifling a violent retch.

Despite the rot that ravaged the dead man's features, Shubazang instantly recognized him as no other than *Ambrose*, the outrider who had also been sent to investigate the raids on the villages of Uncle's Sam's lands.

A television screen in the chest of the medical robot came to life, depicting a pale-faced woman, eyes unblinking and shifting from side to side as it looked through the screen. A mechanical modulator translated its voice:

"Paaathological exploooration 8-6-4, now ennntering the thirrrd hourrr. Specccimen appears physssically normal... but innnternaaal invessstigation of the digessstive tract reveeeals the presence... of a clussster of abnooormal fat reservoirs, along the waaalls of the intessstines. These reservoirs... appear to duplicate the funnnction of a caaamel's hummmp, allowing thisss muuutant to store upwards of a gaaallon of waaattter in its body. This appeaaars to be one of the mooost useful adaptations sooo far exhibited innn a muuutant, no doooubt serrrving it well..."

Shubazang and Gale listened to the slurred voice seemingly coming from the woman on screen. It held no emotion whatsoever, it was utterly cold and detached from its murderous work. Gale was momentarily sent back to her childhood, to the dissection of the gilled mutant for the benefit of her kindergarten class. Even after all these years their mad work continued, the scientific studies never ceased. Even after her people had stumbled and fallen into insanity, they were still hard at work killing and tearing open the poor inhabitants of the surface world to better understand and catalog their infinitely diverse physiology.

"I know him," Shubazang whispered to Gale, motioning to the body on the table. His quiet voice tore her from her trance, but he remained careful not to alert the robot, or the person on the other end, to their eavesdropping. "He was one of the men hired by your father to look into the massacre of Uncle Sam's people... Looks like he got to the bottom of it alright... Cost him his life. Poor bastard..."

Burning Lands

His voice trailed off. Gale moved away, bumping into one of the gurneys and knocking an old rusted scalpel to the ground. It hit the steel floor with a loud, metallic "clang".

The medical robot continued with its task, but the face on the screen went silent for a moment. Gale cringed, and Shubazang drew her into cover, peeking through a narrow space to watch.

The dead eyes of the woman swam around in their sockets, as if whirling about to see every corner of the room.

"Isss theeere annnyonnne theeere?" she asked.

Shubazang pulled Gale further away, until the glow of the robot's optical sensors, the flash of its swift-moving laser scalpels, and the face on the screen were no longer in sight.

"Let's get out of here..." Shubazang said resolutely; Gale agreed.

Shubazang led Gale and Euryale from that place to a deeper chamber, but the horrors did not relent. They leapt back as they almost stumbled into this new chamber, where something awful writhed on another operating table.

Shubazang looked around the corner. There, in the darkness, were two more medical robots, pitted and rusted from such advanced age, working in tandem on the "thing" on the table.

The "thing" was a mass of fused flesh, a boiling blob of protoplasm constructed from tube-grown artificial flesh. The robots stimulated the mass with electric prods, each producing a bright blue spark, that when pressed to the protoplasm caused it to recoil, shiver, and expand a few inches in size. Slowly, with repeated stimulation by electricity, the robots were "weaving" a living, pulsating blob of featureless flesh for seemingly no sane reason.

"That must be some of the protoplasmic flesh substitute mentioned on the computers," Shubazang surmised. "But what are they growing it for? What's its purpose?"

For some reason Gale felt as if she *should* know, as if it was buried at the back of her mind, the purpose for this most unnatural of experiments. She felt a chilling cold, a sickening nausea, and knew it was somehow related to what had happened to her people...

"We've got to destroy this thing!" Gale shouted.

Having escaped the complex of morgues and laboratories, Shubazang moved to a new access door and began to pull it open. He seemed surprised by Gale's sudden determination to destroy the strange wonders that they had so far encountered.

"Why? Imagine it, a *biological* technology!"

"Its *twisted* technology," she shouted back. "Its evil!"

She followed him through the doorway into a dark chamber, its ceiling lights flickering on and off with the same pulse as the place they had come from. It created weird flickering shadows, and only momentarily illuminated banks of lockers, cases and tables. They had finally come upon the much sought-after armory, secured deep in the City's core.

Shubazang began searching the lockers for weapons, power clips, anything they might use. He grabbed a curious-looking grenade and tossed it to Gale, then continued.

"Technology isn't evil, or good, it isn't inherently anything," he said, able to speak freely now that the deafening noise from outside diminished somewhat. "It's just a tool, something we use. It's the people who create it, they're the ones you can judge. Why was something made? What was its purpose? That dictates the intent behind its creation."

At that moment Gale felt a terrible pain shooting through her back. She was staggered by the suddenness of it all. Having trusted in her precognitive senses for so long she was amazed when, looking down, she saw a silvery blade emerging from her stomach. She tried to cough, gasp, gag, but her breath was completely stolen. Mouth hanging open like a suffocating fish she looked over one shoulder and to the creature that held it.

Euryale stared back at her. The silver-skinned android looked down its arm to the wound, then its featureless steel eyes locked onto hers.

At that moment Gale sensed something horrible, something she had only momentarily sensed earlier - the beginnings of a true consciousness inside that android's computerized electronic brain. Crude and clumsy, but it was there nonetheless. Euryale was *alive*. To Gale's empathic mind the realization of Euryale's conscious "awakening" was like hearing a baby's first words, and Euryale's first was the word "hate".

Gale was horrified that the android's first thoughts would be so dark and murderous. The android had only now developed the sentience of a child, at most, immature by virtue of its relatively short lifespan, creating a thing that was unimaginably self-centered, acting purely on impulse.

Euryale looked on Gale with absolute... *jealousy*. And it had picked now to act.

Images flashed through Gale's mind as she touched on Euryale's thoughts. The android was jealous of Gale because of the attention the others had showered on her, putting her at the center of their endeavors. Shubazang had been sent to find her; Rider did all he could to protect her; Tank had died to bring her here. The fact that Gale had swayed Shubazang to *accompany* her instead of *killing* her incensed the android.

Euryale raged at the idea of Shubazang barking angrily at it, while soothing and consoling Gale, even *touching* her... The android seemed to have a plan, rudimentary and simple as it was. Kill Gale, and the attention would return.

When Shubazang turned to see why Gale wasn't speaking he looked completely shocked; his goggles hid his eyes but his mouth dropped in sudden disbelief.

"Euryale! No!" he gasped.

Euryale pushed Gale off its blade and the girl slumped to the side, wheezing as her pierced left lung began to falter.

Shubazang reached for his pistol. It was enough to trigger Euryale into unthinking action, and the android came forward with a step and brought the glistening wet blade back around in a swirl.

Shubazang cried out as the sword sliced off his cybernetic hand at the wrist, cleanly removing the metal extension from the scarred fleshy stump. The hand, and the pistol, fell to the ground with a thud; severed wires sparked and sputtered.

Bleeding from the re-opened wound, Shubazang stumbled back into a bank of lockers with a bang. The door fell open, and a trio of advanced weapons - microwave rifles - spilled out onto the floor.

Shubazang struggled and fell. On the floor he reached for one of the rifles, desperate to defend himself.

A new instinct kicked in, self-preservation. Euryale came forward, finding itself no longer compelled by its master, and brought the blade back down on Shubazang as he crawled, on all fours, towards one of the spinning guns.

Gale looked up and saw Shubazang's head fall from his streaming neck. The boy collapsed in a heavy heap. Blood pulsed desperately from the open arteries, spilling out onto the floor.

Euryale turned away and went back to the hatch. It looked back at Gale, who lay there, struggling in vain to breathe. She would die here, slowly, and in great agony. The android notched its head slightly for a moment, then left, closing the door behind it and locking the latch from the other side.

Having lost Valero in the maze of tunnels, Rider ran into a large chamber flanked on both sides by enormous black windows. Through the dusty glass he saw emptiness; water had once been contained in enormous reservoirs on the other side of each partition, but now these two-story underground tanks were empty, save for a few feet of a churning greenish-brown fluid streaked with ochre and orange swirls.

In the mirrored surface of the glass walls he saw subtle movement, then an orange light. He whipped around with his rifle and prepared to fire.

Valero stared at him, ready to fire as well, gun in one hand and light rod in the other. Both men gasped and rested their weapons.

"What is this place?" Rider asked breathlessly, looking around.

"Don't know," Valero said calmly. "Some kind of water plant. Lots of water down here, it seems."

"Water from the surface," Rider thought aloud. "Used to generate power on the upper levels, then brought to the lake to settle and purify." He looked through the glass again. "Then down here to be stored?"

Valero didn't reply, he simply went to the passage Rider had come from and looked back. "Where are they?"

Rider turned back as well. "Not far behind, I'm sure. We've got to keep mobile."

Valero kept his gun trained on the passage. "Well there's no way out of here. We're stuck."

Rider looked around and with grim realization confirmed that there didn't seem to be a way out. He looked back through the glass.

"That's not water in there," he said. "Its too green..."

Valero didn't seem to care, and kept his eyes glued on the dark passage behind them.

"I'll bet," Rider offered, "that that's not water at all. I'll bet the fools converted these tanks to hold their precious 'Ascendance'. Became so important that they flushed out their water reserves to make storage space for more of their precious drug."

Now Valero looked. "They must have made a *lot* of it."

Rider nodded. "Enough to addict their entire society, enough to keep them fueled for a long time. All other concerns abandoned by the wayside..."

Valero felt fatigue and rubbed his eyes, but quickly went back to cradling his rifle. With growing interest, Rider continued to peer through the glass at the room beyond.

His eyes scanned the several feet of gently lapping fluid, the huge dormant impeller blade that once churned the waters, and lingered on the central column running the entire length of the room. A service hatch sat at the center of it.

"Did you see what they *did* to the old man?" Valero asked over one shoulder. "Goddamn unbelievable. Sucked out his fucking *brains*." Rider chose not to comment. He'd seen it just as vividly as Valero had, he needed no reminding.

Both heard a skittering noise from the passage, echoing down the twists and turns and into their dead-end chamber.

Valero lifted his gun, beads of sweat forming at his brow. "We're cornered..." he whispered.

Both men saw the bluish glow now lighting up the corridor. The tramp of heavy feet, the clatter of squid-like oxygen tubes swaying as they marched forward, the slight wheeze of ancient respirators straining at the air.

Valero threw the light rod down the tunnel so that they might see their enemy coming, until the small plasti-glass rod hit the ground and spun in circles. As it struck the floor and rolled, it illuminated the huge feet and trunk-like legs of no less than a *dozen* of the perfectly-armored Huntsmen, all of whom had been drawn to the sounds of the chase.

The lead Huntsman of this pack stared down at the light rod, its monstrous frame catching the orange glow on its bundles of artificial muscle, its ribs and on the rims of its weirdly rotating telescopic eyes.

"Die, motherfucker!" Valero shouted, and opened fire. Pulling the trigger back while clenching the grip, he brought his other hand around to keep the barrel under control as the ancient Chinese rifle barked out its fitful stream of fire. Flares of light erupted from the end of the weapon as hot lead spilled from the barrel and shot down the passage, filling the tight space with a storm of fast-firing rounds.

The thundering blasts pushed Rider into firing as well, lifting his big-bore sniper rifle and placing it on a large humidifier unit to brace it. He pulled the dusty trigger until the weapon kicked up in his hands, its barrel exploding with flame as it blasted low-drag .50 caliber rounds down the hall and into the advancing ranks. Together they brought a murderous hail of fire down on the approaching enemy, who filled the entire corridor with their massive armored bodies.

Over a dozen spinning bullets impacted against the body of the first Huntsman, striking its chest, arms and legs, triggering its magnetic defenses. Each round struck the rubberized exoskeleton, shattered against the sudden solidity of the fluid within, and bounced impotently off of the monster's armor. Puffs of dust flew off as each round struck the dry, desiccated powered armor, trailing away like smoke. More bullets hit the walls, the ceiling and the floor, kicking up momentary sparks that helped light up the rest of the passage in pulses of white and yellow light.

"Nothing!" Rider shouted as he emptied his five-round clip, but Valero ignored him and kept firing away. Rider turned and brought the butt stock of his heavy rifle against the glass partition of one of the water tanks. The glass immediately cracked, then, as he hit it again, it shattered completely, sending crystalline shards everywhere. As he broke through, an overpowering, chemical odor spilled out into the room, but Rider had already slung one leg over the wall and was climbing into the subterranean reservoir, knee-deep in toxic sludge.

"Valero! Move your ass!" he shouted.

Valero shouted something indistinct but kept firing, exhausting his own clip. Only then did he see Rider pulling back into the tank itself. He moved over to the wall, then retrieved another clip, feeding the fresh ammunition into the weapon.

As the gunfire ceased, the Huntsmen began to move, sweeping down the passage towards their cornered prey. Seeing this, Valero fired again, spraying bullets ineffectively at them, watching sparks fly and the enemy rushing relentlessly through it all.

Rider waded quickly through the chemical slush, splashing it everywhere, until he came to the central column and the rusted hatch that waited there. For a moment he considered what to do, then tossed away the useless rifle and grabbed the hatch's handle with both hands, straining to pull it open.

"Valero, help me out here!"

Only once he'd exhausted another clip did Valero listen, climbing over the low partition and joining Rider in the flooded tank. He rushed over and grabbed the handle as well, relinquishing the glow rod and his own rifle to the depths of the knee-deep ooze.

Together they pulled and pulled, but it was so badly rusted and gummed up it wouldn't budge.

The first of the Huntsmen entered the room they had just left. Its eyes swept around through the darkness, and it saw them. It lifted its rifle and pointed it towards them as they struggled frantically with the door.

There was a crack as the sleek, antique rifle fired, sending a cluster of ultra-thin wedges of soft macrosteel into Valero's side. It almost missed him, but one of the whirling projectiles managed to strike his shoulder, cutting straight through and carving out a hole as large as a man's fist on the other side. The rest of his arm dangled on a strip of meat before it fell completely off, plunging heavily into the pool.

Valero felt the agony but his focus was on something else. Even as blood streamed from the stump of his shoulder he worked his mutant adrenaline to a frenzy, flooding his veins and all his muscles with every bit of strength-enhancing androgens he could muster. As Rider pulled and pulled, Valero used his only remaining hand to help him. His grip intensified, his bones showed white through his pulsing red skin, and with a sudden wrench he yanked the hatch open.

Accompanied by a flood of chemical sludge, draining through the now-open hatch, Rider stepped inside the column, finding a tight shaft leading down. The rusted rungs of an ancient maintenance ladder trailed with the tunnel, vanishing into the wet, odorous darkness below. He quickly looked back at Valero.

"Come on!"

Valero shook his head, slumping weakly until only his head and shoulders were above the chemical ooze. He knew this was his time. Even if the blood loss didn't kill him, the radiation damage that was unraveling him from within would. It was time to let go.

"Get going, Rider," he said, blood trickling from his lips. He reached into the sludge and retrieved the glow rod, thrusting the dim light source into Rider's hand. "I'm staying here. I'm gonna kill at least one of these motherfuckers before I go..."

Rider looked at Valero and saw the determination in his eyes. He needed no second invitation and crawled into the chute. With one last look back at his old enemy he began to descend.

The Major prepared to fire again but its telepathic senses tasted weakness, pain and desperate agony in the air. It lowered its flechette rifle. Then, one by one, more of its kind came into the dark chamber behind it, until Valero could only see a dozen sets of blue eyes beyond the fractured glass.

Valero's vision was fading, but he struggled to remain strong. Under the surface of the slurry he removed his pistol from its holster and kept it at the ready, blindly removing the safety.

The chemicals rippled, tipping him off to the fact that one of the Huntsmen had entered the tank with him. He opened his heavy eyelids and saw the towering beast approaching. The Major put its rifle down against one wall, then came slowly forward.

Valero watched as the thing towered over him. Its bright blue lenses shifted, rotated, stared off in different directions. But he could feel its mind drawn to his angry, fearful thoughts.

The thing reached up with long metal claws and began to remove its helmet. A puff of dusty air escaped when the seal broke and the headpiece came off. Trailing hoses swayed as it began to kneel over him.

Valero stared at the shriveled head underneath, some Ancient warrior, its eyes white and featureless, its mouth already gaping and filled with the broken fragments of obsidian teeth. The mouth opened wider, and it began to moan.

With a last burst of strength Valero quickly lifted his pistol from beneath the water, bringing the barrel right up against the Major's head. Before the creature could recoil in surprise he pulled the trigger, blasting a hole through the Major's forehead and sending a huge glob of corrupted black brain matter, strands of ochre ooze and mustard-colored blood, and brittle bone flying backwards against the wall.

The Major collapsed, dead, the weight of its mighty armor dragging the corpse-warrior beneath the surface of the reservoir's waters.

Valero choked, then managed a weak grin, despite the flood of painful sensations that now began to consume him. He knew there was no escape, and as he surrendered to that realization, another Huntsman entered the tank, drawn by Valero's despair, displacing more of the chemical fluids flowing around him. It came forward, only this time it brought its clawed hand up to his, engulfing his hand and the pistol held in it. With a comparatively gentle squeeze it crushed every bone at once, and crumpled the pistol as well.

His head already swimming in agony, Valero barely felt it. When the creature finally let go, his hand, now fused with the gun in a tangle of shattered bone and crushed steel, fell back into the sludge with an unceremonious splash.

Valero couldn't move. He couldn't fight back. His eyes were slipping into darkness, his lids getting heavier and heavier. But his ears were still sharp. He heard the pop and hiss of another helmet coming off, could smell the dead odors of its face revealed.

He opened his eyes one last time. Before him was a dark-haired woman, a ghastly thing, a female soldier, her face shrunken and her eyes completely rotted away, leaving empty sockets. She moaned like the others, her mouth fell open like a yawning abyss, and she leaned forward to consume him.

Gale was dying. She felt a rush of emotions; fear, failure and desperation. But most of all she wondered what would happen to Rider, once she was gone. It seemed strange to her to focus on such a thing, considering all that they now stood to lose. But she was afraid for his future; even if he survived here, even if he somehow escaped, if she wasn't there to guide him who would make sure he didn't go astray?

Why was his welfare so important to her? She didn't know why, it just *was*.

She struggled to crawl, but every movement invited waves of nauseating, incapacitating pain. She looked back at the sealed hatchway, then over to Shubazang, who lay still and dead. She looked over at his head, which, thankfully, was turned away from her.

At that moment she noticed something spilling the pocket of the boy's greatcoat - several sealed syringes. She immediately remembered the medicine he had taken from the clinic, the stuff that had healed his leg.

She began to push herself along, struggling desperately to conserve her breath, knowing that each inhalation of air was like swallowing fire. Her muscles worked angrily to deny unconsciousness, pushing her forward while triggering new waves of agony. It seemed like an hour passed before she finally came within reach of Shubazang cold corpse. She reached into his pocket and the glass bottle spilled out, rolling in a slow circle before stopping.

She felt weak. There was blood everywhere, hers and Shubazang's. Through hazy eyes she saw her own skin was pale, losing its color fast. She fumbled for one syringe, bit the plastic packaging, and yanked it out.

Her fingertips were numb, making use of the syringe difficult. She pulled the cap off the tip. She put it through the rubber stopper. She vomited. She pulled herself out of it, and then drew the drug back into the syringe.

Losing all feeling she hurried. Her face became hot, she was no longer breathing, and all sound began to fade in her ears. It was a miracle she could still see enough to bring the syringe to her chest. She pushed the needle into the torn flesh surrounding the gaping wound Euryale had left. She felt nothing as she injected herself. She let go and lay there. For what seemed like an eternity.

She awoke, finding herself breathing normally. There wasn't any pain, only a slight disorientation from lying on her side. She batted her eyes, and for a moment found it hard to focus, but soon regained her senses.

She was wary of moving too fast, but her heart was racing. She got up, without any pain at all. She looked down at her chest and saw the hole in her clothing, saw the remnants of blood still clinging to her wetly, but she was okay.

She sat up and looked at Shubazang, then to the weapons scattered on the floor. She picked up the grenade he had given her and put it among her things. She kicked aside her submachine gun and went over to pick up one of the advanced microwavers. Taking it in hand she examined it, looking for the trigger and exploring its complex buttons and switches. She noticed a gaping hole in the grip. This thing needed ammunition like any other weapon.

Stepping over Shubazang's body she looked inside the other lockers and cases, finding another identical grenade to the one Shubazang had given her. She took that too and continued searching. At long last she found a small supply of uniformly-black clips, each no thicker than a television remote. Giving it a try she found one that fit perfectly in the grip of the weapon. As it slid inside there was an electronic "beep" from the gun, and a small green light appeared near the trigger.

She put the rest of the clips in her belt, then turned to the door. She had seen Shubazang do this with a laser; she wondered if she could do the same with this weapon. She lifted the gun and aimed it at the door. She felt uneasy all of a sudden, but pulled the trigger anyway.

The gun shivered for a moment as it projected a thin beam towards the door. Pure heat, invisible to the eye except for the displacement of air as it traveled, like a heat mirage reflecting off the desert sands, struck out at the doorway. There was a spark, then a reddish glow began to appear where the beam bored into the metal. Gale kept the trigger pulled all the way back, and the weapon continued emitting its searing ray, until the very metal of the doorway began to glow brightly like a formless ingot of metal being hammered on a smith's anvil.

After a moment the gun chirped and its power source, now drained, died. The ray dissipated instantly. The door continued to glow, now turning semi-liquid, and from its own weight the metal melted in on itself, until one whole half of the doorway folded inwards.

Gale moved forward, cautiously, and used the butt of the rifle to expand the hole in the door. The metal proved pliable, now that it had been super-heated to extreme temperatures, and soon there was a gap large enough to step through.

She couldn't wait for it to cool. With a deep breath she jumped through, only just barely landing safely on the other side. Standing up, she ejected the dead clip and replaced it with another, then turned her attention to finding the others.

Covered in sticky green and orange matter from the reservoir above, Rider reached the bottom of the maintenance ladder and entered a long corridor. The brownish ooze from above washed around his feet, water-logged his boots and gurgled away through grated drains on both sides of the passage. Down here it smelled of rot and decay, of rust and an overpowering chemical stench. It clung oppressively to him, forcing him to wipe the muck from his face so that he could see and breathe.

Having discarded his rifle he reached down and pulled out his two pistols. He realized they were useless against the Huntsmen, but he felt comforted by them anyway. So he kept them.

To his surprise, the passage he was in was lit; periodically, at least. Small emergency lights ran the length of the corridor, and these flickered on and off, on and off, with precise regularity. Like a heartbeat.

He turned and looked in both directions, but saw nothing down either passage that would make him choose one over the other. Putting away one gun, he then reached into a pocket and pulled out one of the coins he'd taken from the lonely gas station out in the desert. He flipped it into the air and caught it, then opened his slimy fist to look at its silvery face. Regarding the image of some long-dead leader on its surface, he looked to the left and proceeded down that way.

Burning Lands

Gale realized that she might be entirely alone now. Valero and Rider might be dead, or they might have escaped to the surface. Either way she was down *here*, all ties to them severed. Alone.

She re-entered the chamber outside the armory, all flickering and pulsing with power. The ceiling lights shivered on and off, and the walls seemed to hum and throb. She realized that Euryale might be here, hiding, or it might be anywhere, among the miles and miles of tunnels they had already passed through. It could be watching, waiting for the right opportunity to strike again.

She had two things on her side, however. First, Euryale had left her for dead, and if she was lucky the android wouldn't expect to see her alive. Second, the android had as much to fear from the Huntsmen as she did, and if they stumbled into one another chances are Euryale would be destroyed in the encounter.

Gale held the microwaver close and looked around. She felt something there, a sentience again caressing her mind, gently probing her thoughts, listening to her mind work. But instead of fighting it, she listened back. Voices, many, many voices... indistinct, unclear, but ever-present. Like a ghost that still walked these ancient halls, its voice could still be heard if one only listened.

She closed her eyes and let her mind *feel* her surroundings. The voices grew clearer, and soon she could distinguish a direction from which they came.

She opened her eyes and started off down a flickering, dark hallway leading away from the armory, the morgue and deeper underground.

Rider went down one tunnel only to find another ladder, and more shafts leading down. Each time he returned to his coin, letting chance dictate his path. But each time he climbed down he found more access passages, maintenance tunnels and shafts leading deeper. Conduits carrying power cables, sewage, and steam. The inner workings of this underground facility were infinitely complex, like the twisted metal innards of a living, breathing subterranean City.

As he went deeper, the regularity of the heartbeat pulse of lights and subsonic throbbing became more noticeable, and lent more credibility to the idea that this place was "alive". Of course it wasn't, but he couldn't shake the sense that maybe they had unknowingly delivered themselves into the belly of a great beast, and now that they had been swallowed up whole, they would never leave.

Descending one final ladder, covered in sweat and holding a slowly dying light rod, he heard footsteps on metal. There was enough illumination from the throbbing emergency lights that he dropped the rod and gripped his pistols, ready to fire at whatever came at him.

He took in a surprised breath when Gale came into view, her torso covered in red gore and carrying some heavy, advanced rifle in her hands. The flickering light touched on her mess of straw-colored hair, its curls hanging down and almost completely obscuring the emerald hue of her eyes.

"Rider!" she cried out, and ran towards him.

"You're hurt!" he exclaimed, but she shook her head.

"No, I'm okay now. Shubazang's medicine, I took a chance. It worked on me, too."

"Where *is* the tinker?" Rider asked.

She hesitated. "Dead." Then, thinking ahead, "Valero, too?"

Rider was ready to tell her the whole story about Ludd and Valero, but when it came time it seemed far harder than he'd imagined. Instead he merely confirmed with a nod.

"Are you sure?" she asked softly, her eyebrows knit.

"Yes," he replied.

Gale took in a deep breath. "Euryale went insane. It tried to kill me and it even cut Shubazang's head off. It's around here somewhere..."

For a moment Rider looked alarmed, realizing they were now alone. Then he slowly nodded again. "Okay, but at least we're still here. What do you want to do, kid? We can always try to escape..."

She looked at him, her mouth flattening. He forced a humorless grin. "Just kidding."

"Rider," she said, "there's something you need to know. The Brotherhood, they sent us here to capture it, to contain it, to bend it to their will. God knows how they thought I could do that... maybe 'join' with it like it wants, become a living part of it, corrupt it from within... but I won't do it! We have to destroy it, you know that, don't you?"

He looked past her. "I'm with you kid, whatever you want to do."

She looked at him with a sideways glance, unable to tell if he was being sarcastic or not, or even if he was paying attention.

When he realized she wanted something more out of him he looked right at her and held up his finger. "Look, I *told* you those monks were up to no good..."

Gale smiled warmly, comforted by the return of the old crusty Rider.

She looked around. "Look, I know we're close. Really close, Rider. It's hidden, but it wants to be found. It *wants* me to come to it."

"So where is it?"

Gale shook her head. "I don't know..."

Just then they heard a quiet "whoosh" somewhere down the corridor. They both turned and looked back the way Gale had come; a doorway had opened, a door that had been sealed and overlooked, and a dazzling, throbbing light spilled into the passageway. They both stared, aware that this seemed just too easy.

"I'll go first," Rider said at last, taking the lead. Gale was right behind him.

Through the door Rider went, into a room lit by pulses of light. Overhead the ceiling lights were destroyed, the fluorescent bulbs missing, and electricity arched from one socket to another; it was from these that light filled the room. One entire wall was taken up by banks of computer screens and panels. The lights on these flickered and pulsed in reds, greens and oranges to the same rhythm as the arching sparks in the ceiling lights.

Rider looked around but the room seemed empty. Gale entered next, but when she did the screens all came to life, each monitor taken up by a separate face. There were a half dozen of them, two women, four men, including the familiar face of the commissioner. They all filled their respective screens, their features swollen and corpulent, bobbing up and down like boats on a rolling ocean. Blind eyes looked outwards at them, moving mechanically in their sockets, puppet-like and poorly animated.

One of the women spoke. "Gaaailll, yooour faaather's papers maaay have been onnn tooo sommmething..."

An older man spoke as well. "Weee were wrooong to sennnd the Hunnntsmen afffter him..."

The commissioner spoke. "But yooourrr heeere nowww, *little Alice...*"

Then another woman, recognizable as the one seen on the screen mounted on the morgue's medical robot. "We maaade a missstake..."

The commissioner again. "But weee cannn fix thaaat..."

An unfamiliar male face. "Nowww that youuu've commme baaack..."

Rider seemed poised and ready to shoot the screens. Gale addressed them, eyebrows knit in confusion.

"What do you want from me?"

The commissioner's head moved slightly to the left, then the right. His eyes seemed to look right at Gale, then passed over her, looking off in an odd direction. He spoke again, followed by what sounded like echoing whispers:

"The Hunnntsmen are immmperfect... you arrre not... The treatttment your faaather developed... could perrrfect usss alll."

"Yooou hold the keeey!" the first woman spoke. It's face suddenly grinned, a horrible smile that reminded her again of a ventriloquist's dummy, its mouth forced apart at another's whim.

"Joooinnn with usss!" the commissioner whispered. "You beeelong with usss! We are aaall that's left of the truuue human race! Not those muuutants out there! Weee are the hope for aaall humanity!"

Once more Gale had a stunning flashback. Her mind raced back to the clinic, where she remembered her father arguing with the commissioner on the television screen:

"We need to put our minds together to formulate a solution. We need better coordination of each sub-commune's research if we're going to survive this!"

She snapped out of it, just as the commissioner said, *"We neeed tooo put our miiinds... TOGETHER!"*

The floor buckled beneath their feet, taking both by surprise. Rider tipped over and fell as the ground swelled, the metal beneath him fracturing and coming apart. Gale screamed, but it was too late, as something enormous pushed its way upwards, destroying the floor, then descended all at once, taking the shattered remains with it. Both she and Rider fell into the huge hole that it left in its wake, cascading down into darkness.

By some miracle Gale found herself still alive, lying at the bottom of what appeared to be a deep chasm. There was very little light to see by, though the air felt charged with power, causing the hairs on the back of her neck, and the little hairs on her arms, to stand on end. She heard an audible crackle of static electricity burst around the microwaver, which now lay ten feet away in a jumble of broken floor panels. Her body ached, but if she had any broken bones she couldn't feel them.

Head spinning she tried to stand, and saw Rider nearby, already getting to his feet. He was bloody and wounded, but he drew his Micro-Uzi and looked out into the featureless black void that surrounded them. Faint light from the dancing, dazzling computer chamber far above them lit his eyes up, like tiny red lanterns scanning the darkness.

"What do you see?" Gale asked. He was quiet for a moment.

"*Gale...*" he whispered in astonishment, losing his voice. He was looking slightly upwards, his head angled into the blackness above them.

There was a rumbling, as something *massive* moved in the darkness, not far from them. The ground shifted and buckled again, sending vibrations through them both. She heard distant crashes, pieces of the four floors above being knocked about and falling free from their ruined tethers by the creature's movement. She realized that they had plummeted into the deepest part of the complex, its very bottom, where something truly enormous made its lightless lair.

Rider was useless, he was either struck dumb or stunned by what he alone was seeing with his darkvision. So Gale rose to her feet, and fumbled around for something, anything, that could shed some light on their current situation. Cutting her hands in all the debris, she nonetheless found a shard of reflective glass that she immediately lifted. She angled it so that light from above caught its surface, and reflected into the dark void ahead of them.

A weak beam of its light scanned the shadows. She saw movement, vague and undefined at the very edge of her vision. It moved quickly, but it was enough to reveal something *large*. It seemed to react to the light coming near it, slithering grossly and wetly away, moving behind a wall of collapsed metal scaffolding, destroyed supports from the levels above, and rows and rows of meticulously-arrayed computers, monitors and cameras, a complex setup that allowed it, whatever *it* was, to observe and manipulate the entire facility above it. It was buried here, this unseen monstrosity, but even underneath so many thousands of tons of rock and miles of passages and chambers it was still the City's undisputed master.

The commissioner's face came into view, moving sideways out of the darkness into the weak square of light the mirrored bit of glass projected ahead of her. It hovered there, his bloated, unhealthy face undulating from side to side, his eyes looking in all directions. The mouth grinned evilly and spoke.

"Joooinnn with usss!"

At that instant a thousand lights flickered on and off throughout the deep; huge coils of electrical wiring dangling from the ruptured floors above, affixed with old light fixtures hanging nonsensically about at all angles, ceiling lights and computer monitors strung along miles of wiring like lights in Hell's arcade. These all came on, glowing white, yellow, red and amber, flashing and pulsing to some terrible, cyclopean heartbeat.

In the light Gale could see all that Rider had seen. It, what had become of her people, rose fully into view, unafraid now that she and Rider were its captives, now that they wouldn't be scared off by the sight of what it *truly* was.

A gigantic mass of fused *bodies*, a colossal "tree" made of bloated white cadavers with vines and roots of scar tissue (and that hinted-at protoplasmic artificial flesh connecting them all) rose almost fifty feet from the floor of this central chamber and loomed above them. Each body was still somewhat animate, moving and shifting with some sinuous internal motion, like a snake or dragon made from living, breathing, roiling flesh. Each former scientist and citizen was connected to the next by ropes and cables of artificial flesh brewed up in the City's decayed laboratories. What muscular action allowed it to move and lift itself so similarly to a grand serpent was unclear, but it seemed to be made entirely of bodies, even beneath the outer skin of that pulsating flesh-colored protoplasm, for hands and faces could be seen pressing against its hide, momentarily taking shape before vanishing back inside its vast bulk.

Those faces on the outside of the thing looked awful and dead; she saw the commissioner, the men and women who'd spoken to them on the computer screens and dozens, *hundreds,* of others as well. Their eyes blinked like winking, malevolent stars, looking in all directions and taking in everything around it. It was a thousand people united as one, a thousand minds linked through madness brought on by the power of the drug that they themselves created. Together, joined as one, they constituted one gigantic "overmind", an enormous and blasphemous congress of sentiences that generated such immense psychic power that it created its own electricity and had made itself known even to the minds of mentalists a thousand miles away.

The commissioner's face, fittingly, sat at the very tip of the monstrous serpent, with the faces of fellow scientists trailing off from the very top in descending importance. The commissioner looked down at Rider and Gale and saw their looks of horror. The commissioner's head shouted at them from up high.

"We think bettter this waaay, our thoughts shaaare a dirrrect connection! Organic wiiiring, chemical memmmory!"

Electricity coursed across the thing's enormous shape, arcs of white-blue power that crackled and sparked in the weird light.

Rider's first sensible action was to open fire. He pulled the trigger on his submachine gun and watched as the barrel kicked in the air. There was no need to be precise, the thing was so huge that he couldn't miss, but the bullets were insignificant against it, vanishing into walls of bubbling skin and striking at exposed faces. A chemical slurry of Ascendance, a fluid brown and ochre in color, spilled from the wounds instead of blood. The thing had entirely replaced its blood with the drug that had brought them all to this dark and horrifying place. It seemed to recoil from the rounds striking its flesh, but it would take more than a few slugs of lead to injure this monstrosity.

Gale ran for cover even before it began to move. It whipped its "head", just the top end of its mighty length, downward in an arc, sweeping tons of debris aside and towards Rider. Rider saw it coming, heard the thundering crash and the showers of a million sparks, and leapt to the ground, lying prone.

Several tons of fused flesh passed only a few feet over his head; he took a chance to look up as it passed, seeing faces, gaping mouths and maniacal eyes blinking as it soared above him. Air was displaced, making a whistling sound as it went. It was a massive living pendulum, a colossus that had only moments ago intended to crush him with its weight. The odor of ozone swirled around him.

Metal supports and polysteel trestles that once held the floors above came with the swaying creature, knocked free as the thing swung wildly about, coming crashing to the bottom. Tons and tons of metal and stone landed all around Gale and Rider, kicking up clouds of toxic dust, burying parts of the room in a rain of steel.

Gale coughed frantically to clear her airway, but it felt like a losing battle. She heard the floor groan under the creature's great weight and heard rubble from above falling free again. Rider was nowhere to be seen.

As the blasphemous overmind rose up once more, the commissioner shouted maniacally, electricity glowing in his eyes.

"An orrrganic 'super-computer', superiorrr to silicon and microprocessors! The huuuman brain has unmaaatched computing powwwer; you can only imaaagine what we've accommmplished like this!"

Stepping out from behind cover despite its insane rambling, Gale fired the microwaver at the monstrosity. The air rippled as the beam struck outwards, making contact with some part of its hulking mass. The beam boiled its skin instantly, causing it to blister rashly and erupt with steaming fluids. The flesh burned outwards, peeling back away from the contact point as the heavy mass straining within came pouring through the hole, forcing it wider. A few wet, sticky arms dangled limply from the wound, each oozing a drapery of ochre-colored slime. *Its blood was a chemical poison; its innards were parts of human bodies!*

At that instant a voice scratched at the forgotten back doorway to her mind, emanating from a great distance away.

"No! Alive!"

She ignored the command. The Brotherhood would *not* have this thing alive.

The monstrosity seemed to respond, letting off bolts of lightning that leapt from its charged corpse-hulk to metal beams and supports all around. A brilliant flash filled the depths and thousands of sparks flew in cascades from wherever the spontaneous strokes of power touched.

Rider continued to fire, adding his weapon's meager stopping power to Gale's. How he wished he had something more powerful! When at last he'd exhausted the clip, with very little to show for it, he threw the Uzi aside.

The commissioner saw him and smiled evilly, drool exploding from his mouth as his face contorted into a maniacal grin. Power once more welled in his eyes and electricity began to flit and dance across the colossal aberration's hide.

Before he could run for cover an arc of power jumped from the massive creature, accompanied by an audible "crackle", and struck Rider square in the chest, burning a hole through his coat and throwing him back almost a full ten feet into a heap of sharp, stony debris.

With Rider gone, the mighty abomination continued to spew words, the commissioner's head serving merely as a convenient mouthpiece.

"We've fought the drrrug and leeearned to control it! It serrrves us, we donnn't serve it! We're nnnot like the Huntsmen... we're nnnot insane at aaall! And we're close, sooo close, to finishing whaaat we've onnnly just begun! We're ready to aaadvance the time taaable!"

Gale struggled to see where Rider's body fell but there was only smoke and fading sparks. Fearing the worst she cried a garbled cry and leapt up, firing again, discharging another microwave burst that seared the creature's flesh. As the thing moved from side to side with an obscene coiling motion, the ray burned a severe line back and forth across its flesh, zigzagging until it made contact with just one of the many heads studding its exterior. With a grotesque "pop" the screaming human face caught on fire and exploded like a giant cyst, showering the floor with sizzling bone and gore.

"*Nooo!*" the commissioner screamed, and hundreds of others joined him. The room shook with the noise, it rumbled and more debris began to fall from high above.

"*If you wooon't joooin usss...*" he said, his eyes swelling with madness, "*... then off with yooour head!*"

Gale fumbled to reload her expended clip, her fingers suddenly and inexplicably turning to butter. In that instant, the monstrosity produced another arc of electricity welled up from within, shooting it outwards at her like a tendril of living power.

Gale's enhanced reflexes saved her life; at the last minute she rolled behind a wall of collapsed concrete, shielding herself as the finger of lightning struck the ground nearby.

The young woman pulled herself up, keeping to the cover, as the monster rumbled and roared just a few dozen paces away.

Looking to her left, she saw Rider waking from unconsciousness, his eyes fluttering open, smoke still trailing from his chest. In a daze, he reached for a weapon, then remembered he'd tossed his Uzi away. Instead he drew the pistols at his side.

"Rider!" she hissed. Rider looked and saw her, then raised a hand and weakly motioned for her to join him.

Without a moment's hesitation she broke cover and ran towards Rider, who got up with a groan to begin giving her covering fire. But his pistol rounds only vanished ineffectively into the creature's mass. It now came down and rolled after her, a monolithic serpent giving chase to the fleeing girl.

Gale slid behind Rider as he quickly emptied his pistol clips, then dropped down behind the huge rock with her. The thing roared again. It was coming for them; soon there would be nowhere to hide.

Rider contemplated what to do. His weapons were useless, while her microwaver was only slightly more effective. *What could they do?*

Suddenly Gale's eyes widened and she reached down, pulling out both of the grenades she and the tinker had found in the armory. She immediately handed one to Rider. "You're not doing anything with those things!" she shouted, referring to his pistols. "Take this! It's the only thing we've got left!"

Rider cursed and dropped his guns, taking the dusty metal sphere in hand, his hands clasping around the cold, rusted outer case. It looked somehow familiar, this ancient weapon. He stared at the stenciled writing, barely legible, still partly visible on its corroded surface. *M819 NTRN GRND.*

His eyes widened in surprise and recognition.

The thing stopped as it neared the center of the grand chamber, knocking over an array of computers that came crashing down with an explosion of all of its glass screens at once. Sparks singed its flesh, glass fragments buried themselves in its bulk, but it soared upwards, a giant cobra poised to strike its fatal blow.

"*ALIVE!*" came a desperate command to Gale's mind from a thousand miles away.

"NO!" she screamed in her head, a final cry to expel the Brotherhood's mentalists from her thoughts, to bar them from her eyes and ears, to sever their connection and their control over her. In defiance she jumped up, tossing the grenade towards the enormous abomination that loomed in the abyss.

Rider flipped the arming switch on his grenade and, pulling his arm back for just a second, thrust forward and threw it directly into the base of the massive monstrosity. The two spherical devices gleamed dully in the flickering light as they flew together, only finally vanishing as the creature rolled over the two bombs, now angling to bring the top fifty feet of itself down onto them with all the violent energy of a skyscraper coming apart.

Gale thought of the impending explosion, hoped for success, hoped for their lives. Rider worried one or both might be duds, being so rusted and ancient. Unsure as to the outcome, both he and Gale instinctively tore away and ran.

Two muffled blasts exploded through the abyss in quick succession. In that instant, the base of the creature glowed from inside, a veil of orange flesh burning away from within, revealing the silhouettes of bodies, heads and a jumble of limbs crammed together, one on top of another, like multitudes of twins trapped in an enormous womb. Explosive force and waves of intense radiation shook through its bulk. Electricity shot from its body as it buckled and rippled, touching on every bit of metal within fifty feet of it, so that it glowed in the backwash of light and burned in the shower of the billions of sparks that swirled around it.

The thing completely unraveled, shrieking gobbets of flesh, bone and boiling fluids blowing outwards in a gory shower. As the base came apart with the explosive blast of the two neutron grenades, the tremendous mass previously held up by its muscular will no longer had anything to support it. It collapsed, coming undone in layers as each five, ten feet of its body impacted the ground, until it simply crumbled away into a sloppy mass of dead tissue. Lightning scintillated on the remains, crackled noisily through the rivers of Ascendance that spilled from its parts, until it was at last silent and still.

Both Gale and Rider felt soiled by their experience beneath the earth, in the creature's deep subterranean hide. Friends, and familiar faces, would now call the long-lost City their final resting place, along with the monstrosity that had filled these halls with the echoes of its insanity. The tunnels and corridors of the vast underground complex echoed dully as they retraced their steps, aware that there were still dangers all around them. They were exhausted, still nursing bruises from their sudden fall into the abomination's lair, but they were alive, and the greatest threat was now over.

Gale half-expected Euryale to appear out of nowhere, to strike at them from surprise, but the android's emotionless face never emerged out of the shadows. She still kept a watch for the silent phantom, but they seemed safe.

The Huntsmen were still out there, Rider realized, but as they went upwards, climbing ladders and finding their way through the dark labyrinth, they were conspicuously absent. Rider wasn't one to question a good thing, and he hastily scrounged to find more light rods among the emergency cabinets they soon located, one after another, on each level. With newfound light they continued on, sensing that they were not entirely alone, but that they were no longer in danger.

It seemed to Gale that the Huntsmen no longer sought after them in particular; with the "overmind" destroyed, the animalistic Huntsmen ceased to be under its control, and no longer felt the need to continue its mission on the surface, or persecute its

Burning Lands

quarry. Like aimless ghosts they had likely returned to the deepest depths of the City, slinking away into the shadows of its underworks, finding no reason to emerge into the light.

After what seemed like a full day of climbing and exploration, Rider and Gale managed to reach the maze of air filtration systems on the first level of the complex, and found their way out to the weird metal beach surrounded on all sides by the waters of the black lake.

Gale set out to cover the causeway they had only recently crossed, but Rider trailed behind for a moment. He took Gale's microwaver and pointed it at the strange craft that still awaited their pilots, and took aim. With a pull of the trigger he fired at one of the machine's weapon pods, until it became so hot it detonated, igniting the fuel on the tarmac. Within moments it roared into an inferno, and as the fire caught one by one the huge insectoid flying machines exploded. There would be even less for the Brotherhood to inherit.

The elevator still functioned; together they ascended to the surface. As they rode it upwards they wordlessly donned their radiation suits and picked up the Geiger counter. As Rider toyed with it, Gale stared silently at the two idle suits that they would be leaving behind. When the door pulled open they confronted the grand waterfall chamber in all its gray, deafening glory, but were no longer awed by it. Silently they crossed the grand causeway and continued upwards. At long last they climbed the last few rungs of the rusted shaft and emerged into the hollow interior of the great pyramidal mound. Shubazang's rickety Townsman awaited them.

Rider moved to the driver's seat and got inside. Gale was close behind, and stashed the microwaver in the back. As she put it away she noticed something in the sand near the mound's gaping entrance. Heavy humanoid tracks led away from the pyramid and out into the bleak wasteland.

It struck her as ironic; new life *had* been born here. Not the life the Brotherhood had hoped for, but something just as alien. The android, Euryale, had found life here, and was now free. It wasn't a comforting thought. Gale wondered if they would ever see Euryale again, or if it would die out there at the hands of the monstrous mutated creatures that lived here, or if the radiation would shut it down and the android would sleep for 10,000 years until there was no radiation anymore, and awaken to greet a new, future age. It was possible they would never know at all.

She was alone now, an orphan again. Her people, and the glory and hope of the Ancient past they believed they alone embodied, seemed forever gone. Like the mutant survivors who still populated the surface world, the unchanged humans who'd sealed themselves in their secret City had proved just as corruptible, over time, with horrible and disastrous results. If not Ascendance, then some other wild ambition, would have led them to ruin; that just seemed to be the way of humankind. At least now their threat was extinguished, though the dark secrets of the City would still be there, underground, perhaps for someone in the future to stumble upon and ponder over.

Her mother, her father, and her entire people were dead now, just another extinct race that would go unremembered by the survivors of the Twisted Earth. She faced a new world, larger than the City, larger than the camp of a single desert huntsman like

Johnny, and larger than Tucumcari and all the degenerate cities like it. The thought of discovering all there was to see was like a ray of sunshine, and it made her smile.

As for the Brotherhood, only time would tell. She had been their pawn, just like the great armies of Uncle Sam, and Karos too, but in the process of doing their work she had realized their warped plans and thwarted them. What effect it would have on the slow rise of that distant church in the west remained to be seen. She liked to believe she had made a lasting difference. Either way, the future seemed more uncertain than ever.

As Gale lingered near the entrance, Rider got into the vehicle, intent on resting his weary legs. By chance he looked into the back seat where she had put the microwaver, and noticed an old army web belt sitting there, the very one Tank had worn. Tank had put it there to relieve some of his burden when they had first left Tucumcari. It was a sudden and unexpected reminder of the man who had once been a part of their lives... the man who had saved their lives, Rider's and Gale's, long ago in the desert. It was enough to make Rider pause for a moment, then reach out and take it in hand.

Rider leaned into the back seat and picked the web belt up, letting his hand pass over the canvas pouches and burnished brass snaps. Attached to the belt by a loop was Tank's flashlight, dangling heavily. One of the pouches was straining at its button. Rider examined it for a moment, then pulled the flashlight out and held it in hand. For a moment he found himself admiring it for its possible value down the road, as a trade item in some dirty marketplace in some nameless town, but at that instant he felt a sudden attachment to it. As he looked it up and down, he remembered the simple man who had treasured it... and he found it impossible to imagine parting with it. He smiled, put his hand on the button and flicked it, until the beam came on. He clicked it on, then off again. On, then off.

After a while he put the flashlight down and opened the belt's bulging pouch, and to his surprise a half dozen marbles rolled out, spilling onto his lap. In a flood the small spheres bounced, scattering across the front seat and hitting the metal floor of the car with a rattling *tick-tack, tick-tack* sound, until the last skittered and vanished through a nearby grate on the cavern floor. Just as quickly as they had spilled out, it seemed every last marble was gone. Lost forever.

Though he had dropped the marbles as a result of his clumsiness, something was still lodged in the pouch. Rider reached in and, with a firm tug, pulled out what was hidden inside: a rusty, dull straight razor.

Black thunderclouds loomed in the distance, filling the eastern sky. White lightning streaked across this canvas of blacks and grays, but being so far away the accompanying thunder was imperceptible. The Burning Lands were well behind them now.

As if like clockwork the skeleton of the rickety Townsman came to a quiet halt just as the Geiger counter stopped ticking away. Completely out of gas. Rider and Gale sat there or a moment, both of them silent and lost in their own thoughts, then got out. A strong wind picked up and tugged at their suits. Rider pulled his helmet off first, followed by Gale, and in moments they stripped out of the suffocating things and discarded them. The dry desert breeze felt good against their skin.

Burning Lands

They had returned to the spot where their journey into the Burning Lands began. Their horses had gone, all of them except for one, loyally awaiting the return of its Rider.

Gale kicked off the last remnants of her suit as Rider went to the stoic horse and pet it. Twilight had already set in, and as always happened during the gloaming hour his eyes began to glow in varied shades of pink and red. He turned back and watched her, before getting up into the saddle.

"Uncle Sam'll be happy to hear we succeeded," Rider said. "Maybe now his people will finally know the freedom they've been longing for."

She thought about it, but whether or not she could see the future of the natives she said nothing. The *bei man* army had indeed gone back to its native homeland, bleeding away once more into the vast open spaces of the north. Like the minutemen of old who had once defended this land from foreign invaders, Uncle Sam and his people had risen to answer the desperate call to fight for freedom. But now their flags, banners and pennants were stricken, the plains no longer thundered with the boom of drums and cavalry; it was a signal to all, in a sense, a pronouncement declaring the end of what many hoped would be the last great battle for this blood-nurtured land. But Gale didn't seem convinced, not in the least. Hopes aside, there was no guarantee this land would be blood-free for long.

Rider noticed her silence, then changed the subject.

"I suppose we could go east, and leave the desert behind. Or we could try to find that 'mountain kingdom' Ludd spoke of. I guess it's worth a try..."

He stared out at the broad open horizon as the wind picked up. He looked her way, and extended a hand, inviting her to join him, wherever they chose to go. *Together.*

Gale said nothing as she came over, but felt good knowing his sentiments mirrored hers.

THE END

TERMINOLOGY OF THE WASTELAND

Ancients: Few are the historians of the current era who can come close to describing what the times of the "Ancients" were truly like; they were the race of men who existed before the "Fall", before the great war that devastated the world. By the primitive people who now live among the wastelands, the Ancients are viewed almost as "gods", so fantastic was their technology and so mystifying their complex civilization. The survivors of the Fall live among the futuristic wreckage of their world, avoiding the glowing ruins of their cities, gathering their garbage and wistfully wondering what the world was like when the Ancients ruled the Earth.

Brotherhood: A new religion of the wasteland, whose strange robed followers count among them the most deformed mutants and the most powerful *psychics*. The Brotherhood believes the nuclear wars of the past marked the genesis of a new race of human beings that were intended to re-seed the earth with new and wonderful forms of life. The mysterious cult dwells among the ruins of some distant city to the west, but the Brotherhood's robed "monks" are tolerated by the rulers of most trading posts so long as they remain neutral in the affairs of their lands. Not much is known of the Brotherhood's goals, but some whisper they are poised to lead the world into a new age...

Burning Lands (aka *Kui Tu Di*): The Burning Lands dominate the central part of what used to be the American Midwest, a highly-radiated region of land where an inordinate amount of nuclear fallout from the Final War came to rest. The earth here is polluted, its soil deadly and its skies lit by strange auroras visible for a hundred miles.

Burning Lands

Cartel: A powerful merchant house descended from foreigners who invaded America during the Fall, the Cartel is a trade house once rivaled by (but now loosely allied with) the Clean, the wasteland's premier water merchants. The Cartel has existed for generations, profiting from the needs of the desperate survivors of the apocalypse. Their great convoys supply oil, gas and other goods scrounged from the ruins of old cities far to the west, across the Wei Shan, to the people of the Far Desert. With large bases in Styx, Midway and Trade City, the Cartel are obsessed with business and profits but believe their work is important, helping slowly move the wasteland towards rebuilding civilization.

Clean: The Clean Water Clans are the great established power of the Far Desert, all but controlling the vital water trade that keeps the sprinkling of villages and tribes of the wasteland alive. Descended from the Asian invaders who conquered America during the Fall, the Clean have turned their back on the ancient ways, shunning technology (in particular, the use of metal) and building a culture using only "natural" materials: wood, water, clay and stone. These powerful merchants have built elegant fortresses up and down the trade routes, populating them with their illustrious janissaries legions, but from these lavish palaces they issue harsh decrees that affect the lives of many. The Clean believe it is their sacred duty to re-establish law, order and civilization in the wasteland, though this vision is not always shared by their neighbors.

Corium: The cooled, solid remains of radioactive graphite found exclusively among the wreckage of Ancient-era reactors, small chunks of "corium" (as it is known) have become the accepted coinage of the new powers of the desert. Rare and in short supply, corium is used by merchant houses for transactions large and small, as well as to pay their house soldiers and mercenaries.

Fall: The "Fall" is a term used to denote the "End Times" when the race of Ancients fell from their mighty throne as masters of the earth. In truth the Fall was a series of related events, involving the disintegration of society and ethics and a violent, worldwide upheaval that doomed humanity to a slippery slope that ultimately led to a cataclysmic global war. It was during this "Final War" that the world's cities were destroyed, its inhabitants were decimated and the environment was sown with the lasting legacies of radioactive, chemical and biological warfare.

Far Desert (aka *Jia Lang*): The Far Desert is the wide open plain that runs across what used to be northern New Mexico, Texas and Oklahoma. The Far Desert is the heart of a new culture rising from the ashes, primarily dominated by the Clean merchant house and its clients, the tribes and raider enclaves of the wasteland.

Forbidden Lands (aka *Bei Jin Zhi*): This stretch of desert, lying at the foot of the Wei Shan, has long been the domain of raiders and nomads, a lawless country where settlements are temporary and violence the order of the day. Among these wastes the tribal people predominantly reign, as the merchant houses are generally loathe to travel here where there is no guarantee of safety.

Hermavs: "Hermavs" are pitiable creatures born with the shared physical traits of men *and* women. Hermavs are often cast out of their homes when their peculiar deformity becomes known, since many communities consider the presence of a hermaphrodite in their midst intolerable. Driven away and sometimes even hunted for no other reason than their unusual appearance, it is no surprise that these creatures tend to harbor a burning hatred against the rest of humanity. Gangs of hermavs are not unknown, forming destructive and hateful cells among the ruins of some of the wasteland's ancient cities.

Raiders: Long after the Fall of man, the majority of the world is ruled by anarchy. Great gangs of bandits, thugs and killers (known collectively as "raiders") exist outside the few established towns and villages, living by preying on others. There are many raider gangs in the wasteland, both large and small. Some are primitive and others are quite advanced, the latter forming well-armed bands that mount daring raids on the caravans of merchants or brutally slaughter any traveler they come across merely for the water they carry. Some gangs are quite successful and establish a name for themselves in a short period of time, while others burn out or fade away in a matter of years.

Rocky Mountains (aka *Wei Shan*): The Wei Shan comprise a vast mountain range that splits the known world, almost all of it desert, in two. The mechanical, obsessively profiteering culture of the Cartel originates on the west side of these great peaks, while the elegant civilization of the Clean has flourished on the east. The mountains themselves were once a legendary barrier and to this day few dare transgress upon their wind-swept peaks. The industrious merchant houses have established precarious routes, however, useful for ferrying goods back and forth and connecting the deserts of the east with the equally-devastated lands to the west.

Tribal Domains: Beside the Clean and the Cartel lie the domains of the tribal peoples of the Far Desert and the Forbidden Lands, especially in the north, where the influence of the foreign powers is weak. Here the original descendants of America's lone survivors (known in the south as the *bei man*) continue to hold out, clinging to their own lost culture with only a shadowy recollection of the way things once were. Proud and fierce, these tribal people struggle at the yoke of the merchant houses and yearn for the legendary freedom that was once enjoyed by their ancestors.

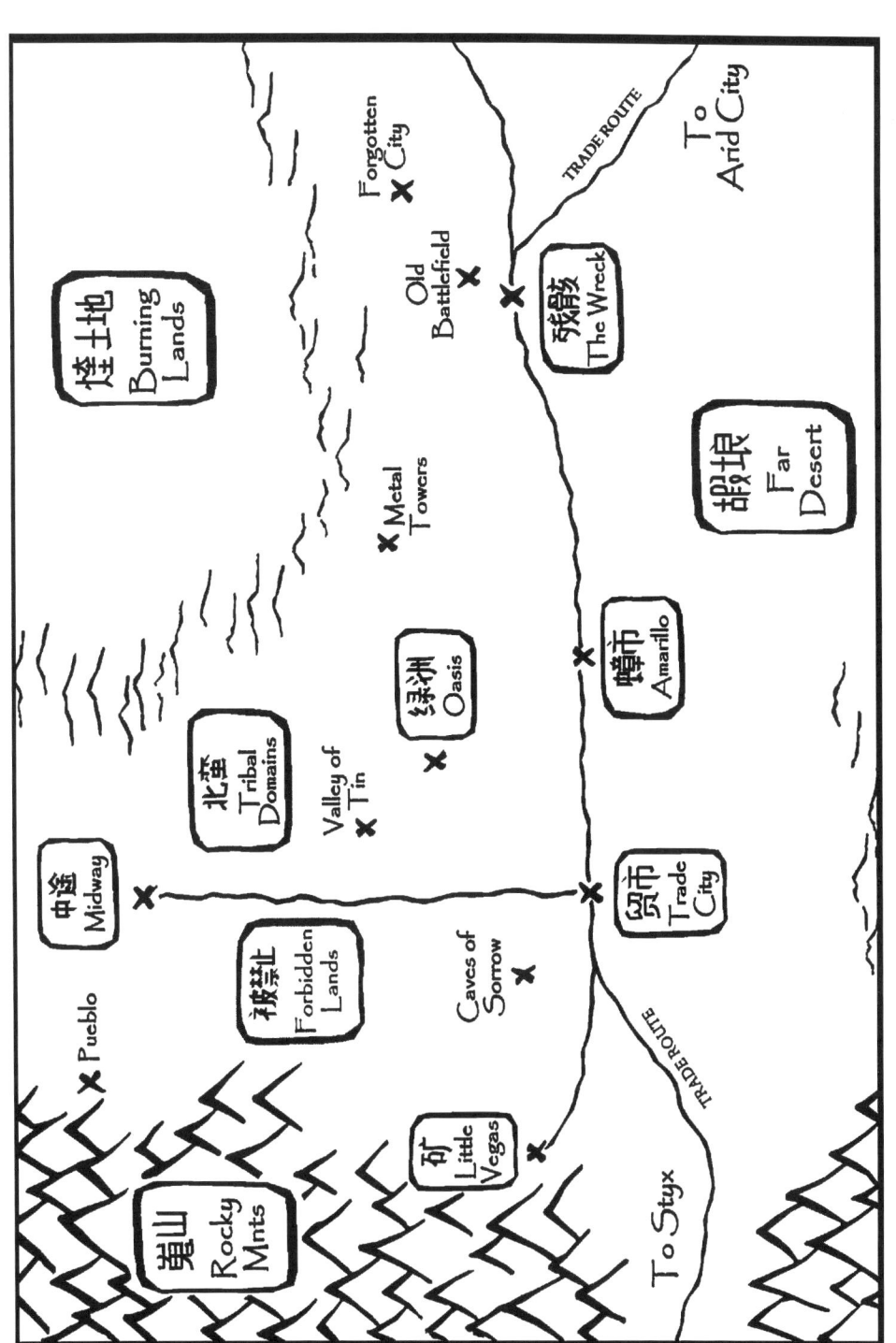

About The Author

Australian-born Dominic Covey has been involved with the "gaming industry" (one way or another) for over seven years. He is best known as the creator of the Darwin's World tabletop role-playing game, and to date has written over two dozen published supplements to support it. This is his first foray into writing novels.

Darwin's World Tabletop RPG

Darwin's World is a role-playing game set in the wild, inhospitable world of mankind's ruin, after a series of devastating wars that brought the human race to the brink of extinction. In a world where radiation has altered the very course of nature, mankind has ceased to exist in its current form. Mutations and genetic variations are the edge separating a species from life and death.

www.DarwinRPG.com